QUEER SQUARE MILE

Kirsti Bohata is Professor of English Literature and co-Director of CREW, the Centre for Research into the English Language and Literature at Swansea University. Her books include *Postcolonialism Revisited: Writing Wales in English* (UWP, 2004), *Rediscovering Margiad Evans: Marginality, Gender and Illness* (UWP, 2013), and *Disability in Industrial Britain: A Cultural and Literary History of Impairment in the Coal Industry, 1880-1948* (MUP, 2020).

Mihangel Morgan was a lecturer on modern Welsh literature, folklore and creative writing at Aberystwyth University for twenty-three years. He won the Prose Medal at the National Eisteddfod in 1993 and has published many poems, stories and novels, including *Melog*, translated by Christopher Meredith (Seren, 2005). He writes a regular column in the Welsh language magazine *O'r Pedwar Gwynt* (From the Four Winds).

Huw Osborne is Associate Professor in the Department of English, Culture, and Communication at the Royal Military College, Kingston. His books include *Rhys Davies* (University of Wales Press, 2009), *Queer Wales: The History, Culture, and Politics of Queer Life in Wales* (University of Wales Press, 2016), and *The Rise of the Modernist Bookshop: Books and the Commerce of Culture in the Twentieth Century* (Ashgate, 2015; Routledge 2019).

QUEER SQUARE MILE

QUEER SHORT STORIES
FROM WALES

Edited By
Kirsti Bohata, Mihangel Morgan
and Huw Osborne

Parthian, Cardigan SA43 1ED
www.parthianbooks.com
First published in 2022
PRINT ISBN 978-1-914595-58-5
EBOOK ISBN 978-1-913640-25-5
Project Editor: Kathryn Tann
Cover design by Syncopated Pandemonium
Cover illustration: Merched Y Beca by Ruth Jên Evans
Typeset by Elaine Sharples
Printed by 4Edge Limited
Published with the financial support of the Books Council of Wales
The publisher would like to thank the Rhys Davies Trust for
support towards the publication of this book
British Library Cataloguing in Publication Data
A cataloguing record for this book is available from the British Library.

CONTENTS

INTRODUCTION

'there was a man in this place one time by the name of Ned Sullivan, and a queer thing happened to him coming up the valley road from Durlas.'

–Frank O'Connor,
The Lonely Voice: A Study of the Short Story (1962)

Frank O'Connor did not share our contemporary notion of 'queer' when he opened his seminal book on the short story with these words. His point was that the short story emerged from communal story-telling tied to a local sense of 'this place' – one's *milltir sgwâr* [square mile] as it is called in Wales. The word 'queer' has changed in meaning over time. From meaning 'odd' and then being used as a term of abuse to describe mainly gay or effeminate men or mannish women, it has been reclaimed. It is now a positive and powerful term to describe LGBT lives and cultures. In a broader sense, it also refers to cultural and critical thinking that challenges received norms, troubles assumptions and creatively upends conventions.

The short story is particularly suited to exploring such queer ex-centric experiences and perspectives. Frank O'Connor explains how, over time, communal, local and usually oral stories—which drew on and reinforced a sense of place and shared experience—evolved into a modern 'private art intended

1

to satisfy the standards of the individual, solitary, critical reader', an art particularly conducive to the outsider experience.[1] The stories in this collection echo O'Connor's contention that the short story 'has never had a hero. What it has instead is a submerged population group ... outlawed figures wandering about the fringes of society [... instilling] an intense experience of human loneliness.'[2] It favours 'tramps, artists, lonely idealists, dreamers, and spoiled priests'; it is 'romantic, individualistic, and intransigent'.[3] In its ex-centric perspectives it has the ability to unsettle, but also to show alternative ways of living.

About a decade before O'Connor's study, Rhys Davies—who features prominently in this collection and who certainly shared some of our notion of 'queer'—described the short story in similar terms: 'In contrast to the novel, that great public park so often complete with great drafty spaces, noisy brass band and unsightly litter, the enclosed and quiet short story garden is of small importance and never has been much more.'[4] This private, intimate and cultivated space needn't appease the views of the wider public market of the novel. Unlike O'Connor, however, Davies sometimes claimed, as he did in a letter to the American author and editor Bucklin Moon, that the short story never entirely lost the qualities of its ancient and communal roots, so that the private and ex-centric tale may also, paradoxically, be the national one:

---

[1] Frank O'Connor, *The Lonely Voice: A Study of the Short Story*, Introduced by Russell Banks (New York: Melville Publishing House, 2004), p. 14.
[2] O'Connor, pp. 17–18.
[3] O'Connor, p. 20.
[4] Rhys Davies, *Collected Stories of Rhys Davies* (London: Heinemann, 1955), p. v. Ironically, none of Davies's most queer stories were included in the 'collected' book.

Short stories, like one's first love, have always remained sweet to me. I like the spread and space of novels, in which one can do much more secret and indirect teaching—and even preaching—and handle themes which make one feel a bit like God, but in the short story one can be, so to speak, more human. There is a fire-side, pure tale-telling quality in short stories and they can convey with much more success than the novel the ancient or primitive, the intrinsic flavour of a race or people.[5]

Davies associates short stories with the personal intimacy of 'one's first love' and opposes them to the God-like preaching of the novel. This intimacy, furthermore, is also the fire-side intimacy of a people connected to a place and a past (which Davies expresses in racialised assumptions of his time). Here the short story is conceived in the tension between public communities and private selves, national belonging and intimate love. So the queer short story of Wales is often doubly ex-centric, expressing national and sexual marginalities that are not always easily reconciled.

The short stories collected here span nearly two hundred years. The earliest—anonymous—contribution is from 1837, the year of Queen Victoria's coronation. The most recent are three new, previously unpublished stories by Dylan Huw, David Llewellyn and Crystal Jeans. Understandings of sexuality and gender have transformed more than once during in this period. In the nineteenth century, gender rather than sexuality was the more rigidly policed element of identity, and so it is apt that 'The Conquest, or a Mail Companion' (1837) portrays dashingly romantic female masculinity in a woman who remains a 'hero' even after we know she is not the gallant young man her

---

[5] Rhys Davies to Bucklin Moon, 31 May 1950, Harry Ransom Humanities Research Centre.

companion believes her to be. Gender is also the focus of Amy Dillwyn's 'One June Night: the Story of an Unladylike Girl' (1883), in which a tomboyish girl (a staple figure of queer writing) tries to fill her father's shoes while reaching across class boundaries. By the end of the nineteenth century, the work of sexologists such as Havelock Ellis and Sigmund Freud had transformed understandings of sexuality and identity. Sex was now more than an act or even a matter of sexual orientation: sexuality itself had become an identity and homosexuality a pathological form of gender and sexual 'inversion'.

Homosexual acts between men were illegal in Britain throughout the nineteenth century, while sexual relationships between women were misrecognised and rendered invisible. As the twentieth century got underway, queer women were increasingly under suspicion while queer men lived at the risk of imprisonment, blackmail, loss of employment, loss of family, and public shaming until well into the twentieth century. The repressive environment, however, also led to alternative spaces of desire and sociability, such as gay balls (as seen in Davies's 'Wigs, Costumes, Masks' (1949)), bachelor apartments (as seen in 'The Collaborators' (1901)), lesbian domesticities (as seen in 'A Modest Adornment' (1948) and 'Nadolig/Christmas'(1929)), erotic tourism (as seen in 'The Stars Above the City' (2008)), cruising parks and 'cottages', gentlemen's clubs and gay and lesbian bars (as seen in 'Muscles Came Easy'(2008)). It also led to literary creativity as writers turned to coded ways of expressing same-sex desire – repeated use of the word 'rhyfedd' meaning 'odd' and 'strange' in Kate Roberts's stories of intense female friendship, for instance, invites the reader to imagine what is not, or cannot be, articulated. The situation began to change in 1957 with the high-profile publication of the Wolfenden Report, which recommended the decriminalisation of homosexuality between two men in private. By 1967, two years before the Stonewall Riots in Greenwich Village, New York, this recommendation was finally passed into law – in large part due to the reasoned and eloquent support and advocacy of Leo Abse, Labour MP for Pontypool.

While a Welsh MP was instrumental in changing the law, and Wales benefitted as part of the UK, it is helpful to understand something of the specific cultural contexts of Wales. The short stories collected here derive from two distinctive linguistic cultures, though the stories, like the cultures, share many points of correspondence. Meic Stephens's *Cydymaith i Lenyddiaeth Cymru* [Companion to Welsh Literature], says that 'It is impossible to begin to understand modern literature in Wales [in Welsh] without paying appropriate attention to the contribution and influence of Nonconformism, and the reaction to it.'[6] English-language literature from Wales also contributed to and was influenced by Nonconformism, but there is a much longer Welsh-language tradition of reading and writing 'in the shadow of the pulpit.'[7] At the end of the nineteenth century and the beginning of the twentieth, Wales was still a predominantly Welsh-speaking country, working-class and chapel-going. People learned to read in the Sunday schools and most reading material was religious in nature. This was due in large part to the fact that the few who had the necessary education and leisure to write in Welsh tended to be mostly ministers of religion. Their work in Nonconformist women's publications such as *Y Gymraes* [The Welshwoman] and *Y Frythones* [The Britones]was often moralistic in tone, on themes

---

[6] Meic Stephens, ed. *Cydymaith i Lenyddiaeth Cymru* (Caerdydd: Gwasg Prifysgol Cymru, 1997), p. 10.
[7] M. Wynn Thomas, *In the Shadow of the Pulpit: Literature and Nonconformist Wales* (Cardiff: University of Wales Press, 2010).

of temperance or, in the mid-nineteenth century and in response to explosive claims in a government report that Welsh women were sexually and morally lax, on the theme of the Virtuous Woman.

The novels of Daniel Owen in the late nineteenth century and Kate Roberts's first collection of short stories published in 1925 were two watershed moments, with Saunders Lewis claiming that the short story in Welsh had 'taken a definite step into the world of artistic creation'.[8] Roberts was a freethinking individual, but even her stories deal with the matter of sex indirectly and arguably all the more finely for that. The lyrical opening sequence of one of her great novels *Traed Mewn Cyffion* [lit. Feet in Stocks, or Feet in Chains] (1934), for instance, opts for a subtle and coded way of telling the reader that her recently married protagonist has just become pregnant. Reticence in the treatment of sex and sexuality was perhaps unsurprising given the scandalised reaction to bolder representations. Prosser Rhys's treatment of the sexual development of a young man, including a (negative) reference to a same-sex experience, had scandalised the Eisteddfod in 1924. Though it won the highest honour, the Crown, the poem was not published again in his lifetime. In 1930, Saunders Lewis published the modernist novella *Monica*, full of brooding dark passion, in which the eponymous character's erotic fantasies and strong sexual desires are the focus of the story. Lewis appealed to the precedent of the hymn-writer William Williams Pantycelyn who had dramatically depicted the sexual nature of humanity in its many variations in *Bywyd a Marwolaeth Theomemphus* [The Life and Death of Theomemphus] (1764) and *Ductor Nuptiarum* (1777). In reminding readers that a writer as revered as Pantycelyn, whose hymns were sung in chapel every Sunday, had written about sex as part of life, Saunders Lewis hoped that this would lead the way to the theme being used more

---

[8] Cited in Stephens, *Cydymaith*, p. 681.

freely in poetry and fiction in Welsh. Indeed, in an analysis of Oscar Wilde, Lewis saw connections between sexual expression and creativity, remarking that 'The years of his intercourse with Alfred Douglas and with London "renters" were the years in which he wrote his brilliant comedies'.[9] Pennar Davies's direct story of same-sex desire, 'Y Dyn a'r Llygoden Fawr' [The Man and the Rat], was published in the journal *Heddiw* in 1941, but for the most part Lewis's hopes were not fulfilled until later in the century, and the word 'pechod' [sin] continued to be used as a synonym for sex.

Pockets of tolerance may have existed in some communities, as Daryl Leeworthy's *A Little Gay History of Wales* has shown, but for many, despite decriminalisation in 1967, the stigma of homosexuality (especially for gay men) continued across Wales and the UK. The AIDS crisis in the 1980s (addressed in John Sam Jones's 'Eucharist' (2003)) led to widespread fear and vilification of gay men, as well as further restrictive legislation by Margaret Thatcher's conservative government, including Section 28 of the Local Government Act (1988) prohibiting the 'promotion' of homosexuality in schools (as seen in 'The Wonder at Seal Cave'(2000)). By the 1990s, partly arising from the political activism born from protesting the poor Conservative response to the AIDS crisis, a more public and organised LGBTQ consciousness began to take shape in Wales.[10] The word 'queer' took on its current political and theoretical meanings; Stonewall Cymru was established in 2003; and the public

---

[9] Harri Pritchard Jones, trans., *Saunders Lewis: A presentation of his work* (Springfield: Illinois, Templegate Publishers, 1990), p. 202. The quote comes from Lewis's 1962 review of Wilde's letters entitled 'Forever Oscar'.
[10] LGBTQ political organisation in Wales goes back to the 1970s, but the 1990s is still a significant period of public political change. See Daryl Leeworthy, *A Little Gay History of Wales* (Cardiff: University of Wales Press, 2019).

imagination of Wales underwent a queering through twentieth- and twenty-first-century cultural industries, education reform, legal reform, and civic and national revitalisation. This history is not, however, simply a case of 'progression' from closet to pride parade. As seen in the later stories in this collection, this latter era of reform is not one of straightforward liberation or progress but increasing complexity and persistent challenges.

Queering Chronologies

While such historical and national contexts are instructive, one must be careful when placing queer texts within them or alongside them. Queer critical historians question whether or not sexual identities can be reliably recovered as we look to the past from our present political position. For instance, one might think of this collection as part of the work of queer 'recovery' of lives that have been lost, hidden and forgotten. This is very important work, but it is often understood in genealogical terms that are at odds with many queer experiences. The nation itself is generally understood in narrative terms, and the story of the nation is often tied to lineage and descent, which is exclusively understood in heterosexual and patriarchal conceptions of time, no less so in Wales' national anthem, 'Hen Wlad Fy Nhadau' [Old Land of My Fathers]. Such an uncovering of the queer past in and through the heteronormative ordering of national time risks reproducing that order.

A book like this one is part of that project of creating a common feeling for the queer Welsh experience, but must also be mindful of the limitations and respectful of the real barriers to conceiving such coherences. As Jeffrey Weeks—one of the most influential historians of sexuality, and a gay activist originally from the Rhondda—has explained:

Identities were important. But they were troubling, and they caused trouble, they disrupted things. We need them to give a sense of narrative continuity and ontological security. They provide meaning and support. They locate us in a world of varying possibilities. They help to get things done. But identities also had their downside: they were limiting, they fixed you, potentially trapped you, even the new identities that emerged in the wake of gay liberation. Identities were not enough – or perhaps they were too much.[11]

Weeks suggests that we must sometimes make the necessary error (what Richard Phillips calls 'strategic essentialism'[12]) of identification. That is, recovery (or looking back into the past to find and acknowledge queer sexualities) is important even at the risk of projecting contemporary identities into the past. These same contemporary identities, conversely, are limiting in the present: one comes out into an identity that makes sense within a dominant heteropatriarchal order. So, as Weeks argues, the task was not to 'celebrate, but to question, not to confirm a settled history but to problematize, not to systematize the past or order the present, but to unsettle it'.[13]

These questions pose problems for the anthologist. There seems to be no ideal way forward, so what compromises does one make in the 'strategic essentialism' of the editor's work? Each story speaks to particular literary, social, historical, political and

---

[11] Jeffrey Weeks, 'Making the Human Gesture: History, Sexuality and Social Justice', *History Workshop Journal*, Volume 70, Issue 1, Autumn 2010, 5–20, https://doi.org/10.1093/hwj/dbq019, p. 13.

[12] Richard Phillips, 'Histories of Sexuality and Imperialism: What's the Use?', *History Workshop Journal*, Volume 63, Issue 1, Spring 2007, 136–153, https://doi.org/10.1093/hwj/dbm004, p. 145.

[13] Weeks, 'Making the Human Gesture', p. 13.

ideological contexts, yet presenting the stories in an unfiltered chronological form might suggest traditions and identities where no such coherences existed. Similarly, grouping the stories by identities—such as gay men, lesbians and transgender—essentialises queer experiences and harks back to the efforts of Victorian sexologists to capture and contain sexual variation by taxonomy. To resolve this conflict between the need for historical reference and the dangers of suggesting limiting traditions and identities, this book dates all stories (and a list of stories in chronological order can be found at the back of the book for those who want it) but organises them in broad thematic terms. Within each theme, the stories are not presented in any chronological order, but with a view to highlighting dialogue across times and places and in the hopes that new and spontaneous connections can be made. We are well aware that these categories are arbitrary and limiting in their own ways. A story like Jane Edwards's 'Blind Dêt'/'Blind Date' (1976),[14] which is placed in 'Transformations', might just as easily be placed in 'Queer Children', as might Rhys Davies's 'Fear'. We placed 'Fear', perhaps provocatively, in 'Internationalisms', a section which could have included Pennar Davies's 'Y Dyn a'r Llygoden Fawr/The Man and the Rat' about a Russian scientist or Thomas Morris's 'all the boys', with its twist on the typical queer plot of going abroad to find sexual liberation. We might also have created other categories, such as 'Working-Class Stories' or 'Queer Artists', but at some point one must choose one's 'necessary errors' and hope for the best.

---

[14] This story was published in English translation in *The Penguin Book of Welsh Short Stories* ed. Alun Richards (1976). The Welsh original was published in a volume of short stories by Edwards, entitled *Blind Dêt* (Llandysul: Gomer, 1989).

Identities

Likewise, we have selected stories on the basis of the content rather than the sexual identities of the authors. A list of biographies that focus on LGBTQ identities in the context of this work might misleadingly create an artificial pantheon of historically representative figures that have been restored to some idealised and essentialised queer heritage. Moreover, can we use a set of historically shifting categories with any confidence, particularly if the people themselves didn't use them? Rhys Davies may have been 'out' to a knowing circle of friends, but can we state with any certainty that he identified as a 'gay man'? In 'Wigs, Costumes, Masks', for example, Mr. Simon has not been identified by the policemen of 1940s and 1950s London, not simply because Davies dared not speak his name in the repressive context of his time, but also because maybe Davies wasn't looking to establish that identity either. It might be more appropriate to see Mr Simon as a decentring figure that makes us less comfortable identifying sexualities of the past. Davies's contemporary, Glyn Jones, shares much of Rhys Davies's queered childhood experiences, as suggested in the long short story 'I Was Born in the Ystrad Valley' (1937) or his bildungsroman *Island of Apples* (1965), and Tony Brown has identified a sublimated homoeroticism in Jones's writing.[15] Nevertheless, Jones was married for sixty years to the same woman, although, only three years after his marriage, he was chafing against the constraints of middle-class domesticity.[16] Evidence of sexual identities, therefore, is ambiguous and

---

[15] Tony Brown, 'Glyn Jones and the Uncanny', in Katie Gramich (ed) *Almanac: Yearbook of Welsh Writing in English 12* (Cardigan: Parthian, 2008) 89–114.

[16] Tony Brown, 'Introduction', *The Collected Stories of Glyn Jones* (Cardiff: University of Wales Press, 1999), p. xxxix.

incomplete, so speculation about writers' sexualities is inevitably far less productive than appreciations of the queer texts they produced. That said, since we are writing in a context where queer lives are still not fully acknowledged, including the deliberate exclusion of same-sex relationships from biographies, it is worth sketching in something of the personal lives of some of the authors who appear in this anthology without presuming to impose categories upon them.

Amy Dillwyn (1845–1935) regarded her close friend as her wife and wrote openly about female same-sex desire in *A Burglary* (1883) and *Jill* (1884), and explored the power of cross-dressing in her first novel *The Rebecca Rioter* (1880). As a successful industrialist in later life, she considered herself a 'man of business' and was known for her mannish clothes and cigar. Bertha Thomas (1845–1918) was part of feminist and female-orientated literary circles in London, including the group associated with the 'Eminent Women' series (to which she contributed a volume on the cross-dressing, cigar-smoking George Sand). Thomas, who never married, was friends with Vernon Lee, Amy Levy (with whom she rode atop the London omnibuses as immortalised by Levy in the queer 'Ballade of an Omnibus'(1889)), and Helen Zimmern, with whom she shared a house in Canterbury. Margiad Evans (1909–1958) had a passionate sexual relationship with Ruth Farr, to whom—along with her beloved Professor (publisher Basil Blackwell)—she dedicated one of her journals. After her marriage, she and her husband kept up a friendship with Ruth. In Bloomsbury, Dorothy Edwards (1903–1934) lived for a time with David Garnett and his wife, with whom Margiad Evans was also friendly (although not during Edwards's time). Edwards maintained close relationships with women she met at university,[17] though her relationship with Kathleen Freeman, another author in this anthology, was bumpy. Kathleen Freeman (1897–1959) taught Edwards Greek at Cardiff University; as her academic senior and social superior (Freeman was very comfortably off while Edwards with only a widowed mother was always short of money), Freeman could exercise somewhat imperious authority. In literary terms, however, Edwards was easily her equal. Edwards's *Rhapsody* was published to acclaim in 1927, the year before Freeman's *The Intruder and other Stories*. Freeman lived with her life-long partner Dr. Liliane Clopet, a GP and author, until her death.[18]

Also making her mark in the twenties with modernist short fiction, in Welsh rather than English, was Kate Roberts (1891–1985). She was at the heart of the Welsh intelligentsia that was forging the new nationalist party—Plaid Cymru—and a new modernist literature. She married Morris T. Williams, the lover of Prosser Rhys, whose 1924 Eisteddfod poem 'Atgof' [Memory] had touched on same-sex desire. In a recent biography of Roberts, Alan Llwyd quotes from a letter of October 1926 in which Roberts recounts the powerful effect of an encounter with 'un o'r merched harddaf y disgynnodd fy llygaid arni erioed' [one of the most beautiful women I have ever set eyes upon].[19] This beguiling woman was the wife of a butcher with whom she stayed after giving a lecture in Pontardawe, and who the following morning kissed Roberts 'ar fy ngwefus' [on my lips]: 'Nid oedd

---

[17] Claire Flay, *Dorothy Edwards* (Cardiff: University of Wales Press, 2011), pp. 74–106.

[18] Deininger, Michelle and Claire Flay-Petty, 'University Connections and Professional Lives: S. Beryl Jones, Kathleen Freeman and Liliane Clopet', *New Welsh Reader*, 119 (December 2018), 29–37.

[19] Alan Llwyd, Kate: *Cofiant Kate Roberts 1891–1985* (Tal-y-Bont: Y Lolfa, 2011), p. 119.

dim a roes fwy o bleser imi. Os byth ysgrifennaf fy atgofion, bydd y weithred hon yno...' [Nothing has given me more pleasure. If I ever write my memoirs, this event will be in them...].[20] Llwyd sees this encounter as an influence on the short story 'Nadolig – Stori Dau Ffyddlondeb' (1929) ['Christmas – A story of two companions'] which is published in English translation in this volume. It was composed around the same time as Roberts's letter and in it Miss Davies bestows a similarly understated but momentous kiss. The story also, as Llwyd points out, explores the choice between same-sex love and conventional marriage which Prosser and Morris would both have to make.[21] Roberts later wrote about male same-sex ties that eclipse a heterosexual betrothal in *Tegwch y Bore* (1967).[22]

The freethinking writer and intellectual, Pennar Davies (1911–1996), also nurtured an intimate connection with a male friend, largely by letter. A theologian and Congregational Minister, Davies was married (with five children) to Rosemarie Wolff, a refugee from Nazi Germany who learned Welsh. As a doctoral student in the late 1930s at Yale University in America, he met and formed a close friendship with Clem C. Linnenberg who would go on to become a successful Washington economist. Linnenberg, whose wife also came from Germany, maintained a lifelong correspondence with Pennar and Rosemarie, sending regular gifts and generous donations to 'The House of Davies'.[23] The short story 'Y Dyn a'r Llygoden Mawr' ['The Man and the

---

[20] Cited in Llwyd, p. 120.

[21] Llwyd, p. 124.

[22] Katherine Mary [Kate] Crockett, 'Rhai Agweddau ar Rywioldeb yn Llenyddiaeth Gymraeg yr Ugeinfed Ganrif', Traethawd MPhil, Prifysgol Cymru, Aberystwyth (2000), pp. 46–48.

[23] National Library of Wales, Papurau [Papers of] Pennar Davies PD2/3 Llythyrau [Letters of] Clem C. Linnenberg [1960]–1988.

Rat'] (1941) was inspired by scientific experiments conducted at Yale while Davies and Linnenberg were students. In 1966 Pennar dedicated *Caregl Nwyf* [Chalice of Passion], in which 'Y Dyn a'r Llygoden Mawr' was collected for the first time, to 'Marianne a Clem Linnenberg, enaid hoff, cytûn' ['soulmate']. His title comes from a line in Dafydd ap Gwilym's poem 'Offeren y Llwyn': 'caregl nwyf a chariad' ['a chalice of passion and love'], while his dedication comes from a poem by R. Williams Parry that talks of walking the wooded path alone or with 'enaid hoff, cytûn', literally 'a special or favoured soul, in agreement'. Davies was a member of the freethinking Cadwgan group; his thinly veiled portrait of that group in the novel *Meibion Darogan* (1961) includes a portrayal of female same-sex desire.

Such visible and veiled forms of male bonding was one subject of Ken Etheridge's (1911–1981) art. His paintings show the influence of queer pornographic art of the 1950s, and his homoerotic 'Rugby Changing Room, Carmarthen' is on display at the World Rugby Museum in the south stand of Twickenham Stadium. As a playwright, artist and poet, he drew on Welsh mythology and symbolism to explore sexual identity in his public work, while his unpublished archives—from which the story included here is taken—show more directly the experience of being gay in a period when homosexuality was illegal.

We cannot, of course, know how any of these now deceased writers viewed their own sexualities at any one point in their lives, still less their changing sense of them over time. Nor can we say that all or any of the contemporary writers included in this anthology identify with the terms and categories that attempt to describe human sexuality currently in circulation. Mihangel Morgan, for instance, has questioned the usefulness of 'queer' for Welsh and Welsh language non-heteronormative experience:

When Queer Nation was formed [in North America] in the 1990s, its founders did not confer with the people of the world, and they did not ask the people of the Rhondda valley if they approved of it. The word 'queer' in South Wales is still an insult and hurtful; hardly anyone there knows that it has been 'reappropriated' by academics... The decision to use the term 'queer theory' was not arrived at by some kind of international democratic consensus; rather, it has been imposed on us through a form of imperialist, American linguistic annexation.[24]

The use of 'queer' has, perhaps, broken out of academic circles and into Welsh popular culture, as exemplified by well-established queer events, such as Aberystwyth's regular 'Aberration' nights, the presence of 'Queer Cymru' on Twitter and the regular Pride Cymru parade. In Welsh *cwiyr*—a homophone of queer which also neatly subverts the Welsh word for 'correct' (*cywir*)—is being adopted by some. But this is not to say that all have embraced the term 'queer'; it is still an uncomfortable term for many. We have used it here for its flexibility and its inherent resistance to taxonomies. Ultimately, while we recognise the value in making queer lives in history visible, we much prefer to let the stories themselves trouble and unsettle one's sense of the sexual past, present and future.

A Note on Form

The formal innovations of the short stories collected here range from a kind of unreliable realism to modernist experimentation,

---

[24] Mihangel Morgan, 'From Huw Arwystli to Siôn Eirion', in Huw Osborne (ed) *Queer Wales* (Cardiff: University of Wales Press, 2016), pp. 67–68.

magical realism and playful postmodernism. A large number of the stories date from the 1920s through to the 1950s, possibly reflecting both the significance of the modernist short story in Wales and the appetite amongst modernist writers to explore questions of sexuality.

The short story is often regarded as a characteristically modern genre with formal features that share many of the characteristic attributes of modernist writing in general, 'particularly the cultivation of paradox and ambiguity, and the fragmented view of identity'.[25] The stories of Glyn Jones, for example, convey a modernist surrealism that refuses a singular, authoritative, rational and external perspective. The lyricism of 'The Kiss' (1936) shifts perspectives in a sensuous and sensual symbolist abstraction. 'The Water Music' (1944) is told through a nearly epiphanic stream-of-consciousness, and both of these stories exemplify the 'inward turn' toward psychological realism. Kate Roberts, Margiad Evans and Rhys Davies write stories whose narrative voices succumb to the partial knowledge of their characters. The revelations, therefore, in such stories as 'Nadolig', 'A Modest Adornment' and 'The Romantic Policewoman' (1931) are never completely exposed, so readers must engage with these subjective experiences and push against the conventions that constrain the characters. In the same way that the techniques of modernist stories refuse 'an ordered approach to fiction and the hierarchical world-view it embodies',[26] these stories of paradoxical repression and revelation challenge master narratives that limit the range of sexual and national belonging. As Adrian Hunter has claimed,

---

[25] Dominic Head, *The Modernist Short Story: A Study of Theory and Practice* (Cambridge: University Press, 1992), p. 185.
[26] Head, p. 186.

The interrogative short story's 'unfinished' economy, its failure literally to express, to extend itself to definition, determination or disclosure, becomes, under the rubric of a theory of 'minor' literature, a positive aversion to the entailment of 'power and law' that defines the 'major' literature.[27]

In Jorge Sacido's words, the short story often conveys the 'subject's experience of a desire which ideology cannot accommodate'.[28]

A second 'wave' of queer short stories at the turn of the century and into the twenty-first arguably corresponds with a surge in confidence and desire to articulate multiple Welsh identities in post-devolution Wales. This second wave varies considerably in form: while 'modern' elements of form and technique persist into the later twentieth and twenty-first centuries, the later stories in this collection are more likely to exhibit a postmodernist play and a critique of the stability of such notions as identity, gender, nation, language, as well as the narratives that uphold them. For example, the future tense point of view sustained throughout Morris's 'all the boys' (2015) gives one the uncertain impression of a possible future outing rather than a confirmed past action. The 'end' of the story is held in abeyance, and one is perhaps doubtful that 'when they cross the Severn Bridge, and see the *Welcome to Wales* sign, all the boys will cheer'. Kate North's 'The Largest Bull in Europe' (2014) has an 'unfinished' ambiguity and symbolist suggestiveness that sits comfortably within the modernist tradition; however, its queer tourist voyeurism stands at an ironic distance from the privileged masculine gaze that dominated ethnographic perspectives in the

---

[27] Cited in Jorge Sacido, *'Modernism, Postmodernism, and the Short Story'* (Amsterdam and New York: Rodopi, 2012), p. 20.
[28] Sacido, p. 7.

early twentieth century. Similarly, Lewis Davies's 'The Stars Above the City' (2008) presents a decentred queer Welsh take on orientalised gay desires associated with earlier queer figures like Andre Gide.

Perhaps the most self-consciously postmodern story in the collection is Mihangel Morgan's ambiguously titled story 'Cariad Sy'n Aros yn Unig' (1996), translated by the author as 'Love Alone Remains'. Presented as reconstructed from Welsh-language letters sent to the author by an Austrian student, and here rendered in English, the story collapses distinctions between fiction and reality, language and experience. The fragments that make up the story have been curated by the silent participant in the correspondence. The sense of curated completion is in tension with the sense of absence and incompletion, so we are left in the fraught spaces in which language only provisionally makes sense of the world (and the nation) and our places in it.

The formal varieties of these stories—whether modern, postmodern, realist or surrealist—address several common themes that we hope will foster meaningful dialogue across the times, places and 'identities' of queer Wales.

Love, Loss, and the Art of Failure

The stories in this first section deal with ways of loving, making contact, and desiring in and alongside queer relationships. Because so many of these connections are made in contexts that are hostile to their expression, many of them are characterised by loss or the fear of loss. The defiant isolation of lovers is matched by trauma, denial, exile and failure. For example, Stevie Davies's 'Red Earth, Cyrenaica' (2018) is a story of repression, trauma and loss, but it is also a love story in both the past and the present in which the wife's love of her husband is more deeply touching for her queer embrace of her husband's pain.

So loss and failure should not be understood in straightforwardly negative terms. When so much of the queer experience is marked by 'failures' to succeed within conditions that are hostile to queer love and queer life, 'failure' may be preferable to success:

> Under certain circumstances failing, losing, forgetting, unmaking, undoing, unbecoming, not knowing may in fact offer more creative, more cooperative, more surprising ways of being in the world. Failing is something that queers do and have always done exceptionally well; for queers, failure ... can stand in contrast to the grim scenarios of success that depend on 'trying and trying again.'[29]

The reward of failure, according to Halberstam, is the escape from 'the punishing norms that discipline behaviour and manage human development with the goal of delivering us from unruly childhoods to orderly and predictable adulthoods.'[30] We see this failure in Kate Roberts's 'Nadolig'/'Christmas', in which Olwen's experience of queer intimacy transforms her impending marriage into a 'grim scenario of success' which will happen *to* her rather than be something she willingly does. When she finally hears her intended husband's shout, 'she felt something like a knife going through her soul'.

Similarly, Glyn Jones's stories present experiences of oddness that defamiliarise the world so that '[e]veryday things are registered, especially in moments of emotion, as strange, as

---

[29] Judith Halberstam, *The Queer Art of Failure* (Durham and London: Duke University Press, 2011), pp. 2–3.
[30] Halberstam, p. 3.

other'.[31] This oddness, again echoing O'Connor, often expresses 'alienation from environment and community',[32] which registers a discontinuity with the dominant forms of life surrounding his isolated characters. In 'Knowledge,' (1937) for instance, an odd and distant collier harbours a displaced intimate sensual knowledge that is suggestive of unspoken desires. In 'The Kiss,' two loving brothers are unafraid to mingle wounding with sensual desire. In a kind of celebratory religious sublimation, the brothers' queer touch bears witness to the shared suffering of industrial labour.[33]

The celebration or moment of articulation of love is contained within several of the stories centred on loss and grief. The opening story, 'Y Trysor'/'The Treasure' (1972), charts a series of 'failures' and losses: the desertion of a cruel husband (a shock to the community, a welcome release for his wife), Jane Rhisiart's realisation that all of her children are selfish, and finally her grief at the great loss of her friend, Martha Huws. This final loss, which she understands as 'the first great sorrow of her life', is also a celebration of 'the treasure' of their intense twelve-year bond. Similarly, death and a possible betrayal of loyalty is the vehicle that provides the final epiphany of a 'secret but weary fidelity' in 'A Modest Adornment' by Margiad Evans.

Kathleen Freeman uses adversity to bring together the protagonists of 'The Fraying of the Thread' (1926). In this story, a young woman embarks on a test of her own faithfulness by wooing a woman driven to the edge of sanity by previous (self-imposed) losses. Freeman's stories engage with ethical and moral standards, outlining a set of personal and spiritual behaviours

---

[31] Brown, 'Introduction', p. lix.
[32] Ibid.
[33] Brown, 'Introduction', p. lii.

worthy of uncompromisingly intellectual, unconventional young women. In this way, her stories have a somewhat Victorian bent, though their structure is modern.

Death and betrayal are the fulcrum on which two contemporary stories by David Llewellyn and Crystal Jeans pivot, though in unexpected ways which are ultimately celebrations of love more than loss. In 'After Steve', Steve's towering presence at the heart of a queer family continues to reverberate after his premature death, so much so that his diminutive coffin is a surprise. Crystal Jeans's contemporary 'Go Play with Cucumbers' displays her typically subversive humour, taking a lesbian cliché and turning it on its head, though Lou's extreme response to the consumption of cucumbers can be read in more obviously Freudian ways.

The final two stories are about getting drunk and not quite coming out. Published nearly fifty years apart, Thomas Morris's 'all the boys' (2015) follows a rowdy stag do to Dublin, while Humphreys's 'A Cheerful Note' (1968) takes us on a trip from an unorthodox interview in which the men are asked to parade their heterosexual prowess to the multicultural environs of Cardiff docks (expressed in the racialised language of the day). It is a geographical remove reminiscent of *Dorian Gray*, in which the ethnically diverse space of the docks is connected with an exotic cocktail of sex, intoxication and danger. In Humphreys, the energy of the docks allows the queer protagonist briefly to upend the heteronormative hierarchy which has defined the evening.

Disorderly Women

The women in these stories are disruptive, disorderly, and often dangerous to the patriarchal social order. Detached, powerful (and occasionally desperate) women invade heterosexual marriages and fantasies proving to make far more attractive partners than the blinkered, arrogant and sometimes violent men who consider themselves the centre of the world.

Jane Edwards's 'Gwahanu'/'Parting' (1980), Rhys Davies's 'The Doctor's Wife' (1930), and Siân James's 'A Most Moderate Lust' (1996) all portray husbands whose wives are moving away from the heterosexual domestic order into alternative relations between women. In 'The Doctor's Wife', the husband fails to see and recognise the queer relationship before his eyes, demonstrating how romantic and sexual relationships between women were socially 'ghosted', in Terry Castle's sense of being only partially perceived, seen but misrecognised, haunting and troubling the security of the heterosexual home.[34] Davies's use of harp music in 'The Doctor's Wife' to symbolise female sexuality (which is contrasted to the 'swelling' phallic masculine music of male-voice choirs), is similar to Dorothy Edwards's expression of queer desire through music in 'The Conquered' (1927). The latter story is told from the perspective of a bookish young man with an aesthetic view of the world returning to the country home of relations on the borders of Wales. Here, he encounters 'a very charming Welsh lady', Gwyneth, with whom his youngest cousin Ruthie has a subtle intimacy. Ruthie, who used to be 'something of a tomboy', clings close to Gwyneth and slyly expresses her love by singing Brahms' *An Die Nachtigall*. The narrator disapproves of the choice of music, but in response he waits for a nightingale in a wood near Gwyneth's house, fantasising about her appearance, thus making clear the meaning of Ruthie's song. Gwyneth favours more lively tunes, singing Schumann's *Der Nussbaum*, a song about walnut blossom mimicking a lover's kiss and a maiden yearning for a declaration

---

[34] Terry Castle, *The Apparitional Lesbian: Female Homosexuality and Modern Culture* (New York: Columbia University Press, 1993).

of love. Ruthie responds by planting a nut tree outside Gwyneth's window, to the bafflement of the narrator. This may well be an allusion to a Bavarian – and wider European – tradition of 'Liebesmaie' in which a May Tree (usually a birch) is left outside a woman's window as a sign of love and devotion. The narrator thus participates in a queer courtship that he never quite perceives, leaving one wondering whether he knows just what is it that he 'wanted to say'.

In Siân James's 'A Most Moderate Lust', a man's mistress and wife grow closer as he grows farther from both. The contact between the two women destabilises the mistress/wife compartmentalisation through which he maintains his definitions of masculinity. When the two women step out of his categories, he is no longer able to see them as complete people, telling himself that they 'don't make up one real woman between them'. As the romantic dynamics in the house slip out of his control, he thinks 'of the time when he had – naturally enough – imagined Rosamund, small and lively, with curly black hair and round green eyes, to be the complete antithesis of his cool and beautiful wife'. Ultimately, he cannot perceive what 'lusts' are satisfied. In 'Parting', on the other hand, the husband thinks too much about the possible intimacies between his wife and her best friend, though he struggles to bring himself to say – perhaps even to think – what, exactly, he suspects. He knows that 'he hated having a drunken woman in his bed', but the obsessive jealousy that mounts as he loses his place in the imagined order of his home is the most destructive force in the story.

In 'The Romantic Policewoman', a gendered domesticity is the fantasy of the queer figure herself. So enmeshed is she in policed gender codes, she deceives herself into viewing her predatory and controlling behaviour as moral rescue. But she, too, is finally far more disorderly than she purports to be, and her intervention briefly disrupts the latent violence that underpins the relationship between Kathleen and Fred Collins.

Transformations

This section deals with the construction and transformation of gender identities. Concerned with clothing, performance, costume, disguise, and embodiment, these stories remind us that '*transvestism is a space of possibility structuring and confounding culture*: the disruptive element that intervenes, not just a category crisis of male and female, but the crisis of category itself'.[35] This category crisis is seen in one of the principal Welsh figures of transformative embodiment, Jan Morris. Morris, whose memoir *Conundrum* (1974) remains among the most important narratives of transsexual experience, is particularly relevant here for the ways in which she figures this transformation in national terms, aligning her gender reassignment with Welsh belonging. The land and myths of Wales, she says, were more accommodating to her changeling experience. In one scene, while she is well into her hormone therapy but has not yet undergone sexual reassignment surgery, she enters the waters of The Glyders and stands 'for a moment like a figure of mythology, monstrous or divine' before she falls 'into the pool's embrace'. Sometimes, she thinks 'the fable might well end there, as it would in the best Welsh fairy tales'.[36] The liquid indeterminacy of landscape and legend accommodates her uncategorised body within what she elsewhere calls 'The Matter of Wales'. In one way or another, all of the stories in this section disrupt and intervene in this 'matter.'

One such national embodiment is found in Jon Gower's

---

[35] Marjorie Garber, *Vested Interests: Cross-dressing & Cultural Anxiety* (London: Routledge, 1992), p. 17 (italics in the original).
[36] Jan Morris, *Conundrum* (London: Penguin, 1988), p. 105.

playful revision of Welsh rugby masculinity in 'A Cut Below.' Rugby, long associated with 'boozy machismo and sublimated homoeroticism',[37] is celebrated in this story for its camp theatricality. The hyperbole of the narrative voice recalls the fireworks, the sparkly face-paint and costumes of the fans, the ritual songs, which are as much part of the national game as what happens on the pitch. The protagonist, Keiron, is the site at which spectacle and sport come into the most destabilising focus. Keiron is a mixture of celebrity mystique, commodity fetishism, and mythic transcendence of the every-day. Before his surgeries, he is a mercurial figure of fame, media representation, cosmetics, and athletic fantasy, ambiguously poised between embodiment and disembodiment:

> Keiron was the embodiment of rugby skill, powered by huge heart and guts, guided by innate intuition and blessed with an ability to read a game like a Gareth, a Barry, or Shane... Keiron was a shape-changer, able to turn from corporeal rugby player to untackleable wraith in a magic breath. An alchemist, too, able to transmute the meatiness of a defense into a whisp of smoke.

In this passage and throughout the story, the embodied experience is changeful and immaterial. However, if the story collapses distinctions between sex, gender and sexuality, it does so while admitting the lived importance of embodied gender. The final arbitrary misidentification of '*his* proper gender' suggests that Keiron is on the cusp of achieving a body that will, when she wakes, be realised.

The cultural authority of Mihangel Morgan's Welsh bard in

---

[37] Mike Parker, *On the Red Hill* (London: William Heinemann, 2019), p. 257.

'Postio Llythr'/'Posting a Letter' (2012) gets a similarly humorous treatment. This story, too, however, has a much more serious intent in redressing the oppressive masculinity within which its accommodating narrator struggles. The story is as much about gender and power as it is about the need for visibility, and both characters may in fact be finding a way out from under the authority of The Bard. Jane Edwards's 'Blind Dêt'/'Blind Date' deals with embodiment and the construction of gender in the context of class. The men the narrator desires are dreamy abstractions of class mobility, and she seems far more interested in women's cosmetics and clothing than she is in sexual intercourse. She is disgusted by both her mother's breast-feeding body and the rural body of her date, but also disappointed by the ill-fitting costume of feminine respectability – the choir dress – in which she dresses up. Her dream of romantic social mobility is also a longing to escape this world of base heterosexual embodiment, despite her (revealing) anxiety over unstable gender categories.

Amy Dillwyn's 'One June Night' is similarly concerned with the social scripts and signs which govern gender identity. The opening reads like a set of stage directions, inviting us to read each prop for symbolic significance. The governess flicks through the fashion pages of *Queen,* while the pupil 'is absorbed in one of Mayne Reid's novels', most of which were adventure stories set in the American 'wilderness'. Rejecting her governess's attempts to socialise her into a superficial femininity, Margery claims a connection with the natural world, which is a masculine space in this story. On hearing some magpies chatter after dark, Margery wonders 'whatever that can mean', to which Miss Stokes retorts 'There's no meaning in all the silly noises birds are always making'. Margery puts her firmly in her place, but the central argument about 'meaning' in the story is over gender (as understood within a specific class context). For Miss Stokes it is 'unheard of' for a girl, still less 'a *lady*', to behave like 'a boy' or to do the work of 'a [game]keeper'. Margery reads her position differently; she is her father's representative as the only member of the family in the house. While her governess regards it a great misfortune that her charge is 'rough, wanting in all gentle and refined ideas, hard, and unfeeling', the story shows Margery to be anything but wanting in feeling. Her compassion reaches across the barriers of class to leave a lasting moral impression on the poacher she has caught, thus demanding a reappraisal of 'the attributes of a true lady'.

Likewise, the legibility, commodification and provisionality of gender are central in Rhys Davies's 'Nightgown' (1942), in which the central character's body is an embattled site of class-based constructions of femininity and masculinity. Dressed and increasingly behaving like one of the monosyllabic colliers she tends, a miner's wife is systematically worn out by an industrial machine that eventually leaves her collapsed and black-faced, like a victim of a mining accident. Her demise is brought on in part by starvation in the cause of purchasing a pristine white satin nightgown she has seen in the window of a drapers' shop. It is uncertain whether it symbolises luxury or femininity, and, of course, the two are closely connected.

A rather different kind of dashing, romantic female masculinity shored up by class privilege is portrayed in 'The Conquest, or a Mail Companion'. Yet another story in which conquest and mistaken assumptions are at the fore, the title of the story is a pun on the apparently 'male' companion on the coach named 'Conquest'. While the end of the story apparently defuses the amorous fantasies of the young girl, she becomes a devoted servant and permanent resident in the house of the female 'hero' with the 'free voice' who first 'rescue[d]' her from the fate of governess.

'Wigs, Costumes, Masks' is set in London when 'the queer was a dangerous incursion into the defining space of Britishness'.[38] This incursion led 'to a culture of knowingness, emphasizing the practical utility of beat officers' immersion in the realities of metropolitan lowlife, crime and vice.'[39] The two detectives investigate Mr. Simon, a costume dealer whom they suspect of some undisclosed crime and whose shop sits in 'a district devoted to the night entertainment of the flesh'. Mr. Simon ultimately eludes their gaze through a fantastic display of theatrical illusion that travesties their rational fact-finding need to place Mr. Simon within clear and criminalised sexual categories.

Theatricality again comes to the fore in 'My Lord's Revenge.' Appearing in *The Weekly Mail* of 1890, this story portrays the *fin de siècle* conflict between, on the one hand, nineteenth-century gender as defined within stable notions of public and private and, on the other hand, sexual, racial, commercial, and aesthetic challenges to that stability. The story revolves around the relationship between Lady Anthony Hopeland, the wife of a Conservative Lord in elected office, and Girly Grey, a beautiful and effeminate actor with a flair for cross-dressing. Girly's threat is evident in his influence on women, for 'he had been the favourite of several posturing, lolloping, Liberty-silked damsels'. The intersection between gender, race, commerce, and aesthetics is signalled by the reference to Liberty silk, which was at the time cashing in on exotic eastern fabrics and designs while collaborating with members of the Arts-and-Crafts movement and figures in the theatre world.[40] Lady Anthony plays 'the boy'

---

[38] Matt Houlbrook, *Queer London: Perils and Pleasures in the Sexual Metropolis, 1918–1957* (Chicago: University of Chicago Press, 2006), p. 24.
[39] Houlbrook, p. 26.
[40] Geoffrey Squire, "E. W. Godwin and the House of Liberty," *Costume* 34.1, (January 2000): 81–99.

to Girly Grey in their quasi-theatrical liaisons, until Lord Anthony eventually returns to put 'his house in order' with the help of his friend His Excellency Kami Pasha. The men hide behind a curtain to witness the gender-inverted playmaking, and Girly (whose gender is never directly redefined) is punished by being sold to Kami Pasha for his Harem in Cairo. This last act of colonialist containment reasserts British patriarchal mastery while simultaneously exiling sexual deviance into the relative safety of exotic orientalist eroticisms. However, like many stories that try to reassert traditional gender categories, this one, too, cannot entirely ease the anxieties it raises. The masquerading Girly Grey is never unmasked; rather, he recedes behind the further mysteries of both the Harem veil and commodity fetishism. This fetishised veil simultaneously reveals and conceals the orientalist fantasies upon which Lord Anthony's equally masquerading performance of his public and domestic power is staged.

The final story in this section, 'The Dead Bear' by Crystal Jeans, sends up the stereotype of the murderous lesbian. In a plot which brings to mind Rhys Davies's novel *Nobody Answered the Bell* (1971) in which two lesbians keep the body of a murdered stepmother in an attic, 'The Dead Bear' combines knowing melodrama – 'Nobody does drama like a lesbian' – with the acutely observed materiality of an early-morning estate after a night getting drunk: 'I head down the path slowly, toward the garage, placing my bare feet down carefully like a blind woman in case I step on glass or shit or slugs.'

Hauntings and other Queer Fancies

The stories in this section exploit the generic strangeness of the gothic, fantasy and science fiction. The gothic has a well-established connection with sexual otherness and queerness, and early gothic writing helped to shape the way we think about sexuality. It is a genre of fear, desire and excess that delights in the uncanny discomfort of crossing the borders between supposedly stable binary opposites. George Haggerty explains that 'the cult of gothic fiction reached its apex at the very moment when gender and sexuality were beginning to be codified for modern culture. In fact, gothic fiction offered a testing ground for many unauthorized genders and sexualities.'[41] The spectral, disembodied, and apparitional have provided ways of writing about same-sex affinities while keeping physical consummation of these desires obscure and immaterial. These spectral affinities offer queer desire as a possibility tantalisingly in view but as yet unrealised. In 'Miss Potts and Music' (1948) by Margiad Evans, the narrator is haunted by the image of a young girl. Constance Potts' gift for music (an artform Margiad Evans saw an articulation of the spirit) breaks through physical and social barriers to touch the narrator like some 'spirit colour'. Ghosts and premonitions bring women together in one of Evans's previously unpublished stories, 'The Haunted Window' (1953) and likewise in Bertha Thomas's 'A House that Was' (1912). In both, the imminence of death provides the impetus for intimacy, while a ghostly image – the beautiful portrait of a dead sister in Thomas and a grotesque picture of sickness in Evans – provides a connecting point within an erotic triangle. Ghostly, artistic collaboration confirms the intimacy between two writers in 'The Collaborators'. The men who share 'a subtle and mysterious aura of mutual attraction, when the world would have looked for a wave of mutual repulsion' find a fraught communion through art and death and through success that is

---

[41] George E. Haggerty, *Queer Gothic* (Urbana: University of Illinois, 2006), p. 2.

also failure. The ghostliness of their bachelor affections is inevitable and impossible, and the double-entendre of the title conveys the criminality from which their death-driven creative consummation both escapes and derives.

Other stories of fantasy, surrealism, magic realism, and dystopian science fiction exploit these genres' tendency to challenge the assumptions of normative 'reality'. In Rosemary Jackson's terms, these stories expose 'the basis upon which cultural order rests'; they open up 'on to disorder, on to illegality, on to that which lies outside the law, that which is outside the dominant value systems' to trace 'the unsaid and the unseen of culture: that which has been silenced, made invisible, covered over and made "absent"'.[42] Pennar Davies's 'Y Dyn a'r Llygoden Fawr' ['The Man and the Rat'] presents a compelling yet troubling portrait of a Nietzschean 'Übermensch'. Commonly translated as 'superman' and associated with eugenicist and fascist strains of thought as suggested in Davies's story, Übermensch also means 'beyond human'. Davies's pairing of his arrogant yet vulnerable scientist with the cleverest lab rat in a narrative that alternates between their first-'person' perspectives, is a comic twist on this, as is the Rat's belief that he is being controlled by entities beyond his understanding. Of course he is, but his confidence that some higher force will rescue him contributes to his final downfall.

Ken Etheridge's 'Nobody Dies... Nobody Lives...' (c. 1950s) contrasts a sterile future world of health and perfection – 'built on the slopes of the highest mountains in the west' – with the vitality of a radical perversion and obscenity. In this

---

[42] Rosemary Jackson, *Fantasy: The Literature of Subversion* (London: Methuen, 1981), p. 4.

questionable utopia, 'the effetism of incurable cancers, which men tried to palliate with obscenities and perversities', have been eradicated, and the 'weak, the perverted, the criminal were not allowed to breed'. The protagonist is queer by virtue of the fact that he is a carrier of just this kind of life-threatening disease, a disease that forces the re-embodiment of the community. In one scene, he encounters beautiful bodies trapped in an ageless, unregenerative heterosexuality in which the dangers of an unpredictable and therefore monstrous future have been eradicated along with the possibility of children and new life. This monstrosity is figured vividly on the mountain where the elderly who cannot let go of the past stand numbed by old pop songs. They are surrounded by a frieze of wild, chaotic sensuality, crossing boundaries of male and female human and animal bodies with orifices confused between 'mouths, nostrils, eyes, and vaginas'. The imagery suggests Etheridge's paintings of the stories of the Mabinogion with their magical transformations. In the end, the protagonist's contamination brings death and therefore life – his perverse criminal corruption becomes the source of life for the young women who feel a 'strange stirring in their bodies' and the young men who 'moved among them, embracing and laughing and touching'. The protagonist's difference forces 'a future that opens out, rather than forecloses, possibilities for becoming real, for mattering in the world.'[43]

In John Sam Jones's 'The Fishboys of Vernazza,' (2003) the sexualising and exoticising gaze of the touring lovers takes a surreal turn as they notice mermen painted on the rocks and

---

[43] Pearson, Wendy Gay, Veronica Hollinger, and Joan Gordon, *Queer Universes: Sexualities in Science Fiction* (Liverpool: University Press, 2008), p.5.

reproduced on rings worn by the handsome young men attending to their needs. The image relates to a local legend: 'when the sea is *tempestoso*, the fishboys come into the village through the *grotto*, and take away... how you say?... They take away the bad boys'. When they ask how bad a boy must be to be charmed away, they are told 'Bad enough that... *lui è desiderabile*'. They soon notice that the young men they desire have discreet gills behind their ears, and the story ends with the entrance of 'the local transvestite' whose black lace panties are 'too skimpy to hide her fishy tail'. This fantasy is played out against the more mundane emotional background of the two lovers' relationship, which is troubled by two irreconcilable visions of gay intimacy. At the end of the story, they begin to trade perceptions but still move in opposite directions. The barriers to a shared life together at home are contrasted to the shape-changing fluidity of the fishboys, which may be nothing more than a reflection of their own desire for a connection that is manageable only when they are away travelling in erotic-exotic landscapes of queer possibility.

Queer Children

This section contains stories of childhood, youth, coming-of-age, sexual awakening, and gender and sexual formation. Queer theorists of childhood like Lee Edelman and Kathryn Bond Stockton have argued that the idea of the child has been burdened with too much meaning as a figure of idealised past innocence, future hope, and developmental normativity.[44] However, stories of childhood lead one backwards from

---

[44] Kathryn Bond Stockton, *The Queer Child, or Growing Sideways in the Twentieth Century* (Durham: Duke University Press 2009); Lee Edelman, *No Future: Queer Theory and the Death Drive* (Durham: Duke University Press, 2004).

adulthood into a remembered strangeness, a state of being before words such as 'gay' or 'straight' had particular meaning.[45] Stockton's description of the fantasy of childhood applies well to these returns to childhood perspectives and the queer possibilities that these returns open up. She asserts that, despite efforts to render the child simple, innocent, pure, and utterly knowable,

> the child has gotten thick with complication. Even as an idea. In fact, the very moves to free the child from density – to make it distant from adulthood – have only made it stranger, more fundamentally foreign, to adults. Innocence is queerer than we ever thought it could be. And then there are the bodies (of children) that must live inside the figure of the child. Given that children don't know this child, surely not as we do, though they move inside it, life inside this membrane is largely available to adults as memory – what can I remember of what I thought I was? – and takes us back in circles to our fantasies (of our memories).[46]

The unrecoverable recovery of childhood in these stories unravels the arbitrary progression toward heteronormativity. In 'The Water Music', Glyn Jones's surreal representation of childhood is conveyed in the immediacy of the present tense, indifferent to the distance in time between the author's writerly sophistication and the child's sensuous experience. Removed from the patterns of the town and the ministrations of adults, the child's imagination swims through a world of boyish play that is indifferent to the boundaries between bodies, animals, nature, and genders. One boy stands 'tall and lovely-limbed... garlanded

---

[45] Stockton, *The Queer Child*, pp. 2, 15.
[46] Stockton, p. 6.

and naked in a dance-dress of sunlight flimsy-patterned with transparent foliage'. Another is as 'beautiful as Sande or some musk-scented princess'. The act of diving is more than a rite of passage or entrance into the brave world of boyish play; it is an act of praise for this crossing of a threshold into ever more fluid, various, and excessive realms of being. Other unruly children are found in Siân James's 'Strawberry Cream' (1997) and Deborah Kay Davies's 'Kissing Nina' (2008). In James's story, the eleven-year-old girl's sexual hungers belie the supposed innocence of children who should have a passion for nothing more than chocolate. The narrator's return to this unforgettable memory reverses the not-yet-straight narrative of child development. Similarly, in 'Kissing Nina', Grace's supposedly more appropriate heterosexual growth is aggressively pushed away. Grace's memory is suspended in the stillness and darkness of her winter kissing of Nina and resists the sexual awakening of spring romance with a boy. In each of the stories in this section, then, the queer child offers other ways of growing up alongside normative patterns and formations of identity.

Internationalisms

This last section takes queer Wales into a wider national and cosmopolitan sphere, where the queer square mile intersects with wider racial, national, ethnic and linguistic perspectives. As Welsh nationhood must be understood in concert with more hybrid, diverse, and global identities, queer Welsh identities occupy ambivalent positions between home and away.

In Aled Islwyn's 'Muscles Came Easy', queerness requires exile and a break from the Welsh past. His queer Wales is a site of irreconcilable trauma, a trauma that seeks no healing incorporation into the nation he once embodied. Lewis Davies's 'The Stars Above the City' also relocates queer desire away from

Wales, which is the site of a failed relationship. The protagonist travels through the multicultural landscape of Morocco while indulging a frustrated and unfulfilling erotic tourism. The story engages colonial exoticism and the history of the Orient as a locale for the projection of forbidden sexualities onto the 'foreign'. The complexities of these exchanges encompass both colonial power and the creation of intimate connections across difference.[47]

This erotic tourism is phobically imported 'home' in Rhys Davies's 'Fear' (1949), published two years after Indian independence, and set on a train to Newport. In one of Davies's most racially perceptive stories, he exposes the fragility of the colonial gaze in the boy's homophobic racialisation of the oriental other. In Mihangel Morgan's 'Cariad Sy'n Aros yn Unig'/'Love Alone Remains,' however, a queer cosmopolitanism crosses nations and languages to make Wales the receptive centre of corresponding cultures. This fragmentary epistolary story challenges narrative coherence while thinking about the nature of story, literature, language, nation and endings. The story carefully works through the development of a queer consciousness in the context of repressive governments, AIDS, and homophobic violence, while also thinking of Wales in relation to other colonial experiences. Its references to the rise of fascism in Europe speak to other stories, such as Pennar Davies's story of 1941, 'The Man and the Rat'. Taken together, the stories in this section place Wales within an international queer hybridity in which sexual identifications expose the limitations and possibilities of national and transnational ones.

---

[47] Jarrod Hayes, *Queer Nations: Marginal Sexualities in the Maghreb* (Chicago: University of Chicago Press, 2000), pp. 23–49.

Parting Words

The stories in this anthology speak to each other in far more ways than we have indicated here, both within and across the sections into which they have been arranged. Though we believe that groups and pairs of stories speak to each other in the order in which they are presented, we hope readers will find their own sparks and echoes in the forms and themes of this wide, yet far from exhaustive, selection of queer short stories from Wales.

LOVE, LOSS, AND
THE ART OF FAILURE

THE TREASURE
(1972)
Kate Roberts
translated by Joseph P. Clancy

For the fourth time in her life Jane Rhisiart was trying to put the events of that life in their proper place. As she was seventy-two years old, there was more of it to be set in place by this time, more events and persons to be moved and distinguished and classified.

The first time she had stopped to reflect on her life was when she was thirty-five years old, the day after Rolant, her husband, left her, an event that gave a shock to the whole district, but not to her. When Rolant disappeared with his wages one Friday pay night, it wasn't a great surprise to her. She was a woman with eyes to see, but with lips to shut tight lest her tongue talk to everybody indiscriminately. Because of her romantic nature, it's true that she took time to see, but when she saw, she saw more clearly than any realist. That's why her husband's disappearance gave more of a shock to the district than to her. That's also why she didn't do anything to try and find him, or try to get anything to support her. She'd rather work ten times harder than before, even, than suffer the quiet, provoking cruelty she'd been suffering from Rolant for years. Some of his fellow-quarrymen knew of some of this cruelty; it was impossible for his partners, and through them, their wives, not to know that Rolant kept back an unreasonable portion of his wages.

In this crisis which was very far away by this time, she had the sympathy of the district, but she didn't want it. She decided to keep on with the smallholding without asking for help from the parish or anyone else to raise her three children. That wasn't easy, not because of the constant battle against poverty – a person often finds peace of mind in poverty – but because Ann, the oldest child, was old enough at twelve to realise her loss after her father's disappearance, since she was his favourite, and had many times been used by him as a weapon against his wife. The boy, Wiliam, who was her favourite, was ten at the time, and Alis, six, wasn't old enough to realise things.

The second time she sat down to meditate on her life was twenty years later, with her children all married, and herself forced to realise that each one of them had disappointed her through their selfishness. Not one of them ever made a gesture to give her any financial help, which they could easily have done. But it wasn't that which had brought her disappointment, but their ungrateful attitude of taking and accepting everything as if she had money for them and not the other way round. Not one of them, not even Wiliam, showed a single sign of thanks or of appreciation. Unfortunately, the three of them were living close enough to visit her every day, and they'd taken advantage of that to pluck her feathers. Taking her butter and her eggs and sometimes paying for them, and more often forgetting to pay on purpose. And her, because of that, forced to ask her customers to look for butter somewhere else. She'd been able to get along better when they were little, than when they'd married and had homes of their own. Not one of them or the in-laws would offer her a helping hand either, but when they had need of help, to her they'd come, and for years she had been blind enough to give it.

But she had a strong and healthy body, a great help in nourishing independence of spirit.

The third time she took a picture of her life was five years later, just after she moved from the smallholding to a little cottage in the village, a few months after she'd become friends with Martha Huws; she was sixty years old at that time. She'd been completely disillusioned about her children by then; she saw that there was no point in holding on to the farm to feed them and their children, and bear their quarrelling and their envy of each other. She saw that she could be fully as well off on ten shillings a week in an unpropertied house, and she was strong enough to go out to work if there were need. So completely had she been disillusioned that she wasn't deceived by Wiliam, who tried to persuade her to invest the money from the cattle and the stock in something he could recommend. She kept her own counsel, and put the money in the bank, after using enough of it to make her cottage cosy.

And here she was today, at seventy-two, trying for the fourth time to set the events of her life in place and in their proper light, and doing it with a heavy and sorrowful heart; not in bitterness like the former times. She was doing it in a very strange place, at the seaside, the day of the Sunday School trip. A fortnight ago Martha Huws, her friend for the past twelve years, had died; and this time her grief was so great that she didn't know how to put her life back together and begin again. Indeed, this was the first deep sorrow of her life.

She'd become friendly with Martha Huws a few months before leaving the farm; it was the desire to be closer to her friend that made her decide finally to move from the farm. She had known her forever, knew she'd been disappointed in love, that was a district story, and had gone to England into service, and returned when she was about fifty-five to live in a small house on her earnings and the small pension she'd had from the last family she served. But Martha Huws was only an acquaintance to Jane Rhisiart until the latter went to visit her when she was ill. And from that hour the friendship grew. Jane Rhisiart saw that day quite a different woman than she had supposed her to be; a woman with an open, intelligent face, beautiful blue eyes set far apart, and thick white hair. She hadn't noticed that when she'd caught a glimpse of her on the bus or in the shop. She could talk to her freely, not an easy task for Jane Rhisiart, and when the sick woman said, 'Come visit me here again,' with such warm earnestness, she decided to go. Talked more freely the second time than the first. By the time Jane Rhisiart moved from the smallholding the foundations of the friendship were down and the two of them were going in and out of each other's houses.

Because she'd been disappointed so many times in those to whom she'd given all her love, Jane didn't rush to pour out her heart to her friend, though she was by nature that kind of person. But she knew by this time what suffering could follow that, when she saw that the taker gave none of the love back. So for a long time she was groping her way tentatively into the heart of Martha Huws, as though she were walking in a tunnel, but Martha's personality soon threw enough light from the other end for her to be able to walk boldly.

The friendship was not without difficulties at the start, but these were from outside. The two of them were going to one another's houses often, and within a year, they found themselves seeing each other at some point every day. It was from Jane Rhisiart's children the difficulties came. They and their children were in and out of her house daily. She couldn't prevent them. And when Martha happened to be there, they would continue to stay and talk in spite of the children's crying and in spite of the taciturnity of the two women. Indeed, Ann and Alis and Wiliam's wife seemed as though they aimed at coming on the afternoons when Martha was visiting Jane. But they had to go home to make quarry supper for their husbands. If Martha came at night, Wiliam or Ann's and Alis's husbands would be sure to come there. That difficulty was overcome by Jane going more often to Martha's house. They wouldn't come there, but once Wiliam succeeded in a plot to go there to fetch his mother, on the excuse that he needed to see her on an important matter. He didn't succeed in getting her out of there the second time.

Then Wiliam went so far as to try weaning his mother from Martha by suggesting vile things about the latter, such as that there was no knowing what her life had been when she was in England. After all, why had her master left her money in his will and a pension? Jane was able to make him look very foolish when she said it was a woman and not a man had been her employer. But, had it been otherwise, it would have made no difference to her by this time. She was too fond of Martha to let any event in the past affect her. All the women could say to reproach her was 'that they might as well not come to visit her now, since that Martha Huws was there all the time.'

'She's not here every day nor all day,' was their mother's answer. They would often find the door locked when the two friends went for a stroll or when Jane went to visit Martha, and that would drive them wild. Wiliam went so far once as to reproach his mother for spending the money she had in reserve to go off with a woman whose history she knew nothing about. And she answered like a shot, that it would be soon enough for him to reproach her for that when she came asking him for something to support her, and that she hoped she could spend it all before she died lest it cause more jealousy among the three of them than there already was.

Wiliam took a great interest in this little sum of money in the bank. He'd suggested many times to his mother that he could have started a little business or raised chickens if he had the money to start, and he was sick of the quarry. 'Yes indeed,' would be her answer, 'a pity you couldn't have saved up when money was easy pickings.' Her friendship with Martha was her backbone for these answers.

And in sitting down and analysing that friendship from time to time it dawned on her that its basis was conversation. She had never before found anybody who could respond intelligently to what she said to them. She'd say something to a neighbour. The other woman wouldn't take any interest or she'd say something stupid, worthless. But with Martha she found from the start a response that had shown intelligence and interest. And that was the beginning of talk, and the beginning of understanding each other, and the beginning of friendship.

Despite that, a good three years went by before Jane could break the ice and could talk about Rolant. He wasn't the uppermost thing on her mind at the time. His disappearance had become something cold and impersonal, and she could talk about him without any feeling at all, not sadness, not bitterness or fondness. Indeed, some of the story seemed amusing by now, such as her knowing what the quarrymen didn't know – namely, that Rolant had used money he kept back to increase his amount for the monthly collection in the chapel, and made himself a laughing-stock to many because his contribution was almost as much as the shopkeepers' and the stewards'.

Martha was able to talk about her own experience of love, but not in as much detail, because there was an element of sadness in what had never reached fulfillment. Martha had had a sudden vision, something like a prophecy, that she would not be able to live with her sweetheart; Jane had seen more slowly and thoroughly. But what Jane liked in Martha was her saying she didn't want to talk about it. And what Martha liked in Jane was that she understood.

They often went for a walk to the mountain, which put the

stamp of oddity on them to their neighbours. To them the mountain was only something that their husbands crossed to the quarry and something that was a sign of rain when mist came to wrap its crown. But Jane and Martha didn't weary of climbing it, and the great thing was to have a lie-down in the heather, and a talk, a cup of tea from a flask, and cake from a paper wrapper.

The greatest thing was the talk. When they went for an outing to Llandudno or Colwyn Bay, walking the streets and gaping at shop windows, the highpoint of the day would come when they went to a restaurant and had a proper meal before starting home, and talked. Neither of them had been able to do this with anyone else before. They thought by now that this was the only way life could still be endured, talking about their experiences – not the experiences of the past, there was no life in those, but their opinions and their feelings about the events of the day, in their village and in their country, and about what they read.

They didn't thrash the youth of today with the cudgel of their own youth's good behaviour, but they rejoiced that they'd lived in a pleasanter age. To the youth of the district they were a laughing-stock with their old-fashioned ways of going for a stroll, of dressing so plainly, of such dignified living, but these young people would have been a good deal surprised had they known the pair were in one thing part of modern life. When they went away for the day, both of them had a little powder in their bags to take the shine off their noses after having too high a tea.

But that was all over by now, and Jane was by herself on the Sunday School trip. A fortnight before, quite suddenly, Martha had left the world that had been so full of her for twelve years. Jane had been with her the night before, and had declared that she was looking pale and tired and offered to stay there with her. But her friend didn't want that. The next morning she was found dead in her bed. Jane's world had fallen apart for days.

Today, at the seaside, she was able to look more tranquilly at the events of the last fortnight, though she was constantly remembering that her friend had been with her on the trip last year. Her memories interwove with the colours of the clothing of children who were playing on the beach and with the millions of pearls that danced on the sea and shone on the sand. She had had a treasure in Martha's friendship, a spotless treasure, the only spotless thing in her life, and no one could take it from her. The string had been broken before it reached the end. But who was to say what the end might have been? Perhaps (but she couldn't think of it), something could have happened that might have made this treasure less spotless.

The minister came towards her and sat down on the rock. He spoke of this and that, and at last he said quite indifferently, as if he'd just thought of it, 'It will be quite strange for you with Martha Huws gone, won't it?' Neither he nor anyone else could understand that this was the deepest sorrow of her life. She was on the brink of telling him, telling how much she longed for and how much she prized the good friend she'd had for twelve years. She wanted to spill that out to someone, just to be able to say it. But she remembered the lift it had given her heart at the Meeting the evening before when a child had said the verse 'And His mother kept all these words in her heart', a verse to which she'd never given a moment's notice. No, she couldn't express to the minister her feelings about what she had lost. Only to Martha could she have spoken of the loss she'd had through the passing of her friend.

THE KISS
(1936)
Glyn Jones

I

A dead lier deep in the coalfield and the cracking darkness filling the pitted earth, stirred out of his first death wanting faintly with two broken hands to push the pitch night back into the stones, feeling close over his face the pressure of the imminent bleak rock, and the water, and the light fingering of the fall earth roofing his grave. His body ached in the ground, groaning with the chill of burial, suffering bitterly from cold and the corruption opening his flesh. As he lay on his back, weary, bearing the cold, watching with the indifference of death but still painfully his stirring bewildered pulses, and the confusion of his nostrils, he could feel from time to time the flicker of his beating heart, tired, uneasy, vibrating like a moth caught under a cupped palm, turning him sick, but at every movement pushing its warm wash of blood farther over the levels of his body.

The darkness is kneeling on my chest, I can't draw breath.

And down into his feet, painfully filling his veins with the blood-froth, and the pods of his rotten cold flesh. Then with a sickness filling his belly and his mouth like bitter water he bent his knees, trying languidly to rise off the rock-slab, but the blood shot up hot through his thighs, molten, mounting like a tilted spirit-bubble through his flesh, sinking his legs out straight again with agony. He groaned and fell back, knowing there was no voice to call him Lazarus out of the rock, to bring his feet rotting with death out on to the grass again. There was only his own heart with its jet of blood spouting full up through his throat into the chill of his skull and now suddenly breaking like a rocket over his brain. And there were whispers perhaps. But slowly, as his perception cleared of the blood-drench, his stroking heart deepened and soft-hooted with more assurance, and soon he could feel the regular beat of his pulses tapping softly like piano-hammers among the bones of his wrists, soothing the flesh, and his hair all over his body beginning to feed again upon his skin. His strength was slowly returning to him, poured into his limbs, his blood was giving it up to him like a grape-wall breathing warm on the hands in the darkness. He was alive again. But even now he could feel a worm deep in his foot, and his hands putrid, enduring cold and death. And when he foresaw the burden of loving and the beginning of speech without judgement, like the difficult cutting of the tongue-string, it seemed one simple act was preferable to many, the dribbling of cut pulses easier than the acceptance of men. But even as he thought it he found himself rising giddily to his feet, unsteadied, with his heart hammering up under the roof of his skull and the blood heavy in his legs. He swayed and had to cling for support to the timbers, blinded and dizzy. But he had to get out. He groped his way in the pitch draught like wading through a current of snow-water to the hips, leaving the coal-fall behind him, making for the old workings that opened out on to the side of the mountain. In his pocket he pushed a piece of the rock that had killed him. When he at last reached the open air and the hard morning sun buffeting his eyes, the blood spouted up from his belly like a vomit, pouring out of his mouth, and he fell on his knees on the grass with his arm over his face. A few moments later, trying to rise, he fainted back on to the grass and lay there at full length in the sun with his stiff beard pointing up in a steep sharp cone out of his chin and the blood running among the coal-dust over his face.

II

The garden looked cold and black, and there was nothing alive in it. There were no weeds on the bready earth, and from the kitchen window the black meagre beds looked sour and poisonous. But right in the middle was a tree like a planted arm. The wind went into the five black branches from the east and the bleak leaves smoked out on the far side, tapping against the wall in a flock and then dropping deflected from the stone-work to the black earth. Darkness was going up the sky like a shutter.

A waking woman sat at the kitchen window. She was dressed in a black gown and a grey woollen shawl, and as was the custom among the women of the valleys she wore a man's cap covering her hair. She seemed to be seeing the garden for the first time, saying to herself:

Are my eyes open or my lids glass?

She watched the leaves jumping up off the garden, pecking at the wall and then falling back to the earth again. She was calculating, a bunch of lines gathered between her brows.

When will I be delivered of this son heavily loading my womb?

Then she laughed because she remembered she was old, the mother of men and women. Her face was thin, and white as an eggshell, but lined almost everywhere as though a broken hair-net were spread over it; and most noticeable were the small sharp lines radiating from the reeving-string of her mouth. Her thin blue lids slid out again from the hollows under her edgy brows, curving forward to cover over her eyes, and along the curved ridge of her nose, and over her cheek-bones, the skin was thin and tight, shining, faintly luminous. And she sat at the window with her mouth open, the naked veins tunnelled blue and prominent along the backs of her hands lying crossed over her lap for weariness.

She wondered how long she must wait for the knocking at her door.

Soon she was able to see nothing out of the window except a narrow tape of cold sky, the blue of clock-hands, showing over the garden wall, with one branch wagging before it still tagged with a few leaves. Her little clock struck hurriedly. The fire got up in the darkness and then sank down again, easing itself like an animal twisting for comfort, and then the night set in.

But even in the pitch darkness the old woman could hear the wind outside gnawing at the tree.

III

Inched against his opening eyelids was a stem growing from the green tangle of grasses. It was a daisy, lifting up the yellow flat catchment of its flower to the sun, gathering the tilted warmth like a funnel, pouring a light-thread down through its thin stem to meet sap that rose up from roots leeching hungrily at the arterial earth. It was a perfect blossom, an ochre disk with petals crowding white and stiff round it pointed with clotted scarlet; and the stem was powerful, flexible, a slender column twisting itself slowly round among the crouching grasses, revolving upon the security of its roots like the ponderous gyring of some machine; it bore its heavy blossom balanced out at the sun as it pivoted steadily round under the weight of the flower, furred all over with a covering of fine silver hairs, shining, delicate, like the silvery invisible shagginess downing the body of a child. The workman, smiling and detached, forgetting in his pleasure his death and his burial, sat up to look at it twisting towards the morning sun. He put out his fingers towards it and saw suddenly the broad backs of his hands thicketed with veins, waxy where there was no coal-dust as the hands of the dead in the sun, and when, instantly remembering everything, he drew them back to his breast he saw the centres of both his palms worn into holes, the flesh gone through into a hole like the thin sole of a shoe. It was terrible to look at, but he felt no pain now, and he was holding the sun hot in his lap. He looked no more over his body. He fell back again and soon he was dreaming of acceptance, seeing the pouring rain falling on to the skin of his shoulders and his arms while he received it through into the inward thirsting parts of his body. And then it seemed he stood alone under the dark glare of a bruise-blue desert sky, while a brilliant cactus growing before him like a green divided fruit on the sand sent a new fleshy shoot growing upward curving towards him from the cleft where it opened out bright green on a pool of sand the sun turned white as salt. And when the sharp spine of the cactus shoot touched his breast he wondered whether he should trample on its fresh green brilliancy or accept it and allow it to penetrate past the protection of his skin into his body. He looked down and gazed with absorption at the spine that had moved upward with such rapid growth and saw it enter his breast-skin like a spear-head; he watched it without resistance slowly blade upward as it grew right into him, tearing off its vivid juicy flesh as it entered. But what the cactus-point found when it had broken into his heart he did not know because it stabbed him wide awake and he opened his eyes to find the daisy with its petals shut into a point and the lovely evening star flickering over the dark valley.

IV

Just outside the village a big square house stood by itself with every window darkened. The night wind rushed at it up the valley with a sound like harsh water, savaging the hedge-bushes and the dishevelled branches of the sumac trees surrounding the garden. Suddenly the door of the house opened and a man ran out bewildered into the night. He ran into the middle of the garden and stood with the light of the open door shining upon him, looking around in a dazed way, bareheaded, bewildered by the darkness, and the wind in the bushes deafening him. A voice from the house shouted that many roads lead out of hell.

The man shivered with the wind and walked slowly out at the gate without looking round. He went in dejection down the road that led towards the village nursing the large bandage of his hand, looking around at the dark valley stretching away on both sides of the road and up at the black slope of the sky ahead with its disorder of stars. When he was beyond the sheltering trees and the house, he found it hard to walk because of the wind, and his hand began to ache although he protected it under his coat from the cold, and soon he was forced to make for shelter towards the roadside where a black lonely tree roared up like a fire in the darkness. But before he reached it the tree spun him a leaf out of the struggle of its empty branches, and as he stooped to pick it up the wind pushed him over as it pushes a candle-flame over on to its back. He lay still in the road unable to move.

V

The workman walked down the slope making for home. As he went along the mountain path, the wind began to rise and the night got colder, the sky quickly filling up with stars. Below him was the valley flooded under soft liquid darkness, black like water, and, above, the body of the mountain out of which he had broken sloped into the night holding up a breast with both hands against the rubbing sky. He came at last to the bows of the hill where the broad valley ahead forked into two and from there he could see a group of shuttering lights, the floating house-lamps of the village for which he was making. The wind was blowing hard, wincing up through the bracken. He hurried down the hill into the darkness, trying to keep his wounded body warm because the wind was flowing so cold, washing low over the curvature of the earth, penetrating his clothes and keeping him back, but even when he got down into the valley it was hardly any quieter. Along one side of the road leading down to the village was a line of naked poplars all shoved sideways, swaying to one side like the long hair of earth blown up erect.

Ahead the white moon laboured slowly out of the ground.

The workman longed to speak again, longed to see the bodies of men and women moving once again with passionate or even commonplace movements as the restless urgency used them, hungered and thirsted to taste with his mouth, longed to smell living bread, to feel fire. If only he could exist to touch flesh with his healed hands, never increasing suffering, in the ignorance of the touched flesh, if only he could give his body to be burnt. At his feet a man lay face downwards on the road clutching a dead leaf in his hand. Over him a charcoal tree screamed, spreading its branches like a menacing bird come down on savage wings at the roadside. The workman turned him over, feeling his breath beautifully warm on his pierced flesh, going among the hairs of his cold hands like an insect and his heart knocking very slowly with the tapping of a knuckle under his breast.

The cautious moon was scattering light, going up the sky like a firework, and the workman recognised his brother.

VI

All actions seemed pitiful, like a cruel fraud. Her passionate body once had been the grave of her child and she had suffered because of it, but when she herself was buried flesh her anguish would mean nothing at all, a wastage of feeling and creation. She felt cheated, bitter and rebellious that enjoyment and suffering were both a fraud.

A stone struck the kitchen door like the peck of a hard beak. The old woman got up and opened it quickly, and stood staring out into the darkness of the garden. The wind rushed past her into the house but she could see nothing in the night outside except the tip of a tree branch above the skyline and the stars looking hard into her eyes. A voice came out of the darkness saying tenderly:

'Mother, don't be afraid, we have come back.'

The old woman recognised the dead voice of her son. A hand struck an aching blow at her throat and she leaned against the open door weak with emotion.

'Don't light the lamps, Mother,' the voice went on gently, 'I am carrying my brother. Make the fire up for him; he is ill.'

The old woman turned back into the house wailing softly to herself:

'My son, my son.'

VII

The village bell struck, starting off another day.

Inside the cottage the mother and her two sons sat down around the table in the darkness while the fire tongued into the chimney and the spittles of the little chewing clock were loud in the darkness. The workman was happy, warm and reposing inwardly, very near tears although the pain had left his flesh. Presently he said to his brother quietly:

'Show me your hand.'

Their mother got up at once when he said it, agitated, her voice protesting in the darkness.

'No, no,' she cried, almost hysterically, 'don't undo those bandages again. You mustn't do it. It is terrible. It is terrible.'

'If my brother is willing I will see it,' the workman said gently. 'Fetch me a candle, Mother. And don't be afraid of an action for healing.'

She turned away and went slowly out of the room beginning to sob, defeated by him, her resistance broken at once, but presently she returned bearing two brass candlesticks which she placed submissively on the table before the two men. Her face was in shadow but they could hear her sobbing bitterly in the darkness, and they knew she was too wounded to say more in protest now. Then, her hands trembling, she struck the matches for them with great weariness, whimpering like a hurt child, and when the candles were lit she turned to the fire with a helpless gesture of resignation and sat with her face averted, renouncing everything, weeping helplessly to herself without hope or remission.

The brother looked pityingly at her for a moment and then as the workman signed to him, he lifted his heavy arm out of its sling and placed the bandaged hand between the candles on the table. It was huge and ugly, shapeless. The workman, bending forward, his eyes showing up very white, shining moist in the candlelight out of the dull coal-dust still covering his face, and his small fibrous beard sharpened from his chin, stared at it with a fascination of pity, the dark hollow mask of his face unrelaxed, intense, close to the two vivid flames and low against the table-board. He stared for a long time as though he were unable to assert himself, not looking at his brother at all and heedless of his mother and her suffering, only gazing at the shapeless wrappings grey on the table with living eyes from the earthy skin of his face. Then very slowly he began untying the bandages. He fingered them with his large hands as though his ministration were sacred, laying them gently aside with slow priestlike tenderness and deliberation while the big shadows twitched behind them on the walls of the room. At first the bandages were clean and unwound easily but when he had taken off the outer layers they began to be patched darkly at intervals with black blood where the bleeding had oozed through and dried, and at these places they began to stick so that he had to ease them gently apart before he could get them off. Love slowed his hands, and the distresses of his brother. But gradually the pile of tangled bandages grew beside the candlestick with the steady unspooling of the hand and then as its flesh was slowly revealed to the air it began to stink into the room.

'Don't undo it,' said the mother, in anguish, her first weeping spent.

But the workman went on steadily unwinding, tender-fingered as a mother in spite of the wounds hindering his blunt hands, taking up the weight of his brother's arm on his hand and twisting the bandages off continually with great care and tenderness. His love-acts were skilful, and soothing to his brother, tender and reverential, and his calm absorption in this eucharistic task seemed child-like and complete. And as he worked steadily at the sticking length of cloth it became blacker and blacker, completely soaked at last with rotten blood, and with the gradual laying bare of the upper hand the stink of putrefaction issuing from it became worse, oppressive, almost unbearable. But the workman went on untwisting in spite of everything although his movements were tiring, and presently after many pauses for his brother's exhaustion, all the bandages were uncoiled into a tangled pile on the table; and, when the soaking undercloths were unwrapped as well and pushed aside, the whole hand lay naked on the table in the candlelight. It was terrible to see, pitiful beyond anything the workman had imagined, and at the horror of it he felt numb, he could only bow his head and remain silent. It was a great heavy mass of black flesh, soft and thick, swollen up with black spongy decay and larger than twice its normal size, showing no trace anywhere of veins or knuckles or the pink shine of fingernails or even of the shapes and divisions of fingers. Beginning from the wholesome pale wrist-flesh and spreading to the farthest tip, it was a shapeless black mass of stinking flesh like some bad inward part cut from an animal, warm and soft throughout, not divided up into fingers at all and with only a small bud of foul black flesh sticking out at the side where the thumb should have been growing. The workman, used to sights of the body diseased and lacerated, had never seen anything so terrible or so pitiful. Beside this putrid rottenness gradually claiming the flesh the wounds he had known were clean, nothing, and looking up at his brother's face his compassion for him was perfect. But there were no tears in his eyes as he looked down again, trying hopelessly to discern in this raw stinking corruption perhaps the ridges of sinews, or the jointed bones of his brother's fingers, or even the three divisions separating them from each other. But it was hopeless. And as he glanced up with emotion, and looked over to where his mother was sitting, he saw she had fallen back across the arm of her chair in a faint with a swallowing vein prominent along her neck; she had fainted without his noticing it, and she lay in her chair before the fire with her face inverted and her hair hanging out of her head like a soft root and a vein gulping uneasily along her throat.

Very tenderly, with tears running down his face, he bent forward and kissed the putrid flesh of his brother's hand.

THE FRAYING OF THE THREAD
(1926)
Kathleen Freeman

'The postman is late this morning,' said John Barton to his sister; he rose and moved impatiently to the window.

'Are you expecting a particular letter?' said Mary Barton.

'No,' he said; and meeting her critical eye, he made an effort after self-possession.

'Do you realise that you are preoccupied in just this way before every postal delivery?' she said, laying aside her newspaper. 'Sit down, do, and forget about it. I don't like it; there is a certain unrestraint about your behaviour that is unlike you; it annoys me. Sit down now, and let us have some bright conversation.'

He sat down, smiling at her ruefully. 'You are right, Mary,' he said. 'I am unrestrained about letters. I can't settle down until the morning delivery has come. Yet I don't know why; I'm not in love; in fact, it's hardly ever a particular letter from a particular person that I expect. Isn't it strange?'

'Perhaps it is; I think I understand it very well; at least, I can supply a similar example. Begin your breakfast – I've finished mine while you've been fidgeting round the room – and I'll tell you a tale – a tale with a moral. I hope it will be a warning to you.'

'Fire ahead,' said he, relaxing into his chair.

In the early spring of this year (began Mary Barton) I took a holiday, you remember, at a small seaside town called Port Hailey, on the coast of Pembrokeshire. In the boarding-house at which I stayed, I met a woman who attracted me. She was dressed in black, except for a white collar and white cuffs; she was handsome, in a severe way; and when she spoke, which was not often, she spoke to the purpose. She and I sat at the same table together with a feeble-minded young man, a jocular elderly man, an affected young girl, and two married women of the pseudo-cultured type. The woman in black and white – well, to turn one's eyes from these others to her was restful, and also stimulating; and when these people broke through her reserve, – you know, they never could bear to leave either her or me outside their incessant interchange of small talk; whenever they saw a vacuum of silence, they rushed in as if by a natural law to fill it with sound, – when courtesy forced her to speak, her sentences came clean-cut and whole from her lips, not patched with 'wells' and 'ohs' and 'I mean to says.' I was surprised to find myself wanting to know her; and one morning, when the others had left the table, and removed their noise to another room, I made advances; I offered her my cigarette-case; and I noticed that the hand she held out was trembling a little. She watched it herself, and frowned; a moment later, when she took the lighted match that I passed, her hand was steady. I was conscious of rigid control working near me unseen.

To bring about what I wished required skill; and as I had nothing else to do, I entered eagerly into the delicate game. In a few days I had earned her gratitude by shielding her from the table conversations; later, with her consent, I bribed the maid to set our meals on a table apart. She began to like me; and as she unbent, she delighted me with her caustic wit, that spared nothing and nobody, not even herself. But she was always holding herself back; and if ever she forgot her vigilance, and let a gleam of youthful fun peep out, a moment later she would remember. She would stop short, and dart a look of fierce dignity at me, as though she resented my having beguiled her into forgetting her reserve; she might have been an Artemis bathing in a pool, and I an Actæon peering at her through the branches. This suspicious attitude hurt me, but it increased my interest. The other guests at the boarding-house had long ago given her up as impossibly difficult, so that I was proud that I had kept my footing so far in those craggy places, and was breathing easily in that thin and chilly air.

If you'd heard the cheerful rot that I heaped on her head! I knew that I was being presumptuous, but it was the only way to deal with her. Every morning when she came down to breakfast a coating of ice had formed; the more she had thawed the night before, the deeper and harder was the frost the next day. I tried the gentle method of melting first; and if that failed, I hewed and battered and crashed my way through; I found it all immensely exhilarating. She consented to come with me for long country walks. She was more at ease in the open air than beneath a roof. When she began to show confidence in me, I caught glimpses of a rare personality and intellect – scholarly, refined and penetrating – almost unbearably penetrating.

After two weeks had passed, she invited me to take tea with her in her sitting-room. I went in a curious state of trepidation. In these surroundings she was different again; there was not a trace left of the ice that had never quite vanished from our previous intercourse in spite of all my hammerings. Before, there had always been a hint of nervousness in her dignity, and it called up in me, the younger, a protectiveness supposed to belong exclusively to you men – the thing you call 'reverence' – I felt, if not older than she, then of coarser fibre, more adapted to endure hard knocks and disagreeable sights and sounds; it seemed monstrous that she should have to hear a loud laugh or a foolish remark; and if anyone had spoken discourteously to her, I should have been ready to strike him. I sometimes glanced at her to see how she took this gallant air of mine; I was afraid she would resent it as an impertinence – I should have resented it in a man – but she never showed annoyance; if she noticed it at all, it merely amused her. But when I walked into her sitting-room on this afternoon, all my brave airs fell away; there was no place for them. She received me with graciousness and ease; it was the ease with which she moved and spoke that changed our relationship; before, I had always felt effort behind that dignity of hers – a nerve quivering somewhere, though willpower and pride kept it hidden. I was amazed, disconcerted and charmed. I sat like a schoolgirl, feeling all arms and legs; I stammered – I, who had boldly put her at her ease over the breakfast-table, and shielded her from the rest of the company! I dropped a scone, buttered side downwards, on to the hearth-rug; my teaspoon fell into the fender; I suffered agonies of embarrassment over an oat-cake that crackled between my jaws like a bonfire of dry twigs. I looked up at her, with burning ears; there she sat in the firelight, gravely smiling, courteous, perfect; she was not merely handsome, she was beautiful; dark hair, clear-cut chin, strong lips – not only a pure and harmonious outline, but colour, warmth and life.

Well, there I sat, shy and awkward, while she in her turn tried to put me at my ease. Gradually I gave myself up to her guidance; I was forgetting myself in the pleasure of being so bandied and led, when from a certain moment the whole atmosphere began to change; her hold on the reins seemed to grow slack; her voice wavered and became forced; conversation ceased with a jolt; and I was conscious for the second time of a nerve quivering somewhere out of sight – an unseen struggle and strain. I looked up at her once more; there was the expression that I knew, that called out of me automatically the desire to protect; I felt as if I had heard a cry of pain, and must be ready to ward off something, I did not know what – something invisible to me – something that had called her to fight; and as she withdrew, I felt I must rush after, and shout and knock and try to force a way after her through a gate that shut in my face.

There was a tap on the door; she put her two hands on the arms of the chair, as if to rise; then she sat back with tightened lips, and called 'Come in.' The maid entered to remove the tea tray; my hostess darted a quick intent look at her, seemed about to ask a question, and then turned away, staring into the fire. The door closed; for some minutes we sat in silence; I timidly tried to take up our discussion at the point where it had been interrupted; but she was plainly unable to give me her attention; she could do nothing but force out monosyllables, and that seemed to cause her pain. I murmured an excuse and rose; she let me go without protest. When I reached my room, I was astonished to find myself trembling and exhausted.

On the next morning, when we met at breakfast, she was less distant than I had expected. Perhaps she was pleased by my prompt acceptance of her change of mood on the previous evening. For the next few days, she came with me on walks and explorations as before; and we sank into our old positions – she into controlled nervousness, with little excursions of wit, and rapid retreats into her fortress of cold reserve; and I to my diffident protectiveness.

On one of these days, when I came down to breakfast, I found her already standing beside our table. Two or three letters were lying on my plate; I glanced at hers; as usual there was nothing; it struck me then for the first time that she never received letters; hitherto it had escaped my notice – it was part of her general aloofness. As I came up behind her, I heard her say to the maid who was laying the table, 'Are there no letters for me?' Her voice was strangely tense. 'Nothing for you, miss,' said the maid. I coughed, and murmured good-morning; an instinct told me not to look at her, and I buried myself in my correspondence. When I raised my eyes, her face was calm and severe as usual; and soon I was hard at my morning task of breaking through the crust of ice that had formed during the night.

It was a wonderful day, I remember, one of those days that the west country often gives us in early spring, a kind day, as we used to call them, – yellow sunshine, rough wind, and a hint of snow in the air. I begged her to come out with me along the cliffs; I said I would carry our lunch on my back, and we would say goodbye to the boarding-house till teatime at least. She consented, – my own enthusiasm seemed to reach and warm her – and out we strode into the bright cold morning. She was young that day; almost playful; we played together in the rare restrained way that was her gift, and of which I could never have enough. As we swung homewards, an hour after teatime, I knew that I had made a real advance; throughout the whole day, she had not once warned me off with that look of suspicious resentment that flashed like a sword between us, and cut the cord of our friendship just when the knot I so laboured to tie was most secure. I was glad and content; I poured myself out in jokes and stories; and more than once I won her rare laugh in answer. But as we turned into the main street of our town, the dreaded change began. An uneasy silence fell; I looked at my watch; it was half-past five. I said to myself, 'She is tired, and no wonder. Tea will refresh her. Good idea; I'll ask her to take tea with me in my room.'

As we walked up the drive, the postman was coming away; we were soon indoors; on the hall table lay a pile of letters. I took them up and sorted them quickly, throwing out two addressed to myself. For the moment I had forgotten her. I looked up to find her eyes fixed on the movements of my hands with an expression that frightened me. I gave a nervous laugh.

'There's nothing for you, I'm afraid—' I began.

She turned away without a word towards the stairs.

'Miss Bellamy,' I called, with an intolerable sense of failure, 'won't you come and have tea in my room?'

'No, thank you,' she said coldly, and left me standing there, with the letters in my hand.

I stayed there for a minute or two, dazed with disappointment. The long evening – how could I face it? And I had thought my day so glowing a success! 'Pull yourself together, you fool,' I said, 'you're getting a bundle of nerves yourself. You spend too much time with that woman; try some ordinary mortals as a relaxation. After all, what is she to you? A chance acquaintance in a boarding-house.'

I heard music in the drawing room. Warmth and comfort – that was what I wanted for the present. They received me among them with interest and respect; they lionised me, a little, as the friend of the superior Miss Bellamy. I sat down between the two married ladies. The young girl began a song – 'Love is of the valley,' she told us to a languorous air. I tried to yield myself up. I told myself that all this was kindly and good, the natural air for the human soul to breathe; the poor human soul was never meant to live on chilly heights alone. It needed contact, close warm contact, with its kind. Here a mincing voice broke in; one of the married ladies was asking me:

'Can't you persuade your friend to come downstairs sometimes, Miss Barton? I'm sure she spends too much time alone. It can't be good for her. But there – she never would unbend to any of us; she's very difficult, isn't she? A very cold nature, I should say.'

The elderly man broke in. 'Oh, yes, she's difficult,' he said, 'but not cold – I don't think so; a stormy petrel, I should call her. Of course she may be different with you ladies, but – do you know, I was coming down the stairs this morning early; I should think it couldn't have been much later than seven; I had had my sleep out, and I thought I'd go out before breakfast, and have a look at the tide; well, as I came down the stairs, I saw our haughty lady standing at the front door, with her back to me; as I turned into the hall, I saw that she was trying to open the door of the wooden letter-box – you know, the first post comes early here, before most of you have your eyes open – so I stepped up to her and said, "Allow me, Madam; perhaps the catch is a bit stiff for your fingers." Well, she jumped as though I'd caught her burgling a safe; she gave me a ferocious scowl that sent shivers down my spine; then she said in a voice enough to freeze your blood, "Thank you – I prefer to do it myself." She pulled out the letters in a handful, flung them down on the hall table, and walked away without glancing at them.'

There was a chorus of 'How rum! How extraordinary!' I writhed in my seat. I longed to knock their empty heads together. To avoid doing so, I got up and walked out of the room, with the words 'mystery' and 'love-letter' ringing in my ears.

Down the main street I went, and dived into the nearest cinema. Yet there too I failed to find distraction. My irritated mind persisted in a detailed review of the glittering day and its sudden end in blankness. It magnified my search for consolation in the commonplace into an unworthy lapse, a disloyalty, almost a sin against an ideal of beauty. Memory mumbled, 'We needs must love the highest when we see it'; sanity kicked its shins and growled, 'Shut up, you fool.' I reeled into my bedroom just before the lights went out, and lay for an hour with throbbing head and staggering heart. At last sleep came.

I crept down to breakfast feeling weak and sore. Miss Bellamy did not appear. A sharp throb darted through my head as I remembered that the day was Friday; on the morrow I was leaving Port Hailey for a week's visit to friends in the neighbourhood. It was too bad, I thought; my last day, and she did not appear. She knew that it was my last day; never mind, perhaps she would come downstairs during the morning; certainly she would be there for lunch. Well, if she came down before lunch, she should not find me. I snatched my stick from the hall-stand, and strode out whistling. I hoped that she would see me from her window, and be sorry... At eleven o'clock I returned, utterly bored with the town, the rocks, the sea and the shore, and lacking the willpower to drag myself off for a longer expedition. She was not there. I sat in the lounge, turning over magazines and illustrated papers, and smoking myself ill; when the lunch gong sounded, I arose with clammy brow and uncertain step. I was the first to enter the dining room. One by one the noisy guests appeared; but no Miss Bellamy. By this time, I could no longer reason. I did not in the least know why I wanted to see her, nor why it should matter to me at all if I never saw her again. I remembered only that when she had left me she had been angry or distressed; whether through act of mine or not I had no idea; but by that sudden withdrawal she had somehow plucked at a nerve in me that throbbed maddeningly, and a blind instinct in me cried out to get her face to face, to find out what had happened. I *must* find out. 'No,' I thought, 'I cannot. I will not go to her room. Pride must keep me away.' I crawled miserably to my own bedroom, pulled down all the blinds, and tumbled across the bed.

At teatime I did not stir. I knew that she never had tea in the drawing room. Six o'clock struck, and I lay still, grateful for the deepening twilight. Half-past six – and there came a tap at my door. A maid entered. 'A note for you, Miss,' she said. I took it; the writing, mingled with black spots, danced before my hot eyes.

It read, 'I shall not come down to dinner this evening; would you care to have coffee with me in my room at half-past seven?' I scribbled an acceptance, bathed my unhappy head in cold water, and dressed shakily. I did not dine; I was afraid of using up the little nerve force I had left. I sat in the darkness until the time came. Then with an effort I rose and crossed the landing.

She was always self-possessed and perfect within her own four walls; she seemed to have shut the door on all disturbing influences. She sat there in the firelight, with books and papers beside her, and her clear voice reached me. She said:

'It is pleasant to see you, Miss Barton. I hoped that you would come and entertain me. Why, you look ill. Come at once and sit down! See,' she said, and she pulled an armchair to the fire. Kindness from her was more than I could bear just then. My eyes filled with tears and I dared not answer. She talked on quietly; as before in that room, she took control, surely and easily, and little by little my nerves relaxed and grew still under her hands. I no longer cared to learn what it was that had perturbed her on the evening before; whatever it had been, its effects were over. She was herself again. I accepted the present hour, and my desire not to disturb it banished even my curiosity. I did not want any clumsy probing of mine to awaken that discord again. Nine o'clock struck, and still we sat in the firelight. She said:

'You are leaving Port Hailey tomorrow, Miss Barton, are you not?'

'Yes,' I said, 'I've promised to go on a week's visit to some friends near here – unfortunately,' I added, suddenly ungrateful.

'Then I suppose I shall not see you again,' she said, 'unless you intend to return here after your visit?'

At this an impulse ran away with me. I said:

'I had half thought to come back here next Saturday, and stay for the weekend. Will you have gone by that time?'

'So far as I can tell at present, no,' she said. 'My movements are a little uncertain; but I should like another two weeks' rest. It is a matter of health; I am recuperating after a nervous breakdown; another fortnight should restore me. Yes, I shall probably be here on Saturday. I shall look forward with pleasure to your return.'

I rose; we shook hands; in a moment I found myself shut out from the warm room, into the draughty moonlit corridor. I made straight for my bed and slept heavily.

On the next morning I breakfasted alone, and caught an early train out of Port Hailey. I felt cheered and invigorated, and my heart warmed towards my friend. She was my friend now, I believed; I sketched plans for the future; ways in which we should take pleasure together danced through my brain. A nervous breakdown, she had said; what had caused it, I wondered. 'Overwork, perhaps,' I thought. 'She is a scholar, it is plain. I will invite her to stay with me this summer. If I were with her I could devise schemes for her amusement – I could shield her from that inimical something that preys on her mind.'

Suddenly an idea came. 'She watches the posts,' I thought. 'Each time she has shown distress, it has been in the expectation of a letter. She is proud; she wants letters, and they never come. Then why shouldn't I write to her? Yes, I will write her an amusing letter every day. I can write amusing letters. She has always found me entertaining when I have talked with her; she will be sure to enjoy the same sort of thing in writing.' The idea delighted me. I pictured her coming down in the mornings and finding my letter on her plate; I saw her face and her faint haughty smile. I made a vow, 'Every morning she shall have a letter, whether she answers or not.'

I did not expect an answer, and I did not get one. All through my visit, which I found very dull, I was sustained by anticipation. I counted the days till Saturday should come, and when it came,

I could hardly bear to wait for the train that my hospitable friends chose for me; I longed to be away in the morning, but I hid my unmannerly impatience, and consented to take a train at three o'clock.

I found the grey stone houses of Port Hailey a welcome sight; I swung lightly up the main street towards the seafront. The boarding-house windows smiled at me; as I passed into the hall, I glanced from habit down at the table. The first thing that I saw was my own handwriting: 'Miss M. Bellamy, at Sea View, Port Hailey.' There they lay, one, two, three, four unopened letters; I had sent seven in all. My head swam as if under a blow. I rang the bell. I said to the maid:

'Is Miss Bellamy in her room?'

'No, Miss,' she said. 'Miss Bellamy left Sea View last Tuesday; she said that we were not to forward any letters – I don't think, Miss, she left any address.' I looked down at my letters. They had seemed good to me when I had written them. I had taken pains to make them amusing. Now I hated them.

I tore them across, and strode out down the street to the station.

I heard running footsteps behind me, and turned to face the little maid.

'Oh, Miss,' she said, 'the lady upstairs, Mrs. Castleton, sent me after you to tell you she's sure Miss Bellamy hasn't left here – she thought she saw her in one of the windows at the Marine Hotel. She thought perhaps you'd be glad to know.'

I thanked her and stood pondering. This time it was not disappointment that filled me – I was furious. I made my decision. I thought, 'Yes, I will go. If she is there I will try to see her. She has treated me abominably. True, I made the first advances, but she accepted them, and she said she would be glad to see me again. I will go. I want nothing further to do with her, but one thing she owes me, and I will have it – an explanation.'

I walked back to the seafront, and into the hall of the Marine Hotel. Yes, a Miss Bellamy was among the guests. I tore a leaf from my pocketbook and wrote:

'If you can bear my presence for a few minutes, I wish to ask you a question.'

The page returned with a note:

'Yes, I will see you if you wish. But you had far better find a more profitable interest.'

As I entered the room, I had an impression of height and coldness. The large windows were open, and they looked over the grey sea. She sat as usual in an armchair before the fire, resting her head on one hand. She turned her face to me; it was paler and colder than I had ever seen it. The fury died out of me; my one thought was, had I the wit to devise a means of slipping past that forbidding barrier?

She disarmed me with a dexterous stroke.

'Come inside,' she said. 'Please do not stand on my threshold glaring at me like a tiger. It is disturbing, and I am not to be disturbed.'

I crumpled up under her ironical smile.

'Why did you go away?' I said. 'Why didn't you leave a message?'

'I went away to escape from your letters,' she said. 'Now surely you see that I am impossible. Please walk away indignant and have no more to do with me.'

I sat down, gaping at her. 'From my letters?' I said. 'Why, what harm could they do you? I meant... I thought... oh, for Heaven's sake, explain a little! I won't go on with this guesswork any longer.'

She raised herself up. 'Miss Barton,' she said, and she spoke every word with close-clipped emphasis, 'I have warned you to seek a more satisfactory interest. But if you persist then I shall tell you the truth. I once said to you that I was recovering from a nervous breakdown. That was an understatement. A worse fear hangs over me, – the fear of insanity.'

'Insanity?' I said. 'Good Heavens, it can't be! Why, you have tremendous willpower – I never saw anyone more self-controlled...' She interrupted me.

'Unpleasantness, Miss Barton,' she said, 'and reality are not, unfortunately, as incompatible as you suppose. At your request I have told you the truth. It puzzles me a little, though, to account for your concern over the afflictions of a person with whom you have had so brief an acquaintance.'

'You must take it for granted, then,' I said. 'Put it down to inquisitiveness or meddlesomeness or anything else you please. Its existence is obvious enough. The question is, are you going to do anything with it? Or do I understand that you find it a nuisance? If so, I won't pester you any longer.'

Her manner changed. She said, 'You shame me. Your forbearance seems to be unlimited, and, yes, your sympathy is precious to me. But I have met with so little genuine friendliness in my life that I think I may be forgiven for being sceptical when its appearance confronts me. Against my will you are forcing me to believe in yours. Would you care to hear my explanation?'

'That's what I've come for,' I said gruffly.

She sat back in her chair, shading her eyes, and looking into the fire. She spoke in a low voice, and without a break, as though she were reading from a book. She began:

'I shall be obliged to give you a brief account of my life. It has been that of a scholar. I have never had to work for my living, and so I have been able to devote my whole energies to learning, and to avoid trivial daily intercourse with my kind. And the average human being has always suffered in my eyes by comparison with the impersonal things with which I live. My

73

parents died soon after I left college; and from my twenty-third year I have lived in the country alone except for a housekeeper and her assistants, who have orders to keep from my ears, at all costs, the squeakings of the domestic machine.

'I did not withdraw from human society all at once. I was always a victim to shyness, but I had a capacity for friendship, and constancy was one of my virtues. During my undergraduate years, I met several people with whom I desired my relationship to continue. For two or three years after we had ceased to meet daily, I corresponded regularly with them, and received their letters with a pleasure intensified by the loneliness of my life, and not to be understood by people whose correspondents are many and carelessly chosen. But the expected happened – the letters grew shorter and duller and less frequent. When we exchanged visits, there would be a temporary flaring-up of the old enthusiasm, but this soon died down, and there came a moment when I saw clearly that nothing but cooling ashes remained. Then I hastened the inevitable end by stamping upon the last stray sparks; I wrote letters snapping off these friendships, that time and absence had worn away to the last strand. And I turned to the Impersonal for consolation.

'And yet, in spite of my joy in my work, I could not eliminate a certain restlessness – a sense of loss. This was always least manageable at the time of the postal delivery; each morning and each evening a rebellious expectation stirred in me at the thought of the postman's approach. I beat it down. But at the sound of his step my body tingled and my heart beat fast. To quiet it was beyond me; and as the thud of the letters sounded in the hall, I could scarcely hold myself down in my chair; I could scarcely wait until the maid went to gather them up. I would hear her slow footsteps along the passage; then there would be a pause; then a still slower return past my study door to the kitchen; or perhaps she would stop and tap; my heart would leap – there was a letter for me after all! But it was never a private letter – always an account, or a catalogue, or a printed notice from a society. A society – what irony! Twice in the day for half an hour this suspense held me, and it receded leaving me with every nerve in violent vibration.

'At last I resolved to take remedial action. The strain on my nerves was destroying my efficiency in the only work at which I cared to be efficient; and though the admission galled me, I had to admit that my efforts at a cure by power of will were proving more and more of a failure. I decided to shut up my house for three months, and travel. On my travels I came of course into constant contact with my fellow creatures, and out of these as before I was able to select one or two with whom friendship seemed possible, and who were not frightened away by my reserve – for reserve was a protective colouring that I assumed through shyness, instinctively, not deliberately, I would have you understand. After four or five months I returned refreshed and hopeful to my work, and for a year afterwards all went well with me. My friends visited me, and I them. We corresponded; my work progressed, and I was happy. But in time their absences grew longer; and in their letters I noticed with dismay the familiar signs of alteration, which human beings, you may have noticed, in their desire to ignore the unpleasant, try to cover up with warmer protestations of regard. Once again I anticipated the work of time, and poured cold water on the cooling ashes.

'Then there followed another period of torture; this time I found my powers of resistance alarmingly diminished. There was no longer any question of controlling the nerves – the whole of my will had to be directed at the control of action. And I must own I failed sometimes even in this. Sometimes I could not wait for the post to be delivered; I would start out in the morning down my garden path to meet the postman. In the afternoon, if my walking kept me out of doors until the hour after tea at which the post was due, I would call at the village post office, in the irrepressible craving for satisfaction. These acts were ordinary and harmless enough, you may say; yes, for other people they are harmless; but not for me; I did them because I could not help doing them, and that makes any act, whatever its own nature, dangerous to the doer. Often when the postman's knock sounded, my maid would enter my study to find me risen from my seat, watching the door in an agony of tension; sometimes I would rush out myself and gather up the letters, only to have to put them into the hands of their rightful owners. Once when I had forced myself to sit still, with clenched teeth, while the steps of my maid passed and repassed my door, an uncontrollable impulse seized me; I pulled my door open, and walking into the kitchen asked her to show me the letters in her hand. Well, the humiliation of that failure made me burn for many days afterwards.

'A series of such circles represents my life history – there is no need to tell you of each in detail. But after every repetition, my will has lost something of its power to combat this obsession; and on the last occasion, I believe I have detected the symptoms of incipient madness. You found me in this place still struggling by change of scene and power of will to retain my sanity. From the moment when we met at the breakfast table I have recognised in you a kinship – that kinship which means the possibility of communication for me. I let myself enjoy your society, your young and happy bearing, and the amusing mixture of solicitude and deference with which you treated me. But I was determined that this time there should be no recurrence of the old torture; there should be no communication between us after we separated. Whether the thread on which my sanity depends will last out my lifetime, I do not know, but from that sort of friction at least, I can and will protect it. It never occurred to me that you would begin to send me letters without arrangement. I had planned to keep within the four walls of my room, where no disturbances could reach me, until your return a week later. Then your letters began to break on me, one after another. On the third morning I left Sea View, giving orders that no letters were to be forwarded to me. This insult, I thought, would sever all communication between us, unless you were of a remarkable obstinacy, a tenacity whose existence in any human soul I had long ceased to believe possible. I expected that on your return you would go away disgusted, without troubling to seek me out. And this, all things considered, seemed a desirable end...' She stopped, and went on in a voice full of effort, 'Will you please leave me now? I will send a message when I feel able to see you again. Then if you think it worthwhile, you can come and make any comments that occur to you.' So I left her.

On the following day at six o'clock, she sent for me. Once again we sat opposite each other in the firelight. She seemed rested and happier; the pallor had gone; there was a fine colour in her face, that heightened it to beauty. She waited for my comments.

'Miss Bellamy,' I began, 'the compliment you have paid me by your confidence is very great. I should like you to know that I regard it as an immense honour. Another thing I want you to know is that all the time I have known you I have hoped for something of the kind. The disturbance of your nerves passed to a nerve in me. Once I made myself ill with disappointment and frustration.'

'Why do you tell me all this?' she said.

'Because,' I said, 'I'm about to lay before you a very audacious request. It is that you will make one more trial of a fellow creature's trustworthiness. You have called me obstinate – could you bring yourself to make use of that obstinacy? Will you admit me to the position of friend, with all its privileges?'

'What privileges?' she said, and there was a hint of alarm in her voice.

'In particular, the privilege of becoming your correspondent,' I said.

There was a long silence. At last she said, 'Do you realise what you are asking? You are asking me to give my hope of sanity into your hands. The thread is all but frayed away... a little more rubbing, and... no, I cannot. I will not take the risk. Why should I trust you more than the others?'

'I don't know,' I said, 'at least, I do know, really. The answer is that I am more deserving of trust. I have a capacity for faithfulness. I think that in your heart you know this already. But I can only give you my word for it, and any evidences that may have appeared to you already. I do realise what I'm asking; I ask you to trust me with just that power. I'll look after the thread; there shall be no more fraying; maybe I'll mend it! It oughtn't to be over-difficult; I'll give you my word always to write on a particular day of the week; suppose I get a letter through to you every Monday morning; then you'd know when to expect them; and you could write to me as often or as rarely as you liked. I'd think it all a great honour, if you'd let me try... I'll come and see you too, if you ask me... and you can come to see me whenever you like; you couldn't come too often!' I stopped, breathless.

She laughed out, with real merriment. 'What an amazing woman you are!' she said. 'For optimism and persistency I've never met your equal. You would think me very misguided and unkind if I refused, wouldn't you? You think it's only right that I should accord you my trust, and let you experiment with my reason, after a month's acquaintance. Well, I give in. Do your worst. Whatever it is, I am sure it will be amusing.'

CHRISTMAS
(1929)
Kate Roberts
Translated by Katie Gramich

On Christmas Eve in 19— Olwen Jones was strolling through the streets of Tre Gaer but felt as if she were flying. From time to time she was so light-hearted that she felt inches taller than she really was. She had that good feeling inside her of having got everything done, having finished sending presents and letters to everybody. Sending presents was a bother, especially at the end of the school term, after marking hundreds of exam papers and feeling depressed at seeing so little of the effect of her labours in the children's work. She had neither the time nor the inclination to go shopping for Christmas presents after working so hard. And yet, presents had to be sent, and like someone who has done her duty, she now felt free and happy.

She looked at everything in this busy little town tonight with that elated gaze. It was raining, but not heavily, just a light drizzle. But despite the rain the town was as busy as if it were a chapel festival day. The motor cars darted through the streets like insects, and the light of their headlamps skated along the street, showing up the dancing raindrops in the air. Their horns screeched impatiently, indeed they sounded just like a man who had lost his temper and was shouting 'Get out of the way!' The light from the windows fell on the faces of people and children, endowing them with a kind of deathly pallor or a strange lavender colour.

The windows were pretty and the children were pointing at them and shouting 'Look mammy, look – a real engine!'

Olwen turned her head occasionally to look at the children who were shouting and now she turned and saw a small boy with a scarf wrapped round his head, his eyes watering from the cold and his mouth from greed, no doubt. She remembered her own childhood Christmases and the warm thrill of happiness that would go through her when she got her Christmas presents – pocket handkerchiefs, more often than not. She could smell those handkerchiefs now – the smell of new fabric, and she could see the 'Merry Christmas' embroidered in their corners in bright colours, with the last letters of the 'Merry' and the 'Christmas' finishing in a little curlicue.

Such were the things running through her mind as she walked the streets. Such things and other, different things. As she thought about these other things she began to feel not quite so happy. Gwilym, her boyfriend, would be arriving in town on the seven o'clock train, and she was walking aimlessly now while waiting for the train to come. As far as Gwilym was concerned she felt happy, but not so when she thought about Miss Davies. Olwen and Gwilym had been going out for about a year and a half, and she knew that he would be asking her to marry him that night. He had already asked her and tonight would be the night when she would give him her answer. She felt perfectly happy because she was going to say yes.

But when she remembered Miss Davies a kind of blackness spilt over her happiness, like a cloud covering the moon. Miss Davies was her friend on the staff of Llanwerful School. And of all the friendships that there had ever been on the face of the earth, this was the strangest in Olwen's view. Miss Davies was fifty-eight and she was twenty-six. When Olwen had first gone to Llanwerful four years ago, she had been in the midst of her grief for her first love, Gruffydd, who had been killed in the War. She and he had been at College together, and the news of his death came in the same week that she heard that she had got her degree. When that last news came, it gave her no pleasure, nor did the news that she had got a teaching post. She had gone to Llanwerful like a person in a dream, and she did her work in the school in the same state. She took no interest in the other teachers. To her they were all the same, except Miss Davies, and it was her age, at first, that set her apart from the rest.

As time passed, she noticed how Miss Davies stood out increasingly from the others. She had no dealings with them, and Olwen began to see how the others often grimaced when Miss Davies was mentioned. Perhaps it wasn't really grimacing, but it looked that way to Olwen. Anyway, it didn't look as if it bothered Miss Davies in the least. She went on with her work with the slow determination of someone who had the end in sight. Olwen felt sorry for her, seeing her labouring slowly up the stairs, and she was sometimes afraid of seeing her fall flat on her back before she reached the top. She thought secretly that she would be like that herself one day perhaps.

And one day something extraordinary happened, in the time called in the county school a 'free period' but which is actually an hour of pouring red ink like the blood of corpses all over children's copybooks. The two of them were sitting there, marking, on a fine Autumn day, with the sunshine streaming in and kindling the auburn in Olwen's hair and highlighting the colourless down on her young flesh. Miss Davies looked at her more with regret than admiration in her gaze, though it would be easy to admire those blue eyes and that hair that danced in the sun. They began a conversation about generalities and before long they got to personal things and Miss Davies found herself doing more than she'd ever done with any of the other female teachers – namely, revealing her secrets to Olwen. She had explained that it was Olwen's sad, kind face that had made her do it. Her story was a familiar one to Olwen, a story such as she had read many times in books. But she knew from the way that Miss Davies told her story that she regarded it as something unique. She had had a lover when she was young, a teacher like herself. She had loved him passionately and he her as far as she could tell. After courting for two years, he married someone else quite suddenly and Miss Davies never saw him again. She had closed her heart to everyone after that, she said. She was one of those who couldn't fall in love a second time. She had worked hard in the school to try to forget, and had given her life completely to her home and the school. Her father had been ill for years and it had been her money that kept the household running. Then her mother had been ill and she had carried on working and giving. After the two of them died she had been totally lost. She kept the house even though it was too big and empty for her by herself. But she couldn't bear the thought of going to lodge somewhere else. Her life now was just a kind of keeping going without expecting or hoping for anything, she told Olwen. She wasn't looking forward to receiving her pension because she had no family or friends to go to and it would be a sad thing to live on in Llanwerful and not go to school.

But she had never met anyone like Olwen who was willing to listen and sympathise like this. And at the end of the free hour, she did a very strange thing – she gave Olwen a kiss on the cheek. Olwen was startled, but she couldn't stop her. She mentioned another thing that surprised her. She knew that her old lover wasn't happy in his marriage, she said. Olwen ventured to ask how she knew that.

'Oh, not through listening to gossip,' she said, 'it's my instinct that tells me.'

Olwen asked no more. But from that moment their friendship grew. Olwen told her own sad story of herself and Gruffydd and his death in the War. And Miss Davies asked her whether she thought she could ever love someone else.

'I don't know,' said Olwen, 'I'm afraid I don't really know myself well enough to be able to tell. Not at present anyway.'

From then on the spinster was transformed in Olwen's eyes. She saw her not as a decrepit woman, but one in the Autumn of her life. And just as she had seen the Spring as beautiful in the past, now she saw Autumn's beauty. From now on, it wasn't just the traces of beauty that were left on Miss Davies's face, but beauty itself. The rich, mature beauty of Autumn. It was true that there were some wrinkles on her face but her skin was still like velvet. And she had never noticed the glory of greying hair before this. Now she felt as if she would like to take a brush to Miss Davies's hair to make it even more like satin. She was invited to her house, and after that, she used to go there often. Everything in the house looked greyish, the same look that Olwen's friend had herself had when she first knew her, a withered look. Thick, red curtains which had lost their colour hung at the windows. An old-fashioned horsehair sofa and armchairs with faded cushions. But Olwen soon got used to them. The warmth of the welcome she received transformed everything. And Miss Davies herself changed. She became more agile, her eyes began to glisten and her hair was more lively.

The friendship grew so that it became a lovely thing for both of them. Not a night passed when Olwen didn't call in on Miss Davies at her house. She would take her crocheting or sewing with her, and often enough a pack of exercise books to mark. They were close enough friends that they could spend an evening together without saying very much. And before she went home Olwen would have a cup of tea and she felt at the time that it was a little bit of heaven to carry her through the monotonous school year. Miss Davies never talked of her lover, but she often spoke about the monotony of her life, and she would finish every time by saying that Olwen had brought so much sunshine into it. And to seal that every time, a kiss on the cheek.

And then Gwilym came into Olwen's life. She had met him on her summer holidays, three years after Gruffydd's death. By now she was certain that she loved him as much as she had ever loved Gruffydd. Though it was different, of course. Two love affairs are never the same. Slowly the gap that Gruffydd had left was closed, and her memories of him were put in the cell where Time keeps such treasures.

*

The night before, Olwen had sent a letter and a Christmas present to Miss Davies. In the letter she had said that she was going to marry Gwilym. She had written the letter hastily. Carried away by her own exuberance, she had poured her joy out over the paper. Miss Davies knew about Gwilym, but Olwen had noticed that every time she spoke to her about him, the old lady didn't seem to listen much. As a rule, she would change the subject. And Olwen believed that she was thinking about her own past courtship.

Tonight as she walked the streets of Tre Gaer she was not so sure. Another possibility seemed to dawn on her, and as she got nearer to the railway station her happiness diminished. A quarter of an hour earlier, she had felt that the town was one lump of happiness and that everyone was looking at life through the same rose-coloured spectacles as herself. But now, no, she was not so happy. She was still thinking of Miss Davies. How would she feel when she received the letter in the morning? She remembered the cloud that came over her face when she had first mentioned Gwilym. She walked on and the magic of Christmas drained away. It was Christmas, Christmas everywhere. Great hunks of beef as big as islands in the shop windows and geese and turkeys with their heads hanging limply over the sills. Those necks could never stretch and make the beaks peck at anyone ever again. Pigs' heads with an orange in the mouth of each, laughing at you. Oh, Christmas was cruel in Olwen's mind by this time, that the poor pig should be made fun of, having something stuck in his dead mouth that he never ate when he was alive, and all these animals killed to supply the desires of man just for one day. This transformation came over her between one street and the next.

By the time she got to the next street, though, she was feeling better. Christmas wasn't as sad as Spring after all. Olwen couldn't bear Spring after Gruffydd's death. Spring just kindled her nostalgia and regret. The smell of bonfires from the heather mountain, deep shadows on the surface of the Menai, and the sound of children shouting while playing in the long evenings – instead of giving her pleasure, they made her sad, obscurely sad. To see everything being resurrected in the Spring except the dead. Christmas wasn't as sad as that. It didn't raise your hopes too high. When you were sad the dark, short days were congenial to your mood. When you were gay the shop windows, children's gaiety, the spirit of present-giving and enjoyment were also congenial. And Christmas was not without hope. It was the birth-time of longer days and you saw the face of a new year.

It was such jumbled thoughts as these that came to her as she made her way slowly to the station. One minute she would be happy thinking of Gwilym and her heart beat faster. But a cloud came over that happiness every time she thought of Miss Davies. The cloud grew as she got nearer to the station. She finally understood what the letter would mean to her tomorrow morning, what her marriage, when it happened, would mean to her. Her legs began to tremble, she felt like Judas, however he must have felt when he betrayed his Lord. She heard the train coming in. When she heard his shout, she felt something like a knife going through her soul. She saw a woman two years off her sixtieth birthday standing alone in her house on Christmas morning and every morning after that, alone against a background of faded curtains and limp cushions.

THE MISTAKE
(1926)
Kathleen Freeman

'I had a letter from a Mrs. Dawson this morning,' said Dr Henry Abel. The letter slid across the American leather of the table towards Miss Hilomax, whose only sign of emotion was an uplifting of the left eyebrow. 'You knew her, didn't you, in your undergraduate days?'

'Dawson?' Miss Hilomax frowned across the pile of examination papers. If you wanted to read Miss Hilomax's soul, you watched not her eyes nor her mouth but her flexible and hard-worked eyebrows. You did not interpret their movements with the obvious code in your hand. Miss Hilomax's eyebrows were much more subtle than that. When her brow was smooth she was feeling clever; horizontal creases meant a fit of benevolence or even tenderness; and the two perpendicular lines deepened when she held in leash a joke. 'Dawson? Yes, that is Helen Calthrop, is it not? What did she want?'

'Some information about a fifteenth-century Latin inscription in a parish church of Nottinghamshire, near her home. I made out some of it – nothing at all noteworthy about it. I must show it to you – where *did* I put the paper—?'

Miss Hilomax's mind did not record the rummaging that followed. She plucked a hair from her right eyebrow.

'Do you remember that woman?' she said smoothly.

'Yes – yes – a clever, dark, bad-tempered-looking girl, wasn't she, with—'

'With a thin strong body, and a fierce chin. Yes. She was extremely cruel, and extremely witty; a delightful companion; I quarrelled with her severely.'

'You quarrelled with her?'

'Perhaps I should have put her into the nominative.'

'I can still less imagine anyone quarrelling with you, unless his heart were set on it.'

'But I was eighteen years old then; I had more dignity to keep up than I have at thirty. You must have a dignity for which to do battle when you're eighteen. Helen Calthrop had a sister of the flaxen-haired sunny type, that loves athletics and has invincible moral strength; sensible and sweet-tempered to outward view, and with more emotion than I ascribed to her while she lived; after she died, I had time to think about her without bias. That girl dominated my life for three years; when she died, and my life temporarily fell to pieces, there was Helen, with her flashing cruel tongue, and her knowledge of all that I thirsted to know – about God and the Greek language, you understand. She was very kind to me; and when she lashed at me, she made the cut seem a tribute to my strength – to my promise. She wrote me letters, too; first of all, caressing my vanity – I showed such promise! – but with the note of personal affection gradually increasing its vibrations.

'Then, just when I had become her attendant to railway stations, her loyal follower, who gladly took on my naked breast the thrusts of her enemies – oh, I "slaughtered them with savage looks," you can guess how! – her confidante – I *thought* I remembered the name Dawson – then she made a mistake, and spoilt it all. She laid on the burden and the whip before the beast was fully tamed. Acts of neglect followed thickly one upon another; and the letters, done hurriedly, showed the seams; I could trace where the desire for my society joined on to the patch of condolence – I still required that; I still hugged my constancy – and the intellectual shot silk, and the thread of satire here and there. I saw the stitches, I tell you. Haste was the only explanation; and of course I pretended that overwork was the cause. But the acts of neglect hammered the truth into me; and the harsh commands "Wait here; go there where I shall be!"'

'Her satellite, yes, yes – the passion for power. Go on.'

'Well, I wrote her a letter, a long clear letter, in which I set forth my difficulty, and the obvious need for some reform. I made it all very plain. I was so crude as to say that I was not one of Nature's born tools, and she was not her sister. I presented her behaviour to her first of all with calm impersonal clarity; then I warmed up to the work; I made it very interesting for her. I thought—'

'You thought she would enjoy it and be interested, and write you a long letter back, weighing all the phenomena, and referring each to its proper spiritual cause. How like you, how delightfully, gloriously like you!'

Miss Hilomax's brows rose nearly to her hair.

'I read it aloud to myself several times. It was stimulating, I still feel. I can't imagine how she refrained from answering it.'

'She never did answer, of course.'

'No,' said Miss Hilomax. 'And so she married Walter Dawson.'

'Yes. I remember, now, hearing my wife's story of a Christmas house-party, at which she and her husband were guests; and how, before that company, she used him as material on which to practise her bitter tongue, and as a servant to do her least bidding.'

'I see it better than that. She tries her power, but the animal is broken in. The zest goes with the going of the resistance. And the bitterness is real – not a display of wit for an audience, but the real impatience of the swift sinewy mind for the adoring heaviness of its inferior. And she said to me once, leaning on the bridge over that little stream the Marly, just below her home on Mynydd Marly; and kicking the moss out of the stones through a hole in the wall, down into the water, "I worship every bit of him.""

Miss Hilomax smoothed down with two fingers the long horizontal crease on her forehead. But for a little while there remained a thread-like line where the crease had been.

A MODEST ADORNMENT
(1948)
Margiad Evans

'Bull's-eyes are boys' sweets', said Miss Allensmoore and popped one in her mouth.

She and Miss Plant had lived together for many years in a cottage just outside a small village. It was difficult to guess whether they liked each other; but they didn't seem to quarrel. They didn't seem to be poor and they didn't seem to be rich: they had plenty of food apparently but no clothes, except what they always wore; and they were squalid, eccentric and original. And rather old.

Miss Allensmoore was a fat black cauldron of a woman frequently leaning on an umbrella. She had a pair of little hobbling feet which turned up at the ends and which were usually bare. Miss Plant had great silky green eyes and soft silver hair with yellowish patches in it the colour of tobacco stain. She was very, very pretty with strawberry pink in her thin face, but in her enormous eyes which were truly half blind, there was a curious sort of threat. But she was the meekest of martyrs. She was an odd rambling creature, always dressed in a shawl and a mackintosh, and she used to pass a lot of pleasant time writing letters to the farmer who owned the cottage asking him to send a man to trim the hedge. They were rather peculiar letters. He kept a few to smile at. 'You are such a shy man,' wrote Nora Plant, 'that I don't like to stop you, although I meet you so often in the lane.'

Miss Allensmoore was an atrocious but, alas, perpetual cook. Coming down the garden path to the door which was generally open, their few visitors always heard furious frying or the grumpy sound of some pudding in the pot, bouncing and grunting like a goblin locked in a cupboard.

Miss Allensmoore also wrote letters which she sent by the baker and always expected to have answered in the same way. She played the oboe. She played beautifully, and she kept a great many dirty black cats.

Miss Plant only kept silence. A sort of blind silence which was liable to be broken at any moment by her falling over something or knocking something else down. It wasn't a quiet silence: and it hadn't the length or the loyalty needed for music. When Miss Allensmoore played in her presence, Miss Plant would sit looking desultory, like a person who is taking part in a hopeless conversation.

The cottage smelled of soot and stale shawls and burnt kettles.

And now it was January and Miss Plant was dying of cardiac disease. And Miss Allensmoore was standing in the garden on a paste of brown leaves, eating bull's-eyes.

It was very cold. On the banks of the steep fields the broken snow was lying like pieces of china. A wind was going round the currant bushes.

'Cold, cold,' muttered Miss Allensmoore looking down at the snowdrops. It would be nice to pick them and have them indoors, she thought. But on the other hand, if she left them how well they would do for the funeral!

'I won't. It can't be long now,' she said.

She breathed a long silent phrase and moved away her hand.

Miss Plant was, in fact, almost through death. At half past three in the afternoon two days later, the district nurse quietly pulled down her cuff. Miss Plant had parted with her dazed, emaciated body.

Miss Allensmoore was again in the garden, picking some washing off the thorns. Suddenly she heard the nurse calling, so she hastened indoors and met her coming out of the cupboard where they kept the stairs.

'It's over,' said the young nurse uneasily.

Miss Allensmoore looked confident and unchanged. 'Oh, don't be upset,' she said. 'What time did she die?'

'Twenty-nine minutes past three exactly,' said the nurse more powerfully. 'Can you give me a bit of help? That bed's so heavy.'

'Certainly,' said Miss Allensmoore affably, 'it *is* a solid bed. Just let me hang these things up before I put them down somewhere and forget them. There's no reunion so hard to bring about as a pair of stockings which has separated.'

It was dark in the narrow rooms. They lit candles and went upstairs. Castors screeched as the bed was moved out from the wall: a flock of birds flew low over the roof with a dragging sound like a carpet being drawn over a floor. The dust could be felt on the teeth. Presently Miss Allensmoore came out fumbling with her candle and dropping grease on her toes. An unfinished smile tinged her face for a moment before she licked it away with the point of her tongue. It was a fat, proud, eternal face, and the little smile gave it a strange brevity. She was thinking Miss Plant would never send things flying again, reaching for others.

But the nurse having finished, stepped back from the candlelight and gazed at the face above the tallowy folds of the sheet. Beneath were the vivid hands, hands in new green knitted gloves, bunched on the breast almost as if they had been a knot of leaves. A woman from the village who used to come to see Miss Plant had made the gloves for her. And she had asked the nurse if she would do her best, please, to see that she was buried in them.

The nurse again went to the bedside and quietly looked. There was a kind of daylight on the face which was the colour of the flesh in that pale, plastered light. Poor Miss Plant didn't look wonderfully young, or beautiful as the dead are said to look: she just looked simple and very, very tired. The nurse sighed as she picked up her case.

She went downstairs. Miss Allensmoore squatted on the fender holding a cup and saucer under her chin. She had lit two lamps which were flaring and she was frying chips on an oil-stove. She got up; her naked feet, dark as toads, trod the hundreds of burnt matches which covered the floor.

'All over now. Funeral Friday,' she announced.

'My God, she's a hard old nut!' the nurse thought. She said: 'I'll let the doctor know. And would you like me to call on Billy Prosser as I'm passing?'

'You mean Mr. Misery. I simply can't think of him as *Billy Prosser*,' said Miss Allensmoore. 'Oh, yes, please, if you would. I'd sooner not go myself.'

The nurse smiled. The village was a great place for dubbing and nick-naming. People called Miss Allensmoore 'Sooner'. It stood for Sooner Not Do Anything.

'If you'd be so good,' muttered she, eating chips. They were long and warped and gaunt as talons, Miss Allensmoore's chips were. She threshed them in her gums and spat them at the cats that caused an idiotic darkness by gambolling before the lamps. Wands of flame flew up the glasses and then shrivelled, while the dirty ceiling swayed with clumsy shadows. And the sagging black cobwebs.

The nurse got ready to go. She sidled away saying: 'Not nervous, are you?'

'Nervous? Nervous of what?' demanded Miss Allensmoore, and she added, 'I've known Miss Plant for a great number of years,' as if that were a perfect explanation for everything.

The nurse went, nodding mildly. Somehow she seemed frightened, Miss Allensmoore thought. In fact she was only relieved, for how dreadful it would be for anybody to have to sit with the old slut in that awful cottage! Every time she walked in the tables seemed more and more crammed with washing up, with crumbs and tea leaves and the hilly horizons of many obstructive meals. And then, the pailsful of refuse, the tusky cabbage stalks, the prowling smell...!

So she was gone. And Miss Allensmoore turned the key on her. Ha! She was alone. Now she would gently, gently put out her hand and take up the oboe. Presently she would play. How beautifully she could play! Between the pieces sighs of joy broke from her and loud words that left holes in her breath.

'Ah – ah – my beautiful – when you sing like that...' And again she would cry: 'My beloved...' Ah, oh – it was the loveliest thing in life, music – the only wise, the only sagacious thing. And afterwards she would play again, until the fire was out and the cats all slept, and something, rain or insects or mice, crinkled in the shapely pauses.

Silence. With her instrument ready, Miss Allensmoore turned to face it. It was to her what the mysterious stone is to its carver who will presently unfurl from it the form which he observes inherent in it. As stone is to the sculptor only a gauze upon the idol of his mind, silence was transparent to Miss Allensmoore. The musicians' dawn she called it. And now she was face to face with the biggest silence she had ever known and all the time the nurse was gathering up this and that she was longing to breathe across it the first dangerous phrase.

With ecstatic anguish she loved the melodious shapes of her breath; she noticed how other people breathed: to her it seemed terrible that most of them used this art only for scrambling about the world and gossiping. Out of breath! She only wished they were! They weren't fit to use the supple air. Or if they were, she reflected sometimes, it was a pity she was obliged to mix such a common medium with her music. For when she played she knew gravity and posture: she felt the formal peace of her heavy body as it centred the encircling grace of Palestrina, Handel, Gluck... Palestrina tonight...

'Art is science,' said Miss Allensmoore, 'there is no sloppy art. There are no sloppy stars.'

She talked to Ada Allensmoore every night. It was no use talking to Nora Plant, anyway, even if she happened to be alive, and she often talked about the stars because for some reason she had decided they were 'scientific and accurate'. In the hours of her playing the universe went round her in satellites of sound, and that irrelevant ingredient, her identity, lapsed into an instinct so rapt and so concise that it amounted to genius. She yielded. She yielded to her breathing, to her transformation. Apart from the Voice, hers, she said, was the most physical form of music. So she gave way, but not lusciously. Always decorously, utterly and unselfconsciously.

Sometime in the night, sitting in her hard chair, her feet crossed, she *noticed* Miss Plant was dead – and then she wondered if one felt dying as one felt music. A giving up, and a giving back, thought Miss Allensmoore. Because she knew the feeling of music was quite different from the listening to it. Of course. Just as different as any two arts could be.

So she laid down the oboe, and she went with a secret intensity to look at Miss Plant who lay hardened to the sudden light in the bed-filled little room.

'Just like a statue of herself,' thought Miss Allensmoore, who had been pondering on stone and sculptors. A statue with hands of vernal green. These, however, she didn't observe. She wanted to ask her a question, and she even prepared a breath for it as for a note, but somehow no question was spoken. Miss Plant's silence had been no more than a continual state of never being spoken to. It was now *her* turn to be superior and uncommunicative.

Miss Allensmoore gazed down upon her friend somewhat severely, as if she were going to lecture her for lying there. Not that she ever had. Miss Plant had been absolutely free. It was just the way Miss Allensmoore looked for a moment. She had, in spite of her chubbiness, strict features, and if momentarily a definite expression replaced her usual abstract glance, it was a disciplinary one.

'But it's nothing after all,' said Miss Allensmoore, her eyes leaving the wistful dead face. And going to the window which the nurse had shut, she opened it, letting in more darkness than her candle could go round. It was nothing.

The nurse had shut the window as she had shut Miss Plant's strange eyes. If they opened now, would darkness come out of them? Ridiculous idea, said Miss Allensmoore leaning out. How a little light does revive one! You feel drowsy and helpless and then someone lights a lamp and then! You're full of energy again.

She saw the lamp from the room underneath shining out on the earth below her. Cabbages had been grown there. There were their gnarled stumps curled like cows' horns. Suddenly she remembered her mother and the way she used to cross the cut stalk with her knife so that in the spring fresh leaves frilled out. Bubbling with green, the garden all round them. And the cuckoo flying over. The sound of summer too in a window which seemed to be its instrument. Rustling rain, and her father's singing...

Beyond the yellow light it was as dark as if one's eyes were shut, and as silent as if a bell had just stopped ringing. Every death brought a little more stillness into the world. But what she couldn't command was the feeling that the darkness was Miss Plant's eyes not seeing—

The village was only a dozen or so cottages all at corners with one another, each one askew, and each one butting into a neighbour's sheds or gardens. The people, primitive, yet not unworldly, entertained themselves with conversation over the hedges while they hung the washing, set rat-traps, or planted their seeds.

Everything was talked over. Yet there was caution and a native secrecy. A person not of their kind might live among them for at least five years before noticing that the sexton in the churchyard gossiped like a sparrow to people in the lane, and even the ringers nodded news under the bells.

And Miss Allensmoore and Billy Prosser the carpenter and undertaker weren't the only people who had nicknames. There was Squatty Gallipot, the fat little shopkeeper, and there was George Ryder, the postman, a tall crooked-headed man whose height and low opinion of himself made him known beyond even his wide and hilly round as Mr. Little-So-Big. The people had, however, a sense of situation and the wryness of circumstances, which at times was apter than the truth. To one man surnamed Beer they had erected a memorial stone inscribed: Tippler of This Parish, which their vicar had caused to be erased, without, however, their permitting it to be forgotten.

The morning after Miss Plant's death a neighbour, calling to borrow something, found Mrs. Little-So-Big with a burst washer and a roaring tap. It was getting light. People were cracking morning wood, carrying pigswill and paddling out to feed the poultry. Mr. Little-So-Big sat in the least wet patch of the already sodden back kitchen, a candle near his feet on the floor, lacing his boots to go and run for help; while the two women with hands reaching out towards the noise, eyed with disdain the bullets of water bouncing madly from the sink all over everything.

'What're we to do?' screamed Mrs. Little-So-Big.

'Tie a scooped out potato over ur,' yelled the neighbour. 'Miss Plant's passed away.'

'Yes, I do know she 'as for I saw nurse go to Misery's. Oh, 'urry you an' get yer boots knotted and go and fetch somebody. No, Nance, I yen't doing anything fancy for meself. Let it run till it do choke itself. Do you s'pose Mrs. Webb do know? I bin to see if I could make her out but them weren't up.'

'Oh, her's sure to know.'

The candlelight swaying in the dank draught of the jet made the nimble lips and eyelids of the women twitch. And a cockerel crouching on the copper among a lot of sacks and boxes leapt dustily and rapped upon the whitening window. The daylight which was creeping upon them seemed to cling about their faces and hair, like a fleecy hood. They wrung their hands busily.

At last Mr. Little-So-Big, tying an audible knot, jumped up, looked grievously at them, put on his hat, and then took it off again to go through the door.

'Him ought to live in a steeple,' said his wife. 'One thing though, the wind do keep 'is 'air short. Oh, come in, Mrs. Webb.'

'Why, what's up yere?'

An elderly thin woman, in a grizzled overcoat was stooping to put a milk tin on the doorstone. 'Why don't you turn it off at the main?' she asked in a shy, rather invalidish voice, which went with her complexion and the sort of pedigree hat she wore.

'Come in – come inside. I've bin three times up the gy-arden to see if you was up. So Miss Plant's dead?' gabbled Mrs. Little-So-Big.

'No!'

'Why, 'aven't you 'eard? It's as true as Satan's false. Yes. Nurse 'ave bin to Mr. Misery's already.'

Mrs. Webb had sat down suddenly on a plain old chair, leaning on the table and arranging her hands finger by finger before her. A nervous colour came into her long cheeks, her eyes filled with tears. Childless, an orphan, a widow, she had been attached to Miss Plant. She had the pallid devoted face of those who naturally develop best in the shade of others. She wore their clothes – clothes which had 'atmosphere' and a vague kind of dignity. Round her neck today she had a little fence of starched net, with posts of bone and a cameo brooch; she was as neat and clean in the early mornings, they said, as if she sat up all night watching that no dust fell on her. But for all her differences (and different she was beside their splashed broadly-shadowed bodies) she was as much one of them as were her speech and her brown sensible hands.

'Yes,' said the neighbour. 'Her's as dead as Sooner baint. Ain't it a pity 'twasn't the other one?'

Mrs. Webb said nothing. She had a sensitive imagination for which common talk was inadequate, and her timid grief was real.

'Maybe Miss Allensmoore 'ool be sorry now,' suggested Mrs. Little-So-Big. 'If you do neglect to do things they do often turn on you at the end. Look at this tap! A was a-dripping all yesterd'y.'

'When did Miss Plant pass away?' Mrs. Webb asked.

'Sometime yesterd'y afternoon I'm told. Ah, poor soul! She's gone. I seen Nurse leaving.'

Mrs. Webb sat up, saying defiantly: 'Well, I be glad for 'er sake: it were time. Her sufferings was bad.'

'Ay, strangled by her own breath,' declared the neighbour. 'And 'twasn't only that...' they cried, 'what a life!'

'Such things. I wouldn't 'ave such things done,' Mrs. Little-So-Big said. '*I'm* not afraid to speak. 'Ow do you think that old baggage spent the night – the first night after Miss Plant died, mind you! Why, a-playing on them bagpipes till three in the morning. I do kna-ow because our Arthur 'eard 'er when 'e went up past after an early yowe 'e 'ad twinning. Ah.'

There was a silence. They rested like people close to a weir breathing the cold, wild smell of running water. Mrs. Webb thought of trees turning ashen, and the drifting, groping winds of yellow leaves. Like most people, she imagined it harder to die after the turn of the days. Miss Plant would never again hear bees in the orchards, the voices of skylarks, the shy singing of waters in the valleys. However, she had no proof Miss Plant had ever heard them...

'Them's educated things though, them musical instruments as Miss Allensmoore do play,' the neighbour was saying, 'spite of sounding like our owld cat a'spaggin' the Vicar's. Some folks do say her's a cleverer woman than us working class do realise.'

'What of it! 'Er be an old turnip for all that and can't 'ave no heart for anything 'uman,' retorted Mrs. Little-So-Big, 'no education can't make up for that, nor change it. Clever! 'Er's no more clever than a dog as has bin brought up to eat bread and butter and chocolate and fish paste. It's a dog for all that, any road, yen't it? I say this: you do kna-ow, Mrs. Webb, after what you told us. Is it educated to sit on top of a great fire a-frying yerself, and let a body die upstairs without so much as a match? Come on now, Mrs. Webb, be it?'

'Pah, education! If that's it I'll wear me eye in a sling,' the neighbour said very angrily.

Mrs. Webb didn't answer. Nervously she danced her fingers on the table. Mrs. Little-So-Big sneezed and wrung her nose in her apron. The cock again scuffled and gave a dusty crow. He struggled for the light and the bright shadow on the water in the butt outside the window. And there suddenly was nothing in place of the cataract. The jet ceased, the tap coughed.

'George 'as turned it off at the main! Now what am I to fill the copper with? Oh, whatever do us women marry for? If I'd another chance I wouldn't pick George out o' a field o' turnips.'

'I want me breakfast,' said Mr. Little-So-Big, walking in.

"Aven't you brought somebody with you? Oh, you 'aven't. Well then, you can go and look for yer breakfast somewhere else. 'Ow am I going to fill the kettle?' his wife demanded.

'There's a bucketful outside,' said Mr. Little-So-Big faintly, 'I pumped it.'

'Oh, tha did? George, where was Miss Plant's part? Where did she come from?'

'I dunno. I never yeard anything about 'er except that daft walk to London she done once, years ago. 'Twasn't from yere she done it, mind. Ah. 'Oo do kna-ow if she done it all?'

'Oh yes, she went to London,' said Mrs. Webb, 'yes, that's true. She told me herself.'

'She did?' The two women looked at her sharply. She had been several times to sit with Miss Plant while she was ill. It was possible she had the secret. There was, they knew, always a secret when anybody died. Especially a woman like Miss Plant, who had never known people. But Mrs. Webb's face was empty. They saw that and went on mutually on a more monotonous level.

'Ah. Yes. Time and agen—yes, time and agen, I 'ave said there weren't anything *to* her. No, as you mid say, there weren't nothing *to* 'er. But that jaunt to London, that's true—'

'As I do kna-ow. Our Arthur, 'e asked 'er once. She said, "Ah, but that was long ago!" So 'e said, "What you done it for, Miss Plant?" "Love and scenery," she said. That was what she said, love and scenery.'

'Eh? Did she now? Did 'er s'y that? Poor thing, 'er 'asn't 'ad a lot.'

'Tchah—women!' Mr. Little-So-Big puffed, and he wrung the cockerel's neck in a decided but rather inattentive manner.

'All right, all right, George. It yen't me as you're strang-ling,' reproved his wife. 'Give yer mind to it, do. 'Tain't as if the bird'll 'elp yer. Ah, if she said that there must a' been a man.'

'I've always thought so,' said Mrs. Webb sadly.

'Huh! It must a' bin Adam then, 'twas so long ago,' the brisk neighbour countered, her eyes spell-bound and her deep pink, old-fashioned workbag of a face gathered tightly round her mouth. 'Miss Plant must a' bin forty or fifty a score years ago, I'll be bound. Not,' she calculated, 'not as any a host of women don't go queer in middle life, as we do kna-ow.'

'Ay.'

'Ah.'

'Oh, they do.'

As they sighed, bracingly, the clock struck. The neighbour stepped startlingly out of a pool, and Mrs. Little-So-Big seizing a house flannel said she mid as well mop up.

'I must do up me fire and make me a seven o'clock pudding,' said Mrs. Webb, rising. And they separated candidly.

A seven o'clock pudding was a recipe for a mixture of currants, apples, suet and flour. It was called that because it was supposed to take all the time from seven o'clock until noon to cook. But it was long after eight when Mrs. Webb sat down in her own kitchen to take off her hat after she had carefully rolled up the blind. Her dog, which had a mouth like red meat, yawned and came and lay down on her feet. Mrs. Webb patted him and then she sat with a sedate gravity on her face worrying a little over what she had told people at different times. She *had* been angry – yes there was no doubt. But she had no wish to set anybody against Miss Allensmoore. It wasn't as if Miss Plant had ever *said* anything. Only the eagerness with which she had exclaimed 'Gloves – I should *love* them. My hands get so cold—' Only that. And yes – but it wasn't much – hadn't she said, 'I don't like music, and I don't like cats'? She certainly had, for Mrs. Webb perfectly remembered it.

That cold bedroom, Mrs. Webb breathed. And Miss Plant

with only a faded old-rose velveteen coat round her shoulders! While downstairs Miss Allensmoore had a fantastic great fire, trained up sticks like some gorgeous climbing flower, right up the chimney. Hadn't she seen her sitting there with her bare legs and her sleeves pushed up, with her fat, soft flesh that looked as if it had been mixed with yeast, all naked, and flushing? Selfish and cruel, that's what she was, and didn't she deserve to be disliked? At any rate, it didn't matter surely? Unless – unless it would have grieved Miss Plant?

Mrs. Webb was uneasy. Not that Miss Allensmoore seemed the one to care or even to notice. Nance and Ellen had been comic, but it wasn't funny really, what they meant. Hostile feelings in the village could be ugly. And ugliest when it was no more than a look... One look, from everybody.

She had unconsciously gathered up a tiny ball of wool – green, the remnant left over from those sad bright gloves, and she rolled it round and round in her palms until it was moist and had a clinging sticky feeling. Tears came into her hazel eyes. Miss Plant had had such lovely eyes! When the lids were quivering, flickering their crescents of lashes against gaunt cheek and brows, they had reminded her of butterflies in summer. It was in summer Miss Plant had walked to London, she'd said. When she told her that Mrs. Webb had seen her in a flourish of dust, dragging past the brambles with their thick pink and white blossom, along some highway hedgerow. And then perhaps stooping to wash her face and hands in a roadside stream with a lovely little fish-shape of clear pebbles underneath the water...

In this way, and in others, she had often 'seen' Miss Plant. She had always interested her imagination. Sensitive, tender, romantic Mrs. Webb, pictured her going those hundred and thirty-seven miles to meet the unheard-of man she adored. Walking because she was afraid to go faster with the fragile words she carried. Looking slowly and quietly about her with her shy, cool, light brown hair stirring, at the earth's monopoly of green...

'Love and scenery,' said Mrs. Webb, feeling for the flour.

'Love and scenery.'

It was strange how certain she had always been of Miss Plant's slow errand long ago, even though she had never before heard her own admittance. It was strange how she guessed at a dominant feeling taken there, a passion which had kept her there, in spirit ever since.

When she had asked Miss Plant why she had gone the answer had been she had forgotten. Mrs. Webb wished she hadn't heard that. If she had sounded bitter and suffering it would have been all right, but she hadn't – she looked and spoke as if she *had* forgotten and was indifferent at it. She was, of course, very near death, though.

London! That was a superstitious long way. Once the women of the countryside had collected themselves and taken a trip there in a char-à-banc. They had seen St. Paul's and the Zoo, and at the end, the Tower. 'Just a broken-down castle like any other round yere,' had been Mrs. Little-So-Big's comment. No one remembered anything very distinctly. The hoardings, the banks of faces, the number of people in a Ladies, a shower, after which one of them had sat down on a seat in the park and dried her shoes with a paper bag – those had been their individual memories, for they weren't old-fashioned enough to be at all aghast, and found London, as a matter of fact, far more like their own cities than they could have guessed.

But Mrs. Webb again was different. She remembered looking at some people sitting on the steps of St. Paul's and wondering if by chance Miss Plant had once sat there to rest and listen to the misty whirr of the world. And at the Tower she thought she had never seen, anywhere, brighter April grass. And (this was queerest of all) when they told her some great man had walked across it to have his head cut off, she had seen not a figure out of a story, but poor Miss Plant, in her old brown burberry, the worsted shawl drawn over her stained white hair, wandering over to the tragic corner as she wandered up and down the hedge the farmer wouldn't cut. She *saw* her. She seemed to quaver across the air, across the sunshine, weaving herself, as it were, *behind* the April light.

Coming home, Mrs. Webb remembered she had taken off her hat and gone to sleep and dreamed Miss Plant was in the next seat, asleep too and leaning on her. Odd, she thought, to dream that someone else was asleep! Odder still that the time should come when she was telling the dream to Miss Plant. Oh dear, she wished she had gone to see the poor woman long before! But she hadn't liked to: it seemed rather presumptuous, for they weren't 'ordinary' folk, and besides Miss Allensmoore was formidable, and, she had been told, unfriendly. But Mrs. Little-So-Big was right: what you neglected turned on you at the end. It made her weep now, to think how solitary Miss Plant must have been. There was something – yes there was – in the way she had jumped at the offer of the gloves, in the tone in which she said she didn't like music – that made Mrs. Webb consider whether she wasn't more like one of themselves really? Only she had got marooned with Miss Allensmoore, who didn't encourage people to be neighbourly and who would, now she was left alone, probably end up as one of those queer women who are found dead one day, dressed in newspaper, after they have shut themselves up for years.

'With seven days' milk sour on the doorstep,' Mrs. Webb exclaimed. The picture was dreadful and she felt quite sorry for Miss Allensmoore, even while remembering the weeks, when alert with indignation, she had waited only for the chance word to speak her mind. But Miss Allensmoore had utterly defeated her by her silence and her acceptance of things. She sat, or she walked about prodding the garden, and that was all. She had a way of standing in the lane just outside the gate with one hand just lifted as if to seize even a robin's twist of song, and catch it, as one squeezes a gnat. She was listening, anyone could see. She listened to every sound as if it were news. And she leant forward meanwhile in the attitude of one who is prepared to grab anything that comes close enough. At Mrs. Webb she even smiled one day when the wind was coming out of the garden, swinging the gate like a white curtain in a window. The smile was even more remote than her speechless indifference to the visitor.

When the pudding was on boiling, peacefully knocking at the saucepan lid in a subdued and proper manner totally opposite to the peremptory frenzies of Miss Allensmoore's fierce creations, Mrs. Webb went and peeped through the window into her orchard. The south-west breeze was blowing, the bare boughs all but knotted against the pane, were full of the village notes of blackbirds and thrushes, and her troop of hooligan young hogs was galloping crazily over the grass under the trees. The weather was yielding, the snow would be melting off the hills, and there would be water over the road for Miss Plant's funeral without a doubt. It was in that orchard, walking up and down, she had knitted most of the gloves, while keeping an eye on a hen who had a mind to lay in other folk's hedges. For several afternoons after having a wash and doing up her grate, she had walked and twinkled her needles until it was time to go indoors again to get her nephew's cooked tea ready. She had knotted the last stitch there, close to the old perry pear and then she had brought them indoors to sew on their backs, at the table, by lamplight, the sprightly woolly flowers that were to bloom in the grave.

Miss Plant must have been *used* to cold hands, Mrs. Webb told herself, in tears again, so that the orchard looked all blurred and warped through the shrunk glass. And the fact that she was apparently determined to be *buried* in Mrs. Webb's gift showed that it was not so much for themselves she wanted them as for what they represented. Friendship. Company, Sympathy. Although she had cried joyously when Mrs. Webb promised to make them. 'They'll be pretty too...'

Mrs. Webb thought they were pretty. Not that she had ever seen Miss Plant wearing them, for she grew worse very suddenly as it happened, and after they were finished and taken to the door she had never seen Miss Plant again. She had given them to the nurse and the nurse had brought back the message: 'Thank you. They're a great comfort. She says she'll never take them off. She wants to be buried in them, she says...'

'Is she – dying then?'

The nurse nodded: 'She may rally but I don't think it's likely now.'

So Mrs. Webb had gone away to wait for the event which was in spite of her foreknowledge such a shock to her. Often and often she thought of Miss Plant lying there under the old dark army blanket which gave her long body the look of a rough image dabbled out of earth. She had known Miss Plant was dying – oh yes. Hadn't she told herself there was a look no one could ever mistake particularly when the face of the sick person was seen in profile? Remembering this and the hair like glass or ice, and the strange fluttering eyes, the shape of which was an intensity in itself, Mrs. Webb felt how easy it would be to see Miss Plant's ghost.

Those eyes! They focussed the tiny room, furnished it; and Miss Plant herself became in some strange way only the brink of them. As she grew weaker, their characteristic, passionate stare seemed to withdraw further and further. Rather than being fixed on distant visions, they appeared to be retreating from everything they gazed on. She would lie and look at the small, low window at the foot of the bed where the wind flopped in the shred of coarse white lace. Close to her hand would be a saucerful of peeled orange left by the nurse, her silver spectacles and the book of Common Prayer. Scales off the white-washed rafters fell in among her hair – thin brittle flakes which Mrs. Webb would comb out, and pick from the bedclothes. Then one day when she was doing nothing at all and thought Miss Plant was asleep she had suddenly been asked if she would read the Litany. That was the time she remembered best. She had gone very red and hasty as she said, Oh dear, to tell the truth she wasn't a very grand reader.

'Not even with my glasses on. And without them, well, I can't read a bull's head from a duck's foot as I say. I expect I haven't been as well educated as you. We all do say you must be very clever to live with a woman like Miss Allensmoore.'

'Why?' Miss Plant asked, as if she were astonished.

Well, I mean she – Miss Allensmoore as do play such educated music! Not that I like it if you can understand me. It's above me. A good hymn now – some of us like that. That's about all. Yes, you must be very clever indeed and I'm sorry I can't read to you. But if it's the Litany you want I don't need to. Shall I repeat it to you?'

Miss Plant looked wondering for a moment. Then she closed her eyes and the two women began to mutter the sorrowful rhythmic words. But in the middle Miss Plant suddenly opened her eyes again and in them was a cunning, confidential look – something sleek and furtive and yet rather defiant.

'I don't like music,' she said shortly: 'And I don't like cats,' she added. 'I wonder if anybody *ever* thinks of me?' she speculated faintly.

Mrs. Webb looked down, sorting her fingers as if they were skeins and making a row of them on her knee. 'I dreamt about you once,' she said. 'It was the night we were coming home from our tour in London. I dreamt you were asleep next to me in the bus.'

'Music's too good for me,' said Miss Plant bitterly, 'and too queer. Did you know I walked to London once?'

'I have heard you did. Whatever did you do that for, Miss Plant?'

'I've forgotten,' said Miss Plant. 'I've forgotten everything about it except that it was one summer, and I used to walk along in the dusk because it was cooler. I saw owls. They were like moths,' she sighed. 'There were bats too and I was always afraid they'd get in my hair. Tell me, Mrs. Webb, do I talk in my sleep?'

Mrs. Webb shook her head. 'I don't know. I haven't heard you. Why?'

'I feel as if I do. I hear myself. I can't change it though—'

'You're free to talk in your sleep if you want to,' Mrs. Webb nodded hotly.

'I saw an old woman,' Miss Plant mumbled; 'it was once when I'd lost the road and I went round to the back of a big house to ask the way. I thought I ought to go to the back for that, but I was so frightened always of dogs! I'm very independent, really, you know and I didn't like asking. I saw such a little old woman, pumping. She had on a skull cap. Yes. A big blue apron with pockets and a skull cap. I couldn't make her understand at all. She kept saying, "The mistress is round the garden, feeding the chickens if you'll just step that way." No, not step, stroll, was what she said. I've often thought she might have been me. How funny to remember that. I'm sure there were only the two of them living there and they both ate their meals in the kitchen together. And it was such a big house! All the beautiful rooms must have been shut up. Lovely furniture and curtains I'm sure. Eh, don't you think so?'

'Very likely,' said Mrs. Webb compassionately. 'Maybe you dreamt it. I know I remember what I dream much better than anything else.'

Mysterious and rambling, Miss Plant shed no intentional secret but lay there talking and letting the irrational light of her sick memory fall here and there on what must have been a coherent life once. And filled with pity, Mrs. Webb tried to arrange her in the bed, to make her eat the eggs she carried to the cottage, warm from the nest, to please and soothe her. Never once did Miss Allensmoore come upstairs. If she had it would have been she who would have been the stranger, Mrs. Webb thought. And she calculated how she would get up and where she would stand when Miss Allensmoore came to the bed. Glimpses she had of her, as she went out, sitting on the fender in the kitchen, nursing her foot. Inscrutable glimpses. That was all. Except the smell of burnt toast, and the sound of the sick woman sighing over herself upstairs.

Yes, it was quite warm for January, said Mrs. Webb, going to look out of her door to see if anyone were about. There would be water over the road, surely. She leant far out, right over her doorstone. She heard the slow shuddering calls of the ewes with early lambs, and a wind which was swift sunlight touched the land as with a white flame. And wasn't that Mr. Misery coming up the hill on his motor bicycle? Yes. He fled past, popping, the silver sidecar flashing a sunspot in her eyes. She listened for the engine to stop, and it did, at Miss Allensmoore's.

Sunlight eddied round the cottage. Through wiry curtain and dusty glass it shone and settled. Under the thinnest shifting film of shadow, it bubbled and stirred like a spring in the wall at the head of Miss Plant's bed. Presently Mr. Misery's stooping head and shoulders obliterated it.

Downstairs, Miss Allensmoore lolled, waiting, turning her

head with a turgid movement on its thick neck as she looked for the undertaker to appear. She had planned the arrangements. No relations, no expense. A walking funeral. But the weather worried Mr. Misery. Did she know floods were already out in the lower meadows, he inquired? Gumboots, snapped Miss Allensmoore, and if there were any mourners, which besides herself there wouldn't be, they could paddle. Personally – here she looked preoccupied and Mr. Misery glanced about him.

'What do you do with yourself all day?' he asked.

'Call the cattle home,' she said lazily. She smiled in her dormant way and added, poking her foot at a cat: 'No doubt you're used to domestic hurly-burlies. Spring cleaning and all that. Now I detest all that sweeping and dusting and polishing. Scrubbing occasionally or washing a floor over I don't mind. In fact it's a sort of pleasure to me.'

'You don't give yourself a treat very often, then,' Mr. Misery observed: ''ard on yourself, aren't you?'

'Witty, aren't you?' she retorted: 'it's your calling, I suppose.'

After she had got rid of *him* she went out and picked the snowdrops. She took them upstairs, putting them in a cup on a small table that looked as if it were made of wet hay. She sat down with a drowsy sigh, blinking as she watched a sunbeam dazzling itself in the mean little mirror. Soon all would be quietly over...

She gave Miss Plant's feet quite an affectionate pat.

A few days later, in her shaggy black, with her healthy wide open gaze which seemed to refuse to mourn, Miss Allensmoore followed the coffin of her friend alone as far as the village. The bearers *were* in gumboots, and, listening to them going champ, champ, champ, along the lane, she smiled to herself.

'A lot of melancholy indiarubber elephants,' she thought, delighted.

But when they came to the village where glass, stone, and slates were giving back a greyish reflection of the flat afternoon light, there was quite a crowd waiting. Quietly, and rather drolly, as if someone else had made up her mind for her, Mrs. Webb came forward carrying a wreath of moss and aconites which she had made the night before. Mr. and Mrs. Little-So-Big and one or two more who were standing by, also wandered up and began vacantly to follow until gradually a funeral shaped itself under the serious and wand-like gestures of Mr. Misery, over whose tall black hat and deft flexions, Miss Allensmoore's ironic eye perpetually tripped in spite of her straightest efforts.

'What can they all be looking so peculiar about? Surely it's what's called a "happy release", she reflected, twirling the identical snowdrops, laughing a little in her bottom chin as she saw aside, other figures trying to catch up. There was a child, alone, who seemed happy, who seemed to think that such a procession must mean a celebration, and who began most respectfully to dance, while all the rest walked silently, with a touch of fame, with transparent gaze and opened lips, as in a story, down to the edge of the thin water where its blue and brownness flowed over the lane.

There they paused a moment as long as a leaf might take to sidle to earth from the top of a tall tree, before the bearers' loaded feet stepped into the flood.

'Oh, will they be drownded?' the child quavered, in her high drawling voice.

As clearly as if the coffin had been glass, Mrs. Webb saw the green hands curled in Miss Plant's breast... she scrounged up her skirts. The water was in truth hardly deeper than the heel of her shoe, but psychologically she seemed to require emphasis.

Miss Allensmoore stopped. What revelation possessed her she didn't, for a moment, fathom; it was something *warranted*, something far too assured in Mrs. Webb's action which convulsed her into perceiving, for the first time, the people who surrounded her.

She stopped. She would *not* share this absurd funeral with that woman or anybody else.

'Can't go any further,' said Miss Allensmoore. 'Here, will you take these?' she addressed Mrs. Webb directly, with a most uncharacteristic courtesy. And she looked past her at the coffin now being slowly borne up the hill, with a terrible expression on her face, like the obstinacy of death. In that second her sight became myriad. She saw Miss Plant, who had somehow at the last moment contrived to amass an undreamed hostility against her. She saw the stupid, avid stares, the dancing child moving only her hands and her eyelids, in her mimicry of joy, the church steeple poking through a hill like a giant darning needle, and five white and golden hens pricking proudly over a swell of winter wheat... She saw the onyx clouds, the beautiful wind that came so suddenly that it was carved like lightning in the silver water fields...

Mrs. Webb didn't turn, so the snowdrops fell on the water and gaily nudging one another, rippled into the ditch.

'Well!' cried Miss Allensmoore furiously. Trumpets of rage and grief sounded for her. She went so pale that many of the small crowd thought she would faint. But not she, not Miss Allensmoore. There, in the middle of them she stayed, staring with paralysed eyes until the coffin and its few followers were round the bend. Then she moved and prodding and pushing the road behind her with her umbrella, she climbed to a point from which she could see them creeping to the churchyard across the ribbed fields.

The church gate was open making a gap in the wide stone wall that was flung like a noose round the top of a hill. And the coffin was being borne forwards like the huge fated black stone that was to fill up the space. On and on they crept....

'That woman—' Miss Allensmoore said to Miss Plant. 'That woman! You *talked* to her. Coming up day after day, lying and spying. Both of you up there *talking*. And who *knows*?' cried she passionately, 'who's to judge? What *could* I do? What use is a wise friend to a fool? People. I hate them! I'd sooner shut meself in and tar my windows than ever endure the sight of one of 'em ever again.'

As she stood on the hill, watching Nora Plant's body being taken to the earth, it was useless telling herself she was going back to silence, useless to say the uproar was over and there would be no more crashes, no more fidgetings, no more nurses and neighbours coming. For the foundation on which she had suffered these things to be, was gone, and nothing was significant any more, and perhaps never would be again. Miss Plant had, she believed, destroyed that profound, if secretly weary, fidelity which had bound them, and in so doing had revealed the astonishing reality of her own quaint affection. She could not speak: her outcry was mental only. There, leaning on her umbrella, she stood, speechless, as when, with her oboe, she turned towards silence with the first low summons to the hordes of sound, as when, all those years ago Miss Plant had come to London just to say to her, 'I can no longer bear to live away from you.'

RED EARTH, CYRENAICA
(2018)
Stevie Davies

After the veterans' reunion, David dreams, awakening in the old anguish. Margie sleeps soundly beside him. *I brought* that *into our bed*, he thinks, *and here it has remained for half a century. There's a self that leaps free of the pieties of married love – a quicksilver, erotic spirit, young through all the years.*

Archaic desires resurface. They were born and should have died in wartime Libya, with Colonel Pitway headless in the desert and the red cave's secret mouth above Derna. The desert brimmed and gushed, in a fortnight's torrential rainfall that engulfed one village after another – Giovanni Berta and Slonta, Tocra and Benghazi. The world turned to a mud-slick.

Demobbed at the end of it all, the men gratefully resumed the customs and certainties of Civvie Street: marriage, kiddies, regular work. What they'd known of carnage and carnality they abandoned in the desert. It was filth, you burned it like the troops' stinking underwear at Derna. With hindsight David came to see the episode with Clem as vagrancy, an aberration. The boy in the dream said to him last night: *When all this is over, darling, we'll make a better world of it.* How wrong he'd been.

The pair came slithering hand in hand down the wadi.

Coupled men with ground-sheets over their heads foraged for firewood through gutted Arab houses. Vehicles sank in a universal bog while engineers and road gangs stained red to the thighs laboured to bridge the floods; planes ditched in sudden ponds; corpses oozed in septic water; radios failed. Such rains had rarely been known in Cyrenaica.

Clem, coming close, breathes freshly on David's face.

II

In the desert, icy night fell in the blink of an eye. Murder paused in the slaughterhouse of northern Africa. In the tank's shelter David lay wrapped in some dead Arab's reeking sheepskin, in a trench dug by retreating Germans. Stars, like jewels on velvet, lit the pallid sands for miles. Craving for his girl Margie, back home, grasped David's heart, a fist thrusting into his tenderest place. An enormous silence surrounded him. The sleep of the world, as it had been before and would be after he was gone and she was gone and the ruined cities were forgotten.

III

White dust misted the desert, up to the height of a man's chest. Into this murk, tanks and lorries belched blue smoke as stagnant oil burned off. Their Colonel had – outrageously – slept in, wearing silk pyjamas. Suede boots scented with pomade like an Italian's stood at the foot of Colonel Pitway's opulent sleeping bag. David's driver, Private Clement Kazarian, said that when he'd delivered the message to the Colonel's tent, the batman shushed him: 'Not until my Colonel has taken his morning tea.' The men chafed, having long since stowed their bedrolls and brewed strong, sweet chai in petrol cans. The line was ready to move. Heat got up and a dreary wind. The Colonel slumbered on.

Later that day Colonel Pitway was dead and already stinking.

The desert drank his patrician blood into its colossal thirst. The column moved past through a graveyard of dead tanks, already half buried in drifting sand. Droves of exuberant Spaghettis cheered their own surrender.

The khaki Padre appeared at the head of Colonel Pitway's hastily dug grave, with five or six men of all ranks. Tears streamed down the batman's face from eyes swollen with weeping. *They shall grow not old.* The Colonel had seemed to the boys already an old man, though he could only have been forty. He'd not been popular. Huntin' shootin' Jew-hatin' type. His head was smashed clear off his body. *As we that are left grow old.* There was no particular sense of horror. A wooden cross cast a shadow. *Age shall not weary them...*

The sequel was a Greek drama all its own. As the funeral party began dispersing, the batman hurled himself on the mound, keening in a voice audible above the din of artillery, the screaming of planes: 'I loved him! I worshipped him! What shall I do now? Where shall I go?'

There were some thoroughly good eggs among the upper officers, men of culture and human feeling. One gentle Major took charge. 'Come along now, my son. You've done all you can for him.' Nobody mocked.

The battalion pushed west. Mussolini's troops ran for it. The pursuers had an open road; their spirits soared. 'To Derna!' Cyrenaica lay on a plateau, with towering cliffs above the dazzling Mediterranean. The Wadi Derna was famed for a waterfall and caves, once the sanctuary of Christians fleeing persecution. The Pass looped down in a series of breathtaking hairpins. A jubilant convoy entered an oasis of pomegranate groves, white colonnaded houses in the Fascist style with neat vegetable gardens.

David translated at interrogations of captured Spaghettis who obligingly blabbed wild, invented secrets. Later he wandered the town, marvelling at its colonial luxury. Officers' beds were laid out with clean linen; gold-laced Fascist uniforms hung on padded hangers. On a white marble mantelpiece a lewd Cupid exposed himself to a naked nymph. Collapsing on a plump mattress, David passed out. For an hour perhaps. Awakening in a state of uncomfortable arousal, he became aware of Clem Kazarian sprawled beside him, dark curls tumbling over the pillow, like David's eight-year-old brother Ned tucked up at home in Truro.

Clem hardly budged as David clambered over him. A Spaghetti officer had bequeathed the luxury of a toothbrush. Swilling from the ornate brass taps – oh, the ecstasy of running water – David spat red mud. He thought of blood on the sheets in Cardiff. For Margie, against all her principles and upbringing, had given herself to him the night before embarkation. With tears. It had not been a huge success. He lay back down beside the boy.

A bird called harrowingly from eucalyptus beyond the glassless window. Bullet holes pitted walls and ceilings; a smashed piano splayed its keys.

He shook Kazarian's shoulder. No response. Wakey wakey! The statuette of Cupid was scarcely more softly suggestive than Clem's full lips, the flush of his face with its dark eyebrows and lashes. On his cheek was a scar like a pair of wings, the relic of a childhood fall from a tree. David's fingertips brushed his driver's forehead; Clem awoke and smiled into his eyes. The cool room held its breath.

IV

Lower ranks under canvas, officers in commandeered quarters, they'd been granted twenty-four hours for shut-eye: bliss for an army that had spent weeks catnapping in trenches. Clean underwear replaced stinking KDs, which were burned. A musical Lieutenant had reassembled the piano in *that* villa. Strains of Schumann's 'Scenes from Childhood' sparked homesickness as David waited outside for his driver.

Clem said, 'Crime to miss the historic caves, sir, don't you think? The chance might never come again.'

'All right but don't *sir* me, for God's sake.'

'Sorry, sir.'

'Give it a rest, Clem.'

'I will, sir, when we're high and dry.'

They climbed a narrow path up the wadi. David, fuddled with fatigue, stumbled along in the rear, his mind full of longing for his mother, brother and sweetheart. Below, lads played cricket on a green sward, a wooden board for a bat. David's heart wobbled wildly.

The sound of hissing and foaming filled the air. The famous waterfall pitched from a salmon-pink ridge into a turquoise pool fouled by debris, the refuse of centuries of trippers. Semi-literate graffiti, ancient and modern, were carved in many languages: tokens of serial pointless conquests by Greeks, Egyptians, Arabs, Ottomans, Axis and Allies.

David must lie down or he'd fall down.

A decaying mouth: the cave's sour breath hit them a yard in. The putrefying carcase of a goat drove them back to the cavernous opening, where they sat above a sheer drop and drank from water bottles. Rain clouds massed. A plane screamed overhead like chalk on a blackboard. Whether this loosened the knot, David couldn't tell. He went to mush. He began, to his shame, to blub, sobs convulsing him, a string of snot dangling from his nostrils.

The eighteen-year-old private says to the nineteen-year-old

captain – and David at seventy hears it from his Truro home, quite clearly, *After this lot's over, there'll be a fairer world, a place of greater gentleness, don't you think so? A Socialist republic. It's all I care about. Well, that and you. We'll make it happen, won't we, darling?*

Clem cupped David's face in both palms, a gesture of boundless tenderness.

When they returned to Derna, the rain was torrential. There'd been a raid: two Stukas brought down. Men fell away before them. For Captain Tremain and Private Kazarian had lost all of twenty-four hours. Nobody said a word. Old Pitway's batman quietly offered chai.

Later, in the Spaghetti billet, David met himself in the shaving mirror, face raw from the boy's stubble. Now he knew. He knew now. There was no quenching a radiant smile at the beauty of his own anointed body, the kindness of Clem's.

V

That was 1941. The Desert Army lost Derna. The Eighth Army took it again in 1942. The length of northern Africa the Allies fought the Axis, east to west, west to east, east to west again. Two years of sun stained their faces to teak. The desert stink became their own smell. Clem had swiftly been reassigned after the Caves episode.

Nothing said.

Fraternising with Other Ranks was the sin against the Holy Ghost. Even a newly promoted young captain was forbidden to consort with a private soldier. After the separation, David demanded demotion to the ranks but his punishment was to remain stranded in the élite, with his soiled reputation. 'Bits of brown', the Tommies called the pansies. But the phrase was spoken with wry fellowship: nobody openly leered or mocked. David wrote to Clem, via his home address. No reply. He wrote again. Nothing. The censors – his bastard fellow officers – were doubtless primed to destroy their correspondence.

By the time David returned to Cyrenaica, Derna was unrecognisable. A bomb site. *That* villa no longer existed. He stood in its ruins. There was no time to revisit the caves, nor in truth was he particularly tempted. Already he was attuning himself to the norms of home and later it was to Margie that he attached a gradually fading ache of intimate loss.

VI

'Poor chap – never made it home. I heard he was ambushed in Palestine at the end of the British Mandate. I'm sorry,' said Colonel Pitway's batman at the reunion, dapper in his decay, a retired insurance clerk. 'You and he were such great pals. Clem was a one-off job, that's for sure.'

He put out a brotherly hand as David turned away, striving to master the decades-deferred sob that burst up from his guts.

Of course the batman had known from the off: who should sniff them out more surely than the unit Fairy Queen? *I loved him!* he'd cried at the Colonel's grave, for all to hear. Throughout his military career Jones would have been joshed, camping it up for all he was worth, giving value. David squirms from the man's complicitous pity, thinking: we were not like you.

Were we? And does it matter? Who cares these days anyway?

In Cyrenaica a match was struck in the dark: some intense but fugitive illumination threw light on nothing beyond itself. No sequel. Or so he grew to feel at the time. Sundered from his friend, David marched through the meadows of Sicily, into the carnage of Italy.

VII

Downpour: the River Truro in spate, the soil awash. Luke, their grandson, who earns a few bob doing the heavier garden work, has left a spade leaning on a tree. David wanders out, bareheaded, in his slippers; finds himself standing ankle-deep in mud. Snaring his hand, Margie leads her husband indoors. She seats him at the kitchen table with a mug of tea and chats about this and that, keeping him in her sights, listening, observing. Through the window David ponders the water-logged trench as he hears Margie on the phone to their daughter: 'Soaked to the skin he was and coated with mud. Seems fine now, bless him. He came back from that reunion rather shaken, you know. And I'm not surprised.' Something in her tone makes David's eyes smart. He has lived mantled in this ordinary affection, eating the everyday food of gods, for nearly fifty years.

Later, in bed, she asks, 'What is it, love?'

'Something I should have explained years ago. A pal from army days, Margie.'

'Yes?'

'Oh, nothing. Just a friend.'

'It's Clem, isn't it? Clem Kazarian. You talk to him in your sleep. Only occasionally nowadays.'

David listens, astounded less by his wife's reserve than by her acceptance. Oh yes, Margie minded at first: the bizarrely broken nights, coaxing her sleep-walking husband back to bed. But then, oddly, she got to know Clem: an exceptional young man. She accepted these trysts as a conversation the three of them shared in the night, a reunion of sorts.

'Don't be upset,' Margie says and cups her hands around his face, in that tender gesture David caught from his lover, brought home to his wife and everlastingly receives back from Clem.

KNOWLEDGE
(1937)
Glyn Jones

On the top of Ystrad Pit three men were repairing the winding rope. It was a lovely sunny morning, blue and fresh, and they worked with the thick black criss-cross shadows of the steel winding-gear falling across them over the sparkling ground, and their fire looking pale because of the strong sunlight, as though it were going out. One of the men was the colliery smith, a grey priestlike old man with a serious, almost mournful, expression, gentle, having the face of one possessing himself completely, claiming nothing. He was grey and clean-shaven, dressed in an old cotton boiler suit of navy blue, and he wore a soiled cap with the peak broken in the middle above his eyes. But although he was old, and his eyes were weary, his body was slim and upright, and the grip of his hands on the stubborn rope was vigorous, as assured and masterful as the handling of a young man; but his face wasn't masterful at all, only kindly and gentle with knowledge. The three of them, the two men and the boy, were working at the pithead and not speaking much, with the cage hitched up in safety above them near the sheaves and the thick steel rope lying coiled over the dusty ground at their feet. They had the stiff brush of strands from its ravelled end fixed securely up like spiky hairs through the bottom of a sort of deep iron cup or inverted bell held in a bench-vice into which the second man was pouring molten lead out of a long metal ladle. The boy apprentice, very dirty with grease and coal-dust, was blowing the fire-bucket from time to time with a foot-bellows to keep the iron crucible of lead hanging over it molten. The man pouring out the liquid metal was the pitman, being responsible for the ropes, and the cages, and the shaft of the pit generally, a big handsome youngish man, with grace in him and restraint, doing his delicate job easily and with perfection. He was using a lipped ladle with a long flat metal handle that he gripped with squares of soft leather, tipping the lead out like water, waiting for it to sink a bit on cooling and then filling it up again to the brim; and he never spilt any, he had done it so often, although once or twice it swelled up like a bubble with the scum cracking on the lister-like curve. He had taken off the oilskins he usually wore for his job and was working in a thin white shirt with his sleeves rolled up almost to his shoulders, and his trousers fastened low about his loins by means of a thick leather belt buckled with two tongues of brass. He was big and powerful, his flesh like most pit workers as white as a girl's in the sunlight, and his arms large and white, and solid, but smooth, not lumped into muscle although they looked capable and were firm with power. He wore a wide strap on his wrist and his hands were big too and soiled, with blunt fingers. He was much younger than the smith but he effaced him with his huge shapely body and his energy. His face was pale and smooth, rounded, and his soft dark hair was cropped short, not moving in the breeze; he was very big, his thin shirt tight on him, and yet he seemed shy, his light eyes troubled a bit from time to time as though he feared being hurt, although not through the body, and his handsome edgy lips were too ready for kindness. He had none of the smith's gentle stoicism and endurance. He knew he could be hurt and he feared it.

The smith was his father-in-law.

Finally the bell-shaped container was completely filled and the pitman lighted a cigarette waiting for the metal to cool before fixing the rope to the top of the cage. It was Sunday and there were no workmen about the colliery, only one or two officials and the lamp man. The boy, who had not long left school, was trying to pitch his cap over the sparrows.

'When are you coming up?' asked the pitman, speaking to his father-in-law.

'I'll come up some night this week, Penn,' he said, stretching out his hand towards the cooling metal. 'Is Gwyn all right?'

'She's all right,' the pitman answered, 'only wondering when you're coming up.'

The old smith smiled; there was sympathy between the two men.

Gwyn was Penn's wife, being eight or ten years younger than himself, a kind of stranger people didn't know very easily, a bit awkward and distant with anyone she didn't care about. People liked her, she was so pretty, narrow, with long straight yellow hair almost golden, cut in a long bob at the back nearly to her shoulders, and growing cropped in a line across her forehead; and she had white skin and spotted blue eyes. But there was something in her people missed, as though she kept something back purposely for herself from everybody. She wasn't easy in her intercourse with people and she flushed readily as though speaking to anyone unfamiliar was a strain, a good bit of a hardship. But inwardly she had the steady unassuming assurance of the old smith, her father. She had no real fear of being hurt at all; she disliked irritating little contacts with people and she avoided them, being at times almost panicky, but she was passionate and she knew she could fight although she never wanted to. Penn understood this somehow and he relied on her, feeling safe with her at his back; she put such spunk into him.

When the metal was cool through and through, Penn got up

the iron ladder on to a platform in the winding-gear high above the open mouth of the shaft that tapered below him like a huge inverted fool's-cap, and clamped the rope on to the cage with two long strips of reddened steel. He watched the spokes of the big wheels above him beginning slowly to move round in answer to his signal, and the thick steel rope dithering like a harp-string as it took the weight of the big iron cage; and then he tested his job himself by getting into his yellow oilskins and being wound down the shaft standing on the roof of the cage. Everything was in order. He called to his father-in-law and started up his motor-bike for home.

II

Penn and Gwyn lived in a pleasant old house belonging to her father, a good way from the pit, right out in the country beyond the edge of the coalfield, with the khaki mountains beginning close behind it. In some ways living there was inconvenient for them because if there was something wrong at the pit Penn had to go out at once, often in the middle of the night and in all weathers, to get to his job somehow. But he had his motor-bike and they thought it was worth it to be out of the dreary shabby town and the smoke and the endless noise. The house was pretty with the bright-coloured painting Penn had done to the outside woodwork, and all the flowers and the trellises; it stood the other side of a brook with a wooden bridge over it, and it had a big garden at the back with fruit trees and roses. Penn spent most of his time growing flowers, particularly roses, and in summer he gave away dozens of bunches to his friends. It was queer to watch him in the rose-garden; he had a large number of little white linen tents, that he could adjust against the sun, clipped onto the supporting stakes of his most valuable rose-trees, and when he looked at the blooms under them he became intent, as though his eyes were seeing past every curled rose-petal, touching the small inner quick and earth-urge that thrust up the stalk and pushed out the shallow petal wrapping from the tiny yellow attachment to the stem; he looked as though he were seeing all over the flower and into the heart of it, right down the thin trunk-stem, knowing the action of its threaded roots, and his big hands went delicately into the thick of a rose bush feeling their way round a flower to pull it back for the loose rose-whorl of its petals, or to scissor it off low down on the stalk. When Gwyn saw him stooping to handle the roses, peering into the tangled bushes at them in his intense absorbed way, so quiet, she felt excluded, strangely out of it. She couldn't see she came in there anywhere, but she loved him for it, shearing himself off like that from time and place, caring about nothing, existing only with the rose between his hands and at peace with it. She was filled with tenderness for him almost to tears, seeing all the latent feeling and power of his magnificent body fused down on this intense observation of an unbudding flower, giving himself up without any reserve of doubt or fear. But she could see there was nothing scientific or curious in his expression; he seemed as though he understood pretty well already, and his look wasn't of inquiry at all, or speculation or even wonder, but just acceptance, and slightly puzzled knowledge. When she saw him like that she was at once filled with pity and tenderness, and she was a bit awestruck as well at the completeness of his withdrawal from everything. She used to say nothing at those times with this awe upon her, but just go back to her house-work again.

It wasn't often she asked him to go to chapel with her. She was religious like her father and went pretty regularly although she didn't like the concerts and the tea-parties; she went and hurried back home again as quick as she could, not very sociable. But the

evening her father came up after work as he had promised she
said, 'Penn, dada and I are going to chapel. Will you come?'

He made a face. 'Oh, I don't know,' he said uneasily. He didn't
like to refuse outright because of the old smith.

'Come on,' she said, 'this once. You always like the meetings
in the weeknights.'

'Oh all right,' he answered. 'I've got nothing much to do, I
don't mind really.'

So the three of them started out, walking.

III

It was still daylight when they crossed the wooden bridge outside
the house, but the chapel was in the town and by the time they
got there it had become quite dark and the lights were lit in the
streets. They went through the wooden door into the warm silent
little schoolroom behind the chapel and separated, Gwyn going
on to sit with the other women near the fire the far side of the
aisle between the benches, and the two men finding seats in the
recess at the side of the wooden door porch. They were early and
there was hardly anybody there, only half a dozen women and
two or three men on the benches near Penn and his father-in-
law, and when they sat down there was dead silence except for
the gas coming hoarse through the rusty brackets sticking out of
the walls and the tack tack of the clock over the fireplace
swinging its quick pendulum behind the little glass window.
Apart from these noises and the sound of the slipping fire there
was a drowsy silence that sank into him throughout the room,
very warm and peaceful, and comfortable. Penn had been once
or twice before but it was always a bit strange to him, the shabby
schoolroom and the few motionless people waiting absorbed in
utter silence for the meeting to begin, because his family was

English really and church, and he had gone there when he was younger. He watched the people coming in, one or two at a time, short people nearly all of them, undistinguished, the majority of the men colliers dressed almost invariably in black suits with their skin pale and shining, looking tight and a bit sickly in the green gaslight. He watched them creaking awkwardly over the bare knotted floor-boards into the shabby vestry and sitting round him, crooked and a bit misshapen some of them, with blue scars tattooed across their hands and their tight shiny faces, not picturesque at all, commonplace, but it was a satisfaction to him somehow to be there touching them, with their rich earthiness warming him through. They sat around him in quiet until they were a good number waiting for the meeting to start, motionless most of the time, some with their eyes shut, solid and finished, wanting nothing; they had been hurt often and had suffered, and they looked uncouth, almost monolithic, with no desire in them, only the warm look of knowledge and understanding. They sat so calm Penn envied them, seeing no bitterness in their easy hands and so much acceptance in the look of their bodies and their clean shining faces. And around them all was the still warm atmosphere, rich and getting drowsy, and the gaslight coming green off the distempered walls.

The meeting started with the young minister reading out a hymn. There was a good number of people present for a weeknight, perhaps thirty, and Penn enjoyed the meeting, especially the hymn-singing; the voices were rich and the words and music moving. He was glad he had come. Usually he didn't like any religious service, it seemed to be about something else, nothing to do with him at all. But he never said anything to Gwyn; he wanted her to go if she liked it.

Then several people prayed and quoted scripture, and one or two spoke describing their experiences and temptations, a sort of confessional. They were good too, some of them, natural actors and story tellers, humorous even, and full of drama and vivid speech. Penn was filled with admiration for them, and contented. But near the end the young minister asked Gwyn to pray. He was a nice young chap, very earnest and hard-working, and Penn liked him, but he was unwilling at once and apprehensive. He wanted to stop her from doing it, it wasn't fair. It was wrong because Gwyn was passionate and would say things to give herself away kneeling on the floor before them all. But her father just bowed his face slowly and waited in silence with his eyes closed, calm and tender-looking, quite unmoved. Penn didn't know really why he was so mad and unwilling, resisting it so much, except that he was afraid of what she would say to hurt herself before them and for a moment he hated all these people sitting round her waiting to hear her reveal herself; it was ugly to him to see them watching the grace of her kneeling body, secretly triumphing over her, hoping to see how her passion would give her away. She began softly, Penn didn't really know what she was saying. She was kneeling with her head bowed at an empty seat, her long yellow hair hanging down from under her blue cap so that no one could see her face at all. Her words were muffled, and from time to time she stopped, and there was silence letting in the sound of the gases buzzing and the eating of the fire and the awkward little coughs breaking from the other women. Penn was white, watching her over his hands, pale and strained-looking with his lips dry. As long as he was watching her he felt he could defend her and justify her, and hold her somehow in his protective control against all these other people. He was afraid to stop looking at her and thinking about her, willing her passionately to hold out against the bitter strength of her emotion and the words surging in her blood; lending her his strength. He was mad against the women near her and his mouth was like fire. He knew how unfair it was to let her kneel down like this; it was cruelty, but he wouldn't let anything happen to her. He could feel rage and strength filling him like a sap rising at the thought of her giving way; he was in a sort of fury, but quiet, knowing she must resist the concentration of so many wills, and he didn't want any longer to stop her; she had to go on and complete her prayer in spite of them while he lent her all his strength. He glanced round feeling powerful with anger and protective tenderness. Then suddenly her body went slack and she began to sob. She faltered in her prayer a bit and finally stopped, her head jerking slowly over the chair; then her body shuddered with fierce weeping. She couldn't say anything any more and she just knelt and wept helplessly with her fingers spread out over her face and her hanging hair rocking to and fro from under her cap. She was shaking right through her body before them all with uncontrollable weeping, making hardly any sound except little choking cries from time to time that broke loose from the strife of her throat. Penn was helpless, feeling nothing clearly, bewildered and helpless. Slowly she got up and sat on the bench, her face bowed over her lap, her shoulders hunched and the sobs still jerking through her like stabs. The silence and the tension were awful and interminable to Penn, who sat on defeated and hopeless, not even wondering how it was going to end, completely empty. Then slowly the young minister got up and gave out a hymn and they sang with spirit as though Gwyn's crying had released purity into the room. But she sat throughout the singing slowly coming back from her prayer with the subsidence of her passion, and by the time they had finished she was calm again, flushed and red-eyed, but composed, gathering her things together to leave. Penn was dazed, it was all so sudden and so hateful. After the meeting he found himself walking home with her through the streets, shining after the rain, and saying good night to her father; not one of them had spoken a word of what had happened. In the lane that led up to their house he stopped her and said:

'Gwyn, what was the matter?'

She laughed and lifted up his hand and kissed the knuckles of his fingers clasping hers. He sounded so sad and bewildered she had to comfort him. She went close up to him not being able to stop laughing, he sounded so tragic.

'It was nothing, Penn,' she said, 'only I love our people and I so seldom show it. Smell the gillies in the garden after the rain. I am so busy fighting.'

She ran on ahead dragging him by the hand. It all seemed so strange to Penn.

EUCHARIST
(2003)
John Sam Jones

Kneeling at the communion rail, I wondered if it had been a free choice. In as much as any choice could be free, I supposed that it was so, but then people are always influenced by outside forces. Social norms, religious myths and beliefs, the political breezes of the age... But yes, loving men in that way, and loving Joel in particular, finally hadn't felt right; out of tune, somehow, with the sacred music inside. The priest, Dafydd, was at the other end of the rail administering the Sacraments. I knew him professionally and we'd even met at a few social events, but our acquaintance wasn't a friendship that could share such secrets.

It had been twelve years since I'd last looked into Joel's open, wise face. We'd kissed and said goodbye again, for hadn't we been saying goodbye for weeks? In twelve hours the plane landed at Heathrow and I'd taken the train to my new home and a new job. We wrote, regularly to begin with, but the letters stuttered into infrequency as time passed. Joel's parish responsibilities had increased, while my own life also took on a crazed busyness as I embraced the challenge of ministering to six congregations.

Mrs Efans, a member at Bethania in the village, had been the post woman for forty years. '*Un o San Francisco heddiw Mr Llwyd*,' she'd say, handing me letters posted in the city that had been my home.

Gwenda, as I was later invited to call her, had taken to knocking my door to hand-deliver in the first weeks after I'd arrived. In her eyes, such regular contact with the new minister back from America gave her status in our isolated, closed community. She had noticed that I wore my shirts open at the chest, that my coffee mugs declared jokey slogans and that I listened to rock music.

I spilled my coffee on reading that Joel was dead. His most recent letter, in July last year, had told of a move to Boston. A letter full of excitement and hope in new beginnings... new movies to look out for and recent productions at the San Francisco Opera. Nothing to suggest a slowing down. Not a hint of ill health. No tell tale signs of being one of the thousands of worried well. The letter from Cheryl was unexpected and, once opened, unwelcome. She'd seen him in November, Kaposi's Sarcoma disfiguring his gentle face and the first signs of dementia cracking his intelligent, sometimes highbrow conversation. He'd died a few days before Easter. I wanted to cry. I wanted to hold Joel within that same strong tenderness we'd shared for nearly four years, to look into his face again and say, 'I love you.' A coffee stain edged further into the whiteness of the tablecloth.

I sought the sanctuary of routine, washing up the few dishes lying used by the sink. I placed the coffee-stained tablecloth in a bucket of cold water. The gas bill was opened and processed for the next Presbytery meeting. I stripped my bed and loaded the washing machine. But as the possibility of routine sanctuary gave way to despair, I sat in the window seat, with its view of Glan y Mawddach and Garn Gorllwyn across the wide estuary, and wept.

With no more tears but a heaviness that was hard to shoulder, I walked up into the hills behind the village and sat searching the waters of Gregennen. I wondered when Joel might have picked it up. Surely since the days of our intimacy? In all the years of celibacy I'd never considered the possibility that the virus might be harboured somewhere in the nucleus of a white blood cell. But now the possibility gnawed.

Walking along the Ffordd Ddu, I yielded to God's embrace and lying in the sun I breathed in the rich smells of heather, bracken and sheep droppings. The Healer, who'd always tended the wounds of my lifetime's struggle with a sexuality that was generally despised and mistrusted, comforted and reassured my troubled mind. The sun warmed my face, inviting my imagination to wander again with Joel in the California sun. The camping trips to Yosemite... the retreats at the house in Bodega Bay where we'd read Anne Sexton and Dylan Thomas aloud to one another to ease the mental fatigue brought on by heavier theological tomes, and where we'd made love in the hot tub on the deck under the stars. I remembered the pumpkin festival at Half Moon Bay; the garlic ice cream in Gilroy that had made Joel sick... and the peace of the Rose Garden in the Berkeley Hills, shattered by the Argentinian students' demonstration against the Malvinas war. And I wept again, but now the tears were less bitter. I had come to appreciate that what I'd shared with Joel had been a rich gift.

That spring evening, in the vestry of Bethania, only six gathered for the mid-week prayer-cum-bible meeting – *y seiat*. We read Psalm One Hundred and Sixteen together. Some of it had come to me, mouthed over and over, during my mind's sojourn with Joel, and again as I climbed down from the hills to the village late in the afternoon. Words that had been the source of comfort and strength to troubled people for more than two thousand years, had also comforted me. Gwenda Efans took her neatly ironed handkerchief from the shambles of her handbag. Wiping away the silent tears she told how she'd recited the same

Psalm, from memory, to her comatose husband in Bangor hospital.

Gwenda's words recalled for me the cavernous pits of grief into which she and many others in my congregations had descended over the years at times of loss. The fatal car accidents; the terminal cancers; the two cot deaths in one family, suicides and so many divorces. I'd walked alongside, and sometimes quite literally held up so many who'd experienced lost hope, uncertain faith and the wrenching hurts of separation. I realised that the news of Joel's death had sparked none of these within me.

The *seiat* ended with cups of tea, relaxed conversation and Dilys Morris-Jones the newsagent's bara brith. After we'd talked, drunk tea, and eaten; all the rituals done, people made their way home. After locking up the building, I walked back to the manse intending an early night.

Cheryl's letter lay open on the table. The sight of it brought Joel back to me. Sitting, watching the lights across the estuary play on the waters of the in-coming tide, I began to make some sense of my feelings. I was sad about Joel's death, but not grieving for him, for hadn't I already grieved the loss of our relationship at the time of my return to Wales? But I was shocked that Joel had been infected with HIV and that he'd developed AIDS. And I was anxious – even afraid, because our communion had been carnal at a time before safer sex and condoms had become routine.

I got the number of the National AIDS Helpline, dialled without hesitation, and spoke with the counsellor. I had to stifle my need to persuade her that Joel couldn't have been HIV positive all those years ago. Her voice was pacifying, but my anxiety only deepened when she said that she couldn't speculate as to when he'd been infected. She talked to me for a long time about testing. The implications of a positive or negative result, how the choice had to be informed, and that before deciding to be tested I'd need to have some fairly clear idea of what I'd do if the result were positive. She was patient and understanding; I could hardly take it all in. She gave me the phone number of a clinic at the hospital in Wrexham where the test could be done. It was past midnight when I hung up the phone.

My blood was drawn off and the small glass vial was sealed in a plastic bag marked BIOHAZARD in bold, red letters.

'It will be a week before the result comes back, Iwan,' the nurse said in broad Glaswegian. 'You do have to come back to get the result. We don't give HIV results by letter or over the phone.'

The doctor had been careful, before taking the blood, to establish that it was legitimate to test me and she'd asked about risky behaviours... unprotected sexual intercourse... shared injecting equipment.

'Risky gay sex then,' she said as she wrote on the anonymous file.

The tears that blurred my vision and forced me into a lay-by on Llandegla Moors betrayed the first conscious realisation that I'd been hurt by the everyday language of the clinic: risky gay sex was an abridged version of all that I'd shared with Joel.

Routine carried me for seven days. The doctor was solemn when she confirmed the positive result of the blood test, and Ali, the Glaswegian nurse held my hand for some time; he was very tender. Somewhere, inside white blood cells, deep within the tissues of my body, there was a piece of biochemical grammar that had the potential to write a sentence in my genes, an instruction that would bring on cell death. The virus, coursing through my blood, waited for tomorrow. As it had done in Joel, tomorrow or some other tomorrow, it would cause my body's immune system to fail.

High above the village I made for the waters of Cregennen

and the solitude that the mountains offered. I yearned for a quietness of mind, but a patchwork of thoughts had been woven in the hours since I'd been told, and my emotions lurched chaotically. Anxiety... confusion... joy... despair. The beauty and quiet of the mountain lake, shimmering in the early morning sunlight, were not infectious, and the thought looms continued to weave. I sought to grasp at the joy that my choice of celibacy now brought. The certainty that the virus, which lay dormant, had infected no one since my return from San Francisco.

'This is the Bread of Life,' Dafydd said, standing before me and placing the wafer on my out-stretched palm. It stuck to my tongue. Somewhere, in the distant cavern of my mind, I heard the echoes of my own prayers over the elements, on the one Sunday in the month that my tradition allowed. 'One Bread, One Body, One Lord of All, One Cup of blessing which we bless.' Anxiety and confusion gripped me as the wine dislodged the wafer from my tongue...

'This is the Blood of Christ.'

Joel came to me, offering comfort. I reached for the warmth of his touch. But the solace of his presence dissolved into the sorrowful words of Cheryl's letter, describing the cancer and dementia that had killed him. I swallowed, knowing that through my Communion, the Body of Christ would become infected. And with a pain that paralysed the thought looms wove into the fabric of my being the first of many malignancies. Joel, too, had been blighted by my love.

THE ANTIDOTE
(1926)
Kathleen Freeman

'Miss Hilomax,' said Dr. Henry Abel, dropping with abandon into the easy chair, and staring morosely at his colleague, 'I have a headache. I am not ready to begin the day's work. Kindly tell me a story.'

Miss Hilomax frowned delightedly, and passed a hand through her hair.

'That is a challenge I always accept. The sudden demand for a story shakes the strongest from the high place of their self-approbation; it is the one service in the game of conversation that is almost never returned. I, therefore, early learnt to return it.'

'Of course. It is like you. But I will praise you afterwards, if the story is good.'

'Wait one moment while I lay the foundations. I have no time to go far for materials; therefore I will sort out the bricks from the pile nearest to my hand – myself and my experiences, you understand.'

'Yes; and how will you select the bricks?'

'They shall come, I think, from the eighteenth year of my life; this is the period that I regard with the greatest interest and the least bias, so that it best lends itself to artistic treatment.'

'Excellent. Now I can lie back and watch the edifice to its completion.'

'Well, then, in the eighteenth year of my life, I was no less intent on the hunt for virtue than I am today; but I was not, of course, a skilled hunter; I rushed up one path and down another, brandishing my absurd weapons; and my elders, looking up from their work at the noise, smiled at my capers. Some smiled fondly, some sardonically; but all smiled. They said, "All young people feel like that; as you get older, you'll learn better." This made me hotly ashamed. I thought they knew where to go when they wanted a virtue; and how to catch it. I wasn't angry because they did not tell me; I was filled with shame, and there was no room in me for anger. But I went on, blundering up and down the different tracks; and I still go on, though with less noise.'

'Ah, you have learnt to stalk,' said Dr. Henry Abel.

'Exactly. Now one of the trails up which I rushed was that of self-denial. In my childhood, that way had been pointed out to me by many people; but it looked so flat and unpromising that I had passed it by for less apparent paths. At this period, it was commended to me again by books; and under their direction I followed it, thinking to catch a big virtue at the end. I went very carefully into the method of advance; by studying them like a craft, I soon learnt all the tricks. Beginning with easy things, like relinquishing the best chair to an able-bodied sister, and choosing the smallest cake from any given plate, I passed on to the more exacting feats. I encouraged the depressed to confide in me, and fixed them more firmly in their depression by causing them to enjoy the frequent recital of it. I allowed the wishes of my friends always to over-ride my own; often I refused to express any wish of my own; and my friends, wearying of the constant labour of decision, began one by one to desert me. I was in an ecstasy; "this," I thought, "is the true way." And there was something in me that longed to abase itself – something that pictured with joy the bowed back and the heaped-up burden, and the tender sadness that would gather in eyes that might have flashed with fighting scorn.

'The person to whom I most desired to exhibit my newly learned craft was of course the human being whom in my heart I called my best friend. This was a woman of my own age, a good-tempered student of science, interested in everything except introspection, and every person – almost – except myself. Me she regarded as a well-meaning young fool, who would have been an entertaining companion save for a deplorable absorption in souls, my own in particular. We did all the usual things together – walked, and played games, and went to each other's houses for tea. I never dared to talk much about my soul. But when the great call came, it was a call to action; and on none of the people within my reach did the results fall so heavily and so continuously as on – let us call her – Frances Benson.

'I shall not recount to you the particular shapes they took. It would distress me; and to imagine them will be no trouble to you. Frances Benson was, I assure you, astonished. She began to cast sharp glances at me; but I only smiled back, with sad and tender eyes. That soon brought matters to a crisis. The immediate cause of the scene which ended our friendship was, I think, an attempt to resign in her favour a place in the County hockey team. She discovered it; and in her just anger she was very brutal; she said:

'"What the devil do you think you're playing at? Do you suppose any decent person will stand that sort of thing going on behind their back? Self-denial, you call it? I call it a streak of servility in the blood."

'Those last words burnt into me long after she had gone away; yet furious as I was under the torture of them, I knew that she had seen clear; in my idleness I had almost sold myself to a devil. And she had pointed her finger at him, and given him a name – a streak of servility in the blood!

'To Frances Benson, as I have said, I had never declared my new-found rule of life; a feeling like shame always prevented me, so surely, so automatically did she register my variations between weakness and strength; and I didn't want to break the instrument! Nevertheless, I had to talk about it; and the cunning devil within me found a listener proper to receive it. There happened to come on a few days' visit to my home a cousin of mine, a woman seven years older than myself, uneducated and sentimental, but not stupid. Her name was Isabel. She had always been interested in me; she thought me very learned and clever; and the shameless naked earnestness of my soul had long been revealed to her. She had written me letters, full of a curiosity, strong but erratic, about souls; hers was an easy-going scheme of life, and her feelings were its arbiters. Did they rush out to that solution? It was the truth for her. Did they turn repelled from that other? Behold, it was false. She came, then; her curious gaze rested on me, and saw the sadness and the purpose; I will not linger over it; three days of her pressing sympathetic presence brought about my downfall; and I poured out to her the whole story of the call and my obedience.

'At the end, I looked up at her; I saw the emotion rush into her face; I heard her say:

'"I always felt that that was the true way – to submit – but you have altered it all, somehow; you have made me sure." And a sick wave of degradation drenched me, leaving me cold and trembling with fear. But it was too late to repent. The mischief was done. In my shame and nausea, I avoided her for the remainder of her stay; but she went away my confirmed disciple.

'You see, then, the hellish punishment that lay in wait for me; months after Frances Benson had shaken me off and gone away; when I was picking myself up from the dust in which she left me grovelling; when my will was my own again, and I had faced my devil, and learnt to bear the sight of his ugly face, and the stirrings of his known and hated form, learnt to watch for his uplifted head, and batter him down again to his dungeon – then, I say, this woman Isabel returned.

'It was the Long Vacation; and for five weeks Isabel was my guest. She accompanied me everywhere; she sat for hours looking at me with reverent eyes; she recounted to me her progress along the path that I had opened up for her; she laid before me her record of faithful service. "I have never forgotten your words," she said. Again the awful nausea overwhelmed me, mingled with pity at the sight of a disease that I had outgrown, and anguish at the thought that through me and no other had the infection passed to her. Nine people out of ten, the strong healthy souls like Frances Benson, would have resisted it, flung it off; why had she, with her terrible susceptibility to just that plague, a susceptibility perhaps in the blood that we shared, why had she of all the world come near and touched me then?

'Could I cure her? I tried, God knows. I gave her fresh air; I played to her brave tunes on the piano. I flooded her with talk about impersonal things, from machinery to politics; I took up a pose of harshness, almost brutality. I rode over her ruthlessly, and tried by rudeness to stimulate her to resistance. But she never resisted; she bore with me patiently. Poke and prod as I might, I could not strike the rock in her nature; I could not get one spark. The rock was all eaten away, and mine had been the hand that months ago had poured upon it the corroding stream of my self-revelation.

'One day, I discovered her in a plot to do me some ridiculous service without my knowledge. I said to her:

'"You must understand that I cannot allow this; you undermine my self-respect; and I resent it."

'"But, dear," she said, "I do so want to do something for you."

'"You want," I said. "Yes, I know." And I told her about the devil. I called him, euphemistically, the centrifugal tendency. She shook her head.

"'It's no use, dear," she said. "I can't see it like that. You've changed; perhaps you've got beyond me; perhaps you're right. But it's too hard for me; I must go along the way I've taken – the way you first made clear to me. I shall always be grateful to you for that."

"'Look here," I said, "I made a mistake then, a damned mistake, do you understand me? And you're making the same mistake; you are doing what I did – simply feeding a hungry devil inside you – the streak of servility in your blood!"

'There was the antidote that had rid me of my disease; I forced it down her throat. Did it cure her? I never saw her again, so that it would be inexact to affirm that it did not. Still you shall have the evidence. Some years later she left England; and on the day she sailed I received a letter which said, as nearly as I remember:

"'Perhaps our lives will not cross again; I want you to know that I shall always be grateful to you for what you taught me. Some day, I think you will return to your old faith; then, dear, come to me.'"

Miss Hilomax raised one eyebrow, and smiled. 'That is all,' she said, 'it was interesting, was it not? The narration of it quite carried me away.'

'My good friend,' said Dr. Henry Abel, 'I was absorbed. But in one thing you fell short of expectation. Your story was not as free from bias as you claimed that it would be. One of your characters I was at several points moved to defend; for you showed in your presentment of it, I think, some injustice.'

Miss Hilomax smiled complacently.

'Injustice?' she said. 'Against whom did I show injustice?'

'Yourself,' said Dr. Henry Abel.

AN ARTISTIC MISSION
(1968)
Emyr Humphreys

The dark auditorium of the small cinema was stiflingly hot. Men sat in their shirtsleeves and the cigarette-smoke ascended like incense into the beam of light from the projection room. Young women with long hair hanging from tilted heads watched the screen with conscious absorption as if they expected to be examined at the end of the performance. It was a warm evening in June. The film was nearing its last climax. A hero was thrusting a heroine up the bell tower to the scene of the original crime. The music was menacing, the actors were sweating with intensity and the camera-work was alive with visual brilliance. The audience was subdued, still, appreciative; except for one exasperated young man in the stalls who wriggled in his chair, gasping quiet protests which failed however to attract the attention of his tall companion who continued to give the film rigid, almost unblinking attention. When the house lights came up, the small young man could contain himself no longer.

—It doesn't have to be like this.

His tall friend was peering about excitedly. He had seen a celebrated ballerina escorted by a handsome young man. People were moving and he wanted to check, wanted to make sure, engrave the vision on his memory.

—It was her, wasn't it?

—Oh for God's sake, Phil. Don't be so provincial.

They shuffled towards the exit, barely taking any notice of each other. Phil's long neck turned frequently as if he hoped to catch a last glimpse of the famous dancer or some other famous person, or of anything, indeed, other than his grumbling friend, to take his attention. Once on the street they were thrown together again, knowing only each other among all the people hurrying purposefully along the pavement.

—Are we going to eat, or aren't we?

—I don't really care.

—Has it ever struck you that people in a cinema audience are ESN?

—What's that, for God's sake?

Phil ran a comb quickly through his thinning fair hair as he glanced at his reflection in a shop window. He was pleased with the fresh appearance of his slub-linen suit. He had been wise to remove the jacket in the cinema.

—Educationally sub-normal.

—Jargon, Phil said airily. Where shall we eat?

—You've just said you didn't care. I thought we'd go home in that case. To my place.

It was clear that Phil wanted to be difficult.

—What about my Turkish *kebab*?

They walked into a dark side-street. After outbreaks and sulky silences the temperature of their emotional relationship found its normal level. They got back to discussing the film they had seen.

—Bombarded into submission by trickery of sight and sound!

—So what, Tony? So what?

Phil executed a few dance-steps and ended up clasping the top of a bollard at the end of the cobbled lane.

—It's all a great big vulgar nothing! That's what. Don't you see what I'm getting at? You're musical, Phil, what about all that cheap and nasty sound repeated over and over again?

147

—Tony! Don't get so serious! Have some sense of proportion.

—About art I am serious. About art, with me, there is no compromise. You know that.

—Yes, teacher.

Phil gave a mocking curtsy. Tony stuffed his hands into his pockets and scowled.

—I don't know why the hell I bother with you.

—Don't you?

Phil smiled and stretched himself to his full height, spreading his arms slowly upward like the branches of a tree.

—I enjoyed it, Phil said. You're such a puritan. What's wrong with enjoying a piece of fantasy? I was moved. I admit it. That poor girl's predicament moved me. I participated. What's wrong with that?

—It's for people with stunted emotions and stunted minds, Tony said. People who need a depth-charge before they're moved by anything. Their emotions are stunted and their minds are blunted by the sterile, monotonous, second-hand living imposed on them by industrial society ... Yes! I do mean it. I've got nothing against the medium. You know that. But the awful uses to which the camera and the microphone are put; when they could be truthful and sensitive. As honest as any poem or novel. This is what gets my goat. And people like you go around making a cult of great slabs of vulgarity, great rubbish-heaps of the garbage of capitalistic fantasies.

—Hey! Steady on. It was *you* who wanted to go in the first place.

—I'm talking about your reactions.

—Look, I came up to town to enjoy myself... And by what right, I may ask, do you pontificate about my reactions when you've no idea what they really were? Here we are. God, I'm dying for a Turkish meal. I really am.

Inside the small restaurant, Tony lapsed into a prolonged sulky silence. When Phil looked about admiringly at the dark young people clustered about a juke-box or at the raw decor of the dim room or sniffed happily at the raisin wine or the aromatic frying from the kitchen, he pulled a piece of bread to bits and stuffed pellets between his own unwilling teeth.

He muttered and Phil looked at him politely.

—Did you say anything?

—We're not really suited.

It was Phil's turn to be irritated and touchy.

—I came up at your invitation, he said.

—I thought you were really interested.

—I am.

Phil now spoke plaintively. Tony having begun to speak was relentless in the pursuit of truth. His small face, under the dark unruly head of curls, was contracted with the effort.

—I thought you had real sympathy. I thought you took my plans seriously. Do you think I was just after your money? That's always the trouble with rich people, isn't it? They always think people are after their money.

—I'm not rich, Phil said.

Tony bared his teeth.

—That's a good one. Only four thousand a year. Only a factory in the family. How much do you think I get?

—I can't touch the capital, Phil said.

—It's all right. Don't get nervous. I just wondered if you had any idea how much a teacher in a London comprehensive school got. That's all.

—If you'd take a job down in Wales…

—A job is the last thing I want. We're just not on the same wave-length.

—I admire your ideas, Tony. I do honestly. And I love coming up to see you.

—Welcome. Share my bed-sitter whenever you like. Bring your mother as well if you like. And your auntie.

—I'm serious, Tony. Honestly I am.

—Are you?

—I had an idea, Tony. I was going to discuss it with you tomorrow. I'll tell you now if you like. A real idea.

—We're not on the same wave-length, Tony said. I can't think how I ever believed we were.

—I thought of you at once when the idea came to me. Shall I tell you?

Tony had begun to eat. Some of his irritation may have been due to hunger. With his mouth full, chewing hard and swallowing, he seemed in a more receptive state of mind.

—It's to do with my aunt in a way. To do with the days when she lived in style. There's an old housekeeper of hers – a Miss Lacey-Lloyd – in an old people's home in Pedrog.

—Where's that?

—In north Wales.

—I know that, Tony snapped. I'm a damned sight more Welsh than you are. I just asked where.

—Awful place it is. I had to take my aunt there, I think it was an old workhouse. Anyway it was awful and I couldn't stand it there really. The atmosphere was getting me down. As you know I'm a happy, gay sort of person really and so much misery, Tony, you've no idea. I'll tell you one thing... I'll kill myself long before I get to that stage. It's the new torture, I think. Prolonged decrepitude.

—What was the idea?

—Miss Lacey-Lloyd remembers so much. She's well over eighty, and she lives and loves in the world before the first world war! At one time she kept house for the Peruvian ambassador in Eaton Square. You ought to hear her talking about getting the grub ready for the grouse-train. And making a wedding cake for a Rumanian princess. And being in charge of forty indoor servants. It's all so vivid to her still. And she looks marvellous, sweet and gentle and a howling snob of course.

—What was the idea?

—Your tape-recorder...

—Ours.

Tony corrected him immediately.

—Here's a chance to make an actuality recording that could grow to anything, in your hands of course. Don't you see what I mean? The core of a theme. Ballads. Pictures. The kind of thing you're after.

—It's been done before.

Tony poured himself more wine from the carafe.

—Not with her, it hasn't, has it?

Phil looked cross.

—I thought it was just the sort of thing you would have liked. After all, anybody over eighty with her experience is unique, I could have taken you there. She'd do anything for me. Talk as long as you like. It's a marvellous spot too. I could get the Bolex mended. Doesn't it appeal to you at all? Not in any way at all?

Tony chewed thoughtfully, as if he were wondering whether or not to please his friend with a sign of approval.

II

The hospital stood on ground that was higher than the level of the main road. It was a grim stone building that had once been a workhouse and everything had been done to make it more cheerful. The walls, which were two feet thick, were painted pink but the windows were often small and above eye-level. The corridors were dark and most of the rooms looked inward, on a tarmacked courtyard where events like the arrival of laundry or bakery-vans, or ambulances or hearses, were eagerly noted by the more vigorous patients.

In the room where Miss Lacey-Lloyd lay there were six cots. Looked at from a low angle they resembled cages. The room was classified as female chronic geriatric. Four old women lay bolstered up on pillows at angles of exhaustion. They were pale, ghostly and clean. The cots were high but the windows were higher and only one gave Miss Lacey-Lloyd a view of the backyard and the letters painted boldly across the yellow side of a large van. She lifted her head to catch as much as she could of the legend within the narrow window-frame as the van reversed slowly in the yard.

A muscular nurse with bare forearms bustled in with a vase of deep-red roses.

—Look at these, she said. Aren't they beautiful? Just look at them. Where shall I put them?

A woman, identified on the card above her head as Mrs Annie Rosina Davies of Tynpwll in the county of Merioneth, groaned as if she wanted more than anything to speak, even under sedation. She was aged ninety-four, and spoke incessantly, sleeping or waking. She had been given a pill to keep her reasonably quiet during visiting time.

There was a transistor set buzzing on the pillow alongside Miss Lacey-Lloyd's head. The transparent earpiece dangled delicately at the end of its lead over the side of the cot. The nurse scooped up the set in her scrubbed hand.

—Don't want this now do you, love?

A nervous smile broke on Miss Lacey-Lloyd's wrinkled face and her eyes peered up out of lids shrunken and sticky with age.

—This old thing?

The nurse held the set near Miss Lacey-Lloyd's drooping nose.

—Want what dear? What is it dear?

The nurse tugged a sheet tight to give herself patience while the old head turned and the old lips trembled.

—I'll have it, tell her!

A savage-looking old woman in the corner had managed to sit up. Her body leaned forward and her bare arms stretched in front of her. She was animated by the prospect of seeing new faces. Her hair and her face were the same tone of grey. She was toothless and her neck was swollen on the left side with a heavy goitre. Her card read Mrs Sophie Thomas, 8 Crimp Terrace, Porthwen, in the county of Caernarvon.

—Would you like some powder, love?

The nurse bent down to bring her head nearer Miss Lacey-Lloyd's.

—A bit of paint and powder. You've got two boy-friends coming you know.

Miss Lacey-Lloyd smiled proudly and nodded.

Mrs Sophie Thomas touched her hair and muttered angrily.

—Stuck-up bitch.

—Now! Now! Mrs T. I heard you.

A huge sigh issued from the wide lips of Annie Rosina Davies, whose bed was opposite Miss Lacey-Lloyd's.

—She's going to start!

Sophie Thomas pointed angrily at the broad head of Annie Rosina Davies lying diagonally on the mound of pillows. Her lips were moving. Miss Lacey-Lloyd placed her hand on the nurse's cool forearm.

—Can't get up higher, dear, she said. I'm very weak today.

The nurse carried the powder-puff and the lipstick in her apron pocket.

—A bit of rosy-cheeks, love. And a dash of eau-de-cologne. That's what the boys like, isn't it?

153

She laughed loudly at her own joke. The fourth woman, a farmer's widow, Mrs Mary Evans of Hafod Lorn, Caregog, in the county of Merioneth, stirred anxiously in the darkest corner of the room. Again the woman with a goitre pointed.

—She wants the bed-pan, Nurse! Mrs Sophie Thomas spoke with authority.

—I can always tell. She'll stink the place out and the visitors here.

Miss Lacey-Lloyd seemed to draw strength from the nurse's attention to her face.

—I don't know what to do about my hair, she said. It's such a mess.

—Bed-pan! Sophie Thomas said holding her hand on her goitre.

—Sorry, Mrs T, the nurse said calmly. She's just had it.

—You wait. Wait till the visitors come...

—Master Philip is very artistic, Miss Lacey-Lloyd said. I think he gets it from his grandfather you know, although his mother of course plays the piano beautifully. Have you noticed her hands? Master Philip's hands are just like his aunt's. I think.

—They're coming!

The woman with a goitre looked around her excitedly.

—I can hear them coming!

—Nurse, Miss Lacey-Lloyd said plaintively, could I have my Spanish shawl, nurse? The shawl Dame Alice brought me. He's sure to notice. These clever people notice everything.

A woman in her thirties, short, aggressive, very stout, marched into the ward with her small daughter at her heels. Her red-faced husband, who looked shy and guilty, followed them from a short distance. They made for the bed in the darkest corner. The man touched his mother's hand. Mrs Mary Evans opened her eyes wearily and closed them again. The family arranged themselves around the bed, conscious of being watched by the woman with a goitre and anxious to group themselves correctly. The son particularly seemed oppressed and uncertain where to look, as if he were directly responsible for his mother's hopeless condition. A motor mechanic, with oil still in the creases of his hands, came carrying his crash-helmet and a bottle of Lucozade to the bedside of his great-grandmother Annie Rosina Davies. He sat patiently by her bed and seemed to be memorising the contours of her large face and her plaits of white hair.

Then Philip and Tony arrived, Philip leading the way. He was wearing peach-coloured trousers and a salmon-pink shirt with a peach-coloured tie. They both trod softly. Philip wore suede boots and Tony wore rope-soled sneakers. The silence of their approach made their advent even more amazing to the people in the ward. Mrs Sophie Thomas covered her goitre with both hands and failed to greet her own visitor, a curate's wife, who brought her a packet of fancy biscuits and four oranges in a brown paper bag.

—Hello, Lacey. I've brought someone to see you.

—Hello, Master Philip.

Miss Lacey-Lloyd shifted up on her pillows, plucked at her shawl and made an effort to smile. Tony, in a black leather jacket and a black shirt, looked down at the old lady and ran his thumb under the strap of the tape-recorder slung over his right shoulder. He nodded at her to show his intentions were friendly.

—If I put the mike on the pillow, he said. The quality isn't going to be much good anyway.

—Auntie sends her love, Lacey, Philip said. She'll be along to see you one of these days.

—I know how busy she is, Miss Lacey-Lloyd said. She's such a good woman. She always loved social work, you know. How is your dear mother?

Philip nodded mutely, smiled and stroked his thin fair hair. The movements of his pale blue eyes were more noticeable because his face was still sunburnt from a recent holiday abroad. Miss Lacey-Lloyd smiled back at him weakly and made an effort at conversation.

—Where are you going for your holidays this year, Master Philip?

—I'm so busy, quite honestly, Lacey...

Tony held out the microphone and lanyard.

—I'd like to try this, Tony said. Do you mind if I put this round your neck Miss... er... Then we could get started.

—This is my friend Tony Jones, Philip said. He's a teacher but he makes programmes for the BBC. He's an artist really. Aren't you, Tony?

—It's nice to have a friend, Miss Lacey-Lloyd said. I've got nobody now you know, not really.

—He'd like to record your talking, Philip said. You don't mind, do you, Lacey?

—What do you want me to say?

Miss Lacey-Lloyd peered from one to the other, anxious to please.

—Count, Tony said. Just count up to ten.

He fiddled with the knobs and keys on the compact machine.

—Well, the idea you see, Lacey, is that you've got this wonderful memory. You can remember so much about the old days, I thought, we thought, Tony thought, what a wonderful programme it would make...

—Yes, Miss Lacey-Lloyd said. Yes. I see.

She seemed to consider Philip's statement deeply, listening to all the implications.

—I'll have to be careful what I say, won't I?

She smiled and the lids stretched over her protruding eyes.

—Oh no, Philip said. No, Lacey. That's just it you see. You can say whatever you like. About anybody. Absolutely anything.

Philip tried to look happy and encouraging. He held up his hand and wriggled the fingers playfully.

—Anything!

—Yes, Miss Lacey-Lloyd said. Yes. I see. It doesn't really matter any more what I say, does it?

—Oh no, Lacey. I didn't mean that. You know what I mean. Remember you telling me about Campbell-Bannerman staying at Plas Coch. And that girl who was so excited. Scalded her thigh with hot soup. Remember?

—I saw the Coronation, Miss Lacey-Lloyd said. The second day. June 23rd, 1911. I always remember the date and I can remember the number of my seat too. No. 101. My lucky number I always call it. No. 71 St James Street. We were all so excited.

—There you are!

Philip turned triumphantly to look at Tony.

—I told you she had a wonderful memory.

Tony made a sign to show the machine was working and that they shouldn't waste time.

—Did your aunt mention my funeral at all, Master Philip?

—Funeral, Lacey! You'll outlive the lot of us! Mark my words.

—She promised me she would make the arrangements with Canon Mathews, but the poor Canon died you see. I hate to trouble your aunt you know but I can't write lying like this all day. Not much else to think about really, Master Philip.

—There, there, Philip said consolingly.

—Oh I don't mind. It's just that it would be nice to know the arrangements were in hand. I bought my grave, you see, in 1936, when my uncle died. It's such a lovely spot. Under a yew-tree with a magnificent view of the mountains... not that I'll see them of course but it's a beautiful thought. I've always liked beautiful thoughts. Old Dean Stocks used to say we can repay God all the blessings we receive by having beautiful thoughts. Do you remember Dean Stocks, Master Philip? He gave you a prayer book for your seventh birthday. Don't you remember? He always used to come down for a week at the end of August. Don't you remember? Before the war of course.

Tony had turned to look at the woman with the goitre.

Her curiosity was making her face twitch as she stretched forward to peer beyond the curate's wife who continued to give her resolute attention. Tony gave Mrs Sophie Thomas a bold wink and this made her cackle noisily and put her hand to her mouth. The curate's wife could no longer prevent herself from turning to see what was happening. Then Mrs Annie Rosina Davies shifted her bulk on her bed and without opening her eyes, began singing.

—Listen!

Tony nudged Philip excitedly.

—She's like that all the time, Miss Lacey-Lloyd said faintly. Never stops day and night, singing or talking. It's terrible really. When you're lying in the dark and trying to sleep. It's really awful. Poor thing can't stop... she ought to be put by herself really.

—Listen!

Tony snapped impatiently and Miss Lacey-Lloyd looked at him in alarm.

—Just listen, he said. It's bloody marvellous. Great stuff.

—What's she singing? Philip said. It's Welsh. I don't understand it.

—God, if I could get a mike round her neck and everybody else quiet... Tony sounded enthusiastic and desperate. He fumbled in a small leather case for another microphone, moving over as he did so to talk to the motor mechanic who was still nursing his crash helmet.

—Is she your mother or something? he said in Welsh.

—My great-grandmother, the mechanic said. She makes a hell of a row, poor old thing. That's why she's here, to tell you the truth. All of us in the same house, you know. We couldn't stand it. Especially my sister Eva. She was courting and bringing her young man in of an evening. It was very embarrassing for her. My mother couldn't bear to see the old lady leave her home, but as my uncle said to her...

—Can I record her? Tony said. Just put this over her neck and let her carry on. That's all. Won't do her any harm.

—Suppose it's all right, he said.

He seemed hesitant.

—Don't know what my mother would say either.

—What's she singing, Lacey? Philip said.

—Just an old hymn.

—Yes, but what are the words, Lacey? What is she saying?

Miss Lacey-Lloyd made an effort to listen.

—It's very emotional, she said. 'The good news has come to our district and it ought to be memorised, Jesus has carried the day and we prisoners shall all be released...'

She coughed and sighed with the effort.

—My chest hurts, she said. I don't want to complain, but nothing seems to do it any good, Master Philip.

—We've got to catch it, Tony said frantically. These things are caught on the wing absolutely. Lift her hand will you... Come on Philip, for God's sake.

He was attempting to take the mike from Miss Lacey-Lloyd.

—The other mike doesn't work. That's what. Come on. Just lift her a little that's all. She's lying on it.

—Hey! Hey!

The woman with a goitre waved her arm eagerly, ignoring the efforts of the curate's wife to keep her calm. All the activity in the ward seemed to give her a new lease of life.

—I can sing, she said. I was in Porthwen mixed choir for twenty-three years. We used to win, everywhere. I know a lot of pieces.

Mrs Annie Rosina Davies continued to sing with surprising clarity.

—'His blood flowed freely in a flood and by its virtue we shall be carried whole, in a wink of time, to the other side – to the other side...'

Tony was beside himself with excitement and anxiety.

—This bloody machine! Whenever you want it, it packs up. What's she done to this mike for God's sake? Has she been chewing it or something?

—It's in every hymn book, Miss Lacey-Lloyd said.

She looked at Philip as if she were pleading for protection.

—She isn't though, is she? Not that woman.

Tony spoke between clenched teeth and Miss Lacey-Lloyd was frightened.

—Steady on, Tony...

Philip searched for the right words to calm his friend.

—Nobody controls that woman or what comes through her lips... oh damn. She's finished!

Mrs Annie Rosina Davies had stopped singing. Her great-grandson was looking at her patiently.

—She'll start again in a minute, he said.

—Will she? Will she?

Tony sounded desperate. The motor mechanic nodded solemnly and within a few moments she began a conversation with herself in a loud clear voice about people and events in a peasant community of almost eighty years ago. Tony listened with an expression of rapture on his face.

—What was that?

He whispered eagerly to the motor mechanic.

—She said 'Ifan is spitting blood' …

—No, Tony said. The other bit.

—'Lumps of bright red lung on the white sheet?'

—Yes. I got that. Who's Ifan?

—One of her children I think, the mechanic said. I'm not sure though. One that died.

—It's all there! Tony said pressing knobs and keys desperately. If I could get this damn thing to work.

Miss Lacey-Lloyd attempted polite conversation with Philip.

—How is your Uncle Daniel, Master Philip? I saw something about him in the paper, didn't I?

—He's fine thanks, Lacey.

Philip took Tony's arm and whispered into his ear.

—What about Lacey? he said. It isn't very nice is it? Bringing all this gear and raising her hopes and all that.

—Just keep quiet will you? That's all I ask, Tony said. Just keep quiet that's all.

—I'm going to sing the alto solo from 'Dwynwen's Maidens'!

Mrs Sophie Thomas covered her goitre with both hands and smiled encouragingly.

—Will that do?

—Just keep your trap shut, Tony said savagely.

Now his machine was working perfectly and he had placed the mike carefully around Annie Rosina's wide neck. She went on talking, completely unaware of her great-grandson watching her intently, or of anything in the ward around her. She seemed to be bringing messages from an idyllic rustic world where young girls were for ever making up their minds to marry handsome young men as soon as they returned from America or foreign wars or coal-mines in the south.

The woman in the dark corner gave a long loud groan. Her son looked at his wife, his face red with embarrassment. His wife whispered crossly to her daughter who reached out for the bell to ring for the nurse. At the same time Mrs Sophie Thomas had rung and the nurse bustled in uncertain who to attend to, clasping her red hands.

—Now then, she said. What's the matter? Who rang the bell? Who rang first? It's like bingo.

—Him!

The woman with the goitre pointed at Tony.

—He's interfering with the patients. Him! That pansy over there. That one. Interfering. We want him out of here.

The nurse looked at Tony and smiled in a friendly way.

—What are you doing, love?

Tony put his finger to his lips.

—You can't fiddle about with patients in bed, love. It's not allowed, you know.

Philip, who had been leaning over Miss Lacey-Lloyd to hear what she was whispering, straightened and began biting his lip nervously.

—Take it off her, there's a good boy. Take it off her. We can't have the whole ward disturbed now, can we?

—Look at his clothes, Mrs Sophie Thomas said. You've only got to take one look at him!

—Master Philip...

—I'm awfully sorry, Lacey...

—Shut up! It's like trying to record in a bloody hen-house.

—And there's his language!

Mrs Sophie Thomas pointed at Tony. Suddenly she began to sniff.

—She's done it!

Her voice was triumphant.

—There you are, Nurse! I told you she would. She'll stink the place out. I told you, didn't I?

—Keep quiet!

The nurse's face was red with anger. The embarrassed son stood up and turned to face the wall. Philip began to talk of leaving. Miss Lacey-Lloyd sank down her pillows and closed her eyes.

—Goodbye, Lacey dear. Take care of yourself.

—Goodbye, Master Philip.

Her voice was faint but firm. She was resigning herself to beautiful thoughts. Philip stepped cautiously towards the doorway and Mrs Sophie Thomas collected all her strength for a last outburst.

—I must order you to take that machine out, the nurse said. Otherwise I shall call the matron!

Tony ignored her order. He stood alongside the great-grandson and together they watched Mrs Annie Rosina Davies's lips move, listening intently. The reels on the tape-recorder continued to turn inexorably like the wheels of fate.

III

The red, two-seater sports car sped along the mountain roads as if making an escape. Philip was at the wheel. He seemed to see nothing of the bleak majestic scenery. But Tony was singing and clearly enjoying the trip. In between songs he drew Philip's attention to the mutations of light on the rocky slopes and the mountain crests and the clouds that raced across the blue sky dragging shadows across the wet peat-bogs and the clear surface of a lake. He shouted out loud lines of ballads that were forming in his head and when he became hoarse he demanded they should stop somewhere and order a pot of tea while he jotted down the new lines. Unexpectedly, Philip drew up in a lay-by that gave a long view of a valley stretching eastwards. Behind them clouds began to gather around the mountain peaks.

—What's up?

Philip's forehead was pressed against the top of the steering-wheel.

—Are you sick or something?

—That woman's voice.

Philip's thin hair was disordered and his face very pale under the tan.

—Marvellous, Tony said. I can't wait to hear it again.

—No. The one with a goitre. When she was screaming...

—Old bitch. Didn't want the injection. You shouldn't have skedaddled so soon. She was foaming at the mouth. Sheer bloody fury. All directed at me. Every ounce of what was left of her life was hate. Hatred of me. There may be a lot of it on the tape. Ward full of snarling and wailing females. What a row, boy. And you should have seen that bloody matron when I told her to belt up. Calling porters and policemen and God knows what to chuck me out.

—I don't know how you can do it, Philip said.

He looked as if he wanted to vomit.

—You wait till I've put a programme together, Tony said. I can just hear the ballads in my head now. You wait. This is art you know. None of your namby-pamby stuff. This is real art. And you've got to be tough and ruthless. My God I'll show them. This is new what I've got. New. Revolutionary. The way I'll handle it. My style. You wait. You'll see.

Philip's head rolled from side to side.

—I'm thirty-one, he said. I'm older than you. Six years older. I see my life stretching in front of me, endless and empty.

—You've got money, Tony said. Lots of it.

He kept his voice deliberately hard and devoid of sympathy.

—Yes but I'm older than you and I'm not qualified for anything. No qualifications at all. I'm just going to live an empty life and grow old.

—It's the same for everybody, Tony said.

—Poor old Lacey. She was my nurse really you know. My nurse.

Tony looked critical but didn't speak.

—I'll never be able to face it, Tony.

He put his hand on his friend's arm and stared at him appealingly.

—Don't let me grow old, Tony. I'd rather you killed me.

He fumbled for his friend's hand and squeezed it desperately.

—It's a pity about the machine, Tony said. The porter dropped it. The tapes are okay but the machine. It will cost a packet to fix it.

—Don't leave me, Philip said. Don't ever leave me, Tony. I need your strength. I'm not strong like you.

—Might be as much as twenty quid...

—That's nothing, Philip nodded eagerly. You ought to have a proper editing machine. For the filming I mean. I thought of giving it you for your birthday but we can get it right away if you like.

A smile broke across Tony's shadowed face. He freed his hand slowly.

—You know, he said, this could be the beginning of a very successful partnership. Philtone Enterprises! How about that?

—Yes.

Philip nodded his head eagerly.

—Oh yes... yes.

—Well come on then.

The red sports car reversed smartly out of the lay-by and roared off to the east.

GO PLAY WITH CUCUMBERS
(2019)
Crystal Jeans

Watching *Blue Planet*. Neon fish living on the seabed, miles and miles down, carrying their little lanterns like monstrous wartime nurses. Lying on the couch drinking cocoa, listening to Attenborough's reassuring voice. But I'm not reassured. She isn't back. Lou. Said she'd be back by ten. Just 'popping' to her friend's house, Kimmy's. She was 'popping' over to smoke her cigarettes and drink her vodka and listen to her talk about the girlfriend who couldn't take a dildo because she'd been abused as a child, and well, she was understanding, didn't want to push things, but c'mon, it'd been, like, five months, just lube up and shut up. That's Kimmy. Lou lets her get away with this kind of thing because she naively assumes that a woman would never be so horrible, not for real, and also, everything Kimmy says is veiled by sneaky layers of irony so Lou can never tell if she's being a prick. I can.

So. Kimmy: twenty-four, pale and clammy with a face like a skinny triangle, a hooked nose, a small Punch and Judy mouth, thick black eyelashes and one of those hairstyles with half of it shaved off. Predatory and man-like, loves turning straight women. Fancies herself a photographer. Likes to take 'tasteful' pictures of underage goth girls with shaven fannies.

'I don't think Daddy's coming home,' I say to Tulip, my black and white Shih Tzu. Tulip licks my knee then rests his chin on his two front paws. I run my finger round the inside of the mug, licking off the bitty cocoa froth. I have a bad feeling in my belly. I try to concentrate on an octopus with an electric-green filament inside it.

Next morning. Trying to get on with things; showering, washing the dishes, brushing the dog's teeth. Lou's phone is switched off. That bad feeling in my belly, a mushroomy feeling.

Around eleven I'm on the couch, TV on, usual late-morning crap, a vacuous redhead going on about prostate cancer. I should be aware of it. Prostate cancer. Me and everyone else should know that it exists. OK. The front door opens and in comes Lou. The first thing I notice, she isn't wearing a bra under her top. Her tits hang low and her pistachio nipples are pointing at the coffee table. Second thing – all her mascara and eyeliner is messed up and smudged – her eyes look like centipedes squished into the ground by a cruel shoe.

I say, 'What have you done?'

She drops to her knees and starts crying and nuzzling my knees with her face. That mushroom feeling in my belly disappears. I still have a bad feeling, but it isn't mushrooms anymore. It's something icy and sick.

'What have you *done*?'

She looks up at me.

'You slept with her, didn't you?'

Just looks at me.

I push her head away and she rolls back onto her arse. 'For fucksake, Lou! You're a fucking tramp!'

'I don't remember any of it! I blacked out!'

'Oh, well that's OK then!'

'Polly, listen to me, *please*.' Eyes so earnest. 'One minute we were just drinking and then...' She cups her face with both hands. 'I just remember coming back to myself, you know, out of the

167

blackout, and she was on top of me, and I freaked out and pushed her off and smashed up her bedroom.' She rolls up her sleeves. 'And I did this.' A few superficial scratches like red biro that's running out. 'I wanted to kill myself.'

'You should have.'

She grabs my knees again and does that nuzzling thing. 'Please. I'm sorry. Please. Please.' And she carries on saying please in a strained crying-voice and nuzzling my lap like a cat with mange on its face. 'It wasn't me. It wasn't me. You know I wouldn't fuck her sober. She's disgusting.' She pulls a face. 'She's dis*gust*ing. I *hate* her.'

I push her onto her arse again. 'Don't tell me what I know.'

Sitting out the back on a white plastic chair, legs sprawled out, Pepsi can on bare thigh. Nice weather – some flat-bottomed cloud here and there but mostly sea-blue sky. I wish the weather was shit. I don't want to be reminded that this could have been a good day. Lounging under a tree at the park listening to reggae on a portable radio. Me and Lou drinking chilled pear cider, her head lying across my stomach.

Deena's dad is trimming his bushes next door. There's the snip-snip of garden scissors and a million birds singing and twittering from his aviary. Deena's attic window is flung open and sometimes I see the swish of her black hair as she moves around inside. Fucking Deena. She's one of those straight women who always flirts with dykes to prop up their own fragile self-esteem. Me and Lou are always joking about one day calling her bluff. Grabbing her head and pushing it down and saying, 'Go on then, eat my pussy if you're so curious.' The garden over I can see the little Spanish girl bouncing on her trampoline. Deena's dad wipes his face, squinting.

I must look terrible. I'm no beauty to begin with, but here I am in a pair of blue gingham boxer shorts, sickly white legs with dark three-day stubble on the calves, a Kenneth Williams T-shirt, the top of his oohing face stretched by my massive tits. Hair fluffy from my shower this morning. New lip piercing all pussy and infected. I look like an ugly dyke. I shouldn't care at a time like this, but there we go.

Lou is inside. Cutting herself probably. She'll come out any minute dripping, Tulip with her. Tulip likes drama. All I can think of is Kimmy's pinched face. I pull a face at the sun and drink my Pepsi. The guy next door, not Deena's dad, the other side – the alky with the English Bull Terrier, he comes out and sits in a dirty red deckchair and opens a can of lager and his dog jumps on his lap and sits looking into the distance with a windswept face both dumb and wise.

I know this is awful, but there's always a tiny part of me, like a lamp in the corner of a very large, very dark room, which lights up when This Kind Of Thing Happens, a part that is happy because I have an excuse to vacate everyday life. The next few days I don't have to bathe or brush my teeth or diet. I get to opt out. It's a small miserable thrill.

Fifth can. Full-sugar Lilt. Still out the garden. Mushy thoughts dripping like thick soup down an hourglass, turned back over, same drip, over and over. It all adds up to this: I should dump Lou but I don't want to dump Lou. We were going to have kids one day. I really don't want it over.

Tulip wanders in and out, sometimes barking at his arch-nemesis the English Bull, sometimes sniffing my ankles with his small wet nose or lying on the grass, panting, surrounded by dandelions and drying turds. Deena's dad's gone inside but the other neighbour is still there with his can. I hardly know this man. Clearly he has a drink problem.

I heave myself up from the chair and go to the fence, which is rotting and leaning.

I lift my can in greeting. 'Hello.'

He nods and lifts his own can. Dark hair and messy caveman stubble, Liverpool strip, worn jeans. His dog comes over to the fence and I dangle my arm down so it can sniff my hand.

I say, 'So what are you celebrating?'

He does halfway between a smile and smirk. 'Oh, you know. Life. Wonderful life.'

'Amen.'

He says, 'Where's your partner today? I assume she's your partner.'

I say, 'What gave it away?' and he laughs. Because I'm an obvious lesbian. Funny. 'She's inside. Feeling sorry for herself.'

'Well good luck with that.' He drains his can and crushes it. Stands up.

I say, 'Can I just ask you a question?'

He looks at me.

'Has anyone ever cheated on you?'

His eyes do a couple of taken-aback blinks. 'Uuh. Sure. Yeah.' I love provoking this reaction from people. Suddenly veering off from small talk, Getting Real. Lou says that I do it because I want to be admired. 'My last girlfriend actually,' he says. 'Woman who used to live here with me? Do you remember—'

'What did you do? Did you leave her?'

He looks at the floor a while, thinking. Comes over to the fence. Spilled food on his top, something brown, like curry sauce, the type you get in chip shops. Dark eyes. He tosses the crushed can into his weedy, flower-less flower border. 'No, I stayed with her. For a while. I shouldn't have done.'

'She cheated again?'

'No. It's just she wasn't really sorry. She had all these

justifications.' He puts his hands in his pockets, takes them out again. 'I wish I'd made her suffer a bit. Earn her forgiveness.' He looks at me. 'I know that sounds horrible.' He looks through me a while, his thoughts in the past. I wonder about his girlfriend. I don't remember her. I do night shifts and sleep most days. Maybe it was her who started up a flower border?

He says, 'Do you watch *The Simpsons?*'

'I used to, when it was good.'

'Did you see the episode where Apu cheats with the Squishy Lady?'

'Probably. I'm not sure.'

'Well Apu is married to Manjula, remember? And he shags the Squishy Lady in the Kwik-E-Mart. And Manjula finds out.' He touches the fence and it gently rattles. 'So she makes up this list of things Apu must do in order to be forgiven. Things like eat a light bulb, change his name to Slime Q. Slimedog. I think he had to get a cartoon published in *The New Yorker* too. So anyway, Apu does these things and Manjula takes him back.'

I say, 'So I should make my girlfriend eat a light bulb?'

He shrugs, laughing. There is something kind in his eyes. Something good and easy. Even while he's talking about vengeance, it's coming out of him like heat from freshly baked bread. For a second I contemplate inviting myself over and having a drink with him, and maybe, at that point when night and drink are mixing like good soup, pulling his dick out of his smelly jeans and sitting on it. Something like that. But I won't do this. Not because I'm incapable of such spite but because I don't like dick enough.

He says, 'Anyway. My two pence' worth. Good luck.' He nods a goodbye and walks away, a little unsteady but not so you'd notice if you weren't looking. His dog follows, wagging its tail, and they go inside. The sun is setting.

On the way to the corner shop I pass an ugly old tramp with a scruffy beard. Swaying, bleary-eyed, carrier bag bulging with cans. He says, 'You look like you need cheering up,' and I say, 'Mind your own business,' and he says, 'Where do baby apes sleep?'

'Don't know. Don't care.'

His smile huge: 'Apricots.'

I say, 'Go and fuck yourself,' and he does a little salute and says, 'Will do.' Which almost gets a smile out of me. I get to the shop, buy some Dr Pepper and a large cucumber wrapped in cellophane. The tramp's gone but there's a puddle of piss on the pavement. Salmon-pink sunset reflected in its surface.

Lou has this thing about cucumbers. She hates them. The taste, the texture. If I've eaten a cucumber sandwich or just had a couple of slices in a salad, she refuses to kiss me until I've brushed my teeth or used mouthwash. She has bad associations. Like once, when she was four or five, she watched a small boy in the playground eating a sandwich. He had a snot bubble. It grew as he ate, a mouldy yellow bulb, till it reached the size of a marble and popped and dripped over his chewing lips. It was the cucumber in the sandwich she could smell the strongest. She threw up.

Bad Association Number Two. Lou came out at fourteen. Everyone knew, the whole High School. She even had a girlfriend, a fat goth who called herself, no word of a lie, Morticia Filth, and they'd hold hands in the street. In the 90s. Pontypridd. Most people left Lou alone because she was weird and angry – she once kicked a boy so hard in his balls he went into shock. So. One day she's on the school bus coming home and there's these bitches from the year above sitting behind her. They're sneaking crisps onto her shoulders and sticking chewing gum in her hair.

She's just sat there all still and charged. I can imagine her eyes growing darker and more psycho with every tentative crisp placement. She's electric sometimes, Lou. When she's mad, she has eyes that would give you cancer if they could. Eyes that spit. And Lou, she gets fucking mad. She spins around and shouts, What the *fuck* are you doing? And the main girl, a sixteen-year-old cunt called Maya, gives her the old teeth-sucking, brow-arching, bitch-eyed head-slant and says, 'Why don't you go play with cucumbers, *Lesbo-Lou*?' And my crazy electric Lou throws herself snarling at Maya – I can just see it – and starts pummelling and scratching and screeching, and Maya doesn't have a chance. By the time the other teens on the bus pull her off, Maya's face is pink and clawed and bloody and Lou has a handful of Venezuelan hair in her fist. 'You fucking dyke!' shouts Maya, crying, as Lou runs down the aisle and gets off the bus. Lou watches it drive off and sees everyone at the window either laughing or flicking tongues between vee'd fingers or staring shocked, and she goes down on her fishnet knees and cries, the long black hair still in her fist.

She's sat at the kitchen table, face blotchy from crying. I drop the cucumber in front of her. Pull a chair out and sit on it so we're facing.

'Why don't you go play with cucumbers, Lesbo-Lou?'

She stares at me. I can't see blood anywhere so either she's resisted the urge or they're on her thigh. 'That's fucking callous, Polly.'

I shrug.

'So you want me to fuck myself with a cucumber? Is that meant to be symbolic?'

'I don't want you to fuck it, Lou. I want you to eat it.'

'*Eat* it?'

I nod.

'So what's that going to achieve?'

'It'll make me feel better.'

'I had no idea you were so Old Testament.'

I crack open a Dr Pepper. 'Well, now you know.'

She says, 'I don't know if I could physically manage it,' and she looks down at the table, a fat teardrop falling from her eye and landing near the cucumber. I feel bad. I feel like I shouldn't be doing this, like doing this is heartless and power-playing. But I also feel like I *must* do this. She looks back up at me. 'I'm not sure I can physically keep this down.'

'Well I'm not sure if I can just forgive you and stay with you.' Another teardrop.

I say, 'Don't you think you should try and earn forgiveness? I'd want to if I was in your place. If that makes me Old Testament, so be it.'

'It makes you kind of sadistic.'

'You're probably right.'

She stubs out her fag and pulls the plastic off the cucumber, palming it down like a foreskin. She sniffs it, frowns. Gets up, looks in the drawer by the sink and pulls out a flimsy Spar carrier bag. Sits down, puts the bag on her lap. Takes a bite of cucumber. Chews tortoise-slow, grimacing. Swallows.

'Nice?' I say.

Her eyes spit at me. 'Fuck off, Polly.' Another bite. 'Fuck.' She does a long wavery in-breath. Swallows. And another, and another. It's slow going. Tulip comes in and puts his paws on her lap. She smiles at him bravely like it's the last time she'll ever see him. The cucumber is half gone. She chews, swallows. Retches once, twice, three times. A lady. Brings the Spar bag to her face and vomits. Water and foam and pale green lumps.

'Ugh.' She looks at me with dizzy pathetic eyes. I look back, cool as a... well. She gags again and more pulp falls into the bag. She makes a little crying sound and picks out a chunk the size of a kidney bean. Puts it in her mouth. Face like a bedpan. She opens her eyes and looks at me with misery, so much misery. Hundred per cent wretched. And then suddenly something passes between us, I'm not sure what, and we burst into laughter, hard, deep laughter which fills the room like a panic of brown doves.

WITHOUT STEVE
(2021)
David Llewellyn

'Come on, Dad. Let's go.'

He looks at us from the bar. Not old, not even fifty, but the last few days have aged him. Hasn't shaved since last week. Same clothes as the day before yesterday.

'Fuck off,' he says. 'The two of you can go. I'm staying here.'

I knew he'd be like this, and I knew exactly where we'd find him. Miles away from home. Up in the valley. Same pub. Always the same pub. One of those places that opens for breakfast, starts serving beer at nine, named after some local hero no one's ever heard of. By half nine there's usually a dozen men in here, by half ten you could say it was busy.

'Brian,' says Gem. 'Come on. Don't be daft. We gotta be there at one.'

As if it's somewhere any of us wants to be.

The others are staring at us now. None of them sat together, each on his own table, turning the pages of a newspaper with one hand and holding onto a pint with the other. One or two of them on their phones. And then there's me and Gemma, dressed in black.

'Dad. You got to come with us.'

He gives me another sulky look. Like a teenager, a wrinkly, drunken teenager. Faded Bluebirds tattoo on his neck. He knows we won't leave without him, but he takes his time. Drags it out long as he can, as if he thinks we'll just turn around and leave him here, when he knows we won't. He stares at me forever before finishing his drink, necks what's left of it in one go. I hold the door open, he gets off his stool, the daylight making him squint like he's a fucking vampire, and I follow him and Gem out of the pub.

He grew up here; one of those valley towns that looks like a fortress. Terraced houses stacked up the hillside with a view of fuck all except what's left of the slag heaps. It's always where he goes, when he wants a drink, when him and Steve have had an argument, a really bad one. He's still got mates up here who'll buy him drinks or let him sleep on the sofa when he's missed the last train home.

The number of times me and Steve came up here looking for him. Steve hated it. Made his skin crawl. He knew what these places are like. I know people say Splott's rough, but up here it's like the Wild West. And Steve couldn't stand going in that pub. Feeling those men staring at him. Because the minute he opened his mouth, they would *know*.

It's a short walk to the train station. The towns in this valley are all the same. One street with three pubs, two of them closed. Two betting shops, a vape shop and a Chinese takeaway. Maybe a little Tesco if you're lucky. Dad always says there was more going on here when he was a kid. There were six pubs, they had a carnival every summer, and none of the shops were boarded up.

We're on the platform when Dad says, 'I needs a slash.'

Gem sighs.

'There's no toilets here, Bri,' she says. 'You'll have to hold it in till we're on the train.'

'I'm bustin'.'

'The train'll be here in two minutes.'

'I'll just piss myself, then, shall I?'

'Wouldn't be the first time,' I tell him.

Gem gives me that look. *Don't be cruel.* But what else am I supposed to be? He used up all my good manners a long time ago. And if Steve was here...

Now, finally, the three of us – me, Dad and Gem – are on a train back to Cardiff, and we're two minutes out of the station when that prick lights up a fag. He takes a drag, holds it as long as he can and lets it out with a moan that comes from the bottom of his guts.

'Bri,' says Gem. 'You can't smoke on here, Bri. *Bri.*'

Dad lifts his head and gives her a look that on any other day would be enough for me to spark him out.

'Dad,' I tell him. 'Put it out, or we'll get kicked off. Come on. Don't be a prick.'

And now he turns that look on me. I've seen it often enough. As a kid, before Mum died, when it was one of him and Steve's weekends looking after me and they'd pick me up from Mum's (Steve never left the car) there'd be something said on the doorstep. Either they were late picking me up or Dad was pissed or both. And he would give Mum the same look. Nothing crafty or hidden about it. Might as well have had the words "FUCK OFF" tattooed across his forehead. And even though Mum could hardly bring herself to say his name I know she'd never have let them look after me if Steve wasn't there.

'Dad,' I say, and he just shrugs and sneers at me, so I snatch the cigarette from his hand, drop it under the table and crush it under my shoe.

'I was fucking *smoking* that,' he says.

There's not many people on the train, but the other passengers are either staring or doing everything they can not to.

'We should have gone to the fucking offy,' he says.

'Aww, yeah, like that's a good idea,' says Gem.

'Yeah? And who fucking asked you?'

Gem takes a deep breath and looks out of the window but doesn't say anything. Out there, it's all brown trees and empty factories.

I lean over so I'm looking him straight in the eye and I tell him: 'I don't care what day it is. You talk to my girlfriend like that again and I'll give you a fucking smack in the mouth.'

Dad says nothing. Doesn't even give me the look. The days when he could take me in a fight are long gone. Neither of us has landed a blow on the other in years, not since I was fifteen, maybe sixteen. So long ago, neither of us remembers what it was over. All I remember now is Steve breaking us up, telling Dad to go to the garden, telling me to calm down. Steve the peacemaker.

'I'm sorry, love,' says Dad, and he reaches across the table to take Gem's hand in his. 'It's the drink, it is.'

'I know, Bri,' says Gem, still looking out of the window. 'Forget about it. It's alright.'

I told her not to come. Four months pregnant. She could do without this. Don't want our nipper getting stressed out in there, I told her. And she's never really seen Dad like this. Knows he likes a drink, knows he's meant to be staying sober. Doctor's orders. My orders. Steve's orders; at least before. But no one's seen him this bad in a long time.

'I'm sorry, love,' he says, squeezing her hand a little tighter. 'You knows I don't mean it.'

The conductor comes along, ticket machine on his hip, and it's obvious he can smell the smoke, but he doesn't mention it. Maybe he knows. Maybe he can tell from the way me and Gemma are dressed, and from Dad's eyes and my eyes and Gem's eyes, and from that pub carpet stink of booze coming off the old man.

Seriously, if someone lit a match...

I buy Dad's ticket and pass it to him, so he'll have it ready for the turnstiles. How does someone even *get* hands like his? All bones and veins. Black hairs down the sides, some blotchy blue tattoos across his knuckles, and every finger and thumb stained yellow.

Hard work, he'd tell me. *That's how you get hands like this. Feel your hands, now feel my hands. That's hard work, that is, son. Something you young'uns'll never understand.*

I never believed a fucking word of it.

He slides his ticket into his shirt pocket and rubs his eyes with his fingers and his eyes look even redder than before. I look over at Gem, nodding to her handbag, and she takes the hint.

'Tissue, Bri?'

Dad nods and sniffs, and Gem nudges the pack across the table. He takes one, wiping away his tears and he blows his nose.

At Queen Street the platform's quiet and I'm glad, because I can picture him making a scene, slipping away, getting on another train and fucking off somewhere else before we can stop him. I'd almost forgotten what he's like without Steve. Like a kid, sometimes. Take your eyes off him for one second...

He starts walking down the steps and there's a gang of lads coming up towards him, talking to each other, not looking where they're going, and it's like they expect Dad to get out of the way, and I'm thinking *move, just move* because if he lets go of that rail there's every chance he'll go arse over tit so *just move* I'm thinking because if one of them bumps into him he'll kick off or he'll say something or they'll say something and he'll kick off and we'll never get to the fucking crem.

I can feel my shoulders getting tense and I want to tell him, I want to say to this lad, 'Excuse me.' But it's like he reads my mind or something, because he gets out of Dad's way without me telling him to, and we get to the bottom of the steps and out through the station without anyone saying anything and without anything happening.

There's a homeless guy outside the station with a blanket over his legs and he takes one look at us and doesn't even say 'Spare any change?' He must have taken one look at Dad and thought better of it, maybe even felt sorry for him, because he can hardly walk in a straight line. It's like he's walking in cast iron boots. Gem hooks her arm around his, to keep him steady, like she's taking her granddad for a walk around the park. And seeing her do that for him, making him look almost respectable.

The love explodes inside me.

Dad's house – already *his* house, not his and Steve's house – is on Ruby Street, in a part of town where all the streets are named after gemstones and precious metals, like a bad joke. '*It's not Splott, it's Adamsdown*,' Steve would say. He was very particular about that. I don't know what the difference is, but he said 'Splott' sounded like seagull shit hitting a pavement, and 'Adamsdown' sounded 'almost bucolic'. I had to ask him what bucolic meant.

He wasn't posh or nothing, but he was brainy. Brainier than Dad, anyway, not that that takes much doing. He pissed all his brain cells up against a wall a long time ago.

The house feels empty. Quieter than I've ever known it. In the dining room the table is covered in white cards; some with crosses, some with flowers. The kitchen sink is full of cups and plates and the bin is full of greasy takeaway cartons and the flowers that arrived after he ran out of vases.

On the mantelpiece there's a photo of the three of us, Steve, Dad and me, down the Gower. We're on that beach with the shipwreck that looks like a dinosaur's skeleton. It was the first summer after Mum died, and I'd just moved in with them. I'm eleven years old in that photo and Dad looks so much younger and happier. Steve in the middle, like a big bear, smiling that gap-toothed smile. We got some funny looks, and I remember Steve saying, 'It doesn't matter what anyone else thinks, as long as you're happy and we're happy.'

First thing Dad does once he's in the house is crack open a can and light a fag; his third since we got off the train.

'You'd better get in the shower,' I tell him. 'The car'll be here soon.'

'Don't need a fucking shower.'

'Bri,' says Gem. 'Not being funny, right, but you stink like a fucking brewery. So get in the shower. I'll iron you a shirt and Kyle'll put the kettle on. How does that sound?'

Dad grunts and moans and shuffles off upstairs to the bathroom.

'I won't have one, mind,' says Gem. 'If I drink any more tea, I'll be busting for a piss all the way through the service.'

I let myself laugh, and Gem puts her arms around me and kisses me, and she tells me everything will be alright, because we can relax now, because we found him, and he's safe.

'We should tell him,' she says, patting her belly.

'Not today,' I tell her.

'Why? Might cheer him up.'

'Or freak him out. Can you imagine him being a granddad?'

Gem smiles one of those sad smiles.

'Give him a chance,' she says. 'But Steve would have been amazing.'

I start looking for clean mugs, blinking away the tears, and Gem goes upstairs to iron Dad's shirt.

Amazing how filthy the house is after only a few days. I should have come around, tidied up a bit, but we've been so busy, with the undertakers and the minister. If Steve saw it like this, he'd scream the house down. No way he'd put up with all those plates and cups and dishes in the sink. No way he'd let Dad smoke in the house, never mind stub his fags out on a saucer.

Tucked away at the back of a cupboard I find the matching WORLD'S BEST DAD mugs I got them both for Father's Day. Only one of them is tea-stained, the other looks brand new. Typical Steve. He probably thought they were a bit cheesy. He liked everything to be matching, tasteful, but when I gave it to him his eyes filled up with happy tears. And he never threw it away.

While I'm waiting for the kettle to boil I look at the photo. The one taken down the Gower. Who took this? Must have been a complete stranger, because it was only the three of us staying in the caravan, but we're all in the photo. And there was a pub up the top, above the beach, with a beer garden looking out over the sea. Felt like we were a million miles away from Cardiff. Steve went to get us some drinks and Dad said he'd have a pint of Coke and some pork scratchings and Steve smiled proudly from ear to ear. He'd gone back inside to get me some crisps when Dad poured a miniature of vodka into his Coke and gave me a wink.

Gem comes back downstairs, shakes her head.

'I'm ironing his shirt in the box room and he comes out of the bathroom stark bollock naked.'

'He didn't.'

'He fucking did. He had a towel drying on the bannister, and he put it around his waist but I saw everything.'

I can't help but giggle, and Gemma starts giggling too. Minutes later Dad comes down the stairs wearing his black suit, black tie and the shoes he only ever wears to weddings and funerals.

'You look smart,' says Gem.

'I looks like I'm up before the fucking magistrate,' says Dad.

'And you should fucking know,' I tell him.

Gem gives me a look and helps Dad sort his tie out.

We've hardly finished our tea when there's a knock on the door. The car's waiting outside. Gem and Dad get in first, sitting next to each other, and I sit in the seats facing backwards. As we drive off Gem holds Dad's hand and doesn't let go for the rest of the journey.

It takes forever to get there. That's the thing with cemeteries and crems, they're always miles away, like we don't want to think about them too often.

'How much longer is this gonna take?' says Dad. 'I thought it was Cathays.'

'Thornhill crem,' I tell him. 'Like Mum's.'

Don't know why I needed to say that. He knows it was Thornhill. And neither of us wants to think too much about that day. I was sat at the front, between Nan and Granch, Dad was right at the back, and Steve wasn't there at all. Nan said she didn't want to upset Mum's brother and sister, Uncle Rob and Auntie Jackie, so Dad was on his own.

I'd never been to a funeral before. I'd seen cemeteries. There's a park, not far from Dad's house, called Cemetery Park, and they've still got some of the gravestones there, next to the basketball court and the climbing frame. But this was different. I knew Mum wouldn't have a gravestone, that we'd have ashes, and that we'd scatter them somewhere she liked.

At least with Mum I knew it was coming. Nan and Granch prepared me for it, when she was in hospital. Said she was going to Heaven to be with her Nan and Granch. And I got to say goodbye. Though it felt weird knowing it was the last time I'd say it, that this was the last time I'd see her, and that this was the last room she'd see.

With Steve it was a phone call. Dad was sober, thank fuck.

'Steve's gone, son,' he said. And the weird thing is, I knew even before I answered the phone, because Dad never phones me. It was always Steve who arranged things and now it was Dad's number and when I saw it on the screen I knew. Collapsed with chest pains, he told me. Taken up the Heath. Dead before they got him out of the ambulance.

'It was his weight, son. I always tells him he should lose some weight.'

As if Dad's the picture of fucking health.

'What song are they playing?' says Gem. 'I forgot to ask.'

'Killing Me Softly,' Dad says, speaking for the first time since we set off. 'Funeral director asked and I gave him the CD. That's Steve's favourite. The Fugees. And we always argues 'cause I reckons the Fugees ain't as good as whatsername. Roberta Flack. My mum used to sing that to me when I was a nipper. But Steve prefers the Fugees, so that's what they're playing.'

'We didn't have songs at Mum's funeral, did we?' I ask him.

He shakes his head. 'That was her family. Only hymns, they said. She wanted Celine Dion. She told me that herself, when we was still together, but they weren't having any of it. Bunch of cunts.'

'Bri!' says Gem. 'You know I hates that word.'

'Sorry, love. But they *were*. If they'd had their way I'd have never seen our Kyle again. They said if me and Steve looked after him he'd end up gay. And you knows that didn't happen.'

There's a look in his eyes, something mischievous. He's the closest thing to sober I've seen him in days.

'When was you two gonna tell me?' he says.

'Tell you what?' I ask him.

'Fuck's sake, come on. I wasn't born yesterday. I noticed the bump when Gem was ironing.'

Even after everything I can't help but laugh. Neither can Gem. As for Dad, he just sits there with a mischievous little grin and tears in his eyes.

We pass through the gates and across the cemetery. Row after row of gravestones, the gravel crackling beneath the wheels. Most of the graves are black marble with gold lettering but one of them is a white marble teddy bear, and when Gemma notices it as we go past I see her shiver.

There's people from Steve's work and some of his and Dad's mates waiting outside the chapel. The hearse is here already, the pallbearers lined up in front of it with their hands crossed. Behind them, through its windows, Steve's coffin seems too small.

ALL THE BOYS
(2015)
Thomas Morris

The best man won't tell them it's Dublin until they get to Bristol Airport. He'll tell them to bring euros and don't bother packing shorts. The five travelling from Caerphilly will drink on the minibus. And Big Mike, the best man, will spend the first twenty minutes reading and rereading the A4 itinerary he typed up on MS Word. The plastic polypocket will be wedged thick with flight tickets and hostel reservations. It will be crumpled and creased from the constant hand-scrunching and metronome swatting against his suitcase – the only check-in bag on the entire trip. He'll spend the journey to the airport telling Gareth, and anyone who listens, that Rob had better never marry again, that he couldn't handle the stress of organising another one of these.

'You should see my desk in work,' Big Mike will say. 'It's covered in notes for this fuckin stag. It's been like a full-time job.'

Gareth will nod and Gareth will sympathise. He'll just be glad to get out of Caerphilly for the weekend; he's been waiting months for this, has imagined how it all might go. He'll take a swig of his can, and look to Rob's father. Rob's father will be fifty-four in two weeks and will think there's something significant about the fact, about being twice the age of his son. He had two kids and a house by the time he was twenty-seven, and he'll think about that as he listens to Larry telling the story about the woman he picked up at the Kings. She'd taken Larry back to her

187

place, and in the middle of the night he'd heard sex noises coming from the room next to hers. Larry said to the woman, 'Your housemate's a bit wild,' and the woman replied, 'I don't have a housemate, love. That's my daughter.'

Hucknall and Peacock, travelling from London, will arrive at Bristol before the others. They'll sit in the bar getting drunk and studying departures screens. Hucknall will have spent the whole morning moaning about the fact they're flying from Bristol, and why couldn't Big Mike have just told them where they're going?

'Bet you it's Dublin,' Hucknall will say, leaning back in his chair, his knees spread wide, his hands smoothing his tan chinos. 'Bet Big Mike's too scared to book somewhere foreign.'

'Don't make a difference to me,' Peacock will say. 'I'll clear up wherever we go.'

When the Caerphilly boys join the now-London ones at the airport bar, Big Mike will confirm that it's Dublin they're headed to. And he'll loudly declare the weekend's drinking rule: pints must always be held in the left hand. If you find yourself holding two drinks, your own drink must be in your left hand. Failure to adhere will result in a forfeit, as decided by Lead Ruler Larry. The boys will all say that's easy, and start suggesting additional rules, but Big Mike will be defiant: the left-hand rule is king.

'You sure no one here's a secret leftie, though?' Hucknall will ask.

'I've done my research,' Big Mike will say. 'Rob's dad is left-footed, but he's definitely right-handed. I made him write his name out earlier.'

When Peacock – with perfect stubble and coiffed hair – goes to the airport bar, everyone will laugh at his shoes that seem to be made of straw.

'Couldn't believe it when I met him at Paddington,' Hucknall will say. 'Doesn't he look benter than a horseshoe?'

'I've seen straighter semicircles,' Rob will say.

Gareth will shout to Peacock: 'Mate, why don't you do yourself a favour and just come out?'

Peacock will stand there, between table and bar, and kiss his own biceps. He'll accept the jibes, and say none of the boys has any idea about style. He'll take the piss out of Caerphilly's clothes shops, and say David Beckham wore a pair of shoes just like these to the *Iron Man 3* premiere. And that will be it: Peacock will be called Iron Man Three for the rest of the trip.

When they board the plane, Larry will tell the air stewardess that Peacock's ticket isn't valid, that his name is Iron Man Three.

When they get to the hostel in Temple Bar – and Hucknall has finally stopped going on about the ten-minute wait for Big Mike's suitcase, he'll ask if Iron Man Three has a reservation.

And in Fitzsimons on the first night, to every girl that Peacock talks to, one of the boys will come up and say, 'Don't bother, Iron Man's gay.'

Peacock will laugh. 'They're just jealous,' he'll tell the girl from Minneapolis or Wexford or Rome. 'They wouldn't know fashion if it woke them up in the morning and gave them a little kiss.'

Gareth, meanwhile, will be at the bar ordering shots. He'll have his arm around Rob and he'll tell him that he loves him, that he's really happy he's happy. He'll make Rob do shots with him – sambuca, whiskey and vodka – and Rob will say he can't handle any more after the apple sours.

'Who's for shots?' Gareth will say, looking around. '*Shotiau?*'

He'll order shots for whoever's beside him at the bar. He'll buy randomers shots. And he'll persuade the English barman to have a shot with him. He's not meant to, but he'll do one just to shut Gareth up.

At a table, Rob's father will have his arm around his son.

'I love Rachel, you know,' Rob will say, his eyes ablaze. 'I really love her.'

'Just pace yourself,' his father will say quietly. 'The boys are getting wrecked. They won't even notice if you don't drink the stuff they're giving you.'

He'll offer to drink his son's drinks; he'll get wasted so that his son may be saved.

Big Mike will be careering around the pub making sure everyone's alright. He'll always have a pint in his left hand. And he'll be going from boy to boy, just to make sure everyone's okay. This first night he'll be torn between keeping steady and getting absolutely bollocksed. He'll decide on ordering half-pints but asking the barman to pour them into pint glasses.

'Dun want anyone thinking I'm gay,' he'll say, and he'll order another pint for Rob, and place it down at his table without saying a word.

And Larry? He'll be getting attacked by an English girl for calling her sugar-tits. When her friends pull her off he'll retouch his hair and say, 'Fair play, my dear, that was lovely. Can we do that back at yours?'

The night will become an ungodly mess. All the boys will be pouncing on each other for holding pints in their right hand, and drinking shots as forfeits, and drinking faster as the night slips by. They'll make moves on girls on hen-do's from Brighton and Bangor and Mayo. By eleven, Hucknall will be puking in the corner of the dance floor, and Rob's father, after a quiet word in Big Mike's ear, will take Rob back to the hostel. Peacock will go missing, talking to some girl somewhere, his deep V-neck shirt showing off his tonely chest and glimmering sunbed tan. And Rob, the groom (lest we forget), will be flat-out on the hostel bed, fully clothed, but shoeless, his father having taken them off while his drunken twenty-seven-year-old son lay half-comatose.

He'll send a text to the boy's mother: *'all gd here, back at the hostel. Rob's safe and asleep.'*

Outside McDonald's, Larry'll coax the boys to take turns hugging the Polish dwarf in a leprechaun costume.

Larry will say: 'Cracking job this would be for you, Mikey-boy.'

Big Mike will laugh and grab at his own hair. He'll slur, 'I'm small. I know I'm small. But at least I'm not fucking ginger.'

Gareth will ask the Polish dwarf if Big Mike can try on his hat, but the man will decline.

'No hat, no job,' he'll say.

So they'll take turns to photograph each other hugging the Polish dwarf in a leprechaun costume. They'll ask a passer-by to take photos of them hugging the Polish dwarf in a leprechaun costume. And when the Polish man points at the little pot-of-gold money box and asks for two euro, Larry will say – actually, Larry won't say anything the leprechaun will understand. Larry will be speaking Welsh. When abroad, all the boys slag everyone in Welsh.

At Zaytoon, Gareth, Big Mike and Larry will queue for food while Hucknall sits on the pavement outside, his head arched between his legs, his vomit softly coating the curb and cobblestones like one of Dali's melted clocks. A blonde girl will ask the boys if they're from Wales. She'll say she loves the accent, and Larry will say he likes hers too – where's she from? But when she answers, she'll be looking at Gareth, not Larry. She'll say she likes his quiff.

'Cheers,' Gareth will say. 'I grew it myself.'

She'll be asking about the tattoo of a fish on Gareth's arm when Larry will tell her that Gareth has a girlfriend called Carly, that they're buying together a house in Ystrad Mynach. The girl will lose interest, not immediately – she won't be that obvious –

but she'll allow herself to be pulled back into the gravitational force of her friends who lean against the restaurant window.

'Cheers,' Gareth will say to Larry. 'You're such a twat.'

'Any time,' Larry will say. 'Have you seen *Iron Man Three*?'

Big Mike will have his hands on the glass counter, his head resting like a small bundle in his arms. Gareth will be looking at Big Mike's tiny little frame, his tiny little shoes against the base of the counter, and Gareth will think he should text Carly back.

'I ain't seen Peacock all night,' he'll say. 'Probably shagging some bloke somewhere.'

Larry will smile. 'Aye,' he'll say. 'Wouldn't surprise me.'

all the boys

Saturday, the hostel room smelling like sweated alcohol and men, heavy tongues will wake stuck to the roofs of dry mouths. Set up a microphone, and this is what you'll hear: waking-up farts and morning groans; zips and unzips on mini-suitcases and sports bags; the library-*shhhhhhh* of Lynx sprays; and the sounds of the bathroom door opening and slamming, its lock rotating clockwise in the handle. Pop your nose through the door, and this is what you'll smell: dehydrated shit mingling with the minty hostel shower gel in the hot, steamy air. And back in the room, more sounds now: the beginning of last night's stories, the where-did-you-go-tos, the how-the-hell-did-I-get-backs and Larry inviting the boys to guess if the skin he's pulling over his boxers belongs to his cock or balls.

Big Mike will be first to breakfast, the others dripping behind. All the boys will be scrolling through iPhones for photos from last night, with Rob's father doing the same on his digital camera. There'll be sympathetic bleats for headaches and wrenched stomachs, with paracetamol handed around like condiments. Big

Mike will be urging the boys to get a move on or they'll never make it to Croke Park. Hucknall will ask why the hell are they going there anyway? And Big Mike, tapping the inventory in its polypocket, will say: 'Culture, mate. Culture.' Fried breakfasts and questions: how's an Irish breakfast different to an English? When you buying the house then, Gareth? And seriously, Peacock, where the hell did you end up last night?

Peacock's story will be confusing and confused. He got in a taxi with a girl, and she was well up for it – he was fingering her in the backseat. ('Backseat?' Larry'll say. 'Up the arse, like?' and Peacock will go, 'No, the backseat of the taxi, you dickwad.') Anyway, when they got to her place she realised she didn't have her keys ('Sure this wasn't a bloke?' Rob will say). So Peacock and the girl walked for like an hour to somewhere – Cadbra or some random place – and when they arrived she told him he couldn't come in because it was her nan's house. She just went in and closed the door on him. When he finally found a taxi, he didn't have enough cash so the driver dropped him off at some random ATM in a 24-hour shop, but Peacock got talking to some random guy about London for ages ('Oh yeah, bet you did,' Gareth'll say) and when he came out, the taxi had gone, so he – ('He's holding his glass in his right hand!' Rob's father will say. 'It's orange juice,' Peacock will say. 'It don't matter,' Larry will say. 'Down it!') – so he found the tram stop and—

'Gay Boy Robert Downey Junior,' Hucknall will say. 'I'm bored now. Worst Man, when we going to Croke Park?'

Big Mike will be glaring. He'll say: 'As soon as you've finished your fucking breakfast.'

All the boys will be surprised and impressed by Croke Park's size, by the vastness of the changing rooms, the way the training centre gleams. When the guide takes them out onto the edge of the pitch, he'll point to the stand at the far end, and tell them about the Bloody Sunday Massacre in 1920, how the British army opened fire on the crowd during a Gaelic football match. Fourteen were killed, he'll say. Two players were shot. There'll be a silence. Rob's father will be nodding – he'll have read about all this in the guide book he bought at the Centra in Temple Bar. Three of the boys will be wearing Man Utd shirts. And the guide will go on, explaining how Gaelic football and hurling – he'll just call it GAA, and it'll take a few minutes for the boys to fully get what he's talking about – are not sports, but expressions of resistance. But they're also more than that, they're not just reactive things. It's in the blood, he'll say. And Gareth will be sort of startled. Something the guide says, something of its tone, will resonate. Though resonate isn't quite how Gareth would put it; he won't even know what he's thinking. He'll just be looking out to the far stand, trying to picture how it all happened.

'They were boys,' the guide will say. 'The ones who fought for independence, they were younger than all you.'

The sky will be white, and there'll be silence and rapture. When the guide leaves them at the museum, Hucknall will say to the boys, 'Fucking hell, I thought he'd never shut up.'

And Larry will put on an Irish accent and go: '*GAA is in the blood.*'

And Hucknall will laugh and go: '*And they killed all our boys...* Yeah, nice one, Worst Man. Most depressing stag do in the world. You got any other crap trips in that suitcase of yours?'

Big Mike will be quiet, he won't know what to say.

'I enjoyed it,' Rob will say, and his father will thank Big Mike for bringing them.

Gareth will send a text to Carly. '*Miss you too*', it'll say.

Peacock will be using his iPhone to check his hair.

They'll get a taxi back into town, then they'll walk around and look at things. Larry'll be in hysterics when he sees the place called Abrakebabra, insisting that one of the boys take his photo next to the sign. They'll walk in a group, taking up half the width of Westmoreland Street, wondering what the hell goes on in the massive white building with the huge columns that look as if they belong in Rome.

'It's a bank,' Rob's father will say, and Big Mike will go, 'No wonder things are so fucking expensive.'

When they pass Trinity College, Rob's father will say there's meant to be a nice library in there, he read about it in his guide book. And Gareth will point ahead at Hucknall and Larry as they eye up a group of Spanish-looking tourists, and he'll say: 'I've got a feeling the boys aren't really in the mood for a good read.'

Before they know it, they'll be in Temple Bar again. In Gogarty's they'll order bouquets of Guinness, and Hucknall will insist that they should have gone to the Guinness Factory instead of Croke Park.

Big Mike will say: 'If you know so much, why dun you be fucking best man?' And the boys will do a handbags-*oooooh*, and laugh until their already-aching kidneys hurt. A greying man on a guitar will sing 'Whiskey in the Jar' and 'The Wild Rover' ('The Clover song!' Peacock will say), and when the boys request 'Delilah', he'll oblige, and all the boys will sing shout along, all the while pushing more pints in front of Rob. Rob will be singing loudest now. He'll have decided that tonight's the night he's going to properly go for it. Leaving Croke Park, he'll have felt something stirring, and he'll have told his father he was ready to have one more final night of going nuts.

Gareth will sing along too, but he'll be thinking of his small bedroom at home, of the journey back to Wales tomorrow night.

'By the way,' Big Mike will tell the group when talk turns to eating, 'before we go for food, we've gotta go back to the hostel.'

'How come, Worst Man?' Hucknall will say.

'Costumes for tonight, butt. And if you call me Worst Man one more time I'm gonna knock you out, you ginger prick.'

'Sorry, Worst Man.'

The boys will be awkward-quiet, and Rob's father will ask where they're gonna get the costumes from. And Big Mike will smile now. He'll say, 'Why the hell do you think I checked in a suitcase?'

'A fucking potato?' Hucknall will say. 'Are you fucking serious?'

They'll all be back at their room, and Big Mike will have his suitcase open on the bed, the bag bulging with bumpy, creamy-brown potato costumes.

'Aye,' Big Mike will say. 'Got a problem with that as well, have you?'

Peacock will take a costume from the suitcase and place it over himself in the mirror. 'These gonna make us look fat, you reckon?'

'No way am I wearing a potato costume,' Hucknall will say. 'We're in Ireland, for fuck's sake.'

'Exactly,' Big Mike'll go. 'They love potatoes. *Dirty-tree potatoes.*'

And the boys will shake their heads, will say all sorts.

'Are they all the same size?' Larry'll go.

'All the same,' Big Mike will say, 'except for Rob's. He's wearing something else. Oh, and you all owe me fifteen quid.'

Rob will beam, his teeth visible, a smile in his voice. 'What the fuck you got me?'

A plunging arm into the suitcase depths and Big Mike will pull out something black in cellophane.

Wordless, he'll hand the package to Rob.

Rob will tear at the cellophane. There'll be some kind of dress: green-and-orange and hideous. It'll take a moment for Rob to click: he's been given a woman's Irish dance costume. There'll be white socks to go with it too.

'*Rrrrriverdance!*' Big Mike will scream, doing an odd, high-kneed jig on the hostel floor.

And all the boys will laugh, and Hucknall will say fair play, that's a good un. And once they see that Rob looks the biggest tit, they won't mind dressing up like potatoes. At least we'll all be warm, Rob's father will say.

They'll drink the cans left over from last night, and Gareth will find himself at the point of drunkenness where he wants to fight. He'll offer arm wrestles to everyone. Using Big Mike's suitcase for a table – and at Gareth's insistence – they'll take turns to lie on the floor and arm-wrestle each other. And when he's not competing, Gareth will come up behind Larry, give him a bear hug and lift him off the ground. He'll do the same to Hucknall and Peacock and Rob. They'll be laughing at first, but by the end they'll be properly pushing him off.

In Temple Bar, with the boys dressed like potatoes and Rob dressed like a female Irish dancer (but wearing his own brown Wrangler boots), they'll argue over where to go for dinner. Foreign girls with dark hair and dinner menus will approach, trying to coax them into their restaurants. Passers-by will cheer and laugh, and tourists – German, American, Chinese – will ask for photos with all the boys. And they'll begin to get into it, begin to feel like Dublin's central attraction.

'We should start charging,' Larry'll say, as Rob poses for a photo with a girl from Cincinnati. 'Two quid per photo, whadyou reckon?'

At some point in the night someone will say that the euro feels like Monopoly money and everyone will agree.

After forty minutes of wandering and arguing, they'll land on Dame Street, at an empty Chinese restaurant.

'Never a good sign when it's empty,' Rob's father will say, but they'll have been walking around for too long, and will be too hungry to go elsewhere. Before they've even ordered, Hucknall will suggest they split the bill. Hucknall is an accountant, Hucknall can afford to say such things. And for reasons beyond them, to save hassle perhaps, everyone will agree. They'll order pints immediately, but the food will take deliberation. They'll all ask each other what they're going to order, as if each boy's afraid of getting the wrong dish, of getting the whole eating-out thing wrong. They'll wind up the waitress who takes their orders, ask her if she'll be joining them for starters, and then they'll make her stand at the table for photos with them all.

The potato costumes will be chunky and clunky, so the chairs will have to be set some distance from the tables, and Gareth will find that to eat he has to lean forward, his back arched like a capital C. His arms will be free, though – he'll have that at least.

'When you buying this place with your missus, then?' Larry will ask.

'We'll see,' Gareth will say, taking a swig of his pint. 'No rush, is there?'

'I heard she wants somewhere by the summer,' Big Mike'll say.

'Carly talks too fucking much,' Gareth will say, and the table will laugh, giddy. Gareth'll say: 'What? It's true. She shouldn't talk about stuff like this with other people. I dun know what's wrong with her.'

Peacock will be smiling like a bag of chips, brimming over, as if he can't believe they're allowed to slag off their partners publicly. He'll think he could handle having a girlfriend if he could just slag her off all the time.

Gareth will finish off his pint and call to the waitress for another. Rob, his arms beginning to itch in the dance dress, will be watching Gareth's left leg. Under the white tablecloth, it'll be shaking.

The boys will chant football songs as they eat. They'll recall stories from school, from holidays, and from other stag trips. And all the boys will laugh as Larry pretends to cry and goes '*I'm soooooo hungry!*' – in imitation of the time Hucknall passed out in Malaga and woke to find his wallet had been stolen. When the boys found him, he'd been walking the streets for three hours and he was a quivering, starving mess. At some point, some food will be thrown at someone. A man and a woman will sit down at a table across from the boys, then promptly leave. Of all the boys, Rob's father will be the only one to notice. But the restaurant manager won't mind the noise because the boys are buying so many drinks and extra portions of egg-fried rice and chips.

'Alright then,' Rob will shout across the table, raising his glass. And it'll take Big Mike and Hucknall to quiet everyone down. 'I should have done this earlier,' Rob will shout, 'but I just wanna say thanks for all this. I know you're all wankers, but I've known you all so long—'

'So he's gonna dump Rachel and marry us!' Gareth will yell, and the boys will cheer.

'Dump the girl,' will come the shout from Larry, and Gareth will shout it too, and they'll both chant the words banging the table. Hucknall will tell them to shut up, and Big Mike will be annoyed because that's his job, really, not Hucknall's.

Rob's father will smile and tell his son to go on with the speech.

'If I could,' Rob will say, 'I'd marry you all.'

'A toast to us!' Gareth will shout. And though his glass will be empty, he'll raise it anyway. And Rob won't realise he never said what he wanted to say.

In Gogarty's, Gareth will be doing his bear-hug-picking-up-mates routine again, but the place will be packed and he'll be banging into everyone. It won't help matters that they're all dressed like potatoes. Big Mike will take Gareth aside and tell him to calm the fuck down.

Upstairs, in the smoking area, Larry and Rob – neither smoke – will be reminiscing.

'Getting older's mad, innit?' Rob will say, taking a swig of his pint. He'll almost have forgotten he's dressed like a woman, and he'll be repeatedly confused by all the looks he's getting.

'Yeah,' Larry will say. 'I can't believe we're twenty-seven. Innit sad thinking about all the things we'll never do? I was thinking about it the other day. Like, at this age, I will never be the victim of paedophilia.'

Rob will laugh and bury his head in his hands. Between his fingers, he'll see the cream foam collecting on the inside of his glass. He'll take a swig and look at Larry. 'Incredible,' he'll say.

'It's not real, though,' Larry will say. 'I reckon we're in *The Matrix*. We're gonna wake up and we're gonna be five years old and it's gonna be the end of our first day at school again and—'

'Yeah,' Rob will say.

'But back to the issue,' Larry will say. 'Any pre-match doubts?'

'What, about Rachel?'

'Yeah. Any niggles?'

'Nah, all good, mate. All good.'

'I dunno how you do it,' Larry will say – and he'll mean it now, he'll be sincere. 'My record is three weeks and four days.'

Downstairs, Rob's father will be standing on a table with a Welsh flag around his head, singing 'Don't Look Back in Anger'.

'I'm telling you,' Gareth will shout at Hucknall at the bar, 'I'm not buying a house.'

'You been with Carly five years now, though, mate.'

'I know, but I'm not buying a house.'

'Look, you bender,' Hucknall will say, 'you can't live at home all your life. I'm spending shitloads on rent in London. I know that. But at least I'm not living with my fucking parents.'

'I know,' Gareth will say, and when Hucknall turns to fetch his pint from the bar, Gareth will put his arms around Hucknall's potato waist, pick him up, and launch him into a group of French guys in the corner. Pints will be knocked over, and Hucknall will be winded. He'll get up, confused, and make apologies to the jostling French men. He'll push his way through, smile at Gareth, and gesture for him to come back. And when Gareth takes a step forward, Hucknall will smack him square in the nose. Gareth will feel the cartilage snap, the muscle tear from the bone, and he'll be buckled over when he sees Hucknall lining up another.

He'll bound for the doors then. He'll leg it out, down the lane, down Merchant's Arch. He'll dodge and weave through the traffic, and lunge up to the bridge. He'll put his hand to his nose and there'll be blood wetting his fingers. He'll keep running until he's on the other side, on Lower Liffey Street. He'll take a seat at the bench.

He'll be sat there, watching the boardwalk, seething and lost, when a girl who's smoking outside the Grand Social will come sit beside him.

'Have a chip on your shoulder, do you?'

'What?' he'll say.

'You're a potato,' she'll say. 'Chips. Potatoes.' She'll look at him, see the nose. 'God, you're bleeding.'

'I know,' he'll say.

The taxis will be piling up beside the Liffey, glowing. Gareth will be staring at them, at the thin whistle of white lights, at the dark night, at the starless sky, at all the people on the boardwalk, and he'll think that only yesterday morning he was leaving his mother's house to get on the minibus. He'll feel small now, as if he's shrinking even, as if he's been dragged down from that vast sky and put here in Dublin, with his past and everything he knows about himself left behind. It's as if they've just brought the shell of his body over to Ireland, as if the rest of him might still be on the plane. He'll realise he hasn't looked up at the girl in some time.

· 'You alright?' she'll say.

He'll pause for a moment, unsure if he'll actually say it. This isn't how he imagined it. This isn't how he thought it all might go. But he'll look down at his bobbly potato body and think *fuck it*.

'I'm gay,' he'll say, and he'll feel there's no returning now.

'Good for you,' the girl will say. 'I was just asking if you're alright.'

He'll shift over on the bench, put a hand on her shoulder. 'No, you don't get it. My friends don't know I am. No one knows.'

'Oh God,' she'll say, watching the blood dribble from his nose, past his lips. 'I bet you're having a long night.'

'Yeah,' he'll say, getting up. 'I've got to go tell the boys.'

He'll leave the girl then, he'll rise, and he'll cross the bridge, and he'll wait at the beeping traffic lights before crossing the road. He'll wipe the blood with the sleeve of his potato costume – red streaks on the creamy-brown. He'll walk through the arch and over the cobbles to Gogarty's. The bouncers won't let him back in because he'll be too drunk, so he'll sit outside on the pavement and ring the boys. He'll call and he'll text, and Larry will come out and Gareth will go to say it, will go to tell him everything. He'll look at Larry, his fringe gelled upwards, and Gareth will open his mouth, he'll go to say how he's been like this since he was fifteen – but Larry will speak first.

'You alright?' he'll say. 'All the boys are off to find a strip club now – are you comin or what?'

There'll be a pause, a moment of nothing.

'Aye,' Gareth will finally say, 'I could probably do with seeing some tits.'

all the boys

They'll wake late on Sunday. They'll be rushing to check out of the hostel. They won't all have breakfast together because the London boys will have an earlier flight. All the boys will hug and high-five, and the Caerphilly boys will say bye to Hucknall and Peacock as the two leave in search of a taxi.

Big Mike still won't be talking to Gareth and there'll be a tough silence in the group until Rob tells them to sort it out cos it's getting depressing. Gareth will apologise for 'ruining Gogarty's', and say he was wrecked, he doesn't remember any of last night now. He'll buy Big Mike a make-up pint and Big Mike will accept.

'Don't get me wrong,' Big Mike will say, 'Hucknall's a prick, but you don't go chucking your mates around a pub.'

Big Mike will say there's still time for them to see a little bit more of the city, but the boys won't be up for it. They've got their bags to carry, and Man Utd are on at 12.30, and can't they just watch the match at Fitzsimons? They're sure the place has Sky.

So they'll watch the United game at Fitzsimons, and they'll nurse slow pints, and they'll keep looking at their phones, sending texts to their girlfriends and wives. They'll decide to leave earlier than they need to because they're just killing time now, aren't they? There's no point waiting around here, they're better off getting to the airport than staying around here. At least they know they won't miss the flight then.

So they'll get the taxi, and they'll wait at departures, and they'll board their flight, and they'll sit there as the plane carries them over the water, over from Dublin to Bristol, and they'll wait at Bristol Airport for their minibus to pick them up, and they'll get on the minibus, and they'll all tell stories about the weekend to each other, and they'll all try to clear up some details that are hazy, like how much did it actually cost to get into the strip club? Did anyone else see Rob Senior on the table in Gogarty's? And Gareth, where did you get to last night, mate? What happened to you?

And when they cross the Severn Bridge, and see the *Welcome to Wales* sign, all the boys will cheer.

A CHEERFUL NOTE
(1968)
Emyr Humphreys

—I got your note.

Glyn Padarn stood, small, breathless and grinning behind the tall man's right elbow. As he waited to be noticed, he glanced down thirstily into the pint pot the tall man was about to raise to his lips.

—Um?

The tall man was vague in an academic way, smiling distantly so that his vagueness should not give offence. Perhaps his exceptional height made him feel remote. His grey curls fanned out behind his head. Had his manner been more decisive he would have looked well in front of an orchestra. He looked down at Glyn over the edge of his spectacles like a professor preparing nervously to interview a student whose name had escaped him.

—I'm Padarn, Glyn said. Glyn Padarn. You sent me a note.

—Ah!

The tall man's face lit up and he stabbed the fingers of his left hand in the air.

—Of course. Forgive me. What will you have?

—A half?

—Make it a pint...

—Oh well—thanks.

The tall man made a sketchy attempt to gain the barman's attention. The club was very crowded.

—I don't know if you two know each other. This is Davies. Davies, this is Padarn.

Glyn stared inquisitively at the man he had been introduced to. It was clear that Davies was equally curious about him.

—I was just telling Davies... barman, barman!

The barman took no notice.

—I was just telling Davies that no one could believe in God any more.

The tall man was watching his reaction closely, so Glyn felt obliged to nod. Davies was nodding wisely too. He spoke with some feeling, but he was suffering from heavy nasal catarrh and the bar was so noisy it was impossible to hear what he said apart from the tall man's name which was Mr Dandel. This was in marked contrast to the tall man who managed to pitch his voice with such precision that if you listened intently every word was audible and somehow the more significant because of the effort you had made to hear. There was no real reason why the barman should not hear him calling. Perhaps there was an old enmity between them. The tall man's manner was a trifle imperious. Or, if he came here regularly, as he obviously did, there was an understanding between them. When it was his turn, the barman was deaf. That could be tested. Glyn Padarn prepared to lean forward and use his own powerful voice to order drinks himself.

—Christianity has had it. It's an unworkable concept. I'm sorry but there it is. Did you say something?

The tall man leaned towards Davies who backed away quickly and shook his head.

—Let's begin at the beginning, the tall man said, if we're going to work together, we've got to know where we stand. My grandmother was riddled with guilt. Riddled with it. From early childhood. It never left her. That's Christianity for you. What will you have to drink?

—I'm all right, thank you.

Davies lifted his glass which was still half-full.

—In a formal interview, the tall man said, people tend to wear masks. Persona you know. That sort of thing. They turn in the light, like things hanging from a ceiling.

He lifted his hand and revolved his wrist slowly to illustrate the visual effect.

—Lots of surface glitter, but quite impenetrable. Dialogue in any sense is quite impossible. Did you notice that Trumper-Thomas wore a wig?

Davies made himself smile because Mr Dandel had indicated he was making a sly joke. Glyn Padarn felt it was time he drew attention to himself.

—I always make a point of being punctual, he said. Try to be creative *and* punctual. That's my motto.

He burst out laughing. Dandel gave a neutral smile, recording an impression of a small, sweating, excited man of thirty-eight and filing it away like a finger print to be taken out and examined with care on some future occasion.

—Let's go and sit over there shall we? Bring your drinks with you.

He waved his glass and then drifted elegantly through the press of people, tall enough to navigate the smoothest passage. He was an impressive figure, a little worn perhaps and untidy but still confident of his own good looks and quiet authority. Glyn Padarn gave a brief bellow and won the barman's attention. He bought a pint of bitter and drank some to quench his immediate thirst and to make it possible to journey across the room without spilling the beer. He looked around hopefully but there was no one in the crowded room he knew. There were no vacant seats at the little tables and there was no sign of Dandel who had sent him such a friendly cheerful little note. He wandered on rather disconsolately, down a short flight of steps, passing a billiard room and another bar which was closed. He found Dandel sitting in a corner of the reading room and as he moved closer he was surprised and disturbed to see that Davies was still with him. He began to take a dislike to Davies. His rust-coloured shirt with the broad purple tie was so consciously arty and he kept pushing a benzedrine inhaler up his right nostril.

—Ah! There you are.

Dandel waved his hands cheerfully.

—Brought your drink with you? Good. Well now. Let's get down to business. Let's get all this mister nonsense out of the way first, shall we? I'm Brian and you call me Brian. That's the way I like it.

He bent forward, smiling, and for a moment Glyn believed he was about to offer to shake hands. Instead he pressed his hands into his stomach and gave a serene belch.

—Tell me one thing, Padarn, he said, for some reason it wasn't mentioned yesterday. Are you married?

—Well as a matter of fact...

Glyn Padarn lifted his glass to his lips and lowered it again.

—I wish I was, but I'm not.

—Pretty good.

Dandel showed all his excellent teeth and Padarn felt he was receiving a considerable compliment.

—He's a lucky chap isn't he, Davies? How many kids have you got? Three is it?

—Four, Davies said.

—I'm divorced, Dandel said. Twice over. But I'm living with a woman who's got two kids of her own. How complicated can you get? Oh dear, oh dear, I must admit it, I'm full of shortcomings. You may as well know it now as later. That's the awful part about interviews. They tell you nothing. They're really no use at all. The way that idiot Bevan kept on asking you if you'd passed your matric...

—There was some doubt about it...

Padarn was surprised to hear Davies speaking.

—He asks the same darn question every interview we give. Then he always falls asleep before the end. Did you notice?

For the first time Padarn realised that he and Davies were candidates for the same post. He rebuked himself for stupidity and lack of perception and began to make a conscious effort to resist the warm atmosphere that Dandel was busy generating.

—I just sit there and let the politicos do the talking, Dandel said. I just sit there and try to keep my mouth shut and watch them trying to play cat and mouse with people's lives. It's quite revolting.

—But...

Padarn searched hard for the right words. Davies started sniffing vigorously.

—Yes, he said, I must admit, so did I.

Dandel smiled at them both, as a child certain of forgiveness will smile at its indulgent parents.

—It's little Gladys, he said. Sweet little secretary she is, but she does get things a little muddled.

—The time?

Padarn was anxious to understand.

—Emotionally. She is such a cheerful little soul. One of her 'I would be delighted if's was it?

Padarn and Davies nodded.

—She's one of life's little optimistic rays of sunshine. To be perfectly frank with you I have the greatest difficulty keeping my hands off her. You're not a queer are you?

He stared unblinkingly at Padarn. Padarn blushed. His round face glowed with indignation and embarrassment.

—Good God no!

Most of all he resented the way Davies was leaning forward with his head a little to one side showing polite, detached interest.

—There you are you see, Dandel said calmly. That's just the kind of question you could never ask in an interview and of course it's terribly important. I've never believed in this business that you can separate your work from what you are; especially in the creative line. In our business your private life shows all over your work.

Davies was sniffing and lifting a finger to make a humble interruption.

—Can I get you something to drink?

—What a jolly nice idea.

Dandel was all warmth and smiling acquiescence. He pushed out his long legs and slouched in his armchair as if he were settling in for a long session. When Davies asked him what he would like he said a double whiskey, and in order to prove that his impulses were naturally generous Davies made Padarn change from beer to whiskey too. When he had shambled off with three empty pint glasses dangling from one of his large hands, Dandel said to Padarn,

—I find him a fascinating chap. Full of very original ideas. His appearance is against him. That sniff for example. And that enormous family. It's my guess that he fights every other day with his wife. Every other week rather. Fight, sulk silence, reconciliation. Cyclical pattern. You can see it on his face. It's worn him down poor chap. Now you've escaped all that.

Dandel gave Padarn a shrewd, keen, look.

—You disapprove.

—Of what?

Padarn was very guarded. He missed not having his pint pot

to peer into. There was nothing in the room worth looking at except Dandel's narrow handsome face under the luxurious grey hair, and the long stare from the pale blue eyes embarrassed him.

—You think its unethical, bringing you two together like this...?

—Well it's not very customary is it?

—Conventionally, no. But I didn't have the impression you were conventional. These foreign trips of yours, for example. And your fluent Spanish. And your deep interest in the ballet. And your devotion to rugby football and typography. And all the rest. They add up to a very interesting man. I'll be absolutely frank with you, Padarn. I just couldn't decide between you two. So what the heck, I said to myself, see them both together, examine them side by side, and if it comes to the push, appoint two assistants instead of one. That would be difficult, of course, but not impossible.

—Here we are!

Davies arrived back with the drinks and a jug of water.

—I was just telling Padarn, Dandel said, there are some who would argue it was unethical to bring you two together like this, but I don't agree. It's fairer to you and it's fairer to me. It gives you a chance to take a closer look at me not only in an 'I and thou' relationship but also in an 'I, thou and him' relationship which is far more practical in daily life. And after all it's me you'll be working with not the appointments committee. Hence those two cheerful little notes from little Gladys. Better than two, separate, hole-in-the-corner, hot-breath confessionals in my view. Don't you agree?

—Yes, said Davies in a louder tone than Padarn had heard him use before, I think I do.

—It's the way I like to work, Dandel said, well out in the open. I'm the kind that never bothers to shut his office door. Here's to us then, the creative and the exploited! United we fall...

All three laughed, swept up suddenly by a reckless gaiety. The alcohol too was beginning to take effect.

Padarn continued to laugh on his own account, an explosive cackle that surprised and amused the other two.

—It's only once I've been taken for a queer before.

—Tell us about it.

Dandel made a generous gesture, ready to give Padarn all the patient hearing his story might need.

—An American bird in Portugal, Padarn said. Beautiful figure. We bathed in the nude together. By moonlight. It was damned cold too. Those blasted Atlantic breakers.

Padarn paused to recapture the atmosphere of that time and place.

—Well go on then.

Davies looked as if Padarn could tell him something he was anxious to know.

—They had a flat in Sintra. She and her husband. He was sleeping upstairs. There we were, down below in the kitchen. She was cooking me an enormous steak.

—Yes?

Davies found it difficult to endure the long pauses.

—He was upstairs...

—You said that.

Davies was watching him carefully.

—Well how could I do it? With the husband upstairs. She was very annoyed I can tell you.

Davies looked relieved.

—What's the point of the story? he said.

—No point at all. She just said I was queer, and I didn't bother to contradict her. I never finished the steak either. This was three years ago. He was a jolly nice chap. I wasn't going to... you know with him upstairs asleep. Was I?

Davies nodded approvingly but Dandel continued to sit in silent judgement.

—Let's have another drink, he said.

—I'll get them this time.

—No...

Dandel went through the motions of protest.

—I insist!

Padarn spoke loudly, in a manly, almost parade-ground manner.

—Same again?

When he had hurried himself off, Dandel said to Davies

—What do you think of his story?

—Seems a decent sort of chap.

—Yes.

Dandel paused significantly, so that Davies who was fidgeting should give him closer attention.

—On the other hand it could be true. He had a greater affection for the husband than the wife... However let's not hold it against him. He's a very likable little chap. How tall would you say he was?

—Oh...

Davies hesitated.

—About five foot six.

—Um. That's pretty small isn't it? The assertive bantam class. But we won't hold it against him. You know the set-up?

Davies tried not to look puzzled by the rapid changes in Dandel's talk.

—We're independent of the government but responsible to it. Something between the BBC, The Arts Council, The Tourist Board and the Distillers Company! We manufacture and sell Welsh spirit! I'm in charge of the design side. You got all that?

—I wasn't clear about the office routine...

—I insisted on that, Dandel said. I told them quite bluntly I run my own office in my own way. If you don't like it I said, you can get rid of me. That's your privilege. But as long as I'm in charge, internal affairs are my province. He didn't like it.

—Who?

Davies lifted his eyebrows helpfully and combed prematurely thin hair back with his open fingers.

—Crunch.

—Who?

—Crunch. S. T. Z. Watkins esquire. We were at Oxford together. I still call him Crunch. He didn't like it. Did you notice at the interview he never opened his mouth? Not once. Did you notice that?

—Well... yes, now you mention it.

—There you have it. In a nutshell. When everyone else is shooting his mouth off, old Crunch is silent. Plotting away. Waiting his chance. He's always been like that. I'll be absolutely frank with you Davies. I've known Sammy Crunch for nearly twenty years and I've never once ever... not once... not even once... heard him utter an original idea. Not even an original thought. He is one of those clever parasites that live off the work and originality of others. A natural exploiter. And fate has so arranged matters that I am responsible to him. Can you imagine it? The massive irony. Ah, here he comes!

Padarn was moving as quickly as he could, smiling at the load he was carrying and at the companions he was carrying it to; eager to be convivial, a man of a naturally jovial disposition, the drinks he was providing were warm symbols of his good-natured friendliness towards his fellows.

—I saw old Benny in there. Benny Valentine. You know, the outside-half. Wonderful chap, old Benny. I had no idea he was in your organisation.

Dandel took his drink and showed by a slight frown that he had sad thoughts about Benny.

—Poor bastard, he said. I tell you this in the strictest confidence. You would hardly credit it. He earns little more than a good typist. It's a bit of a scandal in my opinion. They use his name and the good will that goes with it and that's all they pay him. Of course it's all Crunch's fault.

—Who's Crunch?

Padarn settled his broad buttocks in the seat of his chair. Whatever the outcome now, he was prepared to enjoy a long session of drink and gossip.

—S. T. Z. W., Dandel said. He sat on the Chairman's right at the interview yesterday. You may not have noticed. He didn't say much. The one with the long thin lips and beady eyes. Our controller. Your controller and mine. Crunch.

—Why Crunch?

Padarn gave the onomatopoeia the full benefit of his rich voice.

—Something he said at a political meeting in 1949. Somebody in New College got to hear of it. The name stuck. It was bound to stick really. It's so appropriate. I've never seen a man so calculating. An operator. Never does anything on impulse. Drinks very little. Can't afford to risk getting drunk. It's amazing really. I've watched him you know, having one with the boys: the way he manages to slide off after about twenty minutes. It's always twenty minutes. Not fifteen or twenty-five. Always twenty. Never does anything on impulse as I say. Not a thing. He works it all out. Spends all his time plotting.

—Doesn't sound my type at all, Padarn said. He looked challengingly at Davies.

—Nor mine, Davies said hastily.

—It's a tragedy he should be where he is. But there we are.

We've got to live with it. He's very careful with me of course. I've known him since Oxford. He treads very carefully with his old friend Brian. Mind you, if he saw a chance, he'd put the skids under me as fast as you could blink. But he knows I'm watching. In my cosmology, he's the very devil.

Padarn and Davies laughed a little uncertainly.

—I suppose you think I've got a fixation about him? Dandel gave both of them a searching look.

—Well, Davies said.

—Well what?

—Well, I know I would.

—Would what?

—Get a fixation. I've got one already. There's a chap in our office. Gassy Watts. Pinches my ideas regularly. I can't do a thing about it. He's married to the boss's daughter.

—What about you?

Dandel wanted a reaction from Padarn.

—Can't say I've ever experienced it really.

—You've always been inclined to avoid responsibility.

—Me?

Padarn didn't wish to be cross-examined by Dandel or anyone in the middle of enjoying his drink.

—Marriage, for example? And a chap with your qualifications. You could be earning twice the money. I'm not trying to be personal. These are the questions we've got to face up to and answer.

Davies was nodding wisely and Padarn felt resentful.

—If we are going to work together, the collaboration must be pretty total. How far do you trust people?

—I like to trust everybody, Padarn said.

He took a drink and tried to gauge the reaction.

—I know it's a weakness, he said, elaborating a little. I suppose I'm too easy-going. But I couldn't bear to spend all my time worrying and scheming and plotting. I like to do my job, enjoy doing it, and then go out and enjoy myself even more if I can. That's the way I like it.

He finished his drink with a mildly defiant flourish. Dandel looked at him with silent admiration.

—That's very appealing, he said. Very appealing indeed. Will you excuse me? I must go and have a pee.

In this way Davies and Padarn were left alone together, facing each other across the low table like tennis players, uncertain whether or not to knock the ball about while waiting for an elderly referee unexpectedly taken short in the middle of a match.

—It's a funny set-up, Padarn said.

—What is?

—The organisation. What's it for? What does it do?

—You could say the same about lots of organisations. Look at the BBC for example.

—Oh I don't know. The old corporation isn't so bad. A very benevolent employer.

—Why are you leaving then?

Davies couldn't resist a quick smile of triumph.

—Who said I was leaving?

Padarn was ready to defend himself. He wanted Davies to understand that although he was by nature easy-going, good-natured, he had learnt enough about life not to allow himself to be pushed around or even taken advantage of by more selfishly orientated persons. It was the time now to demonstrate swiftly that he was as subtle as a snake when he felt like it.

—You know what he's up to, don't you?

—Who?

—Dandel. Head of Design and all that. He's playing us off against each other. He's not called the designing head for nothing.

Padarn chuckled, willing to relax now he had made his point. Davies looked very anxious. He relapsed into a very local accent.

—You're right, boy, he said. That's just what I've been thinking.

—Do you want the job?

Padarn was frankness itself and Davies couldn't help trusting him a little.

—The money's good, Davies said.

—More than you're getting?

Padarn was ready to help and to enjoy being helpful.

—I'll never get a partnership, Davies said. Gassy Watts will see to that. The idea is to keep me in a little room, unqualified and underpaid, spawning out new ideas every week for the greater glory and the greater income of the firm. I've got four kids to think of.

Padarn wanted to show he was genuinely sympathetic.

—Don't show him you're in a weak position. Dandel I mean. I don't trust the bugger, quite frankly. Now you take my advice, negotiate from strength...

Davies looked at him so long Padarn began to blush.

—If I take it, he said, you won't get it.

—Never mind about me! It was you I was thinking of... You just show you are doing him a favour... act as if you didn't really need it anyway... oh hell. What's the use. Let me get you another drink.

—It's his turn, Davies said.

—Damn, so it is! Just sit there looking at your glass like this.

Padarn gave a wriggle and settled himself into a meaningful pose, gazing at his empty glass. Davies giggled and did the same. Then nervously he said,

—Oh what's the use. He's got us over a barrel. It's my turn.

—What a world, Padarn said. The reason I want it is pique. I've been passed over for promotion in the corporation. Not that I wanted it. But I did want to be considered.

Davies shook his head sympathetically and said,

—If it wasn't for the kids, he said, boy, I tell you I'd be on the next boat to Morocco.

—I've been thinking of going there!

Davies smiled sadly. Padarn was full of a charming excitement.

—No, seriously. It's my hobby you know, foreign travel. It's what I live for really. Why don't you come with me? I had a marvellous time in Granada four years ago. I went to Seville you know for the Easter Fair. Fabulous, Davies. I'm not exaggerating. And there was a bird there from Sweden. Anette her name was, her father was in shipbuilding, specialising in ice-breakers as a matter of fact. I rather fancy myself as a bit of an ice-breaker myself... marvellous girl. Built on ample proportions, plenty to work on... No, seriously, Davies. Why don't you come with me?

—I would love to... Davies was openly wistful.

—Willie can't come this year. Willie Daniels. Works in Town and Country Planning. We went to Montenegro together. Had a marvellous time. And Greece the year before that. He's got married and he's painting the bedrooms, poor sod. 'I promised Dilys I'd paint the front bedroom'... She's got him bleating like an old sheep... I'm conscious of it you know. I'm the last one. The one left behind. Gwyn, Rowley, Tal and now Willie. All of them married. It's like the end of an era.

—I know what you mean, Davies said. Padarn brightened up.

—Come on now. What will you have? Same again? Look, Davies, I've just had a great idea.

Davies looked up expectantly.

—Let's walk out on him!

—On Dandel...?

—It's not my line of country but I can see right through it. He wants one of us or both of us to crawl on his side. There's a battle going on in that office and he wants to make sure of the man who gets the job. Don't you see it?

—You might be wrong, Davies said. I thought there was some sense in what he was saying, about getting to know the person you might be working with for the rest of your life.

Dandel came back, fresh and friendly.

—Sorry to leave you chaps! Had to make a quick telephone call. This woman I'm living with she's worse than a wife. Gets ever so worried if I'm late getting home. Now what's it to be?

—Whiskey again, Padarn said promptly. Whiskey all round.

Davies looked nervous.

—Fine. That's fine.

Dandel went off murmuring as if he were memorising an order. Padarn chuckled and rubbed his hands.

—It's no use being pushed around, he said.

—I don't think he meant it that way, Davies said. I may be wrong of course...

—All this business about Crunch, Padarn said. You can see it written all over him. He's got to the stage where he can see Crunch behind every tree. That's the reason for this meeting. To get one of us, at a disadvantage, to swear all sorts of loyalty-oaths.

—Do you think so?

Davies was deeply worried.

—Coming from a private firm you might not know this... You get this kind of enmity in these big organisations. Nothing quite like it. You can walk down a corridor in the middle of the morning and hear them sharpening their knives. They put a lot of creative energy into it. This Crunch you see. To Dandel, he's a sort of devil. An embodiment of evil... if you...

Dandel came back very tall and carrying the drinks with great care, clearly unused to such a manual operation. As he sat down, Padarn said,

—We were thinking of moving on.

Dandel was taken by surprise. So was Davies.

—Steady on, Davies said trying to be jocular.

—To the docks, Padarn said. I know my way around there. Would you like to come?

—This is interesting.

Dandel smiled mysteriously into his whiskey glass.

—I didn't think it would happen this way. People are fascinating, I must say.

—I'm not people, Padarn said. I'm Padarn.

—Of course you are, Dandel said. And I'm one of the few people who can vouch for it. I studied your application and your testimonials. I know your date of birth and the nationality of your father and mother.

Padarn's face was flushed.

—The way I look at it, he said, you need us more than we need you.

—I don't follow that, Dandel said.

—This is all highly unofficial, Padarn said. Isn't it?

—I made no secret of the position.

—Suppose one of us went to the controller, Crunch as you call him...

—Ah... that was a risk I was prepared to take.

Dandel remained calm.

—I reckoned that with men working on the creative level, artists in effect, there could be a genuine degree of frankness... I thought you agreed about that?...

He was looking at Davies.

—Yes I did, Davies said.

—I think you ought to know, Dandel said, that brother Crunch – and the appointments board for that matter – are well aware that I am acting on my own initiative. There are good reasons for this. Two or three men working on the same creative design, as I see it, they have to be able to crawl in and out of each other's vests.

—I don't see that at all, Padarn said.

He sounded stuffy, standing on his dignity.

—Who are the people best able to invade your private life?

Dandel was exultant, but firmly reasonable.

—Your friends of course, he said. Isn't that what friendship is all about? The people you confide in, warm to, close up to...

—I'm not sure that I favour mixing business and pleasure, Padarn said. I like to choose my own friends in my own time in my own way.

—Very good.

Dandel sounded full of admiration.

—Very succinct expression of nineteenth-century individualism. You're a bit of a fossil old boy, and I admire you for it.

—A fossil?

Padarn was indignant again.

—Of the nicest kind. A natural conservative with anarchic, artistic leanings.

He smiled engagingly and Padarn smiled back.

—We've got to peer into each other's psyche. Something exciting will be sure to emerge. Now then, if it's the docks you want, it's the docks you'll have. I'll order a taxi. Had you noticed *that* by the way? Not one of us owns a car. Artists you see. Not to be tied down by material goods, washing cars on Sunday mornings.

—I can't afford one, Davies said.

—All right, old boy. Don't spoil it.

Outside the moon was shining and even the shopping centre of the city looked exciting. Dandel ventured to slap Padarn on the back and Padarn chuckled loudly to show he didn't mind. The taxi-driver had a morosely expressed sense of humour and once in the back of the car the three were filled with the party spirit.

—We'll go to the Golden Goose, Padarn said, and make the

darkies sing Welsh hymns. The manager is an old friend of mine. Sea-faring man trapped on land by a weak heart and a demanding wife... No! Better still! There's a club behind, a place for African dances. You never saw anything like it. I'm a member. I'll get you both in.

While Padarn was negotiating their entry Davies and Dandel put in a good deal of drinking. The little pub was crowded and singing was already in progress. They were pushed close together and they smiled into each other's faces, swallowing whiskey whenever they were at a loss for something to say.

—Poetry is my true vocation, Dandel said.

—Eh?

Davies could not hear and yet he nodded as if he understood.

—Alcohol brings it back to me. And singing. I remember it. A sort of drunken stupor of holiness. Do you know what I mean? An exultation. A giving out of music in return for some nameless blessing. Do you know what I mean?

—I always liked making things, Davies said. Even when I was a kid. Making things with my hands.

—The divine flash, Dandel said. Nothing else like it. To know you've got it. Here.

He tapped his chest gently with the tips of his fingers. The noisy chorus in the saloon drowned most of what they were saying.

—Making and building, Davies said.

He repeated the words and they smiled at each other.

Padarn took hold of their elbows and dragged them down a dark passage to a narrow lift that only held three people. A muscular negro with a Welsh accent was in charge of the lift. He and Padarn appeared to be old friends. Padarn pushed Dandel and Davies in the lift and said he would follow. Dandel made a joke about being elevated and they both giggled helplessly and the negro smiled as he closed the lift gate. For a while as they waited upstairs in the stifling darkness the only music to be heard was the beating of a drum; they were a little afraid. Fierce-looking men jostled them and wherever they stood they seemed to be in somebody's way. But Padarn joined them grinning and gleaming with sweat in the semi-darkness and they were reassured.

Under a spotlight a negro girl was dancing with an astonishing mixture of physical discipline and abandon, to the ecstatic rhythm of a drum. Padarn pushed the two tall men nearer and the performance was so rhythmic and so sustained that it seemed to pass outside time. There was no means of telling how long they had been watching or how long the girl had been rocking her beautiful body so close to the floor. Dandel, Davies and Padarn merged into the circle of people watching. They seemed to become thinner, like figures in a frieze given shape and importance by the attention they paid to the sacred ceremony. The girl lay on the floor, panting, exhausted, giving off a strong smell. No one moved. Everyone seemed filled with reverence and respect. Outside in the harbour there was a blast of a hooter to say the fog was gathering in the channel. The silence and the stillness seemed to solidify around the beating of the girl's heart. Then suddenly a drunken sailor toppled against an upright piano in the corner of the room and noise broke out again. The girl opened her eyes and the ritual, or whatever it was, was over.

Dandel wanted to play the piano.

—When I was at Oxford, he said to Davies, I was in constant demand.

He got his fingers to the keys, but an angry young negro pushed him away.

—Black power, Padarn said gleefully.

He borrowed a pound from Davies and fixed them up with more to drink. He knew his way around very well and Dandel seemed impressed with his social gifts and the way he managed to persuade people to do what he wanted. Davies said he wanted beer to quench his thirst and in no time Padarn got someone to deliver three pints on their tiny table. He took a long swig and then got up and merged into the crowd, and in a few moments they saw him dancing with a white woman who was tall enough to look over his head. As he came near them he steered the woman's hand under their noses so that they would see her wedding ring. Dandel wanted to dance but Padarn introduced the woman to Davies and forced him to shuffle off with her.

—Look at him! Padarn said. Looks just like the back of a vintage car, doesn't he? Real nineteen-twenties, baggy pants and all. What'll you have? It's on me.

—Rhythm was part of my vocation, Dandel said. I'd have been in a chair by now you know if I'd stayed in the academic world. I did my thesis on Philips. Ever heard of Philips?

—Can't say that I have. I'm thinking of southern Italy next year you know. Brindisi, Lecce, Tarento. Down in the heel.

—Virgil, Dandel said. I used to be hot on Virgil. Just my cup of tea really. Pagan, Imperial, Mediterranean and all that stuff about bees. Great chap Virgil.

—Why don't you come with me? Padarn said. You'd have the time of your life. Nothing like it you know: opening your bleary eyes south of the Alps. Just that glimpse of snow and then everything jolly like the sun of Italy, *vino* and oranges and uniforms...

Padarn lifted both hands and snapped his fingers as if they were castanets.

—I thought you were Spain, Dandel said. Bull-fights and all that...

—You're coming then, Padarn said, reaching up to slap Dandel on the back. All the way there and maybe all the way back. Great! You've made a very wise decision and you won't regret it.

Davies had rejoined them. He looked worried.

—He pushed me, he said. Big black chap. Is he a boxer or something?

—That's the husband!

Padarn collapsed with laughter, but Davies still looked worried.

—Said I'd got to clear out. How do we get out of here? How did we get in in the first place?

—Oh damn, Padarn said. I'm sorry but you've got to admit it's funny.

—He'll be after me, Davies said. He said he'd give me sixty seconds to get out. Said he'd knock my block off.

—Impatiently, Padarn pushed his two companions towards the lift. He gave the doorman-operator a ten-shilling note and within a few minutes the three of them were standing in the empty street. They wandered on to a narrow bridge, crossing a deep channel between two dry docks. The shadow of a ship in a nearby berth was huge and romantic in the moonlight.

—Right, Dandel said stretching himself happily, where next?

—It's getting late, Davies said trying to read the time on his wristwatch by the light of the moon.

—It's a wide, wide, world!

Dandel stretched his arms and gazed lovingly at the silhouette of the ship. They moved across the quayside to peer down into the water. They appeared now as three men who had been friends for years and not three who had met for the first time that evening. Padarn asked Dandel if he would care to go aboard ship. They walked backwards and forwards trying to read the name of the ship on the starboard bow. Padarn was pretty certain he knew the captain. He shouted out the captain's name and Davies became nervous.

—It's a German ship, he said. From Hamburg. It's getting late.

—Now don't worry, Davies, Padarn said. You worry too much. Let yourself go.

They found themselves leaning against a bollard. Dandel gave a huge yawn and slithered down so that his long back was resting against the cold iron.

—She'll skin me, Davies said.

—Who'll skin you?

—Iris. My wife. It's her day for selling pamphlets tomorrow.

—Pamphlets?

—She gets the kids off to school and then she goes out selling pamphlets. I've got to get home.

—I'll come with you, boy, Padarn said. Explain all. All is forgiven.

—She'll never forgive me.

—What?

—I told her a lie before we were married. I said I was qualified. She'll never forgive me.

Padarn stretched out his arm compassionately and patted Davies on the shoulder.

—Miserable bugger aren't you, he said.

—Some weeks she won't speak to me, Davies said. She leaves my meals on a tray outside my bedroom door. If I earned a bit more, things would be better.

—That's marriage, boy.

—I was hoping you'd like to hear the story of my life, Dandel said.

He was trying to light a cigarette untidily and dropped his box of matches on the ground.

—I'll tell you anything you want to know. Absolutely anything.

—Loneliness, Padarn said. Loneliness, that's my trouble. My landlady's little dog shat on my hearthrug yesterday. Now look here Mrs Jones, I said, is nothing sacred? D'you know what she said? She said I encouraged it.

—You interview me, chaps. That's the idea. Ask me any damn thing you like... something interesting will emerge!

Dandel waved his arms generously.

—I'm not drunk, he said. I'm serious. Go on. Ask me.

—You should get married, boy, Davies said to Padarn. Have a houseful of kids. How do we get out of here?

—There was this bird, Padarn said, in Vienna. God, she was lovely. We sat all day in the coffee-houses, talking. In the early spring. We saw a wedding in Semmerling. A lovely wedding. A peasant boy and girl. Near the house where Schubert was born. So I said to her, what about us? And we kissed there and then. In the middle of the street. That's life, boy. That's what I call life.

—Why didn't you marry her?

—I went back there, two years later. With a bit more cash. All set to do the right thing. She'd moved, gone away. Married an Italian, believe it or not. She couldn't wait. They never can, can they? After all I wasn't worth waiting for.

—I'll have you both, Dandel said. Both of you.

They looked down at him pityingly, because he looked more drunk than they were.

—All I ask, brothers, is that you keep Crunch out of my hair. Give me a few ideas once a quarter for the programme meetings and if you can spare the time, poison my Catholic wife.

Padarn looked at Davies. He was being stern and shrewd.

—I can size a man up, he said, if you give me time. It's what a man is, in himself, apart from his job. That's what counts.

—I'm nothing, Davies said. Husband plus father of four plus job plus nothing. See how I work it out? 'Take away the height take away the weight, take away the house take away the mate...' Get it?

—Come on, Dandel said. Ask me something. Come on.

—You know what we've been doing, boy, Padarn said. We've been wasting our bloody time. It's not his decision.

Dandel was struggling to get back on his feet.

—I'm concerned with humanity in its widest sense he said. I said this to Crunch in our last quarterly meeting. Wales as such means nothing to me. Just give me the means to create. That's exactly what I said.

—You can stuff your bloody job up your jumper, Padarn said, as far as I'm concerned. Where are we?

—Don't you know?

Davies looked horrified.

—Now don't you worry, boy.

—Well I am worried, Davies said. She'll skin me. You don't know Iris.

—You can trust me, boy, Padarn said. I'll get you home. I'll just tap the back door and I'll say 'Iris, my dear, I've brought your good husband home...' I've done it before.

—I'm worried, Davies said. I'm really worried. She'll skin me.

—Now come on, boy. I'll see you right. Take my word.

He took Davies by the arm and they moved back along a tramway with Padarn pointing to the tracks, saying they would lead them back to the road leading to the city. Dandel followed them at a distance, swaying in the moonlight and talking to himself.

DISORDERLY WOMEN

THE CONQUERED
(1927)
Dorothy Edwards

Last summer, just before my proper holiday, I went to stay with
an aunt who lives on the borders of Wales, where there are so
many orchards. I must say I went there simply as a duty, because
I used to stay a lot with her when I was a boy, and she was, in
those days, very good to me. However, I took plenty of books
down so that it should not be a waste of time.

Of course, when I got there it was really not so bad. They made
a great fuss of me. My aunt was as tolerant as she used to be in
the old days, leaving me to do exactly as I liked. My cousin Jessica,
who is just my age, had hardly changed at all, though they both
looked different with their hair up; but my younger cousin Ruth,
who used to be very lively and something of a tomboy, had
altered quite a lot. She had become very quiet; at least, on the
day I arrived she was lively enough, and talked about the fun we
used to have there, but afterwards she became more quiet every
day, or perhaps it was that I noticed it more. She remembered far
more about what we used to do than I did; but I suppose that is
only natural, since she had been there all the time in between,
and I do not suppose anything very exciting had happened to her,
whereas I have been nearly everywhere.

But what I wanted to say is, that not far from my aunt's house,
on the top of a little slope, on which there was an apple orchard,
was a house with French windows and a large green lawn in front,

and in this lived a very charming Welsh lady whom my cousins knew. Her grandfather had the house built, and it was his own design. It is said that he had been quite a friend of the Prince Consort, who once, I believe, actually stayed there for a night.

I knew the house very well, but I had never met any of the family, because they had not always occupied it, and, in any case, they would have been away at the times that I went to my aunt for holidays. Now only this one granddaughter was left of the family; her father and mother were dead, and she had just come back to live there. I found out all this at breakfast the morning after I came, when Jessica said, 'Ruthie, we must take Frederick to see Gwyneth.'

'Oh yes,' said Ruthie. 'Let's go today.'

'And who is Gwyneth?'

Jessica laughed. 'You will be most impressed. Won't he, mother?'

'Yes,' said my aunt, categorically.

However, we did not call on her that afternoon, because it poured with rain all day, and it did not seem worthwhile, though Ruthie appeared in her mackintosh and galoshes ready to go, and Jessica and I had some difficulty in dissuading her.

I did not think it was necessary to do any reading the first day, so I just sat and talked to the girls, and after tea Jessica and I even played duets on the piano, which had not been tuned lately, while Ruthie turned over the pages.

The next morning, though the grass was wet and every movement of the trees sent down a shower of rain, the sun began to shine brightly through the clouds. I should certainly have been taken to see their wonderful friend in the afternoon, only she herself called in the morning. I was sitting at one end of the dining-room, reading Tourguéniev with a dictionary and about three grammars, and I dare say I looked very busy. I do not know where my aunt was when she came, and the girls were upstairs. I heard a most beautiful voice, that was very high-pitched though, not low, say:

'All right, I will wait for them in here,' and she came into the room. Of course I had expected her to be nice, because my cousins liked her so much, but still they do not meet many people down there, and I thought they would be impressed with the sort of person I would be quite used to. But she really was charming.

She was not very young – older, I should say, than Jessica. She was very tall, and she had very fair hair. But the chief thing about her was her finely carved features, which gave to her face the coolness of stone and a certain appearance of immobility, though she laughed very often and talked a lot. When she laughed she raised her chin a little, and looked down her nose in a bantering way. And she had a really perfect nose. If I had been a sculptor I should have put it on every one of my statues. When she saw me she laughed and said, 'Ah! I am disturbing you,' and she sat down, smiling to herself.

I did not have time to say anything to her before my cousins came in. She kissed Jessica and Ruthie, and kept Ruthie by her side.

'This is our cousin Frederick,' said Jessica.

'We have told you about him,' said Ruthie gravely.

Gwyneth laughed. 'Oh, I recognised him, but how could I interrupt so busy a person! Let me tell you what I have come for. Will you come to tea tomorrow and bring Mr Trenier?' She laughed at me again.

We thanked her, and then my aunt came in.

'How do you do, Gwyneth?' she said. 'Will you stay to lunch?'

'No, thank you so much, Mrs Haslett,' she answered. 'I only came to ask Jessica and Ruthie to tea tomorrow, and, of course, to see your wonderful nephew. You will come too, won't you?'

'Yes, thank you,' said my aunt. 'You and Frederick ought to find many things to talk about together.'

Gwyneth looked at me and laughed.

Ruthie went out to make some coffee, and afterwards Gwyneth sat in the window seat drinking it and talking.

'What were you working at so busily when I came in?' she asked me.

'I was only trying to read Tourguéniev in the original,' I said.

'Do you like Tourguéniev very much?' she asked, laughing.

'Yes,' I said. 'Do you?'

'Oh, I have only read one, *Fumée*.'

She stayed for about an hour, laughing and talking all the time. I really found her very charming. She was like a personification, in a restrained manner, of Gaiety. Yes, really, very much like Milton's *L'Allegro*.

The moment she was gone Jessica said excitedly, 'Now, Frederick, weren't you impressed?'

And Ruthie looked at me anxiously until I answered, 'Yes, I really think I was.'

The next day we went there to tea. It was a beautiful warm day, and we took the shortcut across the fields and down a road now overgrown with grass to the bottom of the little slope on which her house was built. There is an old Roman road not far from here, and I am not quite sure whether that road is not part of it. We did not go into the house, but were taken at once to the orchard at the back, where she was sitting near a table, and we all sat down with her. The orchard was not very big, and, of course, the trees were no longer in flower, but the fruit on them was just beginning to grow and look like tiny apples and pears. At the other end some white chickens strutted about in the sunlight. We had tea outside.

She talked a lot, but I cannot remember now what she said;

when she spoke to me it was nearly always to tell me about her grandfather, and the interesting people who used to come to visit him.

When it began to get cool we went into the house across the flat green lawn and through the French window. We went to a charming room; on the wall above the piano were some Japanese prints on silk, which were really beautiful. Outside it was just beginning to get dark.

She sang to us in a very nice high soprano voice, and she chose always gay, light songs which suited her excellently. She sang that song of Schumann, *Der Nussbaum*; but then it is possible to sing that lightly and happily, though it is more often sung with a trace of sadness in it. Jessica played for her. She is a rather good accompanist. I never could accompany singers. But I played afterwards; I played some Schumann too.

'Has Ruthie told you I am teaching her to sing?' said Gwyneth. 'I don't know much about it, and her voice is not like mine, but I remember more or less what my master taught me.'

'No,' I said, looking at Ruthie. 'Sing for us now and let me hear.'

'No,' said Ruthie, and blushed a little. She never used to be shy.

Gwyneth pulled Ruthie towards her. 'Now do sing. The fact is you are ashamed of your teacher.'

'No,' said Ruthie; 'only you know I can't sing your songs.'

Gwyneth laughed. 'You would hardly believe what a melancholy little creature she is. She won't sing anything that is not tearful.'

'But surely,' I said, 'in the whole of Schubert and Schumann you can find something sad enough for you?'

'No,' said Ruthie, looking at the carpet, 'I don't know any Schumann, and Schubert is never sad even in the sad songs. Really I can't sing what Gwyneth sings.'

'Then you won't?' I said, feeling rather annoyed with her.

'No,' she said, flushing, and she looked out of the window.

Ruthie and Jessica are quite different. Jessica is, of course, like her mother, but Ruthie is like her father, whom I never knew very well.

Next morning, immediately after breakfast, I went for a walk by myself, and though I went by a very roundabout way, I soon found myself near Gwyneth's house, and perhaps that was not very surprising. I came out by a large bush of traveller's-nightshade. I believe that is its name. At least it is called old man's beard too, but that does not describe it when it is in flower at all. You know that it has tiny white waxen flowers, of which the buds look quite different from the open flower, so that it looks as though there are two different kinds of flowers on one stem. But what I wanted to say was, I came out by this bush, and there, below me, was the grass-covered road, with new cart-wheel ruts in it, which made two brown lines along the green where the earth showed. Naturally I walked down it, and stood by the fence of the orchard below her house. I looked up between the trees, and there she was coming down towards me.

'Good-morning, Mr Trenier,' she said, laughing. 'Why are you deserting Tourguéniev?'

'It is such a lovely morning,' I said, opening the gate for her; 'and if I had known I should meet you, I should have felt even less hesitation.'

She laughed, and we walked slowly across the grass, which was still wet with dew. It was a perfectly lovely day, with a soft pale blue sky and little white clouds in it, and the grass was wet enough to be bright green.

'Oh, look!' she said suddenly, and pointed to two enormous mushrooms, like dinner-plates, growing at our feet.

'Do you want them?' I asked, stooping to pick them. 'Oh yes,' she said; 'when they are as big as that they make excellent sauces. Fancy such monsters growing in a night! They were not here yesterday.'

'And last week I had not met you,' I said, smiling.

She laughed, and took the mushrooms from me.

'Now we must take them to the cook,' she said, 'and then you shall come for a little walk with me.'

As we crossed the lawn to the house she was carrying the pink-lined mushrooms by their little stalks.

'They look like the sunshades of Victorian ladies,' I said.

She laughed, and said, 'Did you know that Jenny Lind came here once?'

Afterwards we walked along the real Roman road, now only a pathway with grass growing up between the stones, and tall trees overshadowing it. On the right is a hill where the ancient Britons made a great stand against the Romans, and were defeated.

'Did you know this was a Roman road?' she asked. 'Just think of the charming Romans who must have walked here! And I expect they developed a taste for apples. Does it shock you to know that I like the Romans better than the Greeks?'

I said 'No,' but now, when I think of it, I believe I was a little shocked, although, when I think of the Romans as the Silver Age, I see that silver was more appropriate to her than gold.

She was really very beautiful, and it was a great pleasure to be with her, because she walked in such a lovely way. She moved quickly, but she somehow preserved that same immobility which, though she laughed and smiled so often, made her face cool like stone, and calm.

After this we went for many walks and picnics.

Sometimes the girls came too, but sometimes we went together. We climbed the old battle hill, and she stood at the top looking all around at the orchards on the plain below.

I had meant to stay only a week, but I decided to stay a little longer, or, rather, I stayed on without thinking about it at all. I had not told my aunt and the girls that I was going at the end of the week, so it did not make any difference, and I knew they would expect me to stay longer. The only difference it made was to my holiday, and, after all, I was going for the holiday to enjoy myself, and I could not have been happier than I was there.

I remember how one night I went out by myself down in the direction of her house, where my steps always seemed to take me. When I reached the traveller's-nightshade it was growing dark. For a moment I looked towards her house and a flood of joy came into my soul, and I began to think how strange it was that, although I have met so many interesting people, I should come there simply by chance and meet her. I walked towards the entrance of a little wood, and, full of a profound joy and happiness, I walked in between the trees. I stayed there for a long time imagining her coming gaily into the wood where the moonlight shone through the branches. And I remember thinking suddenly how we have grown used to believing night to be a sad and melancholy time, not romantic and exciting as it used to be. I kept longing for some miracle to bring her there to me, but she did not come, and I had to go home.

Then, one evening, we all went to her house for music and conversation. On the way there Ruthie came round to my side and said, 'Frederick, I have brought with me a song that I can sing, and I will sing this time if you want me to.'

'Yes, I certainly want you to,' I said, walking on with her. 'I want to see how she teaches.'

'Yes,' said Ruthie. 'You do see that I could not sing her songs, don't you?'

In the old days Ruthie and I used to get on very well, better than I got on with Jessica, who was inclined to keep us in order then, and I must say it was very difficult for her to do so. When we got there, right at the beginning of the evening Gwyneth sang a little Welsh song. And I felt suddenly disappointed. I always thought that the Welsh were melancholy in their music, but if she sang it sadly at all, it was with the gossipy sadness of the tea after a funeral. However, afterwards we talked, and I forgot the momentary impression.

During the evening Ruthie sang. She sang Brahms' *An die Nachtigall*, which was really very foolish of her, because I am sure it is not an easy thing to sing, with its melting softness and its sudden cries of ecstasy and despair. Her voice was very unsteady, of a deeper tone than Gwyneth's, and sometimes it became quite hoarse from nervousness.

Gwyneth drew her down to the sofa beside her. She laughed, 'I told you nothing was sad enough for her.'

Ruthie was quite pale from the ordeal of singing before us.

'It is rather difficult, isn't it?' I said.

'Yes,' said Ruthie, flushing.

'Have you ever heard a nightingale?' asked Gwyneth of me.

'No,' I said.

'Why, there is one in the wood across here; I have heard it myself,' said Jessica. 'On just such a night as this,' she added, laughing, and looking out of the window at the darkness coming to lie on the tops of the apple trees beyond the green lawn.

'Ah! You must hear a nightingale as well as read Tourguéniev, you know,' said Gwyneth.

I laughed.

But later on in the evening I was sitting near the piano looking over a pile of music by my side. Suddenly I came across Chopin's *Polnische Lieder*. It is not often that one finds them. I looked up in excitement and said, 'Oh, do you know the *Polens Grabgesang*? I implore you to sing it.'

She laughed a little at my excitement and said, 'Yes, I know it. But I can't sing it. It does not suit me at all. Mrs Haslett, your nephew actually wants me to sing a funeral march!'

'Oh, please do sing it!' I said. 'I have only heard it once before in my life. Nobody ever sings it. I have been longing to hear it again.'

'It does not belong to me, you know,' she said. 'I found it here; it must have belonged to my father.' She smiled at me over the edge of some music she was putting on the piano. 'No, I can't sing it. That is really decisive.'

I was so much excited about the song, because I shall never forget the occasion on which I first heard it. I have a great friend, a very wonderful man, a perfect genius, in fact, and a very strong personality, and we have evenings at his house, and we talk about nearly everything, and have music too, sometimes. Often, when I used to go, there was a woman there, who never spoke much but always sat near my friend. She was not particularly beautiful and had a rather unhappy face, but one evening my friend turned to her suddenly and put his hand on her shoulder and said, 'Sing for us.'

She obeyed without a word. Everybody obeys him at once. And she sang this song. I shall never forget all the sorrow and pity for the sorrows of Poland that she put into it. And the song, too, is wonderful. I do not think I have ever heard in my life anything so terribly moving as the part, 'O Polen, mein Polen,' which is repeated several times. Everyone in the room was stirred, and, after she had sung it, we talked about nothing but politics and the Revolution for the whole of the evening. I do not think she was Polish either. After a few more times she did not come to the evenings any more, and I have never had the opportunity of asking him about her. And although, as I said, she was not beautiful, when I looked at Gwyneth again it seemed to me that some of her beauty had gone, and I thought to myself quite angrily, 'No, of course she could not sing that song. She would have been on the side of the conquerors!'

And I felt like this all the evening until we began to walk home. Before we had gone far Jessica said, 'Wouldn't you like to stay and listen for the nightingale, Frederick? We can find our way home without you.'

'Yes,' I said. 'Where can I hear her?'

'The best place,' said Jessica, 'is to sit on the fallen tree – that is where I heard it. Go into the wood by the wild-rose bush with pink roses on it. Do you know it?'

'Yes.'

'Don't be very late,' said my aunt.

'No,' I answered, and left them.

I went into the little wood and sat down on the fallen tree looking up and waiting, but there was no sound. I felt that there was nothing I wanted so much as to hear her sad notes. I remember thinking how Nietzsche said that Brahms' melancholy was the melancholy of impotence, not of power, and I remember feeling that there was much truth in it when I thought of his *Nachtigall* and then of Keats. And I sat and waited for the song that came to

'...*the sad heart of Ruth, when, sick for home,*
She stood in tears amid the alien corn.'

Suddenly I heard a sound, and, looking round, I saw Gwyneth coming through the trees. She caught sight of me and laughed.

'You are here too,' she said. 'I came to hear Jessica's nightingale.'

'So did I,' I said; 'but I do not think she will sing tonight.'

'It is a beautiful night,' she said. 'Anybody should want to sing on such a lovely night.'

I took her back to her gate, and I said goodnight and closed the gate behind her. But, all the same, I shall remember always how beautiful she looked standing under the apple trees by the gate in the moonlight, her smile resting like the reflection of light on her carved face. Then, however, I walked home, feeling angry and annoyed with her; but of course that was foolish. Because it seems to me now that the world is made up of gay people and sad people, and however charming and beautiful the gay people are, their souls can never really meet the souls of those who are born for suffering and melancholy, simply because they are made in a different mould. Of course I see that this is a sort of dualism, but still it seems to me to be the truth, and I believe my friend, of whom I spoke, is a dualist, too, in some things.

I did not stay more than a day or two after this, though my aunt and the girls begged me to do so. I did not see Gwyneth again, only something took place which was a little ridiculous in the circumstances.

The evening before I went Ruthie came and said, half in an anxious whisper, 'Frederick, will you do something very important for me?'

'Yes, if I can,' I said. 'What is it?'

'Well, it is Gwyneth's birthday tomorrow, and she is so rich it is hard to think of something to give her.'

'Yes,' I said, without much interest.

'But do you know what I thought of? I have bought an almond tree – the man has just left it out in the shed – and I am going to plant it at the edge of the lawn so that she will see it tomorrow morning. So it will have to be planted in the middle of the night, and I wondered if you would come and help me.'

'But is it the right time of the year to plant an almond tree – in August?'

'I don't know,' said Ruthie; 'but surely the man in the nursery would have said if it were not. You can sleep in the train, you know. You used always to do things with me.'

'All right, I will,' I said, 'only we need not go in the middle of the night – early in the morning will do, before it is quite light.'

'Oh, thank you so much,' said Ruthie, trembling with gratitude and excitement. 'But don't tell anyone, will you – not even Jessica?'

'No,' I said.

Exceedingly early in the morning, long before it was light, Ruthie came into my room in her dressing-gown to wake me, looking exactly as she used to do. We went quietly downstairs and through the wet grass to Gwyneth's house, Ruthie carrying the spade and I the tree. It was still rather dark when we reached there, but Ruthie had planned the exact place before.

We hurried with the work. I did the digging, and Ruthie stood with the tree in her hand looking up at the house. We hardly spoke.

Ruthie whispered, 'We must be quiet. That is her window. She will be able to see it as soon as she looks out. She is asleep now.'

'Look here,' I said, 'don't tell her that I planted it, because it may not grow. I can't see very well.'

'Oh, but she must never know that either of us did it.'

'But are you going to give her a present and never let her know who it is from?'

'Yes,' said Ruthie.

'I think that is rather silly,' I said.

Ruthie turned away.

We put the tree in. I have never heard whether it grew or not. Just as the sun was rising we walked back, and that morning I went away.

THE DOCTOR'S WIFE
(1930)
Rhys Davies

When Dr Morgan married Phoebe Pryce, the harpist, people in the Valley thought of the match as an idyll and expected to see them settle down to a long and happy life together.

The doctor was admired as a clever man. He had a pleasantly bullying way with patients, gruff and hearty with the men and domineering with the women, so that everyone had confidence in him. His rough didactic manner as he talked boldly and energetically to them made their illnesses seem more important. It was nice to have such a large influential looking man bothering in such a masterful way about them. He took an interest in the local governing bodies, too, and had his say in no uncertain fashion; people said he would go to Westminster in the end. There was scarcely a political or local council meeting that did not contain his large red fighter's head, but he said things in such a magnetic way, with jokes stuck here and there, that no one could resist him. And when a local personage was buried he was always the most distinguished man in the funeral, in his frock-coat and top-hat, a stern gravity spread over his healthy face.

He was thirty-six when he married Phoebe, and so was long past the nonsense of youth. She, however, was twenty-four, and a demure eagerness had not yet left her pretty face. She would turn her head, her green, uncertain eyes glistening, her lips parted, as though she always expected to see or hear something remarkable from the persons who came to the house.

The house became a social centre in the Valley. The doctor had dozens of male friends, and since he became married they brought their wives and there were little gossipy parties, the men at one end of the big drawing-room talking politics and golf, the women, some of whom brought embroidery or knitting work, at the other end, where Phoebe's harp stood. Sometimes she played the great gilt instrument, that stood so aloofly against blue curtains, though the guests always became a bit fidgety if the piece of music was too long, accomplished as Phoebe was.

She loved her harp. It had never been necessary for her to earn her living playing it and she had a sentimental and romantic regard for the ancient instrument. When she played for charity at concerts she always wore a white satin dress, and her long graceful arms, as she pecked at the strings, were like the necks of swans lifted to the music. She seemed to dream over the thing in impassioned poses, and she liked best the languid reflections of Debussy's music.

Perhaps she thought Dr Morgan, with his boisterous health, would rouse her to a vitality she lacked. In any case, he was a 'catch' and took her away from the refined shabbiness of her vicarage home. Their wedding was a big and picturesque event in the Valley.

'Now, Phoebe,' said the doctor heartily, 'you're going to be a new woman. I shall take you to pieces and build you up again. A doctor's wife must be an example to the place.'

It was true he kept her physical health in good order, for she had suffered from one or two minor complaints, and indeed, no woman could have had a more conscientious husband, medical attendance apart. Perhaps he was too conscientious, in his polite, if voluble, manner.

For after a couple of years she began to wilt, like a frail lily in a boisterously playful wind. She became quieter, and the demure eagerness in her face was replaced by a kind of inquiring expression, as though she were puzzled at some vague abstraction in her mind. Dr Morgan gave her the best and most cunning tonics in his surgery, and even deprived himself of many a meeting so that he could take her for airings in the car. And she took to going oftener to her harp. Indeed, it wasn't unusual to find her seated at it before breakfast, playing to herself some dim old solo that the doctor thought trash: his attitude to the harp had never been very benevolent. Her pensive little silences during a party were very noticed too.

The women said she ought to have a baby. One, who wanted to be her friend, suggested it to her.

'Oh no!' said Phoebe in quite a startled way. 'I don't want a baby.' She looked hurt.

She was roused to some interest by the formation of a Dramatic Society.

The idea had been suggested by a newcomer to the Valley, Agnes Wright, an unmarried woman of thirty who had come to the place in connection with some social work for refining the colliers' families, running a club where the wives could be taught new methods of living. Phoebe agreed with Miss Wright that the upper class of the Valley also needed new interests. They planned concerts of chamber music, but the reception of the first was so bleak that they were abandoned, just as the circle for the discussion of modern literature ended in whist drives. In music nothing but swollen floods of sound from male-voice choirs roused these people of the mountains to any emotion. The Dramatic Society, however, met with some approval. *The School for Scandal* was the play chosen.

Phoebe was attracted to Agnes Wright. Miss Wright was a

sturdy handsome woman with strong cheeks, clear pale-blue eyes and good vigorous limbs. She had a liking for rough expensive tweeds and Scotch jerseys. Her voice was clear and wholesome, and what she said was always definite and to the point. People thought they could trust her. She was a lady and she could sing, in a voice of strange haunting charm, the sentimental ballads of several nations. The doctor said she was an accomplished woman.

He encouraged her friendship with his wife. A strong personality such as Miss Wright possessed, a personality in which feminine intuition was blended with a masculine decisiveness, was what his wife needed in a friend, the doctor thought. Miss Wright called nearly every day, and those afternoons in which she wasn't at the house, Phoebe spent at her rooms. It was always 'Miss Wright said this or that' now. The doctor listened and approved, though after a few weeks he began to weary of never hearing any opinion but Miss Wright's.

He watched his wife's face glow into a kind of roguish eagerness. She began to dress her hair in a different way and to paint her lips; she bought daintier and more expensive clothes. And her everyday manner to him became exceedingly pleasant and amiable. He began to bestir, smartening his own appearance and doing as much as possible to look younger. He sent her loving and secret glances across the table at dinner and sometimes patted her hand in an understanding and deferential way. He was still waiting for her.

'Phoebe is a different person since you became her friend,' he said to Agnes Wright.

Agnes lifted her clear pale-shining eyes to him. There was always a subtle touch of homage in her manner towards him, which he accepted in a gratified and jovial way.

'I understand her,' said Agnes Wright. 'She has never had a woman friend who had a sympathy with her.'

'She talks of nothing else but you and that play you're producing together,' said the doctor teasingly. 'I feel I ought to be jealous, you know, she has so little time for me now. But since you are her friend I know she'll be safe and taken care of.'

The pale gleam behind Agnes's eyes became brighter as she looked into the doctor's eyes. Her strong handsome face was lifted up close to his and he thought there was something queer about her expression, a flash of something that repelled him for the moment. She seemed to be searching him too, her gaze went into his mind. Then she withdrew that gaze and laughed her clear wholesome laugh.

'Of course,' she said, 'but of course. What could happen to her?'

'Oh, you play-acting people have a reputation,' he answered, teasing. 'How do I know what flirtations go on with all those young fellows in the company. The rips some of them are, to my knowledge. After all, I'm only a staid and settled old bloke now, only a husband!'

'Phoebe,' said Agnes with decision, 'is not at all likely to flirt with any young man.'

He looked at her with gratification. 'That's true, I feel that's true,' he said. 'I do believe she's really in love with me alone, in her own queer way.'

'Yes,' said Agnes Wright, fingering some lace on her well-shaped breast.

'You feel that too!' he said eagerly. 'You women always know about each other.'

'Yes, usually,' she answered, turning her head to where Phoebe stood, with her hands crossed on her throat, talking quite gaily to one of the matrons of that evening's gathering. 'And she does look much happier now, doesn't she?' she added, with some pride.

The doctor's voice became rather unhappy. 'If only she were stronger in her physical health,' he said in a secret undertone. 'She can't stand much, you know.'

Agnes lowered her voice too in gentle sympathy. 'She's such a dreamer, a kind of poet!' she said. 'She's one of those people who seem to live in a different world from our ordinary coarse workaday one.'

'I'm so fond of her!' said the doctor plaintively.

As the months passed he began to think he had cause to complain. There was no doubt that Phoebe had improved in physical well-being. He could find nothing wrong with her at all. And she seemed so very contented. Selfish, he began to think her.

'But, my darling, I love you,' he would repeat again and again. 'Why are you so quiet?'

'I like being just quiet,' she said. 'You know I'm happier like this, quiet.'

He thought himself too much of a gentleman to fume and be angry with her. Once he did let the word 'selfish' slip out at her and she began to weep, so that he felt himself a beast and a ruffian.

And so, baffled and annoyed, he retired into himself and became suspicious.

'I wonder has she a lover!' he said to himself, and could not think it possible. The damage to his conceit he worked out in the council meetings and with patients. People said he was a man with an iron will who would always get what he wanted: he spoke with such thunder in the meetings and bullied his patients with such determination... His golf, too, was discussed with marvel.

He was easily the most admired man in the Valley, preachers excepted.

Again and again he tried to warm Phoebe's wintry cold heart. Sometimes she stirred and kissed him with a soft and slow pressure, a fragile kiss that was so typical of her that it almost irritated him. Then she would lean back from him and sigh and dream. He would become almost maudlin in his appeal to her.

It was her air of gaiety and content during the day that puzzled and angered him. He never forgot his suspicion. Sometimes he really decided that she had a lover. Then his blood fumed, and he would shut himself in his surgery or go out to play an angry and accurate game of golf. 'Who can it be?' he would growl to himself. 'If I find any fellow hanging round her I'll break his bloody neck, I will, sure enough.'

He thought of appealing to Agnes Wright for advice and help. But she was such a devoted friend of Phoebe that he knew her sympathy would not be for him. They were always together. More than ever, he thought, a trifle savagely. Probably plotting against him. Perhaps Agnes Wright was even assisting Phoebe in a love-affair with some young good-for-nothing chap. By God! he was suddenly clear about it. Phoebe went twice a week to tea at Agnes's rooms and he had noticed she always came back looking particularly happy, a little excited flush on her cheeks.

The thought persisted, though sometimes, looking at Phoebe's gentle soft face, so sweet in its luminous purity, he could not believe she could be so sordid and so cruel to him. He watched her after her return from her next visit to Agnes's rooms. Yes, she was certainly gayer and sweeter-looking and her eyes seemed wide with a soft ecstatic joy. Her manner to him, too, was almost humble, and she asked him how he felt, what he would like for Christmas, and told him how much nicer and younger he looked since he had clipped his moustache short. The suspicion returned. Her niceness to him was so obvious.

'What do you two women,' he asked, 'talk about that you can stand seeing each other so often?'

She turned her head to him quickly, her face wakened. He watched her.

'Agnes,' she answered after a moment, 'is a woman in a thousand. Her life has been so varied, she is always interesting. Other women are boring compared with her.'

'H'm,' he half-sniffed.

'You've said yourself she is an exceptional woman,' Phoebe said, quite self-possessed now.

'Yes,' he answered. Anger began to flood his veins. 'But she's inclined to be domineering and possessive. You've become an echo of her lately. Surely you don't want to be the echo of anyone? Can't you be yourself?' And he added, putting a shade of warning into his voice, 'No doubt you find her useful though.' His big fighter's face became red as he struggled to say something biting, something that would make her realise his suspicions. 'You two in those rooms of hers, heaven knows what ideas she puts into your head. All I know is that you are not quite the sweet girl I married.'

She was looking at him in such a startled way, and such an expression of fright suddenly passed over her face and was suppressed that instantly he decided his suspicions were well-founded. She had a lover! His body became rigid, his thick neck stiffened, he flashed her a look of furious indignation.

'Something has happened, hasn't it!' he said angrily.

'Arthur, what are you saying!' she cried. Her face paled, she swayed, and then as quickly, her eyes searching his face, she recovered and smiled at him appealingly. 'Oh, you silly darling, why do you try to hurt me? Of course nothing has happened. What could? I do believe you're jealous of Agnes. All right. I won't see her so often.'

'I'm not jealous of Agnes,' he said, beginning to sulk, turning his head from her, and laying his rigid fists on his knees.

'Well, what is it then?' she demanded with such an appeal of innocence in her voice that he began to doubt himself again.

He would not answer. She had to go to him and caress him out of his sulking. Her thin hands were perfumed, the nails long and magenta, her lips were painted a bright red, her eyelids darkened. He suddenly gripped her passionately over the hips and drew her upon him. She submitted, closing her eyes and limp in his arms.

'Breathe,' he whispered, 'breathe.'

Her little lips parted and uttered a soft sigh. She lay quite lax in his hard grasp. As suddenly as he had gripped her he threw her away to a corner of the sofa.

'You're like a dead woman,' he said.

She opened her eyes then. But they seemed sightless as they looked at him drawing away. Sightless and not her own. She lay still. She seemed to be in a dream. Such indifference of him was manifest in her that he had to go out of the room to prevent himself striking her and uttering the abusive name that rose to his lips.

Disconsolately he told himself that he was certain of her infidelity now.

Who could the young man be? Somehow he felt certain that it was a young man. His hands clenched in rage as he went over the list of possible lovers in the place. None seemed of great account as men compared to himself. After all he was the best-known and most admired man in the Valley. Ah! To think of it! Some young rip laughing at him behind his back. How could Phoebe be so cruel to him! He felt that his dignity as an A1 man, as he called himself, was set at naught.

Frigidly, a coldly heavy expression on his face, he went down to dinner. The pit engineer and his wife were guests, and after dinner more people were coming in for music and cards. During the meal he talked to the engineer in a strong and dignified way of political matters, putting the women out of his consideration. He said things of great weight. He hinted that he was determined to reach Westminster. Indeed, one felt it was only a matter of time and choice before he would be in Downing Street. His healthy red face, with its fine width of gleaming brow, going bald now, expressed a clean trustworthy character of the best British breed. His voice boomed out heavier and heavier as the meal progressed. Anyone could see what a man of character and strength he was. And people had almost abject faith in him, he knew. As, the women gone, he lit his cigar and pushed out his stomach, he felt he could achieve anything.

Later, in the drawing-room, he kept a watchful eye on Phoebe. Two or three of the young men from the Dramatic Club had arrived and they were talking and joking with Agnes Wright and Phoebe together at one end of the room. Ah! that young fool, Emlyn Walters! He had noticed how friendly the fop had been with Phoebe and Agnes Wright lately. He had found books inscribed with the initials E.W. about the house. Books of poetry too! Ha! The doctor's lips made a gibe of contempt. Emlyn Walters was just the kind of sloppy good-for-nothing to get round women. And he wrote verses which were published in the local newspapers.

The doctor watched them closely. Yes, Emlyn Walters and Phoebe did exchange secret glances and laugh together a great deal. They were always looking at each other too. Agnes Wright sat back in her chair and smiled at them benignly. Such outrageous conduct he would never imagine in his own house! Suddenly he strode over to the group.

Emlyn Walters glanced up at him inquiringly. He looked so cheeky, the doctor could have thrown him out of the house there and then. He was a slim fair young man with delicate feminine features and hair longer than a man's should be. He wore a scarlet tie and a big Egyptian ring. The doctor's nostrils quivered in contempt. He was rather at a loss to know what to say for a moment or two. Then he blundered out:

'What are you talking about all on your own? Come, Phoebe, mix up with your other guests.'

'Oh, go away, Arthur,' said Phoebe. 'We're trying to allocate the characters for our next play.'

'You seem to be enjoying it,' he said, pursing his thick lips. 'Quite a lot of fun you're getting out of it.'

'It is rather funny,' said Emlyn Walters in his flippant voice, 'to think how certain characters would turn out when handled by the wrong people. Yourself as Bottom in Midsummer Night's Dream, for instance.'

'H'm,' said the doctor, 'h'm.' He turned his back on the young man and drew a chair beside Agnes Wright. He wasn't going to be pushed out, he'd show them he was boss in his own house.

'Now, Phoebe, what about your harp?' he demanded with an attempt at breeziness. 'Give people a rest from talking.'

'I don't want to play my harp tonight,' said Phoebe with playful peevishness. She leant and put her hand on Agnes's arm, lifted her face beseechingly to her friend. 'You go to the piano, darling, and sing us some ballads.'

'All right, dear, presently,' said Agnes in a warm affectionate way, looking at Phoebe with a glint of amusement in her eyes.

While she sang, Phoebe closed her eyes and dreamily blew clouds of cigarette smoke out of her nostrils. Agnes's voice became plaintive and sentimental. The doctor sat and looked stern. If only he knew for certain, if only he knew. He'd whip the affected miserable little fop. If it really were Emlyn Walters, who looked and behaved, he thought, like a nancy-boy! It was awful to think of it.

He determined to find out if the young man was present at Agnes's rooms when Phoebe went there. He'd pay a surprise visit the next time. In any case he'd show that he intended to keep an eye on Phoebe. Something was going on, he was quite certain now. Some young man, by hook or by crook, was having a proper affair with Phoebe. It was disgraceful, the way she was treating him, her husband, of late. Not many men would stand for it. They'd separate. But he loved Phoebe, and she was young and easily led. She'd make foolish mistakes. He would overlook them if she'd come back to him properly.

So in the early evening of the next Wednesday he quietly opened the gate of the villa where Agnes lodged and tiptoed up the little front garden. He knew Agnes had the front-room downstairs as a sitting-room. A light burned there, and the curtains were drawn. He paused at the window. It was a dark wintry evening. Cautiously he searched round the window for a chink in the curtains. He found one that admitted a view of most of the room.

He drew back and went back slowly and softly to the door. His head hung down a bit sheepishly. He felt he had intruded on something rather beautiful where he had no business. He realised the close friendship that existed between Agnes and Phoebe. It was nice and unusual to see two women so fond of each other. And he admired Agnes as a fine social worker, in spite of her over-shadowing of Phoebe's personality. He had seen them, through the chink, kissing each other in such a sweet way. He felt ashamed. He would, however, go in, he would be very nice to them. He would forget his suspicions for a moment. He knocked.

The landlady admitted him and took him immediately to Agnes's sitting-room. Agnes jumped up from Phoebe's side and, straightening her hair, made an exclamation of happy surprise. Phoebe looked rather startled, crying:

'Arthur, you!'

'I was passing here coming back from a patient,' he said untruthfully, 'and thought you'd like me to take you home. The car is there.' He rubbed his hands before the fire. 'Nice and comfy place you have here, Agnes.'

Agnes was darting about getting fresh tea-things out. 'You must have some tea,' she cried almost shrilly. 'To warm you up. It'll only take a minute to make. Yes, you must have some. No trouble, no trouble.' Her strong cheeks were red, her manner excited. The doctor decided he liked her more. 'She is flattered at having me here,' he thought, noticing her unusually excited manner. 'Poor thing, I think she's destined to be an old maid. A pity. She's well made enough, and ought to have some blood in her, I should think.'

'He really doesn't want tea, Agnes,' said Phoebe in a tone of quiet reproof. 'Don't fuss over him.' She sat back on the sofa calmly now and lit a cigarette.

But Agnes made tea and fetched cakes for him and gazed up eagerly into his face while he sipped, and listened attentively to his talk. And he accepted her deferential homage with an agreeable smile. Presently she went back to sit beside Phoebe and looked her old capable self.

The doctor, however, did not abandon his suspicions. Perhaps Phoebe met her lover in some quiet backwash among the hills, perhaps during her occasional trips to Cardiff, perhaps even at his own house. His various interests took him away nearly every afternoon. Phoebe had the house to herself nearly all day.

Sometimes he wanted to shake her violently, she looked so happy and amiable. How in Heaven's name could she be so happy when she was depriving him of his own content? She was quite heartless. Heartless in a disgusting way. She seemed to care not a jot about him. He continued to grizzle at her. A little look of pain would cross her face for a moment, but she would make it quite definite that it was impossible for her to be the woman he wanted. Then afterwards she would be so pleasant to him, socially. 'Perhaps it's my fault,' he muttered to himself. 'Perhaps I am unusually masculine.' Phoebe looked so pretty and fragile he felt he would be blamed if the conflict became a public scandal, a separation.

Then he caught Emlyn Walters alone with his wife at the house one afternoon. Sitting together, too, in an indolent attitude on the sofa, a wanton laughing look in his wife's eyes. The doctor instantly felt they had been laughing at him. He stood, stern and silent in the doorway; he had come back unexpectedly from a meeting. Emlyn Walters rose and greeted him, an impudent smile on his silly feminine face. The doctor growled:

'You look a pretty couple there.'

Phoebe laughed. By God, how she laughed. He could have struck her.

'Have the other councillors been irritating, Arthur? Really, dear, you shouldn't come back looking so upset.'

'I want to see you alone,' he told her grimly, not advancing into the room.

'Good-bye, Mrs. Morgan,' lisped Emlyn Walters affectedly, taking her hand and bending over it.

The doctor's eyes glittered. He wanted to lift his foot and kick the sloppy imp out of the house. He stood aside and turned his head away as the young man, wishing him good-bye, went past. Afterwards, the door closed, he advanced towards Phoebe, his thick lips protruding rigidly.

'Really, Arthur,' said Phoebe, with a sudden burst of temper, 'your manners are impossible. How dare you behave like that!'

'How dare I,' he stormed, 'how dare I!' He began to splutter.

'In my own house, under my very nose, one might say, carrying on with that—' He stopped to control his voice.

Phoebe was staring at him with a horrified expression. She opened her mouth to speak, but he waved his arms and burst out:

'I've suspected it for a long time. I've seen how it's been going on. Flirting and laughing with young men, and treating me as you do. You've got a lover. That's what it is. That's what's wrong with you, that's why you treat me like you do.' He stared at her with a malignant glitter in his eyes and his voice rose. 'You're one of those false women that pretend to be so holy and far above the common herd and all the time you're just filth underneath. I know your sort. I can see through you. Ha, you thought I was a fool, didn't you, a blind loving old fool. I've noticed these goings-on for some time, let me tell you.' He thumped his fist on the back of a chair. 'It's all got to stop, d'you hear? I've had enough of your nonsense. No more of these parties and Dramatic Societies, no more good-for-nothing people hanging about my house. It's got to stop.' He finished sharply and looked at her threateningly.

She sat quite still in the corner of the sofa. Her pretty face was like an astonished child's, her lips were parted. And her eyes were bright with a look of wounded innocence. His stormy fury was quite new to her. He waited for her to speak, continuing to look at her threateningly. Then she said in a quick startled way:

'Arthur, whatever are you saying! You're mad. A lover, indeed! Do you realise how insulting you are? I've never heard such a vulgar lot of trash.' Her voice began to rise angrily. 'How dare you speak to me like that! You're insanely jealous, nothing else, though why, I don't know. I've heard enough. Go away and calm yourself.' And she looked at him with contemptuous disdain.

'You order me about!' he fumed, thrusting out his big red head, that seemed swollen with wrath, 'I'll—'

She rose and walked to the door. His eyes followed. He wanted to bear her away and crush her into his arms. She heard his excited breathing. She walked out with dignity. He sank into a chair and his face snarled. Somehow he felt she had been triumphant.

After all, he had no real proof that she had been faithless to him. But he had an unbounded belief in his own perception and keen instinct for fathoming guilt and secret behaviour; his success in the world had been partly due to that talent in him. Phoebe's complete behaviour pointed to the existence of a lover. Her lack of passion for him, her social amiability, her secret gaiety, her well-being, when before she had been so puling, her liking for young men such as that sloppy-romantic Emlyn Walters and other play-acting fellows – what would any man think?

His fury began to burn out. Perhaps, after all, she had not been unfaithful technically. Well, if she would be nice to him and try to begin their married life all over again, he would be forgiving and forget all. The past would be abolished entirely if only she would come adoringly to his arms. He would go to her now and try to persuade her, he would be tender and gentle. Since his outburst he felt a load had been taken from his mind. The air in the house felt clearer. The quarrel had been bound to happen; he would make her see that.

But he could not find her anywhere. The maid told him she thought she had heard Mrs. Morgan go out. A fear gripped his heart. Had she left him? Had he said too much, insulted her? He sat down, overwhelmed. Surely she had not left him. He could not bear the thought. His sweet Phoebe, that he had maligned in his mind, perhaps very unjustly.

He guessed she had gone to Agnes Wright. He took comfort as he thought of Agnes talking to her, certain of what she would say. Agnes, a mature woman of the world, would send her back. She would calm and soothe her distracted friend, she would make Phoebe see where her duty lay. He thought of Agnes's kind handsome face, her vigorous personality, her clear wholesome voice. A woman one could trust, a steady reliable woman, intelligent and well-read. He had never heard her utter any of the rubbishy modern notions of free and easy marriage morals. She was a true-blooded British woman. He grew confident that Phoebe would be back before dinner.

She came back. He went to her room and stood looking at her with a disconsolate appeal in his face.

'Phoebe,' he said, 'let us begin our life over again.'

He had expected to see marks of stress on her face. Tear-stained eyes and trembling lips. But she looked just the same. There was happiness in her face. Perhaps it was because he had come to her in this simple apologetic manner. He went close to her.

'My dear,' he said, 'my dear! You knew it had to happen, didn't you?'

She looked at him and was silent. Her sweet face was quite happy. But her eyes were mysterious. He suddenly dropped on his knees before her and held her legs tightly, looking up imploringly.

'Oh, my dear, we must be kind to each other,' he said loudly, emotionally. 'Forgive your old jealous husband and be considerate of him. You remember how you used to curl up in my arms? Can't you do it again, can't you? Oh, my dear, you must.'

A shadow came over her features.

'Arthur,' she said, 'get up.' He rose obediently.

'I want to hear no more of this,' she said evenly. 'It has been disgraceful, but we won't discuss the subject any more. Now I want to wash and do my hair before dinner.'

He stood back and began to look sulky. But perhaps it would be best to leave the subject now, disappointing as it had turned out.

'But I can't promise to let it stand at this,' he said in a hurt voice, going to the door.

All the next few days she was unapproachable. Her manner frightened him, but he believed she couldn't keep it up for long. On the following Saturday he came home from his afternoon golf and found a letter on his dressing-table. He stared for moments at her handwriting on the envelope, and an ague shook his limbs. Then furiously he tore the letter open, and, the blood in his ears, read:

'Dear Arthur,—

I have come to the conclusion that we had better part—if not for always, at least for a long while. I am far from happy with you now and I want to see how I'll be alone. I am going to stay with Agnes at her flat in London; you can tell people, if you don't feel equal to telling them the truth, that I am spending a holiday with her, needing a change. I enclose her address, but I warn you it's useless thinking that you could come and argue with me. If I want to return I'll write and ask you if you are willing to have me back. Agnes will take care of me and I expect I shall help her with her social work in the slums of London.

Phoebe.

P.S.—I may need my harp, so if I send for it I shall be grateful if you will see that it is packed carefully.'

Such a sense of desolation came upon him that his fury died out and he could only sink into a chair and hang his head, breathing stertorously. His dear little Phoebe gone! She had run away from him. Him!

For days he brooded in acute melancholy. He wondered if Phoebe's letter was a deception and she had eloped with a young man: he made discreet inquiries as to who had left the place of late. He came to know that Emlyn Walters intended leaving shortly to go on the stage. And all his suspicions returned.

He wrote her a letter:

'My Own Darling,—

You have broken my heart. How can you behave like this to me? Surely it can't be that your affection for me has died entirely? You have never given me much opportunity to show how much I cherish you.

I feel you are to blame for all that has happened; you have never tried to understand me. I cannot bear to think of your living in London, doing social work in dirty slums. You know you are delicate and very likely you'll catch any disease that's hanging about. Still, it is a comfort to know that you are with Agnes. She is a capable woman, you are in good hands, I know. But surely she must see that you are doing the wrong thing. I will write her too. As for the harp, please don't send for it. I treasure it and I feel you are here when I look at it, that at any moment I will hear music from it and your dear hands. Come back, come back, I am fretting for you.

                    Your husband,
                    Arthur.'

The weeks went on and she did not return. The doctor, concealing his broken heart admirably, never talked of her, but became even more masterful and didactic with his patients and in committee meetings. He always had his way. He caused a new town-hall to be built, he had swimming-baths and new libraries made, he kept the rates moderate and became a magistrate. His practice increased, he employed two young doctors. People respected his trouble and Phoebe was never mentioned. He continued to send her pathetic appeals and once asked her if she had fallen in love with another man, adding masterfully, 'But I warn you I'd thrash his life out if only I could lay my hands on him!'

PARTING
(1980)
Jane Edwards
Translated by Mihangel Morgan

The driver behind him sounded his horn. He waved his fist at him before realising he'd just driven through a red light. It wasn't the first time. He had to be more careful. He held the steering wheel tighter, leaning forward, willing himself to concentrate on the road; following the instructions of that song Enid used to sing when they were courting. How did it go now? Slow down, slow down – green light. He smiled: why was he slowing? A green light gave him the freedom to go. *Keep your mind on your driving, keep your hand on the wheel...* Yes, that's the song. He tried to hum it but couldn't remember the tune.

He reached Bryniau Road, a fine wide long street, with solid houses built in the thirties on both sides and plenty of trees and bushes in the little gardens giving the area a prosperous look. There was something growing there every season of the year – a sign of careful planning. Enid knew all their names and he loved listening. The charm of the names – the laburnum, the silver birches, the lilac and the fuchsia bushes, the rhododendron and the camellia, the peony, rainbow colours; but he couldn't tell one from the other. Today the leaves had started to fall, playfully descending as if they were enjoying their demise. Surely that was like dying. A splash of colour followed by a joyful dance. He shut his eyes. He thought of death and depressing things too often. A young man just turned forty-two he should be full of energy and plans for the future. He hit a pavement. No harm done, he was going too slowly. What a stupid thing to do – driving with eyes shut. He could have killed someone – that boy who was riding a bike down the street with his feet on the handlebars. An equally stupid thing to do.

As he approached the drive of his house he felt his muscles tightening and the sweat collected around his collar. Given half a chance he would turn back.

He swore under his breath. The white Dolomite was still there. He gathered his case and his mac from the back of the car and he walked stiffly towards the door. It was an unnatural attitude since he was in the habit of dropping his shoulders. He searched his coat pockets for a key before recalling he didn't have one. He rang the bell long and loudly. It was insane – ringing the doorbell to gain admittance to his own house. He'd have to have a word with Enid on that matter. She'd have to do without keys for a day while he got copies made in town. Between the Dolomite and the keys he was a talking point for the neighbours. He rang the bell furiously.

Rhodri opened the door, grumbling because he'd had to leave his television and his toys. He rushed back to the living room, slamming the door after him. He took off his hat and placed it on the hook in the clothes cupboard and hung his coat on one of the pegs. There was a smell of fur in the cupboard – a nice warm smell, a rich smell. He'd promised to buy a fur coat for Enid some day, but with the rise in interest rates and the cost of hiring, that day moved further and further away. Damn inflation! Damn Menna for flaunting her wealth. He pulled furiously at the fur with the intention of ripping it.

A barbaric act. He petted the mink back into place allowing his head to rest for a second against the lovely softness.

The kitchen was brightly lit; that sort of yellow light that gives the skin a sickly tone and shows up every wrinkle. The formica table had been laid for one, and at one corner sat Menna swinging her long legs back and forth. She smiled at him without uttering a word, and he smiled back except that the smile didn't reach his face. 'You're late,' his wife said. 'We've eaten, we were famished.'

She pulled out a plate of salad covered with clingfilm from the fridge and plonked it in front of him. He knew before tasting it that there was too much oil on it. That wasn't good for his health. 'I had salad for lunch too.'

Menna laughed, adding to his misery.

'That's how to lose weight.' She sat in the chair opposite watching him eat while Enid continued to wash the dishes or to do something around the sink. The silence deepened his feeling of discomfort. He had the feeling that he had interrupted a fun conversation – one that for some reason was not fit for his ears. And now everyone looked to him to engage their interest. The great entertainer himself! He resisted. Why should he break the ice? Next minute he heard himself asking: 'How is Wil?'

'Ok, fine as far as I know. I never ask.' Menna chuckled. She had good teeth. Took advantage of every opportunity to show them off. He couldn't help but appreciate what sort of relationship existed between her and her husband. He had to be a bit of an oddball himself. He'd seen him once or twice driving a Rover around town, but he would be hard pushed to recognise him if he came face to face with him.

He pushed his plate aside not having touched the salami and the lettuce. He needed something warm. He looked at his watch to avoid looking at Menna. 'Where is Catrin?'

'Out playing.'

'She should be in. It's getting dark early.'

'I told her to be back before six.'

'It's quarter past...'

'Coffee?' Menna got to her feet. 'I could do with another one.'

'Please.' She had a strange accent – a mixture of South and North. Affected.

'What about you, En?' She was the one who asked. She was in charge of the house by all appearances, deciding mealtimes. Taking up his wife's time. But Enid was not bothered: she grinned happy with the attention. She turned her head away, her smiles did not include him. He swept his hand over his forehead where the ache was.

'Are you doing anything tonight?' Enid was asking.

'I was going to write the report...' Her face dropped. 'I don't have to do it tonight. Tomorrow night will do. Why?'

'Menna is going to the White Hart and wondered if I'd like to go with her. There's a folk group from Brittany singing there tonight.'

'You go, you two go by all means.' He was surprised by his generosity, the enthusiasm that hid the anger. Menna smiled triumphantly. Why did she always smile so much, he wondered. Someone had told her she was attractive, probably. Even he couldn't deny that. She had charmed him with her smiles at one time. And he, such an idiot, had tried flirting with her. But she hadn't wanted any of that: she was a different person beneath the smiles. He felt ashamed now that he had made such a fool of himself – bringing her to his home like this.

'I must get myself ready.' She picked up her gloves and threw on her cardigan. Enid took her to the door and he eavesdropped on them. He couldn't make out a word they were saying but he understood the laughter. He got the feeling (mistaken of course) that he was the object of their amusement. He gripped the corners of the formica table tightly. He'd had enough of the situation, more than he could take. He'd have to have a word with Enid before things went too far.

'Enid... Enid...' His voice claiming her.

'I'm coming now...'

'Don't be too long or you'll be late for the pub.'

'I'm behind already.' She took off her apron and flung it on the table.

'Sit for a minute.' More command in his tone than encouragement.

'What's worrying you?' It was obvious from her voice and her eyes this was not the time for a discussion. (Is there an ideal time?). He shut his eyes – this wasn't going to be easy.

'I just feel...Well, just feel, have been feeling for some time, actually, that our marriage is getting a bit shaky.'

'Don't talk daft.'

'There's a rift, an estrangement, between us. How can I explain it?'

'It's in your head. We never quarrel, never argue.'

'We don't talk either.'

'And whose fault is that?'

'You're not short of words when you're with Menna.'

'She has more things to say. Anyway, women's talk is different: we have more things to talk about.'

Something inside him exploded and yet when he opened his mouth to speak his voice was flat and reasonable. 'I'm fed up, that's all I can say, I'm sick of having her in my home every day of the week. A man wants a bit of peace when he gets home from work.'

'Childish.' She got to her feet to leave and went to the mirror to look at herself.

'Since when is expressing an opinion childish? Surely I have the right to say what I think in my own house.'

'Don't raise your voice you'll disturb Rhodri.'

'Damn Rhodri!' He stood behind her snarling in the mirror.

'Shame on you speaking like that about your son.' She stared coldly at him before walking out.

He followed her to the foot of the stairs and called. 'And I want a hot dinner and pudding when I come home tomorrow. Is that understood? Is that clear?'

He went to bed early with the intention of reading, but he couldn't concentrate as he was listening out for the sound of the Dolomite. In the end he switched out the light and pulled the blanket over his face. He decided to sleep. He looked at his watch. Half past midnight. Where had she been? What had they been doing at this time? He bit his tongue rather than asking and she made no effort to enlighten him.

He watched her undressing in the mirror, and in his nervous, drowsy state he had the feeling he was watching a woman he didn't know – a shapely one, with loose morals. An exciting experience. She was too tired and groggy to make love. But he insisted on having it his way, he forced her to comply with him. And now he was plagued with guilt. Oppression never leads to affection; the intercourse had not brought them even a little bit closer. Yes, he felt ashamed. He sought comfort playing with her hair and pushing himself into her arms but she was dead to the world. The smell of cigarettes and drinks came from her. He turned on his side – he hated having a drunken woman in his bed.

Taken the kids to the pictures. See you about 9. Your food in the oven. F.

He re-read the note and gave a sigh of satisfaction. How nice – going to the pictures. It was such a family activity. Family. Familial. Yes, that was the word.

A smile spread across his face. Yes, it paid for a man to raise his voice from time to time. He opened the oven door and looked with pleasure at the baked potato and the rice pudding. And the icing on the cake was to have peace to eat without that Menna eyeing him with every mouthful he took. Thank god. He ate with relish.

He decided to write to his parents: something he hadn't done for ages since it was so much easier to pick up the phone. But this evening he would write. He had a hundred and one things to say but when it came to putting it down on paper, the movies was the main thing on his mind. And his good mood started to evaporate.

He drew back the curtain a little to spot the car. The most ugly Dolomite in the whole world. How naive was he, so unsuspecting to think they'd gone on the bus. Family night, damn it! The blood beat in his temples! Calm down now, calm down. This is how people have heart attacks. He was too quick to get stirred up and angry and to lose his temper these days, and that was unfamiliar to him. He heard the sound of laughter and good nights. That meant she intended to go straight home. He was grateful.

Rhodri and Catrin rushed in with their eyes sparkling. They insisted on telling the plot of the film. He sat on the edge of his chair to listen carefully though he couldn't make head or tail of the story as they both spoke over each other jumping from one scene to the next.

'You're tiring your dad. Come on, bedtime.' Enid stood over them still wearing her high heels.

'No they're not tiring me. I've had a quiet little evening. What were you saying now, Catrin?' He ignored his wife. There'd been too much of that lately: *Leave your father alone. Don't irritate him, he's tired.* To begin with he'd been grateful to her for being so considerate but most recently he'd begun to be suspicious of her motives.

'Dad, you're not listening,' Rhodri cried.

'Go on with the story, butty, I'm all ears.' He tried to get them both on his lap but they were too big for that. He decided to exchange experiences with them – telling them about some of the films he'd seen in the Arcadia when he was a boy. 'Cowboy films. Just six old pence we paid to go in.' They turned up their noses, they were too full of themselves.

'That's enough for tonight, you can finish your story tomorrow,' said Enid. And this time he didn't stop her.

He noticed that she'd changed from her tight skirt and blouse to jeans and slippers. She looked different – untidy, but more like the old Enid. She went straight to the drinks cabinet and poured herself a vermouth.

'I'm thirsty. It was horribly hot in the cinema.'

'You drink too much.'

'What?' She raised her eyebrows. A nasty expression, frivolous.

'You're drinking more than is good for you.'

'This,' she held the glass high, 'this is the first I've had for ages.'

'Last night. What did you drink last night – lemonade?'

'Last night?' The eyebrows again.

'Yes, last night. In the White Hart with Menna. Don't say you've forgotten such a memorable evening.'

'We went to hear the folk group.'

'You had something to drink too.'

'We did... yes, but that was different. Everyone drinks in a pub.'

'There are dangers. It can turn into a habit.' He bit his tongue. What was wrong with him? He was irritable, all he did was make reproaches and bicker all day long. Earlier he'd been in a good mood – earlier was a thousand years ago.

He went to the cabinet and poured himself a whisky.

WARNING. Don't drink on your own. Don't drink if you're depressed or in a bad mood. Where on earth had he read those words? A women's magazine, he guessed. One of the numerous magazines that showed the way to paradise on the one hand and the dangers along the way there on the other hand. He poured himself a big glass.

'And what sort of evening did Menna have?'

'Okay. Okay, as far as I know. She laughed enough.'

'That sort of film was it? I always thought you didn't like children's films.'

'I don't. But since Menna had kindly offered to take us, I didn't want to disappoint the kids.'

'No.' He turned the whisky comfortingly around his tongue. Amazing how much confidence a little of this gave a man. 'I just don't understand what her husband makes of all this.'

'Wil.' She stretched out the name giving her time to judge what direction the discussion would take.

'Wil. Yes, that's his name, you say. What does he think of all this wandering and gallivanting?'

'Nothing.'

'Nothing?'

'He doesn't care. He's never at home to care.'

'Very convenient.'

'He travels around with his work.'

'He's not on trips all the time, surely.'

'No...'

'More reason for Menna to stay home to keep him company.' He poured himself more whisky. 'Tell me, why don't they have any children?'

'I've never asked. Perhaps they don't want children. Not everyone's the same.'

'Quite true... yet odd that one of them doesn't want any.'

'Children wouldn't fit in with Wil's lifestyle. He likes his freedom.'

He laughed with derision. Wil would have the baby but Menna was no mother. He couldn't picture her tied to the house with a herd of children. She was far too fond of her freedom: thinking nothing of gallivanting, partying and shopping for fine clothes. Of course; she could afford to do that on her salary. There was no sense in the situation, a woman earning more pay than a man. Another example of something that grated on him. 'If Menna wanted children no wizard could prevent her. Wil would have no choice.'

'If it worries you so much, why don't you ask them?'

'Perhaps I will.'

'Why not phone now, strike while the iron is hot. Ask them to come over for a meal one evening. How would Saturday suit you?' She sprang to her feet eagerly.

'Any night suits me.' He tried catching around her waist playfully as the drink eased the anxiety in his mind.

'Stop it. There's a time for everything.'

'Why don't we make up?'

'Make up? What are you talking about?' She pushed away the hand that was creeping up her blouse, and turned on her heel.

She spoke on the phone for ages. He didn't follow any of what was said. But he understood the laughter alright, and that hurt. Other people's laughter shut him out, hit a sensitive nerve in his nature. Her face was flushed and her eyes glowed when she came back.

'Sorry. Men apologises from her heart, Wil can't come. He's arranged to go to the Canaries with some seventeen-year-old bimbo.'

Bimbo. Common ugly word. His Enid using such a word. Enid who was always so well-spoken, so respectable. She must've glugged down the vermouth. And he wasn't with it either. He started to drink his third whisky or perhaps this was his fourth. 'Well that's just great. Sensible too.' A quarter of a whole bottle, that's how much had gone.

'Men wants to come.'

'Men is *not* coming.' He thumped the coffee table so that the glasses jumped. 'Her feet won't come over the threshold.'

'But I've just asked her. I can't withdraw my invitation.'

'Why can't you? What's so special about her that you can't withdraw your invitation?'

'I've given my word.'

'But I haven't given *my* word. This is my house and I'm the one that counts.' He raised his fists unconsciously. 'And I don't want to see the old bag here ever again. Do you understand me... Well, do you understand me?'

'I understand but that doesn't mean that I agree.'

'You've got to.' The blood rushed to his forehead and exploded. He hurled the glass from his hand leaving shards underfoot. Enid bent down to clear it. Such a mess. Such destruction. 'Enid.' She raised her head to look at him without saying a thing.

'I'm sorry.' He took hold of her arm. 'Sit down, I'll clear it.' But she baulked. Suddenly he was consumed by fatigue. He threw himself clumsily onto the armchair. He closed his eyes.

'I'm sorry about the glass. I'm sorry about my tantrum. I don't know what's come over me lately. I'm sorry, I'm sorry, I'm sorry.'

'It's okay.'

'I'll buy a glass to replace it for you.'

'Crystal? Do you know how expensive it is?'

'I'll buy you a set. I know I have many faults but love of money or miserliness was never one of them.'

He heard a sound like thunder through his head. He opened

his eyes to see Enid clearing the pieces of glass with the Hoover. There was blood on her hands.

'Enid.' His voice pleaded for comfort. 'Enid, will you forgive me? I haven't been half well. My nerves... I must be suffering from...' He didn't finish the sentence.

She put her foot on the button to switch the machine off and straightened herself. She looked at him and told him she was leaving him.

'You're leaving me.' *Leaving me* his headache said.

'Yes, I'm going to leave you and I'm taking the children with me.'

'Oh, are you indeed! You're not so stupid as to think you can take the children away from me. No court of law would allow that. You would have left me. And anyway I would absolutely refuse to let you have the children.'

'I don't doubt that. Talk is easy. Who would look after the children while you're at work? Who'd feed them? Who'd wash and iron their clothes? Who would take them here and there? Who would be at hand day and night to attend to them?'

'I could make arrangements.'

'Arrange what? With whom? Your mother? She's riddled with arthritis, too frail to move. And you couldn't afford to pay some woman with the mortgage being so steep and all.'

Typical – they discussed the kids before going to the root of the matter. And Enid was crafty too, throwing him off course. He was a coward too.

'I'm sure I'd get someone. And don't you think for a moment, my lady, I'd be prepared to pay for your upkeep.'

'There'll be no need for you to maintain me. I've got work.' She smiled to show this gave her great satisfaction.

'Surprise surprise. And what place, if I may ask, will you be gracing with your presence?'

'Tour de Luxe travel agency on the Queen's Road.'

'Very nice.' Now it was his turn to enquire who'd look after the children.

'No need for you to worry, it's all set up. Men and I are sure to get through it. The children will love it: it's not as if they're going to be with strangers.'

Men. Men. Menna. He covered his face with the cushion. His worst fears had been realised. Why couldn't he lose his wife to another man... but to Menna...! He made the noise of a dog howling.

He found his wife in the spare bed. She lay there as if she were expecting him. She looked at him with her innocent blue eyes. The blood shot to his head and he raised his hand to smooth away the pain. And he hit her. Over and over mercilessly. He blamed the drink and retreated to his own bed and went straight to sleep.

The first thing the next morning Enid was in the doctor's surgery. From there she went to the solicitor to show her injuries and set up a divorce.

A MOST MODERATE LUST
(1996)
Siân James

It was a small private ward with pale pink paintwork and pink floral curtains. The bed and the armchair were covered in a deeper pink.

'How pretty,' Laura said. She sat gracefully at the bedside, letting her coat fall open as she sat. Her coat and dress exactly matched her wheat-coloured hair.

'I loathe pink,' Rosamund said sharply. Though feeling at a disadvantage, she was far from cowed. She was, after all, a very attractive woman. Her white satin nightdress had insets of handmade lace.

Laura's eyes, having already registered the Reger nightdress, rested on the enormous bunch of bright pink tulips on the glass and chrome table, conspicuously the only flowers in the room. From Philip of course.

'I hope you don't mind my coming. I've been worried about you. Honestly. And Philip's been quite frantic.' The ugly, ill-chosen flowers made her feel particularly generous.

She freed the bunch of hot-house grapes she had brought from its several layers of tissue. It was a large, well-shaped bunch, but not large enough to be ostentatious. Absently she picked a pale, almost milky fruit from the underside of the bunch and handed it to Rosamund who accepted it with neither visible surprise nor thanks.

'He wasn't frantic,' she said, 'not at all. Just a bit fussed.'

Laura's fine eyes narrowed. An apt word. It summed up her husband. A middle-aged, handsome but fussed gentleman, whose hair, moreover, was getting rather thin on top.

Rosamund studied the grape she had placed on the palm of her hand. It was a very pale blue, like the veins of her wrist. 'Don't you hate me then?' she asked gently, a little nervously.

'I did at first,' Laura admitted, 'though not a lot. Especially when I realised he didn't seem to want a divorce.'

There was a short pause. 'But don't you want to get married?' she asked then. 'Don't you need a man of your own? Or is that being old-fashioned?'

'He's very fond of you. And proud of you. Don't underestimate yourself.'

They smiled at each other for the first time, the splendid bunch of grapes between them.

'I don't think you love him very much,' Laura said. With some deliberation she chose the largest grape from the very top of the bunch and ate it gravely. 'But then,' she said, 'I don't suppose I do either. I mean, not the great all-absorbing love one always hopes for.'

Rosamund sighed, seeming to agree with her. She ate the small sour grape Laura had handed her and grimaced like a child. There was something child-like about her. 'It's partly habit now,' she said. 'Like marriage, I suppose.'

'At least you have your career,' Laura said.

'Yes.'

'When I first met you at that Christmas party, I didn't like you at all. I thought you were... well... rather brash.' As she spoke, Laura pushed the bunch of grapes towards Rosamund as though to mitigate the sting of her words.

'I was very nervous. Perhaps I was over-compensating. It had only just begun then. Just a week or so I think. And after all, you were his wife.' She plucked off several of the choicest grapes. Her smile was either thanks... or apology.

'He didn't like it much when you took that job in Saudi Arabia a couple of years ago,' Laura said. 'To be honest, I thought it was all going to end then.'

'So did I. I cried a lot, I remember. I think I must love him, you know. I certainly cried a great deal at that time.' Rosamund seemed surprised to remember her tears.

'Oh, endings always bring out the most exaggerated feelings,' Laura said. 'Whenever I've been on the point of leaving him, I feel so emotional and helpless and weak that I always stay. Of course, I love the house very much.'

'It's a beautiful house.'

'I didn't realise he'd taken you there,' Laura said, a shiver of ice in her voice. 'When was that?'

'Sorry. Just once or twice when you were in Greece last summer. I didn't touch anything valuable, I promise you.' Rosamund tried to be frivolous.

'You don't care for antiques, I suppose?'

'What makes you say that?'

'Architects usually like great square white ashtrays and spotlights and stiff flowers bundled into acrylic jars.'

'I loved your house. You have exquisite taste.'

'Thank you.' Laura was mollified. 'I have a shop, you know, but I always keep the best pieces for myself. You have a flat, I think, in Battersea.'

'Yes. No square white ashtrays though. No acrylic jars.'

'Do you have any family? Philip told me about your mother dying last year. I was so sorry.'

An orderly brought in tea on a bright pink plastic tray. A minute or two later, she came in again with an extra cup and saucer.

'I'll pour,' Laura said. 'Have you any family?' she asked again.

'One sister, one brother-in-law, two nieces and a nephew. They live in Australia.'

'What very dark tea. Not so much strong as sinister. Is it always like this?' Laura placed the cup and saucer carefully within Rosamund's reach. 'How long do you have to stay here?'

'The last stitches come out tomorrow. Another two or three days after that, I think.'

'When the phone rang that night, do you know, I was quite certain it was you. I woke up and just knew.'

'I'm sorry I disturbed you. I hadn't anyone else to ring. Philip's number was the only one that came and I was shivering too much to handle a directory.'

'I went in to wake him and told him who to ring and what to do. Do you know, he'd never even noticed that you were looking ill. I'd noticed it at that reception we all had to go to and told Philip so then. But I suppose he thought I was being spiteful... You know.'

'I'm nearly forty,' Rosamund said, quite suddenly.

'What of it? I'm forty-six in August. Though I'd never tell anyone else... I thought you were much younger though,' she added.

She remembered the time when Philip had first mentioned the new woman in the office. Five or six years ago. 'Very pretty,' he'd said. 'Not a beauty like you, but certainly very pretty. A bit like that Romney portrait of Emma Hamilton.'

They looked at each other kindly. Rosamund put her cup back on the tray and settled back on her pillows, suddenly very tired. She closed her eyes.

'Come and stay with us when you come out of hospital,' Laura said. 'No, I mean it. You'll really need to be looked after for a while. I have nothing much to do, I only do an hour or two at the shop these days. Say you'll come. Please. It'll be so... so convenient.'

They looked at each other and suddenly they both laughed, they laughed out loud and laughed again. They gasped for breath and then started again, laughing till the tea tray rattled on the bed. They both became ugly, their faces distorted. It was the sort of laughter that doesn't often happen after childhood and which brings all the intimacy of childhood back with it.

'Oh stop it, stop it,' Rosamund shrieked at last, violently pushing the bedclothes and the tray away from her. Laura pressed the bell and went on pressing it.

'Whatever's happened?' the nurse asked. Rosamund was very pale and her face was wet with sweat and with the tears that were running down her cheeks.

'I'm afraid I'll have to ask you to leave,' the nurse whispered to Laura, as she took Rosamund's pulse. 'Something seems to have upset her.'

As Laura walked down the corridor, she could hear Rosamund's laughter starting up again.

From the first Philip was both irritated and embarrassed by the situation.

Rosamund was introduced to their friends as Laura's cousin, Laura inventing a whole childhood they had shared, even producing snapshots showing the two of them in sunbonnets. 'She was such a pretty little thing,' she would tell everyone, 'even Cook loved her better than anyone else.'

On Tuesdays and Fridays, the evenings that Philip used to spend with Rosamund, Laura made a point of having to go out somewhere, so giving the lovers a chance to be on their own.

'The position is quite intolerable,' Philip said one evening, as soon as Laura had left them. 'I know she wouldn't be capable of planning this just to spite us, but if she had, she couldn't be succeeding better. We're both on edge. It's quite monstrous.'

'I can't see that. Not at all,' Rosamund said. 'After all, the situation has been more or less like this for nearly five years. Laura and I have often met and been quite civilised to each other. This isn't so very different, is it? Anyway, it's only for a short time, only till I'm well enough to start work again.'

'Oh God, when will that be? I know Anthony's pretty fed-up with having your clients breathing down his neck all this time. When will you be well again? Oh Rosamund, will it ever be as it was before all this happened?'

'I don't know, Philip. Perhaps this is giving us time to take stock. Perhaps we should...'

But Philip suddenly advanced upon her, pulling her into his arms. He kissed her more and more ardently. 'I need you, Rosamund. I need you. This simply won't do.'

'We must get married,' he said then, thoroughly roused and at the same time worrying about his rapid heart-beat and jerky breathing, Rosamund's sudden illness having given him the first intimations of mortality. 'This won't do at all,' he repeated, his hand on his heart, 'I must regularise my life. We must get married. There's no other way, no other option.'

At last, Rosamund managed to heave him away. 'You seem to have forgotten about my operation,' she said crossly, 'and furthermore you seem to have forgotten where we are. Sit up, Philip. I'll stay here until the end of this week, then I'll return to my flat. But while I'm here, I'm Laura's cousin, so don't embarrass me with any more of this wild behaviour. And please don't say another word about us getting married because we both know it isn't feasible. Now I'd like a large whisky, please.'

When Laura returned at eleven o'clock, she was surprised to find that Philip had gone out.

She and Rosamund had a nightcap together and talked.

Rosamund spoke of the time she had been unfaithful to Philip during a holiday in Spain. Laura revealed that she had men friends; one a retired major who took her for lovely meals in country clubs, the other a literary gentleman, the grandson of a famous poet, who took her to lectures and museums and pubs. Both relationships were platonic.

'They restore my self-confidence, I suppose,' she said. 'Anyway, I seem to need them. Both of them.'

'How sad life is,' Rosamund said. 'We all seem to be filling gaps. Aren't there any relationships that are complete? Really complete? I've never found one. What about you? When you and Philip were first married, what was that like?'

'Disastrous. For both of us I think. For the first year or two, he seemed to think I was some sort of faulty engine he could get going if only he tried hard enough and often enough. When he finally gave up, things got much better.'

'He's pretty insensitive. When I met him first, he seemed courteous and considerate. I was sick of men who pounced and he seemed different. When it was too late, I realised that he was only more experienced in his timing.'

'He'd become fairly experienced by the time he met you... oh, I hope you don't mind my saying that.'

'Not at all. I gathered quite soon that I wasn't, by any means, his first girlfriend.'

'No. And some of them were rather frightful. Poor Philip. At least I was never ashamed to be associated with you.'

They smiled at each other again; they had become sad, even sentimental.

It was after one when Philip came home. He was very drunk and they both scolded him.

'This is an impossible bloody situation,' he said to himself when Laura and Rosamund had taken themselves off to bed. 'They don't make up one real woman between them.'

As he worked savagely at his drawing-board, he thought of the time when he had – naturally enough – imagined Rosamund, small and lively, with curly black hair and round green eyes, to be the complete antithesis of his cool and beautiful wife. 'Neither of them,' he told himself gloomily, 'could satisfy even a most moderate lust.'

Some time later, he marched noisily up to his bedroom, casting neither a thought nor look towards mistress's room nor wife's. The next morning, in spite of a vicious hangover, he set off to the office almost an hour earlier than usual.

On the last day of her stay, Rosamund seemed more loath than usual to get up. 'What a beautiful house this is,' she said when Laura arrived with her breakfast tray at eleven o'clock. 'I *have* been happy here. It's so warm and silent and luxurious. I don't at all want to leave.'

'Stay,' Laura said, her voice harsh with sudden excitement. 'I certainly don't want you to go. Why shouldn't you stay here with us, live here with us? There's masses of room. What could be nicer and more natural for us all? Please stay. Please. Philip will get used to it. He'll have to get used to it. After all it was he who brought us together, wasn't it? And we need to be together, don't we?'

Rosamund fell back onto the bed and they looked at each other as though for the first time.

Words, like a host of angels, seemed to be hovering in the air above them, but they only looked at each other and let them go.

After a few moments, Rosamund stretched out her hand to Laura, who snatched it up, lacing the fingers into hers.

THE ROMANTIC POLICEWOMAN
(1931)
Rhys Davies

Policewoman Dobson paced and re-paced a length of the Embankment with a fixed mechanical gait that betrayed how bored she was. Her numb face was vacant with boredom too. Only when a male drunk swerved almost into her a hot and cross look came growling into her pale green eyes.

'Beg your pardon, mate,' said the drunk, touching his hat.

She gave him a curt and warning nod and passed on. If she had been a P.C. she'd have put the fear of God into that sot. Beastly pigs that men were.

No one new about tonight. There was the skinny old woman on her usual seat, her newspaper-swathed feet thrust into a rush bag, her face gently asleep; there was the one who ate orange peel and smoked a clay pipe; and there too the one who always soberly greeted her with 'Good evening, my lady.' No one new to talk to and cross-examine.

A cold wind swirled up the river and tugged at the heavy folds of her serge skirt. A draughty night. She really ought to have put on those woollen underthings, now that winter had arrived and it seemed that she'd have to stay on this beat. It was damp too near the river. Not that she wasn't strong... She might even be called hefty, she thought suddenly and feeling even more cross: she never suffered from anything except a cold in her nose now and again.

One thing that ought to content her was the fact that she was doing good work. Many a girl she had rescued and handed over to the proper hands. Young helpless slips of things that ought never to have left their homes in the country. Some of them were orphans like herself. But she, she had always been able to battle with the world. And always she had wanted to rescue and uplift those of her sisters who had not come through as successfully as she had.

Pausing for a minute under a lamp-standard, she told herself again that she ought to be grateful. She was doing useful, even noble work. Yet... yet it was not quite satisfactory to her, it was not *quite* what she wanted. The Force was so impersonal: rules and regulations were such cold dead things. Having to hand over those young girls to a set of iron rules. She merely had to search for the unfortunate poor little things, a strong firm arm of the law, gripping and carrying them off: then they disappeared from her ken. There was not the *humanity* in it that she had wanted.

Still, she ought to be grateful. She had her own nice bed-sitting room now, and plenty of clothes. Sometimes, if they had a day off together, Policewoman Hood would come to have tea with her and then they'd go down West together to a cinema and, afterwards, supper in the Regent Palace. Different from the days when she had been a housekeeper in the middle of Cornwall and when you looked out of the door there was nothing but miles of wild, wet moors.

Once more she paced the distance between seven lamp-standards. She always made it seven. And sometimes – foolish girl that she was, she smiled to herself – she would not, *could* not indeed, tread on the divisions of the pavement flags, so that her usual long and severe stride became a hesitant and rather crazy toddling. Undignified. She would pull herself together after a while, hitching her belt tighter and looking round suspiciously for any bad characters hanging about.

Sighing, she rested again under the seventh standard, and began to use up the time by planning what she'd do tomorrow, her day off. Policewoman Hood was on duty, so she would be alone. It was beastly being alone for a whole day. Well, she would go down to Wright and Carter's Sale and have a look at the tweeds; she wanted a coat and skirt. And she'd have the coat cut in that simple man-like style that she saw so often nowadays. With a shirt and collar and tie to wear with the suit, she'd be chic. Yes, she would arrange it all tomorrow – it would take up the whole day. Then she'd go to the upper-circle of the Gaiety to see Betty West in *Put Two and Two*, lovely actress that she was.

Her gaze was suddenly arrested by a smallish figure in a buttoned-up raincoat sitting on the far-side steps of the Memorial, facing the river. A girl. Her shoulders were crouched, she looked as though she wanted to hide. Policewoman Dobson, her face alert now, walked across to her. After a moment's examination, during which she had to decide whether to be sharply officious or tactfully enquiring, she said quietly: 'Now, Miss, you can't sleep there, you know.'

A pair of frightened brown eyes stared up at her, and the thin body in the raincoat shivered. Good skin, very little makeup, not more than twenty-one, the better type of working-girl, probably unemployed, looks as though she's run away from home, apparel quite good at one time – Policewoman Dobson registered the girl in a glance. Quite pretty, too, and helpless-looking. Ella Dobson said:

'Haven't you anywhere to go?'

Still the palpitating eyes peered up. Policewoman Dobson added more briskly:

'Come now, I wish to help you.'

'I want to stay here,' said the girl, a little sulkily. She looked away. Her delicate brows quivered.

'Can't you pay for a bed?' demanded the policewoman, but with a promise of gentleness in her voice— 'haven't you any money?' The girl shook her head. A tear darted out of her eye.

'You know, I'm here to look after people like you. To see that no harm comes to you. Now—'

'There are people staying out down there,' half-sobbed the girl, sweeping her trembling hand towards the Embankment.

'They're hardened cases, they choose to sleep out. They can afford a bed, usually. But you're different. Now, there's a home—'

'I'm not going to no home,' said the girl with sudden trembling violence. 'I've got a room to go to if I want to. But I don't want to go there neither. I want to be alone—' Emotion overcame her and she began to sob.

Ella Dobson hesitated, staring at the young girl. Then she said, soothingly, patting the trembling shoulder:

'Now, now, my dear, what is it?'

Bursting with a nervous need to express her violence, the girl sobbed out her story, the policewoman asking cautious questions at intervals. She had come to London six months ago, from Luton, with a young man who, apparently, was a bookmaker, though she had no proof of it. They were going to be married at a registry office. But he had kept putting the ceremony off – and that evening she had heard that he was married already: a girl in a café over the Elephant and Castle way had told her. And he had been cruel to her two or three times, he had even beaten her once, just because she burned a steak.

'The wicked beast,' she finished with fierce emotion.

'Aye,' agreed Ella Dobson austerely, 'a lot of them are that.' She stood looking down warmly at the fragile girl. Poor young thing. And such prowling ruffians about. She suddenly said, 'Look here, I want to help you – not only is it my job but I'd like to help you personally. So I won't do anything official. I shall be off this beat after about another hour. Then you can come to my room, if you like, and have an egg and some nice hot buttered toast and then a sleep.'

The girl's face was confused with distress and fear. 'I can't go back to Luton,' she whimpered.

'You mustn't go back to that man, my dear, either,' Ella Dobson said. 'He'll let you down sooner or later – that type always does. I've known dozens of them.'

'I dunno what I shall do!' cried the girl. 'Life's horrible, that's what it is – horrible.' She rubbed her hand under her nose like a child.

'Cheer up,' said Ella Dobson. 'I'll be your friend. Now, you can't sit there, you'll catch your death in that thin coat. There's a respectable café up the road, open all night. Go there and have a plate of soup.'

'I only had a shilling when I came out, and that's gone now,' the girl whispered.

The policewoman took a shilling from her pocket and pressed it solemnly into the girl's hand.

'Be outside the café in an hour's time and I will meet you.' It would be a test of her honesty and her willingness to accept protection. The policewoman told her where the café was, and the girl, who was calmer now, and grateful, trudged off. An azure tam-o'-shanter was stuck school-girlishly on the side of her soft fair hair.

Ella Dobson watched her cross the road, and her heart was warmed. That was the sort of person she liked helping – sweet tender young things just reaching the danger-point where, if they were not rescued, they'd become coarse and hard. She would do her best for the girl if she showed herself honestly willing to turn over a new leaf. It would be like looking after a daughter, Ella Dobson assured herself – yes, it would be like caring for a pretty and sensitive child of her own.

With a renewed energy she paced again down and up past the seven lamp-standards. Her boredom was gone: she began to plan several kind actions for this young girl, providing the little creature showed a proper interest and willingness to remain respectable – for undoubtedly she was already a fallen girl. A fallen girl... Ella Dobson sighed. It was frightening to think with what ease girls took the first downward step. Why, even she, years ago, had half-listened to an auctioneer down in Torquay who was separated from his wife. But she had always distrusted men. Always.

The hour passed cheerfully – except for a slight throb of fear that the girl would not keep the appointment at the café. But somehow Ella Dobson felt she would be there, and when at last, with a foolishly loud-beating heart, she approached the café entrance and saw the little thing waiting inside the doorway, her face broke into a tender smile, which the girl shrinkingly returned. 'I must get her to lose her fear of me,' thought the policewoman. 'It's my uniform. I'll take it off when we get home and wear my Chinese dressing-gown.'

'There you are!' said Ella Dobson cheerfully.

The girl handed four pennies to her. 'The soup was only eightpence,' she whispered.

Honest as myself, Ella thought. 'What's your name, my dear?' she asked gently.

'Kathleen,' said the girl, after a moment's hesitation. And Ella tactfully decided not to ask for a surname just then.

She decided to afford herself the luxury of a taxi, and within a few minutes they were at home in Bloomsbury, in a tall clean house in a Square. Ella had a pleasant room, large and bright with chintz, and there was a cupboard that served as a larder, and another full of clothes. Kathleen sat stiffly on the edge of a chair, her brown eyes round and very observant, while Ella, after lighting the gas-fire, unbuckled her belt. Dawn was just beginning to break.

'I must get this uniform off,' said Ella, entirely the chatty woman now. 'It's that stiff and heavy, it'll be a relief to get into something soft.'

Kathleen followed every movement, staring at each piece as it was removed – the business-like belt, the ominous whistle and chain, the great tunic and greater skirt, the tall strong boots. But there was no truncheon and no pair of handcuffs visible. Then the girl's eyes became rounder as she saw the delicate rose and pink silk of the policewoman's underthings. Ella, noticing her naive surprise, said with a whimsical smile:

'I do like pretty undies, I can't resist them. The only thing, it's getting so cold on that beat down on the river that I shall have to wear wool soon. I get catarrh so quickly in the winter. There now, that's better.' She had taken from the cupboard a green wrap embroidered with writhing gold dragons and scarlet chrysanthemums. Her big strong head emerged from the garment like an emperor's. She could look very forceful.

'Now for a bit of breakfast,' she said briskly, pulling out a gas-ring. 'Would you like to make the toast, dear, while I see to the eggs and tea?'

Presently, under the shaded light, the breakfast table looked very inviting, bright with good flowered china and a yellow-checked cloth. Kathleen's face began to soften. But her lip trembled now and again, bitterly.

'It's nice to be somewhere clean and cosy again,' she said. 'I thought I was going to have a little flat like this when I came up to London—'

'Why did you stay with that man so long?' Ella demanded with sympathetic indignation. 'Treating a refined young girl like you so coarsely!'

Kathleen looked down into the fire, averting her face. But Ella caught the look of strange, hunted fright that had passed over her eyes.

'He...' the girl whispered, 'he could be very nice sometimes. It was only when the other boys, his rough friends, took him away and he came back to me after drinking with them... then I couldn't manage him.'

Ella declared in a loud decisive voice:

'He'll leave you, he'll leave you in the lurch sooner or later. He'll disappear.' She leant forward and tapped the girl's knee. 'Then, what will you do? Oh, my dear girl, the next step is so easy! The fallen women I've had to deal with – it breaks my heart when I think how easily they've gone down just because their balance has been upset by some man they'd been fond of. Lost women! Two or three years of it, and then what happens to them?' Her voice sank into a dramatic whisper. 'I couldn't tell you all I know. But sometimes I want to pray to God to send down fire and brimstone over this foul city, it would be the only way to make it clean.' She sat back breathing heavily. Then, observing that the shrinking fear had returned to the girl's face, she smiled, encouragingly and affectionately.

'But there!' she continued, peeping into Kathleen's cup— 'more tea, dear? ... There, *you've* got a streak of refinement in you that'll keep you safe. It's what made you run away from your seducer.'

'But what am I to do?' Kathleen cried in a soft wail. Her hands and her voice trembled from the nervous storm that had passed through her.

'That,' said Ella briskly, 'we can leave for the time being, until you're calmer. You must stay here with me for a while. You'll be company for me when I'm off the beat, and the room is large enough for two, surely?' She waved her hand towards the walls.

'The divan is a wide one, as you can see.' She held up a finger banteringly, and with her other hand fumbled in the pocket of her wrap. 'Don't think because I'm a stern policewoman, I don't indulge. But only three a day.' She produced a packet of cigarettes. 'Will you have one? They're Turkish.'

Kathleen's thin brows quivered. 'You are kind to me,' she said, hesitatingly... 'I don't know why you should be so kind to me.'

Ella thrust out her strong hand and laid it with an honest grip on Kathleen's knee.

'It's because,' she said in a ringing voice, 'all my life I've had the interest of my sisters at heart, my sisters that have made little errors, have gone blindly into a path the end of which they cannot foresee. I am devoting myself to an ideal.'

Kathleen's eyes began to palpitate again. 'You won't send Societies after me, will you?' she whispered. 'Societies and Guilds and the like.'

'Not I,' said Ella staunchly. 'I am a policewoman, but I have a soul of my own too. You shall be my private little charge, I shall be your protectress.'

II

And from that day life for Ella Dobson became really worth while living. Day followed day, and still, when she came off the beat, little Kathleen was waiting for her, had not run away. She hadn't misjudged the girl's honesty. Breakfast was always ready, too, and the room kept tidy and cosy. So much better than coming home to an empty cold room. And after breakfast and a chat they would go to bed and sleep until nearly midday. Ella said once, with brisk decisiveness:

'A friend of mine. Policewoman Hood, might take it into her head to call. I shall tell her you are a friend's daughter from

Winchester, to save a lot of bothering explanations. You see, she's the kind that does everything officiously, she's all for rules and regulations, to the letter. She has no imagination – you know the kind. But in case you'd be nervous, I shall do my best to prevent her coming.' She smiled cheerfully at Kathleen. 'Why, dear, how well you're looking already, well and happy.'

Which was not strictly true. Kathleen was slightly fatter, the hollows of her cheeks not so evident, the droop of her thin shoulders not so dejected. But she seemed quite without gaiety or hearty good spirits: she did not talk very much, but sat under Ella's torrents looking evanescent and non-committal. At the warning about Policewoman Hood she betrayed signs of agitation.

'Perhaps I'd best leave you now,' she murmured.

Ella stiffened alertly and demanded, 'Where would you go to?'

'Oh, there's no need to bother about me. I shall find something.' The pretty and quiet oval of her face betrayed nothing of any scheme she may have been forming.

Ella bent her body almost with a click as she sharply sat down beside the girl and grasped her hand.

'I will not hear of it. You'll be ground down by this wicked city. You want a sincere and respectable friend to look after you for at least a year.' What she wanted to say was that she intended kneading vigorously the soft and pliant character of little Kathleen. To raise up a fallen girl – could any intentions be more glorious and honourable?

Was there a flicker of alarm in Kathleen's eyes? But she so constantly dropped her eyelids! Only when conversation was trivial would she look directly into Ella's own eyes – and then not often. Was it shame? Ella told herself it was shame. 'She's ashamed because she's been a wicked girl and fundamentally she's respectable. Her sin weighs on her mind.'

'You never think of that man now, do you, darling?' Ella asked, accusative in a bantering fashion.

Kathleen, after a nervous start, slowly shook her head.

'He has probably,' said the policewoman, 'picked up some Piccadilly tart by now. That kind of man likes a change often.'

'He...' began Kathleen, her delicate brows darkened, 'he seemed to be in love with me.' Her voice died away in a tremor.

Ella broke into a kind of hysterical guffaw that was meant to be an affectionate rejection of such a sentimental idea as Kathleen had just uttered. But the girl suddenly looked very sulky, and for an hour or so she scarcely spoke. That afternoon Ella took her out and bought her a coat in Oxford Street, after which they had tea in the Trocadero, followed by a cinema. Kathleen made mild protests at the expense, but Ella swept them away with grand gestures of dismissal.

And after all, Ella thought as she paced her beat, she was getting a good return for the expense – not that she begrudged a penny of it. To have this girl to look after and bring back into her original sweetness – it gave a meaning and a mission to her life, which had been bleakly empty before. She was a saviour and a good friend. And she *would* succeed. It maddened her to think that such a pretty and fragrant young girl could be so sordidly mishandled and ruined by low-down ruffians of men. Moreover, she was succeeding... A small, mysterious smile jumped across her lips for a moment. And as she passed along the beat her gait became swaggering.

To warn Kathleen, Ella told herself, of the horrors that might befall her should she return to immorality, she took the girl for one or two evening excursions to the haunts of cheap prostitution, including avenues of Hyde Park where horrible drabs plied themselves for a shilling or two – or so Ella said, balefully informative, and adding, 'They only last for a year.'

'Don't some of them,' Kathleen said, 'do well for themselves?' There was a certain amount of knowledge in her cautious voice.

'A select few,' answered Ella sharply, 'that have great personalities and beauty make a few thousand perhaps and marry into the upper classes, but ordinary women like you and I would be more likely to find ourselves up at Marylebone for soliciting.' She occasionally thought it necessary to deliver a hefty blow, in maternal fashion.

Kathleen was an observant and interested spectator on these excursions. In fact, she seemed to take a quiet pleasure in them, and appeared to be quite at home in the squalid coffee-bars and eating-houses to which Ella, in her efforts to frighten, took her. She never shrank from even the lowest of them. But though she gazed and was aware of everything, she vented no opinion, no comment, no criticism. 'Is she really daft?' Ella asked herself once, looking secretly at the pretty face. 'Is she just a doll?' Her determined loyalty made her add in haste, 'She's merely a child, that's all, a child struck dumb by things she doesn't understand.'

That Kathleen had something on her mind, nevertheless, was betrayed by her habit of talking in her sleep – talking in a restless, fretful manner that sometimes ended in sobs. Ella strained to listen but there was little coherence in what was said – all she gained was that Kathleen had gone to have a coffee in a shop in Ely Street and had met Patsy there, and that Fred was the name of the lover, and that when they were in Luton things had been all right.

And as the second week wore on, Ella bloomed with a new vigour, almost a kind of luxuriance. Florid, some would have called it. There was a good healthy flush in her cheeks, a bright roll to her eyes, a deliberate self-confidence in her movements, that told of a mind fully and happily occupied. The habitúes of her beat were often surprised to be treated to a joke from her –

though sometimes it was a piece of kind moralising or a slice of uplifting philosophy; and it was rumoured among them that she had won a sweepstake.

Policewoman Hood never called – somehow Ella manipulated that. And Ella never talked of the official details of her job, or of her colleagues. 'No,' she said once, in reply to a tentatively curious enquiry from Kathleen, 'when I am home with you I want to forget my work and be myself, a plain domestic woman.'

The passivity of the girl delighted her – she spread herself over it with a large good will and an exuberant luxury that seemed very successful. Kathleen never contradicted, was never stubborn or obstinate. She dutifully read the historical romances, written in safe and chivalrous style, on which Ella fed her own taste for fiction. Often, though, she would drop her book or her sewing and stare into the gas-fire with a fixed tense look that took away all the softness of her face and made it seem horrible to the ever-watchful Ella. Horrible and – yes, sinister. Ella presumed that some dark memory of her evil life with her lover came back to her in these moments. She would lean forward, pat the girl's hand, look yearningly into her face, and just whisper gravely, remindingly:

'Kathleen, don't forget I am your friend.'

III

Then, one foggy and unpleasant morning, Ella returned from the beat and found her room desolatingly cold and silent. No Kathleen in a soft wrap kneeling before the fire making toast, no purring warmth in the room, no hesitating voice asking something deliciously trivial. The policewoman stood shuddering in the doorway, her eyes straining into the dark grey room, her head moving round with a slow heavy movement of pain. After a minute or so she frantically switched on the light and darted to the mantelpiece, where a note stood propped against the black china cat. With a slight groan she fell into a chair and read the letter.

Dear Friend,

I am now going to leave you, you have done a lot for me but my place is not here, I belong to somewhere else, which I can't help now. Perhaps someday I will be able to repay you for all you have done and if I can I will send you the money for the coat. We have had some good times together and I shall often think of you, you have taught me a lot, and you must forgive me for making off like this but I could not argue with you face to face.

From your friend,
Kathleen.

No address, no information as to her plans. Ella's first emotion after reading the note was one of intense anger. 'Slut, harlot,' she cried aloud, and beat her fists on her knees in fury. Then she sprang up and looked in drawers and the cupboards – but nothing had been stolen.

She stood in the middle of the cold room, a stark and stiff figure struggling to master the storm that was swiftly gathering in her. Then she fell on the divan, plunged her face into a cushion and broke into weeping. Gaunt silent weeping that sprang over her body in horrible undulations. After a while she rose, lit the fire, and mechanically prepared to make some tea and a bit of breakfast. Her face became set into a hard sullen determination.

Was she going to abandon her high-minded work of rescue because of this little set-back? Not she. She'd find that girl again, if it took her months. The Elephant district, Ely Street, a café where

Kathleen had met a girl called Patsy – ha, clues enough. She knew these districts and the clans that met in their pubs and cafés. Iniquitous places where crime and vice flourished. She'd bet she could land that lover Fred for something or other – he sounded like a rogue. And, as a scheme of detective work formed in her mind, she almost regained her old swaggering confidence. Only, as she looked round the room and felt its silence, and saw the empty chair where Kathleen was wont to sit, and the cold flat width of divan, her upper lip trembled cruelly. She was going to do such things for that girl – educate her, refine her, make her a useful member of society, and she was going to give her a watch when her birthday came, and take her to Paris for a weekend in the Spring – yes, a lot she was going to do. Well, she'd do it yet, she *would*. Up, Ella Dobson! Was she going to allow the forces of evil to snatch back that sweet young girl? No – a thousand times no.

So that very day, after a short troubled sleep, she took a trip to the Elephant. She did her best to alter her appearance as much as possible, painting her face and trying to look wicked – it would be no good searching for information if she looked like a policewoman in civilian clothes. And she did not want the official assistance she could have demanded: she had too much love for Kathleen, she told herself.

After some tribulation she found Ely Street – it was beyond the Elephant district – a low dark street of unsavoury doorways about which shrill-looking women hung in gossiping squalor. Cards advertising bedsitting-rooms to let were stuck in windows. A slim cat-like young man in a tight-waisted overcoat slithered out of one of the houses, tasted the air with an absorbed expression, his tongue licking quickly out of his smiling mouth, and glided with a lithe step up the street: looked like a... but Ella coughed over the thought, walking indignantly past the stale, evil dwellings.

Yes, on the corner at the end of the street was a café – one of those rude smelly bars where massive doughnuts and coconut cakes are piled in the window, under showcards describing beef-tea and mineral-waters. There was also a large plate containing a coil of dolorous-looking sausages with a couple of greenish-pink tomatoes balanced on top. Ella glanced inside and saw the café was empty. In any case, she had to hurry back to Bloomsbury now – her time was up. She'd have to wait until she had her evening off: night would be the time to go and sit in the café.

And the contemplated search kept up her spirits, excited and thrilled her, so that only at odd moments was she conscious of the bitter throb of anguish in her heart. But it was there – and when she became aware of it, she wanted to do some wild damage to the world. The habitúes of the Embankment became alarmed at her harsh manner. Her very feet, striking the pavement, seemed to ring with an implacable anger.

IV

Again she made the sordid journey to Ely Street and at seven p.m. was seated at a table covered with peeling oil-cloth. Her hat was set at as jaunty an angle as she dared: rouge flamed untidily on her cheeks, which burned of themselves in feverish excitement, and her lips and eyes were loudly painted too. A yellowish fur curled round her neck and sprang friskily halfway down her back. She looked like a woman who was determined to go wrong at all costs. Carefully concealing her finnicky nausea as a cup of ochre-tinted coffee and a doughnut were set down before her, a look of piercing archness darted out of her eyes at the bar-keeper, who had brought the dishes.

The only other person in the café was a corpse-like man huddled in a corner.

'I haven't been round these parts for a long time,' said Ella chattily.

'No?' said the bar-keeper stolidly. He had a dull pasty face.

'Perhaps you can help me,' Ella went on, her affected voice becoming mincing with girlishness. 'I am looking for a comfortable bed-sitting-room. Can you recommend any address?'

The bar-keeper scratched his nose. 'Plenty of them round about,' he said, 'up and down the streets. Mrs Weeks, number thirty here, lets 'em.'

He seemed unsuspicious. She went on smilingly:

'I used to know a young couple living round here, but I've lost touch with them. She's a thin girl with a small face. Kathleen and Fred were their names.' With a business-like gesture she dug a knife into the doughnut. 'I don't suppose you know them by any chance?'

He wiped a part of his dirty apron over a puddle of tea on the oil-cloth. 'Kathleen and Fred Collins? – why yes, a young pair that are in here nearly every night now. Just come back she has from somewhere.'

Ella clapped her hands in delight. 'Oh, I shall be glad to see them again. Tell me where they live.'

'Ah, that I don't know,' said the bar-keeper. 'Somewhere hereabouts, but the house I don't know.'

Ella continued hurriedly, 'About what time do they come in here then?'

He began to move wearily away. 'The chap,' he grunted, 'comes in here with a bloke or two after the pubs close and then she comes to fetch him, that's what it is.'

'Have you,' asked Ella sweetly 'some chocolate biscuits? I'll have some, please.' He brought them. She went on brightly, 'And Patsy – do you know Patsy?'

'I *did*,' said the bar-keeper, and looked at her rather sharply now.

'Poor Patsy,' sighed Ella intuitively, 'I'd like to see her again.'

'Then you won't for six months,' he said with asperity. 'She's up at Holloway.'

'What did she do?' asked Ella, horror writ large over her face.

'Lifting, with a gang of 'em,' he said. 'And she owes me a bill too. You a friend of hers? Twelve bob she owes me, for fags and suppers.'

When he had gone away she sat stiff with triumph. A pack of thieves and burglars, pickpockets and ponces – this place shrieked of them. Of course Fred was one of them – Patsy had known about him, and out of a fit of jealousy or spite had told Kathleen. Send him for a stretch and she'd capture Kathleen.

All the evening she loitered about the main street of the district – loitered, indeed, so obviously and peeringly, that once or twice a policeman looked sharply at her painted face. She wanted to have Kathleen alone for a few minutes if possible before she joined her lover – to warn her that Scotland Yard knew all about Fred. Long before ten o'clock she took up a stand in a dark corner opposite the café, a corner whipped by an icy wind that had arisen. But determination and excitement kept her warm. She saw herself as a Knight, a Crusader, a succouring angel carrying a banner: she became exalted and enraptured as she waited amid the thrashing winds. Hers was more than a mission, it was a sacred duty. Ah, if only she had the divine courage and strength to rush upon Kathleen, bundle her into a taxi, and hold her by force in some pleasant spot until the sweet girl was persuaded that a respectable life was best after all! But that she couldn't do. In these days one just had to be crafty.

Ten o'clock striking from the steeple! Ella swayed expectantly on her heels.

Only two people had gone into the café, two men. Perhaps one was Fred. But a few minutes later three men and a girl came along the street. The girl was Kathleen! And she was walking arm in arm with one of the men. 'Damn,' Ella breathed. And Kathleen was tittering and smiling up into the man's face. Ha, they had taken her to drink in pubs, had they – the sots, the hooligans, the criminals! Ella's fury burned up anew.

And it was her fury that stiffened her legs and carried her across the road to march boldly into the café. But she did not lose caution. She entered the café as though it were the Regent Palace and, without looking at anyone, sat at a table by the door. There were only four or five people in the place, at the far end near the stove. Her plan was to beckon to Kathleen and have a quiet conversation with her.

Gazing round with a dignified examination of the café, she saw Kathleen rise from her seat, a startled look on her flushed little face. Ella smiled pleasantly and lifted a finger to call her. But Kathleen seemed unable to move. And now one of the young men at their table was asking something of her, glancing inquisitively at Ella. Ella beckoned more insistently, hurriedly. But she was disturbed and angry to see Kathleen turn to the young man and murmur something to him. He sprang up like a flame, and Ella saw a pair of fiery blue eyes stare at her.

He advanced to her. She saw a good-looking, athletic young man advancing with a tense determined tread that made something in her shiver: his shapely face was taut and menacing, and even his sharp crisp hair seemed to spring with anger. Ella tried to pull herself together. Bah, one of those odiously handsome fellows that girls of a soppy age adore. But a rough, a hooligan, a nasty slummy tough. Ella stared back at him with a certain amount of righteous bravado. She had forgotten the crude, smudgy make-up on her face, that made her look like a blowsy tart.

'So you're the skirt that tried to pinch my girl, are you!' he said softly, having pulled up dangerously near her.

Ella quickly mastered the foolish panic that had risen in her. She scarcely heard what he said. The bar-keeper had come to the table too: she ordered a cup of tea. And to the young man she rapped out:

'I wish to speak to Kathleen for just a few minutes.' She leant her head past his menacing body and made another beckoning call to her.

'You lay off my girl, d'you hear—' he began to bark.

But Kathleen was coming towards them now, hesitatingly. The young man swung round and scowled. Kathleen hung back in uncertainty, gazing with dilated eyes at him. Then he said, oh, so softly! his voice like honey:

'Now, Kath, you leave her to me.'

Ella was shivering again. But again she sharply reminded herself of her sacred mission, her duty to a lost young girl. She called emotionally:

'Kathleen, remember your God, your home, your poor mother: think of your future and what waits for you if you allow this man—'

'Shut your jaw, you mangy old cat,' snapped the young man. 'And let me tell you a thing or two—' But Kathleen had come up to him and placed a restraining hand on his arm. He turned and gazed down into her eyes. They seemed alone together for an eternity. Silent. And Ella could not still the trembling of her knees now. She wanted to avert her face from the intolerable exhibition the lovers made in those few savage moments. Then Kathleen whispered, restrainingly, but fearfully:

'She is my friend.'

Ella started again into vigorous indignation: it was as though she heard a trumpet-call. She cried yearningly to Kathleen:

'Listen now, listen now before it is too late. My dear girl—'

The young man banged his fist down violently on the table, so that the cup of tea that had been placed there jumped.

'God Almighty, I've had enough of this,' he snarled. 'Policewoman or no, I'll let you know what I know—' He lowered his face, alive with a derisive contempt, and began to hiss almost into Ella's mouth words that turned her to stone. Kathleen shrunk back, white and helpless. He finished with an epithet that turned Ella's blood cold with a fear new to her. Then he lifted his shoulders, flashed her a look of warning, and stretched his arm protectively to Kathleen. They left the café.

She sat gazing before her as if stricken. For some moments there prowled in her eyes the terror of the revelation. Her mouth was dry, and mechanically she put out a hand to lift the cup of tea before her, but her strength seemed to give out as she lifted it, and the cup crashed to the table. For a moment or two she stared at the mess in a stupor. Then, feeling the movements of the bar-keeper near, she started into life again, threw back her head, and stood up. Her jaw became set, sternly, her face was impenetrable. Tossing the bar-keeper a coin, she went out.

THE DEAD BEAR
(2021)
Crystal Jeans

Sal is looking through my CD collection. She's on her knees. Her jeans are drooping down and I can see the top of her arse.

Sal is my girlfriend. Real name, Sarah-Ann Lewis. Goes by her initials for the sake of androgyny and because she has a thing for Kerouac.

I think she's wonderful.

She's from the valleys but doesn't have a Welsh accent. She's twenty-one. Sometimes she looks like a boy and sometimes she looks like a girl. She has the odd pretentious outburst – the first night I met her she jumped on a bench in Queen Street and started reciting poetry in an earnest, angsty voice, and I had to tell her to shut up and get down. But secretly she is down-to-earth.

Sal is the singer in a screamy punk band called The Physicists and her voice sounds like smashed glass and screeching brakes. I don't usually like screamy punk, but she has the sexiest scream in the world.

Sal is so punk rock that she pisses herself on stage. She's the real deal.

But the best thing about Sal is she thinks I'm wonderful.

'Pixies or Madonna?' she says.

'Pixies,' I say.

'Madonna,' says Ashley.

Ashley is a childhood friend of Sal's. He is a gentle manchild with a love of badges and alternative British comedy. His head is massive and round and his small-featured face sits in the middle, like the yolk of an egg, proportionally speaking. He has thick eyebrows and a beard and his mouth is a tiny crescent. He looks exactly like the little boy from *Up*, all grown up and gay. Ashley is sometimes called Bear because he is a big hairy man who fancies other big hairy men. Though, more accurately, Ashley is young and therefore a cub.

'Bone Machine' comes on. Sal sits on the bed next to me and kisses me on the temple. It's only been six months and we're loved up. Ashley rolls his eyes. The first time me and Sal slept together Ashley was asleep on a sofa at the other end of the room. Except he wasn't really asleep, and he heard every disgusting slurpy noise.

Sal shakes her empty can in my face. 'I want more drink.'

All the shops are closed – it's gone midnight.

'It's gonna have to be the Jamesons,' I say.

My nan keeps a bottle of Jamesons whiskey in the liquor cabinet downstairs for her brother, Paddy, who looks exactly like Hoggle from *Labyrinth*. Whenever me and Sal run out of drink we sneak downstairs and steal it. Then, the next morning we get some more from the shop and put it back into the cabinet when my nan's not looking. We do this almost every week. Sometimes twice. It's not cheap.

I go downstairs and get the Jamesons and the Canada Dry my nan has with her brandy. When I come back up, Sal is playing the guitar. Ashley is sitting on the floor, cross-legged. He's watching Sal and fiddling with an old cinema ticket, folding it smaller and smaller. He has a sliver of a smile on his moon-face.

I pour drinks for us all. We listen to music and talk. After a while I pass out on the bed.

It's still dark when I wake up. The TV is on silent, its light flickering on the wall and the carpet. The room has an empty feel to it. But it isn't. Sal is sitting in the corner, by the door. She's clutching her knees. Her eyes are huge and intense.

'Sal. What's wrong?'

It takes her a while to realise who I am. 'I dunno. I dunno.' She shakes her head.

'Where's Ashley?'

She shakes her head again. I look around the room. There's his black trainers, big as bread loaves. His house keys, attached to a Count Duckula keyring. His satchel, covered in multicoloured badges. His phone. The empty bottle of whiskey.

'Where is he, Sal?'

Her eyebrows crinkle – she looks like she's been tortured for hours. 'I don't know.'

I slide off the bed and signal for her to move so I can get out the door.

She looks up at me, kohl-smudged eyes staring. 'Just don't look in the attic,' she says.

'What?'

'Just don't. Don't look in the attic.'

'What the fuck, Sal?'

She tightens her hold on her knees and starts rocking like some textbook lunatic.

'What have you done, Sal? What the fuck have you done?'

Keeps on rocking.

There's a small door next to my bed. My room used to be the attic. Then it got turned into a proper room. There's still a bit of old attic left, behind a partition wall. Dusty, insulated, filled with old crap. I don't want to look inside. There might be a dead bear in there. I open the door. A stale, cold draught whispers past.

'I said don't look in there!' shouts Sal.

'Why? What's in there?'

She starts crying. I grab the torch by the door and click it on. I aim it inside, poke my head in. It smells like old damp wood and dust. It smells cold. There's heaps of junk. Binbags full of Christmas decorations. Old stuff of mine – artwork, boxes of X Files comics, serial killer magazines, old clothes. No corpse. I look at Sal crying and feel a mixture of things – pity, love, fear, horror, sadness. Mostly I feel gutted. My girlfriend is possibly unhinged, and not in the fun way I'd grown to love. Maybe she's killed someone tonight. I feel sick.

'Sal. Sal. Look at me.'

Her eyes are so miserable it breaks my heart.

'What have you done with him? You might as well tell me cuz I'm gonna find him anyway.'

'I don't know. I don't remember. I'm *pissed*. I'm sorry, I'm sorry.'

'Move, please. I need to get out. Fucking move!'

It suddenly occurs to me that I'm shouting at a dangerous person. I imagine her jumping at me – lips twisted, eyes screaming – and smashing my head against the wall again and again and again until my brain fluid dribbles out. I take a step back. But all Sal does is crawl away from the door on her knees.

I run down the stairs. The second floor of the house is rented out by Brian, a sixty-year-old Cockney milkman who smokes fifty Richmond Superkings a day and whose death rattle wakes me up some mornings. He's at work now. I check his bathroom and kitchen, the only rooms he keeps unlocked. No Ashley. I go downstairs. The living room is empty, the conservatory too. I go in my nan's bedroom. Her TV is so loud it hurts my ears. She's in bed, asleep, her rumpled face poking out of the top of the blankets like Little Red Riding Hood's nan. Her cat and dog are asleep by her feet. I turn off the TV.

Which leaves the garden and the garage. I find a torch and take it outside, panning the pathetic beam across the grass. Nothing. I light up the corners. Nothing. I head down the path slowly, toward the garage, placing my bare feet down carefully like a blind woman in case I step on glass or shit or slugs. I get to the garage.

This is the last place he could be.

The dead bear.

I push the door open and flip the ancient, grimy light switch. As always there is a delay, and then the garage lights up. It's old and dirty and grey and cobwebs clog the corners and cling to the rotting rafters. It has the same smell as the attic. A vague draught swirls. Junk, tools and gardening equipment line the walls.

Ashley is not here.

What do I do? Ashley is gone but he's left his shoes and his house keys. Ashley is gone and my girlfriend's a fruit loop. Ashley is gone and maybe he's dead.

Or maybe he's dying. Maybe Sal stabbed him. And then she dragged him with her superpsycho strength into the attic, but he crawled out, gasping, out, out, along the bedroom floor, to the door, and Sal didn't notice because she was too busy foaming at the mouth, and now Ashley's dying in some quiet lamp-lit street in the Heath area.

This is ridiculous, I think. Sal is not a killer.

But on the other hand, these things do happen in real life.

People kill each other. People go nuts.

I've only known Sal six months.

I go to the living room, pick up the phone. I dial 999. It rings once, twice, then a click.

'Which service do you require?' A man's voice.

'I don't know. Um. The police, I think. But maybe an ambulance too. I don't know.'

A pause.

'Is this an emergency?'

'Uh. I think so. I don't know. It might be a massive emergency. But also it might not be. Sorry.'

'That's OK. Where are you now?'

I give him my address.

'Can you tell me the nature of the incident?'

It spills out fast, and some words bump into other words. I tell him about the mania in Sal's eyes, and the empty house, and Ashley's trainers. '... and, like, why would she say something like that? "Just don't look in the attic." It's fuckin' weird. Excuse my language but she's *done* something to him. I mean, why would you *say* that?—' And suddenly I'm crying into the mouthpiece. High-pitched, whimpery crying. 'I'm sorry,' I wail. 'But I love her!'

I'm gutted. If she is a killer, I'll have to dump her. And it's been going so well.

The man clears his throat. 'Can I just ask if alcohol has been consumed tonight?'

I sniff. Wipe my eyes. 'Yeah. Some.'

'OK. Just had to ask.'

I hear footsteps and the living room door handle starts turning. I quickly slam my body against the door and hold on to the handle. 'It's her! She's trying to get in!'

'Calm down. An officer is on their way over.'

'Crystal, what the fuck are you doing?'

'Go away, Sal!' To the man: 'OK. Hurry up.'

The handle yanks around in my hand. I hold on.

'Crystal! Let me in!'

'If you feel threatened,' says the man, 'then I advise you keep the door closed.'

Sal throws her shoulder at the door. 'Let me in!'

'I'm just gonna hold on,' I say to the man on the phone. 'Thank you.' And I hang up.

Sal is silent for a while, then I hear a dull thump, like she's thunked her forehead against the door. 'Crystal, just let me in.' Her voice is tired.

'I've just called the police. They'll be here soon.'

'What? Why the fuck have you called the police?'

'Because you killed Ashley, you crazy bitch!'

'What are you *talking* about?'

I wedge my foot against the door and stretch toward the liquor cabinet, opening it and taking out my nan's Courvoisier Cognac. I take a gulp. 'Because that thing you said. About the attic.'

'What thing?'

'"Just don't look in the attic." Like some fucking mental... person.'

'Well I don't know why I said that. I was wasted.'

'And suddenly you're sober?'

'No. Just let me in. Please.'

'So what happened with Ashley then?'

Sal sighs. 'I don't know. I don't remember. We were drinking. Ashley got weird. I dunno. Something about ... I dunno. That's all I remember. Something happened but I don't remember. He got weird with me.'

I drink some more brandy. 'Why would you say that thing about the attic? I just don't see why you would say it.'

'I don't know!' She's silent for a while. I drink some more.

'Crystal,' she says. 'I love you.'

I slump against the door. 'I love you too. This is horrible.'

'Let me in,' she says.

And because I'm tired and lovesick, I do. And she looks normal now, if a little rough. We hug and kiss and share my nan's brandy. I call her a nutjob and she nods like it's a sad truth. And now she's here, in person, I think it's ridiculous that I ever thought she killed the bear.

The doorbell rings. It's a police officer, a young blond man with chapped lips. I invite him in. We stand in the hall. I tell him the situation. Sal looks at the floor when I mention the crazy attic talk. 'But he's not in the attic, and I think she was just having some weird black-out moment,' I say. 'From the drink.'

The officer nods like he understands, he understands only too well. 'So where's Ashley now?' he asks.

'He could be anywhere,' says Sal.

'Where does he live?'

'Caerphilly.'

The officer huffs out a laugh. 'I doubt he's walked home then.'

We shake our heads, smiling. How strange it is that we are doing polite smiles, after all that.

'The only thing I can do at this point is drive around the block and the streets nearby. It could be that he's wandering or lost. He's probably sober by now.'

'I'll come with you,' says Sal.

I have a sudden mental image of Sal plunging a pencil into the side of his neck while he shifts gears, a small spurt of blood coming out, his fingers scrabbling at the wound. But that's only because I've seen too many films.

'I'll stay in case he comes back,' I say.

Sal and the officer go out the front door. It is black morning. Quiet – no wind, no traffic. I go upstairs and lie on the bed. And I remember what one of my old bosses used to say:

Nobody does drama like a lesbian.

It's half five when Sal comes home. She's alone. No Ashley, no policeman. For a second I picture a pencil jutting out of a throbbing, fresh-shaved neck, and then it's gone. Sal looks tired – pale, porous skin, multiple lines under her eyes. She's almost sober now. She has a slip of paper and a glossy leaflet about missing persons that the policeman gave to her. We must ring up if we haven't heard from Ashley in twenty-four hours. She lies on the bed next to me and closes her eyes. I make rollies for us. I'm licking the Rizla of the second fag when I hear a dog barking. Jack – my nan's ancient, foul-smelling mongrel.

Maybe he can hear Ashley outside?

Me and Sal run downstairs. Jack is skidding around the tiled floor of the hall on his neglected Velociraptor claws. His hollow barks ring out and echo. He sees us and wags, his head hanging to one side because of the stroke. My nan comes out of the living room, wearing a puffy orange anorak and a grubby, turquoise Naff Naff tracksuit and some court shoes. She has a dog lead in one hand.

'Mornin', she says, walking past us. 'Come on, Jacky.' She goes out the front door and the dog follows, his head flopping around like a bendy saw. It's getting light. Birds are twittering. Me and Sal stand on the step outside and light our fags.

'You didn't believe me,' says Sal. She's looking up at me, bramble-eyed.

'Well, you said that weird thing about the attic. "Don't look in the attic." What was I supposed to think?'

She glares at the smouldering tip of her roll-up. 'You were supposed to trust me.'

'Sal. I've only known you six months and you went all crazy on me. Don't get pissy. You went really *weird*. You weren't *you*. You were like something out of a bad film.'

I cross my arms and frown. But I feel guilty.

Maybe she's right and I'm a terrible girlfriend.

We smoke in silence. And then – trundling up the tree-lined

street is Ashley. His hands are in his pockets. He is wearing white sport socks on his feet.

He reaches us. Stops. Somehow manages to look up at us even though he's much taller. His expression is one of child-like guilt.

'Sorry,' he mumbles.

'Where have you been?' I ask.

'Walking. Round town.'

Sal takes a step and slaps him hard across one cheek and the sound is as harsh as a struck cymbal. Ashley's tiny mouth trembles, his face crumples, and he starts to cry.

Sal walks back in the house and goes upstairs. I follow.

TRANSFORMATIONS

A CUT BELOW
(2012)
Jon Gower

Despite a whirling wind which threatened to throw the rugby posts into the air like chopsticks Keiron Lye put in another performance of a lifetime. Yes, another performance of a lifetime, outstripping even his own abundant excellence, in the face of a mid-Wales monsoon, where the rain and wind hurled buckets of water into the players' faces. They were drenched in a way more profound than any one of the bedraggled supporters could remember. It was wetter even than that fabled trip to Nantyffyllon where Hughie the prop almost drowned in a ruck when his head was forced down into a huge puddle on the halfway line.

Holding his head up as best he could in a wind which wanted to bend his spine into a sickle, Keiron scythed in from the touchline, cutting through the defensive line like heated cheese wire through margarine. There were so many flailing arms reaching for him he felt like a man snorkelling among octopuses. Four very experienced players were made to look like lumbering dolts as he jigged and weaved through the spray. Keiron finally palmed off Resolven's full back, who fell down in an awkward pantomime motion.

There were old men in the crowd who thought they would take their last ever gasp watching Keiron play. He was excitement on legs. Their hearts raced at the mere sight of him. One of them had to clutch his chest cage, so severe was the thrill of one of his tries, catching a grubber kick from one of the centres and making a dummy pass before outflanking three men in a line by running the long way round them, leaving him with a good five clear yards between his touchdown and the nearest trailing opponent. He was a player with southern hemisphere skills: you couldn't laud him with much greater praise. He was good enough to be selected by the All Blacks.

Keiron was the embodiment of rugby skill, powered by huge heart and guts, guided by innate intuition, and blessed with an ability to instantly read a game like a Gareth, Barry or Shane. He easily matched any of the greats and, by now, even this early in his career he almost casually surpassed them. Keiron was wondrous. Keiron was a shift-changer, able to turn from corporeal rugby player to untackleable wraith in a magic breath. An alchemist, too, able to transmute the meatiness of a defence into a wisp of smoke. And he was surely going to be picked for a Welsh cap now that one of their scouts was in the crowd.

Keiron had blazed in Newtown for almost a season but because he didn't play for one of the big sides he was under the radar for a bit, a comet unreported until the local paper started to put him on the front page. Then a BBC reporter churned out a pretty ordinary piece of TV about rising rugby stars, which included some amateur footage of Keiron's coruscatingly good second-half try against Nantyffyllon, which despite the rain-which-should-have-stopped-play was a classic. Other badly framed shots recorded his crunching tackles, including upending a sixteen-stone forward and tossing him into the mud like a doll.

His teammates carried him off the pitch at shoulder height. They enjoyed having him in the team. He made them enjoy the game more, gave them power, bestowed, well, virility; even if he himself was disarmingly effete. He'd slathered on all sorts of poncy unguents: patchouli oil content, jasmine scents and you might catch a glimpse of frilly underwear.

Off the pitch he was disarmingly camp in his manner, as 'camp as a row of pink sequin tents' according to one piercing wag. At the start of his first season some of the grizzly old buzzards who'd been playing for the team for years and years took offence at Keiron's lack of manliness. But he won them over on the pitch. As he ran tiny clumps of grass thrown up from his studs sprayed behind him as if he were sowing seeds of future greatness. He chinked. He wove. He was majestic.

One Saturday he single-handedly racked up eighty-one points during the course of a heatedly violent game, scoring one try that seemed to defy gravity as he floated over a Resolven player and drifted down like dandelion seed to score. Who else could invoke comparisons with dandelion seeds when he drifted in from the touchline? Or similes involving peregrine falcons when he flew in to make the hard yards? Or have staid commentators suggesting that he ran like a man able to outpace his own shadow. One fan gave him a boot with silver studs. Real silver. No kidding.

There's a drunken panoply of post-match rugby club beer, but among them Keiron was as unexpected as monkey fern orchid growing out of the centre spot. Keiron identified perfumes, singling out individual scents he picked out from the olfactory orgy that was the Saturday night crowd, when the players' wives turned up for the disco. He would name them without shame and with unerring accuracy. Daisy by Marc Jacobs. White Jasmine and Mint Cologne by Jo Malone. Cristalle by Chanel. L'Air Du Temps by Nina Ricci. Stuff by Chloe, Madame X, he'd get it every time. Nail it. He could have made a living out of this ability, found a niche on TV somewhere, as he inhaled deeply and identified which celebrity perfume was on a girl's skin. The players watched him, bemused and impressed as he named each woman's perfume in turn. Mariah Carey, a saddo's down-at-heel and frumpy smell; Christina Aguilera, a seductive little number which proved just how far the girl from Staten Island had come since the days when she appeared on TV on the *New Mickey Mouse Club*. Keiron knew the back story as well as the most avid reader of *Hello*.

In the air tonight: Christina and Britney and Jennifer Lopez, Gwen Stefani, Paris Hilton and even Sarah Jessica Parker.

The forwards started betting on him getting one wrong. His fellow backs backed him to the hilt, until there was a pot of over three hundred pounds resting on his naming the perfume Mart the butcher's wife was using. It wasn't one he recognised at first. It was expensively vulgar, more skunk than musk.

'It's that new line from Chanel – Gymnopédies, I think,' laying on a laughable Breton onion seller accent as he said it.

And before he could be probed about the actual name Mart blurted out the word 'Gymnopédies' and by then all were roaring with delight, especially as Watkins, the ageing centre, said that the backs had won fair and square but the winnings were all going behind the bar to be drunk with abandon.

'To salve your weary souls, gentlemen,' he said, lifting a pint pot to a tumultuous cheer.

Keiron sat down with his rugby friends and tried to concentrate on what they were saying in their cups amid the din of disco music. But his mind was far away. He was thinking about his forthcoming sex-change operation. In an opulent Harley Street consulting room an Australian doctor made absolutely sure he was decided on this course before starting his hormone treatment to enlarge his breasts. The doctor had even taken him out for dinner afterwards. All part of the service.

Keiron wanted to tell them, he really did, but he knew that

things would never be the same. They'd probably never want to play the Perfume Challenge with him ever again. And never allow him to disgrace a rugby field. It was one thing to accept his odd ways, it was quite another to play with a girlie.

That year the Six Nations competition started on October 8th with Wales pitched against their deadly rivals, England. It was an old saw that Wales and England still went to war for eighty minutes. Keiron Lye scored a try which earned a place in the pantheon, shrugging off three tackles, outpacing a full back who was renowned for breakneck speed and doing a ceremonial forward roll before grounding the ball. On the Sunday he went quietly into the clinic for a bilateral orchiectomy where he had both testicles removed.

He'd told the coach he wasn't coming for training on Monday, citing personal reasons. His consultant had told him to rest for six weeks but Keiron, headstrong with pain, ran out for a full session on the Tuesday, even though he might have burst all his stitches. He deftly avoided tackles, gritted his teeth and made damn sure the team doctor didn't get within a diagnostic mile of him.

In the changing room he kept his shorts on and said he was going to shower at home, and no one thought twice about it. Other than the coach, who had noticed how he winced more than once when running, and who had also noted that his running style was less graceful. After three more training sessions he felt obliged to ask Lye what was going on. Keiron was disarmingly frank.

'I'm in the process of changing gender. I've been on hormones for eight months now and during the Christmas break I'm due to have a penectomy...'

'Is that...?'

'It is.'

'Jesus H.'

'And that'll be followed by a vaginoplasty...'

The coach counted to six, a calming device.

'What is that exactly?'

The coach blanched when it was explained to him, and this was a man who'd been with the Territorial Army to Helmand province in Afghanistan, worked in a field hospital where unspeakable injuries came in on convoys and Apache medivacs.

'But the good news is I'll still be able to play.'

The coach bit his lip. He wasn't so sure. He did, however, know he was talking to the greatest player in the history of the game, Keiron Lye, who was already set to eclipse all the significant point scorers; Keiron, who never missed a kick, whatever the angle, who almost always scored once he had the ball in hand. There was an unstoppable force about his running, as if a deity had put on togs. As if a man in a chariot with blades on its wheels was facing an opposition of tulips. He made it look that easy.

The two of them decided that they would have to tell the chairman, then the team and then the world.

The W.R.U. was rugby union's equivalent to an in-growing toenail – old, encrusted and irritating. The emergency board meeting was in state of collective catatonia, especially after the physio started to explain some of the procedures that would change Keiron into a full woman.

Chairman Gwilym Morthwyl Prosser, still drowsy from the previous evening's whiskey, managed to bumble to the heart of the matter:

'Is he allowed to play for us, as a woman, that is?' Charles Eminent, Q.C., had a voice desiccated from his time in ancient European libraries, pursuing his passion for medieval bestiaries. The law, for him, was just a means to an end, a way of bankrolling his time among the strange animals that wandered the corners of old vellum manuscripts.

'It's such an unusual situation that there isn't anything in the statutes at any level,' said Mr Eminent, exhausted from so much legal spade work.

'And will he be, well, equipped for the challenges of the modern game?' asked Prosser, looking for a way out. He always felt like a vole in a room full of buzzards. His were antiquated, reactionary views but he felt he represented the fan in the street. Once upon a time he did, but then came electric light, the dawn of flight and the suffragettes.

Gerry Harthill, the physio, reminded the board that women were stronger in many ways than men.

'And he's growing breasts, I understand?' asked Prosser. 'That will be a distraction, if nothing else.'

'I've discussed that aspect of things with both him and the other players...'

'And...' prompted Prosser. 'They say no one fancies him!'

The laughter dissipated the tension in the room. Not that it was strictly true. One of the second row players had caught himself looking at Keiron a bit too often. Something about his eyes, and the softness of his skin.

The press conference was electrifying. Barely had they got to the substance of the event before one of the shabbier papers sent a cohort of reporters, armed with cheque books, to ferret out lovers, winkle out one-night stands of his. But Keiron had been celibate for a long time, and before that he'd had one long-term girlfriend who had become a nun. She lived on a holy island and sent him cards at Christmas and Easter that she decorated herself with dried seaweed. Keiron had a fleshy memory of her wearing a basque and wondered what God made of her then.

At the news editors conference at the British Broadcasting

Corporation they were having conniptions over who should be covering this most delicate phase of Keiron Lye's transformation. Should it be the Health Correspondent or was this a story for the Chief Reporter? With his head in his hands, the editor of Radio Wales News pondered how they were going to deal with things. In a recent phone-in there'd been a strong wave of protest against intruding in the man's private life, and he was finding it hard to explain how any coverage of the sex change was going to be in the public interest. The editor regaled his colleagues with a tale about the war years when the BBC sent out truth to fight the Nazi propaganda machine. One night a stentorian newsreader announced to the People of Free Europe, 'Good evening, this is the British Broadcorping Castration'. How appropriate.

Around him there was a scrum of competing voices. Ian Bridei, the head of the Political Unit was making reference to a poll which suggested that were Keiron to stand for election in his native Newtown he would win with 98% support.

'There's something Messianic about it, there really is. He's more than just a rugby player; he's the fullest expression of people's desires and the oath finder to how to realise them. Even soccer fans love him. Even people who hate rugby and all other sports love him. He's the most quotable sports player in the history of any game, and even though what he's doing flies in the face of the most fundamental machismo at the heart of rugby all the men love him and all the women love him. Should the Iranians launch a missile strike against Israel it would have to take second place on our news agenda to Keiron's tackle, as it were.'

They decided to do a live outside broadcast from the car park of the clinic and started making calls to get permission to park the satellite truck. Keiron's op was happening on the same day as a Welsh game. It had a certain elegance.

Marrying a steady hand with an accomplished eye, the glinting blade of the scalpel cuts through the flesh, the tiny pipette vacuuming away the blood. The surgeon cuts against the grain of the flesh, as if preparing carpaccio from Keiron's muscular brisket. High-class removals, that's what the anaesthetist calls it.

Without their star player, their dependable totem, Wales only scraped a win against an Italian side that had all the power of a Panzer division in their forward line. At half time the LCD display pumped out the message 'Get Well Soon'.

Outside the clinic, the chief reporter studies the unfamiliar lexicon she is going to use for the first of her live broadcasts. There are the unchangeable facts such as the Adam's apple, the one thing Keiron can't change other than shrink it in size, and then there are all the other options such as 'suction-assisted lipoplasty of the waist, rhinoplasty, facial bone reduction, the conventional face-lift, and blephroplasty'. As stories go this one was supremely different, she had to give him that. She mouthed the words again. Ble-phro-plasty. On in five.

Six hours later and the effects of the gas had worn off. Keiron, in his private room, reached between his legs. He was as smooth as a Gilbey's match play rugby ball. There were three weeks to go before the next international and he was determined to play, against medical advice, without insurance if it came to that.

Wales' next game was a clash of juggernauts: Croker Park in Dublin. On that fateful Saturday the Irish were taking no prisoners and were going to take Keiron out. They were sick to the gills of hearing about him on TV and radio. They knew he'd been advised by all the medical staff not to play so soon after the operation but he'd said, with a cocky arrogance, that he'd take just one precaution, namely that he wasn't going to be tackled by anyone. Which was a big ask of anyone, especially as he was a marked man. Man? Huh! The Irish coach had found himself in a vat of hot water when he suggested that Wales was starting with just fourteen men. Keiron was impervious to such bear baiting. In the changing room before the game Keiron asked if anyone had any objections to his putting a hundred points on them.

'I'll need all your help, mind. I'm still a bit delicate after the operation so if you could just block a few tackles when they're coming my way that would be just hunky dory.' His team members surrounded him as a phalanx and said they'd defend him to the death. It was a capacity crowd and they were expecting such a gargantuan TV audience that the engineers in the control room of the National Grid were predicting a huge energy drain at half time as kettles went on across the land. An economist on Radio Wales predicted that the equivalent to eleven million pints of beer would be drunk in pubs, clubs and homes across the land. He also surmised a slump in economic productivity on Monday should Wales win and a worse slump if they lost.

The Royal Welsh Fusiliers band couldn't be heard above the hubbub. All of the television commentary focussed on Keiron and for the BBC coverage they'd taken the unusual step of ascribing two cameras just to him, so they could follow his every move. The crowd had made placards to show their support. 'She's the Best', said one. 'Never Miss a Try', said another.

When the teams took to the pitch there was an unearthly roar.

When Keiron came out, already a little curvy from the hormones, the Welsh fans drummed up ecstasies. During the warm-up many in the crowd scrutinised the images of him on the big screen, curious to see the physical changes and, most importantly, because of a nervousness that 'losing your tackle means losing your tackle' as one newspaper pundit put it.

The Irish side had marked him for as many bone crunchers as they could mete out. It wasn't just his fiery skills they wanted to dampen down but also the buzz of idolatry that was generated around him. If they could break him they could break the team. It was a brave move and an unpopular one. But first they had to catch him. From the opening whistle, when Ireland's kick-off ball landed squarely in the cradling arms of one of the Welsh props there was a confidence about the Welsh team that verged on a swagger. They ran forward with fluency and took risks as if these were the closing moments of the match, not the opening salvos of what settled into a fully fledged physical game at the first set piece. The Irish scrum seemed like an advert for steroids, their legs pedaling like cyclists and the front row pushing forward in an outrageous muscle surge. The Welsh pack wasn't just taken aback but were taken back, losing fifteen yards because of this almighty push. The ball sped out and would have passed deftly all along the back line until Keiron managed to intercept a pass and started a slightly loping run with the crowd baying him on. He had caught the Irish napping. To the delight of the Welsh fans Keiron had enough time to do a little twirl and allow his behind to offer a hint of a waggle before putting Wales' first points on the board. And then, in an expression of excitement lifted from the manual of football hysteria, the Welsh players queued up to kiss him and both the irony and unity of the gesture wasn't lost on the crowd. Fifteen men. Fifteen men.

By halfway through Wales were a scarlet flow of jerseys queuing up to penetrate the Irish defensive line, which held solid until Keiron chipped a ball over their heads, to be picked up with the dexterity of a basketball star by his best friend Martin. He landed on the touchline and threw Keiron a theatrical kiss, which was the moment above all others that showed how totally the team accepted him. They couldn't treat him as a woman yet, but they could show their team mate a good time, even as they took on the reigning world champs. It was like a first date.

The Irish came within a centimetre of replying with a try but had it disallowed by the fourth official. This might have been the thing that stoked up the spleen, this might have been what caused the Irish wing, Andy Shankleton, to stop a charging run by Keiron by bringing his knee up into his groin, which not only crumpled him but caused a rivulet of red to run down one thigh. The crowd was in uproar and the doctors couldn't sprint on fast enough for them, especially as the BBC had by now mixed both of the dedicated cameras, which intrusively showed a man in agony on a stretcher dripping blood. Such was the fury of the crowd that when Shankleton was peremptorily sent off one of the crowd threw a thermos flask at him, which hit him on the head and nobody was that shocked.

On television half time had precious little analysis of the game itself. Everyone wanted to know how Keiron was and the pitch-side commentator went to stand outside the medical room. A minute before the second half resumed the Welsh team came out of the tunnel with Keiron leading in front, where the captain should have been. The play-side reporter tossed a question at him, asking him how he was and he quipped, 'Guess I won't be having children now, Sharon,' which was relayed to a delightedly relieved crowd in the stadium and to millions of viewers who took a huge collective sigh of relief. It was also revealed that Hemmings the captain had voluntarily given Keiron the captain's shirt as he thought that would rack up the pressure on the green shirts even further.

Down to fourteen men the Ireland team struggled to keep the ball and deal with the fact that they were booed at every turn. The gap between them opened to over fifty points and the crowd wanted to pile on the humiliation which was now being doled out because of the heinous act against Keiron. Keiron who, three minutes before the final whistle, ran almost the whole length of the pitch and made a point of making sure that every Irish player was in the tally of those who wanted to catch him, but he ran rings around them all. He ran with joy and humour and when he finally touched the ball down as if it were an egg, and took a careful curtsey just before an Irish player came in late towards him, it was the best moment in the whole history of rugby union. Everyone agreed, apart from the sullen Irish.

That night, when an Aral sea's worth of ale was downed in the city, surgeons were working to contain Keiron's blood loss. There had been a news blackout on how serious things were. By three in the morning, they had managed to staunch the flow but not enough to stop Keiron announcing his retirement from his bedside to a friendly reporter who needed the money such an exclusive could generate.

'I want to quit while I'm ahead,' said Keiron before he fell back into an opiate-determined dream, in which he danced a funny sexy jig in a gold lamé dress on a big glass stage, and the crowd of seventy-eight thousand rugby fans roared at him as he started his slinky, sensual dance to the accompaniment of a Donna Summer clubmix, which blasted out of the stadium P.A., a resounding celebration of his proper gender.

POSTING A LETTER
(2012)
Mihangel Morgan
Translated by the author

When I married the Bard I knew he was no ordinary man. Well, he was a poet wasn't he? He won the Chair in the national Eisteddfod when he was very young. Nevertheless, I had hoped to have quite a conventional married life; raising two or three children and becoming a Nain later on. But the Bard made it clear from the start there would be no children.

'Why?' I asked, a fairly reasonable question, to my mind.

'There is no greater enemy to poetry than nappies drying in the bathroom. Not to mention the cry of the infant in the night. I can't sleep as it is – I haven't slept properly for ten years.'

'But,' I said, 'it's perfectly natural.'

'A Poet's work, Megan, is to rise above nature. That is why a poet was put on earth.'

'But you're famous for your verses about the spring and the birds and the fox,' I said, after all I was young at the time and still felt I could reason with him.

'You do not understand poetry, Megan. When I sing about a fox or a swallow or about ducks it's not about those creatures I'm writing but about other things. The fox is a metaphor. It's similar to algebra.'

'Algebra is those triangular things?'

Yes, I was inexperienced. But I didn't realise that at the time.

That's what naivety is – imagining you know everything when you know nothing. And of course, when we married no one spoke of that sort of thing. No, not algebra, but about married life, of what takes place between husband and wife, or, in my case, what was not taking place. Over the years I learned that the only child I would have was the Bard and that taking care of him would be more work than raising a houseful of children. I came to terms with the fact that the only thing like grandsons and granddaughters I would have were his poems, though I would receive no acknowledgement. After all a poet is a capricious unpredictable creature. The slightest thing makes him pout and extinguishes the Muse. In order for him to produce poems he has to have the same food at the same time every day, he has to have a quiet corner in a special separate room, and woe betide me or anyone else who goes near him, let alone interrupts him when he is in the process of creation.

'I don't like new food,' the Bard once said when I bought a cheese that was not the usual kind by some oversight, 'I don't like anything new. I don't like any change. I don't like people. I'm not a family man. I need silence.'

How many times did I have to turn visitors away? Even his own relations? And they also were Bards, some of them.

He had to have special pencils, and special paper, in order to write his poems. And who was it that had to go to town to buy these unusual things? Me. And there would be ructions if I came back with the wrong things.

Looking after his Muse was as difficult as cosseting some tender, rare plant. The smallest thing could make that plant wither and shrivel. He went on a bardic strike for many years. But I was not the cause of that, fair play, but some disagreement with the college where he worked. They did not consider his poetry to be of equal importance to academic research.

'Philistines!' he said. 'What do they do academic research on? On poetry! Who creates poetry? Poets! Who studies poetry? The researchers!'

As if I were disagreeing with him! I soon learned that my function as wife to a Genius was to agree with him in everything.

But the bardic strike ended, as you know, and he published his second book of poems. He only ever published the two volumes, after all the care and attention and coaxing I devoted to him. Was it worth all the trouble? Well, those that know better than me are of the opinion that some of his poems are immortal masterpieces. But the Bard would have given anything to be immortal in place of his poems in spite of his hope that his work would be remembered. His fear of death overwhelmed him. He worried so much about dying that he couldn't live. That's why the third volume never came and nothing of worth after that second one.

But there's a side to his life that most of you know nothing about. I alone, and a few of the villagers, probably, knew about this. But perhaps there are secret sides to the lives of every poet – indeed, I would say there are secret sides and mysteries in the lives of human beings too. I'm sure I'm correct in saying that.

Anyway, one day I'd been to town to buy the special foods and goods that were essential to this way of life. And for some reason I got back home earlier than expected – possibly the shops had been less busy than usual so that I hadn't had to wait long to be served. I went into the kitchen and there was the Bard sitting, wearing one of my best dresses and earrings, a necklace and a pair of my shoes (he had tiny feet). What did I do? Well, I altered the dress so that it fitted him better.

I knew there was no point ranting and shouting and calling for a divorce; wasn't this yet again part of him, part of his make-up that contributed to his Genius?

Some of you perhaps will find fault with me, because instead of insisting he kept this thing under control, what I did was urge him to experiment with hats, frocks, cosmetics. Since his Muse had to all intents and purposes died (this was after publishing the second book and he was drawing towards the promised age) there was nothing else left to nurture except his new interest – cross-dressing. That is how I looked at it, anyway.

He had a better figure than I did, so I bought clothes for him from a catalogue by post. He liked bright colours. A frock with big roses on it was his favourite; this was in the mid-nineteen fifties, remember. In his female attire he didn't look like a real woman, it has to be said. He was the spitting image of his old aunt, his mother's sister (she didn't look like a real woman either). But it didn't matter to him. The clothes and putting on makeup gave him a tremendous thrill. Only once or twice a week did he Dress Up. And when he did this the Bard no longer existed; he was Laura. I daren't refer to him by his own name; it was Laura who came to tea or called for a bit of gossip, and I was Laura's friend. He spoke in what he considered to be a woman's voice. He moved like a woman, he drank his tea like a woman and sat like a woman, or according to how he believed women did these things. Of course, to me, as a real woman and his wife, he was nothing like a woman at all. But I didn't disillusion him. I never corrected or judged him. It was all a sort of game to him that gave him a special pleasure. Indeed, thanks to Laura, I think those last years were the happiest in his life.

But he had – or rather, Laura had – one wish that weighed upon him, or her, namely to go out for a walk in the world in the form of Laura. The Bard knew and I knew how dangerous that would be. For months, even though Laura alluded to the subject frequently, we did our best to rein in the urge by not pursuing it. If Laura were to raise the question of what to wear when going for a walk I would show frocks in the latest catalogue to her and choose something new to buy. When Laura spoke of her desire to walk down the street like everyone else I would offer her another cup of tea and a piece of cake.

But the Bard was ageing, indeed he was an old man by this time with snow-white hair and his skin like chalk. The end was drawing closer and he knew that better than anyone. The worst thing about this was that his fears were to some extent accelerating the inevitable.

One evening Laura had turned up for supper. This was strange since Laura was a creature of the afternoon as a rule. She was eager to get something new to wear (strange how Laura acquired new clothes more frequently than the Bard's wife) so we went through the catalogues carefully until Laura picked out a custard-yellow coloured frock – it made me feel sick, but there you go, rarely did my taste and that of Laura overlap when it came to clothes – and so we filled in the order form and put that with a cheque in the envelope with a stamp.

'Well then,' said Laura, 'I might as well post this now, don't you think?'

Suddenly I saw his strategy, Laura's strategy. It was a dark winter's night. If she wore my coat and one of Laura's own hats (there were plenty of those by this time) and went out to post the letter, who would notice? I considered the matter for a while. Yes, there was an element of danger, but what was the worst that could happen?

'Go then,' I said, 'go quickly and don't speak to anyone. Post the letter and come straight back.'

And Laura went out to post the letter. I sat in the kitchen waiting for her return, on pins. I sighed with relief when I heard the key in the door.

'Everything ok?' I asked nervously.

'Everything ok,' Laura said, 'it's a lovely fine evening. If I were a poet I would write a poem about it.'

'Did you see anyone?' I asked as Laura hung my coat on the peg.

'Yes, one or two.'

'You didn't speak to anyone, did you?'

'Yes of course, I said "Good evening!" There's no need to be impolite, is there?'

BLIND DATE
(1976)
Jane Edwards
Translated by D. Llwyd Morgan

I've borrowed this frock from Gwen; it's a pink one with a mauve velvet ribbon around the waist. Everybody knows it's a choir frock, but it's prettier than the one I've got, though it's much too big and miles too long. I've been standing for hours in the glass, studying myself, turning and twisting the frock all ways to see if I can make it look better. Gwen has warned me not to pin it in or tack the hem. It's that sort of material that shows everything.

'What if we lapped the waist like this over the ribbon,' said Gwen, 'and pretend that it's a blouse and skirt you've got.' But to no avail. 'Don't worry,' said Gwen. 'I'll lend you my high heels. It won't look so long then.'

'I'm not size fours yet,' I said peevishly.

Then we heard Margaret's voice talking with Mam in the kitchen. 'Comb your hair and tell her you won't be two hoots,' said Gwen.

Margaret had on her brand-new frock not yet out of its creases. A yellow one, with butterflies. 'Pretty. New?' I asked.

'From the club,' she answered, 'a big parcel from Littlewoods arrived on the L.M.S. yesterday.'

'Lucky you,' I said, turning to look at Mam.

She was feeding the baby, and struggling to tuck one breast under her clothes before getting the other one out. Her teats were long and red and dripping. I really don't know why she couldn't have gone into the parlour to feed. I'd say *teats* was the ugliest word in the world.

'You've had a bath,' I told Margaret, seeing her nose shining and her blonde hair a cluster of curls on her shoulders. She lives in a council house. About a year ago all the council houses got a bathroom with hot water heated from the fire, and a toilet with a chain outside. We get our bath in the wash-house every other Saturday when Mam puts a fire under the boiler. It's ever so warm there. You can't see farther than the tip of your nose for steam. Dad still holds that there's nothing like a bath in front of a roaring great fire. But Mam says this is more private, and that it's important for us to keep with the times. 'That costs money,' says Dad. He's an old spendthrift. He'd be astounded to know that the bath costs three pounds ten. Mam pays half a crown weekly, by postal order.

'Where did you get that pink lipstick?' I asked Margaret.

'Borrowed some from Helen next door,' she said. 'I'm going to buy some next time I go to Woolworth. Outdoor Girl: only costs tenpence.' I'd be ever so glad if Mam believed in buying a new one instead of that red thing that tastes old like Adam.

'Are you ready now?' Margaret asked. She was looking at her watch as if she was on tenterhooks.

'What's the hurry? Nothing calls,' said Mam.

'Doesn't she know then?' said Margaret when we were out of the entry.

'Gracious me no, or none of my feet would be out. Does your mother know?'

'She never bothers.'

We walk for a while without saying a word. That's the effect talking about mothers has on you.

Margaret said: 'That pink suits your suntan.'

'It's a bit big though.'

Margaret is a tall well-built girl and I'm a small skinny scrag. And when we walk together everyone turns his head to look at us. But because it's Saturday night there aren't so many about. Neli Harriet as usual is in the telephone kiosk. 'Looking for lovers, that's what she's doing,' said Margaret, 'they call it Neli Harriet's bungalow.'

Then Deina Jones Tyddyn toddles out of her house, a stained shawl over her shoulders. She stands stunned-like in our path, thrusts her nose out into our faces. 'And where are you two going on a Saturday night like this, all made up as there never were a pair?'

'Date,' Margaret boasted.

'Points at your age! Home scrubbing floors or learning verses, that's your place. Does your mother know?' she asked me.

'She will now,' said Margaret, stepping out of her way.

'Is that a choir frock you're wearing?' she asked, feeling the stuff with her forefinger and thumb.

'Cheek!' I said to Margaret.

'A real busybody.'

It was beginning to get chilly by now. The sun had gone behind a cloud, and a breeze was blowing a leaf or two across the street.

'Where's that pretty green frock with the long sleeves you had?' said Margaret.

'The one that made a paper noise? Gone too small.' It was Bill who liked that frock. 'I like your frock,' he said one afternoon as we stood by Nelson's Tower looking at the others throwing stones into the river. 'It makes a noise like tissue paper.' His voice was different as if he were hoarse, or as if it were nearly breaking. 'Mam made it,' I said shyly, and left him. We didn't speak to each other for weeks afterwards. And we're still a bit bashful.

'I've got a pen-friend,' said Margaret. She pulled a piece of paper from her pocket. 'Through Radio Luxembourg. Perhaps I'll write to him tomorrow. Terry's his name, Terry Wayne O'Brien. Here's his address.'

'I like your handwriting,' I said.

'From London.'

'So I see. Gee, you've got good handwriting. Much better than mine. Everyone's saying you should have passed scholarship.'

'No one to push me.'

A kick for me, that one.

'Would you like Terry to find you a pen-friend?'

She was saying the name *Terry* as if she'd known him all her life. I honestly didn't like the way she said it.

'I wouldn't dare. Mam would half murder me.'

'Needn't worry. He could put his letter in with Terry's. We wouldn't be any the worse for trying. Perhaps he'd get a student for you.'

A student. Like Mr Harrington, who came to teach us Scripture and biology. Mr Harrington from somewhere far away like Surrey, his hair yellow as gold, his eyes blue and soft. Mr Harrington who was always so kind and tender. Mr Harrington who would duck under the desk every time he heard an aeroplane. Mr Harrington.

Margaret said, 'You're very quiet.'

'I was thinking.'

'Thought so. Perhaps you're nervous.'

'A little.'

'You're shivering.'

'Cold.'

'You should eat more. I get two dinners every day. School dinner and another when Dad gets home.'

That's why she's bonny. I can't stand food. That's why I'm scraggy. 'Perhaps I better nip home and fetch my cardigan.'

'There's no time. The boys won't wait for us. Hey, do you like my scent? It's Evening in Paris.' She lifts her hair so I can sniff behind her ear.

'Mmm... nice. Nain had some of that from Auntie Meri as a Christmas box. A small blue bottle with the Eiffel Tower on it. Nain only uses it for chapel. Two spots on her handkerchief.'

'You're not supposed to put scent on clothes.'

'Leusa says the nuns say that only people who don't wash use scent,' I said, to stop her having the last word every time.

'Huh! They need it. Do you know what I hear?'

'What?'

'That they go to bed in their clothes.'

'Never!'

'Do you know what else I heard? They daren't look at themselves in a glass or in a shop-window, or look at their breasts when they change underwear.'

'I don't either,' I said shyly.

'Well, you should. How will you know one isn't bigger than the other? Or that you haven't got three like that woman in the *News of the World*?'

The *News of the World* is terrible. It's got stories to raise the hair on your head, and keep you awake all night. True stories about women turning into men and men turning into women, and every calamity that could hit you.

I've got goose pimples all over me. My inside is shaking like a jelly. My feet are like ice blocks and my scalp is tight and hard. My nose is red. Red and ugly as usual.

I said, 'What about turning back?'

'Turning back? No fear. Afraid or something?'

It's easy for her to talk. She knows this Frank boy. Been with him before. But not one of us has ever seen Henri, though she seems to think he's a farm-hand.

A farm-hand! My dreams don't include farm-hands. My dreams turn round students. Tall handsome students with long scarves around their necks. Students with piles of books under their arms. Merry, noisy students like those I see from the bus at Bangor. Nice respectable students – ministerials like the ones who come for a walk with us to Llyn Rhos Ddu before evening service. Like Mr Harrington.

'How old is this Henri?' I asked as we neared Fern Hill.

'Same age as Frank, I suppose.'

'How old is Frank?'

'Twenty-one.'

'Twenty-one? Heavens above, that's old.'

'You've moaned enough about schoolboys being too young for you. Don't worry. Everything will be alright as long as you don't let him put his tongue in your mouth.'

'Put his tongue in my mouth? Ugh!'

'It's a boy's place to try, a girl's place to refuse him.'

'Does Frank try?'

'Every boy tries.'

'What did *you* do?'

'Tell him not to.'

'And he listened?' If anyone tried it on me he'd never see the colour of me again.

'Of course he did. Do you know Olwen? Do you know what Olwen did to a boy from Llangefni way last Saturday night?' She looks into the quick of my eyes and smiles. 'She bit off a piece of his tongue.'

'Bit it off?' I can't swallow because there's a lump like a potato in my throat.

'He had to go to hospital for four stitches.'

I feel quite ill, am cold all over from thinking what I'd do should this boy Henri try such nonsense. Henri's a silly name.

An old-fashioned, ugly name. A name to put anybody to shame. How can anybody with a name like that be handsome?

'Why?' I asked coyly. 'Why do boys want to put their tongues in your mouth?'

'To make you sleep, of course.'

'Oh!'

'And while you're asleep they lift up your clothes, pull down your knickers, and give you a baby.'

I feel my legs giving under me. I feel my inside caving in. I was always a one for jibbing it.

'I'm not coming,' I said, looking in the roadside for a comfortable place to sit.

'Don't talk rot. Come on,' said Margaret, taking hold of my cold hand with her warm white hand. It was like a picture of a hand in a catalogue.

'I'm shivering,' I said and showed her my arms. 'Look how cold I am. I'd better go home before I catch pneumonia.'

'You won't, stupid. Henri'll warm you up like a piece of toast. Anyway, it's too late for you to turn back now.'

It's never too late. Never ever ever too late. I can run as if the devil himself was after me.

'I can hear the motor bike coming,' said Margaret. 'It's them, I tell you. Here, straighten your frock.'

It's Frank who owns the motor bike. 'Hello, girls,' he says after slapping the pedal with his heel and raising his goggles to have a look at us. He's trying to smile like a film star.

'Here's my friend,' said Margaret, laughing and winking at me.

'Henri, give Mags your helmet, and then we'll leave you two in peace,' said Frank.

'You needn't go,' I said sheepishly.

But away they went, and before I knew where to turn I was in Henri's arms, my head out of sight in his armpits. And I'd have stayed there all the time, even though his coat was coarse and smelled, like someone's breath in the morning. But in a while he asked, 'What about a kiss?' 'What about a kiss?' he said a second time, and put his thumb under my chin.

He had a red face and red hair and a voice that made you think of manure and pigs and muck-raking and the like.

'You're much too tall for me. I've got a crick in the neck,' I said, fed-up with his wet kisses.

'What about going to lie down in the fern?' he said.

Only lovers with bad intentions lie in the fern. 'We'll sit on the roadside,' I said.

And there we sat for I don't know how long without speaking or looking at each other.

'A motor bike's lovely.' Margaret said after the boys had turned for home. 'Would you like to have a go some time?'

'You were a long time,' I said, close to tears. 'I'd got tired of waiting for you.'

'You've got grass stains on your frock,' she said. 'Grass stains are difficult to get off. Your mother'll be raving when she sees it.'

Mam was in the wash-house carrying hot water from the boiler and was in a lather of sweat.

'Where have you been, girl?' she asked, though she couldn't see anything through the steam.

'Only for a walk,' I said, 'only for a walk.'

ONE JUNE NIGHT: A SKETCH OF AN UNLADYLIKE GIRL
(1883)
Amy Dillwyn

CHAPTER I
A Magpie's Chatter.

It is about half-past nine o'clock on a fine evening in June, and two ladies – one middle-aged, and the other a girl of between fifteen and sixteen – are sitting together in the handsomely-furnished drawing room of a country house. Their mutual relations are those of governess and pupil. The elder lady is engaged in studying the *Queen*, whilst the younger is absorbed in one of Mayne Reid's novels. They do not wear evening dresses; some outdoor garments deposited in a corner of the room show that they have just returned from a walk this beautiful summer's night, and have not thought it worthwhile taking the trouble to go upstairs and perform a fresh toilet before bedtime.

Perfect silence reigns both within and without the house, when suddenly the harsh chatter of a magpie disturbs the prevailing stillness. The girl puts down her book, and listens. The sound is repeated. She rises, and goes to the open window, exclaiming,

'Now I should just like to know whatever that can mean?'

She was speaking to herself, having quite forgotten there was any one else in the room; but this her companion did not know, and naturally supposed the remark to be addressed to her and to demand a reply. What difference a bird's cry could make to any sane human being was quite beyond her comprehension, and she was inclined to be annoyed at being interrupted for such a trivial matter when she was in the very midst of a most graphic description of the last new fashion in mantles. Consequently there was a shade of irritation perceptible in her voice as she answered,

'Mean? Why, what should it mean? There's no meaning for all the silly noises birds are always making, and persons in their senses never try to account for them.'

'Don't they, indeed!' returned the girl, with a smile. 'But anyhow it can't be natural for birds to be kicking up a dust after they've gone to roost. You bet there must be something up to make a magpie chatter like that when it's going on for ten o'clock at night. Hark! There she is at it again.'

'Margery, I must insist on your paying more attention to what I have so often told you about not talking slang,' said the governess. 'You use expressions that are utterly unsuitable for the lips of a young lady; "you bet", in particular, is intolerably vulgar and repulsive to refined ears. But pray what should there be "up", as you inelegantly call it?'

'Ah, that's more than I can say, Miss Stokes,' replied the pupil; 'all I know is that at this hour it's a magpie's normal condition to be asleep, and that if she isn't then there must be some out-of-the-common reason to account for that out-of-the-common fact. What that reason may be I can't tell by intuition; so I'm just going to give a look round and see if anything's wrong to have routed out that bird.' And as she spoke she took up her jacket and hat, and began to put them on.

The idea horrified Miss Stokes to such a degree that she fairly dropped the *Queen*, and started up out of her easy-chair.

'Going out! – at this time of night? Nonsense!' she exclaimed. 'And to do what is a keeper's work, too! It's out of the question. It's quite unheard-of for *any* girl, still more for any *lady*, to go out alone at night in that sort of way just like a boy; and I positively cannot allow anyone in my charge to behave in such an extremely unladylike manner.'

Margery was quite undisturbed by this speech, and smiled pleasantly as she went on buttoning her jacket.

'I'm afraid, though, you'll have to allow it this once, Miss Stokes,' said she tranquilly. 'Really I'm awfully sorry to vex you in the matter, but I don't see how I can possibly help it. Of course I must see to things being right now that Papa and all the rest of us are away, and I'm the only one of the family left at home. If he were here I know he'd be off like a shot to find out what set that old magpie chattering so late; and so, as he's away, I'm bound to go instead of him. And how can it be unladylike, since I do it, and I'm a lady? Don't worry yourself; I'll be back directly.'

With these words she disappeared out of window, leaving Miss Stokes to reflect sadly over the evil fate that had chanced to give her the charge of such a girl as Margery Castlemartin, who was not only willful, but also strong, active, and daring beyond the wont of other girls, who regarded the whole race of governesses with profound, though good-humoured, contempt. Poor Miss Stokes would sometimes be quite in despair at her independent ways of going on, and had more than once thought that she really could stand it no longer, but must give up the situation, well-paid and comfortable as it was.

What was she to do with a headstrong tomboy of a girl who insisted on turning out in this way at night, merely because some stupid bird had woke up and made a noise? No other young lady would ever have dreamt of such behaviour, Miss Stokes was sure; and yet Margery quite took it for granted that she was only doing the most natural thing in the world! That was always her way, though; whatever unheard-of thing she might do, it was sure to be done in the most perfectly matter-of-course fashion, and as if there could be no possible doubt as to its propriety. What a misfortune it was for the girl to be so like a boy, and to care for nothing but running, jumping, riding, and all kinds of rough outdoor amusements! It necessarily made her so terribly unfeminine, hard-natured, and unsympathetic. Unladylike, rough, and wanting in all gentle and refined ideas, hard, and unfeeling – that was Miss Stokes's verdict upon Margery. And Miss Stokes was a person who prided herself much upon her knowledge of the nature of girls, and was convinced that she could not possibly be mistaken in her judgement as to the character of any one with whom she had spent a couple of months; indeed, she considered this infallible insight of hers to be one of her great recommendations as an instructor of youth.

To be unladylike was, in her eyes, a crime of enormous magnitude. This for many reasons but especially because she held a very decided opinion as to the softening, elevating, civilising, and generally beneficial influence which it was the special mission of ladies to exercise over everyone with whom they came in contact; and she deemed it wholly impossible for an unladylike lady to fulfil this mission. Therefore such a girl as Margery, altogether hard and masculine, was obviously failing to carry out one of the greatest objects for which she had been put into the world, and was an individual whose ways of going on were to be deplored by all right-minded well-bred ladies.

For a few minutes after the girl's departure Miss Stokes fidgeted about the room, meditating over these things, and wondering uneasily if it could possibly have been part of her duty to have accompanied Margery on this nocturnal expedition. But it was too late to go now at all events; and before long she found her mind becoming sufficiently calm to allow of her again settling down into her easy-chair, where she was soon once more happily absorbed in the account of new mantles in the *Queen*, from which she had been disturbed by the eccentric behaviour of the unmanageable pupil whose return she was now awaiting.

CHAPTER II
What Made the Magpie Chatter.

In front of the house was a terrace, and round the terrace ran a stone parapet which had a flight of steps descending it on one side. Of these steps, however, Margery did not avail herself, because they would have taken her a few yards aside, and it was her custom always to go by the shortest and most direct route to whatever object she had in view. Therefore she sprang on to the top of the parapet, dropped lightly into the field beyond, and made straight towards the plantation whence the magpie's note of alarm appeared to have issued.

Not for a moment did it occur to her that there was anything odd about her proceeding, and that she was not behaving exactly as anyone else would be certain to do in similar circumstances. The case seemed to her a perfectly simple one. She being the only member of the family who was at home just then must necessarily be the guardian of the place, the person on whom devolved, as a matter of course, the care of Papa's interests during his absence. And as it was obviously injurious to those interests that there should be nocturnal disturbance of the covers and plantations – whether by means of human beings or vermin – therefore it clearly was her duty to sally forth and give a look round the grounds, as Papa himself would do if he were at home.

She reached the plantation to which she was bound without discovering anything to account for the magpie's disturbance, and there stood still and listened for a minute, but heard nothing save the rattle of some poplar leaves clattering against one another in the night breeze, and the whirr and cluck of a distant night-jar out on a mothing expedition. After deliberating whether to get over the fence and enter the plantation, or to skirt round on the outside, she determined upon the latter course, and began walking noiselessly along the hedge, with her ears on the alert for every sound, and her eyes straining into the dim light to try and distinguish objects at a distance. She had proceeded thus for a short distance when, in turning a corner of the fence, she suddenly found herself close to a man kneeling on the ground who was in the act of setting a rabbit wire, and had a couple more wires and a big stick lying beside him.

So quietly had she come that the man did not discover her presence, and continued his occupation. And now, an unexpected difficulty presented itself to her and made her pause. She had always had a great ambition of behaving in a thoroughly correct and business-like manner in all circumstances of life; and as she beheld this man in the act of committing that heinous crime, poaching, it all at once struck her that she did not really quite know what was the proper way of addressing such an offender; it was an experience that had not before come to her. At first, therefore, she did not speak, but stood silently watching him, and endeavouring to recollect how she had heard her father accost trespassers, which would, she thought, be a safe model for her to imitate on the present occasion. Then she said severely,

'Who are you? And what business have you here? Don't you know that these are private grounds?'

Until she spoke the man had no idea that he was not alone, and at the first sound of a voice he sprang to his feet in alarm, ready for instant flight. But, on seeing who the speaker was, he changed his mind. He had never supposed it possible for a girl alone to venture to address a man in this way as boldly as if she had a whole army to support her, and he hardly knew whether to be most angry, astonished, or amused at her audacity.

'Wot's that to you, young 'ooman?' he replied. 'I've as much business 'ere as you 'as – and more too, like enough.'

'No, you have not,' returned Margery with dignity, 'for this land belongs to my father, Sir Glendower Castlemartin. You've no business here at all, as you know very well; and you are still more wrong to be setting wires. What is your name?'

The poacher laughed.

''Ookey Valker, Eskvire, is the address to find me whenever you wants to drop me a line, my dear,' replied he.

His insolent familiarity of manner gave her a shock and made her very indignant. She was still but a child, and her youthful simplicity had fancied that he could not fail to be awed at finding himself detected by one of the rightful owners of the soil whereon he was trespassing. Owners, too, to whom it had belonged from time immemorial – since the Deluge, Margery had no doubt (indeed, there would to her have been nothing absurd in the idea that Shem, Ham, or Japhet, whichever had been her immediate ancestor, had been settled on the estate even before the Flood, and returned to it again as soon as ever he left the Ark). But, instead of being awed, here was this poacher presuming to give a false name, and taking the liberty of calling her 'my dear'! O that she were a man, like Papa, and able to knock the villain down, or shake him, or administer some other immediate personal chastisement for the insult offered her! Her blood boiled at the miserable impotency of her sex, which compelled her to endure such an affront without instant retaliation. For unusually strong though she was as compared with other women, yet she knew that any average man would, of course, be far more than her match in physical force. Therefore it was in vain for her to insist on his giving his real name if he chose not to do it; and, perceiving this, she discreetly let that point alone, and merely answered,

'You'd best be off from here at once, or you'll be taken up.'

'Taken up!' echoed he derisively. 'Lor' a mussy! You wouldn't never go for to do that, my dear, I'm sure. Not if I didn't choose to be took, anyhow!'

His rudeness and disrespect were intensely irritating to Margery, who could by no means understand how a man like this should remain absolutely unimpressed by hereditary dignity and importance of position such as hers.

'You do as I tell you, directly,' said she sternly, 'unless you want to be put in charge of a keeper.'

This reminded the poacher of something he had hitherto forgotten, viz. that there was a possibility of her calling out and summoning assistance. Determined to stop this danger, he raised his bludgeon ready to strike her, and growled out fiercely,

'Just you dare bring a keeper on me, that's all! I'd knock yer down as soon as look at yer; and I'll do it, too, if you makes a noise. I'll soon quiet yer if you goes a hinterfering with me!'

They were standing very near together, so that she was within easy reach of the great stick that was lifted threateningly over her head. And all of a sudden there came upon her a sense of fear, of a longing to start back out of reach of the weapon, and to run away. Never had she experienced such a sensation before in her life, and it gave her as great a shock as though a douche of freezing water had come upon her unexpectedly. At the same moment, however, was also vividly present to her mind the disgrace of cowardice, and the unutterable contempt with which she had always regarded it. The latter feeling counteracted the former. The fear of openly incurring the reproach of being a coward predominated over the terror that had nearly made her one, and she stood her ground as steadily, to all appearance, as though she knew nothing of any sudden, shameful impulse to take flight, and remove herself to a safe distance from the formidable bludgeon that menaced her.

It was at this critical moment that the arrival of a third party completely changed the aspect of affairs.

CHAPTER III
Capture.

The new-comer was a keeper named Tom Beynon. He, like Margery, had been attracted by the magpie's untimely chattering, and had come to investigate the cause. Entering the plantation on the side opposite to that where the poacher and Margery were, the sound of their voices had directed him towards them, and he now jumped over the hedge close by. The sense of relief which she experienced on seeing him seemed to her unbecoming and humiliating. She could not help being glad, and yet at the same time was half angry with herself for being so. But though vaguely surprised why Tom's advent should evoke the contradictory emotions of rejoicing and dissatisfaction of which she was conscious, yet there was no opportunity for indulging in mental analysis to account for them at the present moment. The poacher took to his heels, with Tom after him; and, of course, Margery followed to see what would happen next, so the three went steeplechasing over the country at full speed.

Fence after fence was jumped or scrambled over anyhow in the dim light, and several fields had been crossed without much alteration in the distance by which the two men were separated; when the poacher came to a small open ditch, which he did not notice. Putting his foot into this he fell down, and the sudden check to the speed at which he had been going made him roll over and over, so that he could not regain his feet before Tom had had time to reach and seize him. He made a violent effort to get free, but the keeper was the bigger and stronger man of the two; and the poacher, finding it was useless to resist resigned himself sullenly to his fate.

Margery had kept well up in the chase (though not without considerable detriment to her garments as she forced her way through the hedges), and arrived panting at the spot just as Tom addressed the captive, whom he grasped tight by the arm. 'What's your name,' asked Tom; 'and where do you come from?'

The man made no answer so Tom gave him a rough shake and repeated the question.

'William Williams, then,' answered the poacher sulkily, 'and 'tis Aberwen as I lives at.'

'O, you come from Aberwen do you?' said Margery, who knew something of that village. 'And whereabouts do you live there?'

The man looked curiously at her for a moment, and then replied, with a sudden alteration of voice and manner which now bore no trace of his former insolence or sulkiness. 'Just beyond the Farmer's Arms; and, indeed, lady, I'm a honest man, and never did sitch a thing as this before in my life, and wouldn't 'a done it now but for bad times as drove me to it. A wife and eight young uns to feed, and me out o' luck about getting work, was bad enough to begin with; and when the missis fell sick on top o' that 'twas worser still; and I've bin that put about with the trouble as I didn't know which way to turn. Polly's the eldest, and she'll only be nine come next Christmas; and there's bin no one but me and 'er to do for all the rest; and there's the 'ouse and the childern to see to, and the missis to 'tend as well, for she's bin that bad she can't rise up off her bed to get herself a bit nor a sup nor nothin'. Not able to eat a mossel she've bin for days till to-day, and this morning the fancy took her she could eat a bit of chicking if so be as she should 'ave it. It went to my 'eart not to 'ave it to give 'er when she wanted it, poor thing! but chickings isn't for poor people like we, with no money.

'Then it come to my 'ead as maybe a rabbit would do every bit as well. I know there's many'd sooner 'ave rabbit than chicking any day – just the same nice white meat, and more taste to it too. And so 'twas that as brought me 'ere now, lady, though I'm in a fret and fidget all the time for fear as the missis may be wantin' somethin', with me away and no one there to give it 'er. For Polly 'as to work that 'ard all day that sometimes, when night comes she sleeps like the dead, and there's no such thing as to waken 'er. 'Tis a terrible trouble to me to think as 'ow they may be wantin' me at this very minnit, and to know 'ow 'ard it'll be to them to get on without me. But there! I know as I can't expect for you to let me go free and go right back to them. Only if you did, lady, I'd be more thankful than I can say, and I'd promise faithful as you shouldn't never see me 'ere in this way again. And now you knows every word of the truth, lady; and I 'umbly asks your parding for not tellin' of it to you when fust you spoke to me.'

To this speech Tom Beynon listened with growing impatience. The great variety of excuses and pleas for release which he had heard during his official life as a keeper had made him extremely sceptical as to the truth of such things, and he supposed that this man's story must be as untrue as the rest; but it was not so much on that ground that it aggravated him, as that it was addressed to Margery, who, being young and inexperienced, might perhaps be impressed by it. Supposing she were to order the poacher to be set free, what was he, Tom Beynon, to do? She would, in that case, be interfering, in his opinion, in a matter that was quite out of her proper jurisdiction; but none the less would she be the present representative of his master, and, as such, entitled to

respect and fealty. Even though she was but a child, and herself
subject to a governess, yet he recognised her as, in a way, being
his mistress. There could not be a doubt, to his mind, that all
sporting and poaching concerns should be governed exclusively
by males, and he was certain that she ought on no account to
interfere with those matters; but, at the same time, if she *should*
be so wrong-headed as to do so, he did not quite see how he
could oppose her without appearing to fail in his duty towards
the master, to whom he owed allegiance. Therefore he was
anxious to cut short the appeal to her feelings, which might
perhaps result in placing him in a dilemma.

'Come, you,' said he, beginning to walk away smartly, and still
keeping tight hold of the poacher's arm. 'Your sort do always find
plenty to say for themselves, I know; but we aren't going to stop
here all night listening to your stories.'

Margery had quite forgotten, while the poacher spoke, that
he might perhaps be telling lies; but she was reminded of that
possibility by Tom's short speech – which nevertheless seemed
to her decidedly harsh. However, she made no remark, and set
out with the two men across the field, fully engaged in trying to
make up her mind as to what Papa would think the right thing
to do if he were there.

She knew that Papa hated poaching – so much so, that from
her earliest childhood she had imbibed the idea of its being one
of the greatest of offences, and never, on any account, to be
treated lightly; but she knew also that he was good to people who
were sick and in trouble, and would be sure not to want her to
keep a man away from a sick and helpless wife. But then, what if
the man's story were untrue? She had often heard Papa laugh at
soft, credulous people who believed whatever they were told, and
shrunk intensely from the idea of incurring that ridicule.
However would she look him in the face if she were to be guilty

of such a piece of folly as to let herself be gammoned by the first lie told by a poacher taken in the act of poaching?

Then there was another consideration also. No doubt, as the sole member of the family then at home, she had a right to expect her orders to be obeyed implicitly by all the servants. But in spite of her full belief in her own authority, she yet had some dim notion of the possibility of what was passing through Tom's mind. She could not help feeling that for her to order the release of a poacher on her own sole responsibility would be a very bold step. Though she did not actually believe that Tom would venture to disobey her, still, supposing he *were* to be so presumptuous, might not that act of rebellion be less inexcusable in such a case than it would be under any other circumstances? It was evidently better not to give an order at all, than to give it and have the mortification of seeing it disobeyed. No doubt, disobedience to constituted authorities, as represented in her person, would be a crime of which Papa would have to be informed as soon as he should return home; but in order to insure the offence being visited with due punishment, it was clearly advisable not to issue any commands that he would not be certain to approve of. And would he approve of the release of this poacher?

As she walked along, turning over these considerations in her mind, and gradually arriving at the conclusion that, on the whole, she had better not have the man set free, it suddenly struck her that meanwhile she had given no directions about what was to be done with him at present, and was allowing Tom to do what he liked, without taking any steps to ascertain her pleasure upon the subject. Obviously this was quite *infra dig.*, and on no account to be tolerated; but as at the same time she felt somewhat puzzled to know how the prisoner ought to be disposed of for the night, she condescended to take council with the keeper before issuing her instructions.

'What had we best do with him for to-night, do you think, Tom?' she said, with all the air of one who perfectly believed herself to be sole arbitrator of the poacher's fate.

'Well, 'tis late to go to the poliss-stashun to-night, miss, whatever,' replied Tom; 'I was think to go to the big house. We can lock he up there saff enough till to-morrow.'

'Ah, yes, that'll do very well,' she answered; 'bring him along to the house.'

And having thus, with her own mouth, ordered what was to be done, she felt satisfied that she had duly fulfilled the responsibilities of her position, and kept up proper appearances, by not allowing it to seem as if an underling could venture to act independently when in the presence of one of the members of his employer's family.

CHAPTER IV
Released.

By the time the trio had reached the house, Tom felt pretty easy in his mind again. He, as well as the other people in Sir Glendower's service, was quite aware that Margery was in the habit of promptly putting into execution whatever project she might have formed, and he therefore concluded that if she *had* been foolish enough to have any idea of interfering with the fate of his captive, she would have done so before now. Notwithstanding this confidence of his, however, Tom thought it just as well to try and confirm her in her disbelief in the poacher's story, and took the opportunity of her wishing them good-night to observe that it was 'bound to be lies – every word of it;' to which the only reply she made was an indefinite sort of sound that might mean anything, and left him quite in the dark as to whether she took his view of the matter or not. Then they separated. The prisoner was refreshed with tea and bread-and-cheese, to enable him to support the rigours of captivity, and was then taken to a small strong room, tied up so as to have no chance of escape, and locked in. Tom, as soon as he had seen his charge thus securely disposed of, went off joyfully to the pantry, to be entertained with strong beer, narrate at full length every detail of the adventure, and enjoy that temporary consequence which was the natural result of his having had a bit of a scuffle, from which he had come off triumphant, and having something to tell which there was an audience anxious to hear.

Meanwhile it may very likely be imagined that Margery hurried off to allay Miss Stokes's anxiety about her, and inform her of what had occurred. That, no doubt, was what she ought to have done; but, truth to tell, she had at that moment utterly forgotten all about the governess's existence, and went straight up to her own bedroom without one thought of that lady, who might have sat up long enough in the drawing-room awaiting her pupil's return, if an unwonted sound of voices, opening and shutting of doors, and general stir in the back parts of the house had not given her an idea that something out of the common must be going on, and made her ring to inquire into the cause of the commotion. By the footman who answered the bell she was informed that Miss Margery and Thomas Beynon had caught a poacher, brought him to the house, and locked him up, and that afterwards Miss Margery had gone to her room and rung for her maid. On hearing this, Miss Stokes uplifted her hands in holy horror, and hurried off to find her young charge – being drawn thither by natural curiosity and desire to have a full, true, and particular account of what had happened; and also by a sense of duty and belief that she was bound to lose no time in pointing out the general unseemliness of Margery's behaviour. Miss Stokes felt thoroughly scandalised to think that a pupil of hers should have got mixed up with a poaching row, and was still further aggrieved at the girl's unceremonious departure to bed without having given herself the trouble of making known her return to her anxious governess. 'It all comes of her unladylike tastes and habits,' meditated Miss Stokes as she proceeded upstairs. 'By having to do with keepers and poachers, and suchlike, she has grown utterly hard-hearted and callous to the feelings of other people. I'll speak to her about it, but I'm afraid it's not much use. I doubt whether I shall ever be able to teach her to have the instincts of a lady, or one spark of consideration for other people. She's so unsympathetic and insensible that she never gives a thought to what anyone else may be feeling, and I really often doubt whether she's got any heart at all.'

Not much satisfaction did she get out of Margery, for the girl, who at all times hated any sort of fuss or gushingness, was just then in a particularly uncommunicative mood, and wanted to go to bed. She told very curtly all there was to tell, apologised for not having remembered Miss Stokes was in the house (an unflattering truth which scarcely did much to smooth down the poor lady's ruffled sensibilities), and got rid of both governess and maid as quickly as she could. Having done that, she went to bed.

To be in bed, with her, generally meant the same thing as to be asleep; but on this night slumber seemed resolved not to visit her couch. Somehow or other she could not by any means manage to lie still, but kept tossing and turning from side to side, and going over in her mind the events of the evening.

In the first place – and she blushed with shame at the recollection – her heart had quailed with downright physical terror, and she had actually felt inclined to run away from a danger! It was hateful to have to think such a thing of herself, and she tried to imagine that she had perhaps been mistaken as to her own sensations. But no; they were too recent and vivid for there to be any doubt about what they had been, and her honesty left her no choice but to recognise the unwelcome truth. Must she then believe herself to be that most contemptible of things, a coward? Was it only owing to her never before having been in real and immediate danger that she had not sooner discovered this disgraceful, miserable truth?

And then, as from this her thoughts naturally passed on to the man who had frightened her, and to the account he had given of himself, she began to feel uneasy. What if the story had been true, after all? Tom Beynon thought not; but why should Tom Beynon be likely to know more about it than she did? He wasn't infallible. And supposing the poacher's story to be true, could it possibly be right of her to have allowed him to be kept away from the home where he was so sorely needed?

Visions rose before her of what his cottage would be like, and of what was perhaps at that moment taking place there. She saw a poor, rough, dirty place, with the mistress ill, and no care-taker save little nine-year-old Polly. The child slept heavily, worn out by work and worries beyond her years. The mother lay helpless and parched with thirst, calling feebly for water, trying vainly to rouse the exhausted child, and hoping at every sound that it announced her husband's return. But hour after hour drags wearily on, till the night is past, and yet he has not appeared. And when the new day begins, and still he stays away, what is poor, overworked, little Polly to do? There will be the fire to make and breakfast to prepare (if indeed there be any materials for that meal in the poverty-stricken house), and there will be a sick mother and seven little brothers and sisters to nurse, dress, and take charge. How is it possible for a child of nine to cope with all this work single-handed?

The idea of Polly's difficulties and the sick woman's sufferings haunted Margery's brain with increasing vividness. She could neither forget it nor go to sleep, and at last it oppressed her past endurance. These people's troubles would be all owing to her – all caused by her hard-heartedness in having retained the house-father as her prisoner. Had Papa heard the man's story she was quite sure he would have been touched by it.

It was impossible to lie there any longer, feeling herself such a monster of cruelty as she did; so at last she got up, dressed hastily, and went softly downstairs, carrying a lighted candle. The house was quite quiet, for everyone had gone to bed by that time; and she reached the room where the poacher was confined without meeting any one on the way. The door was bolted and locked on the outside; but as the key had been left in the lock, she had no difficulty about opening the door and going in.

The thought of the woes of his family had been enough to keep her awake; would it have done the same for him?

No. He was fast asleep, half sitting and half lying on a bench against the wall, in an attitude as comfortable as bonds permitted. She went up and laid her hand upon his shoulder. This awoke him, and he stared stupidly at her and all around him, trying to recollect what had happened and where he was.

'Don't make any noise,' she said; 'I've come to send you back to your wife and Polly and the rest of the children; for I'm sure they won't be able to get on without you.'

The man looked intensely puzzled for a moment; but he had recovered his wits and was thoroughly awake by the time she finished speaking, and then the look of bewilderment was replaced momentarily by a queer expression of amusement. This expression, however, she did not notice, having begun to undo his fastenings, and being far too much engrossed in her occupation to attend to his face. So eager was she to set him at liberty at once, and put an end as quickly as possible to the misery that his absence from home might be causing, that her fingers quite trembled with impatience whenever they met with any knot that was tighter than the rest, and harder to undo. At length the last cord was undone, and she led the way silently towards the house-door, whilst he followed her. The door was secured by a bolt, bar, and lock, which she proceeded to open, taking the utmost care, as she did so, to make no noise. An ordinary observer would certainly have deemed this anxiety for secrecy a little strange on the part of one who claimed supreme authority in the place; yet had any one attributed her precautions to the fear of being stopped if overheard, she would have indignantly denied the supposition. Why should she be afraid of any interference? Was she not, for the time being, absolute mistress of the house? And who, therefore, could presume to gainsay whatever she chose to do? In spite of this confidence, however, it is possible that some shadow of doubt as to her own power may have lurked in the recess of her bosom, and influenced her without her knowing it; for certain it is that she took as much care to move quietly as though she had been a thief breaking into the house; and as she might perhaps have been a good deal puzzled to account for this curious fact, it was probably fortunate that there was no one there to cross-question her on the subject.

The fastenings being all undone, she opened the door, and as the man passed through she held out something towards him, saying hurriedly and rather nervously,

'O, by the bye, here are a couple of shillings to buy a chicken for your wife, or anything else she might fancy.' Then, seeing that he drew back, and seemed unwilling to take the money, she feared she had offended him, and added, still more nervously, 'You don't mind my sending her a little present, do you? And please tell her how very sorry I am that you have been kept from her tonight. I do hope she hasn't wanted you while you've been away.'

He was standing in the doorway, with his head turned away, so that the light from the candle in her hand did not fall upon his countenance, and thus she did not see the look of uncertainty and confusion that crossed his face at that moment. His hesitation was soon over, however, and he accepted the money with the words, 'Thank you, lady; you are very good.' But there was an alteration in the way in which he spoke, as though something unexpected had moved him in earnest, and made him ashamed of himself, and his tone had a ring of genuine respect and feeling that it had lacked before.

Having said this, he disappeared into the star-lit darkness, whilst Margery fastened up the door again, and returned to bed to sleep the sleep of the just.

There was a fine to-do next morning when the prisoner was missed. As for Tom Benyon he could hardly contain his wrath within bounds upon hearing what Margery had done; he felt that he had been unjustly defrauded of what was a keeper's natural prey, and bitterly reproached himself for not having 'taken that there potcher straight to th' stachun th' night before, no matter for it's being late. Then he'd a been saff where no woman can get at him.'

Poor Margery! After all this it was certainly hard upon her when subsequent enquiries revealed that no one answering to the poacher's description was to be heard of at Aberwen or elsewhere in the neighbourhood, and she perceived with dismay that the first thing she would have to tell Papa on his return home would be how ill she had filled the place of châtelaine during his absence, and how easily she had suffered herself to be gulled by a lying rogue. Even rough Tom Beynon was capable of appreciating how galling the position must be to her, and could not help being sorry for her, even in spite of his wrath and his conviction that it served her right, and that a mess of some kind or other was always sure to result when women meddled in affairs connected with game.

Miss Stokes, however, was less soft-hearted, and remained absolutely indifferent to the discomfiture that Margery felt so keenly. A girl whose nature was so hard and unladylike was clearly beyond the pale by which sympathies should be limited. It never entered the exemplary Miss Stokes's mind that there was any possibility of Margery's standing in unconscious need of such things as comprehension, sympathy, and consideration; or that there was a likelihood of her being the better for having them, even though she did not herself know it. Miss Stokes would have treated with scorn the suggestion that she had, in this case, thrown away a fair opportunity for exerting that beneficial influence which she considered to be one of the essential attributes of a true lady; whilst her unladylike pupil, having had a chance of the same kind in her dealings with the poacher, had turned it to considerably better account.

Yet it was a suggestion that might not have been so far wrong for all that.

NIGHTGOWN
(1942)
Rhys Davies

She had married Walt after a summer courtship during which they had walked together in a silence like aversion.

Coming of a family of colliers too, the smell of the hulking young man tramping to her when she stepped out of an evening was the sole smell of men. He would have the faintly scowling look which presently she, too, acquired. He half resented having to go about this business, but still his feet impelled him to her street corner and made him wait until, closed-faced and glancing sideways threateningly, she came out of her father's house. They walked wordless on the grit beside the railway track, his mouth open as though in a perpetual yawn. For courting she had always worn a new lilac dress out of a proper draper's shop. This dress was her last fling in that line.

She got married in it, and they took one of the seven-and-six-penny slices of the long blocks of concreted stone whipping round a slope and called it Bryn Hyfryd, that is, Pleasant Hill. Like her father, Walt was a pub collier, not chapel.

The big sons had arrived with unchanged regularity, each of the same heavy poundage. When the sex of the fifth was told her, she turned her face sullenly to the wall and did not look at him for some time. And he was her last. She was to have no companionable daughter after all, to dote on when the men were in the pit. As the sons grew, the house became so obstreperously male that she began to lose nearly all feminine attributes and was apt to wear a man's cap and her sons' shoes, socks, and mufflers to run out to the shop. Her expression became tight as a fist, her jaw jutted out like her men's, and like them she only used her voice when it was necessary, though sometimes she would clang out at them with a criticism they did not understand. They would only scowl the family scowl.

For a while she had turned in her shut-up way to Trevor, her last-born. She wanted him to be small and delicate – she had imagined he was of different mould from his brothers – and she had dim ideas of his putting his hand to something more elegant than a pick in the pits. He grew into the tall, gruff image of his brothers. Yet still, when the time came for him to leave school at fourteen, she had bestirred herself, cornering him and speaking in her sullen way:

'Trevor, you don't want to go to that dirty old pit, do you? Plenty of other things to do. One white face let me have coming home to me now.'

He had set up a hostile bellow at once. 'I'm going to the pit. Dad's going to ask his haulier for me.' He stared at her in fear. 'To the pits I'm going. You let me alone.' He dreaded her hard but seeking approaches; his brothers would poke jeering fun at him, asking him if his napkins were pinned on all right, it was as if they tried to destroy her need of him, snatching him away.

She had even attempted to wring help from her husband: 'Walt, why can't Trevor be something else? What do I want with six men in the pit? One collier's more work in the house than four clean-job men.'

'Give me a shilling, 'ooman,' he said, crossing his red-spotted white muffler, 'and don't talk daft.' And off he went to the Miskin Arms.

So one bitter January morning she had seen her last-born leave the house with her other men, pit trousers on his lengthening legs and a gleaming new jack and food tin under his arm. From that day he had ranged up inextricably with his brothers, sitting down with them at four o'clock to bacon and potatoes, even the same quantity of everything, and never derided by them again. She accepted his loss, as she was bound to do, though her jutting jaw seemed more bony, thrust out like a lonely hand into the world's air.

They were all on the day shift in the pits, and in a way she had good luck, for not one met with any accidents to speak of, they worked regular, and had no fancies to stay at home because of a pain in big toe or ear lobe, like some lazybones. So there ought to have been good money in the house. But there wasn't.

They ate most of it, with the rest for drinking. Bacon was their chief passion, and it must be of the best cut. In the shop, where she was never free of debt, nearly every day she would ask for three pounds of thick rashers when others would ask for one, and if Mr. Griffiths would drop a hint, looking significantly at his thick ledger, saying: 'Three pounds, Mrs. Rees, again?' her reply was always: 'I've got big men to feed.' As if that was sufficient explanation for all debt and she could do nothing about it; there were big, strapping men in the world and they had to be fed.

Except with one neighbour, she made no kind of real contact with anyone outside her home. And not much inside it. Of the middle height and bonily skimped of body, she seemed extinguished by the assembly of big males she had put into the world off her big husband. Peering out surly from under the poke of her man's cap, she never went beyond the main street of the vale, though as a child she had been once to the seaside, in a buff straw hat ringed with daisies.

Gathered in their pit-dirt for the important four o'clock meal, with bath pans and hot foods steaming in the fireplace, the little kitchen was crowded as the Black Hole of Calcutta. None of the sons, not even the eldest, looked like marrying, though sometimes, like a shoving parent bird, she would try to push them out of the nest. One or two of them set up brief associations with girls which never seemed to come properly to anything. They were of the kind that never marry until the entertainments of youth, such as football, whippet-racing, and beer, have palled at last. She would complain to her next-door-up neighbour that she had no room to put down even a thimble.

This neighbour, Mrs. Lewis – the other neighbours set her bristling – was her only friend in the place, though the two never entered each other's house. In low voices they conversed over the back wall, exchanging all the eternal woes of women in words of cold, knowledgeable judgement that God Himself could have learnt from. To Mrs. Lewis's remark that Trevor, her last, going to work in the pits ought to set her on her feet now, she said automatically, but sighing for once: 'I've got big men to feed.' That fact was the core of her world. Trevor's money, even when he began to earn a man's wage, was of no advantage. Still she was in debt in the shop. The six men were profitless; the demands of their insides made them white elephants.

So now, at fifty, still she could not sit down soft for an hour and dream of a day by the seaside with herself in a clean new dress at last and a draper's-shop hat, fresh as a rose.

But often in the morning she skulked to London House, the draper's on the corner of the main road, and stopped for a moment to peer sideways into the window where two wax women, one fair and one dark, stood dressed in all the latest and smiling a pink, healthy smile. Looking beautiful beyond compare, these two ladies were now more living to her than her old dream of a loving daughter. They had no big men to feed and, poised in their eternal shade, smiled leisurely above their furs and silk blouses. It was her treat to see them, as she stood glancing out from under Enoch's thrown-away cap, her toe-sprouting shoes unlaced and her skirt of drab flannel hanging scarecrow. Every other week they wore something new. The days when Mr. Roberts the draper changed their outfits, the sight of the new wonders remained in her eyes until the men arrived home from the pit.

Then one morning she was startled to find the fair wax lady attired in a wonderful white silk nightgown, flowing down over the legs most richly and trimmed with lace at bosom and cuffs. That anyone could wear such luxuriance in bed struck her at first like a blow in the face. Besides, it was a shock to see the grand lady standing there undressed, as you might say, in public. But, staring into the window, she was suddenly thrilled.

She went home feeling this new luxury round her like a sweet, clean silence. Where no men were.

At four o'clock they all clattered in, Walt and her five swart sons, flinging down food tins and jacks. The piled heaps of bacon and potatoes were ready. On the scrubbed table were six large plates, cutlery, mugs, and a loaf, a handful of lumpy salt chucked down in the middle. They ate their meal before washing, in their pit-dirt, and the six black faces, red mouths and white eyes gleaming, could be differentiated only by a mother.

Jaw stuck out, she worked about the table, shifting on to each plate four thick slices of bacon, a stream of sizzling fat, ladles of potatoes and tinned tomatoes. They poked their knives into the heap of salt, scattered it over the plate, and began. Lap of tongue around food was their only noise for a while. She poured the thick black tea out of a battered enamel pot big enough for a palace or a workhouse.

At last a football match was mentioned, and what somebody

said last night in the Miskin taproom about that little whippet. She got the tarts ready, full-sized plates of them, and they slogged at these; the six plates were left naked in a trice. Oddments followed: cheese, cake, and jams. They only stopped eating when she stopped producing.

She said, unexpectedly: 'Shouldn't be surprised if you'd all sit there till doomsday, 'long as I went on bringing food without stoppage.'

'Aye,' said Ivor. 'What about a tin of peaches?'

Yet not one of them, not even her middle-aged husband, had a protuberant belly or any other signs of large eating. Work in the pit kept them sinewy and their sizes as nature intended. Similarly, they could have drunk beer from buckets, like horses, without looking it. Everything three or four times the nice quantities eaten by most people, but no luxuries except that the sons never spread jam thinly on bread like millionaires' sons but in fat dabs, and sometimes they demanded pineapple chunks for breakfast as if they were kings or something. She wondered sometimes that they did not grind up the jam pots, too, in their strong white shiny teeth; but Trevor, the youngest, had the rights to lick the pots, and thrust down his tongue almost to the bottom.

At once, after the meal, the table was shoved back. She dragged in the wooden tub before the fire. The pans were simmering on hobs and fire. Her husband always washed first, taking the clean water. He slung his pit clothes to the corner, belched, and stepped into the tub. He did not seem in a hurry this afternoon. He stood and rubbed up his curls – still black and crisp after fifty years – and bulged the muscle of his black right arm. 'Look there,' he said, 'you pups, if a muscle like that you got at my age, men you can call yourselves.'

Ranged about the kitchen, waiting for their bath turn with

cigarette stuck to red-licked lower lip, the five sons looked variously derisive, secure in their own bone and muscle. But they said nothing; the father had a certain power, lordly in his maturity. He stood there naked, handsome, and well-endowed; he stood musing for a bit, liking the hot water round his feet and calves. But his wife, out and in with towels, shirts, and buckets, had heard his remark. With the impatience that had seemed to writhe about her ever since they had clattered in, she cried:

'What are you standing there for showing off, you big ram! Wash yourself, man, and get away with you.'

He took no notice. One after the other the sons stripped; after the third bath the water was changed, being then thick and heavy as mud. They washed each other's backs, and she scuttled in and out, like a dark, irritated crab this afternoon, her angry voice nipping at them. When Ieuan, the eldest and six foot two, from where he was standing in the tub spat across into a pan of fresh water on the fire, in a sudden fury she snatched up the dirty coal-shovel and gave him a ringing smack on his washed behind. Yet the water was only intended for the dirt-crusted tub. He scowled; she shouted:

'You blackguard, you keep your spit for public-house floors.'

After she had gone into the scullery, Trevor, waiting his turn, grunted:

'What's the matter with the old woman today?' Ieuan stepped out of the tub. The shovel blow might have been the tickle of a feather. But Trevor advised him:

'Better wash your best face again; that shovel's left marks.'

From six o'clock onwards one by one they left the house, all, including Walt, in a navy-blue serge suit, muffler, cap, and yellowish-brown shoes, their faces glistening pale from soap. They strutted away on their long, easy legs to their various entertainments, though with their heads somehow down in a kind of ducking. Their tallness made it a bit awkward for themselves in some of the places down in the pits.

Left alone with the piles of crusted pit clothes, all waiting to be washed or dried of their sweat, she stood taking a cup of tea and nibbling a piece of bread, looking out of the window. Except on Sundays her men seldom saw her take a meal, though even on Sunday she never ate bacon. There was a month or two of summer when she appeared to enjoy a real plate of something, for she liked kidney beans and would eat a whole plateful, standing with her back to the room and looking out of the window towards the distant mountain brows under the sky, as if she was thinking of Heaven. Her fourth son Emlyn said to her once:

'Your Sunday feed lasts you all the week, does it? Or a good guzzle you have when we're in the pit?'

She stood thinking till her head hurt. The day died on the mountain tops. Where was the money coming from, with them everlastingly pushing expensive bacon into their red mouths? The clock ticked.

Suddenly, taking a coin from a secret place and pulling on a cap, she hurried out. A spot burning in her cheeks, she shot into the corner draper's just as he was about to close, and, putting out her jaw, panted to old Roberts:

'What's the price of that silk nightgown on the lady in the window?'

After a glance at the collier's wife in man's cap and skirt rough as an old mat, Roberts said crossly: 'A price you can't afford, so there!' But when she seemed to mean business he told her it was seventy bob and elevenpence and he hoped that the pit manager's wife or the doctor's would fancy it.

She said defiantly: 'You sell it to me. A bob or more a week I'll pay you, and you keep it till I've finished the amount. Take it out of the window now at once and lay it by. Go on now, fetch it out.'

'What's the matter with you!' he shouted testily, as though he was enraged as well as astonished at her wanting a silk nightgown. 'What d'you want it for?'

'Fetch it out,' she threatened, 'or my husband Walt Rees I'll send to you quick.' The family of big, fighting males was well known in the streets. After some more palaver Roberts agreed to accept her instalments and, appeased, she insisted on waiting until he had undraped the wax lady in the window. With a bony, trembling finger she felt the soft white silk for a second and hurried out of the shop.

How she managed to pay for the nightgown in less than a year was a mystery, for she had never a penny to spare, and a silver coin in the house in the middle of the week was rare as a Christian in England. But regularly she shot into the draper's and opened her grey fist to Roberts. Sometimes she demanded to see the nightgown, frightened that he might have sold it for quick money to someone else, though Roberts would shout at her: 'What's the matter with you? Packed up safe it is.'

One day she braved his wrath and asked if she could take it away, promising faithful to keep up the payments. But he exclaimed: 'Be off! Enough tradesmen here been ruined by credit. Buying silk nightgowns indeed! What next?'

She wanted the nightgown in the house; she was fearful it would never be hers in time. Her instinct told her to be swift. So she hastened, robbing still further her own stomach and in tiny lots even trying to rob the men's, though they would scowl and grumble if even the rind was off their bacon. But at last, when March winds blew down off the mountains so that she had to wrap round her scraggy chest the gaunt shawl in which her five lusty babies had been nursed, she paid the last instalment.

Her chin and cheeks blue in excitement, she took the parcel home when the men were in the pit.

Locking the door, she washed her hands, opened the parcel, and sat with the silk delicately in her hands, sitting quiet for half an hour at last, her eyes come out in a gleam from her dark face, brilliant. Then she hid the parcel down under household things in a drawer which the men never used.

A week or two later, when she was asking for the usual three pounds of bacon at the shop, Mr. Griffith said to her, stern: 'What about the old debts, now then? Pity you don't pay up, instead of buying silk nightgowns. Cotton is good enough for my missus to sleep in, and you lolling in silk, and don't pay for all your bacon and other things. Pineapple chunks every day. Hoo!' And he glared.

'Nightgown isn't for my back,' she snapped. 'A wedding present for a relation it is.' But she was a bit winded that the draper had betrayed her secret to his fellow tradesman.

He grumbled: 'Don't know what you do with all you take out of my shop. Bacon every day enough to feed a funeral, and tins of fruit and salmon by the dozen. Eat for fun, do you?'

'I've got big men to feed.' She scowled, as usual.

Yet she seemed less saturnine as she sweated over the fireplace and now never once exclaimed in irritation at some clumsiness of the men. Even when, nearly at Easter, she began to go bad, no complaint came from her, and of course the men did not notice, for still their bacon was always ready and the tarts as many, their bath water hot, and evening shirts ironed.

On Easter Bank Holiday, when she stopped working for a while because the men had gone to whippet races over in Maerdy Valley, she had time to think of her pains. She felt as if the wheels of several coal wagons had gone over her body, though there was no feeling at all in her legs. When the men arrived home at midnight, boozed up, there were hot faggots for them, basting pans savoury full, and their pit clothes were all ready for the morning. She attended on them in a slower fashion, her face closed and her body shorter, because her legs had gone bowed. But they never noticed, jabbering of the whippets.

Mrs. Lewis next door said she ought to stay in bed for a week. She replied that the men had to be fed.

A fortnight later, just before they arrived home from the pit and the kitchen was hot as a furnace, her legs kicked themselves in the air, the full frying-pan in her hand went flying, and when they came in they found her black-faced on the floor with the rashers of bacon all about her. She died in the night as the district nurse was wetting her lips with water. Walt, who was sleeping in a chair downstairs, went up too late to say farewell.

Because the house was upside down as a result, with the men not fed properly, none of them went to work in the morning. At nine o'clock Mrs. Lewis next door, for the first time after thirty years' back-wall friendship with the deceased, stepped momentously into the house. But she had received her instructions weeks ago. After a while she called down from upstairs to the men sitting uneasy in the kitchen: 'Come up; she is ready now.'

They slunk up in procession, six big men, with their heads ducked, disturbed out of the rhythm of their daily life of work, food, and pub. And entering the room for the last view, they stared in surprise.

A stranger lay on the bed ready for her coffin. A splendid, shiny, white silk nightgown flowing down over her feet, with rich lace frilling bosom and hands, she lay like a lady taking a rest, clean and comfortable. So much they stared, it might have been an angel shining there.

But her face jutted stern, bidding no approach to the contented peace she had found.

The father said, cocking his head respectfully: 'There's a fine 'ooman she looks. Better than when I married her!'

'A grand nightshirt,' mumbled Enoch. 'That nurse brought it in her bag?'

'A shroud they call it,' said Emlyn.

'In with the medical benefits it is,' said his father soberly. 'Don't they dock us enough every week from our wages?'

After gazing for a minute longer at the white apparition, lying there so majestically unknown, they filed downstairs. There Mrs. Lewis awaited them. 'Haven't you got no 'ooman relation to come in and look after you?' she demanded.

The father shook his head, scowling in effort to concentrate on a new problem. Big, black-curled, and still vigorous, he sat among his five strapping sons who, like him, smelt of the warm, dark energy of life. He said: 'A new missus I shall have to be looking for. Who is there about, Mrs. Lewis, that is respectable and can cook for us and see to our washings? My boys I got to think about. A nice little widow or something you know of that would marry a steady working chap? A good home is waiting for her by here, though a long day it'll be before I find one that can feed and clean us like the one above; she worked regular as a clock, fair play to her.'

'I don't know as I would recommend any 'ooman,' said Mrs. Lewis with rising colour.

'Pity you're not a widow! Ah well, I must ask the landlady of the Miskin if she knows of one,' he said, concentrated.

THE CONQUEST,
OR A MAIL COMPANION
(1837)
I. H.

The hero of the following sketch, though now too wealthy to incur adventures such as the one I am about to tell, is, in other respects, so unchanged, that our fair Amalekites will readily guess who sat for this portrait, even if they have not previously heard the tale from the original's own lips:

Beneath the starlight, uneclipsed by gas (December, 1818) the Conquest night coach stopped to change horses, at its first stage out of London, in a dull little town, whose name I spare; nor shall I say whither the vehicle was bound; enough that its journey was to last from nine till twelve, three dark and drowsy hours.

'Ve takes up 'tother hinside here,' said coachee, 'come, marm.'

An elderly man led to the steps of this equipage a weeping female, in flimsy, spoilable array. While her luggage was hoisted he placed a large heavy flail basket on the seat, saying, 'Well, Ethelinda, you won't be quite alone. Sir, any attentions you—'

'I'll take every care of the lady!' replied a free voice, as the capped, cloaked, and comfortered personage, who sat with back to the horses, held out a thickly-gloved hand, to help and hasten Ethelinda's entrance. She sobbed 'good by,' and was driven off; but soon, over her tear-wiping kerchief, strove to ascertain whether her fellow passenger was likely to afford her one of those stagified romances of which she had read and dreamt, long and often. Brief, fleeting, 'few and far between,' as were the glimmerings that aided her feminine scrutiny, they, by degrees, informed her that her opposite neighbour was still young, not too tall, with a dark and bright complexion, prominent profile, black curls, and short whiskers, deep set, swarthy eyes, that seemed to light up the obscure, as would those of a dog or cat, yet very steadfast withal.

'As an old traveller,' said, at length, the proprietor of these noticeable orbs, 'I always take this side, because women usually prefer the other; but now with your leave, I'll cross, that my cloak may have the honour of falling at your feet; no matter how we look, on these occasions, so we are but warm enough.'

The interminable, fur-lined folds, so concealed the figure of their wearer, that not even the tip of a boot could be seen. They were now officiously adjusted round the knees of Ethelinda, and a large shawl wrapped over her shoulder, by this *beau galant*.

'Apparently,' he resumed, 'ma'amselle is unused to the road.'

'Quite, Sir, I assure you,' sighed Ethelinda, 'to *public* conveyances. Next to one's own carriage, which can't always be spared, a postchaise is best; but to travel all night by the mail—'

'Our leathern convenience has not even that dignity,' said the stranger, fixing his peculiar eyes upon her; 'yet many gentlewomen now go about alone, by stage; 'tis economical, and avoids fuss.'

'True,' coincided the damsel errant, 'but—really—for a young, a single lady—to be thrown—unprotected—with an unknown—'

'Nay,' laughed her hearer, 'that unknown is bound to protect her. If, during our trip, any intruders arrive to mar the tête á-tête, they shall not obtrude their flatteries on you while I am by, even if so inclined, which 'tis just possible they might not prove.'

Ethelinda felt she knew not how; and called herself '*faint*.'

'What d'ye mean?' asked her new friend, 'on *this* side? Why—hah! You heroines are always unpoetical. Let me drop some *Eau de Cologne* on your handkerchief, the only thing to use and, here, take a cayenne lozenge, my dear!'

'You are very good,' faltered Ethelinda, between love and fear.

'I,' continued the other, 'can't, even at sea, forgive the "inglorious slaves," as Byron calls them—who that could sketch or scribble but *would* be well to gaze, listen, breathe, sing, dance, on deck? I'm a capital sailor, and shipboard always gives me an appetite, even for the homeliest fare!'

'Indeed? Perhaps then—even—' hesitated Ethelinda, half turning towards her panier, but the hardy tar rattled on.

'Now one has nothing to put up with on land in that regard. Inns would lose – what now they have a *right* to expect – our custom, if they did not furnish good refreshments; though they charge highly for the accommodation but persons of *our* caste, my love, could not, of course, be either so stingy, or so vulgar as to burden ourselves with substantial cates, such as nobody can require during the hours usually devoted to rest; one might as well lie with sandwiches and Madeira, cake and Cognac, under one's pillow.' He adjusted his stock, and drew up his collar in spite.

Poor Ethelinda actually feared that awful eye through dunnest night (wicker-work and brown paper) had seen – or that Roman nose smelt – the hoard of cold pork, gingerbread, and 'ardent spirits diluted,' which now she dared not offer to Monsieur, nor taste herself, nor even own.

'Still,' pursued the provoking one, 'that I may not lose your conversation by a doze, I must resort to *ma tabatiere*, if you please. I promise not to smoke.'

He explained the mystic phrase by taking a pinch of snuff from a small silver box, as the lady tittered forth.

'No, pray don't smoke, sir; for though Pa sometimes indulges in a cigar, Ma and I never let him bring it into the drawing-room.'

'Well,' rejoined the incognito, 'tomorrow I shall be in the atmosphere of home, with which tobacco's fumes may blend, and no lady's leave asked.'

'Bless me,' exclaimed Ethelinda (we may guess how sincerely) 'I hoped you were – at least – a married man.'

'Not I, though, perhaps, every man should marry at my age.'

'La! Sir, you make me curious – to know the age when a gentleman ought to take a wife.'

'Oh, if you want to know my years, child, I am nearly six and twenty, which, I presume, is full ten years older than I am at liberty to call *you*, eh? Come, ladies are invariably candid on this subject.' He brushed up his curls maliciously.

'I will be so at any rate, sir; I am just of age, so all I have is at my own disposal.'

'Ha! Then beware of fortune hunters! Talking of hunters, oh that I were exercising my limbs on the back of mine instead of being cramped in here! Do you ride?'

'Donkeys, by the sea-side, sometimes.'

'Ay, at Margate your *very* fine folks quiz that place unjustly. I've had many a capital swim there, and such walks! I'm a desperate peripatetic; are you?'

'Sir, I—' Ethelinda did not know.

'Nay, don't be ashamed! Remember Queen Caroline was a pedestrian, as well as Davie Deans' bairn.'

Whether she *was* that unintelligible something, or which Queen Caroline was meant, the half-frightened, half-affronted maiden could not tell; but, resolving to tax her taxer's generosity, said,

'I should not be ashamed of owning anything that was true to a perfect gentleman like yourself.'

'You are *too* civil,' he laughed, 'I fear I shall disappoint you before we part, or on better acquaintance.'

'Sir,' faintly articulated Ethelinda, but the gentleman, seeing at the inn door where now they stopped a couple of fine spaniels, was whistling to them instead of heeding the lady.

'They remind me of my own dogs,' he cried; 'have you so much as a bit of biscuit with which to coax 'em near us?'

Ethelinda reluctantly produced a slice of pig-impregnated bread from her store, with which the merry wayfarer fed the animals from a manly, yet neither a large nor a coarse hand, decked with many a ring. Again they started, and he now enquired,

'Do you go all the way to—?'

'Not quite. I am about to stay some time with a friend of Pa's. But – you will excuse me – how very well you whistle! I am so fond of music; are not you?'

This was saying anything to blink the question.

'When 'tis music indeed,' replied he of the forage caps, 'I love, though I but imperfectly understand it; yet hate to have my ears bored by Misses who attempt French and Italian songs knowing as little of the sound as the sense, in every way. From the very parlours behind shops issue the discords of these would-be *cantatrice's*. If tradesmen's daughters are to gain their bread by teaching, let them be thoroughly taught first. But tell me – I know most families on this road – is the friend you visit the rich Mrs. D__, the fashionable Lady Y__, that charitable spinster Miss F__, or the *so-called* CLEVER Mrs. M__?'

'So-called!' repeated Ethelinda, unguardedly. 'Is she not clever, then? I heard that she was very severe.'

'Umph! If it be she to whom you go, I am surprised at your asking her character of me,' equivocated the stranger.

'Oh, sir, Papa has long had her husband's acquaintance, but I never yet saw her. Is she not extremely proud, satirical, strict, and—'

'She is a sworn foe to vanity, affectation, and deceit; so she ought to be, as she educates her own children – though, as the eldest of the four is now seven years old, she has just engaged an assistant, who was to have been on her post two days since.'

'Think, *dear* sir!' nearly wept Ethelinda, 'how humiliating must such a situation be to a girl of any appearance and feeling, accustomed to all the comforts of home.'

'May be so, *ma chère*; but this person owns to thirty, is very plain, the daughter of an humble tobacconist, and leaves a home which is anything but comfortable. Waste not your sympathy in judging her feelings by your own. The character her father gave his customers to procure this place, and your account to me of yourself, marks the strongest possible contrast between my fair Ethelinda and Esther Humphries.'

The poor maiden burst into tears, sobbing out,

'Oh, sir, though I couldn't resist the temptation of your politeness to make the most of the first and last such interview that I can ever hope to enjoy, yet, as soon as I found you were a friend of that lady's, I resolved to trust.'

'Or rather, you knew that I must soon learn the fact. Well?'

'Well, sir, Father only calls me Ethelinda, to quiz my liking for novels. Poor man because he saved and spared to give me a boarding-school education, he insists on my accepting this offer, and has vouched that I am fit for it; but, oh sir! It is a sad pilgrimage for me; no friend to read my heart, to rescue me at the precipice's edge; I go a victim to the sacrifice, a bear to the stake – a beast to the slaughterer!'

'Ay, *that's* something *like*,' commented her hearer; 'but don't cry so I'll rescue you; you need not fear – you shall never be a governess!'

'Sir,' ejaculated Miss Humphries – visions of rank and matrimony still floating in her brain – 'how, sir?'

'Quite honourably; you shall find a matron in *my* house, though it lacks one just now; but till *you* become a bride – tell me honestly – is it teaching or service you shrink from? What can you do to merit such a sanction?'

'Any thing – every thing! Make gowns, caps, bonnets, wash lace, dress hair, keep accounts; – who would not rather be a lady's maid than a governess?'

'Very few waning flirts, I should hope – but – hollo! Coachman! Remember where you put me down. Mr. M.'s__ the Nest – you know,' he craned from the window.

'I does, bless your voice,' shouted back the driver.

What! Was this Mr. M. himself? – but no, he had said he was a bachelor. Ethelinda dared not speak; she peered over her companion's shoulder, and listened to his panting breath, as a light flashed across the road. The carriage drew up, its door was opened, the steps fell; a servant, lantern in hand, came from the garden of a *cottage ornée*, followed by a gentleman, leaning on a stick. The gathered-up cloak now betrayed the petticoat of a dark cloth habit, and the supposed hero leaped out, clamouring,

'Dear Frank! The ankle better? How are the youngsters? Bring in Humphries; boxes too, Matthew. Alight, my girl, and make yourself at home!'

So vanished Ethelinda's fairy dream. Her conquest had been achieved by the equestrian Mrs. M., who had gone to town on business for her husband, as he had recently lamed himself in a hunting leap. Though she had no desire to be taken for a man, or her side curls for whiskers, she would not undeceive the blunderers; especially as she suspected, from the *locale* at which the young lady joined her, that this might be the very female whose disposition, for her children's sakes, she thought it her duty to ascertain.

Esther, though no longer lady's maid, yet lives with Mrs. (now Lady) M., her own woman, to Sir Frank's French cook, who yearly imports foreign snuff for his father-in-law, and Paris romances for the too susceptible Ethelinda. She still, though devoted to her mental, exemplary, and kind-hearted mistress, calls horse-riding, and its masculine costume, 'dangerous and unmerciful for fine women.' I am, though not in her sense of the words, inclined to say so too.

WIGS, COSTUMES, MASKS
(1949)
Rhys Davies

Although it was not an evening for loitering, they remained in the vicinity of the florist's window, apparently aimless, occasionally passing a remark to each other, and not particularly noticeable to the street's day-time workers hurrying past hunched in their own warmth, anxious to escape the thinly muffling fog.

Shops closed one by one, window lights switched off, and even the Gipsy Palmist drew down her upper-floor blind; though under a sudden illumination behind a revolving glass door a waiter took off his table-laying apron and smoothed his hair, and from the florist's window massed saffron and tawny chrysanthemums, dark red carnations, a tub of violets, vases of livid orchids still brilliantly shed colour across the black pavement. A first lady of leisure appeared from nowhere, hesitated outside the chemist shop, looked sharply and accurately at the two loitering men, and disappeared.

'They'll be closing in a minute or two, Frank,' remarked the younger-looking man. 'Doesn't look as if he's going in this evening.'

'What's to stop him going in after closing?' Frank said, pulling up his raincoat collar over a scarf.

'He always goes in as a customer. Expect he is a customer... Besides, isn't Simon going to that big charity ball tonight?'

'It doesn't start till ten,' Frank said, sunk stolidly in their mission. 'Stick it, Jimmy boy; expect we'll have to go to the treat later.'

Both had the rather blank but positive-bodied aspect of ex-athletes, all their power once given over to a taut physical development which now ran to mere size. Their strong-jawed faces became bluishly cold as they waited. No one entered the shop across the road. But it was an erratic establishment, and unusual in its trade: a shop in the kingdom of pleasure, though some of the faces in it were of a saturnine and even tragic significance – just inside the door a masked headsman of the guillotine could be seen looking speculatively at a skittish pink Columbine. Light still burned inside.

The street, intersecting a district devoted to the night entertainment of the flesh, began to assume something of its customary raffish atmosphere. Luxuriously purring cars drew up for parking and furred women alighted and disappeared with escorts into the fog. A saxophone, muted by distance, sounded a tuning-up wail. And the girls whose beat lay in the street began to flower like hardy annuals that could be left out safely in the cold. But these were troubled by the presence of the two men.

Perhaps because of the carefully-empty scrutiny they received, they moved at last, crossing the road with a neutral insouciance. The one called Frank turned the handle of the shop door. It opened and they walked in.

A single plain-shaded light burned in the shop's depths, over a desk at which, incongruously authentic in this place, a clerkly-looking woman sat filling entries into a book from slips of paper. Drab and workaday, she did not look up for some seconds. But enough light was thrown into the crowded shop's expanse to disclose that this clerk and the two men were the only persons of their utility period and class present.

Queen Elizabeth sat there on a throne, dressed to receive at least the French Ambassador, her handsome brocades and ropes of pearls perhaps too garish, the pointed face, and even the little hands, too rigidly shrewish. A blackamoor arrayed in scarlet and Prussian blue grinned impudently at the two men while, perched above him, a huge extravagantly-coloured parrot watched them in petrified silence. Everlastingly smiling, a polite Chinaman stood with hands inside the sleeves of a pretty kimono, quite at home with his companion, a high-wigged Western lady in a lilac crinoline, who peeped over her fan at the intruders. But most splendid of all was the Fairy Queen whose butterfly wings had carried her, in her rose-tulip bodice, pale green gossamer skirt and starlit shoes, to a dais for their inspection; charmingly, she wanted also to touch their raincoated shoulders with her silver-blue wand. Withdrawn into the background other presences watched; a Roundhead, a Puritan, a Jack-of-Spades, a monk, a Plantagenet king.

'I like the fairy.' Frank's massive jaw, fit to withstand dangerous blows, moved in a hard murmur.

'Makes you remember Christmas is just round the corner,' Jimmy remarked, looking around pleased.

High under the ceiling, groups of strident faces hung, laughing, weeping, fire-cheeked, pig-spouted, bearded. And, adjusted on stands over a draped table, heads of hair – ringlets of glossy gold, Apollo clustering curls, long generous plaits – testified to the truth that art can always set nature's deficiencies at naught. There were various odours in the shop, of thick dust, stale pomades, insect powder, singed hair and old mouse-traps.

The clerk lifted her pebble glasses. 'What d'you want? It's long past closing time. We close at seven!' She slammed the ledger shut.

'We would like to see Mr. Simon.' Frank's conciliatory tone sounded woodenly untrustworthy.

'He's busy.' She got down from her stool and limped towards them, right hip protruding under her black overall; she peered dartingly, with a natural but unpersonal spite. 'We can't take any more orders for the Ball. Too late. We've had a busy day.'

'We have to see Mr. Simon privately,' insisted the man.

'What about?'

'Tell Mr. Simon we would like to see him for a few minutes.' And the elder of the two disclosed their identity.

She glanced at them sharply, then said: 'Well, it's a pity you couldn't come during business hours.' She bolted the door, went back to the desk and pointedly locked a drawer, and, limping at her customary grudging pace, went up a ponderously curved staircase such as is seen in an old-fashioned draper's shop in a country town. At the top she switched on a light and, coughing, disappeared. The men were left for several minutes.

'You can come up,' she shouted down the staircase.

Over the banister of the first floor a horse's head glanced down amiably at the mounting intruders. The clerk stood scratching her scalp with a pencil. Beyond her in the dimly-lit showroom a prince of some highly decorative court lifted a deprecating hand. But, from inside a little crystal and gilded coach drawn by a painted pony, an over-winsome girl bowed to the visitors. Sitting on an enormous pumpkin, a patched clown did not cease his argument with a tall-hatted witch whose single fang jutted over her lip evilly. Marie Antoinette stopped on her way to a soirée expecting, not surprisingly, to be admired. One disgraced figure was completely shrouded in a grey sheet, only its silver-buckled shoes visible.

'This way,' said the woman; 'and I hope you won't keep him long; I've got to lock up.'

They passed a purple-draped table holding a royal crown and sceptres, too brilliantly jaunty for mortal head and hands, and a

casket pouring a torpid opulence of crusty gold chains, linked
jewels needing vitality, pearl collars, diamond tiaras, ruby girdles
awaiting the blood heat of wearers to spring alive. The men
glanced in automatic interest at the jewels, with a quick attention
soon dismissed. Respectable felt hats in hand now, they followed
the clerk up another staircase. She pointed to a half-open door
marked 'Private' and left them. They walked in.

'Good evening, gentlemen,' said Mr. Simon. 'What can I do
for you?'

He might have asked it – even dressed in this rajah's
scintillating golden tunic and jewelled turban with a pear-drop
opal lying on his forehead – on a hundred thousand occasions.
To celebrities having strict business with his calling, to others
wanting his aid in escaping reality for an evening, perhaps to
legitimately crowned heads seeking incognito. His own regal
courtesy, the formal *grand seigneur* manner, aided his not
unattractive grotesqueness. He was a stumpy tub-bodied man,
with a large greasily flabby face – in which, however, intent eyes
could focus sharply from within pouches of slack dead flesh...

Did those restless eyes look too rigidly at the two callers? For
a moment too long? Were they indifferent enough?

'You'll excuse us calling so late.' The florid one called Frank
still spoke with that doubtful obsequiousness; the younger one
hung uncommunicative behind him, listening with a not-
listening expression.

'Please take a seat. As you see, I am trying on a costume. What
do you think of it? ... Old in this business though I am,
gentlemen, I still find relief in changing my own identity for a
night.'

The large room seemed used both for business and
domesticities. A kettle steamed on a gas-ring, a wooden bowl
on the table contained a substance like gluey porridge: there was

a swivel-glass, a page's wig on a hat-stand, a box of grease-paints, a teapot, masks, chairs heaped with silken garments of carnival hue, another casket spilling over-opulent jewellery. The tight canvas body of a wax-headed figure, male-faced, stood nude and wigless. In a corner a spiral staircase led to the top floor.

'Pretty!' Frank indicated the casket of jewels. 'Fit for a queen.'

Mr. Simon whinnied. '*I*,' he said, with a struttingly mock majesty, 'am wearing nearly all those tonight.'

He was known for his pranks. People expected him to be outrageous. Even in his shop-owner's formal black coat and baggy striped trousers he did not belong to the precise realism of the day and always there was about him a hint of the pantomime kingdom. But squat Simon shaking a head-dress of unclean ostrich feathers at a masquerade, or arrayed as a ferocious oriental despot with a jewelled dagger – his favourite identity – evoked delighted belief among his hordes of friends and customers. They did not like him to exist as a business man – and, indeed, to receive a bill from the improbable creature, king of a waxen nation bewigged by his own talented hands, was unnatural. His commercial affairs were never in healthy condition: the ferocity of the oriental despot was counterbalanced by a royal generosity – particularly to the young, the talented, the 'artistic'.

The visitors sat down on dirty cane-seated chairs, while the rajah readjusted his enormous pearl-entwined turban before the swivel-glass: his slackly hanging cheeks were roguishly pink, a greasy hue. The visitors had not replied to his first enquiry, and he proceeded, with a sociable skittishness as if they were old friends: 'As I am to be a rajah tonight I had thought to inject my skin with a dusky tint, but then I decided a pink and white complexion would be nicely *perverse*... do you agree?' He had a mannerism of exaggerating certain words, his cunning old eyes widening child-like.

'You're an expert, Mr. Simon,' Frank complimented.

The rajah flung a rope of rubies agilely across the turban. 'I must be allowed my *debauchery*,' he whinnied. 'Tell me, gentlemen' – he turned, courteously interested in these authentically solid visitors – 'what are *your* debaucheries? ... Don't tell me you're heavy betting men!' he exclaimed, going shrill. 'Gamblers bore me... don't bore me, *anything* but boredom! ...and I *can't* stand horse-races, though the costumes of the jockeys are charming... Well,' he postured at the glass again, 'I think this will do... I'm only rehearsing,' he explained; 'it's early.'

Frank shifted on his chair and said doggedly: 'We've come looking for facts, Mr. Simon—' but paused again, looking from under his lids.

'Ah... facts!' The rajah seemed to be judiciously savouring the term, while the men seemed to be feeling a way with cautious patience towards further utterance, Jimmy's eyes still observing in that non-observant way of his profession. 'Facts!' continued the rajah, in the silence. 'What are facts?' Pointing to the nude wax-headed figure, to the casket of jewellery, to the raven-black page-boy's wig, he asked: 'Would these be called facts? For me, yes. Reliable facts. The same as a glass eye is more of a fact than a real eye: *it lasts*, gentlemen.'

'Do you know a man called Calvert... Elmer Calvert?' Frank asked suddenly. And, bright with concentrated search, the two pairs of eyes became ranged full on the rajah.

'Calvert... Calvert.' He stood ruminating, a not very clean paw fumbling into the casket of jewellery. Was the meditation moments too long? 'Is he a customer of mine? I have so many!'

'He's been seen going in your shop several times.'

'Then obviously a customer. What did he want?'

'Do you know him, Mr. Simon?'

'Is he on the stage? – the name seems familiar... Or did he want a costume for a dance?'

'Or a disguise?' Jimmy allowed himself this lapse from his impersonal watching; he seemed even to favour a grin.

The rajah waved a hand from which swung a gilt and amethyst girdle. 'All my creations are disguises, gentlemen! Can you blame people for wishing, whatever their sex, to escape themselves for an evening? It's a healthy instinct! ... I,' he declared, 'would entirely welcome a law decreeing that everyone in this country placed himself in my hands for one night out of every fifty... For instance,' and those haggard eyes, so perversely child-like, considered them appreciatively, 'you two gentlemen – I could transform you into magnificently barbaric Royal Guards of Queen Catherine; your faces would become so Russian that your own wives wouldn't recognise you, and just think what *refreshing* escapades that might lead to!'

'You're fond of a joke, Mr. Simon,' remarked Frank, who was unamused. 'But let's get on about this Calvert... Do you know him?'

'A middle-aged chap with a hook nose,' broke in Jimmy, adding surprisingly, 'and a past.'

'*That*,' said the rajah, 'we all have. A past – where would we be without one?' He suddenly drew his short bumptious body up and pounced: 'Are you suggesting that I turned his hook nose into a snub? Impossible! For special occasions I've worked wonderful miracles on the general appearance of people, particularly of society ladies, but you're asking too much of me! No, no!'

'I didn't say anything about a snub nose,' said Jimmy, a trifle aggressive but, on the whole, maintaining his peaceable inscrutability.

'Do you know Calvert?' asked the other, leaning forward and

twiddling his slouch hat. A double telephone bell began to ring distantly, above the spiral staircase and somewhere below.

'The name certainly means something,' the rajah agreed. 'I must consult my books, muddled though they always are... You know I had a fire here in July, gentlemen? I lost all my records and books, and five thousand-worth of stock destroyed... *Where* is that woman?' he grimaced, becoming highly distracted by the ringing. '*Annie*,' he shrieked.

'You've had two or three fires here in your time, haven't you?'

'Keeping an establishment of this kind is *playing* with fire,' declared the rajah, as the ringing ceased.

'I have now forbidden smoking in the basement showroom.' The laden turban tilted dangerously as he bent to lift a bottle of whiskey and two glasses out of a theatrical basket. 'I have a strange dream sometimes; I dream that my teasing models play tricks on me when my back is turned; especially a Huguenot lady – I've now locked her away in a cupboard, though she is one of my masterpieces, almost as good as my Queen Elizabeth. I worked very hard on her, and I don't mind *admitting* that she's got – *yes*, human hair, gentlemen! I bought a quantity in Poland a few years ago; in certain districts there the poor people shear the hair of their dead women and sell it... Help yourselves, gentlemen; it's a bronchial night. You'll excuse me not joining you, I have a poor head for it, and a poorer stomach... an *ulcer*!' He widened his eyes importantly. 'Due to worry, my doctor tells me; taking things too seriously.'

The visitors looked as if they debated within themselves, but Frank, as the telephone began ringing again, stretched his hand to the bottle.

'*Annie*!' shrieked the rajah. 'Where is she? ... I *hate* telephones. They ring and ring here at all hours, especially from the Profession. At their beck and call! ... *Annie*! And I warrant it's only for a stick of grease-paint or a spray of tea-roses... She's gone!' he screamed. 'Excuse me a moment, gentlemen.'

Hissing and spitting, he waddled to the spiral stairs and bulkily began to climb. Even the jewels of the turban and tunic seemed to shoot out ferocity. Disappearing, he took all the room's vitality with him; the air was drained of colour and heat.

The callers, expression still dismissed from their faces, glanced at each other. The ringing ceased but no voice could be heard from upstairs. And the atmosphere of busy premises closed and deserted for the night began to press into the silent room. Frank got up and, glass in hand, examined the autographed photographs and the letters from stage celebrities framed on the walls.

'Queer old codger,' Jimmy remarked.

'Ha! Artful as a cage of monkeys.'

'Childish with it, though.' The younger one, not to be taken in by antics, nodded his head sagely.

'All this lot,' Frank, with a large gesture which included the framed celebrities, became garrulous, 'got something childish in them. I've seen a deal of them, off and on, enquiring and interviewing. They don't seem to grow up properly, only one part of 'em does... Many's the time I've wondered if it's because they're always dressing up and acting in all these Shakespeare plays, always murdering and so on... getting crime on the brain.' He stared hard at a famous Hamlet. 'When I've gone interviewing them, they just don't seem to understand crookedness properly; sometimes I've had to speak like a school-teacher. Anybody would think their brains just can't cope with the laws of the land. More than once it's struck me that they're just naturally loose, in a dotty sort of way... not developed,' he insisted.

'Look how they're always hopping in and out of the divorce court too,' Jimmy agreed. 'Then there's the—' Something bumped on the floor above and, glancing at each other, they listened alertly for a minute. But there was nothing further to interest them.

Frank sat down again; he refused to take more whiskey and, after his knowledgeable tirade, remained pondering. Jimmy lit a cigarette. The silence became more oppressive. And after about half an hour Frank restlessly got up. 'What the devil does he think we're here for – fun?' he frowned, went to the spiral stairs, and called up sternly: 'Mr. Simon!' There was no reply. He called again, without result.

'Absent-minded, I expect,' Jimmy said, faintly ironical. 'Forgotten we're here. Taking a nap before the Ball, perhaps.'

But Frank became decisive. 'Well, let's go up. This time we'll do straight business... He ought to be on the blinking stage himself,' he muttered, climbing.

They stepped on to a large landing piled with cardboard boxes: there was a table on which lay a few stalks of large over-blue delphiniums and a frying-pan containing an uncooked mutton-chop. Between the boxes a door stood open a few inches, a soft red glow behind it. 'Mr. Simon?' called Frank, and pushed open this door – there were two others – without further preamble.

And there was Mr. Simon calmly sitting at a table concentrating on some documents lying before him. But he had changed out of the rajah's costume, and now, in his rusty black jacket and stiffly formal if soiled white collar and cuffs, was the well-known figure of the shop below. The room was heavily furnished in a middle-class Victorian style, solid with mahogany sideboard, enormous vases, a sofa, basket chairs, oil-paintings of cattle and shaggy dogs. A portable electric stove burned in the hearth: on the mat in front of it a black cat lay asleep. Though the light coming from a red-shaded lamp standing on the mantelpiece was distant from him, Mr. Simon sat engrossed in his papers and did not look up at the intruders. There was a telephone on the sideboard.

'We can't wait any longer, Mr. Simon,' began Frank curtly. 'We got one or two questions to ask you.' Uninvited, they sat in the basket chairs at either end of the hearth: they could see, under the table, the red wool socks on Mr. Simon's shoeless feet.

Mr. Simon did not deign to reply: no doubt he was offended by this rude entry into his private quarters – he often was very haughty. 'I believe,' resumed Frank, slightly raising his voice, but still somewhat conciliatory, 'you know this Elmer Calvert quite well—' His head swung round to his companion.

Jimmy, evidently a cat lover, had leaned down to stroke the sleeping beast: after a caress along its back he picked it up. And immediately dropped it. The body fell to the mat with an unnatural thud.

'What's the matter?'

Jimmy picked up the cat again and displayed its under-part of flat plywood. The thick black fur was without gloss; the eyes stared glassily wide open. Frank gave a thin laugh, and turned again to Mr. Simon. 'You do like your little joke, don't you?'

'He does,' ominously remarked Jimmy. He rose and quickly crossed the room to Mr. Simon, paused a moment the other side of the table, and growled: 'Yes, you do, you nasty old crook!'

'Jimmy,' mumbled Frank, faintly astonished, 'here!'

'For two pins I'd bash your greasy old pan in, see!' Jimmy shook his fist towards the aloof Mr. Simon. 'I've a good mind to poke your sly old eyes out—'

Frank, now disturbed by his colleague's rage, hastened across the room. But not before Jimmy had leaned across the table, gripped Mr. Simon by his iron-grey hair, and pulled the wax head halfway out of its chest socket.

'By God!' breathed Frank.

'I've told you before,' his colleague turned, grinning, 'you need glasses, Frank. Soon as I came in I was suspicious he was just acting at reading those papers, in this dim light... But fancy making a waxwork of himself! What for, I wonder? To scare burglars off?'

'Or leave it to the country in his will.' Frank had recovered from his own little shock. 'The blighter's got a tip-top opinion of himself.'

After this they went without delay or hesitation into the two other rooms, a bedroom and a kitchen, but there was nobody to be found and nothing to interest them. Frank opened an enormous wardrobe, but Mr. Simon was not crouching inside; or under the four-poster. Obviously the old rascal had gone down the spiral stairs while they were addressing his familiar in the living-room: the fire-escape ladder was tucked secure against the landing skylight. A characteristic jest.

Yet Frank's frigid expression seemed to denote that the prank might hold a sinister implication. Was Mr. Simon trying to elude them? To decamp? Jimmy smiled faintly as they descended to the ground floor. In the room below the spiral staircase the casket of jewels was empty.

And still at her desk sat the clerk, writing while she bit at a sandwich from a paper bag before her. Flung across her shoulders was a hank of reddish old fur.

'Where's Mr. Simon?'

The pebble glasses flashed. 'Heaven above, I've taken you to him once – what d'you mean "Where's Mr. Simon?" *That* was Mr. Simon.'

'I know,' said Frank, patient, 'but he's not there anymore. Not the Mr. Simon we want.'

'Well, if he's not there he's gone, hasn't he?'

'Didn't you see him come down?' he demanded, stiffening.

'No, I didn't. I've been out to get these sandwiches from the coffee-bar... Mr. Simon is a very busy man, he has dozens of people bothering him here every day, dozens and dozens. It's a mania with some of them, to see Mr. Simon. This place is like a public infirmary sometimes.'

Jimmy, hovering behind, chuckled. 'As there are two Mr. Simons,' he said, 'I expect the bothers are halved.' The Fairy Queen's wand almost touched his fog-stained slouch hat. And the clerk gave vent to a little squirting noise like laughter, flashed her pebbles in his direction, and resumed her writing.

A pierrot with a bicycle-handle moustache, who stood with observant discretion near one of the exits from the floor, had not danced. But his Cavalier companion, somewhat untidily bearded, took the floor zealously – he had boldly accosted a straw-skirted Honolulu maiden in the bar – though he too seemed to keep a private eye open for any misdemeanours around him. There were three Cavaliers and several pierrots on the floor.

The charity affair, by virtue of which many woe-begone old people would benefit, seemed a success. The King of such fêtes – and he insisted on dancing, in a jigging style, despite his old shopman's flat feet – was gorgeously present. Jewel-covered, he received a full homage of delighted affection. Half the costumes whisking over the floor had arrived from his royal closets; those bunchy ring-encrusted hands had 'created' (as he was given to say) all the best wigs. Besides, he was so easy with his bills.

Cherished Simon, the liberating magician! Arms lightly embraced him, many a celebrated lip was pressed to the coarse old cheeks, excusably rouged. The gold tunic, alive with myriads of cleaned stones, the pearl-entwined turban with its aigrette and diamond brooches; the pear-drop, the dozen rings, and especially the genuine-looking gold and amethyst waist-girdle, evoked hoots of delight. Fingers touched his accoutrements. Was he real? The profane face looked compounded of old dead mysteries and crafts. And he did not seem quite his usual dependable party-self tonight: some of his subjects remarked on it.

But these inhabitants of history, tale and legend, or persons become for an illicit night the creatures of their dreams, spread an atmosphere of enchanted liberation as they fled through shafts of changing tints. An expensive cream-faced band-leader whirled high above a bank of showy flowers, insisting on energy. In a curve of gold and crimson boxes matrons and settled gentlemen, visited occasionally from below, sat like a row of busts. A real if minor Royalty was present.

'Simon! Simon, my sweet!' Like an emptying of a giant cornucopia, the dancers were pouring into the corridor. A girl from a Turkish harem flung herself, attar of roses rising from the confectionery of her hot bosom, on the rajah, and drew back scrutinising: 'Why, darling, aren't you well tonight? Your cheek is cold!'

'Angela... !' He panted a little. Then the dulled eyes flickered into vitality, widened; he bridled up to perform the characteristic strut, to say the expected piece; he glanced about him as if for an audience. 'I am *never* well, my dear; I am a frail little straw *buffeted* about. A delicate little *waif.*'

'You're a scandalous waif, Simon, so they tell me,' she giggled. 'Oh, I'm always hearing such wicked tales of you!'

The turban shook as he preened himself. 'Very, very bad ones?' he purred. '*Wonderfully* bad ones?' In the crowded bar his eyes darted restless over his nation. He tweaked the cheek of a tall Medici prince and, starting back horrified, pointed to his forehead: 'Your join! It's dreadful. One of my finest wigs and you just *throw* it on your head. Don't you dare come in my shop again! ... Well, gentlemen,' the preposterous head turned with a rapid stagily grand patronage, its owner entirely stimulated now, 'still looking for facts?'

'Yes, Mr. Simon,' said the moustached pierrot. Behind him the Cavalier, bumped by a Czech peasant girl carrying a glass of lager, brushed drops off his ill-fitting costume.

'Surely you have been pulling Christmas crackers too early?— you should have come to me for that moustache! And it's askew... allow me... there! But a moustached pierrot! ... it's *inartistic*! Pull it off!' The expert's eye, flashing malign fire now, pounced on the Cavalier. 'And that costume—*where* did you get it, sir? The buttons! Out of period! Why wasn't I consulted?'

The Cavalier, however, looking coolly at the indignant rajah, said: 'I asked the other Mr. Simon for a fact or two, but couldn't get any sense out of him. Might as well have spoken to a cat.'

'There can't be two Mr. Simons,' tittered the pretty Turkish odalisk, and took the rajah's arm, it seemed protectively. 'Not two of you, my sweet... Who are your nice friends?' She looked at them curiously, uncertain of the alien air they seemed to exude.

'Angela,' he lowered his voice dramatically, 'we must be careful... *They're public executioners!*'

'Oh,' she shrieked, 'how wonderful! You know everybody... Hangmen!' She looked at them palpitatingly, half-enticed, half-disbelieving. The rajah's extensive circle was known to contain very peculiar members.

'Mr. Simon likes his little joke.' And the pierrot, unamused, added obscurely: 'But facts have to be faced.'

'Not here,' entreated the rajah, and the odalisk, as if a cold draught blew into the excitedly vocal room, contracted her silver-netted shoulders and drew back a step; 'not here. There's not a fact in the place. Isn't everyone wonderfully happy?'

A Gipsy, great gold hoops swinging in his ears, captured the odalisk, thrust a drink into her hand, addressed her with amorous familiarity. The pierrot taking advantage of this, remarked solidly: 'All the same, Mr. Simon, we would still like to have a word with the Mr. Calvert we mentioned.' His eye greyly chill as an oyster, roved a moment over the masqueraders. 'If we could see him, Mr. Simon,' he invited, 'it would be best for *you*, in the long run. Is he here?' The Cavalier stood watching and listening.

It seemed a portentous moment for the rajah. His face seemed unable to decide what expression it could assume. The eyes blinked rapidly, the rouged old cheeks hung with a clay-like lifelessness, the fat unctuously tittering lips fell silently loose... But this was only for a few seconds. Outraged, he drew up his stumpy body and, while the diamonds in the shaking turban shot fire and the pear-drop leapt, he threw out his hand in dismissal.

'My good sir, you speak in *riddles*. I should be much obliged if you stopped this ridiculous pursuit of me.' His tongue snacked offended against the roof of his mouth.

'Very well, Mr. Simon.' The pierrot, regretful but ironical, nodded.

'Riddles, riddles... !' With his squat but vivid majesty, ring-crusted hand waving before him, the rajah broke a passage through the crowded costumes, and refused to be detained by his smiling courtiers. A camera was focussed on him, he graciously hesitated, there was a lightning flash, and he proceeded in a waddling sweep to the circular hospital-green corridor. '*Simon!*' voices called, affectionate but disregarded. A fox-trot sounded a distant recall of the dancers.

He was seen in one of the boxes gesticulating, as though still upset, to a little party of appreciative friends. But he soon descended from this isolation – perhaps his duties as potentate of such revels weighed on him – to the midnight-packed floor, and danced with a Louis XVI coquette, holding out her hand with an irreproachably accurate ceremoniousness. The moustached pierrot stood idly at the main exit. But the Cavalier had found another ready partner, and, with a little grin, seemed to be constantly manoeuvring her into the rajah's wake. And once more the painted old face became bellicose and haughty. As soon as the music stopped he abandoned his coquette on the floor.

The lovely odalisk, whom he had liberally dressed for grander occasions than this; hurried after the provoked figure. 'My pet! ... Who are those two terrible men?' She sounded indignant.

'Angela,' he panted, fingers pressed glitteringly to his chest, 'my poor little bird of a heart! ... I ought not to dance. Am I *purple*?'

'No.' But she drew him to a seat. 'There they are again!' The Cavalier had joined the pierrot: they stood looking across at Mr. Simon.

'Hounds!' he squeaked. 'What a *naked* face that pierrot has! ... So bare and elementary; I want to work on it.'

'Who are they?'

'So rude,' he whispered... 'Coming here! I left them the person they required.' Lusciously, as the lamps poured an azure moonlight, the band floated into a waltz. 'They and their horrible facts!'

'What?' she asked, giving him a sideway glance.

But he rose, quivering, scandalised, his fingers pulling her warm peach-soft hand. They disappeared into the moon-blue throng. Heedless of her protests, he waltzed with abandon, swaying his turban to the lollipop music. Observers, becoming alive now to a new event in the life of this character of the town's most gossiping parish, thought he was drunk. His partner warned him that she could hear his heart; he squeaked that he could no longer afford to own a heart... He would not stop; he loved a waltz. But when the music lapped into its caressing finale he broke away from her, whispering something incoherent. And as a rosily pale light flooded the throng – they were clapping for an encore – the oriental despot, looking mortally offended, was disclosed butting a way again through the rabble.

He was seen dodging through the dingy green corridor in unregal haste. Pulling at his ropes of pearls and rubies as though they choked him. Shiftily glancing behind and around him like an incontinent person at the mercy of a high-strung temperament. Again he would not be detained by persons wishing for a grotesquery from the wonderful old buffoon. He disappeared. And was found later drinking champagne in the bar. But once more he fled.

And there was a final glimpse of him silently squatting, with a docile air of being under protection, in the back corner of a box, behind a placid dowager strongly brocaded, her adolescent niece in innocent white, and a Mephistopheles who beat time to the music with a very long cigarette-holder. He sat there for some time, eyelids closed and chest sagging, looking like a deposed monarch.

The pierrot, followed by the Cavalier, jumped out of a taxi without his moustache, paid, and crossed the street. Hatless and wearing raincoats over their costumes, they skipped into the florist's deep doorway, and stood peering upwards. The street was deserted, though at the lower end, where it ran into a brighter-lit throughfare, an occasional figure passed vaguely through the thin russet fog. Even the most undefeated of the street's walkers had recognised the first uneasy stirrings of another icy day and gone home. All the buildings were blind and dead.

But in one of the two windows of the top floor over Simon's shop there was the dimmest illumination behind the curtains. Frank crossed the road and pressed, high beside the bevelled glass panel of the shop door, a shy dusty little bell-push. It seemed to possess an active resilience. Hidden in the doorway nearly opposite, Jimmy still looked up. Nothing happened. The pierrot, trousers snowy below the raincoat, pressed the bell again, kept his finger on it; waited, without result. Then he walked up to the telephone-box on the corner of the intersecting street, came back to the florist's, and grunted: 'No reply.'

'There was a shadow,' said Jimmy, gazing up.

'He's there all right,' Frank declared, as though he possessed second sight. 'You'd think he'd have more sense than to behave like this; the shop's got to open in the morning, I suppose.'

'Perhaps Culvert is there with him... I'll be glad to be shot of this job.' Jimmy shivered. 'He's a bit too wily, with his tricks and jokes, and laughing at us.'

'Laughing! Not him. He knows he's got nothing to laugh about.' Frank crossed to the door again and held his finger on the bell, drew it away, pressed with a long insistence – until Jimmy hurried over.

'Someone is moving up there; there's a shadow. Moving about quickly.'

But no one opened the door. 'Go back—' Frank, for some reason, had begun to whisper. And he pressed the bell yet again – perhaps only too well aware of the effect of a persistent door-bell on worried nerves.

And presently, peering into the shop from the side of the thick glass panel, he gave a low calling whistle. Jimmy hurried over and bent at the other side of the glass.

'God!' Frank whispered. 'Is he doing it again? ... Get to the phone-box, quick,' he suddenly ordered.

Through the glass, low in the shop's black depth, they had seen a small candle-dim flame. It walked over the floor in a circular motion, shrank for a moment, seemed to gutter out – then leapt into a tall narrow tongue of dazzling yellow. It curved over high, like a cornet, haphazardly illuminating the whole interior. Elizabeth could be seen sitting unconcerned on her throne; the Fairy Queen stood smilingly poised with her wand; and none of the other figures, limelit for a moment, looked flurried yet by their danger. Then the interior was quenched in darkness... and, with a more vivid certainty, became resplendent from a brisk flare in another direction. Frank helplessly rattled the door-handle, banged testingly on the glass panel.

Jimmy ran back from the telephone-box, shouting: 'The first floor's alight too!'

'He's mad! Does he think he'll get away with it again?— specially now... Get something to break in this glass—down there in Herring Yard.'

Jimmy fled to the ancient cobbled cul-de-sac; in a few moments he returned with an empty dust-bin, which smelt grossly. They crashed its rim into the glass panel. After the shattering noise, they could hear the whisper of flames, and a soft undertowing crackle. And for seconds they stood in abeyance before the threatening scene within, a totally abnormal scene, horrid yet almost festal, which surely lay beyond even their jurisdiction.

The whole interior was dazzlingly illuminated from a blowing curtain of fire in the background. Faces shone colouredly bright and alive in the radiance. The central Elizabeth, cheeks beginning to sweat, seemed as if at any moment she would draw her handsome grey and silver skirts away from the sprites of flame maliciously dancing on the ground towards her throne. On her dais the Fairy Queen began to quiver in precarious doubt of her power over this excessively boisterous event – and, even as she hesitated, the nearby little blackamoor's scarlet drawers caught fire, and the parrot, overcome by the dazzle and heat, fell off its perch. Above, the clusters of masks began swaying agitatedly.

The dust-bin crashed against the panel's jagged edge. Bursts of thin smoke, heat and odours, blew out. Frank was yelling now. A fire can unsettle the most phlegmatic of persons.

'Come out, you old devil!' he roared through the door, and put one leg over it, but stopped astraddle the door as a horse's head, cut off at the neck, tumbled in flames down the staircase. Jimmy gripped his arm.

'We can't go in there – the firemen will be here in a minute. The first floor's ablaze.' Frank withdrew his leg, cursing. Was he to be robbed of his prey? Jimmy reminded him that Mr. Simon could get out by the fire-escape in his flat. Were they to risk their lives in what seemed a deliberately fired building?

The few minutes that had elapsed since they saw the first snaky flame seemed like half an hour. When would the firemen arrive, with their estimation of what to perform? 'A place with this stuff in it will go up quick as muslin,' Frank shouted, just as the first engine, brakes cumbersomely grinding, rounded the corner below.

For those last instants they stood staring through the doorway like a couple of stolid boys excited by a magical transformation scene in a pantomime – now half-hidden by bluish smoke which coiled green-streaked up the staircase, then revealed in brilliantly garish clarity by plumed flames of chemical hues. Deserted by their master – where, oh where was he? – the forlorn figures were moving in doomed alarm, staggering, crumbling, collapsing. Though Elizabeth's body remained intact in its stiff jewel-sewn clothes, a terrible disease was attacking her face and hands; half her jaw had disappeared, the nose was flattened, and from her diminishing hands drips of buttery matter stained the precious fabric of her skirt... then, as her rival in splendour, the Fairy Queen, butterfly wings plucked from her, slewed over on her dais in a swoon of defeat, she, the only figure to prevail against destruction, looked for the last time on the anarchy around the throne – her eyes fell out of their fading sockets and disappeared into the flames writhing up her skirts. Already the Fairy Queen was consumed in a coffin of tinted flames. Over the floor ran fire-licked screams of vari-coloured matter, like the blood of jewels, and from the high air the companionable clusters of disembodied faces separated and slowly floated down in the loneliness of death. Out of the odours of smoke, charred garments and burning wax came, pungent and dominant, the smell of sizzled hair. The whole interior, a chamber in the happy dwelling of fantasy, was irremediably alight now. Yet there was something kindred, not dismaying, in the fiery carnage. The old magician knew what was proper.

'Hell,' cried Jimmy, delighted, and almost with respect for the grand gesture, 'he's done for himself this time!'

'He's barmy *and* a tyke.' Frank sneezed and turned, curt and official, towards the arriving engine. 'They'll get him.'

Clasped solid to their ponderous red and brass vehicles, which were arriving one after the other now, factual in steel and thick tunics, axe-weaponed, rope-hung, the rescuers took possession. Frank, after holding brief consultation with an officer, withdrew with his colleague to a point of vantage: they kept observation on the dim flat roof. The first floor was blazing, smoke pouring from the shattered windows, and already a radiance skulked behind the second-floor windows. But in those of the living-quarters above there was darkness. A few spectators had run up with the engines: three policemen held unflurried converse with Frank and Jimmy.

Then, from the ground floor, came a new crisp little roar. And through the smoke-cleared doorway could be seen, for moments, a squat doll-like creature of fire, faceless in its gown of flames but with a churning kaleidoscope core, like a heart in solid conflagration. Even as the group looked at this mystic figure-piece, an unknown native of the flames, it exploded into hyacinthine glory, self-consuming, a phoenix death, a bursting figure crested with curly feathers of reddish-purple and footed about by swarming dragon-tongues eyed like the tails of peacocks: it gave a last flare of violet, gold and rose, and vanished into ashen smoke.

Jimmy's smile, his face changing from rosy health to a lard-like blob in the leaping and withdrawing illumination, seemed nervous. 'It wasn't old Simon himself, was it?' he asked. 'Perhaps he wanted to go up with all his folk.'

'The best thing he could do,' Frank remarked. 'But I expect it was some pot of his greasy chemicals.'

'It wasn't Simon,' said Jimmy, and pointed up.

They were standing in the florist's doorway. There were shouts. The policemen were keeping the increased spectators beyond the firemen's province – the engine-jammed, hose-entangled roadway where they trod brisk and bulky in their thigh-boots, sliding ladders off the engines, bending at a pavement hydrant, uncoiling more ebbed grey piping: indubious realities to rescue the last remnants of pleasure in the establishment of illusion. The shouting, excited and thrilled, increased. A tilted ladder extended upwards in smooth deliberate efficiency: but too late.

Mr. Simon had appeared in a window of his flat; had thrust up its lower frame and leaned out. Had hysterical fright possessed him at last? Was the fire-escape jammed under his skylight – the old man become too overcome to manipulate it? His two pursuers stared up, arrested – yet in their faces a release like gratification. From the spectators there were louder cries, almost of ecstasy. A fireman had begun to climb the ladder. But Mr. Simon, ignoring the ladder tilting up towards him, or unable to see it, slowly bent over the window-sill, hung over it for a moment in suicidal peril... and descended head foremost, hit the ladder, turned a slovenly somersault against its rungs and, while firemen leapt, rushed towards the road. Down to the solidity, the malevolent facts, the punishment below.

Frank and Jimmy picked their way over the hoses. Spectators had broken loose and dodged among the engines and pump-trailers towards the group crouching over the water-running gutter of the pavement. A fireman had left the bending group and, tightening his chin-strap, hastened back impatiently to his pump-operating: others followed to their important tasks. The colleagues thrust their way in among silent spectators. Looked down at the well-known figure of the shop sprawled on his back across the watery gutter, one baggy trouser-leg rucked up and revealing a long sock of warm red wool on the shoeless foot.

Mr. Simon seemed little damaged by his fall; though his head, the neck as if dislodged from its security, lay at an unnatural angle on the pavement. In the glassy wide-open eyes, flame-illumined, a cunning gleam seemed to linger. He lay like an intoxicated man who had been galvanised into sudden activity, but had collapsed from it. No one touched the figure. The spectators peered down at it in astonishment, and the colleagues went back at once to the florist's doorway.

A peremptory voice ordered a clearance of the dangerous pavement: after the appalling moment the policemen became authoritative again. Simon's celebrated establishment, its gorgeous stock so eminently combustible, was beginning to purr with an additional golden energy.

MY LORD'S REVENGE
(1890)
Anonymous

'What has become of Girly Grey?'

Several people asked the question, but no one supplied the answer. None knew, few cared. He was not the sort of fellow you would trouble about, a poor actor, an effeminate dandy, and a prig. He had his successes, notwithstanding. He was held in high esteem by a set of long-haired men and short-haired women, who perverted art and canted concerning culture. He was the leading spirit in a company of languishing lop-sided amateurs, and he enjoyed the reputation of being loved by a lady of title.

The idea of any healthy, sane woman falling in love with Girly Grey seemed too ridiculous, but there was no denying the fact that he had been the favourite of several posturing, lolloping, Liberty-silked damsels, who affected sickly aestheticism, and for whom a man with virile mind and body was a thing too desperately real to be tolerated at any price. The ladies of a theatrical company in which Grey had once travelled through the provinces declared that he wore stays, and the green-room jokes anent his feminine appearance and nature were so frequent that he had become known generally as 'Girly'. On the bills and programmes he figured as Mr. G. Grey. He may have been given in baptism the name of George, or Gideon, or Graham, or Gilbert, for all I know. A chorister christened him Girly; everybody knew him as Girly, and, to tell the truth, he seemed quite proud of the appellation.

His latest affinity – to use his own word for his amorous relationships – was Lady Anthony Hopeland, a member of the Attic Mummers, a band of aristocratic and incompetent dramatic amateurs. He had assisted them in producing a Roman tragedy in the drawing-room of a duchess, and had taken part in the representation of the Midsummer pantomime, 'Little Goody Two Shoes; or, the Goose with the Golden Locks,' in the middle of Barnes Common. In this piece Lady Anthony had played Little Boy Blue, and lovely, indeed, had she looked in her turquoise silk tights.

The Goose with the Golden Locks had been represented by Girly, for whom the performance had been a fateful one. Lady Anthony had found this pale-faced actor, with his hairless cheeks, his watery eyes, and sensuous mouth, his fawning sentimentalism, and his sham poetry, such a contrast to the robust manhood of her husband that she had at first sought shelter by his side from the rough and impetuous attentions of her lord and master.

Lord Anthony was a man of deeds, not words. There was little nonsense about him; a keen sportsman, a travelled gentleman, a Conservative by birth and conviction, fearless in danger, outspoken in argument, noble in bearing, brave and straightforward. When first they met, she, then a fresh, active girl, had regarded him as an ideal man. It was not until a year after her marriage that she had fallen under the influence of the culturists, who cling, for monetary and other selfish reasons, to the skirts of London Society. Lord Anthony was in Parliament, and she was left to herself a great deal – more, indeed, than was good for her. Her husband was glad for her to find amusement, play-acting was fashionable, and he saw no harm in it. The result was that, before long, the bright, well-dressed, intelligent woman was transformed into a limp, clinging creature with tousled hair and unutterable languors. Lord Anthony saw the change, and could not but recognise that some other mind than his own was exercising its power over his wife, but he was much occupied at the moment, for having accepted a vacant Government office, he was obliged to go down to his constituents and seek re-election. He saw no immediate domestic danger, and after the struggle was over he would be able to give more time to his wife, and should soon shake the foolery out of her, as he expressed it.

Meantime the intimacy between Girly and her ladyship had intensified. People began to talk, for in her husband's absence the actor was continually at her house. She soon recognised that hers was the stronger nature of the two. She called him by his soubriquet, and after the open air exhibition of her charms had even told him always to call her his 'boy'. She caressed him, petted him, provided him with money, and on one occasion made him dress up in one of her costumes. She loved to rehearse scenes of plays with him, she taking the male and he the female part. There was some secret mysterious tie between them. Whatever it may have been, it is not our business here to inquire. It certainly seemed pitiable that this living woman, in whose veins ran the vigorous blood of ten county families, the wife of a man descended from heroes – almost a hero himself – who would have fought for his rights and defended her honour against all the world, should fall to the degradation of linking herself, by some unnatural bond, with such a thing as Girly Grey. Let base-born, ill-bred women sicken on their morbid imaginations, and feed their sexless desires, if they will, but the thought of the once fine, vigorous woman, Lady Anthony Hopeland, making simpering love to the elegant, emasculated fop with curled hair, painted eyes, and powdered face, was one to weep over.

She had already loosed the tongues of scandal when her

husband returned from the North. He had been elected by a large majority, and was in the best of humours, looking forward to the putting of his house in order with bright hopes. Unfortunately, on his way home he called at his club, and the first man to greet him was his cousin.

'Well done, old fellow; we all congratulate you. It was a real victory. But, Anthony, I'm deuced glad you're home again.' And he took him aside.

They talked earnestly together for some time. At the end of the interview, Lord Anthony, looking sad, but with a most determined look on his face rose to leave.

His cousin accompanied him into the hall.

'I know I've pained you, Tony, old chap but you were bound to hear it, and I thought it best you should hear it from a pal. Of course you can stop the nonsense at once; the fellow isn't a man, and probably there's no harm done. The worst of it is the servants have got hold of it. Before you do anything you ought to speak to Jevons.'

Lord Anthony was not in the habit of discussing family affairs with his servants, but Jevons was a very old and faithful attendant, and from him he learnt nearly all the truth.

He dined at home, alone with his wife. She was conscious-smitten, and tried her best to be at ease. He had never been so attentive and tender. He asked her about all her doings, and evinced quite an active interest in her theatrical successes.

After dinner he continued the subject.

'By the way,' he said, 'what did you say was the name of the clever young actor who assisted you?'

'Mr. Grey,' she answered simply, flushing slightly.

'I should like to meet him. Could you get him to come to-morrow evening?'

'To dinner?'

'No; I may not be at home. Drop him a pretty little note asking him to look in during the evening.'

Lady Anthony went to her desk and took out some paper. She seemed agitated, and hardly knew how to write a stiff formal letter to her lover.

'You need not be embarrassed. I'll tell you what to say.' Lady Anthony took up her pen.

'Begin, "My sweet Girly".'

Lady Anthony could hardly believe her ears. Was her husband jesting? What did he know?

She looked round nervously; there was a gleam of triumph in his eyes.

'Go on,' he said, and she commenced to write in terror. '"The ogre has come back, but it is alright. He wants to meet you. Come to-morrow evening at nine, and we shall have two hours to ourselves first – Your Own Boy." That will do nicely. Address the envelope.'

She obeyed and he touched the bell.

He then wrote a short note himself. It ran as follows: 'Dear Pasha, – Just returned. Have some fun for you. Reserve to-morrow night. Shall be at the club at four.' He addressed the envelope to 'His Excellency Kami Pasha, Hotel Metropole'. And he gave the two letters to the servant who answered his summons to be posted at once.

'What are you going to do?' at last Lady Anthony summoned courage to ask. 'Kill him?'

'Oh, no; surely you are not selfish, you will admit me to the entertainment. Your friend shall play and dance to me as well as to you. I am a judge of pretty women; I will tell you what I think of his makeup. And remember this, he is to dress and act exactly as he has been in the habit of doing in my absence. If there is nothing wrong between you – and I have made no accusation –

you will surely not object. But I mean to know the truth.' Before his strong will she was powerless.

The next evening Girly was punctual. In the room, into which he was shown, all the articles for his masquerade were laid out, and a pencilled note, 'For the last time'.

When he was dressed Lady Anthony entered, but she had lost her usual gaiety. She was, in fact, more dead than alive for she knew that her every word was being heard, her every movement being watched by her husband.

'Why, my Boy, what is the matter? You have been crying? And haven't you one kiss for your Girly? Has the Ogre been cruel? Oh! how can he ill-treat my Boy like this,' and he put his arm round the half-insensible woman to support her. 'If he were only here.'

'He is here, madam!' and Lord Anthony, followed by Kami Pasha, stepped from behind a heavy curtain. 'What do you want with him?'

Poor Girly let his burden fall, and slunk across the room towards the door.

'You cannot leave, madam; I address you as "madam," for such I presume you are, since I see you in woman's attire. Your few words are sufficient to show me exactly the position in which you stand towards my wife. I cannot find terms to describe the baseness of your conduct. Were you a man I should call you out and shoot you. As it is, you deserve to die. But I give you a chance. If you wish to have your life spared you must pay me at once, on the spot, five thousand pounds!'

'Five thousand pounds!' cried Grey, half-hoping that Lord Anthony was jesting. 'I have not five thousand pence in the world.'

'That need not trouble madam,' interrupted the Pasha. 'I am in London recruiting my harem. I will buy madam for five thousand pounds.'

'Sell myself?'

'Certainly, I will give five thousand pounds, and pay the sum now to his lordship in order to save your life,' and he took out his note-case.

'Otherwise you die!'

Girly began to realise that the two men were in earnest. He glanced at the poor, miserable woman crouching on the floor, and he felt that his hour of punishment had come. He was too weak to protest, and he had no chance of escaping in the clothes he wore.

Two of the Pasha's servants were summoned, and he was carried off in a close carriage.

Some people say he is now at Cairo, but the question, 'What has become of Girly Grey?' remains unanswered.

HAUNTINGS AND OTHER QUEER FANCIES

MISS POTTS AND MUSIC
(1948)
Margiad Evans

I push away a bundle of letters, post-marked, slightly muddy. It has been wet for so long. In the orchard this morning the raindrops were no longer running off the slippery leaves: they were no longer visible but had become part of that dull, dark green glaze which is the old summer's surface. The rain had become part of the air, had disappeared and been absorbed into it.

And it still falls, at times heavily. It is a material then. In the bus I was thinking, why, you could almost build a house with it. Having observed this to no one in particular but unaccountably loudly, I felt mad. Well, there go the letters. Now, I can really begin to write if there's anything left over...

But can I? Looking at those trees can I concentrate on this rather stately balanced article? Surely there is a child swinging in the branches? She – it is she – hangs and kicks her dangling legs: her long light hair held back by a band of ribbon, is woven like a cocoon among the three-cornered leaves. It *is* she whom for some reason I suddenly remember – Miss Potts? Of course not. The wind is between the lonely wet branches shaking them, and the low dark twilight is coming on cloudily, or I might think the flaxen moon made her hair. I think of Hardy's exquisite poem:

My fellow climber rises dim
From her chilly grave—

423

Just as she was, her foot near mine on the
bending limb
Laughing, her young brown hand awave.

Many winds and winters are in those lines, which, like all real
memories, hold much more of oblivion than remembrance. Not
that Miss Potts was ever a fellow climber of mine, or as far as I
know, anybody's else's. In fact the question is, did she ever climb
at all? That's what I am trying to decide.

But surely there *is* a child in the tree. Questioning the
direction of darkness which is behind that tower of hustled leaves
I ask, are you Miss Potts, are you dead, are you a success or a
failure, what did you do at Weymouth and why do I remember
you tonight?

If she is Miss Potts I don't see her often but I know that she lives
somewhere up in Lindenfield outside the town, with her
grandmother, her widowed mother and her aunt who teaches me
music. Her name – well, it is never anything but Miss Potts to
me and to all the other children who learn the piano from her
aunt. It is in scorn of her isolation and her umbrella that we call
her so. She wears white socks and she must be about twelve years
old. Her cheeks are a round, sober pink, her fair, floppy hair is
banded back, her mouth, not very originally, is a button, but a
button sewn on very tightly. Precociously it has the pout and the
quivering disdainfulness of an artist, for Miss Potts is already a
solid instrumentalist. Her touch is formed. She is said to be a
genius. I have not, at the stage when she might have been
imagined swinging herself, ever heard her play, but at the time
when the piano was to me a noisy bore, Miss Potts was said to
use *both* pedals.

Of course when we hear this we know we are hopeless. But

that which is so sickening and altogether incredible is that she plays the violin too. The violin is her real forte; and yet as a second course she beats us all at the piano. Or so her aunt says.

Oh, how I hate music lessons and Miss Potts, *and* her aunt who looks an exact embodiment of somebody or other – or rather two somebodies as it has taken me years to realise. Combining Rossetti's Beata Beatrix and my own idea of Sherlock Holmes, I have the most perfect projection of her. A long, long throat, a big clever nose, a thin ethereal face with ascetic and romantic eyes, that was B.B.S.H. when I was ten. She looked a saint of music and her niece was her novice. But with her nostrils down on her fiddle she became pure Sherlock Holmes. Later on when I was sixteen I had another music mistress – a Miss Townsbridge, a black-eyed, hoarse, cheerful woman, who exercised the most amazing vocabulary of tone upon the violin, and who possessed a sheer mathematical knowledge of theory which made her a genuine mystic and initiate of her art. She used to do her shopping during my lessons and dump her damp bag of fish and watercress on the top of the piano where B.B.S.H. used to keep an unfurling rose in a silver vase. Miss Townsbridge used to declare that music such as mine required judgement at a distance.

I was going to write by that time Miss Potts had quite gone from my conscious memory, as she and Beata Beatrix, the mother and the grandmother had left the town years before. However, if I have forgotten her it must have been about then that remembrance revived with the letter I found and read about them being gone to Weymouth. That letter which has in a sense kept her continuous and connected the thought of her forever with wet esplanades and a snail-coloured sea...

Why I thought of Miss Potts and my music lessons when I looked at the tree was because it is a birch. Birches grew outside the room where B.B.S.H. taught us. (Her name was Miss Amy Holman.) A pattern of tombstones, a diagonal path, green turf and the aerial trees filled the Georgian window. I can see those grey-green three-cornered leaves now. The room was up a flight of stone stairs, over a school. Outside on a long, ugly landing was a yellow pine bench where sometimes the next pupil sat with her music case and sweetie bag, kicking the wall.

Perhaps, too, my being in the orchard this morning unconsciously opened my mind to her image. Down there with the smell of the long grass and nettles and the horse mushrooms under old perry and cider trees the sense of an intimate past is always more powerful than anywhere else: under those trees my childhood grows over me; and to-night especially I can suddenly see myself with my friend Marian in my aunt's orchard.

We were feeding the ferrets which lived in a box nailed to a pear tree, Marian carefully holding up the saucer of bread and milk while I opened the cage for her to slip it inside. The ferrets stank and we were afraid of getting bitten: they undulated in their straw, and their sensitive, wincing nostrils and eyes opened and shut like stars.

Marian was the same age as Miss Potts. She had a large shining white face with clean open pores all over it, like the ostrich's egg in my aunt's bedroom. Her hands were red and blue and her hair cold-tea coloured and growing in a bunch over the middle of her forehead. She was my great friend because she was utterly different from me – tidy and quiet and concisely mannered.

'Mother is going to ask Miss Potts to tea,' said Marian.

'Oh, Marian,' I groaned. We all groaned when Miss Potts was mentioned.

Then I tried to envisage the arrival of Miss Potts and B.B.S.H. at Marian's father's shop. Would they walk up the alley under the barber's-saloon to the family door? Or would they, furling their umbrellas, step into the shop as if they were customers? I decided they would go to the door. I saw them with the little black coffins that held their fiddles, turning to look at each other on the threshold just as Marian's mother opened the door to admit them. But I couldn't see them going in. They would *not* go in. No, in my vision they would not. There, dressed for some reason as once perhaps I had really seen her, in a fine pale pigeon-grey dress with a soft white collar and a damson dark rose, stood Beata Beatrix with her peculiar ecstatic smile, holding Miss Potts by the hand as I had sometimes seen her do when they walked quickly across the churchyard to wherever they were going.

Suddenly I knew they wouldn't go at all. They were only *asked*. And I believe they didn't. I believe I can remember Marian muttering, 'Too grand' when I inquired.

'Do you know what's going to happen to me one day?' I said, after we had fed the ferrets and pulled to pieces all the Jew's-ear fungus we could find: 'Shall I tell you? One day *I'm* going to play the violin. I know I am! Better than Miss Potts. Miss Potts will sound awful after me.'

'I bet she sounds awful now,' said Marian.

'Ah, but you wait! This is really *going to happen*. You see. One day when I've been out all day, miles and miles and miles and I'm hot and thirsty and lame with blisters – I shall come to a cottage and I shall stop. It'll be an old man who'll ask me if I'd like a drink. And he'll take me inside. And there hanging on the wall—'

'Hanging on the wall...?'

'Hanging on the wall there'll be an old, old violin, covered with dust. Nearly black with age and the strings broken. I shall say, do you want that? No, you can have it: I'll give it to you. It belonged to my grandfather and he's dead and I can't play it so you can have it—'

'But neither can you.'

'I shall learn. I shall take it away and have it all my life and it will be in my grave with me, so there, Marian B.'

'You always talk about being dead,' cried Marian. 'But what about Miss Potts?'

'Miss Potts! Oh, *Miss Potts*. Nobody'll listen to *her*.'

I cannot see the tree any more. It's quite dark now, but out there behind the candles it is swinging the wind like a child on its branches. And what I wonder is – did I ever with my eyes actually see her in the birch trees? And again jumping off a tombstone, and running along the churchyard wall as far as the iron lamp? When I hear again her spirited voice – the only time I *did* hear it – passionately raised against us who were baiting her – 'I'm *not* crying. My nose is going to bleed!' – I can believe that she did these things and I saw her. But who can tell me? I don't think I saw half of what I remember, and I may have dreamed or imagined it. Certainly it seems real. Terribly, noticeably real. But then so does the dark red car going swiftly along without a driver, but containing a man asleep in the back with his head on a white bolster. I feel that I saw that: it was the kind of car that generals used in the last war, but its reality never convinced anyone except myself. I suppose it was one of those intense, psychic impressions very young children receive and isolate in their minds from time to time. However, don't let me patronise myself: at ten years old I had a good deal of penetration and independence. My reaction to B.B.S.H., for instance, was one of stubborn dislike in spite of her fascination and the atmosphere of admiring emotion she caused among some of her pupils and all of the grown-up people who knew her. Simply, the more they raved over her looks, her music, her cleverness and her brilliant ill-health, the more certain I was of her – what shall I say – her secret levity, her contemptuousness. And the formidable drive, the *will* of her.

Nothing in fact that I should have disliked if she had let it be obvious. It was the sighing – the false exhaustion...

One day she told me – I thought maliciously – that Miss Potts was playing the Moonlight Sonata. She was sitting beside me at the piano, her great coil of wistfully romantic hair falling down her neck. I asked:

'Why can't I learn it? I like it.'

She sat up and stretched; her limp but beautiful body seemed to yawn: '*You*! Ha ha. My dear—' and she looked at me with thoughtful hate, 'there are *immense difficulties*. You don't realise—' She sighed. 'Constance is – well, she's remarkable.'

And she spread her thin hands in the tenuous way she had...

And then there was that dreadful music competition. We – the dozen or so pupils – all had to play the same piece. Miss Potts was the sure winner. Why she was included – but she wasn't. *We* were included, because she couldn't win without us. That was what we decided, anyway.

Ten girls and two middle-aged little boys waited outside Beata Beatrix's room that afternoon, quietly and carelessly playing Puss-in-the-corner. When we heard footsteps coming we flew and sat upon the bench. We giggled, we whispered as Miss Potts's grandmother arrived, as one by one we were called in to play. The game went on tensely; the cotton smell of our clean frocks mingled with the sharp one of glazed music rolls and satchels, the pattern of the piece now faint, now desperately bold, occurred and ended. I remember I hung out of the dull window and watched the swallows threaded in a double row on the telegraph wires, and the old almswomen in their tiny courtyards down below carrying their coal buckets into their doorways.

Miss Potts didn't sit with us. About halfway through she came. She wore gloves and she walked through us haughtily; and she knocked on the door. Then she stood, hand and forearm uplifted, posing complete indifference. It was easy. Her back was towards us.

But, oh, she would have made an artist! Why hasn't she? The tap, the listening hand – the feet a little tilted on the toes... Lord, what hadn't those three women taught her! There was a giggle after the door had shut. Somebody said: 'I say – the Light of the World!'

Slowly we nodded our heads.

We waited for her music. Until it came, we nodded, not looking at one another, but muttering her name all down the bench where we were now sitting: 'Miss Potts, Miss Potts, Miss Potts, Miss Potts, go dots.'

Down and up the length of the bench, her name went, like a scale of chords, the way of a ritual of magic. Separately we had all undergone the ordeal of Miss Potts, but now it was we who were unanimous...

When she began to play I found no one to look at. And suddenly I wanted a face who would meet my eyes and my astonishment. For without premonition how could I have been prepared? *Astonished* – I was so astonished that I might have been picked off the bench and set down in the middle of the churchyard without noticing I'd moved. And my chest felt blank, not uncomfortable, but simply empty, as if I had no breath and no need to breathe. I had expected there would have been *some* likeness to our playing. Some recognisable equality. But there was none.

The piece sounded as if it had never been played before.

Miss Potts might have been thinking it to me as she played it. It seemed as if I could see the arch of the notes in the air through the thick red panels of the door, definite and lovely as the swallows strung on the telegraph wires, but of some unknown spirit colour resembling white gold...

As playing it was a boundary, Miss Potts and the grown-ups on one side, ourselves on the other.

The others went on muttering faster and faster. The spell was turning into a game. But all of my mother in me possessed me to listen, and when the music was over, to watch the door.

When it opened and she came out, I was more confounded than ever, for she dropped her silly gloves and she stooped and fished about, looking exactly as I felt I looked when my aunt made me sing to people. Her music might be grown-up but she wasn't. And nobody ever was nearer to plain crying.

'Miss Potts, go dots,' sang somebody, changing the game back to a taunt.

Oh, I felt sorry for Miss Potts! I felt sorry for her in the way children do for one of themselves when they see through adult cunning. It was in the vehemence of triumph she had been included among us and now she had to face us. I felt that blindness one gets behind the eyes after a shock or an accident like falling down or cutting your finger – something instantaneous which is there to protect you, but which bewilders you too and makes you wonder how it happened.

Instead of running past us she stood there staring. The tears started to crawl out of her eyes.

'She's going to cry-ee!'

The faces swayed forward.

'I'm not crying! My nose is going to bleed!'

She twisted her shoulders – she was gone; part of her face that I had seen was a fierce red and white, one suffused eye glaring over the handkerchief.

'Ha, ha, ha!' we laughed. 'Ha, ha, ha. Hush, hush.'

Another one was called.

Remembering that afternoon, and the way she used to walk whenever I saw her, always between two women as though the world were a slender path endlessly enclosed – I wonder more than ever whether she was secretive, found things dull, hid from everybody the laughing foot on the bough and the hand that shook the birch leaves into the movement of climbing smoke. But my Miss Potts Collection is after all so slight! There is no guessing. And probably there was nothing, nothing at all interesting, one way or the other. Six years passed. B.B.S.H. had been gone a long time and Miss Townsbridge with her bursts of shopping and her boredom was teaching me technique which I couldn't translate into action. Searching back, I cannot find a trace or a murmur of her remaining.

Yet she did that once come back. When I read the letter which was going to be burned on my bonfire. She came, as she has come tonight, abruptly, not with a speech, but with a certain astounding brevity, like a ghost story in a newspaper.

The letter fell off the wheelbarrow out of a heap of papers, music and magazines I was trundling through the snowball bushes. I picked it up and read it: it was signed by Amy Holman. It seemed I could actually hear the voice of the writing and see it spoken out of Beata Beatrix's frail profile. She had been rather a friend of my aunt's; after they had gone away she had written a few times.

'My sister is rather worried about Constance.'

(Constance – Constance? Oh, Miss Potts.)

'My sister is rather worried about Constance. She and my mother have taken her away to Weymouth where my sister hopes to settle if they can find a small flat, and if the air does Constance good. But so far they are having nasty wet weather. And Constance is so devoted to her music that there is no holding her back.'

That letter was the very last I ever heard, the final mention in my life of any one of them. I have never heard that Miss Potts *died*, nor for that matter that she lived. She has not become a celebrity. But I wonder, did they settle? Did they ever find anything to hold *them* back? I can imagine them living in that small flat for the rest of their lives. Sometimes I see her one way, sometimes another. Now she is growing unobtrusively older between them: walking along the esplanade in that kind of seaside rain which seems to oil the roofs and the waves, glancing occasionally aside uneasily and rapidly at the swishing, dishevelled beach, the whorls of clinging, shining shells... And then another time I am sure she gave up music and took to lipstick and dancing and marriage with the rich proprietor of a garage, storing her fiddle on the top of a wardrobe and allowing the women a pension of moderate affection only. Nothing lonely, slow or wistful after all. In fact, it's quite probable that I have been close to her without recognising her: have passed her in some park, sitting in the square shadow of a statue, reading, watching the birds and sometimes vaguely lifting the direction of her face towards the band under the cupola, to whose rosy music she feels so placidly and distantly related.

Yes, I wonder.

But it is so late that even the moths have ceased to butt at the candles and with folded wings have settled in little chequered lumps on the curtain, like limpets on a dark green rock.

I'll go to bed. Wind, tree, darkness and Miss Potts are all inscrutable.

THE COLLABORATORS
(1901)

Anonymous

I

Arthur Pagewood and Henry Varcoe had become close friends and intimates, although their acquaintance was by no means one of long standing. In fact, it had commenced about twelve months before the period at which our story opens in the smoking room of a Westminster club of which they were both members.

They were Varsity men – Pagewood hailing from Exeter College, Oxford, and Varcoe from Gonville and Caius, Cambridge – and moreover litterateurs in a small way. Some startling and unconventional short stories, of the decadent type, from the pen of Pagewood which had appeared in a certain eccentric magazine whose life had been a short and merry one, had caused a considerable flutter in the dovecotes of Philistia; and Varcoe had contributed to the still surviving 'Tyburnia' six or eight fugitive sketches of London life, admirable in style and technique, but lacking in power of 'vision' and imagination.

Extremes meet, they say; and Arthur Pagewood and Henry Varcoe, contrasting strongly in physique and line of thought, separated by nature to all outward appearance as widely as the poles, had not been long in each other's society before they became conscious of a subtle and mysterious aura of mutual attraction, when the world would have looked for a wave of mutual repulsion. Each man was, as it were, the complement of the other.

The romantic friendship which resulted presently led to a literary partnership.

The collaborators scored many successes, but they were, after all only minor ones. Each had a soul above the short story – which is often regarded as the most effectual test of literary ability – and each aspired to produce a work which should make Stanley Weyman and Conan Doyle tremble for their laurels.

One breathless evening in late August, when the Parks were deserted and Pall Mall and Piccadilly disconsolate, Arthur Pagewood, in his usual casual way lounged into his friend's Bayswater chambers, and, flinging the soft felt American hat which he always affected upon the table, while he jerked the butt-end of a cigar out of the open window, threw himself listlessly into an easy chair.

'Varcoe,' he said, fixing his bright eyes eagerly upon that gentleman's face, 'I have been haunted by it in the visions of the night. It will make the world grow pale – readers with delirious horror, rivals with delirious envy.'

'You mean the plot of our projected historical novel, no doubt,' said Varcoe with his accustomed phlegm.

'Why what else would rouse my enthusiasm in this weather? I have the "root of the matter". But to attempt to develop it here – in London – in this stifling, pestiferous atmosphere, with the thermometer at 80 deg. in the shade – would lead to ruin, disaster, idiocy, and asphyxia.'

'What do you propose to do, then?' inquired his coadjutor rather ruefully, for he by no means relished the abandonment of his cherished idea.

'Briefly this: to "fly these cruel lands, this avaricious shore" –

pray excuse mixed reminiscences of Virgil and Savonarola – "and seek larger ether", larger inspiration, and local colouring.'

'A brilliant project, indeed!' cried Varcoe, affected by the other's enthusiasm. 'But can't you tell me something more about the plot?'

'Not here – not here, my friend. The city dust would besmirch, the brazen glare of the city streets would scorch the radiant butterfly wings of the Iris of my fancy. As I have said, William de la Marck is the hero. For the rest, let it suffice that the leit-motiv is the old, yet ever new one of a "woman weeping for her demon lover". Once more I adjure you not to be alarmed, for I pledge you my honour as a literary Bohemian that there is not a souneon of Moore's "Love of the Angels" nor a trace of Maturin's "Melinott the Wanderer" in my highly original plot.'

'Have with you, then, Pagewood. I place myself unreservedly in your hands. You have a right, I suppose to play the autocrat, for you supply the literary "hegemonic spark". Let us see. This is Monday. Well, I shall be ready to accompany you in your quest of the "larger ether" and the "local colouring" on Wednesday.'

II

From place to place in the picturesque woodland Ardennes district did the friends wander through the shortening days of the golden autumn. Adhering to their programme, they made a pilgrimage to Liege, followed the windings of the Meuse, visited grey old Namus perched above the river, stayed for some days at the Tete d'Or in lovely Dinant, and explored the grottoes of Hun. But their steps always gravitated towards the forest, and when its greenery had given place to russet they settled down at a sleepy little hotel in St. Hubert, which, as every Belgian traveller knows, lies in the very heart of the Ardennes.

Now, Pagewood was eccentric – eccentricity, we know, is the hall-mark of genius – and cherished some peculiar fads, which he had been known to sacrifice on the altar of friendship, or even on that of love. The most aggravating of these fads was a literary one, as Varcoe had learnt to his cost. You might urge him with the most frenzied entreaties, you might demonstrate the utter futility of his line of action, but you could never induce him to disclose the denouement or peripety of a story until its conclusion was virtually reached. 'I must keep the bonne bouche for the last' was his invariable reply to the remonstrance of Varcoe on the subject. Men may and do laugh at fads, but they often lead up to strange and unpleasant consequences – a truism destined to receive a specially melancholy exemplification in the present case. Arthur Pagewood was by no means a strong man; the fiery and ceaseless workings of his soul had already well-nigh frittered out the frail constitution which he had inherited from consumptive parents. To make matters worse, he was one of those Quixotic individuals who scorn to adapt their clothing to the weather. Cold blasts were not unknown in the Ardennes in October, but Pagewood rejected an overcoat as effeminate. The consequence was that during a walk one day, when the wind blew from the east, he contracted a severe chill. Pneumonia set in, and in less than a week Henry Varcoe stood weeping bitterly, for all his Anglo-Saxon phlegm, over the corpse of a friend whom he loved as few brothers are loved.

This, then, was the end of all their pleasant intercourse. Thus had their partnership terminated. The bright star or fancy was extinguished, the sparkling foam of imagination choked up for ever. Those eyes, eternally closed, would never again thrill him with the impassioned fervour of their gaze; that white cold, delicate hand would never again hold his own in the grasp of friendship. And what of the dream of literary distinction, than which none other is more fascinating? Death, grim harlequin of life's pantomime, had smitten the illusory fabric with his icy wand, and the glistening rainbow battlements, the golden towers, the fairy cupulas, had trembled, tottered, fallen in ruin, like so many stage properties beneath his resistless hand. Neither man nor angel could rear again the palace of delight in which the vanished spirit had so revelled.

Cut is the branch that might have grown full straight,
And burned is Apollo's laurel-bough.

III

Henry Varcoe was stricken to the heart by the death of his friend, and yet he could not tear himself away from the scene of his loss. Some spirits are so constituted, and they suffer most acutely of all.

Alone he roamed the dreary and sodden woodlands, now thickly carpeted with fallen leaves, missing his dear companion at every step; alone at night in his solitary chamber wherever his eye rested he was reminded of Pagewood. On the mantel lay his favourite meerschaum; the few volumes which had accompanied his wanderings – Homer, Dante, Shakespeare, AEchylus, Schopenhauer's *Parerga* – were ranged on a shelf hard by; and on a small in a corner of the room was deposited the treasured MS whose progress had been interrupted by his death.

That chief d'oeuvre, Varcoe feared, would never see the light. His mental powers were in abeyance – under eclipse. More than once, when the burden of his lonely sorrow had seemed utterly insupportable, he had sat down and tried to write; if for no other purpose, at least to distract his thoughts; but his brain was torpid and barren, no ideas would come to him and the useless pen was quickly laid aside in despair.

The master hand which had so jealously retained the clue that led through the labyrinthine maze of the plot right to its heart lay stiff and cold in the grave. Varcoe might have been hypercritical, too distrustful of his own powers, but no solution – only a few, indeed, occurred to him – of the mystery hanging around the fate of the hapless heroine who had surrendered herself, body and soul, to the embodied demon. William de la Marck, commended itself to him as satisfactory, or even remotely probable. And then he caught himself wondering whether there was out in the vast unknown universe a mystic treasure-house wherein were deposited those thoughts of the mighty thinkers of the earth which seemed to perish on their decease, and wishing that, if such there were, he knew the open sesame that would compel it to disclose its secrets. Musing thus, he bethought him of Lytton's *Pausanias*, of Dickens's *Edwin Drood*, of Louis Stevenson's *St. Ives*, and then, looking back through the centuries, of

Him who left half-told
The story of Cambuscan bold.

All these inspired ones, like that Pagewood whom he mourned, had wended their way to the 'bourne from which no traveller returns,' and others had endeavoured, with scant success to place a coping-stone shaped by alien hands upon the fabric which the mighty dead had left unfinished, and which they alone could have adequately completed.

One night – it was November, and the rain, driven by violent, intermittent squalls, beat furiously against the casement – Henry Varcoe, as if in protest against the wild weather, his own gloomy thoughts, and no less gloomy surroundings, braced himself up for a supreme effort. He read and read again the latter part of the MS; he tried to think whether the dead man had ever dropped a casual hint which might lead him to the discovery of the intended denouement; he marshalled for the hundredth time before his menial vision the various possibilities of the case. All was in vain; his brain whirled like a lonely sphere of fire, desolate, unproductive, tormented.

He buried his face in his hands, and moaned aloud, 'Oh, Pagewood! Pagewood! friend of my heart. I have lost you, and with you, I have lost all – hope, energy, intellect. I am not man enough to complete the monument of your genius, which owes so little to my poor efforts. And yet how gladly would I give my life, my soul, to place before the world – not, Heaven knows, for my own sake, but yours – in a manner worthy of you, our last labours.'

The bells of the Abbey Church of St. Hubert, which was within a stone's cast of the hotel, at this moment, in tones muffled by the battling wind and rain, slowly chimed the midnight hour.

The last stroke was still vibrating through the troubled air, when the door of the chamber was noiselessly opened, and a tall, cloaked figure as noiselessly glided in and took the seat at the table before the open manuscript which Varcoe had been perusing. The visitor next, with a well-remembered gesture, flung off his broad-brimmed felt hat and seized the pen which had so lately fallen from the watcher's nerveless grasp.

From his post beside the stove Varcoe gazed in much terror upon the features of the newcomer, which were fully revealed by the removal of his headgear. The face he beheld was, and yet was not, the face of Pagewood. It was a livid and horrible mask, which simply reproduced and travestied, as a wax replica might have done, the cast of his features as his friend remembered them in life, but left them utterly devoid of expression. Sorrow and joy were equally banished from the passionless lineaments of the dead; and in those fixed and glassy eyes there was neither speculation nor recognition.

Varcoe, naturally a strong man, and by no means given to sentimentality and imaginative crazes, was now an altered being. He was unnerved by the constant presence and tensions of his grief, his prolonged vigils, his utter loneliness in a foreign land, and the gnawing haunting sense of a complete paralyses of his literary powers, and, consequently of his literary ambition. The sight of the melancholy apparition, which seemed unaware of his presence and yet bent upon the performance of some important task, so wrought upon him that his consciousness forsook him, and he slipped helplessly from his chair to the ground in a deep swoon.

When Varcoe came to himself the weird eidolon of what had once been Pagewood had vanished. Time had not stood still, although he had been unconscious of its progress, for the candles on the table burned low in their sockets.

Feebly he arose, and fearfully he drew near the open manuscript. He remembered that the instant before he fainted he had seen the shade take up a pen and bend eagerly over it. Judge of his amaze when he beheld page after page, from the point where the narrative had broken off, filled with the handwriting of his dead friend! Was he waking or dreaming? That night, at all events, he would not – he could not – sleep.

He replenished the stove, procured fresh candles, and addressed himself to the perusal of the concluding portion of the MS.

The story was finished! Yes, finished by the hand of the dead, which had dispensed with his feeble help.

The plot culminated in scenes suggestive of the lurid splendours of the Hindu Padalon when the doomed Kehama made his descent thither. The mystic and terrible things of the spiritual world were, for once in the history of literature, described by a spirit. The frantic efforts of the wretched Yolande, the heroine to rescue the demon soul of the outlawed William de la Marck, whom she loves in spite of all the threats and judgments of the angry heavens; the supreme sacrifice which her luckless passion claims and receives; the ghastly horrors of that night when the nameless tragedy is consummated and the silver planet of love is quenched, as it were, in a lake of blood and fire; all these things were portrayed in words and imagery that lived, that breathed, that stood out as grim, objective realities from the pages, like the ghostly pylons of Karnak silhouetted against the pure indigo of the midnight Egyptian skies – the words and imagery of a spirit, redolent of that higher sphere wherein spirits exist.

When Henry Varcoe had ceased reading, the hair on his head stood up, he was bathed, despite the warmth of the apartment, in a cold sweat, and his countenance was as livid as had been that of his phantom visitant.

Some lines traced on the last page of the MS now arrested his attention. They ran thus:

'Our collaboration, the action and reaction of our spirits each upon the other, seemed to, but, did not cease upon my death. The agony of your heart, the cry of your sorrow, the bitterness of your disappointment – these are influences that reach from earth to other worlds, and they have brought me to your side to-night.

'The story, which was begun so gaily and hopefully has, alas! been finished by the hand of the dead. You can use it or destroy it as you please. To me it matters not; for to me earthly triumphs are indifferent. But remember that conditions are annexed to your choice, whichever that may be. If you destroy it your life will be as that of others – the normal threescore years and ten; if you use it, unparalleled success – which your collaborator is not destined to share and enjoy – awaits the book and its author. But then you must die, in the zenith of your fame, a year after its publication.

'Ponder and choose. In either event, beloved friend,
Be thou assured I shall not fail
To meet thee in that hollow vale.'
That night Henry Varcoe made his choice.

The grand sensation of the Christmas literary season that year was *A Romance of the Ardennes* written in collaboration by Arthur Pagewood and Henry Varcoe. Edition after edition was called for and exhausted. The glories of the popular Corelli waxed pale and were eclipsed by the splendour of its success. It took the hearts and souls of men captive, and yet it was more 'triste et terrible,' more awful in its diablery, than the weird masterpiece of the uniue Maturin. It was a wail from the regions. Of eternal dolour – a wail in which was heard the death-shriek of a woman's love, which had vainly essayed to plumb those sunless depths.

The world, of course, knew that Arthur Pagewood was dead; but it looked for other work from the pen of his brilliant confrere. The world was disappointed. Long ere it had ceased clamouring for fresh editions of *A Romance of the Ardennes*, Henry Varcoe had re-joined that friend to immortalise whose name he had cheerfully laid down his own life. Those who had bent over the pillow of the dying man to catch his last words had seen a smile light up his face as he faintly whispered –

'Be thou assured I shall not fail
To meet thee in that hollow vale.'

THE HAUNTED WINDOW
(1953)
Margiad Evans

Miss May Hill was ordinary. She often told herself so looking at
her pot-plants or the red rubber tubing on the sink taps while
she washed up her two plates. It was beginning to rankle for she
liked reading Tchekov. And the people in those stories – well!
They laughed, they cried, they had hysterics in public, they said
(and wore) the most amazing things. They nearly all had pistols.
And though they talked endlessly of morals they didn't really
bother whether they were married or just living in sin. They
talked – 'just as Father was for ever talking about the weather.
No wonder I'm so boring! But at least he had to think whether
to cover the bookstand or not.'

Her father had been a dealer in second-hand books. He had
done very comfortably. When he had died she had sold the shop
and bought a house in Acacia Avenue. She was quite well off and
fairly happy but as she approached forty she sometimes felt like
accusing him of a lack of excuse for her existence. Her mother
she remembered only as a grumbling noise in a scullery.

Morals would be more interesting to talk about than the
weather or food, she thought. But she daren't begin such
discussions even with herself because she didn't know what it was
like to be immoral. 'And you should always first do what you
afterwards say no one should ever do' she concluded. So her life
didn't brighten. She always met the same people in the same

roads carrying the same baskets full of bread and fish and darning wool.

One evening when the two plates were still dripping May Hill went out into the back garden and sat down under a lilac tree to read *Rudin*. It made her cry: 'but what's it all about?' She saw that Rudin was a big eager lazy child, and finally he brought the answer:

'He was just afraid of growing up and being ordinary and that's why he made such a fuss. Pretending.' And she leaned back in her deckchair and stared at her lawn bristling with buttercups, the half-shut daisies shimmering in the long soft grass like white pebbles in some divine stream. And suddenly because somehow Rudin had *pretended*, she was aware that her neglected garden was far more beautiful than her neighbour's mown lawns and regiments of flowers: that there was, in the season, at certain moments, nothing that was ordinary, and she remembered, frightened, how she had dreamed last night she'd heard the nightingale singing in a willow tree: and now she wondered was it too early, or had he really sung in those cypresses at the bottom of the garden which were so still, so dark, so upright that she could see the light-coloured moths weaving around them. Just as if she were watching the pattern of light flowers being laid over the dense background of a carpet.

She sighed, took up *Rudin* and read till she could see no more. Then she went to bed. Quite as suddenly as she'd thought she'd heard the nightingale in the middle of her sleep, she saw those fat shopping bags and baskets filing past her without any hands to carry them. Bread, meat, onions... she woke – damn! Tea, the most ordinary reaction to nightmare, she decided must be made; and while the kettle boiled she did commit eccentricity for once – she put on a coat and went outside, flicking the light on in the front room so that she could see her way down the path. She was muttering as she moved sleepily towards the gate of her suburban home:

'Must've been getting on my nerves for a long time. My nerves, my nerves, it's living alone. I'll look at the light. No, I'll listen to the trees.'

The night was sharp as it often is after a hot day. High up in the tree tops of Acacia Avenue (Silver birch and plane) a breeze was shaking out a small noise like the jingling and rustling of a bunch of keys. This housekeeping noise in nature itself was inexpressibly dreary to the haggard May Hill. Even the dark night was middle-aged and dull. She turned back to her door.

And then so decisive, so dreadful and impossible was the picture she saw for an instant through her lighted front window, that she had only time to fall at her own feet as it were, in a faint of pure shock. Hope came round with her... Perhaps a policeman would walk up the road and ask her about the open door and the light. Then she could say to him, 'Look in there Officer! who's that woman? I don't keep lodgers. Turn her out. She's no *right*—'

It was a very large, fat face like a dropped plum with a whitish bloom as of powder or sheer decay over the purple features. It was leaning on a plump fore-arm, on a cushion, at the end of her sofa. A thermometer stuck out of the lips. Beside it, a yellow and white curly mongrel terrier stood with its forepaws on the cushion. From its open jaws came the movements of barking, but no sound from the ghost dog disturbed Acacia Avenue. Such a face as this woman's is only seen when the person is surely near death: it was unrecognisable as a person, as a particular person any more. The electric light made the whole scene abominably clear and detailed. She saw that the cushion was her amber satin one, that the sofa drawn close to the Victorian bow-window, was her own which she had had reupholstered only three months ago, in beige brocade. There wasn't a corner of darkness, of inexplorable scenery in this terrifying spectacle. May Hill stared at it gulping and shuddering but without any sensation of being looked at or looked back at, any more than if it had been 'the Flicks'.

No policeman came. She felt the gravel from the path in her folded body and clothes. An intense cold, the cold of shock which is like an abyss grew on her. She pulled herself upright and staggered into the house.

She drank the tea, swallowed aspirins and then sat in the kitchen until the neat blue sky of morning showing her the bows of swallows against it, filled the kitchen with daylight. Only then did she dare to put her arm round the open door of the front room and switch off the light.

She did two brave things that day: she looked into the front room and found every piece of furniture in its right place, the sofa against the inner wall under the corner cupboard with the cushion on it, where the sun couldn't reach and fade the new brocade, and she looked carefully at her own face in the glass. Here the furniture was all moved, the features sunk, the eyes as though arrested by fright: since this was, in vain to comfort her self with the undisturbed front room with its massy Constable prints, its brass fender and coalscuttle, the vase of daffodils on the table in the window centre arranged just as she'd put them, one by one, her head on her shoulder and her tongue curled round her front teeth. Twice she looked into this empty room and twice she looked at herself. 'You look *dreadful*' she said; 'no more aspirins and tea and no more ghosts or you'll go potty. Out into the garden and then bed at eight o'clock.'

Rudin fell off her lap as she sat in the garden with her sunglasses on. Never would she go into the front garden again after dark and look into that window with its waxwork exhibition of the dying. Never would she go into that room at all. What, she asked, as she crept about the back part of her house, could have brought it all on? A nervous breakdown she supposed. For she made an appalling discovery – if she looked out of the window she invariably saw a funeral at the gate, motor hearse, coffin, flowers and a short train of mourners' cars – while if she looked *in*! Ah she didn't. For two days May Hill ate nothing but some stale scones. With a face as desperate as hers she daren't go out.

On the third a visitor came. Her knock was a like a chirrup. She was a small, plump blonde woman in the grip of high heels and corsets – so unemphasised in looks that her mascara was like the underlining in black ink of a word in pencil. She was May Hill's nearest friend and she was 'psychic'. She gave a shriek which smelled of violets: 'My dear! You must be ill – your aura!'

'It's better than the rest of me, however awful it is,' May Hill said forlornly. It was understood by her friend Flora Vickson, that May Hill's aura was a lovely blue one, uncomplicated but profound – 'the *mystic* blue'. May Hill didn't believe she had one, and she added miserably: 'lumbago'.

'That's it then, it's positively *red*. Danger, danger. Come and sit down and tell me.'

Mrs Vickson was very shrewd inside her little fur coat. May Hill said to herself: 'No fear. I'm not telling anyone in case I'm mad, not even if my aura sets me on fire.'

Yet before she could stop herself she'd burst out crying: 'Oh I've got a nervous breakdown. What does a woman do when she's got a nervous breakdown?'

'Nothing, and you haven't got one, May,' said Mrs Vickson becoming absolutely natural and sensible: 'if you had you wouldn't tell me, you wouldn't know!' They argued; May Hill felt better.

'Well come and have a look,' she said. She led Mrs Vickson

into the front room: 'There, look out of the middle window. What's there?'

'Why – why May? I was just going. I only called to bring you this little book *Healing by Health*. Oh! Who's dead?'

Mrs Vickson was just pulling on her mesh gloves. 'You cruel thing – your poor daffies are dying they haven't any water. I can't go now. I can't walk out in the middle of a funeral, but I *must* say they might pull up outside their own door.'

May Hill lay down on the sofa and shut her eyes. Mrs Vickson's voice seemed to be going round her in circles and getting nearer the floor. But she managed to answer: 'It must be for next door.' After a few deep breaths she managed to stand up and look over Mrs Vickson's shoulder. There it was – the light oak coffin, the hale sun, the chrysanthemum wreaths. She said 'My sight's not too good, Flora. How many cars are there?'

'Three,' Mrs Vickson said, 'why don't they go? Everybody's ready.'

Mrs Hill also saw three cars. But she knew the house next door had been empty for weeks. She stared silently over the frost work lace curtain wondering if the sensation in her head meant that she was going mad, or just her hair turning white.

After a decent pause Mrs Vickson said she thought she might be going now without disrespect.

May Hill didn't try to stop her. At least Mrs Vickson had *seen* the thing.

The worst part of her front room window being haunted, she found, was the extraordinary longing she felt to stand looking in and out of it. She loathed the funeral – and she came to have a purely malicious hatred for the yellow and white ghost dog with his jaws forever jerking in an unheard yap. Two or three nights later a policeman on patrol saw her door open and light in the front room. He walked into the garden and found May Hill lying unconscious on the path. She didn't come round, and her pulse was like a leaf blowing, so he sent for an ambulance. May Hill woke up in hospital.

She passed a great many days there telling the House Physician that on no account must she ever acquire a yellow and white dog: 'under *no* circumstances Doctor,' she said, sitting up in bed in a pink dressing jacket which Mrs Vickson had brought to her, with several sexy novels, a pot of jam, and a remarkable book on self-vision which she asked the Ward Sister to keep away from the patient, 'under no circumstances whatever, R.S.P.C.A. or not, you understand?'

'Yes.'

'I simply won't have it.'

'No.'

The spring backed away like a wave, then surged forward. Neighbours came and mowed May Hill's beautiful dandelions and daisies. The shadows of birds flew straight upwards from the lawns into the leafy boughs – all along Acacia Avenue there was a faint banging and clashing of greenery. All the houses and gardens lay sunny but spotted with shade and all were netted together by the shades of branch, leaf and bole. The tulips, like cups lifted at a tea-party, turned this way and that as the breezes swayed conversationally in the air. The House Physician sent for a psychologist: 'You *like* asking questions. I don't. Such a lot is chucked at me if I didn't get rid of it in golf I'd go crackers. Find out why she's afraid of this yellow and white mongrel.' The psychologist couldn't and didn't. Not from May Hill. She just shut up her mouth in a way that told him how much there was behind it and how tight she'd got her teeth in it. She said she knew what *he* was.

'Well,' they said, in consultation: 'we can't help her here, not with our shortage of beds. Would she attend as an out patient?' She was asked. She would not. She had thrown away the sexy novels and was reading Tchekov again. The word 'ordinary' had changed like a bus board destination into the word 'normal'. And it seemed to her the most beautiful and sublime destination and voyage in this world.

'In this world. In this world.' The phrase started her repeating it aloud for three more days. The other patients were annoyed. One, a woman, supposed to be dying, threw a shoe at her. She sent for her relations. They sat round the death bed bulging out the curtains like a cricketers' tea inside a marquee. Every now and then an eye stuck at May Hill through a slit. As she passed her bed one of the visitors muttered to May Hill: 'You're mad. Nuts, Crackers, off your chump, and they ought to kick you out.'

The Staff who were worried but conscientious, agreed. They begged May Hill to go home, but never to live alone again. When she refused, they suggested she should be a voluntary patient in a mental hospital. She shrieked with laughter for the first time: 'Go into a Bin because I've got haunted eyes – because I'm psychic! Yes, that's what being psychic is – having haunted eyes!'

The House Physician, a young Highlander, listened to her and afterwards seized the psychologist. 'Look, I don't know if it will work,' he exploded. 'Maybe it's not hallucinations. Psychic is only a modern hotch potch term for the second sight. I've a grandmother has it – only hers works backwards. Saw Killiecrankie. She's eighty-five and still goes on the tops of buses. You English! Why do we Scots have to think for you!'

'Possibly,' answered the psychologist, 'because you can't think for yourselves. Thanks though, it could be, though I don't understand what we can do.'

'Do? Hasn't she a friend, that violet-smelling woman? Not a stupid creature for all her looks; get her in. Give her a lead, confide in her man if you must. Miss Hill must be moved to a small room by herself. Your part is to listen.'

'Mine is to listen, thine is to sing!'

The next day on a radiant afternoon tea was carried in to Miss Hill and Mrs Vickson. In the corridor outside the psychologist had his ear flatter to the door than nature had fitted it to his head. The cleaners who hissed up and down the hospital all day with scrubbing brushes had been sent from this undignified scene by the Sister-in-Charge. The conversation, manipulated by Mrs Vickson, began disappointingly for May Hill wanted to talk about Tchekov.

'Well, May, if you will read such rubbish,' Mrs Vickson's tones, pitched for the other listener, were shrill: 'Why, I can't even pronounce his name!'

'Check-off. Think of Check-up,' said the mad one; 'he's a Russian. They're all psychic you know. To think I wanted to be like them! It's my punishment.'

There were polite sounds of sipping, and then Mrs Vickson's voice said:

'After all, May, it's very wonderful. Why don't you get it photographed for the *Psychedelic Times*? Why don't you go home? There's nothing the matter with you now.'

May Hill said something inaudible, which Mrs Vickson took up: 'Frightened? You! When it's such a wonderful wonderful case. I'm not frightened.'

'It's not your funeral,' May Hill said sullenly.

'Ah,' Mrs Vickson's tones were soothing as well as intelligent; 'I think I see.'

'Yes, it's me looking out of the window – it's my hearse! Oh it doesn't look like me, but I'm very ill. You can see, I mean, I shall be, and Die.'

'Well it might be,' Mrs Vickson admitted strenuously through bread and butter: 'but obviously it's a very old you, as you say. And you've got to die, May, the same as me' – Somehow she sounded virtuous – 'I mean Pass Over. Where you'll be so *wonderfully* free, so happy!'

Miss Hill wailed: 'I *want* to go home. But I hate that dog. As soon as he comes into my life I shall know that the end's started.'

'You can't stay here forever,' Mrs Vickson pointed out, in such close sympathy with the psychologist that he nearly danced in the corridor.

'No. I don't know what to do,' May Hill said resignedly, 'I've always been so normal so ordinary. Now if it were you, Flora. Oh Flora, come and live with me. You've seen it too – I should be quite easy with you seeing it.' This upset the psychologist who was beginning to utter 'Case of pure obsession.' Two people couldn't be obsessed. Besides he couldn't imagine a Mrs Vickson obsessed even by herself. While he thought, there would have been silence in the room, if it hadn't been for Mrs Vickson tapping her marquise ring on the locker until she said: 'I can't commit myself yet, May. It might work. The lease of the flat is up – and there's an intense, but not too intense sympathy between us – and we're both psychic too. I must say that once your attitude to our Helpers on the other side – was – was – or would have been – against it. But that's different now. Thank you, May. I'll think it over. Cheer up, dear.'

The psychologist signalled to a nurse. She went in and told them the visiting hour was over. The conversation was reported to the House Physician. 'Both seen it, eh? Well man I'm interested. That woman's got to be up and dressed this evening. I'm taking her home. Sister told me they'd eaten enough tea-cake for half a dozen.'

'It's a risk, Sir.'

'Everything's a risk. That woman, according to my surroundings as a child, is quite normal. She's seen a ghost. My grandmother saw one every day – a woman with white gloves, sitting on the doorstep. No one else saw her. But she'd lived in the house before us.'

'Someone else has seen this one.'

'Well, she doesn't count. She isn't in hospital after it.'

The psychologist hovered. 'I'm afraid I don't believe in ghosts as such.'

With a sardonic smile the Highlander remarked, 'You believe that everything's inside the mind, nothing out.'

'That's it, roughly.'

'Then,' said the House Physician, 'I can't compliment the mind on the conception of Matron. Oh, yes, she's alive and doesn't count as an argument, but so's a ghost you know.'

About nine o'clock that evening when the light seemed weary and dreamy and the cuckoo was sounding one long bell note inside the metal range of hills, the House Physician led May Hill up to her gate. She was stricken and trembling as he opened the gate and asked her to look up. She wouldn't. She cowered. 'Miss Hill, don't let me down,' he begged her, 'all right, I'll look.'

'The middle of the window,' quavered Miss Hill. He saw only the cotton frocks of abandoned furniture, but he said sharply:

'Someone's at home!'

'What do you mean?' May Hill leaped at his arm like a madwoman.

He pointed to the window. 'Who is it? Someone waiting for you?'

'Oh yes doctor, she's waiting for me. Has she got the thermometer in her mouth?'

'Yes,' said the House Physician not knowing whether this was right or wrong: 'let's go in.'

May Hill picked a petal off her coat: 'So you can see her too?'

'Yes I can see her. I think she's a ghost – if necessary. Now sit down on the step and give me your key.'

Millions of petals flew by and settled like light in a new place. When he opened the door she walked in and they went and sat in the kitchen and drank tea.

'This is a doctor!' she thought, amazed. 'No wonder women marry them!'

They talked until it was dark. She told him everything, even how much she hated the dog. Then he got up: 'Now I'm going into that room. No I don't want you. Stay here. Ye have the second sight Miss Hill. Ye'll see a lot more ghosts in your life. For the Lord's sake don't make such a fuss about 'em.'

She heard him walk along the hall and the front room door click open. One last time she'd gone in, she'd come out with her tongue bitten... there was a terrific crash. She jumped up and ran into that room without anything in her to think with. There was a large rent in the glass of the middle bay. The House Physician was grinning and being affected when by himself was muttering: 'there's a wee cannie man!'

May Hill said, 'You've broken my window!' She scratched at him, steadied herself, and was staring at a funeral with a hole in it. Where the glass was shattered, the greater part of the hearse, coffin and flowers had vanished. The other details were as clear as ever. She was less struck by this than by something else:

'How can we see it in the dark?'

He was still grinning.

'We're psychic. Haunted eyes don't need light. I threw a book at it,' he added with pride. May Hill was too busy throwing everything else that was hard and heavy, to reply. When the whole of the glass from the middle window was lying broken on the floor and the garden, and the space showed her only unoccupied darkness, she stopped. 'Gone!' she shouted, and she folded her arms and laughed – hard.

'Yes, and I never saw a thing, and my grandmother's been dead these ten years!' reflected the House Physician. 'Psychology is strong stuff. And I must be gone too,' he said aloud: 'Miss Hill I believe you're cured of what's called an obsession. For heaven's sake don't walk about in here or outside before someone's cleared up, or we shall have you in hospital again, sewing your feet on. You'll go to bed now and take some aspirin. No, I don't think you need anybody with you. We'll just turn the key on the outside of this door. Ye don't want a burglar walking in on ye. Goodnight.'

As he drove off he reflected that he was certainly taking a grave risk with a patient. But not so grave, thought he, as calling in a psychoanalyst, and perhaps an alienist and having a woman end up by being certified.

He had certainly seen nothing. His story of the lady in white gloves struck him as a literary masterpiece until he remembered his Roman Catholic grandmother who certainly, according to her beliefs and inclinations was going to survive *passing over*, as they called it. It wouldn't be nice meeting her after this... yet he chuckled. As he expected, the hospital saw no more of May Hill.

When the last and latest apple bloom had faded and all the rose had gone from the sky, she felt lonely. She knitted, she read more Turgenieff, but it wasn't enough. So she rang up Mrs Vickson, who was vivacious and wanted to know if she really might come and live with her friend 'for a teeny weeny while. Top-knot is very good.'

'I'd love you to, Flora,' Miss Hill sounded excited: 'but it's gone. You must expect anything but dullness and poor old ordinary me. Who is Top-Knot?'

'I'm never dull,' her friend answered happily, 'with so many interests on both sides. Top-Knot – you'll see – I've been taking the most wonderful astral journeys and now they tell me I'm to take a course!'

'How nice!' said May Hill.

Flora Vickson came in a taxi a week later. She had three trunks, a medicine chest and Top-Knot. May Hill didn't notice him until she had drawn her friend inside. He was a yellow and white mongrel puppy.

'Oh, May don't send him away,' said Mrs Vickson with tears, 'he's out of the dog's home. If I send him back and – and nobody else takes him, they'll *put him to sleep*. I love him so much.' May Hill kissed her friend and patted the bouncing young dog: as Mrs Vickson wept she saw a mauve tinge on her friend's plump brightly lit face. It showed even under her whitely powdered complexion. She said: 'Nonsense! I've got over all that, Flora! *Of course* he'll stay with us.'

And she felt on her features that irrepressible grin of triumph the tenderest-minded can't help when having been plagued for weeks, they find dead in the trap, its neck squeezed, a fat mouse. She almost said: 'You won't be frightened, Flora. You're going to be so *wonderfully* happy and free.'

A HOUSE THAT WAS
(1912)
Bertha Thomas

... Where we sang
The mole now labours, and spiders hang.
Thomas Hardy

It was Ivy Harvey, a girl from Kansas, aged two-and-twenty, just disembarked on European shores.

Her parents had treated her to a trip to England, and she was taking it, alone and as unconcernedly as though it were a mere run from London to the Isle of Wight.

The liner *Recordiana* set her down at Fishguard, South Wales. 'Land of a hundred castles,' read Ivy from her guide book. 'Say, I'll stop and sample one or two of these before I jog on.'

Now Ivy had never seen any ancient thing in her life.

But before she was two days older she had viewed a cathedral whose bells were ringing in King John's time, a palace where men feasted in the days of the Black Prince, mysterious carved stone wayside crosses of untold antiquity, and castles such as made of all the wildest romances she had ever read and laughed at so many bits of real life.

On the third afternoon – the morning had added a Merlin's cave and an Arthur's Stone to her Welsh records – she stood on the ramparts of Carreg Cenen, a ruined fortress great in story, back to the legendary days of the Wizard and the Warrior King, and looking as though sprung by magic from the precipitous rocky steep whence, from miles afar, it arrests the attention.

Such tokens of things that have lasted – of continuous life and action unbroken from generation to generation – to the Britisher mere common objects of his country – were fascinating novelties to Ivy, half-mazing her with wonder and enjoyment.

'I must grab on to that London express before breakfast tomorrow,' she said, contemplating the rare and splendid panorama of mountain crags and evergreen pastures looking as if they were just created, 'or I'll be staying here till I die! I just can't believe these things have been round here all these ages – and I never dreamt!'

Now to get back to the Glendower Arms, Llanffelix, five miles by the high road. Striking a bee-line across country, Ivy walked for two hours up and down deep land dips, numerous and undiscernible till you came upon them as crevasses in a glacier; then followed a fisherman's path by an alder-fringed brook to its full stop near a cottage farm, buried like a hermit's cell in a shady, sleepy hollow.

'Well, I've loafed about a might sight,' she sighed, 'and all to end up with this shallow! Hey, my dear boy in the barn there! I want the way to Llanffelix – if there is one.'

The dear boy carefully shut all of him but his head and scowling face into the barn. But Ivy was not to be taken in by that scowl. 'It just yells at you, "There's a stranger and an enemy coming along. Shoot or hide!" But it means, "This young lady is about to address me in English, a foreign tongue with which circumstances have prevented my becoming sufficiently acquainted to enable me to reply with suitable fluency and ease."'

So Ivy smiled her winningest, and cooed entreaty, 'Llanffelix – where?'

He pointed to the setting sun, bawled something uncatchable, and bolted himself securely into the barn.

Facing westward, Ivy explored two hilly fields, with no discoverable outlet till a kink in the hedge disclosed a little spiked iron gateway, as it were, into private grounds, and alongside a brick-walled enclosure.

'That there's a large cabbage-patch,' reasoned Ivy. 'Should belong to a white man with an English tongue in his head.'

She broke through into the grass-grown glade – ringed with forest trees, gay underfoot with yellow Turk's-cap lilies and blue wild hyacinths – and stopped short, met by something more beautiful than the loveliest dream.

A tiny path slanting steeply and straightly upward, between two thin files of over-shadowing fir, ash, and sycamore, with an undergrowth of rich-flowering laburnum, whose branches, meeting overhead, fanned a complete golden avenue, radiant, dazzling, for as far onward as eye could reach.

'Oh, but this is Fairyland!' exclaimed Ivy. 'Fairyland, saying, "Come and find me." Wait, I'm coming.'

She wanted a peep through the dilapidated doorway into the herb garden. Paradise forsaken and run wild. A hedgehog was sunning itself on a low stone bank; a snake and a lizard slithered away at her tread: 'Impish elves in disguise,' her roused fancy suggested. Or spirits of departed presences revisiting in these lowly shapes, their old haunts. Who knows?

'I'm just gone silly,' she told herself. 'But don't tell me I'm here in one and the same world as the Kansas Cowboys' Club at the Crack Ball Splitters.'

Onward she climbed under that golden arcade. The laburnum clusters, hanging thick as grapes in an Italian vineyard, almost touched her head, half intoxicating her with their fragrance, mingled with scents of hawthorn hedges in the fields beyond. A slit in the leafy screen startled her with a sudden passing glimpse of Carreg Cenen Castle, looking, by some trick of atmosphere, thirty miles off instead of three – dark, rugged, angular, like some mighty monster couched there and waiting to spring.

Atop she found a little shrubbery gate. Close before her loomed the rough-cast walls and gables of a house, ancient looking and grey.

Turning to say goodbye to the golden avenue, Ivy distinctly saw, or thought she saw, an ugly, hobgoblin-like thing – black monkey or mannikin – picking his way upward in her wake. Fancy, at her tricks again! Nothing but the wriggling shadow of a dark bush in the breeze. 'Git! You bogey man!' quoth Ivy, indignant though half scared by an illusion born, perhaps, of that sheer craving for crude contrast that drove court-beauties of old to keep apes and black dwarfs at their sides as a set-off to their charms.

Past a shrubbery that was all blossom and no shrub, she slipped furtively by the veranda front, and round the angle to the drive and entrance door of solid oak under a pointed wooden porch. Ivy pulled at the old bell knob. But none answered.

Glancing up at the chimneys, 'Smoke means fire,' she said hopefully. 'Fire means man,' and rang again. Still nothing happened.

Came a faint shuffling as of slippered feet; a hand groped at the latch, and the door was opened to her.

II

By a dead woman! So it struck her. A corpse-thing. Ivy stood aghast, spellbound with horror, or she would have turned and fled from the shrivelled, vanishing-looking shape, huddled in a loose wrapper, the parched, blanched features, sunken eyes, and dishevelled hair, as it were, of a death's head, hastily enveloped in an old woollen shawl.

Then, as she stood her ground, she perceived that those eyes were regarding her intelligently. She there was still living, though perhaps dying. Anyway, she looked at it; and compassion forbade Ivy to flee.

'Oh, please excuse,' she stammered out, 'I've missed my way from Carreg Cenen, and thought to ask it. It's a long distance from over there. I've disturbed you... I never meant...'

Voice and nerve failed her to go on.

'What! Have you walked from Carreg Cenen?' said the Grey Lady kindly. 'You must be very tired. Would you not like to rest yourself for a few minutes? Will you come in?'

Ivy, who was quick-witted, had recovered herself. 'I was a sheep to be scared so just because she looks a bit ill.' 'Oh, I'll be pleased to,' she responded aloud. There was nothing so terrifying here after all when you came to look. The wasted features were delicate, the eyes came to life as the lips spoke. And Ivy had caught a glimpse of the old-world house interior.

'I'm raging to see inside,' she thought. 'Just the quaintest old tenement! With the dearest old lady ghost hanging on to it!' For that it was the lady speaking was as obvious to her as, to the lady, that Ivy was an American girl on her travels. Such mutual introduction seemed enough, and she stepped into the little hall.

Ravishing to Ivy beyond any millionaire's palace was the simple, sober symmetry of a Welsh country house – the old oak flooring, settle, chest, and woodwork. 'Those fixings were sawn before ever the *Mayflower* set sail,' she thought enviously. 'And that oak staircase I'd love to carry straight off to Kansas City. Ho! The lady ghost has a flesh-and-blood maid, at all events,' as a female domestic showed herself at a doorway in the passage, eyeing Ivy unpleasantly.

A handsome but evil and insolent face that gave her a turn, like the scarecrow her imagination had conjured up in the Golden Avenue. Better the Grey Ghost by far, Ivy felt, shut in with her now in the sitting-room opening on the veranda, a room whose faded, decaying upholstery and tottering furniture seemed, like its occupant, perilously nearing its end.

Like to like! Ivy's young eyes flew straight to the one thing bright and beautiful here visible. A vignette portrait in pastels of a young girl that hung over the fireplace.

Such a girl! Coils of Italian-like dark hair crowning a brilliant young face, vivid-complexioned and of thrilling vivacity. It shone there like a jewel in a vault. What was it sent the visitor's eye rebounding to the withered visage beneath the shawl, wondering doubtfully? The Grey Lady shook her head...

'My sister Julie,' she said, 'who died in May.' Lingeringly, as to herself, she added, 'The May after that likeness was painted.'

'What eyes!' murmured the fascinated Ivy. 'They dance, they sing. Yet – she died?'

The grey face smiled wistfully, the white lips let fall:

'Here where we were born and brought up – so suddenly – as by the visitation of God – she was taken... Over forty years gone by.'

'And you, you poor old dear, have you been mouldering here ever since?' Ivy wondered on silently. But she said, regarding the lovely hill-and-dale prospect from the windows, 'What a beautiful place this is, and how happy you must be to live here and have all these enjoyments without the seeking!'

'While I,' the other resumed unheedingly, 'who had gone hence to be married at the New Year, was never to set foot in the old home again till... yesterday, was it? No, longer ago than that, but not much. One forgets. Few here now remember me or my dear – my lost husband.'

'A widow, then,' thought Ivy pondering. 'And she – Julie?'

'Never a bride!'

Ivy, startled at the prompt reply, perceived she had been thinking aloud.

'Forgive me if I seem impertinent,' she said. 'But when people are nice to me as you have been I get interested in them, forget my play talk and company manners, and long to know what their lives are and all that they do and have done.'

She could not keep her eyes from that face on the wall there – 'So fair and morning-eyed!' 'She is beautiful,' she let fall.

'I was not,' said the Grey Woman. 'And yet—'

'It was you he preferred.' The words sprang spontaneously from Ivy's lips.

The strangeness of it, that they two, only just met together, two with half a century and the ocean between their ages and their homes, and who did not know so much as one another's names, should be discoursing thus, was unfelt by both, as though mutually hypnotised. Ivy's sympathetic little soul went out to the lonely invalid. While to her, the native born, the Spirit of Place was calling back the remote facts that had determined her life's course, and moving her to relate them to this eager and attractive listener who had dropped, as it were, from the clouds.

'We were not brought up orderly – not like other girls. Father and Mother had poor health, and lived in a way of their own to humour it. Their dress and habits were peculiar; they kept odd hours, paid no visits and received none. My Frankie and I used to meet by the stealth in the lanes after dusk, till the whole countryside rang with our romance, shocked out of measure.'

'Why?' asked the New World maiden naively.

'Well, it was not customary,' her hostess explained with a passing smile. 'Only farmers' or labourers' daughters did such things, and it was many generations since our husbandmen

ancestors had struggled up into the ranks of the gentry. People
wrote to tell my mother of the scandal. It had to be stopped, and
we were forbidden to meet. Frankie and I stopped it. We ran
away.'

'Oh, well done!' came from the impulsive Ivy. She thought a
good deal. The narrator pursued.

'Julie was against it. She said, "He is delightful, but he will
make you miserable. He must. He was known for a waster and a
free-liver." I said, "You wait here for your saint and prince. He
loves me. And I? By him I stand or fall. But I think I believe...
that together we shall stand." Then she helped us. Had she lived
she would have agreed that I was right. And yet,' in an undertone,
distantly, 'Julie was not quite wrong.'

Ivy felt as if between two phantom-like presences. For Julie
there opposite, so fair and free-hearted in her unspent youth,
radiant with energy and the joy of life, seemed every bit as real
to her as the shadow-woman in the chair, the woman with the
shrunken, marred visage, stamped with the wear and tear of a
long and chequered life – joys of the sweetest, sorrows of the
sharpest, the tribulations and ups and downs of a life lived out
bravely to its desolate end. 'Game to the last bunch of feathers!'
thought Ivy, admiring the spark of Julie-like animation
smouldering in those dimmed and dimming eyes. Sister souls,
Julie and she. But what an unspeakable gap between their
destinies! Which, now, was the more blessed?

III

Here a piece of buxom humanity – the sinister-looking maid-
servant Ivy had caught sight of in the passage – came sauntering
past the veranda. Her watchful stare inside was as purposely
insolent as a grimace. The lady rose sharply, opened the window

and stepped out to give some peremptory order. The reply it provoked Ivy did not catch, but it seemed of the box-on-the-ear, slap-in-the-face temper. A moment's altercation followed, then the maid walked away, but the little passage-at-arms had upset the old lady. With difficulty she got back into the room, a ghastly pallor on her cheek, a glassy look in her eyes. She staggered and fell. Ivy caught her in her arms and lifted her on to the sofa, shocked at finding but a mere featherweight to lift.

'Fainted. Now if I yell for help,' Ivy reflected, 'it will only bring back that devil of a woman – enough to kill her outright.' Without an instant's hesitation she went into the passage and through a door into the servant's quarters, and faced the demon in her kitchen den.

'Some water for your mistress,' she demanded. 'She has fainted.'

'My mistress, indeed!' came the answer. 'I take no orders from her – nor from you – whoever you may be.'

'I give no orders,' said Ivy, promptly. Her sharp eyes had immediately detected a brandy bottle half full on the dresser.

'But a thimbleful of that – if you can spare it – with some water, will bring her round. I would save you the trouble.'

She had scored – got what she wanted; and in a few minutes had revived the prostrate invalid, who struggled to a sitting posture with a bewildered look round. 'You were taken bad,' said Ivy soothingly, 'and just toppling over when I caught you. I thought if I called your servant you might be annoyed.'

The lady shuddered. All that was left of her seemed to cling to the kindly girl. 'Appallingly weak and just terrified of that woman,' thought Ivy, perplexed and concerned.

'Not my servant,' she was told. 'She and her husband stayed on in charge here after the last owner's death, and my coming displeased her, for good reasons of her own. A strange breed too; no native here.'

'Well, I tell you our home helps in Kansas don't spoil us,' said Ivy feelingly, 'but that type makes me feel boiling inside.'

The Grey Ghost smiled. The eye-spark flickered again and in a few minutes she seemed to Ivy about as much alive as before. Presently, to their mutual surprise, the maid-demon brought in the tea, for which previous order had been given.

'Brazen thing!' thought Ivy; 'she just wanted to know what we were doing. She can't look me in the face, though. I'd give anything to see the inside of her head.'

Recalling that tea with the Grey Ghost, Ivy could think herself the dupe of false memory, though every detail of it is as clear to her mind's eye as a Dutch picture seen under a triplex American arc.

'She who had just now seemed utterly broke in spirit and body seemed to grow almost fit again,' so Ivy afterwards described the scene, 'as she went chattering on at a great rate, telling me heaps and stacks of things – her life's tale, but all in scraps, like nuggets. A grey bundle of energy, sunk in the chair, she held me fast by a moving show of pictures in the web of her life.'

'A web of tangled yarn,' from the leaving of her home, with one irrevocably dear, chronically undeserving. One with lofty ideals, good gifts, and right intuitions, yet in conduct falling often below the level of the despised Philistine. One to wreck the life of a feebler partner – their life's voyage together a twenty years' venture – but whose bark her unflagging spirit and resource had kept afloat to the last. Children born and reared to become fresh springs of joy and of anguish; bright hopes gleaming and ending like rockets; poverty that failed to depress, windfalls that failed to enrich; a haphazard existence spent chiefly abroad – for cheapness – births, sicknesses, deaths; a troubled sea out of which in her widowhood she had drifted into a quiet backwater in a foreign town with a beloved son, the last survivor of her offspring, not one of whom were built for a long span, alas!

If, after losing him, she had gone on living, it was from habit only.

And now the old home, passed long ago into the hands of distant kinsmen, had reverted to her ownership, heavily mortgaged and valueless, a prey to be handed over to the speculative builder – a mock heritage that had brought her hither from the little German capital where she still sat mourning for her best beloved. She was wanted here to order and to rule, but had arrived to succumb only, and to vanish.

Every once in a while the graveyard shadow crept over her countenance, wiping out the life therein. She thrilled it back till the thread of reminiscence was ended, leading her on to where Julie had lain these many years.

IV

For it was only a flare-up after all. Back came that mortal pallor, never more to be driven away. The maid-devil re-entered stealthily. 'Oh mercy!' moaned poor Ivy, to whom the room seemed full of shudders. When that hard, cruel, handsome face had removed itself, together with the tea-things, the invalid, with a final effort to rally, said feebly:

'It's poor hospitality I've shown you, young lady!'

'Why no—quite a flourish tea, you mean,' said Ivy cheerfully. 'But I'm troubling you.' The Grey Ghost rose totteringly – Ivy helped her back to the sofa, where she lay unable to speak or to stir, Ivy now fully alive to her own predicament. Alone in a strange house with its dying mistress, an utter stranger. Ought she not properly to withdraw her interloping presence? 'And leave her with that she-devil?' her nominal servant, the real mistress and tormentor of the moribund lady of the manor. 'The idea makes me sick. But I must call someone.'

She moved, but the quick, appealing, detaining hold taken of the little dainty hand was heart-rending. 'Hark you,' said Ivy, steadily. 'Strike me dead if I leave you alone with her! Let me go. I'll polish her off, that I swear.' Gently disengaging herself she went quickly back to the dragon's den and asked her:

'Where is your husband?'

'And what do you want with him, pray?' demanded the woman, incensed.

'I want you,' said Ivy, 'to tell him to go straight to Llanffelix for the doctor, and not to come back without him. The lady here is perilously ill – dying, I fear.'

'Oh these old people!' was the rejoinder. 'They give a lot of trouble! Why can't she die and have done with it?'

'Mind you,' said Ivy, restraining herself, 'I am staying at the Glendower Arms in the town. If you refuse to take my warning and my advice – well, it shall be known there; and you will be blamed, should this poor lady die unattended.'

The shot had told. The hostelry was one of standing. County families stayed there. Ivy might belong to one of these for all that the house-servant could tell. She went out into the yard. 'Nat!' she shouted peremptorily. An absent-minded, subdued-looking Welshman emerged from the shed where he was chopping wood. Ivy stayed to hear the message given and see the man start, nothing loth, on his errand to the town. 'Urgent, mind!' she called out after him, and turning her back on the wife flew back to the faded parlour where the lady lay in a stupor. But she stirred faintly, and her eyes glimmered consciousness at the girl's approach. 'I don't know who you are,' she said, 'but it seems to me I have been entertaining an angel unawares.'

'She's slipped back a few paces since I left the room,' poor Ivy observed, dismayed. She was sinking fast now. Restoratives avail not where nothing is left to restore. Immeasurable to Ivy was the hour and a half that she sat there, by the light of a solitary candle, watching the departing spirit, herself on the verge of collapse under the nerve tension of the closing scene of that strange afternoon. Only Julie, who could never grow old, seemed to become more living, beaming joy and welcome down on the sister, worn and widowed, who was coming to meet her. This that was happening was not a calamity or a tragedy, but a change. So felt the looker-on.

At intervals she spoke, in broken accents; but through those disconnected utterances ran a traceable thread. Not death, but life taking lingering leave of her; the latter years the first to slip away – widowhood, motherhood, wifehood – as a tale that is told. Then the love romance of half a century away.

'He says there's none he'd rather meet 'neath moon or star,
Than me – of all that are!'
she said slowly, not loudly, with an emphasis that rings in the girl's ears to this day.

Lastly, the old home life with Julie in the House that Was – things from the very Back of Beyond of memory; snatches of talk and Jest. She saw Julie everywhere – in Ivy – in the picture, fitfully recalling little happenings, follies, drolleries, things childish, even babyish, trifles every one, yet undying, as are things felt in the beginning, when God created the heavens and the earth; and those young things questioned not but that for themselves and their pleasure they are and were created.

At length, when Ivy was feeling almost as old as her charge, came the relieving sound of wheels on the drive and an arrival. The Satanic servant woman, in the guise of a pattern parlourmaid and with the mien of a ministering angel announced, 'Dr Edwards.'

At the sight of the strong, benignant, prosperous, and fatherly looking professional man, Ivy was herself again at once.

In a word or two she explained her position. A stranger to the patient, she was none – little though she suspected it – to the Llanffelix medical magnate. The pretty little American girl staying at the Glendower Arms had been the three days' wonder and talk of the town, and he accepted her accidental presence here without surprise. Then he looked at the inanimate form on the sofa, put his finger on the flickering pulse and shook his head, saying:

'Her life is over. Only her wonderful spirit has kept her here in this world so long. There is nothing to be done – nothing.'

He seemed at least concerned for the young lady herself, nerve-worn and wearied out. 'You must get home,' he told her. She hesitated, then came out with it:

'I have vowed not to leave her alone with that – that creature; I mean with nobody to moan to but that servant-woman. They had a little wrestling-match a while ago that ended disastrously, in a faint.' She looked at him significantly and saw he understood.

'We feared as much,' he sighed. 'But it was difficult; it seemed that it needed a stranger and a foreigner like yourself to interfere to protect her. But the man Nat, though a booby and a chicken-heart, is a good fellow, and I got enough out of him to make me bring a nurse along with me – one who knew her and whom once she knew – Ruth Harris, the daughter of old Betty who nursed them both.'

'Both?'

'Both.'

He was looking at Julie's face in the portrait, fixedly, intently, as though it meant something to him. Might his boyhood's romance, perhaps, lie buried in the grave with her? – a student lad's adoration – a mere jest, perhaps, to the beauty there in the pride of her youth? Ivy wondered, but she never knew.

'I am sending my servant back to Llanffelix with an order,' he said. 'He shall drive you to the Glendower Arms.'

'If I am of no service here,' Ivy assented. 'Only... that serpent – that hateful woman...'

'Shall not come near her. You may trust Ruth not to leave her for a moment, and I myself shall stay on for as long as may be necessary.'

Ivy bent down and kissed the pale, fine forehead, then turned to go. The doctor shook hands with her, saying emphatically: 'You have done a beautiful thing, young lady – a thing for which I would thank you, as would not a few others that are left, right heartily, did they but know – softened the last hours of one of the cleverest and most charming women that they ever knew.'

Ivy drove from the door, her memory indelibly impressed by the image of the Lady of the House that Was. She never recovered consciousness, Ivy heard on the morrow, but died at dawn, so quietly that to the watchers the moment was all but imperceptible when she crossed the border into the Land of Memory.

THE MAN AND THE RAT
(1941)
Pennar Davies
Translated by Mihangel Morgan

The Man

Is it completely impossible for you to come here to visit, right now? I think that's the only thing that saddens me – your constant absence. If I were to think of those evenings in Odessa – what pain, what yearning possesses me. Something draws me, relentlessly and without mercy, draws me towards you. There is no remedy for me but your love, your body, your presence. Come if you can, come at once. Even if you are beginning by now to forget me (but that *cannot* be true!) think at least about the interesting experiment I'm in the process of organising now. It would be full of interest for you. You'd really like Repin in any case. He is the cleverest and smartest rodent I've seen for some time. He learned to pull that lever a thousand times quicker than the others. Indeed, he's started to pull the lever *twice* at a time so that he gets two rewards at one go and so conserves his valuable energy. That's a genius for you! In comparison, the other two have average intelligence. Maliafin looks much more stupid than Fasnezof as he is so fat and lazy. Fasnezof is the fastest *runner* I have, and an attractive rat, I believe – that's to say from a rat's perspective! But Repin is closest to my heart! – apart from you, my friend who is *in* my heart at all times, day and night, and reigns there...

The Rat

I don't like this new world, not very much. It's far too clean, too hard, too cold, too easy to live in it! Simply pulling this thing, and running across the smooth cold floor, and receiving good but monotonous food from that big thing there. This is no way for a rat to live. Where is the stuffy air and the darkness and the dirty water? Such things are exciting in comparison to the smoothness and uniformity and the endless brightness that surrounds me now. I'm so irritated seeing a disgusting reflection of a rat following me everywhere – in the floor and in the big thing that gives me food. I'd love to live a normal life again. This is no life for a rat.

The Man

...Thankyou, Michail, oh thankyou for the promise. But hurry, my friend, hurry. My heart awaits. I think of you as I go to sleep at night and when I get up in the morning. There is always room for you in my bed – and there is a place for nothing besides you in my heart. And the experiment gets more exciting every day. We have put the three rats in the same case now, and they have now become *viciously* ravenous. Fasnezof the great runner and the *beau*! – has gone insane with hunger today. He's been attempting to jump through the glass case. He's lost his senses entirely. The three of them have tried to eat the lever and the cylinder which contains the food. But Repin is the wisest of them by a long way. He clearly *knows* in his *mind* that it's pointless to waste time on the cylinder; he has been concentrating on the lever the entire time. The other two have pulled our lever twice or three times, but, of course, the piece of food is eaten every time before the operator of the lever can run back to the cylinder! Maliafin was the first to give up on the work, the lazybones. He had waited at the cylinder for hours, expecting the tidbits that fell to him sometimes following Repin's experiments. I'm afraid he's a parasite by nature, a *petit bourgeois* almost. And he's as fat as a capitalist too, fair play to him! He's a bad influence on Fasnezof I'm afraid. Fasnezof has been a disappointment to me. He gave up on reason and common sense and cooperation soon after Maliafin, and yet he was the first to become confused by starvation, and to attack the glass and the aluminium in a sort of ravenous greed. I had thought there was more stability in him. By the way, there was such an expression of disappointment on his face after he pulled the lever the first time and ran to the cylinder to see the bit of food disappearing into Maliafin's mouth! You would have laughed. But Repin! Repin is the rat for me. He was the last to lose his mind to madness, and I'm sure that it was the panic of the others that caused it. He was also the first to regain his sanity and begin working with reason and seriousness again. And he's working in the right direction. He's been working harder by far than the others put together. That is how intelligence and genius have to dedicate themselves to the service of society! So stupidity and poverty of mind take advantage of our intelligence and genius. We are the Repins of society, and millions of Fasnezofs and Maliafins exploit our energy and wisdom. I have been reading the book of the old superstition recently. And I noticed this truism: 'If any man desire to be first, the same shall be last of all and servant of all.' It isn't fair. Bring your comfort to me Michail...

The Rat

I must have food. I must have food. Food is life. I must have food.

Someone must have arranged things to be this way. Our agonising condition is no accident. It must be that someone, someone completely incomprehensible, outside our lives, someone who enjoys our agonies and our stupidity and our foolish selfishness. The situation is too despicable to be accidental. If I pull this thing here, the others will get pieces of food from that big thing there. If the fat rat pulls, I and the fast rat will get the food. If the fast rat pulls, then there's a chance for the fat rat and me again to have food. The one who does the work does not get the profit. How despicable, what a curse. The worker does not get fed. And therefore my fat companion and my fast companion will have given up working. The idiots: can't they see we will perish unless we cooperate? I may produce food for them; but they must produce food for me too. That much is obvious: but they are too daft and too stupid to understand. I've wasted too much time already trying to make them get it. I have pawed their bodies; I have bitten their tails; I've *endeavoured* to lead them from the big thing there to this small thing. But they can't understand. They're too dull. Every effort was in vain. Instead of cooperating they prefer to attack me, and to get at me, and to chase me. The fools! The morons! They deserve to starve and die.

But who takes pleasure in our tribulations? Oh, starvation makes me confused. Great Shiny Thing, give us this day our daily bread. Starvation is like a crazy rat inside me, biting and biting.

The fools! I'm ready to work for all of us, but they have to keep at least a little food for me. But they're too silly and too limited and too greedy to appreciate my value – when I die from starvation. But now they continue to eat every morsel of food that comes out of that big thing there as a reward for my work. Every scrap has gone before I can reach it. The situation is perfectly horrible. More than likely, it will be me, the most sensible, who will be the first to die.

Someone has to save me. I must have food. Life is food.

But I must save myself. If only I could run a thousand times faster than my swift friend! If only I could snatch a bit of food sometimes before my fat friend can get his teeth into it!

Oh I have a plan – yes – a hope – salvation! A rat cannot eat more than one piece at a time. One rat, one turn, one morsel.

And therefore, every time, there has to be one portion for the fat one and one portion for the quick one and one for the brainy one! One, one, one. One, one, one. One, one, one! And while the fat and the quick are eating their pieces, there's a chance for the brainy to run and grab his piece. I have to do the work of three rats each time.

It's better than starving.

One, one, one.

Click, click, click... click, click, click... click, click, click.

The Man

...Michail, friend! The miracle has happened. What a brain he has – what intelligence, what a genius! If only you were here to see it! Repin – my hand shakes with joy and agitation – it's hard to write! My hero Repin – he pulls the lever *three times* every time now. *Three times*! Isn't he brilliant, noble, sublime? Is this not the entire hope of life on earth? Three times. Don't you see? While Fasnezof and Maliafin eat their pieces, one piece each, Repin has time to run from the lever to the cylinder to snatch the other piece. That's the only way he can get food, since there's no such thing as cooperation in his society. The only way. But isn't it an *achievement*? That a rat can think like this. You have the brilliance of a genius here. But the social morale of Maliafin and Fasnezof is quite hopeless. They don't do a *thing* to help Repin. They wait at the cylinder and eat – that's all. The *canaille*! The scum! The fat cats! The thieving bastards! The rotten fat rats! The putrid, diseased, stinking, poisonshits! Repin had worked hard for them for a whole hour. An hour! Think of it! But I want to take Repin out of the case soon. It will be interesting to see what Maliafin and Fasnezof will do without him. But my heart leaps when I think of Repin. Such a pity you couldn't come! But come, Michail, as soon as you can, and put an end to this enormous yearning that abides within me.

The Rat

What an enormous relief to get out of that oppressive atmosphere. What has happened to the morons, I wonder? How nice to have some different food.

The Man

...It was heavenly to receive your letter and the beautiful photograph. Your beard is growing well. But woe is me: it will hide some of the most attractive parts of your face. Woe is me, indeed! And who is the girl who is with you? A fellow officer, probably. Do you like working with women? I hate seeing women smirking and giggling around the workplace. They are so uninteresting. I have to disappoint you about the experiment. Fasnezof has not followed Repin's example. He did pull the lever, but only once each time. And of course, the piece had gone each time too before he reached the cylinder. Once, indeed he pulled the lever twice and so he got a bit. But that was a fluke, no doubt about it. Fasnezof's plan to begin with was to run as fast as he could in order to beat the old fellow Maliafin, but he couldn't run fast enough. Then, realising he couldn't reach the cylinder in time, he begun to *attack* Maliafin. Viciously! But Maliafin can defend himself excellently, it seems. Then in time, Fasnezof madly attacked the cylinder, as before, the idiot. But he's exhausted now, and he's lying quietly on the floor of the case, gazing at the cylinder. Maliafin hasn't left the cylinder at all! In the meantime, Repin is happily resting, his belly full of food and satisfaction. I will put him back in the case with the others shortly. I wonder if he will feed the others! He's not starving now.

But remember, friend, I am starving, wanting to see you and hold you. The photograph has caused a craving in me. Can't you come, Michail?

The Rat

Oho! Here I am on the cold, smooth floor, under the Great Shining Thing. And here's my fat friend and my fast friend lying under the thing that gives food. That's their regular place! I wonder if they're starving? I'd like to have a few bites before resting again... click, click, click... They're *terribly* hungry. They rush at the food insanely. I'm not very keen on this food here. The others gobble it up unhesitantly... click, click, click... Yes, the food is bland. I'd rather rest than eat now, rest and watch my starving companions. If they want more food they'll have to work for it... But here they come to me and paw at my body. They're asking for food, poor things! Both of them. Is it laziness or stupidity that stops these rats from working themselves to get food? Perhaps laziness *is* stupidity. Well I'm prepared to give them a little help. But just a little! ...click, click, click... click, click, click, click...

The Man

P.S. – Your second letter has just arrived. I must admit your news is a surprise and a disappointment to me. I feel as though I have lost someone who was very dear to me. I can do nothing but grieve for you, Michail. But that's it. Be happy. I can't imagine you living with a wife, and I have not dared to look at the photograph again. I fail completely to understand this thing. That's the truth. I can't understand. Why? That's the unanswerable question. You've left me, gone out of my abnormal, struggling, electric life and become part of that normal, strange, meaningless world which is beyond my comprehension and understanding. I don't know what to say. And yet – bless you, Michail...

The Rat

Here they are, coming after me again. They want more food. Well, the fools have to work. Why should I be a slave to them? If they come after me, I can run away. Both of them must learn to earn their own food...

Here they come! What a hunt! The fast one can run like the wind. There's fun in a hunt. The wretches! The fools!

The Man

...Michail, how lonely I am! Why have you done this?...

The Rat

Better for me to give them food, after all. But this fast runner here has gone mad, and is trying to kill me! I've had it! Why does such awfulness happen? Someone must be watching. But he's got hold of me, his teeth sink into my neck. Save me, save me! Whatever you are, save me!

The Man

P.S. again – Michail, this is the last letter you will ever have from me. This is the last letter I will write. I see there is no safe place for genius to abide in society. Genius is an abnormal thing, and the normality of society is opposed to it. When I was your love, I had a sort of society of my own, and it was possible for me to challenge the normal world and its nasty enmity. But now you have a woman in my place. I stand alone against the world, and the world is stronger than me.

Even Repin has gone. While I was writing this letter, Fasnezof attacked him. I've just seen the consequences. Repin's body lies on the floor of the case near the lever, and Fasnezof is ripping him ferociously. Hatred gone mad – that's Fasnezof now. The scene is revolting and terrifying. I feel sick after looking at it. Repin is not moving at all.

I will stroll over to the steep cliff at the other side of the forest tonight. Do you remember? Our cliff? I will never come back.

NOBODY DIES... NOBODY LIVES...
(c. 1950s)
Ken Etheridge

The young man crossed the polluted rivers and plains and came at last to the New Atlantis after the disaster of the bombs.

The city, golden and white in the morning glow, was built on the slopes of the highest mountain in the west. For a moment the mirrors that caught the solar rays and provided its heat and power flashed and blinded him. He shielded his eyes with his hands and stumbled forward to the portals. After a brief interrogation the guards took him in, stripped him of his stained and dirty clothing, made him shower and gave him a new tunic and a pair of shorts. They looked at his identity disc, which said simply DIRK and phoned to the civic police.

Dirk soon found himself facing Aaron, one of the Elders. He was impressed by the old man's long white hair and beard, the healthy colour of his cheeks and his sinewy build.

'I am Aaron, and Elder of the City. Where are your papers?' Dirk showed them.

'And the all-clear card?' went on the old man, scrutinising the papers. 'You are clean?' He raised his eyes for a moment. He liked this tall, young man with the bold, dark eyes and the long hair.

'Yes.' His eyes flickered on the lie, but the other did not see them, busy as he was with the papers.

'The mountains protected us. We survived,' said the old man, as if reading the questions in Dirk's mind. 'Why did you come here?'

'To see.'

'Then you shall see.'

They went into the street.

Dirk saw the clean plastic cubicles, arranged in irregular terraces on the hillside. They were spotless, set in green lawns and gardens. Funicular railcars were suspended above the wide streets, connecting them with parks, shopping centres and theatres and stadiums. He was shown sports arenas, grassed with nylon sward of permanent green with every facility for refreshment and hygiene. All the seats were kept at an even temperature by nuclear power, that also operated the lighting and the mechanisation of the chainstores and the arenas.

Not one car could he see.

'We banned cars a century ago,' said the old man. 'My grandfather just remembers them. Transport lorries, too. We do not need such monsters to assault our ears and our noses. Lifts and funicular cars carry all our needs.'

'I see no children.'

The old man smiled.

'Children? We decided not to have any more at the beginning of the twenty-first century. We could not feed and clothe them on the produce of the state. What need is there for children when everybody lives forever?'

Dirk looked amazed. 'You mean—?'

'We have conquered all known diseases. We have combated decay of the body and the mind. Nothing can kill.'

A laughing party of young people went by, the youths kissing and fondling the girls.

'I don't understand,' said Dirk. 'You said that there had been no children since the twenty-first century. And now we are in the twenty-third. Who are these young men and women, then?'

'They are all a hundred years old.'

'And still healthy and amorous?'

'Of course. They make love. There are no consequences.'

'The women look deprived.' He pointed to a few sitting in the shade of a banana-tree. One had a plastic doll in her arms, crooning to it and rocking it gently. Another had a cage with a bird, another a spider in a glass box.

'The pets take the place of the children,' Aaron said.

Dirk said, 'You cannot eradicate the instincts.'

'They can be conditioned. Come. There is more to see.' He led the way to a funicular car, talking as they went. 'You are still harassed by memories, young man.'

'How else?' Dirk sighed. 'So much of the twentieth century affected my family. Nuclear fallout mutilated the genes that made me.'

'Ah yes. The western world was festering from the wounds of three world wars, feverish from the effetism of incurable cancers, which men tried to palliate with obscenities and perversions. Men at the end of hope always crawl back into the dirt.'

'Perhaps we were too much occupied by wealth.'

'Gold and a lust for gold gave a false sense of security. An art obsessed with trivialities is no less unreal. You cannot live forever on the fat of the spirit, fed too long on centuries of creative work from the Dark Ages. A nation of dwarfs cannot breed giants. The people hid their heads in despair, drugged and drunken, fleeing the disaster they knew would come one day.'

Dirk smiled. 'Are you perfect in the New Atlantis?'

He looked again at the ordered and fruitful landscape. The healthy men and women and the clean streets that smelled like a hospital ward.

The old man gave him a sharp look. 'If you mean we have no mentally-retarded here. You are right. The weak, the perverted, the criminal, we do not allow to breed. Such charity in the twentieth century was a confession of weakness, robbing humanity of the wealth of mind to save the unsaveable and the untouchables. There is no love, where love embraces weakness; there is no charity when charity spares the ugly and the diseased; there is no wealth, where wealth of the material and the physical is squandered on worthless projects. All true wealth and the saving of it must lie in wisdom. And it is not wisdom to protect them or to excuse them in the name of charity. Your Carpenter of Nazareth was altogether right or righteous.'

Dirk listened with due humility, realising that the evident truth of his assertions could be seen all around.

'Another writer of the twentieth century,' went on Aaron, 'if you forgive my quoting from that barbaric and decadent age, said that evil is as much a manifestation of God as the good. But he forgot to add that man – at least the godlike part of him – is himself like his Creator; he has a goodness and divinity in his nature, and he has the ability to change the world in the light of that reason.'

'And that is what you have done?'

'We have tried. First by curing the evils – disease and destructiveness – mischief of the mind.'

'And achieved the good life?'

The old man hesitated before replying, then said,

'The healthy life.'

'Of the body and the mind?'

'Both, we hope. You cannot divide them.'

Dirk looked again as a group of young athletes walked past. They were as beautifully proportioned as Greek gods in the statues of Praxiteles. They walked with light and easy grace. They held their heads high. They had nobility and good looks. But their eyes were empty.

Then a team of players came out of the gymnasium. They wore

only the briefest of shorts, their limbs and bodies tanned and oiled. One was carrying a ball. Dirk went over to him.

'What game do you play?'

'Basketball.'

Dirk looked at them. They were all identical in build and features.

'Will your team win?' asked Dirk.

The young man smiled, shook his head. 'We know we shall not. Our talents have been calculated by the computer to the last ounce of strength and initiative. The other team will win today.'

'Then why do you play?'

'It is something to do.'

'It's a change from making love,' laughed another. 'What is the point of pouring sperm into a woman who will never breed a child?'

They ran on, passing the ball to each other.

'Come on, fellers,' shouted their leader. 'There's a nellie* to the stadium.' They ran to the helicopter station.

Aaron sighed. 'He's young?'

'How old?'

'Just ninety.'

'Come. There is more to see.' He led the way to a funicular car that went up to the hillside.

Dirk watched the passing landscape, fascinated by the well-ordered fields of grain and terraces of vines and oranges and peaches. Surprised at such variety, he turned to Aaron, who answered before he spoke:

'We regulate the temperature by the use of mirrors and gauges to suit the trees. Water is stored in the large reservoirs you see in the valleys and piped as required.'

---

* Short for 'omnellicopter,' an omnibus helicopter.

'I see no workmen,' said Dirk.

Aaron chuckled. 'That's a very archaic notion. If the machines can be invented to do those routine jobs, why employ a man?'

'But if machines do all the work, what do men and women do?'

'Oversee. Carry out adjustments and repairs. These are very few really. The machines more or less run themselves and are computerised to do repairs.'

'Receiving instructions, too, I suppose?'

The old man nodded. 'From central control, which watches over them carefully.' He stopped talking then, as if afraid to reveal too much.

They were now almost at the summit. They went out, and Dirk saw what he thought at first was a large compound with ornamental walls of wood. On closer examination, he saw that they were plastic, modelled to suggest in a semi-abstract way figures and animals. The grotesque, zoomorphic forms mingled with almost realistic limbs and torsos that were cleverly pierced with oval and circular holes that might be mouths, nostrils, eyes or vaginas. Pillars with conical, rounded ends and pairs of appended spheres suggested the male. Tendrils and spirals suggested locks of hair, and here and there running balls in grooves and whirling miniscule droplets of silver and gold and pearl darted and drifted, now quickly, now slowly, forming ever-changing patters of colour and form. Warm tints and cold counterpointed the erotic connotations, and subtle textures of wool and fur and bristle pelts caressed the smooth limbs, giving infinite variety.

When he raised his eyes to view the landscape beyond, he realised that what he thought were trees were in truth the heads of hundreds of people, massed together. Grey, white, off-white and silver blond, they stood shoulder to shoulder quite nude, men and women with shining elderly faces. As he watched, a crane-like device hovered over them and a jet of warm, perfumed vapour shot out. They uttered little cries of joy, lifting their hands and faces to the sky.

Dirk looked at his guide for an explanation.

'The perfumed jet comes over twice a day to cleanse them of physical impurities. The troughs at the sides catch the runnels, and the effluence is channelled to our factories. There the useful greases are siphoned off and stored. Some are changed into animal food or into oils and soaps and perfumes.'

'How old are these people?'

'A hundred and fifty. Some are a little older.'

'Can they do no work?'

'No. But they enjoy life.'

'Doing what?' asked Dirk.

'Nothing.'

'That must be very boring.'

'Not at all. Listen.'

Music came over the loudspeakers, soft and gentle at first, then getting louder and louder for more dominant moods. The crowd swayed to the rhythms, everyone in his or her separate but identical dream, the minor gracenotes and thirds lending themselves to subtler thoughts. Arms were raised and fingers moved tremulously as if playing the notes on imaginary instruments. A few voices improvised words. Old love-songs, romantic ballads, pop tunes from ancient times and rock from the savage centuries had now a nostalgic charm. Everyone seemed happy.

Dirk looked up the hillside to another compound, almost on the summit. On the unprotected shelves of rock and the precipices beyond the shelter of the weather-resisting envelope, stood icy skerries and glistening white boulders of virgin snow.

Wind-whipped frosty flakes whirled into the sky shining like a new milky way. Some of the eyes of the very old people were fixed on the driven snows as if mesmerised by the moving torrents that lacerated the blue sky and formed and reformed crystalline patterns in free-forms and ferns and fronds and spangled wheels. All were reflected in the eyes of the very old, fascinated by the proximity of the everlasting cold that only science held at bay.

The walls of the compound were very quietly coloured. Barely distinguishable were the tints of palest pink, mauve and clover, broken up by the ecru, ochre and cream of the basic fabric of the stockade. This was only waist high, but none of the inmates had the energy or inclination to move outside. They watched for a few moments.

'The D.C.'s have no desire to move outside,' said Aaron.

'D.C.'s?'

'The double-centuries. Happy to recline at ease.'

Dirk looked at the white-haired crowd. Relaxed they certainly were with their faces turned now toward the tent of illuminated nylon that hung over them. Films of ballet, theatre plays and Westerns from the dark ages lured the viewers to form little groups to watch the films of their choice. Pivoted metal arms moved among them and threw out fruits, drinks, sweetmeats and stimulants at a touch.

'To each his choice,' said Aaron. 'What more could they want?'

Dirk was silent.

'They live in an eternity of pleasure. Nobody dies.'

'And nobody lives,' added Dirk, going nearer and scrutinising the face of one old woman. She reached out a hand and touched his face. Others did, too. And others. A sigh went up among them. Their forms trembled and swayed like a field of corn, when a summer breeze blows over.

Dirk stood for a moment, letting their fingertips touch him.

Aaron gave him a sharp look, hustled him back down the path and into the car.

As they descended to the lower slopes, Dirk looked about him. Little valleys of indescribable beauty could be glimpsed through the windows, trellises of vine, lemon, and orange-grove hung with golden fruit, apricots and peaches, villas and follies and baroque palaces cunningly reconstructed, the walls festooned with bougainvillea of every hue from heliotrope to rose pink and flame and trailing passionflowers and roses and lilies and exotic blooms he had never seen before raised their heads to exhale delicious perfumes. Soft music played in a minor key.

'Is the music for the workers?' asked Dirk.

'No. For the plants. They grow better with music. They're particularly fond of Beethoven and Bach. Perhaps the counterpoint in these echoes the effect of the leaves and sprays. They respond to voices, too.'

'Do the girls sing to them?'

The old man shook his head. 'No. The singing is recorded. It can be dangerous to mingle with them. Some of the plants have acquired a taste for blood.'

Dirk shuddered and drew back.

'How do you protect the workers?'

'The harvest is not collected by hand.' He pointed to a nearby grove.

A cleverly designed machine moved down the terraces, equipped with long arms that had metal claws. Coming to a tree, it stopped, groped among the foliage, grasped the fruit, gave it a twist and a tug and dropped it into a container that moved along a belt to a waiting receptacle. This, when full, detached itself and moved to a factory where the fruit was jammed or puréed or stored for eating.

Similarly, a perfume-detector projected its mechanical nose along the banks of flowers and herbs, plucking a bloom here and rejecting there and filling the baskets in its trolley. This machine carried out the whole operation of selecting and distilling. Cachets and phials of perfume appeared in its boat, and a hoard of butterflies hovered over it, descended, and expired, killed by a lethal ray from another aperture. Red admirals, fritillaries, peacocks with golden eyes on their marron and purple plush wings, and swallowtails swanking their indigo trains in a suicide sweep.

'Insects we do not like,' said Aaron. 'They travel widely and may bring infection.'

'How can you detect it?' asked Dirk uneasily.

'We have ways.'

'To preserve the New Atlantis in health and perfection?'

The old man looked at him, puzzled by the doubting undertone.

They went down in silence. Dirk was afraid to voice his uneasiness. It was all too perfect, he thought, too rich, too satisfying. He thought of the squabbles for food and shelter and the most elementary needs of existence in the devastated lands he had passed through. He thought, too, of the hardy spirits who had survived with a kind of grudging admiration. Life had been hard, but it had been fun. Wasn't it Heraclitus who had said that we only appreciate the little successes and happinesses because we have had so many failures and sorrows? The struggles and the hatreds, however, wore you down. He would like to rest now.

'It is an ideal place,' he said when they alighted. 'I would like to live here.'

'If you are accepted.'

'By whom?'

'By the rulers.'

They had stopped before an impressive building of granite in the main square.

'Would you like to meet them?' asked Aaron, as the young man stood awestruck before the massive portals. He seemed undecided.

'Your thoughts are still back in the primeval slime,' said the old man. 'You are unable to appreciate the virtues of the New Atlantis.'

Dirk bridled at his obvious scorn.

'What have you produced here?' he cried.

'The perfect city-state with health and comfort for all, and with plenty to eat and drink. Eternal life, too.'

'And for the mind? The heart? The spirit? Where are your Michelangelos and your Shakespeares and your Mozarts? Does perfection lead to creativity?'

Aaron was silent. Then he said, 'We can only hope.'

'For danger. And death. Are not these the spurs for great art?'

The old man's eyes flashed angrily, 'That is blasphemous talk!'

'Is it? Blasphemy is a sin against religion. You have none here.'

'The State is our religion,' he said coldly.

'Do you pray to it? Light candles?'

'The candles are in our hearts.'

They had gone in by this time. A flicker of discontent ran through the computers in the entrance hall.

'Have they hearts?' asked Dirk. 'Has any one here?'

Aaron looked mystified, shocked, as if Dirk had uttered a dirty word. He made a gesture and they walked into the hall. The inner doors opened as they approached. There was still no one in sight. Dirk looked at his companion. The old man made a gesture toward the dais at the end of the hall. It was dominated by a great computer equipped with panels on which rows of figures and symbols, continually changing into new formulae and equations, dazzled the eye and the mind with the rapidity of their responses. Aaron waved him on, then stopped. A dozen smaller computers ranged against the wall seemed to be troubled by Dirk's presence. One emitted a shrill squeal of alarm as he passed.

Dirk walked on. When he neared the dais, the Chief Computer gave an angry buzz. The symbols and figures raced into new computations. Red lights glowed. An arm came out with a sensitive nozzle, which probed all over his person.

Aaron watched with growing concern.

When the Chief Computer had digested the data, it issued another warning of danger on all the windows of sight, sound and touch. Red danger signals flared on all of these. High-pitched pips broadcast a warning that none could ignore.

Aaron drew back.

'You lied to me!' he shouted. 'You are not free from contamination!' He turned to read the figures. 'You bring danger. Why did you lie to me?'

'If I had not, I'd have been prohibited from coming here.'

The Chief Computer now whirred into action, calling upon an army of crab-like machines to attack the intruder, their steel mandibles reaching toward him menacingly.

Dirk ran. Out of the building, across the main square and up into the hills he raced. Turning into an orchard, he paused for breath.

It was peaceful there. Only the fruit-gathering machines went about their task purposefully, quietly, probing and grasping and plucking the fruit. Dirk ran on, coming to a vineyard. He plucked some grapes and ate them, went on refreshed, listening to the soft music that soothed a little his frayed nerves.

The computerised machines had stopped.

The music changed to a menacing tune. The vines shivered and seemed to tense again. Their leaves took on a malevolent, metallic sheen, darkening to a poisonous blue. Two strong tendrils shot out towards him. Dirk did not see them until they had closed about his neck. Other branches enclosed about his arms and legs. He could not move. He struggled with the tendrils and branches, tried to tear them away. The music crescendoed to a savage intensity. He could smell the fresh sap rising in the vines. The heady stench almost suffocated him.

Then the fruit-picking machines closed in on him. He broke loose from the vines at last and ran. Two other fruit-picking machines came in from a side path and barred his escape. They were on all sides now, their machinery ticking furiously, their mandibles opening and closing as they came nearer. One nipped his arm. Another his thigh. A third probed and groped and gripped his testicles. He screamed and tried to escape. Another brought its metal grips close to his head, groped and probed around his eyes, found a grip and tore and wrenched at his eyeballs. Two others had a grip of his torso. A large claw grasped his left buttock, another his right. They probed and grasped and pulled... part of what were once Dirk's body and limbs disappeared into the maws of the collecting machines.

Attracted by the scent of blood, an Emperor Butterfly hovered and perched, savouring the young man's torn flesh for a moment, before it, too, was dismembered and devoured.

Aaron watched and laughed.

His merriment soon gave way to alarm.

A wave of terror had spread over the hillside enclosures. The elders were rocking and wailing and tearing at each other in a frenzy. He watched in horror.

Higher up the mountain, the double-centuries were swaying and tottering. Their hair fell out like the hair of a rotting skull in a grave. The flesh scaled away from their bones, so that fingers that had erstwhile played arabesques to melodies and flowers, now plucked grisly gracenotes and staccato tattoos from the agony of their dying.

A high keening came from the mountain. The host of elders swayed like a field of grain before a storm. Swayed and disintegrated, heads drooping, torsos folding over like paper figures in a flame and arms and legs crumbling into dust. Only the hands fluttered wanly in the evening light for a second or two, then they also lay still. The cleaning jets made their routine visit. Soon nothing was left but the busy and garrulous rivulets that appeared to be clotted with dead leaves.

A crowd of younger men had gathered about Aaron.

'Soon,' he said, 'we will have to breed again. There will be children to replace the dead—'

'And adventure and death!' said a young man.

The elders laughed and cheered for the first time in their lives. The women danced, throwing away their captive insects and birds, feeling a strange stirring in their bodies. The young men moved among them, embracing and laughing and touching them amorously.

THE FISHBOYS OF VERNAZZA
(2003)
John Sam Jones

Giacomo's knowing smiles and attempts to engage them in broken English don't entice them to dawdle in the Bar Gioia, not even with all the fidgety-fingered cradling of his crotch, as is the way of so many Italian boys. They know that the hike from Monterosso to Vernazza will take at least a couple of hours so they can't indulge in Giaco's flirting or linger over their sticky pastries and cappuccinos. If they miss the train they'll have to wait another hour and that will certainly mean they'll be cutting it fine. Shôn smiles his cheekiest smile and asks Giaco if he'll be behind the bar later... And so it's agreed that they'll come back and drink *sciacchetrà* with him after they've eaten dinner.

From the gloomy station building that smells rancidly pissy, the passengers that alight the train spill onto the narrow, sun-soaked promenade. Geraint and Shôn stroll beneath the neatly trimmed oleanders, the leaf cover just thick enough to diffuse the sun's warmth and allow them to feel the autumn's chill. Every now and then, Shôn darts from the purple shadows and leans out over the balustrade to ogle the few dedicated sun worshippers that lie in skimpy trunks on Monterosso's sandy beach. Geraint would like to do the same, but it isn't in his nature to be quite so open about his attraction to other men. Knowing this, Shôn describes the delights that he sees (or just imagines) in clipped, crude morsels: 'Nice ass on that one... Oh God, there's one over there who's got pecs to die for... And this one here's got such a packet.' Geraint feigns disdain at the teasing and wonders if Shôn has plans to cop off with some handsome Italian. Then, for a few minutes, he considers his place in Shôn's life, despite promising himself that he wouldn't allow such introspection to spoil their time together.

He doesn't like to think of himself as Shôn's fuck-buddy, though that's how Shôn describes their relationship whenever Geraint tries to pin him down. He considers it such a vulgar term, and so American... and it hardly reflects the reality of their nights together when mostly they just cuddle. He's Shôn's teddy bear really, but Shôn's image of himself is far too butch to allow for such a passive interpretation of their liaisons. Geraint doesn't know how much longer he'll let him continue to shape this part of his life. Monogamy and a joint mortgage on a three-bedroomed semi, preferably with a garden, is what he hankers for... a quiet and secure marriage. But they retain their separate lives, their separate flats, their separate circles of friends, and come together only once or twice a week, and for holidays, because that's what Shôn wants. So Geraint takes what he can get; after all, Shôn is a lot of fun to be with... he's gentle, kind and generous (which tempers the bitchy streak), and when a teddy bear to cuddle is the last thing on his mind, their sex is pretty accomplished. Shôn is the only man Geraint has ever loved. And in four years Shôn has never so much as whispered to Geraint that he loves him.

'What about him?' Shôn quizzes, pulling Geraint back from the edge of pensiveness.

'You're like a dog on heat,' Geraint jibes.

The track ascends quickly through the terraced vineyards taking them along uneven pathways that crown the dry stonewall; and up crude, steep steps that connect the terraces.

The vines have been recently stripped and most have been pruned back ready for the winter, their few remaining leaves blotchy with red and gold. The grapes, the *albarola, vermentino* and the *bosco* wither and wizen in some shady spot, a vital step in the process of turning them into *sciacchetrà*. The trail takes them past isolated huts that defy the precipitous gradients with stubborn sturdiness. Around these now forsaken vinedresser's shelters, clumps of prickly pear rear up like tethered, menacing beasts, to deter the inquisitive rambler from exploring. Where the terraces have been abandoned and recolonised by native heathers and squat pines, the *maquis* has reclaimed the derelict refuges.

Above the vineyards, a sea of white-crested turquoise a thousand feet below them, the path, though obvious enough, is rough. Gouged into the face of the mountain, the original course is obstructed time and again by boulders from rock falls. Where landslides have gashed the sea cliff's contours, haphazard cairns mark an imprecise direction across the rock fields.

'You'd think they'd have put a sign up about the condition of the path,' Geraint carps.

'There was one,' Shôn says dismissively, 'but you've got to have a bit of adventure in your life. Besides, the Australians I was talking to last night when you were reading your book said they'd walked it, and once we've crossed the ridge we get back onto the terraces.'

Where the vines begin again, the descent becomes vertiginous. Geraint stops every few minutes to curse his new varifocals and their tendency to blur the irregular steps unless he looks directly down at his feet. Pausing on a bluff, he takes in the view: Vernazza, hanging on its rocky spit around an almost circular harbour, looks like a child's model village, the pink and lemon and ochre of the tall, narrow, green shuttered houses adding to the toy-like quality. Shôn bounds on ahead and after ten minutes or more, Geraint finds him slouched against a rocky outcrop.

'What do you make of this, then?' Shôn asks, pointing at a carving in the rockface.

'Mermaids,' Geraint quips with delight.

'That's what I thought, but...'

'Right... they're boys!'

'Exactly... three cute mermen. I wonder what it's all about?'

'Probably some local legend,' Geraint shrugs. 'The artist was no amateur.'

'It's good, isn't it?'

They come into Vernazza by a lane behind the octagonal domed church, where washing hangs from clotheslines and spider plants hang low from balconies of potted scarlet cyclamen. They find the small terrace of the Ristorante Belforte at the top of the uneven steps at the end of the harbour wall, just like the fetching older couple they'd befriended on the train from Genoa had described: four tables, decked with pink linen cloths and napkins, polished silver cutlery and crystal glasses that glint in the glorious October sun. Shôn, his scientist's eye trained to observe the merest details, gestures to Geraint that they should sit, as there's no evidence that the splashes from the waves can reach them. Despite Sol's benevolence since their arrival in the Cinque Terre, Neptune and his sirens have been irritable, the sea choppy... squally even; rough enough for the ferryboats that connect the five villages to have abandoned their erratic schedules and for the smaller fishing boats to have remained at anchor. Waiting for *il cameriere* – the waiter – whom the old queens on the train had said, with the campest affectation, was *molto delizioso*, they watch the translucent, azure waves rupture into cascades of glistening diamonds as they fold heavily onto the rocks not ten metres below them.

Between glances at the menu, Shôn takes in his surroundings. Over Geraint's shoulder he has a view of the harbour. The fishing boats, brightly painted in red and blue, are pitched by the swell, their short masts tracing the fingerprint whorls on the harbour cliffs where some ancient sea god's hands once moulded the strata. Wherever the rocks give way to vegetation, agaves cling like stranded starfish. Higher up, between prickly pears and heather, an errant bougainvillea bleeds its loveliness from a deep gash. And he thinks of Geraint, and whether he should commit himself.

With a lyrical *ciao*, the fingers of his left hand indolently sinuous at his crotch, *molto delizioso* interrupts Shôn's reverie. Shôn studies the boy's felinity as he approaches their table. There's a grace in his movements that pleases the eye and suggests he might be a dancer. His arms, the muscles defined beneath a smooth chestnut-shell skin, are strong; the sort that take your breath when they embrace you. The features of his face are more Abyssinian than Siamese, and framed by thick black hair, sleek and worn unfashionably long. His smile, in so proud a face, seems slightly mocking but there's a seductive stealthiness in the charcoal of his eyes that quickens Shôn's pulse. In a fleeting thought, Shôn concludes that Geraint, alongside one so dangerously desirable, is too safe... too dependable, and altogether too tame.

Between them they have enough Italian to recognise that there's a choice of local fish on the menu, but they enjoy the boy's attention and pretend to be stupid Brits abroad, coaxing him to translate *pulpo*, *totani* and *acciughe*. They ask for octopus and squid with potatoes *alla genovese* and freshly caught anchovies with lemon. As he writes the order on his pad, Geraint notices the silver ring on the waiter's index finger.

'I've never seen anyone wearing a ring there before,' Geraint says after *molto delizioso* goes back into the restaurant, rubbing the index finger of his right hand between the two end joints.

'It's called the middle phalanx,' Shôn says, a bit like a lecturer in an anatomy class.

'Well... whatever... it's still a strange place for a ring.'

'What's even more strange is the pattern and figure engraved on it,' Shôn scoffs.

'I didn't notice,' Geraint submits.

The boy returns, places a rustic loaf of bread and a jug of wine on the table, and disappears again through the curtain of corded beads that keeps the flies out.

'It's a merman,' Geraint offers, surprised.

As he clears their table, and just after he's asked if they want an *espresso*, Shôn asks him about the carving on the rock above the village.

'You mean the... fishboys?' he hesitates. 'You call them fishboys in *Inglese*?'

'It's a good enough name,' Geraint quips.

'You been to the *grotto del Diavolo*?'

'The devil's cavern? No.'

'Sometimes, when the sea is *tempestoso*, the fishboys come into the village through the *grotto*, and take away... how you say?' The charcoal embers in his eyes glow. 'They take away the bad boys.'

They laugh at his fishy tale and Shôn, catching his eye, teases, 'And just how bad does a boy have to be to be charmed away by the fishboys?'

'Bad enough that... *lui è desiderabile*,' he says with an inscrutable smile and carries the plates away.

'He's quite a story teller,' Geraint says as the curtain of beads clacks. 'Bad enough that you're desirable indeed!'

'He is pretty desirable,' Shôn quips.

'Yes... and did you see how he hid the ring on his index finger in his hand when you asked about the carving?'

'I wonder,' Shôn muses. 'When he leaned over to pick up the

plates his hair fell forward. He's got a strange mark behind his ear, all feathery and reddish purple... just like a fish's gill.'

They eat ice creams on the *piazza* that fronts the harbour and then cross into the purple shade and take a narrow street made even narrower by stranded fishing boats, hauled from the sea for repair or a coat of paint. Geraint gawps at the large, ugly fish being laid on the marble slabs outside the *pescheria* by the fishmonger, fresh from his siesta. Shôn gawps at the fishmongers apprentice, a tall, awkward youth with a cheeky smile. As the boy stands before the open refrigerated display counter arranging rose-coloured fish with golden streaks around a hand-written sign that reads *Triglia*, Shôn thinks that in a year or two, when he's filled out a bit, he won't be unattractive. The boys hands are bloodstained and scaly and a silver ring glints on the middle phalanx of his right index finger... and when he turns, Shôn makes out the curious purple mark behind his ear. So the boy's potential has already been realised. Further up the street the cobbles are drenched in an arc of sunlight. Enjoying the warmth of the sun they peer into the *grotto del Diavolo*. Shôn wonders if the fishmonger's apprentice and the waiter put up much resistance when the fishboys of Vernazza lured them into the devil's cavern.

After a long shower, Shôn sneaks into bed beside Geraint, rousing him from his nap. They cuddle for a while and watch the sun set in a haemorrhaging sky and then they make love, their crazed delight inspired by their holiday mood, the gorgeous waiter and his fable. As their sex gives way to slumber, Shôn supposes that life with Geraint might be worth a try. Watching the last smears of blood fade into the gunmetal sky, Geraint decides it's time to get off the emotional rollercoaster of the half-life he shares with Shôn.

Later, at the Bar Gioia, Giacomo pours three stout goblets

sciacchetrà. The silver ring on the middle phalanx of his right index finger catches the light as he tilts the bottle. They raise their glasses, and swirling the richly amber, slightly viscous wine, they toast '*Salute!*' Geraint's senses fill with curiosity and cocoa, apricot and Mediterranean herbs. Shôn is aroused by his lusty thoughts of Giaco.

'It's a very good one, no?' Giacomo enquires, his round, cheery face filled with pride. 'Is the one my mother makes... much better than the one you buy in the tourist shop.'

'It is very good,' Geraint ventures, his gaze drawn and held in the questioning blue-green of Giacomo's eyes.

'You want to buy *sciacchetrà* you come see me before you go back England,' Giaco says when he's peered too long into Geraint's confusion.

'We will,' Shôn says stressing the *we*, jealous that Giaco seems more interested in Geraint.

Giacomo returns to their end of the bar after serving a giggly teenage couple.

'Can you tell us anything about the carving in the rock above Vernazza?' Geraint asks.

'We couldn't find anything about it in the guide book,' Shôn says, competing for attention.

'I don't know,' Giaco says with a shrug. 'I never walked on this path.'

'It has three fishboys, like the one on your ring,' Shôn accuses.

Giacomo holds up his finger and looks, almost seriously, at the silver band.

'Is a very cheap ring from a shop in Spezia,' he says, smiling. 'Is very fashionable to have a ring here,' he adds, rubbing the middle phalanx with his thumb.

For a while, they watch Giaco's every move as he serves more customers further along the bar. A larger than life, blonder than blonde girl sweeps into the Bar Gioia with smiles and *ciaos* for everyone. Shôn observes her carefully and deduces that she's the local transvestite. She rests her ample breasts on the bar and reaches over to kiss Giaco, ruffling his sandy curls with her crimson nailed fingers. Her skirt rises as she stretches. Geraint and Shôn are distracted by her black lace panties, which are too skimpy to hide her fishy tail.

QUEER CHILDREN

THE WATER MUSIC
(1944)
Glyn Jones

Shall I dive, shall I dive? Behind me the patterns of the coloured town I left lie spread out in the green valley like a carpet taken out on the grass for beating, and I race down the sunny slope out of sight of it. I am a flier with the wind rushing under the bony arches of my wings, I am a white gull, I am two hundred gulls, I am the gull-shower of snow in sunshine, and the whirled flakes of summer whitening the world. I turn my beaked face and out of a bright eye I see beside my head, rigid and purposeful, my crooked wing with its piled-up foam-crest of feathers broken wave-white along its ridge in the speed-created wind, I see the few cricketing children dwarfed in the tree-surrounded meadow and the grannie in black who minds their picnic fire, and the column of wood-smoke upright in the odorous air of the field. Beyond the curtain of foliage surrounding the oval meadow glitters the curve of the river in silver patches, poured like a flat snake among the trees, sundering the rooted feet that crowd upon its bank. And beside the river's biggest pool rises the grey diving-rock, the stone in the sunshine pale as coltsfoot leaf but felt-smooth and smouldering warm to the fingers. Shall I dive, shall I dive?

As I stood by the little sherbert shop at the cornfield gate and looked over the wheat, a large broken-hearted bird came crying inland on long transparent wings like knives, radiant as fine

507

sailcloth or sunlit snow. He was a beautiful gull, and after circling came to rest on one leg like a wineglass on the gatepost beside me. He had a lovely white neck and the sun-kindled curve of his swelling breast gleamed white as the milky dazzle of coconut kernel in the sunshine which he faced. Over his powerful boxer's back was spread a mantle of smooth dove-grey feathers, and below the glitter of his theatrically darkened eye-disc he had a brilliant broom-yellow bill, long, curved and tigerish, with a blob of blood-orange red painted near the nostrils.

'Gull,' I said in bad Latin, 'why have you left your green egg?' – 'Wha, wha, wha,' was his reply, as he folded up his webs and flew off rapidly up the valley ahead of us. Shall I dive?

Now I am across the scented meadow and through the partition of trees, I climb the high grey diving-rock and see the bathers undressing on the cliff-shelves opposite or already swimming in pure water. I greet twenty boys from my crocketed pinnacle, waving towel and black triangular slip, hailing red-tied Thomas as comrade, a ginger boy with freckles and the blue eyes of a black kitten as neighbour Williams, and having to cry 'Gracias' to the pale and orphaned Scabbo Ball, who, wishing me well, addresses me with a bow as señor. The water beneath is limpid, the pebbles and the sandy bottom waver under it, smoothly it flows over them like flawed glass. Shall I dive with the speed of the gull or like the capering swallow who plunges with shut wings?

Below me among the rocks is the perfectly fitting pool, large and circular, with the sun shattered upon its surface; there is the voluminous river cataracting down the grey limestone steps in crystal fans and ferns and luminous ice-sheets and floods of clear rock-varnish, and bunches of glass bananas; there is the dim tunnel that receives the sliding river in a long sealskin volute out of the dazzling floor of the pool, the down-drench of birch-boughs and the green masses of beech-leaves sleek under the smooth glove of the sunshine are arched over the glossy water. The broad scarlet towel-stripe glows unbearable as ruby on the grey rock, the black-slipped boys in naked groups lounge white and delicate in midday moon-flesh, and warm, on the sunlit shelves of the little cliff. Rosie Bowen the bootmaker's boy, begotten of mild mother and boxing-glove burning sire, ignoramus, *victor ludorum*, stands in the water severed at the knees, with half-revealed distaste upon a dunce's countenance of endearing and transcendental ugliness. As he ponders, somebody throws a pebble into the water, and his back is splashed.

'Ay Scabbo,' he shouts without looking round. 'I'll dig you in the chin.'

And then he slowly advances over the velvet-growing stones like a thief among snares or a sufferer from foot-warts; with the pool-water chilling his bandy legs he is hesitant as Dic Dywyll, reluctant and maladroit now, no reckless Christmas morning plunger to be met with an ice-hammer in his pocket on the track to the frozen tarn. He toes the slippery pool-stones in his path, each bearded with a long phlegm of green weed, into the water as clear as crystal he peers with the intensity of a louse-hunting mother examining the hair of her dirtiest. By spreading to the sun his boxer's ape-arms, powerful and muscular under their gleaming ginger fell, he achieves for a moment the unstable balance of the tightrope artiste. He is an indifferent concealer of his dislike of this element in its icy mountain freshness, unwarmed by equatorial current or outpoured boiler-water from the pit-head engine-room, but gradually he sinks into the depths of the pool, the blackish birthmark on his leg is submerged, the rings spread from his hairy thighs, and finding with his soles a rock-slab in the river bed when the water is around his waist, he crosses his arms in respite on his chest, and tucks into his armpits his yellow iron-mold hands – because he would smoke tea-leaves, or seaweed or even india rubber. His abnormal homeliness in the pool is as rare as great villainy or genius. Upon his giant head is sewn a dense fibrous hump of coconut hair; his cheeks even now are tomato-red, and his protrusive lower jawbone with the liquorice stumps of disordered black teeth gapes open like a half-shut bottom drawer. Were I to dive and come up beside him, before punching he would stare with the incredulity of Gerallt's soldier voiding a calf. Dare I dive into this huge water?

Under a tree with the curving tail of a branch hanging down over the water stands Arthur Vaughan Morgan, Rosie's friend, tall and lovely-limbed, forgetting now the humiliation of battered teaspoons and the charred cork for a knob in the broken teapot lid; he leans garlanded and naked in a dance-dress of sunlight flimsily-patterned with transparent foliage. And Evan Williams, the third of The Three, his hair corrugated like biscuit-paper, surreptitiously unrobes behind a jut of rock, concealing thus the unique and resourceful fastenings of his broken underwear. He removes last a sort of check bodice with a frilled waistline. He has orange-golden hair and orange-golden freckles you couldn't put a pin between. He does not wear the black school bathing triangle but a scalene slip of his own devising fashioned from a pair of bootlaces and a folded red handkerchief covered with white polka dots. That Sterne-visaged grammarian, our English master, who annihilates me with sarcasm when I audibly praise heaven for prose-writers who use two words where one will do, yet reads aloud with approval to the assembled form my essay upon the virtues of our native land. 'Glory be to the Isle of the Mighty for her ponds and the pools of all her rivers,' he sneers, 'for Pwll Wat, and Pwll Taf and Pwll Tydfil. And for her lakes, for Llangorse and Llyn y Fan, and for Llyn Syfaddon lovely under Dafydd's swan.'

'Let there be praise also for the pools of the Po and for the waters of Lake Titicaca,' Evan whispers behind my blushing ear.

'Praise her for her towns and villages and her ancient divisions, praise her for Gwynedd and Powys and Dyfed and Morgannwg. Praise her for her lovely names, for Llanrhidian, Afon Sawdde, Fan Girhirych, Dyffryn Clwyd. Praise her for Rhosllanerchrugog—'

'And for Llanfairpwllgwyngyllgogerychwyrndrobwllandysiliogogogoch,' softly intones Williams to a mutilated version of 'Hen Nhadau'.

'Let us praise her for Lleyn and Llanelly, for Dinas Mawddwy and Dinas Powis, for Cwm Elan and Cwm Rhondda, let us praise Tresaith equally with Treorky and Penrhyn Gŵyr equally with Pengarnddu.'

'Let us praise Moscow equally with Little Moscow,' growls Evan, 'and Llantwit Major equally with Asia Minor,' and the only thing to do is cough.

Now Bolo Jones the overman's boy, togaed in many towels, wishing to show Arthur little Dai Badger denounced as Catiline and indignantly interrogated as to when he shall cease oppressing the people, shouts down, 'Acker, Acker, look at this.'

Arthur, dappled under his hanging bough, ignores him.

'Acker Morgan,' shouts undaunted Bolo again from his proscenium, a grey ledge of rock six feet above the water, his arm outstretched in indignation towards the singing Catiline.

Arthur frowns, examining his nails. He is a cock with a high comb. His three sisters are knowing and fashionable, they have haughty expressions but short legs.

'Ack-er,' shouts Bolo once more, loud above the cries and the chorus singing and the low roar of the river rushing into the pool with the splash of water washing itself all over.

Arthur turns towards him. 'My name is Arthur,' he says testily. 'Arthur – heroic and European. Arthur Trevelyan Vaughan Morgan.'

Bolo Jones drops his towels, claps his hands to his head and collapses backwards into the pool.

And dare I dive from this height into the water?

Rosie Bowen is swimming. He has waded up to the foot of the cataract and now, using a breast-stroke, proceeds kicking with the help of the current down the middle of the water. His swimming is laborious and convulsive, like a frog who has swallowed a handful of lead-shot, but everyone remembers Imperato's and his head is not pushed under. On the lowest ledge of the cliff opposite, Phil and Sinky swing a grinning Dai Badger to and fro by the wrists and ankles, while Scabbo, his body white as pipeclay, gives them orders. 'Away with him,' he cries, 'cast the perjured caitiff into the roaring torrent of the river.' – 'The traitor says he cannot swim, my lord,' says Sinky. 'Clearly,' answers Scabbo, 'here is a fine chance to learn.' Dai bounds outwards, he enters the water in the button of a ragged bloom of spray. Bleddyn Beavan who has just climbed out to watch crouches smiling in a sleek skin with his toes gripping the rock brink, his hands on his knees and a thread of water running back into the pool off his chin. All of us in our form have a firm and scientifically accurate knowledge of our physical genesis because his father is Doctor Gomer and Bleddyn will lend you his medical books at tuppence a week. Shall I dive?

When I was small and dirty, with a quilted bottom to my trousers, I wanted only to learn swimming. Out of my big brother's book I spelled this sentence: 'The action of the frog should be studied and imitated.' On washing day I mitched and went up Cwm Ffrwd, croaking about by the river like a frog. At last I found a big green one weighing a quarter of a pound. I put him in my cap to bring him home and he didn't like that because my cat used to sleep in it every night. My mother had two tubs of clothes-water in our back and I put him in the one for the flannels. I made him swim about in the warm water among the shirts and the nightgowns, and soon I could swim lovely. When I heard my mother coming I put him down the lavatory and poured a bucket of water on top of him.

That evening I went up the pit-pond on the tips where the collier-boys used to swim dirty. I climbed on to the timber balks and dived in. When I woke up a big crowd of men was carrying me home across the fields on a stretcher. I thought I had been punished for drowning the frog who had taught me to swim. At home the doctor said, 'And last week he pulled the coping of the Methodist Chapel wall on his chest.'

The same summer my mother took us to the Wells for our holidays. I borrowed tuppence off my brother and went for a swim in the open-air baths. I had never been to a baths before. The water was black and crowded with people. I dived in at the shallow end. This time when I came to I was stretched out on the mohair couch in our lodgings with my skin cold as glass and a big smooth lump like a teacup on the front of my head.

And now dare I dive?

Behind me across the meadow, I see through the trees the luminous green slope where I was a rugger-running gull, tilted to the sunglare, the grass seething in the summer sunbeams vivid and crystalline, the brightness glowing over the kindled surface with a teeming lustre of intense emerald as though the grassy fabric were a sheet of transparent crystal evenly illuminated with rays of pure greenish fire from beneath. And over it goes my gull, rigid and ravenous, crying 'Wah, wah, wah'. He is beautiful enough to be addressed by the wandering scholar who said, 'Lovely gull, snow-white and moon-white, immaculate sun-patch and sea-glove, swift-proud fish-eater, let us fly off hand-in-hand, you are light on the waves as a sea-lily. My grey nun among sea-crests, you shall be my glossy letter, go and carry a *billet* to my girl for me and win distant praise by making for her fortress. You shall see her, Eigr-coloured, on her castle, gull. Carry her my note, my chosen, go girl-wards. If she is alone do not be shy of talking to her, but be tactful in the presence of so much fastidiousness. Tell her I shall die without her and look, gull, tell her I am over head and ears in love with her, that not even Merddin or Taliesin desired her superior in beauty. Gull, under her tangled crop of copper you shall behold Christendom's loveliest lovely – but she'll be the death of me if you bring no for an answer.'

'Take my boots off when I die,' sings Dai Badger, shaped like a ship's anchor floating on the surface of the pool.

'Take my boots off when I die.'

The butcher's cart and bill-heads of Dai's father bear the slogan, 'Let Badger be your Butcher,' which seven-syllabled line in the opinion of that erratic but pithy critic Evan Williams, contains more poetry and *cynghanedd* than the similarly hortatory but more famous words of the High Priest of Lakery urging us to take Nature for our Teacher. For Evan, who always hears of such things, has solved the riddle of Hamlet. The clue lies, he maintains, with the hidden character called Pat, addressed directly only once and that in the tortured reflection of young Denmark – 'Now might I do it, Pat, now he is praying,' but whose machinations and subtle influence have confounded three hundred years of criticism. Shall I dive now like a glider of the boughs?

Dai Badger is again on the shelf, juicy-nosed, counting his tail-feathers after his ducking and the bravado of his song. He spots me watching him across the pool and wants to know if I will come over the mountain with him tomorrow. 'To where?' I ask cautiously. 'One A one b one e one r one d one a one r one e,' he cries at breathless speed. 'Will you?' He is a fabulist and claims to be in love with the vicar's Swiss maid there, who is indeed a nicely shaped young woman but twice his size. I make an excuse and he sings a wicked ballad describing his passion for her foreign body. He feels no *pudeur* at our natural out-curves and tuberosities and his naked belly now is tight as a bagpipe with lyricism. But Rosie Bowen, hearing him, spits into the water; he has coconut hair, an undershot jaw, and, to a god's-eye view, a hump like a bosom on his back; he spits copiously and without displaying muscular action, projecting a large and heavy gob down-stream with a twitch of his face, sending it flying in a sweet curve from his immobile face.

And now shall I dive?

Arthur leaves the shelter of his tail-shaped tree and stands among the swimmers on the soaking ledge like a patrician candidate heroically facing the malodorous citizens. Flicker, our mathematics master, who declares so-and-so to be an outstanding this, that and the other, if he would only more frequently 'duck his nut,' is despised by Arthur, the inelegant phrasing, bad breath and linoleum waistcoat of this unpleasant sciolist deeply offend him. 'Here is a clever chap,' sneers Flicker, distributing the marked examination papers after his terminal test, 'Arthur Morgan, the famous mathematical genius. He can solve a quadratic equation in one line! Stand up Morgan! You cooked the answer!'

'I didn't,' says Arthur with dignity.

'You did,' shouts Flicker, reddening and bulge-eyed.

'I didn't,' says Arthur.

'You did,' shouts Flicker.

'Oh, all right,' says Arthur sitting down. 'I'll give you the benefit of the doubt.'

But he is teased because Bolo Jones has his photograph taken in his first long-trousered sailor-suit, with a cane whistle on a cord and a fouled anchor worked on his front.

Below me where the water is quiet, foam in clusters of pappus and pints of cuckoo-spit and fine meshes of foam thin as beer-froth float on the dark water; under the overhanging boughs of the boy-bodied beeches and the cataracting birches, a broken mesh of reflected gold is thrown up in the gloom, the network of uneasy golden light on the under-branches is torn apart and joined up again as the green liquid glass of the water is splashed and the sunlight scattered. A breeze starts, the wind is handed on from tree to tree, I hear near me the first soft clatter of the poplar leaves. Soon the swimming will be over and I dawdle and have not dived. Rosie retires shivering in the hot sunshine, cold beyond the reach of wine or smith's fire. Evan says a swig would be welcome as hail in hell and Dai Badger shouts, 'I feel poppish too.' They dress and leave together for the widow's shop at the cornfield gate where on a piece of torn cardboard, for the information of picnickers, is chalked the message – 'Hot water sold here. Pop round the corner.' I must dive.

Shooting down the silky chasm of my plunge, with my soles to the brilliant county blue and the cortex of that highly convolved and dazzling cloud, I shall be the gull off her olive egg, the diving gull from the covey dawn, the herring-gull or blackback falling like large snow off the roof of the world. Rosie is a powerful land-animal, Evan charming and unawakened, Arthur learned in Latin, beautiful as Sande or some musk-scented princess; but I am the finest swimmer in this water and the only person who knows what a *vidame* is. My lungs are full, with hirundine screamings I hurdle hedges, I plunge performing the devil-dive of a star. I bomb the water blind and all images are shattered in my head. I sink and soon it is silent there, the dark beards of the stones wave as though in the breeze and the small grains of sand bowl in the current along the bottom of the pool. My breath rises like anchor-bubbles through the water green as glass edges, I lie like sand-eel, water-snake, or Welsh Shelley under the ten-foot slab of transparent green, watching it reach the world of my God whom I continue to praise, whom I praise for the waters, the little balls of dew and the great wave shooting out its tassel; I praise him for the big boy-bodied beeches and all the trees velvet in sunshine and shying like mad when the grass is flat under the wind; I praise him for the blooms of the horned lilac, for the blossomed hawthorn with the thick milks of spring rising over her and the blood-drop of ladycow bled on the white lily. I praise him for the curving gull, and brown coat of the sparrow and the plover with wings like blown hair.

I praise him for words and sentences, I praise him for Flicker Wilkins and for Arthur Vaughan Morgan and his sisters in fashionable hats like low buckets; I praise him for Bolo Jones and Dai Badger and Scabbo Ball, and for Scabbo Ball's auntie who keeps the weighing machine and has green glasses and one hand. I praise him for the golden freckles of Evan Williams as much as for Rosie Bowen who suffers a traumatic malformation of the jaw.

I praise him for the things for which I have not praised him and for the things praised only in the pleats of my meaning.

I praise him for his endless fertility and inventiveness, that he stripes, shades, patches and stipples every surface of his creation in his exhaustible designing, leaves no stretch of water unmarked, no sand or snow-plain without the relief of interfering stripe, shadow or cross-hatch, no spread of pure sky but he deepens it from the pallor of its edges to its vivid zenith. I praise him that he is never baulked, never sterile, never repetitious.

There is praise for him in my heart and in my flesh pulled over my heart, there is praise for him in the unnecessary skip of my walk, in my excessive and delighted staring, in the exuberance of my over-praise.

And when I dive, I shall feel the ice of speed and praise him, the shock and tingle of the gold-laced pool and praise him, the chrism of golden sunshine poured on my drenching head again and praise him.

I dive into the engulfing water, praising him.

THE FORMATIONS
(2021)
Dylan Huw
Translated by Mihangel Morgan

Salt on the frame of the Margarita glass, clasped by the red fingernails of a wrinkled hand – and wise eyes, rich and sad, looking into my naïve glare:

'Do you know what it is you want yet, Oli?'

A flurry of memories; two characters, the end of an evening. Me and her, Oli Gwilym and Elisa Gaynor, for a night.

*

Elisa Gaynor was a *brave* woman, my mother would say.

'Well, Elisa Gaynor looks *brave* tonight, doesn't she!'

'We're acting *brave* tonight, are we, Miss Gaynor?'

Elisa Gaynor had lived a lot of life. That much was obvious to anyone, even to me, even then. That's why Mam and Anti Magi and their ilk would belittle her, openly, with that specific smugness that derives from having lived a life more correctly than others. Having lived a lot of life was something to be ridiculed.

My entire understanding of Elisa Gaynor had been coloured by this kind of euphemism.

She had long divorced from my great uncle, yet she still moved within our circles, while existing beyond them. There, in our lives, as a figure, an image, a phantom, that appeared at parties and occasional events, not to be heard from otherwise. She was different to the other women I knew back then; her perfume was stronger. A figure, not a person. Elisa Gaynor: a woman.

To a boy like me, a boy older than his years, on the brink of experiencing an attraction to colour and feeling that was different from that of other boys, but a boy nevertheless, she stirred something that I still can't describe. Her *seperateness*. Her *chutzpah*.

That night, the night of the old world, the night of the formations, is impressed upon my imagination after all the years, all the experiences I have lived since then. Too many for one man, for one boy. I remember the smell of her perfume, yes, the salt on the glass, her wisdom. No one was ever as wise as Elisa Gaynor seemed to me that night.

I recall her sitting there, at the bar, her back towards me. I was twelve, thirteen, perhaps – a child, but with intimations of enthusiasm and curiosity about to reveal themselves, about to explode, complicating everything – and it was wedding season. We would be invited to all the weddings in those days, all the sad, decadent weddings held in our remote, privileged milieu. And me, I was a golden boy.

I was fetching a drink for Anti Magi. Anti Magi was not a *brave* woman, but she was a woman with a fondness for an open bar.

Elisa Gaynor was lost in a one-sided conversation with the barman, her words slipping unsteadily from her mouth, the barman blushing, but playing his part. I remember him as well as I remember her that night. His white shirt was stuffed tightly into his trousers, revealingly tight – almost certainly the wedding venue had provided his outfit, a summer job perhaps, a gap year.

I stared at his skilful hands preparing another cocktail for the brave woman in front of him, as he kept his boyish eyes fixed on hers, her reciting half jokes and old stories about the old times. The drinks in his hands would mix in ways I'd never seen before, their colours bleeding into one another, creating dances, harmonies.

I must have been staring for some time, transfixed by the handsome barman's dexterity, because Elisa Gaynor turned to me, forcing me to order.

I asked for Anti Magi's drink.

'*Bachgen Eirlys, ie?*'

'Yes.'

'And you don't want to sit and have a drink with Elisa Gaynor?'

I looked up at the strange figure sitting on the high stool, leaning on the bar, her face covered in expensive makeup, her smile warm and terrifying at the same time. I looked nervously to the barman.

'And an orange juice for me please.'

She asked me what I had done with my summer; did I have a sweetheart; what had I thought of the bride's gown.

I would give short answers, unsure, polite, and she would respond to each one with some story from her life, some character she had known, a memory, a romance. Her life in the city in the fifties, her travels around the world as a performer, her third marriage and her fourth. I got the impression the barman had already heard them, but was happy to do so again.

The discussion continued this way for some time, as she finished another drink, and a second and a third. I didn't get to say much; strange how the conversations one half listens to and quarter understands are often the most memorable.

*

521

Elisa Gaynor got drunker and drunker, as I stared, taking her in, with a mixture of fear, admiration and pride at being in her presence.

'What year are we in?'

The barman cast me a look. I wonder if this scene impressed itself in his memory the same way it did mine.

There was silence, neither of us knowing how to respond, the words falling, now, from her mouth, inelegantly, senselessly, her eyes almost rolling.

'Do you know what you want yet, Oli?'

I didn't know how to react, as you might expect. I got the impression even then that she was asking me a hundred things at once. But I knew the answer.

'I want to dance.'

She looked at me as if I hadn't understood the question.

'I've known a lot of dancers, Oli. You'll need to be strong. Are you strong, Oli?'

'I don't know.'

She laughed.

'Be a dancer, Oli. Be the best dancer there ever was.'

Her tone now had changed, the words weighing strong and defiant on her lips. 'And never look back.'

The bubbles swirled in her drink as she poured more into the glass, creating formations in the liquid, that dance again, that revelatory dance.

'You're different to everyone else here. You're nothing like Mam.'

'Your mother is a... healthy woman, Oli.' I had never heard the word *healthy* said so disdainfully. 'You'll see soon that there are other ways to live life, other ways to be healthy.'

'She says you've seen too much life.'

I don't know what possessed me. But Elisa Gaynor appreciated my frankness. Was this what it meant to be strong? My young mind was tired, attempting to catch up with the discussion, the night, the memories.

'Your mother is right, I'm sure.'

She noticed me staring at the bubbles in her glass again, their swift, strange dance, their graceful new formations.

'Two more,' she yelled at the barman, 'and that's it.'

He couldn't say no to her; I couldn't imagine anyone saying no to Elisa Gaynor. The young man's face, staring at her, then at me, the golden boy, is one of that night's most unshakeable images. He poured two drinks, one for me and one for Elisa Gaynor, looking around nervously to make sure no one had seen.

'What do you say to the nice man, Oli?'

I couldn't move.

'Thank you.'

I don't recall the taste, but I recall the sensation – the bubbles hitting the back of my throat like a knife, dancing bitterly within my body.

'I better take this to Anti Magi.'

The taste of the drink still filled my mouth.

'Give her my regards,' Elisa said sarcastically, downing her drink in one. She laughed, and I laughed too.

She picked up her bag from the floor and pointed to her jacket, which had been hanging from her stool. I held up the jacket and draped it around her shoulders as she stood. 'A pleasure, Mr Gwilym.'

'Be the best dancer, Oli Gwilym,' she said. Her perfume and the weary look in her brilliant eyes as she said this to me haunt me to this day. 'Never look back.'

With that Elisa Gaynor, the phantom, the brave woman who formed me – with one conversation, a drink, a lived life's wisdom – disappeared from my life, without looking back.

STRAWBERRY CREAM
(1997)
Siân James

I was eleven that summer, but according to my mother, already moody as a teenager, 'What can I do?' my constant cry. 'I'm bored. What can I do?'

'There's plenty to do. What about dusting the front room for me? Your grandmother and your Auntie Alice are coming to tea on Sunday.'

I hated our front room which was cold and shabby, the furniture old-fashioned, the ceiling flaking and pockmarked with damp and the once mauve and silver wallpaper faded to a sour grey and wrinkled at the corners. Our whole house was depressing, each room having its own distinctive and unpleasant smell, the front room smelling of mushrooms, the living room of yesterday's meat and gravy and the back-kitchen of Oxydol and wet washing.

'Dusting doesn't alter anything,' I said.

I expected my mother to argue with me, but she seemed too dispirited. 'I know it doesn't,' she said. And then, 'Just get yourself a nice library book and pretend you live in a palace.'

Was that what she did? She was always reading; two and sixpenny paperback romances with fair-haired girls standing on windy hills on the covers, their skirts gusting out prettily around them, their long tresses streaming behind, but their makeup immaculate.

Once I'd tried reading one of them. *Caterina breathed in as Milly tugged at the corset strings around her waist. 'Tighter,' she commanded sharply.*

'Yes, Miss Caterina,' Milly murmured in a humble voice. She loved her mistress with a blind adoration and wanted nothing but to serve her.

I continued the story in my own way. *Milly squeezed the juice of the deadly nightshade into her mistress' drinking chocolate and chuckled as she imagined pulling the strings of the shroud tighter and tighter around the tiny waist.*

I was fiercely egalitarian. My dad was a farm labourer and he had the same attitude, speaking to his boss with unconcealed disdain. 'You want me to do... what?'

'Don't you think that would work?' his boss would ask.

'Of course it wouldn't bloody work, but I'll do whatever you tell me. It's all one to me.'

My mother served in the village shop for two pounds ten a week and she was pretty cool too. I don't think she ever demanded a decent wage, just helped herself to groceries to make up the deficiency, mostly items that fitted neatly into her overall pockets. We were never short of packets of jelly, cornflour, mixed herbs, caraway seeds. Or bars of chocolate. That summer, Cadbury's Strawberry Cream was my passion and she brought me one every single lunchtime. And every afternoon I'd snap the bar into eight squares, sniff every one, bite a hole in the corner and very slowly suck out the oozy pink cream, afterwards letting the sweet chocolate casing melt on my tongue. Sometimes I could make it last a blissful half-hour.

My father's boss, Henry Groves, had a daughter called Amanda who was three or four years older than me and went to a boarding school in Malvern. I'm sure she wouldn't have chosen to spend any time with me had there been any older and more sophisticated girls in the village, but there weren't; she'd knock on our front door and stand there silently until I condescended to go out with her.

We usually walked along by the river, kicking at stones and muttering to one another. 'What's your school like?' 'Deadly. What about yours?'

'Deadly.' We had nothing to talk about.

We could never think of anything to do either. What was there to do? The sun beat down on us mercilessly every afternoon, the hours stretched out long and stagnant as sermons; I felt dusty and dried-up as the yellowing grass on the verge of the path.

'Don't you have any adventures at your school?' I asked her one day. 'Don't you have midnight feasts and so on? Pillow fights in the dorm?' I wanted some sort of conversation; lies would be fine by me. Her eyes narrowed. 'What rubbish have you been reading? How old are you anyway?'

'Thirteen.' She looked across at me. I was tall and sturdy for eleven. She was small and, I suppose, rather pretty; a turned-up nose and so on, floppy hair and so on. My God, she looked a bit like the lovesick girls on the covers of my mother's Mills & Boon. Why was I wasting my summer afternoons with her?

'Well act your age then. Pillow fights! For God's sake!'

I tried again. 'Do you have a boyfriend?' I asked.

She gave me a friendlier look. 'That would be telling.' I was definitely on the right track.

'I'll tell you if you tell me,' I said, trying to recall conversations I'd overheard on the school bus; a fierce, fat girl called Natalie Fisher, who was about fifteen I suppose, but looked thirty, who was always whispering loudly about 'doing it'. I could pretend I was 'doing it' with Joe Blackwell who sometimes helped me with my science homework.

'You go first,' she said.

'I've got this boyfriend called Joe Blackwell.'

'And?'

'He's tall and he's got red hair and millions of freckles. Quite attractive.'

'And?'

'And... and we "do it" sometimes.'

She was suddenly looking at me with alarming admiration; her eyes dilated and her lips moist. 'Go on,' she said.

'Nothing much more to say. Your turn now.'

'Let's cross the river. It's more private in the woods. We can talk better over the other side.'

We hadn't seen a soul all afternoon, but if she wanted to cross the river I was quite prepared to wade across with her. It made a change.

We took off our sandals and splashed across. The sky was white and glaring, the stones in the riverbed were hot and sharp.

'These are my father's woods,' she said.

There was no answer to that. I knew as well as she did whose bloody woods they were. 'This is where Joe Blackwell and I... you know.' I said. It seemed a way to get even with her.

'Show me what you do,' she said, moistening her lips again with the tip of her small pink tongue. 'Show me how you do it.' She sat on the ground and pulled me down with her.

'I can't do it with a girl,' I said, my voice gritty with embarrassment.

'Yes you can, of course you can. Don't you think I know anything?' She was opening her dress and pulling me to her. 'Do you like my breasts?' she asked, tilting them up towards me.

I hated breasts. My Auntie Alice was always getting hers out to feed her baby, great mottled things, large as swedes, but more wobbly; I hated having to see them, the shiny mauve veins; the pale, wet, puckered nipples.

Amanda's breasts were different, small and delicate, creamy as honeysuckle, pink-tipped. She snatched at my hand and placed it over one of them. It seemed like some small, warm animal under the curve of my palm. 'What now?' she asked. 'What do we do next?' Her voice was creaky like the hinge of a gate.

Her nipple hardened under my touch. I felt shivers go down my body like vibrations in the telegraph wires. I closed my eyes as my fingers circled over and over her breasts. 'We have to do this part properly first,' I said.

I peeped at her face. Her eyes were closed. She looked like the picture of St Winifred in church; as though she was seeing angels.

'Now what?' she asked again. I lowered myself onto my elbow and licked her nipples, one after the other. Her eyes flicked open in surprise. 'Licking?' she asked.

'Licking,' I said firmly. 'Don't you like it?'

'I think so. Do you?'

The shivering started up again, it was lower now, my belly seemed to be fluttery as a nest of fledglings. 'Yes, I like it.' I tried to sound non-committal, but suddenly I was lifting her towards me and sucking, sucking her little round breasts.

'That's all I know,' I confessed at last. Other images which were beginning to besiege my mind seemed altogether too bizarre. 'I don't know the rest of it,' I repeated.

I thought she'd be annoyed, expected her to fasten up her dress and flounce off. She wasn't, though, and didn't. 'Well, we can do this part again, can't we?'

And we did. We did it again and again all through the last dog days of that summer. Every fine afternoon we'd set off wordlessly along the same path, crossing the river at the same spot, lying down under the same trees, finding the same stirrings of pleasure.

At the beginning of September, it got damp and cold, the leaves lost their lustre, the birds grew silent, the woods began to smell of rust and wet earth and we realised that our time was running out.

'I'm going back to school next week,' Amanda said one Friday afternoon, 'so I suppose we'd better say goodbye.'

I raised my mouth from her breast and sat up. 'Goodbye,' I said. I felt something almost like sadness, but wasn't going to let her know.

'Perhaps we'll do the other part next year,' she said. 'Perhaps.'

I never saw her again. Before the Christmas holidays my father had found a better job and we'd moved from our horrid old house to another that wasn't quite as horrid, and my mother worked in an office instead of a village shop.

I went to a different school and forgot Joe Blackwell. But I never quite forgot those afternoons with Amanda: my strawberry cream summer.

THE WONDER AT SEAL CAVE
(2000)
John Sam Jones

Gethin stacked the returned books and wondered why Mr Bateman always seemed to do his marking in the middle study bay; why not the staff room, the small 'prep' room at the back of the biology lab, or even one of the other bays? Quite often, when he was putting books back in the geography section, nearest the study area, they'd smile at one another. Sometimes, if there was no one else in the library, they'd talk – but only if Mr Bateman initiated the conversation. Gethin liked these talks; he liked it that Mr Bateman seemed interested in what he was reading and what films he'd seen, or what he thought about mad cows, adulterous royals, and the war in Chechnya. Sometimes they even talked about football. When Gethin turned up for his library duty he found himself hoping that he and Mr Bateman would be alone, that there would be plenty of geography books to shelve, and that they might talk.

Mr Bateman was his favourite teacher; he was most people's favourite really. He got angry sometimes and shouted a bit, but he was never sarcastic, which seemed to be the weapon most of the male staff used to intimidate their classes into some kind of order and control. And he always made biology interesting, even if there were lots of facts that had to be memorised. He was the kind of teacher most students wanted to do well for, to please. The exam results pleased everyone; there were more A grades in biology from Ysgol yr Aber than from any other school in Wales and the school's record of success in biology was always used by the Welsh Office to challenge the cynicism of those opposed to Welsh-language science education.

Mr Bateman had learned to speak Welsh; perhaps this was what Gethin liked best about him. Very few of the English people who'd settled in the area had bothered to learn the language, but he had, and Gethin was hard put to detect an ill-formed mutation or a confused gender; Mr Bateman spoke better Welsh than many native speakers and Gethin admired him for the respect he'd shown to the language and culture of his adopted home. And there was football too; Gethin thought highly of him for that! Mr Bateman had grown up in Manchester and everyone at school knew how fanatically he still supported his home team – United, not City. Gethin supported Liverpool and went to some home games with Mel Tudor, Me I-siop-baco as everyone knew him, who had a season ticket at Anfield.

Gethin carried the Welsh novels back to their shelf wondering if he dared start a conversation with Mr Bateman. He needed to talk to somebody. The school summer holidays had been such a mixed time; although he'd been confident enough of good grades, waiting for the GCSE results had found him lurching between the certainty of staying on at school to do his A-levels and the uneasy emptiness of 'what if?' It was then that 'the other thing' bothered him; it had been there for ages, of course, but 'doing well in your exams' and 'going to university like your brother and sister' had been a sufficient enough screen to hide behind. The kiss on *Brookside*, outing bishops and the debate about the age of consent had made the screen wobble a bit, but he really hadn't allowed himself to think very much that he might be, or what that might mean, until those moments of uneasy emptiness had folded over him. And now he knew that he was and he needed to talk about it.

He'd tried to talk to his sister. Gethin had stayed with Eilir in Liverpool at the beginning of July; he'd tried talking to her after seeing the film, but she'd seemed so taken up with her patients, her new boyfriend and the hassles she and her flatmates were having with their landlord about the fungus growing on the kitchen wall. It was because she'd been so preoccupied that Gethin had spent his time in the city alone and had the chance to go to the cinema on a rainy afternoon. He'd read a review of *Beautiful Thing* in the Guide that came with Saturday's *Guardian*, and when he saw that it was showing at the ABC on Lime Street he'd loitered on the opposite pavement for almost an hour trying to muster up the courage to go in. It was the rain that eventually sent him through the glass doors into the garishly lit foyer of the cinema to face the spotty, many ear-ringed boy in the ticket booth who dispensed the ticket with a wry smile. Gethin had panicked, interpreting the boy's smile as 'I know you're queer... All the boys who come to see this film on their own are!' Only after taking his seat in the darkened auditorium did his panic subside.

It was a love story: Jamie and Ste, two boys his own age, falling in love with one another. There were no steamy love scenes and but for a fleeting glance at Ste's naked bottom there was no nudity, so Gethin got few clues as to what two boys might actually do together. When Jamie and Ste ran through the trees chasing one another and finally embracing and kissing, Gethin had become aroused; he'd wanted to be Jamie in the film – to be held and kissed by Ste... He'd wanted his own mother to be as accepting as Jamie's and he'd wanted a friend like Leah to talk to.

Outside the cinema it had stopped raining so Gethin decided to walk back to Eilir's flat near Princes Park. Wandering along Princes Avenue, he came to understand that something had changed in his life and nothing would be the same again. Behind the screen that he'd erected to keep himself from thinking about 'the other thing' he'd felt closed in silence – a silence which had left him anxious and uncertain, even fearful. But the screen had been pulled away by Jamie and Ste and their story had begun to give that unspeakable part of Gethin's life a shape. For the first time Gethin really understood what his father had so often preached to his congregation – 'that stories give shape to lives and that without stories we cannot understand ourselves'. Of course, the Reverend Llyr Jones had a certain anthology of stories in mind for giving shape to lives and Gethin knew that his father wouldn't include Jamie and Ste's story alongside those of Jacob, Jeremiah and Jesus. Llyr Jones wouldn't see the two boys' story as a 'beautiful thing'.

Gethin recalled that Sunday during the age of consent debate. His father, in a fiery sermon, had exhorted the congregation at Tabernacl (Methodistiaid Calfinaidd – 1881) to write to the local MP urging him to vote against lowering the age to sixteen. Gethin remembered the discussion over the roast beef after chapel, his father – with all the authority of an M.Th. and a dog-collar behind his words, saying that homosexuals were sinful, and his mother – in her calm 'I'm the doctor and you can trust me' manner – saying that they were disturbed and needed psychiatric treatment.

Crossing Princes Park, Gethin sat by a reservoir of the city's debris that had once been a lake. He watched a used condom navigate its course on a stiffening breeze through the squalid waters between the half-submerged skeletons of an old bike and a supermarket trolley until it came to lie, stranded on the shore of an abandoned pram. He thought about his father and mother; how he loved them – but how he now didn't think he knew them at all. If he told them about the film – about Jamie and Ste and about what he now knew to be true of himself, would his father's love be acted out in some kind of exorcism and would his mother want the best medical care with visits to some psychologist? Gethin wondered if their love and trust in him were deep enough to challenge thirty years of belief in Calvinistic Biblical scholarship and 1960's medical science?

A doll's arm reached from the crib of slime in which it lay, grasping an empty sky; Gethin wondered if his reaching out would be as futile. Back at the flat, Eilir wanted to talk about her first AIDS patient – and about the fungus on the kitchen wall...

Mr Bateman looked up from his marking and smiled at Gethin; he smiled back and mouthed a silent greeting which Mr Bateman returned. Gethin put the dozen or so geography books back on their shelf and turned to talk to his teacher, but his head was already back in his books. With no reason to linger by the study area and insufficient courage to go up to Mr Bateman and ask if they could talk, he went to fetch the remaining pile of returns and went to the science section at the other end of the library.

For some weeks after his stay in Liverpool, Gethin had tried to prop up the screen which Jamie and Ste's story had so successfully toppled. The hikes and bike rides he and his friends had arranged made hiding from the dawning truths of his life easier, but he couldn't escape the knowledge that in all games of hide-and-seek, that which was hidden was always found. Then there had been the tense days leading up to the exam results, and those few exhilarating hours which high achievement and congratulation had brought. His course of A-level study was set, and before the trough of anti-climax swallowed him he got caught up in all the preparations for Enlli. Ever since he could remember, the whole family had spent the week of August bank holiday on the remote island. Everyone had thought that this year would be different – that Seifion, Gethin's brother, wouldn't be able to come home from America; but then Seifion had phoned to say that his newspaper needed him back in London for the first week in September, so he'd be with them after all. For a whole week, Gethin packed all the provisions they'd need on the island into boxes which were then wrapped in bin bags to keep everything dry during the trip in the open boat across the sound. At least this year they didn't have to take all their drinking water too!

Their week on Enlli was, for different reasons, special to each member of the family. His mother liked the peace and unhurried simplicity of life without electricity and phones, cars and supermarket queues – and patients! She'd sometimes come in from a walk and say things like 'Life here makes you question so much of what we think is important on the mainland...' to anyone who happened to be in earshot, but such things were said in ways which beckoned only the responses of her own thoughts. Ann Jones would bake bread every day and gut the fish that Seifion caught in Bae'r Nant at the north end – things which Gethin never saw his mother do at home. His father spent hours alone reading and meditating; on his first visit to the island, more than thirty years ago, Llyr had found a sheltered cove near Pen Diben, at the south end beyond the lighthouse. It was to the cove that he retreated, drawn back by the whisperings of Beuno, Dyfrig, Padarn and other long-dead saints, to be with his thoughts and God. Seifion liked to fish for bass and pollack, and in the last years, since his work had taken him to places like Sarajevo and Grozny, he seemed to use his time on Enlli to find some peace inside himself; by the end of the week he'd be lamenting his choice of career in journalism and wishing he could stay. Eilir painted and enjoyed long talks with her mother; but mostly she painted. And for Gethin the island was where wonders unfolded. He watched grey seals and built dry stone walls; he looked, late into the night, for Manx Shearwaters in the beam of a torch and watched for flocks of choughs. Over the years he'd talked with the marine biologists and the botanists, the geologists and the entomologists that stayed at the Bardsey Bird and Field Observatory and accompanied them on their field trips. For Gethin the island was a living encyclopaedia of the natural world.

On the evening before they crossed over to Enlli the whole family had lingered at the supper table. Eilir had unfolded the saga of the last days of the fungus on the kitchen wall and Seifion had told them stories about New York – the unbearable August heat, the congestion and pollution caused by too many cars, the crumbling health care system – about which he'd been doing a piece for his newspaper... Then Eilir had talked about *her* AIDS patient; Ann had wanted to know if they were using the new combination therapy in Liverpool, the one she'd read about in the *BMJ*. Seifion told the grim details of a visit to an under-funded AIDS hospice, run by a group of nuns in Queens, where people died in their own filth. Eilir couldn't speak highly enough about the loyalty and care her AIDS patient's partner had shown and how impressed she'd been with the faithfulness of her patient's gay friends. 'Homosexuals are still the highest risk group then?' asked Ann. Both Eilir and Seifion tried to say something about how it was behaviours that were risky, and that the notion of risk shouldn't be pinned onto groups of people like a badge, but their words were lost as the talk shifted from health care to homosexuality. Llyr didn't believe that God was punishing homosexuals through this disease, but that the disease was a consequence of their sinfulness and the biggest lesson to humanity from the whole AIDS crisis was that if we chose to flout God's law some pretty catastrophic things would happen. Seifion talked about two gay friends, one from university days and the other a journalist; coming to know these two men had made Seifion rethink his position – the position he'd grown up with – Llyr's position. Seifion didn't think, any longer, that being gay was sinful. And wasn't all the work with the human genome project going to reveal that sexual orientation was genetically predisposed? If that were true, then gay people were an intended part of God's creation. Llyr had said that even if science did reveal the genetic basis of sexual orientation, that didn't make homosexual acts any less sinful; the Bible was clear that sexual intercourse between a man and a woman in marriage was what had been ordained; celibacy was the only acceptable lifestyle for homosexuals, as it was for all unmarried people.

Perhaps Gethin imagined that both his brother and sister had blushed on hearing this; he knew that he'd blushed as soon as they'd started talking about homosexuality. He'd thought that he might clear the table while they talked, to hide his anxiety and embarrassment, and yet, the things that Eilir and Seifion had said had been interesting and positive. Before falling asleep, he decided that he'd talk with Seifion in the morning when they drove together to Porth Meudwy at the tip of the Llyn.

Waiting on the pebble beach for the two rowing boats to carry everyone and everything bound for the island across the bay to the larger boat in the anchorage, Gethin considered his disappointment. Who was he most disappointed in, himself or his brother? Seifion had said it was a phase that he'd pass through; he'd even shared with Gethin that he and two other boys, when they were about thirteen, had 'played' with themselves and had competitions to see who could do it quickest and shoot highest. When Gethin hadn't seemed convinced, Seifion talked about a sexual experience with a French boy during a language exchange when he was about Gethin's age; they'd shared the same room for the whole of Seifion's stay and done things in bed together; none of it had meant that he was gay. Gethin hadn't tried to explain what he knew to be true; but then – he didn't have the words to give it any shape, and alongside Seifion's experiences Gethin had nothing to share – just an intuitive knowing, without form or outline – without a voice.

Bugail Enlli rounded Pen Cristin and came into calmer water. The sound had been wilder than Gethin could remember and everyone was soaked. The two Germans left behind by the Observatory boat had sat next to him and in the first minutes of the crossing, in the relative calm of the Llyns' lee, they'd introduced themselves. Gethin, filled with the confidence of his A*, had said 'Hallo! Mein Name ist Gethin Llyr'; he'd tried to explain that it would probably get rougher once they got into the channel and that it might be a good idea to wear the waterproofs that were tucked through the straps of their rucksacks. Bernd, the one Gethin supposed was about his own age, speaking in English that was better than Gethin's German, had said that it was his first time on such a small boat. When all the conversations had submitted to awe at the waves and silent prayers, Bernd wove his arm through Gethin's to stop himself being thrown around so much. Later, standing side by side on the uneven jetty in the Cafn, passing all the luggage from the boat along the line to the waiting tractor and trailer, Gethin and Bernd talked easily. The German boy was impressed that Gethin had been to the island every summer; he asked about its wonders. Did Gethin know about the Seal Cave? He'd read all about it; was it hard to find? Gethin said that it was, but that he'd take him there if he liked.

When Bernd came to Carreg Fawr later in the day to find Gethin, Ann Jones, who'd been kneading the first batch of dough had tried to explain that she wasn't Mrs Llyr, but Mrs Jones – but he could call her Ann anyway. Bernd, in his confusion, had said that in Germany it was impossible for children not to carry their parents' family name. Ann had done her best to explain that her three children were named according to an old Welsh tradition whereby sons were known as 'son of' and daughters as 'daughter of' – so Eilir was Eilir Ann and Gethin was Gethin Llyr. Though Gethin had gone fishing with Seifion and Ann didn't know for sure when they'd be back, Bernd stayed with her at Carreg Fawr and she told him stories about the island; he especially liked the idea that they might be stuck there for days if the weather turned bad. When Gethin and Seifion returned with three large pollack, more than enough for supper, Bernd and Gethin went to climb all 548 feet of Mynydd Enlli; from the 'mountain-top' Gethin could point out interesting places and give Bernd his bearings.

The hour after all the supper things had been cleared away was quiet time. Gethin had never thought to question this, it was part of their life on Enlli; an hour in silence to listen for the wisdom of the twenty thousand saints and God. The last quarter of the quiet hour was evening prayer and they all came together in the small front room; sometimes this was silent too, and at other times someone would say whatever their day on the island moved them to say. Gethin thought about Bernd; when he'd put his arm through Gethin's, on the boat, he'd become aroused... He'd had an erection. The memory of it now – before God – left him filled with shame. It would be hard to live as a homosexual in a world with God, Gethin thought, but how much harder would life be without God?

Eilir and Gethin were eating breakfast when Bernd turned up at Carreg Fawr. 'Today we explore Seal's Cave, ja?' he'd asked. 'Wenn du willst', Gethin had said... If you like! They put some bread and cheese in Bernd's rucksack and set off to explore the east side of the mountain. Ann shouted after them that they needed to be careful on the sheer slopes above the sound; the last thing she wanted was to scramble on the scree to tend broken legs!

From high up on the north side of the mountain Gethin spotted Seifion, fishing from a shoulder of rock in Bae'r Nant way off below them. As they came over to the east side they saw a man sunbathing; he mumbled something about being careful on the narrow paths. Across Cardigan Bay, Cader Idris proved a worthy throne for its mythical giant and the blue of the sea was spotted with bright sail-cloth. When the path dropped away steeply, Bernd betrayed the first clue that the expedition was more dangerous than he'd anticipated; 'You're sure this is the right way, Gethin? If we fall here then – das issues...!' Gethin reassured him and suggested that they ease themselves down the steep, scree path on their bottoms. After ten minutes they reached Seal Cave.

Bernd looked disbelievingly at Gethin... 'But this hole... it's too small... you're sure this is the place?' Gethin remembered that he had thought the same thing that first time with Seifion. 'It's just the entrance that's small, then it opens out...' And Gethin disappeared into the blackness with 'Come right behind me. You can hold onto my leg if you're frightened...' Then he felt the German boy's hand around his ankle. Halfway along the pitch-black tunnel Gethin heard the wheezing and snorting of the seals echo from the underground chamber. He whispered into the darkness behind him that if they stayed as quiet as possible they wouldn't scare the seals. When they both finally pulled themselves from the tunnel onto the wide, flat rock and looked down into the cave, well-lit from a large jagged opening just below the water's surface, they saw two seals basking on the rocks just feet away and another deep in the water, an outline against the water-filtered light. They hardly dared to breathe and marvelled at the wonder of it all.

After ten, perhaps fifteen minutes, Bernd had asked, in a whisper, whether they could swim with the seals. Gethin remembered that he and Seifion had swum in the cave a few times, but that the seals were usually frightened off... 'We can try...' Gethin whispered back. Bernd stood up and as he took off his clothes Gethin saw that his body was already that of a man. 'Come... let's swim...' he whispered, beckoning Gethin to undress. Gethin followed him into the water. The two basking seals snorted, wriggled from their rocks and dived deeply, circling them both before making for the underwater exit to the open sea. The boys were enthralled and hugged one another, each discovering the other's excitement. They swam together... touching... exploring one another's bodies... and they kissed.... On the wide, flat rock above the water they lay in one another's arms for a long time, their bodies moving together. Bernd's sigh, when it finally erupted from somewhere deep inside him, echoed around the cave before dying away into Gethin's low moan.

During the quiet hour that evening, Llyr told them the story of Saint Beuno and the curlew; he'd watched the birds for most of the afternoon, breaking off the legs of small crabs before swallowing them. According to the legend, Beuno, in the years before coming to Enlli to die, had lost his book of sermons overboard on a stormy sea crossing; in some despair, he arrived back at his cell in Clynnog Fawr to find his sermons, pulled from the sea and carried back to him by a curlew. It was a story Gethin had heard every summer on the island, but then, of Enlli's twenty thousand saints, Beuno was his father's favourite. Gethin's mind wandered to Bernd and to Seal Cave and now, before God, he wasn't so sure that it was the 'beautiful thing' it had been that afternoon.

Later, feeling heavy with a guilt that only Welsh Calvinism could bestow, Gethin left Carreg Fawr in search of some distraction. Near Ogof Hir he looked for Shearwaters. Beuno came to him... And then there were two others, perhaps Dyfrig and Padarn, but their faces were hidden under their hoods... And there were curlews; lots of curlews. Startled by the swiftness of their appearance, Gethin dropped his torch; the glass broke as it hit the rocks and the beam died. The blackness of the night wrapped itself around him and, through the curlew's melodic 'cur-lee', Beuno whispered his wisdom. Gethin didn't want to hear words of judgement and condemnation and he hit out at the three robed figures, shouting at them to leave him alone. Their robes and whisperings folded over and under him and, quiet in their embrace, he was carried back to Seal Cave. Beuno spoke through the whisperings of the other two in a babble of Latin and Welsh, Greek and Hebrew, and though it sounded odd, Gethin understood. Bueno wept for all the men down the centuries whose lives had been tortured by self-hatred because they had loved other men. 'The glory of God is the fully alive human being', he'd said, 'and as it is your providence to love men, love them well, in truth and faithfulness... Where love is true and faithful, God will dwell... *Ubi caritas et amor, Deus ibi est...*'

The bell rang and as Gethin watched Mr Bateman pack away his books he decided that his need to talk might keep until another day. They both reached the library door together and with a broad smile, Mr Bateman asked, 'What sort of week did you have on Bardsey?' Gethin replied he had a lot to tell and offered to help set up some apparatus in the lab during the lunch break. And so Gethin got to talk.

Mr Bateman listened as Gethin explained that he now realised he was gay and understood that he needed some support, but he interrupted Gethin when he started to tell him about Bernd and the Seal Cave... 'I don't want to know if you've had sex with boys,

Gethin; that would put me in a difficult position...' And he explained about the school's policy on sex education and the laws which guided it; 'I'd be expected to inform the head if I knew that one of our pupils was having sex below the age of consent... And the school policy doesn't really give me much guidance on how to talk to you about gay issues... Can't you talk about this with someone else?' After a long silence Gethin said that he didn't think there was anyone else, but that he didn't want to put Mr Bateman in an awkward position either, and he left the lab feeling down and lonely.

That evening, when the loneliness became too deep, Gethin told his parents he was gay. Ann said she'd ring one of the psychiatrists at the hospital. Llyr knew of a healing ministry on the Wirral that had some success in saving homosexuals. They both wanted the best for him. *Ubi caritas et amor, ubi caritas, Deus ibi est.*

Later that evening Kevin Bateman talked with his brother's lover, David, about what support he might offer Gethin, 'You could suggest that he phone the gay help-line in Bangor...'

Kevin Bateman then wrote Gethin a note to say that he was sorry for letting him down and he put the phone number David had given him clearly on the bottom... *Ubi caritas et amor, ubi caritas, Deus ibi est...*

KISSING NINA
(2008)
Deborah Kay Davies

Grace first fell deeply in love when she was ten years and six months old.

Until then she had only been practising, going through the motions. Not that she knew many of the motions. She could only watch TV kisses on other people's televisions, and her own parents never would kiss, that she knew for definite. Grace had thought about the best ways to kiss for a long time, long before she was ten even. She had started by kissing her pillow, at night. Instinctively she made her mouth as delectable as it could be, as soft and eager as she knew how. She took time to close her eyes, concentrating on the fall of her eyelids. She knew how they gleamed damply as they lowered; she felt them cooling as the night air breathed on them. She was aware of the way her thick, spiky lashes would first touch and then mesh together.

There came a time when pillow-kissing was not enough. Grace thought about who would be willing to practise with her; she needed a person to kiss. She had to be sure that kissing a particular friend would, in itself, be pleasant. It wasn't easy to choose someone, but Grace knew that, of all her friends, Nina was the only one suitable.

Nina was very pretty. The same build as Grace, with heavy, auburn hair that always felt cool. The sort of hair that wouldn't stay in hair-clips or ribbons, but dead straight, poured down

Nina's back. Of the two, Nina was the leader, and so it was arranged. All through the quiet evenings, in the autumn and winter before the spring that led to Grace falling in love, while they were supposed to be doing school projects, she and her friend Nina tried out all the different sorts of kissing they could think of.

Nina kissed with a sweetly martyred air, eyes wide-open and vacant. Grace loved to kiss Nina's chilly, unresponsive lips. She began to take care about where she stood when Nina kissed her. She liked to lean against the bedroom door, back and shoulders cushioned by the soft, dark-red towelling of her dressing-gown. Before Nina started to kiss her, Grace would hold the edges of her dressing-gown sleeves tightly in her fists. Not long after Nina began, her kisses as light as falling icing-sugar, Grace would murmur against her mouth, harder, Nina, do it harder. She'd feel a weakness spreading down through her chest, a pleasure shivering on the very edge of fear, which centred in a thick knot between her straining legs. Each time, just before she felt she must fall to the floor, Grace would push Nina away and jump onto the bed. Nina's hair, falling forward on her face, trembled as if it were alive. Avoiding Grace's eyes, she'd go back to her books.

Years afterwards, the memory of the waiting stillness of the house, the warm, musty air of the bedroom, the way the darkening sky pressed itself like a lost, lonely dog against the windows, and most of all, Nina's wide-open eyes, candid as a baby's, were still vivid to Grace, and seemed part of the spring she first fell in love.

It was the end of January when Grace found out about kissing with tongues. She'd heard about it before in school but wasn't sure if it was true. Finally she was convinced that people really did it. Now Grace felt shy about telling Nina. The early evening, while she waited for Nina to come to study, seemed to go on and on. She thought about this kissing with tongues. She imagined how she and Nina would do it, what it would taste like. She was unsure of Nina's reaction. She might get mad, tell Grace to grow up. She was anxious about her parents; she could never be entirely confident that one of them wouldn't come into her room without knocking, with a drink or something to eat. Grace's sister was another big problem. Even though she now had the tiny box room for her own, she was always finding reasons to slide into Grace's bedroom.

But everything was perfect this evening. Tamar was staying at their grandparents' house, where she could watch television. She'd been talking about a pop band she was mad about called the Bay City Rollers. She'd even got herself a Rollers tartan bobble hat and smuggled it into the house. She kept it under her mattress. Grace imagined her now, sat on the sofa at Gran's with her hat on, watching the band play. Grace's parents were intent on tidying-up in the lighted greenhouse. From the landing window she could see them hunched over pots and sacks. There was no danger of them coming in for hours.

Nina listened calmly as Grace explained about the new kissing. She asked Grace to swear she was telling the truth. They decided to do the new way of kissing that night. It was Grace's turn to kiss first. Nina's lips seemed different to her, hot and salty. She could feel Nina's lop-sided smile. Grace licked the smiling side of Nina's mouth and found the tip of her pointed tongue. To Grace, the taste of Nina, the feel of her sharp teeth, was delicious. As she pushed her tongue into Nina's mouth, she felt as if her whole life was concentrated there. She didn't want to stop. Nina's arms slid around Grace's shoulders, and they lay down on the bed.

In the warm quiet of the bedroom the radiator ticked. Snuggled on the pink candlewick bedspread, Nina and Grace felt suspended, waiting. They lay on their sides facing each other. Nina's breath, smelling as sweet as shortbread biscuits, lifted Grace's fine blonde fringe. They were quite still. Nina's brown eyes looked into Grace's blue, and Nina brought Grace's head close to hers, resting their smooth foreheads together. Can you read my mind? Nina said, and closed her eyes slowly, luxuriously. Linked at the mouth, they fell asleep. Grace and Nina did not talk to each other about the kissing and lying together. To them it was simple. They were very careful, even so, to keep it as their own special thing, something to be protected. But as spring slowly approached, and the evenings started to grow lighter and milder, they did not see so much of each other. There were so many other things to do outside. Soon the times they had spent together in the autumn and winter became part of the past – half-remembered, barely believed.

Grace loved to swim, and spent her Saturday mornings at the pool. Nina hated the water and never went anywhere near it. There was a particular boy at the pool, called Kit, whom Grace began to think irresistible. Secretly, she watched his elegant diving. She loved the way the water ran off his back, the way it made his pale hair darken, how he swam without splashing. She knew he watched her too. They didn't talk to each other, but gradually they began to swim together. Underwater they circled each other, slick legs twining. Once, Kit pulled her under towards him, where the water was six feet deep, and Grace silently slid down the length of his body, following its contours with her hands, her hair undulating above her. They looked at each other's eyelashes studded with seed pearls and watched the tiny bubbles escaping from between their lips as they smiled, the sound of the deep water like the pulse of some huge marine creature in their ears. They were evenly matched, alike in build and colouring.

One day, after they had silently swum together all morning, Grace found Kit waiting for her outside the swimming pool. He asked if he could walk her home. Grace smelt the chlorine drying in their hair; it made her dizzy. She held his hand, and they walked home together. At Grace's house no one was in. The air inside felt heavy and waiting, strange, like the rooms of a holiday home in winter. Grace felt like a visitor, no longer bound by the familiar rules that applied when her family was at home. She felt confident too, unable to put a foot wrong. The possibilities of the empty house seemed limitless.

Grace led him up to her bedroom. The winter bedspread had been replaced by a light cover, splashed with lime and yellow. The curtains sighed, lifted by a breeze from the open window. Spring sun slanted across Grace's legs, and she felt the familiar tightening and breathlessness in her chest. She sat on the bed and drew Kit down beside her. He smiled, the freckles on his nose stretching, and offered his lips. His kiss felt as sweet and smooth as a green grape. Grace drew back, recalling a hot, salty mouth on hers, and looked at the closed bedroom door. She remembered the warm radiator ticking on winter evenings, the cool hank of shining hair that slipped forward to bump her cheek, the shaggy embrace of her dark-red winter dressing-gown against the door. The light in her room was too bright. Grace shivered. Closing her eyes, she clenched her empty fists and firmly pushed the boy away.

INTERNATIONALISMS

FEAR
(1949)
Rhys Davies

As soon as the boy got into the compartment he felt there was something queer in it. The only other occupant was a slight, dusky man who sat in a corner with that air of propriety and unassertiveness which his race – he looked like an Indian – tend to display in England. There was also a faint sickly scent. For years afterwards, whenever he smelled that musk odour again, the terror of this afternoon came back to him.

He went to the other end of the compartment, sat in the opposite corner.

There were no corridors in these local trains. The man looked at him and smiled friendlily. The boy returned the smile briefly, not quite knowing what he was thinking, only aware of a deep, vague unease. But it would look so silly to jump out of the compartment now. The train gave a jerk and began to move.

Then, immediately with the jerk, the man began to utter a low humming chant, slow but with a definite rhythm. His lips did not open or even move, yet the hum penetrated above the noise of the train's wheels. It was in a sort of dreamy rhythm, enticing, lonely and antique; it suggested monotonous deserts, an eternal patience, a soothing wisdom. It went on and on. It was the kind of archaic chant that brings to the mind images of slowly swaying bodies in some endless ceremony in a barbaric temple.

Startled, and very alive to this proof of there being something odd in the compartment, the boy turned from staring out of the window – already the train was deep in the country among lonely fields and dark wooded slopes – and forced himself to glance at the man.

The man was looking at him. They faced each other across the compartment's length. Something coiled up in the boy. It was as if his soul took primitive fear and crouched to hide. The man's brown lips became stretched in a mysterious smile, though that humming chant continued, worldlessly swaying out of his mouth. His eyes, dark and unfathomable, never moved from the boy. The musk scent was stronger.

Yet this was not all. The boy could not imagine what other fearful thing lurked in the compartment. But he seemed to sense a secret power of something evilly antipathetic. Did it come from the man's long pinky-brown hands, the sinewy but fleshless hands of a sun-scorched race? Long tribal hands like claws. Or only from the fact that the man was of a far country whose ways were utterly alien to ours? And he continued to smile. A faint and subtle smile, while his eyes surveyed the boy as if he contemplated action. Something had flickered in and out of those shadowy eyes, like a dancing malice.

The boy sat stiffly. Somehow he could not return to his staring out of the window. But he tried not to look at the man again. The humming did not stop. And suddenly it took a higher note, like an unhurried wail, yet keeping within its strict and narrow compass. A liquid exultance wavered in and out of the wail. The noise of the train, the flying fields and woods, even the walls of the compartment, had vanished. There was only this chant, the man who was uttering it, and himself. He did not know that now he could not move his eyes from those of the man.

Abruptly the compartment was plunged into blackness. There was a shrieking rush of air. The train had entered a tunnel. With a sudden jerk the boy crouched down. He coiled into the seat's corner, shuddering, yet with every sense electrically alive now.

Then, above the roar of the air and the hurling grind of the train, that hum rose, dominantly establishing its insidious power. It called, it unhurriedly exhorted obedience, it soothed. Again it seemed to obliterate the louder, harsher noises. Spent and defeated, helplessly awaiting whatever menace lay in the darkness, the boy crouched. He knew the man's eyes were gazing towards him; he thought he saw their gleam triumphantly piercing the darkness. What was this strange presence of evil in the air, stronger now in the dark?

Suddenly crashing into the compartment, the hard blue and white daylight was like a blow. The train had gained speed in the tunnel and now hurled on through the light with the same agonising impetus, as if it would rush on for ever. Spent in the dread which had almost cancelled out his senses, the boy stared dully at the man. Still he seemed to hear the humming, though actually it had ceased. He saw the man's lips part in a full enticing smile, he saw teeth dazzlingly white between the dusky lips.

'You not like dark tunnel?' The smile continued seductively; once more the flecks of light danced wickedly in his eyes. 'Come!' He beckoned with a long wrinkled finger.

The boy did not move.

'You like pomegranates?' He rose and took from the luggage-rack a brown wicker basket. It was the kind of basket in which a large cat would be sent on a journey. 'Come!' he smiled friendlily and, as the boy still did not move, he crossed over and sat down beside him, but leaving a polite distance.

The staring boy did not flinch.

'Pomegranates from the East! English boy like, eh?' There seemed a collaboration in his intimate voice; he too was a boy going to share fruit with his friend. 'Nice pomegranates,' he smiled with good-humour. There was also something stupid in his manner, a fatuous mysteriousness.

The basket lay on his knees. He began to hum again. The boy watched, still without movement, cold and abstract in his non-apprehension of this friendliness. But he was aware of the sickly perfume beside him and, more pronounced than ever, of an insidious presence that was utterly alien. That evil power lay in his immediate vicinity. The man looked at him again and, still humming, drew a rod and lifted the basket's lid.

There was no glow of magically gleaming fruits, no yellow-and-rose-tinted rinds enclosing honeycombs of luscious seeds. But from the basket's depth rose the head of a snake. It rose slowly to the enchantment of the hum. It rose from its sleepy coil, rearing its long brownish-gold throat dreamily, the head swaying out in languor towards the man's lips. Its eyes seemed to look blindly at nothing. It was a cobra.

Something happened to the boy. An old warning of the muscles and the vulnerable flesh. He leapt and flung himself headlong across the compartment. He was not aware that he gave a sharp shriek. He curled against the opposite seat's back, his knees pressing into the cushion. But, half turning, his eyes could not tear themselves from that reared head.

And it was with other senses that he knew most deeply he had evoked rage. The cobra was writhing in disturbed anger, shooting its head in his direction. He saw wakened pin-point eyes of black malice. More fearful was the dilation of the throat, its skin swelling evilly into a hood in which shone two palpitating sparks. In some cell of his being he knew that the hood was swelling in destructive fury. He became very still.

The man did not stop humming. But now his narrowed eyes were focussed in glittering concentration on the snake. And into that hum had crept a new note of tenacious decision. It was a pitting of subtle power against the snake's wishes and it was also an appeasement. A man was addressing a snake. He was offering a snake tribute and acknowledgment of its right to anger; he was honeyed and soothing. At the same time he did not relax an announcement of being master. There was courtesy towards one of the supreme powers of the animal kingdom, but also there was the ancient pride of man's supremacy.

And the snake was pacified. Its strange reared collar of skin sank bank into its neck; its head ceased to lunge towards the boy. The humming slackened into a dreamy lullaby. Narrowly intent now, the man's eyes did not move. The length of tawny body slowly sank back. Its skin had a dull glisten, the glisten of an unhealthy torpidity. Now the snake looked effete, shorn of its venomous power. The drugged head sank. Unhurriedly the man closed the basket and slipped its rod secure.

He turned angrily to the boy; he made a contemptuous sound, like a hiss. 'I show you cobra and you jump and shout, heh! Make him angry!' There was more rebuke than real anger in his exclamations. But also his brown face was puckered in a kind of childish stupidity; he might have been another boy of twelve. 'I give you free performance with cobra, and you jump and scream like little girl.' The indignation died out of his eyes; they became focussed in a more adult perception. 'I sing to keep cobra quiet in train,' he explained. 'Cobra not like train.'

The boy had not stirred. 'You not like cobra?' the man asked in injured surprise. 'Nice snake now, no poison! But not liking you jump and shout.'

There was no reply or movement; centuries and continents lay between him and the boy's still repudiation. The man gazed at him in silence and added worriedly: 'You going to fair in Newport? You see me? Ali the Snake Charmer. You come in free and see me make cobra dance—'

But the train was drawing into the station. It was not the boy's station. He made a sudden blind leap away from the man, opened the door, saw it was not on the platform side, but jumped. There was a shout from someone. He ran up the track, he dived under some wire railings. He ran with amazingly quick short leaps up a field – like a hare that knows its life is precarious among the colossal dangers of the open world and has suddenly sensed one of them.

THE STARS ABOVE THE CITY
(2008)
Lewis Davies

The piano was old. The lid shut, smeared with dust. Thin light cut into the foyer from the bay beyond. Anthony had spent months dreaming of the Intercontinental. Its green shuttered terraces looking down onto the port. He had arrived at the site of one of his dreams.

A porter appeared and picked up his rucksack. It was light and the man smiled. He indicated that Anthony should follow him. The hotel opened out along wide corridors. He noticed with some disappointment that the carpets were worn, and there were prints of palaces on the walls and an English huntsman with hounds. The room was on the second floor. It opened onto a balcony guarded by iron railings. He looked out over the bay, which curved away to the south. There were fishing boats out beyond the headland. The porter was waiting in the room. Anthony fumbled in his pocket. He only had euros. The man smiled. He passed him two euros.

'Euros are good here.'

He waited for the stillness of the room to reach him. He wasn't quite ready to face the city again, but he had promised a man at the port who claimed to be a good guide – 'official, sir' – to meet him at 5 p.m. There was enough time to sleep. He tried to imagine himself back, as the sounds of the port rose up past the balconies. Gulls, lorries reversing, a ship leaving. The sounds of a world moving.

He woke to a loud knocking at the door. He spun, unsure of the room. His hands grasping at the sheets. Then his memory caught him. He waited as his heart calmed. There was a knock again.

'Monsieur, your guide?'

He was aware of his crumpled trousers and shirt as he answered the door. He blinked at the porter. The sun was hurting his eyes.

'*Dix minutes, d'accord?*'

The porter smiled and turned away.

The medina proved more than expected. More than he had read about. He didn't realise that a return to the past could be so swift. A surge of life swept into him. The flux of people, living, eating, working in the shaded passages cut out of what seemed the solid life of the city. He had a few offers of things he didn't need but the guide seemed to deflect most of the attention. He appeared to know many of the people who smiled at him. It seemed he had been telling the truth about being an official guide. The guide's name was Mohammed. At least it was one of his names. Anthony suspected he had used it as the easiest one a European might pronounce. He was an old man. Over sixty with tight-cut silver hair. He wore a well-tailored suit and carried an umbrella to protect himself from the sun. He kept it furled in the medina but carried it with a quiet grace that seemed to protect him from the rush of the city.

Mohammed recommended a restaurant and waited while Anthony was served a 'traditional meal'. He was the only customer of the restaurant.

'You are too early for dinner and too late for lunch, but we'll serve you anyway,' the waiter laughed.

The tour continued after the meal.

'It is quiet in the afternoon. Evenings are better. Now people rest. But I will take you to an emporium.'

At the emporium he was introduced as 'Mr Anthony', as if they should know who he was. A silver tray carrying a heavily sugared glass of mint tea was presented to him. He sipped delicately. He wasn't sure of the etiquette. There must be an etiquette. He was invited to sit down as the theatre of carpets was revealed to him. A thrilling display of four different types of rug and carpet was presented by a tall lithe man in a black singlet. His muscles flexed as he unfurled each new display. The commentary was provided by the head of the emporium. Anthony kept his eyes down, trying not to give himself away. He wanted to buy a carpet. It would look good in the flat. There was more space now. He wondered what Jac would have done. Anthony had never been good with salesmen. They sensed a weakness in him. A desire to please. To be helpful almost whatever it cost him. He looked at the man in the vest. There was a sheen on his skin from the heat even in the cool of the emporium. But he knew he simply couldn't buy a carpet on his first day. He bought a blanket. It was the cheapest woollen item in the shop. The man who had served him the tea shook his head sadly as he took his money. He could sense that what Anthony really wanted was a full-scale, two-hundred-and-fifty-thousand knot, five-hundred-euro carpet. Jac always said he wasn't assertive enough, didn't make demands. Anthony had always found when he made demands he lost things, friends, lovers. He had lost Jac. Jac would have bartered the carpet down to two hundred euros and made the salesmen feel he was doing them all a favour by buying it from them.

He paid the guide off after the third carpet shop.

He followed one of the alleyways back to centre of the medina. It was a Sunday night and children were playing football in the small spaces between the houses. As he walked he had glimpses of lives he could never see in the veiled portals, warm kitchens, the flavours of food high in the air.

He remembered their kitchen in Cardiff. He had loved to fill it with recipes from countries he had never visited as if with alchemy he could produce them to share on order. He loved the programmes on the television that told you how to eat and live. He liked that. He liked the surety of it.

The night was beginning to fold around the city. He walked down the Petit Socco. The chairs were filled with dark men looking out at the moving street, just looking. A shudder went through him. He found a chair at Café Tingis. He looked out. Watching. Men in hooded gowns. Women clothed tightly against the world of men, pale Europeans in the coloured clothes of the young and rootless.

A waiter brought him a coffee. He had asked for it in French. He could order food in French. It was a small miracle of his education that he could actually remember words from a classroom twenty years before. The evening filled in the spaces. He began a postcard in his mind. Dear Jac. On the Petit Socco, you would like it here... Dark men with smiles in their eyes. I'm speaking French badly again... sorry, bad French.

Jac had always laughed at his pronunciation. He would write the postcard in the morning. He should be able to get stamps in the city.

A man in a white shirt smiled at him from the crowd. Anthony smiled back. The man waved and began walking towards him.

Sun filtered into the room early. He remembered the bar he had been persuaded to try for one drink. Hardwood, dusty sawdust floor. The smell of hashish. He checked his face. No marks. He could walk away from this.

He packed quickly. The man at the reception took his money without comment. They had refused his credit card, so he'd been forced to withdraw money from a cashpoint. He walked back up the Petit Socco, through the medina to the new town. It had been new in the 1920s when the French had planned it. There was a Café de Paris, and Café de France, along a Boulevard Pasteur. He was tight with sweat from the climb up the hill with his rucksack. There were no offers in the early morning. It was too early for business. He settled into a dark leather chair and withdrew into an order for black coffee with a croissant. He had always liked croissants since his first visit to Paris as a sixteen-year-old. To him they tasted of opportunity and a delicious sense of guilt in the morning. He had visited the *cimetlière* with Jonathan. He was rather horrified when Jonathan produced a lipstick from his pocket, covered his lips with the darkest red and kissed the statue above the grave they had both come to see. He had heard Jonathan stayed in Newcastle after university. They had kept in touch for a few years. It seemed a long way back now.

He wrote a postcard to Jac. It didn't say anything. He signed it, *With love from Anthony. Always.*

The bus was half-full. He had expected it to be old and battered, but it was new with good seats and air conditioning. He sat next to a man who spoke good English. He was going to Chefchaouen. He worked for the Banc de Maroc. He was going to explain a new computer system to the manager in Chefchaouen. He usually travelled by train, but there was no train to Chefchaouen. Anthony was glad of the information. The man had two children.

His wife was expecting a third. Life was good. You worked hard, you enjoyed life. What did Anthony do? Anthony wasn't sure about that. I write – write what? For the television. Films? No. Not films. I write down ideas for television. Shows. Programmes. You get paid for that? Usually. Are they popular? They don't usually get made – I just come up with the ideas.

The man looked at him. He wrote ideas for shows that never got made.

The open fields passed the windows. Men riding donkeys, sunflowers about to open, a grey reservoir. Travel made him think of home. His work. Jac.

He had started writing plays for the theatre. They had been well received. He was young and the reviewers were generous in small papers. He would get better, write better plays with more complex plots. But he didn't get better. He found that after the third he had very little more to say. He worked for television instead. He wrote treatments for new shows that went into development or were offered to digital channels that no one watched. It had allowed him to live for six years in the city he had shared with Jac. It had paid for holidays to Barcelona and New York. It had never felt like much money. But he was happy. Jac was with him. They had partied. They had friends around to dinner. He felt like he was living the life he had wanted as that sixteen-year-old in Paris.

That was nine months ago. Before the money came. A treatment had been made into a show. It was called *Fantasy Shop*. It allowed people to indulge. That was its hook. It had been franchised. He had had to employ an agent, and the agent had employed a lawyer on his behalf. He had earned money. A lot of it, very quickly. There was still a cheque for $260,000 due to be paid. His accountant had suggested waiting until the new financial year to accept payment. His tax bill had frightened him.

Surely he couldn't be giving that much money away in tax? Where would he get it from? The accountant had reassured him. Then Jac had left him.

The man took out pictures of his two healthy children. Their bright eyes stared out at the bright lights in the photographer's studio. He noticed they were well lit. The photographer had known how to light children, how to get the best from their youth and clear skin. A kind of hopefulness.

The bus stopped at a service station on the brow of a hill.

The man from the bank invited him to share a table.

'My name is Abdul. Yours?'

'Anthony.'

'As in Cleopatra, yes?'

Anthony looked blankly at the man. 'The play. Shakespeare?'

'Sorry, of course. I was... a bit out of context.'

The station was crowded, full with families and travellers. The man from the bank had a certain stature that Anthony found attractive. He seemed at ease. A waiter arrived promptly to take their order. Abdul switched into Arabic to order his food. There was a rush of words Anthony found strangely familiar. The sound of the language was rather beautiful. The two men then looked expectantly at him. There was no menu: the butchered side of a cow hung down from the rafters next to the kitchen. Anthony didn't eat meat. He had given up meat five years before on one of Jac's fad diets. But he had surprised himself and stuck to it, which was more than Jac did.

'The fish is very good. Trout.'

Anthony was grateful for the advice. He smiled up at the waiter.

'*Un poisson, un café au lait, s'il vous plaît.*'

The waiter retreated to the kitchen.

'*Parlez-vous français?*'

'*Non. Un peu.*'

'It is a fine language. I lived in Marseille for two years. Before I was married of course.'

'You were able to travel there?'

'To work, yes. *La vie est très cher là-bas.*' He looked at Anthony and then added, 'Otherwise it is too expensive.'

'You didn't think of staying?'

'No. Why should I? My family is here. I was a young man. I wanted to see another country, that is all.'

The fish arrived. It was grilled dark under a fine spiced flour.

The afternoon lengthened as the bus climbed through the valleys that fed into the mountains. He was surprised how green the land was. He saw people on the land, farmers and shepherds, and they were making the most of the land. Cultivated plots stretched up into the hills. Small herds of goats and sheep tended by a shepherd seemed to be travelling up and down the valley. He had expected Morocco to be red with sand dunes. It was ridiculous, he knew, but everyone had a mental image of a country built on something, words and pictures, and through these the country had been categorised, the deserts, palaces, dark men. He could see the men.

The night in Tanger. The bar was not what he was expecting. The man at Tingis had suggested they should go for a real drink at Deen's.

'My name is Haroun. You will like Deen's. It is for you.'

He knew the name. It was in the *Spartacus* guide: 'Just the most lively place in Tanger. Bank clerks and diplomats. Careful after dark.'

He followed Haroun up the Petit Socco and across the square. The road narrowed, and they cut back on themselves down a side alley. A simple sign marked 'Deen's – Prix 10 Euro'. He thought about turning back. Jac blamed him for giving up on things. He took out his wallet and passed the money to the man on the door. Haroun didn't pay anything. The light was low and a heavy Europop beat pushed through the air. There was red lighting and flashing fairy lights. He could just make out the rows of men sitting at the fringes of the room. He could feel their eyes on him. He shouldn't have come in. Haroun took him to a table.

'I'll get us a drink?'

Anthony nodded and Haroun disappeared into the gloom. The music began to eat into him. He wished himself smaller.

A man sat down opposite Anthony. He spoke in what could have been German. Anthony smiled back nervously.

'You are English?'

Anthony nodded. He had explained too many times the subtle differences between Welsh and English.

'I am sorry. I thought you were German. My name is Rashid.' He smiled.

'Anthony.'

'You are here on vacation.'

'Yes.'

'Good. I like to meet people on vacation. I get to improve my English. I work in a bank. I need to speak to people. You are a very attractive man.'

Anthony blushed. He had never been called that before. People were usually more subtle or honest.

'Do you have a boyfriend in England?'

A waiter arrived with two drinks. They looked like spirits, probably vodka. Anthony took one of the glasses. His new companion waved the waiter away.

'I don't drink. Because I am a Muslim.' He laughed. 'Maybe I shouldn't be doing this either.' The man raised his eyebrows in a way that sent a shiver down Anthony's spine. He had never been good at this part of the game. He took a sip of the drink. It was vodka. He then swallowed the remainder. He felt the liquid caress his throat, urging him forward.

In the alley he kissed Rashid. There was no one around. He could feel the urgency in the man's caress. In the club Rashid had been confident but now, back in the reality of his city, he was scared. They could both go to jail for this. As Anthony pushed his hand hard onto the man's cock, he could feel the soft, wet warmth of his semen immediately, the tensing of his body as he came, lost in the desire and finality of the moment. Rashid pulled away.

'I am sorry.'

'It's OK. It's my turn now, though.'

The man shook his head. The situation catching up with him. He straightened his trousers, re-zipping his fly.

'I go now.'

'No, not yet.' The man turned and began walking away. 'You can't.'

But he quickly merged into the shadows. A cat scuttled past him. Anthony looked up. He could see the stars above the city.

Money had always been difficult for Anthony. His father worked at the steelworks. He had been a chemist. Anthony was twelve before he realised his father had more money than other boys' fathers who also worked at the steelworks. His family holidays were package tours to hot places in Spain he couldn't remember the names of. His father changed the family car every few years for a new model. Always something built by Leyland. His father had attempted to push him towards science. Medicine would have been a good career option. Anthony was 'being offered chances that I couldn't dream of'. Anthony had wanted to go to art college. They compromised; English with Drama at Leeds.

University was fun but not too serious. After Anthony finished the degree he forgot about money. He wanted to write plays. His father wanted him to get a proper job. Something with a career plan and a pension. Playwright seemed impossible. There were no playwrights in Llanelli. Surely he could write plays in his spare time. The Llanelli Players were always looking for new people.

Anthony forced his way through a series of grim restaurant jobs until he was finally made assistant manager at Pizza Express. He had been good at it. His father saw hope in the title of Assistant Manager. Anthony was now in the restaurant business. When he visited his mother in Llanelli, people still asked him how the restaurant business was going. He met Jac at Pizza Express. They had both been serving tables, sharing the tips. One night after work they ended up back at his dreary flat off Cowbridge Road. They opened a bottle of Mesquite. Jac had stayed. He wanted to know what Anthony was going to do. Anthony showed him his work.

Jac forced him to request an interview with the literary manager of the Sherman Theatre. It had a reputation for new plays. He had sent a play in six months previously but had received no reply. The literary manager was a thin uninspired man in his early thirties. He flirted hopelessly, almost desperately, with Anthony. A week later they offered him a contract of production. Sometimes you simply had to stand up for yourself. It seemed a long time ago. Anthony knew Jac had changed his life.

His father had never really accepted Jac. He was civil but cold. It was all a bit beyond his experience. He had wanted grandchildren. Anthony was his only child. Anthony didn't hold it against him. His father was a good man. There were a lot of people at his funeral.

Then there were six years of each other. Their own world.

The money had come as a surprise. The unexpected rush of it. His first commissioned play was worth six thousand pounds. He had lived for a year and a half on the money. Now in Asilah he was embarrassed by it. He had recently bought himself a new car. A Volkswagen Beetle with huge headlamps that looked like eyes. He looked at the car in a way that unnerved him, the sixteen thousand pounds of shine, curves and metal transferring itself into an expression of his wealth and well-being. He'd heard Jac's new boyfriend drove an Astra. This knowledge gave him a perverse enjoyment he was deeply worried by.

The bus had passed men on the side of the road. They were riding donkeys or herding goats. They didn't seem as if they could be part of the same world.

They arrived in Chefchaouen in the late afternoon. It was a town trapped at the blind head of a valley. The mountains continued up into the clouds beyond the blue terraced streets. His hotel was optimistically called The Parador. It had a swimming pool that was tacked onto a slope beyond the garden with a view down into the valley. But a thin mist drifted down from the mountains and no one used it. Anthony shared the breakfast room each morning with a party of Americans. They were old but seemed healthy with fine skin and bones carrying them well into their seventies. They talked to each other but ignored Anthony. He attempted to start a conversation each morning but was met with only polite short replies.

The town reminded him of a hill station he had visited for a week in India. It had the same narrow, terraced streets. But here there was more space, fewer people. He was offered more mint tea and a lot of grass. Most of the young Westerners seemed to be here for the marijuana. He had avoided it in college. It was a type of penance he was happy with. Jac had sometimes brought some home, and they smoked it late at night with the windows open, listening to the sounds of the city at night. He always felt slightly ridiculous smoking. The unusual touch of the rolled paper filled with dried plants. He liked the smell better. The sweet promise of it. But here he refused the offers.

He bought more things he didn't need, copper bangles, postcards, odd-looking wooden boxes that reminded him of cuckoo clocks without the bird. He was reduced to giving some away to the children who accosted him for money. The begging here was only half-serious. Here the children had homes to go back to.

He met the man from the bank for tea. The visit was going well for him. He had finished the training and had a day spare to be a tourist.

'Sometimes it is good to have nothing to do. Just to be? Don't you think?'

After three days he caught another bus back down to the coast at Asilah. It had an appealing write-up in his *Lonely Planet* guide, although no mention in *Spartacus*. He wrote another postcard to Jac but didn't post it. He found a hotel on the seafront. Huge blue waves rushed in across a wide-open beach. He could feel the sea in the air and the history in the stones of the old town. Portuguese, British, Spanish and French had all fought over this piece of the world. He had often stayed in places where the Portuguese had built forts. They had a lovely way with stones and the sea. The town had charm. Tree-lined boulevards backing away from a promenade lined with restaurants that served fine French coffee.

He spent a day on the beach. He was resisting the urge to check his email account. He was hoping Jac had written but was afraid he had not. It was a couple of weeks now. He had come to see him off on Cardiff station. It was as if he were performing some last duty. A final leaving. Jac had taken a day off from the new Coffee Republic he was managing. Anthony couldn't believe how miserable he felt. He had watched Jac from the train. He could see Jac's relief, as if he had become a burden. The whole thing had become a burden. The expectations of happiness. Maybe he wasn't meant to be happy.

A group of students were playing football on the beach. A sharp wind blew in off the water. But the players seemed to be able to tease the ball between them, as if it were an object of their own will. They were all lithe men who moved with a grace that was beautiful.

The ease with which he could remove himself from his world caught him. The money he had at home was enough. Here it seemed like too much. He thought about Rashid. The first night in a new country, a strange new man. He had been waiting for him at the top of the alleyway. He was more composed. His suit pulled tight around him. He could sense he wanted more.

'Maybe we can walk together?'

He had taken him back to the hotel.

'No one will know you.'

It hadn't taken long in the room. He was young, inexperienced, still scared. Anthony had brought his own condoms. Rashid's skin was rather beautiful, brown and tight across his chest, his buttocks small, feeling full in his hands. Anthony felt desire even as he was thinking of Jac.

Rashid lay on the bed afterwards covered in the smells of sex, smiling, open. Anthony felt the guilt swallow him again. He walked into the bathroom, closed the door, took a shower. When he returned to the room Rashid was dressed.

'You want me to go?'

'It is probably best.'

His face lost its hopefulness.

'Wait, I will give you something.' Anthony reached for his trousers on the floor. He took out his wallet. As he offered Rashid fifty euros he felt the sting of his hand sharp across his face.

'I am not your boy.' He spat at his feet and left.

In the afternoon he returned to his hotel room. He made love to Jac's memory, the white, starched sheets sharp and exciting on his own skin. It was a relief to come on his own, without any guilt. He fell asleep into the deep heat of the afternoon. The music of God woke him. It was a beautiful sound. He began to cry.

LOVE ALONE REMAINS
(1996)
Mihangel Morgan
Translated by the author

In 1986, when I was living in Cardiff I met a young student from Austria who was studying English. We became friends and he learned Welsh very quickly; he was a gifted linguist. After returning to his own country he wrote to me from time to time. A selection of extracts from those letters is what follows.

Apart from his studies in literature he refers to his time as *Zivildienstleistender* in a mental hospital and to a period on stipend which allowed him to spend some time in Berlin.

When he was unsure of the Welsh he would put in English in brackets with a question mark. As I didn't understand German, English usually, was the bridge between our two mother tongues. He did not write Welsh like Sir John Morris-Jones, needless to say. I have not changed his Welsh much, except to change the order of a few sentences where the thought was not entirely clear and to correct spelling and mutations.

Where part of a letter is omitted I use [–]. In the first letter to me Wolfgang quoted from a poem by Gwynne Williams, namely, 'In the Memorial Service for Philip Larkin' (*Pysg* [Fish], 1984, page 104; a book I gave him as a present on leaving Wales). The part that is quoted is a translation and paraphrasing of Larkin's words and I have taken them as the title for this selection of letters. Although there is a sentimental ring to the lines Larkin's poem is not at all soft; see 'An Arundel Tomb'.

Innsbruck
19. 10. 86

Dear M –
  because
  love
  alone
  remains
  of us
  each one
    Gwynne Williams

Letters are always late, too late, so you are always reading my past. Letters need immediacy. A letter is inadequate in place of the presence of a person. My thoughts will seem very unsteady and changeable. But I try to adjust. Things move quickly and change appearance with speed. I live in a constant time lag.

I got your letter today. Thanks so much. I enjoy your letters. You become present out of them. I can almost hear your voice. I got the Welsh Grammar about a fortnight ago. I hope it helps to improve my Welsh.

[–]

I am reading *One Hundred Years of Solitude* by García Márquez at the moment.

Warmest love forever
Wolfgang

Götis
2. 11. 86

Dear M –

Thanks for the letters and the poem and the photo of Morrissey. Only a photo of you would've made me feel happier (do those words make me an 'arse licker'?)

[–]

When I was in Cardiff I got the feeling I had been reborn – or born for the first time. There I began living my life. There I took responsibility for myself and the few people that I love. There I began to open myself up like a box of secrets. I would go beyond the scope of a letter (unless I went to write one as long as *Alexis**) if I were to relate all the things I got from Wales. I was so happy. Life was as perfect as it could be and then I had to come back to Austria, a country I could no longer think of as my mother country.

M – you wouldn't believe how naive people are here. Their lives are so narrow; school – work/money – family/church – death. And they fail to understand anything outside that framework. Homosexuality is not a *possibility* here. I wear my pink triangle. No one reacts. No one knows what it means.

[–]

I've been reading a book of poems by Ingeborg Bachmann. She's Austrian. She died in her bed that burned because she dropped a cigarette on it.

[–]

I'd like to meet you in Paris, I'm looking forward to it. I'm trying to improve my Welsh.

Best Wishes
Wolfgang

---

* *Alexis*, a novel by Marguerite Yourcenar in the form of a long letter by a man to his wife confessing that he is gay.

Götis

18. 2. 87

Dear M –

I'm pleased to hear you've found a new flat. Do you have a phone? (Linguistically this question is very complicated because the answer 'yes' would not be enough; it's an enquiry in disguise to get your phone number!) It would be easier and quicker for me to arrange to come to stay with you by phoning.

[–]

A Cheyenne Indian came to see us. He spoke in English and in his native language which I loved hearing very much. Cheyenne of course is incomprehensible to me; it's more like a strange music. I preferred hearing the poems in the original language in order to better appreciate the lovely rhythms, whereas his English poems sounded like poor translations. His poems are incredibly simple. He says: 'Poems are distilled stories, we come to understand who we are through the process of imagining. Poetry is an expression of the imaginative process. I use a range of techniques to spark the opening of our memories'. I got the feeling that he was very mystical. Breezes represent the spirits of the dead relatives. Animals are personified or they are allegories. I see a resemblance between the Indians and the Welsh. Many Indians carry their roots in their hearts while they are bogged down by the White Man's System, like the Welsh by the system of the English.

[–]

Best Wishes
Wolfgang

Innsbruck
[no date]

Dear M –

Are you familiar with the *Last Exit to Brooklyn* by Hubert Selby? It's a *harrowing* book on the whole but one of its most interesting aspects is the chapter with a 'queen' as the main character. The way she speaks and thinks is so right (to me, that is). I wonder where the author got his material, the 'evidence' – is he gay himself I wonder? I'll send extracts with my next letter, perhaps, to see what you think. I won't recommend the book though it's brilliantly written since some cruel scenes are hard to read, unbearable, perhaps.

Take care, enjoy yourself and don't be boring (this is a quote from your letter).

Loving wishes as usual
Wolfgang

[card]

Innsbruck
28. 4. 87

Dear M –

Heartfelt thanks for letting me stay with you. The time was very important to me, and has changed me, has made it easier for me to live. It's important to me and makes me feel happy to know that you are my friend.

Warmest love
Wolfgang

Innsbruck
19. 5. 87

Dear M –

Everything is quiet in Austria. Our president [Waldheim] forgets everything that it's better to forget and hopes that we will do the same as him. He's getting more and more unpopular. I'm waiting for some nutter to kill him.

I've been thinking of a plot recently. I'd like to turn it into a (short) story or a poem (but I don't write poetry).

Two people meet after a long time. But they haven't lost the connection with one another – actually, perhaps they've come to know each other better – and yet separation is deceiving. The one's feelings towards the other are not challenged by the living *alter ego*. So the One Other (The Other) turns into an intercorresponding object for their hopes, their dreams and their desires. Let's assume they are both weak, easily hurt and odd in their own individual ways – let's call them *idiosyncratic*. How are they going to communicate and break out of their self-deception? Let us imagine also that the two love each other but in different ways and for different reasons and that they are unable to give physical expression to their love. Let us understand that they cannot wish for the act of making love. As they are like this, what will be the consequence? How will this be interpreted by the one and the other? As they are constricted by themselves is there a way for them to break through? Can the friendship survive?

You have to admit that this plot has a life of its own and the conclusion could be manifold. The sad ending would be: their friendship turns sour and comes to a complete end, in spite of their love. But I hate endings like that and I'm struggling hard to think of something better. As the characters change the story

577

changes – so the sketch of their personalities is blurry. If their natures were fixed I would have no hope. I prefer to be hopeful.

[–]

It's late and the Föhn (the warm wind) has made me tired. I 'feel' the weather – the weather is low and I'm low too and I don't mean that metaphorically. Most people have a physical reaction to the Föhn-weather.

Dearest love
Wolfi

Innsbruck
8. 7. 87

Dearest M –

[–] There's another person I'd like to tell you about. Christina, she comes from Spain, she lives in the Basque region. She's full of life, domineering, generous, she goes over the top (especially with alcohol and tobacco) and she's fascinating. She's full of stories and she is herself a living story. She's been all over Europe and she hates Innsbruck so much. She showed me that the Austrians are full of problems that are not problems at all. People here begin many sentences with 'the problem is...' Wherever you go people are discussing problems. According to Christina the Spanish worry less about the cause of things but treasure the beauty of the moment. It's a different way of looking at things. A friend of a friend of mine, Maturot, comes from Thailand and people there also focus on the beauty of the moment. Their native literature has a different purpose. Our literature, usually, and in general, tries to explain and to reveal, whereas their literature deals with beauty.

But our analytical and destructive way of looking at things holds too much power as if it enables us to control nature better. Whorff studied the Hopi language and came to the conclusion that the way people think is structured by the quality of their language. In Hopi days are not counted in our way because, to them, each day is brand new, completely different to the one before. It reminds me of a piece of graffiti I saw a while ago – *what does it mean 'what's the time?'*

I'm reading *The Man Without Qualities* which starts well but which is a drag now and I have about 1,500 pages to go!

Lots of Love
Wolfi

P.S. If you have time read *The Man Without Qualities*, especially chapter 8 which says so much about Austria. There are just 2–3 pages to this chapter. That's Musil at his best.

Innsbruck
30. 12. 87

Dear M –

Thank you for the pink dinosaur. He is protecting me.

[–]

If I hadn't have got that *stipend* I would've thought they were homophobic. It's hard to resist the temptation to use 'oppression' as a weapon. That's what blacks did until recently: 'If you don't do what I want, you're racist'. Women still do it. Every minority uses it. I am a minority but I'm pissed off when I catch myself doing it. The trouble with setting oneself as a minority is that your personality gets reduced and the aspect in focus overwhelms every other aspect.

[–]

I'm still working on my dissertation on *Last Exit to Brooklyn* (Hubert Selby Jr.). I'm under pressure now as I have to finish it within a week and all I have is a scattered collection of ideas. I've read a substantial number of articles on the book and it's remarkable how many *emotional outbursts* were caused by the novel. It was banned in Britain in 1965 because it was considered pornographic and *obscene*. I wonder if it's available there now? It's shocking how *blatantly* the critics reveal their prejudices and their *ideologies* in writing about this book.

Lots of love
Wolfi

Innsbruck
10. 1. 88

Dear M –

Thanks for the first letter of the year.

[–]

I have finished my dissertation (more or less) on *Last Exit to Brooklyn*, and feeling fairly satisfied with my work. Our general topic is *urban fiction* and I have been somewhat critical of other people's presentations so far. It makes me mad when the only reaction people have to works of literature are *moral judgements*, the expression of counterfeit feelings said to have been caused by the novel, *truisms* such as: I was horrified/ I was shaken to the core/ *I was deeply moved*... It was wrong to have... He shouldn't have... This is a novel against materialism (isn't all serious fiction anti-materialist?) What a waste of time! But after all my criticism (which could not be heard in the seminar every time, I have to admit) my presentation had to be special.

[–]

To the majority of straights homosexuals are just straights gone wrong, even to the liberals.

[–]

According to the post-structuralists people exist through language – the language 'thinks' them. Post-structuralists do not aim to establish a coherent ideology, rather their object is to locate power and to expose it, to reveal structures, to show things interact, and react. Everyone is his own revolutionary.

Perhaps this letter is confusing but these are the things that concern me at the moment.

Dearest love as always
Wolfi

Innsbruck
25. 1. 88

Dear M –

I got your letter this morning. I have an exam on Thursday so this is just the start of a letter.

Thanks for designing the cover of *Pentackle* – it's excellent for our newsletter and everyone likes it.

Of course I'd like to meet you in Berlin. I will have to *rent* a room there for a month, anyhow, so you'll be able to stay with me there, more than likely. I'm sure you'll like Berlin as much as Paris.

[–]

I've re-read your letter. Your experience with the *transvestite bricklayer* sounds *incredible*. Philip Roth wrote an article about the problem contemporary writers have in facing reality – reality is always further ahead (?) than fiction, which is much more 'plausible'. There you have the proof!

I have to tell you about the sad ending of my love for George. After a year of *throbbing heart* and *jelly knees* every time I saw him, I decided it was time to do something, so I asked him to come for a cup of coffee. Before long we were both intimate. We were talking as if the year had never happened. Before Christmas I went to see him again but it was awkward, and another thing, I realised we were talking on different levels. Our two worlds were no longer connecting. Anyway, everything was ok until he mentioned he had taken a new lover after I had stopped seeing him. From that moment I saw the *not-so-gorgeous* and *not-so-charming* side to him and the *spell was broken*. What's strange – now that I have no interest in him, he's showing interest in me! Not only do our two worlds fail to connect, they have two separate timetables! I can't take him seriously now and the last time I saw him I just made fun of him.

[–]

Today is the day of my exam. I got up at 6:30 to look over my notes. I'd like to get a question on the post-modern short story. I'd love to write on that subject more than anything. I know it's always possible to write *something* but I don't want to write just to *fill up pages*.

I went to see a film from the '60s of *Ulysses*. Quite good. Bloom was good and it must've been a fucking hard part to play. Dedalus was *boring*. Molly Bloom's soliloquy was brilliant. There was a sort of earthy feeling, sensuous and something a little grotesque about the film. Have you read the book? Some parts of it are *hilarious*.

By the way I used the word 'fucking' because of something a friend said to me. We were talking about all the ways you can say go away in English and I said there was nothing as strong as *fuck off* in German. And she said, 'Yes, there's not a lot of fucking in German'. I agreed, of course. I remember reading somewhere there's a Celtic root to the word 'fuck'.

[–]

I got the question I had hoped for. Shattered now.

Lots of love

Wolfi

Here's an addition to my letter – extra ideas –

I've already mentioned *Last Exit to Brooklyn*. Selby understands that people's reactions to each other are based on power and that people are also trapped by 'visions'. I would say 'theories about life'. These visions tell people what to look for, what to hope for, what to shrink away from, etc. They arrange people's worlds; that's their map through life, telling what roads to follow. Georgette's story in 'The Queen is Dead' had a profound effect on me because so much of it is in me. She is in love (?) with a wild, violent 'John'. You know the *type*. '*Georgette was a hip queer... feeling intellectually and aesthetically superior to those (especially women) who weren't gay (look at all the great artists who were fairies!)*'. In this story (which surprisingly awakens the sympathy of the reader towards her) the vision gets shattered and ceases to be. Now, the point is that these visions are 'given' to the people (for example, mother, wife, real man) they are 'prefabricated individualities, and in accepting them and internalising them people become estranged from *themselves*. In an article on the book Frantz Fanon is quoted as saying that people have internalised the linguistic and cultural 'codes' of the oppressor. Through bestowing prefabricated individualities upon people they become predictable and they are controlled from within. The problem with these visions is that they are fixed and inflexible and the individuals do everything within their power to maintain them. The visions start to take on a life of their own until they start to govern those that are taken up by them. I believe people try to *manipulate* 'reality' in order to protect their visions or sometimes they go mad. Visions are important but they have to be flexible and they must come from within.

Take care, fondest wishes
Wolfi

[no date, no location]

Dear M –

Have you heard about the elections in Austria? The main winner is the party that is said to be made up of Nazis. They've gained 7% extra of the vote. It's dreadful and I don't believe it. The Greens have also got a foothold. After the election the leader of the Greens called the leader of the Nazis a 'demagogue' and compared things to the 1930s. And she also refused to shake hands with him.

Best wishes
Wolfgang

[no date]
Innsbruck

My dear M –

This will be a short letter. More of a message, really.

On Friday I fly to Crete for a week to relax. So I thought maybe you'd like to relax too, since you're teaching all those people. I have a £10 note left after the last time I stayed with you. I'd like to send you this so you can go out for a meal with someone you like and enjoy being with. I'm not sure you can buy a meal for two with £10 but it's a contribution. Of course you're free to go with anyone but I'd prefer that you didn't go with Gloria – he's *boring* and a phony. Nor Stewart you used to share a flat with – he's worse! It would be nice if you could go with someone you love, or at least someone you haven't been out with but you've always wanted to go on a date with.

So off I go to Greece. Who said *'there's nothing like tourism for narrowing the mind?'*

Best wishes
Wolfgang

Innsbruck
15. 2. 88

Dear M –

Just back from Evelyn's home where I saw Waldheim's address to the nation. It's weird because he's so convinced that the 'minority' of radicals that oppose him are just a spiteful gang that want to overtly run the nation. He believes he's doing a great favour to Austria by carrying on as president. Waldheim argues he's been elected for 6 years and it would be undemocratic for him to step down before the end of that time. At this time Austrians are so busy playing with words and deeds that people can't understand each other. Was Waldheim's 'ignorance' a sort of amnesia or was he lying? Did the report on his past show that he was innocent or prove he was a liar? The meaning of democracy in Austria has become clearer: everyone who is against Waldheim or who protests is 'undemocratic'. Guilt has been redefined in several uses too: Graff argued it couldn't be asserted that Waldheim was guilty unless it could be proven that he had killed six (!) Jews with his own hands. (Why six I wonder? Why strangulation?) Waldheim said that knowing about an atrocity is not the same as guilt. I have always thought that if my neighbour, for example, beats his wife and I know but don't do anything, I would also be guilty of the consequences. Austria is a divided country because of Waldheim. Perhaps the time will come when it will be dangerous to let people know if you are for or against Waldheim. In his speech Waldheim charged Austrians (the politicians in particular) to stop criticising him because only then could other countries be expected to cease blackening our country (or him, rather!).

I hate him and everyone that supports him through ignoring the evidence.

People don't see the general in the specific. Most Austrians realise that anti-Semitism is unacceptable (hopefully), but it's quite commonplace to hear people speaking against the Turks. Xenophobia is rife in Austria. But people fail to see the common factor between those two things.

It's obvious to me that Thatcher is a fascist but people don't see it because they haven't dug deep enough under the face of fascism into its mechanism.

Lots of love
Wolfi

10. 3. 88

Dear M –

[–]

I delight in letting people fall into their own mental traps. These traps say a lot about how a person's mind works. That's the plain truth. If I say to my sister-in-law I'm going to meet up with Margarete tonight I know, of course, where her mind goes. Most thoughts follow 'old grooves' (like the 'old grooves' of *Rhigolau Bywyd* by Kate Roberts).

That's what I like about *Last Exit to Brooklyn*: it depicts some of the main grooves of society while throwing an artistic light onto them so that the reader can see them for the *cul-de-sac* they are. That's the main appeal of the novel probably.

[–]

Since you mention Kafka – have you read 'Bartleby' by Melville? That's a Kafkaesque story, but it predates Kafka of course. It's about Bartleby the scrivener who takes work while refusing to do more and more duties by using the words 'I would prefer not to'. It's a great piece of writing. The story is told from the point of view of the employer who is at a loss as to know how to deal with the situation.

[–]

Best Wishes
Wolfi

6. 4. 88

Dear M –

No, I'm not surprised that you are 'besotted' with 'Bartleby' and it's one of your favourite stories. Yes, I agree it's a masterpiece and there's some mystery in its power. Bartleby himself reminds me of the Indian in *Moby Dick* who refuses to do things and refuses to communicate until he commits a sort of non-violent suicide by his own willpower. And of course the business at the end with the 'dead letter office' brilliantly closes the story leaving us with a sort of conundrum. It's all so convincing that we want to know 'is this based on a true story?' (as we ask after reading *Moby Dick* too). And what happened to Bartleby to make him so estranged from people? I have a friend who works with people like that; he has mentioned one case of a young man (in his early twenties I think) who has taken to sitting bent over refusing to speak to anyone or do anything. No one knows why but it's thought that he was abused when he was young. But to come back to 'Bartleby', I believe the secret to the story is the narrator, the 'rather elderly man' who is thrown off balance by Bartleby. Melville gives very little information about him since he concentrates on his workers and Bartleby in the narrative. But Melville alludes to many things. The man himself admits to being 'eminently safe'. And everything points to him being unmarried. And there is not one female character in the story. I don't see this as particularly misogynistic but rather as an attempt on the part of the author to create a single-sex literary world – it is generally believed that Melville was a closeted homosexual. And many strangely erotic things take place in the story. What exactly was Bartleby doing in the office 'in a strangely tattered déshabillé... approaching nudity'? Though the narrator says 'was anything amiss going on? Nay that was out of the question. It was not to be thought for a moment that Bartleby was an immoral person,' the idea has crossed his mind. And near the end the old man offers to take Bartleby to live with him – but Bartleby refuses, of course. The truth is that the old man has fallen in love with the young man otherwise he wouldn't have tolerated his behaviour for long, he would have sacked him at the start. Well there's a simple interpretation based on unacademic guesswork. And this letter is in danger of becoming an essay.

Regards
Wolfi

Berlin
1. 5. 88

Dear M –

And so my third week in Berlin begins already and the idea of having to leave within a fortnight breaks my heart. I'd love to stay.

I don't know what makes Berlin so attractive. I feel that people really appreciate freedom here since they believe they are surrounded by the land of the enemy. And as homosexuality is one sign of freedom it is tolerated (though it is not fully accepted) by the majority in Berlin. Here I feel I have equal status with the straights as gays are so visible here.

[–]

I have been in a gay sex shop for the first time ever. Full of excitement. I want to see things. Up to now I have spoken against things without coming into contact with them (not to mention experiencing them). I was (I am, really) nervous and tried to hide this nervousness behind morality. I now see that this was fear. When I went into that sex shop my heart ran wild. I've decided to watch one pornographic film to the end – though I'm not sure I will be able to overcome my frustrations. It's important to me. Berlin opens up new vistas to me. I want to explore my morality and test it against 'reality'. Like the hardcore magazines I saw; they're repulsive and yet exciting in a strange way. They have disturbed my imagination like a nightmare (perhaps I am overdramatising the effect slightly). I want to see a variety of gay people.

[–]

Everything here is in a state of *flux*. You should come to Berlin once to experience this. My life in Innsbruck was *clotting*.

I'd love to see you more often to talk to you. I'd like to travel through Berlin together to discuss the place. So there we have Paris and Berlin on our *agenda* now. Will we ever go to these places together, I wonder? I hate the thought of being buried in Innsbruck for months to come.

Here I am in Berlin – JOYFUL. Lots of love; fond wishes
Wolfi

Innsbruck
18. 5. 88

Dear M –

[–]

I often think that people who 'drop' their friends as soon as they find a lover are stupid and not worth keeping as friends.

[–]

Berlin was a strange place. The first week was dreadful. Looking for a room, familiarising with the library and the people there, feeling the city. But I was lucky. Markus, my first landlord, was friendly and kind. One night we both talked about all sorts of things – that I was gay; he knew from the start, though he was not gay. That night I 'broke in' to Berlin. I went to all sorts of places – cafés, bars, discos. I was eager to see and to remember. I wanted to lose some of the burden of my upbringing. I went into gay porn shops: revolting, exciting. Even the 'raw' magazine is erotic. Eroticism permeates the place since it is 'consecrated' to pure sex. After a fortnight I wanted to experiment. So I prepared myself to go to a disco (that I didn't particularly like) and I went with an unremarkable guy I wouldn't have taken any notice of under normal circumstances but I was keen to have sex with a person I didn't want to go with. We went to an 'hour motel' and I made him feel great like a prostitute pleasing a customer. Then there were only pornographic films left and it took me four weeks to get over my *barriers*. Then, after that, I went to this place which was exciting, hot, wet, like in dreams – but pure fact – and I was there myself. Everyone separate but aware of what was going on. He came to sit near me and he was sexy. I watched him instead of the film and he watched me. We went for a walk, he spoke little. He created desires in me which were satisfied there and then. His name is Georg and he's just 21. I don't know much about him except that I long for him – his heart, his body, his dick. So we were together for a few hours, very few, some twenty hours, before I had to leave for Innsbruck. Isn't it incredible that I had to meet a guy in a gay porno cinema of all the places in the world? It's so unlikely it's romantic!

That's Berlin for me. No wonder I want to go back.

Lots of love

Wolfi

Innsbruck
19. 7. 88

Dear M –
[–]
It's time, I didn't want people to 'like' *Last Exit*, but I had hoped
it would prove *important* in their lives, relevant. Assuming every
novel asks to be read in its own particular way, I looked for a
reading that went along with its 'aim'. You see, the novel was heavily
criticised by many critics. But I believe that when people react in
such an extreme way to a novel it obviously contains aspects of
their *psyche* they don't want it to acknowledge. This novel, it seems,
is a dangerous threat to the fragile balance of many people. I don't
'like' *Last Exit*. The first time I read it I almost felt sick. In trying
to understand it, and making it important to me, I succeeded in
removing its 'kick', and also, I changed my way of seeing things.
                    Wishes
                    Wolfi

[no date, no location]

Dear M –
I bought a pile of hardcore magazines in Berlin and I posted
them to myself in case I got caught at customs. I labelled the box
'Academic Material' – what else?
Before I went to Berlin I accepted the feminist take on
pornography – that is it's disgusting as it exploits people. Now, I
see that is true of heterosexual pornography that uses women but
the same thing is not true for gay porn at all. There's a world of
difference between gay pornography and straight pornography.
It is obvious that models in gay pornography are not being used
against their will. These men want to show themselves in front

of the camera, they are happy to do so, or, otherwise, they wouldn't be able to 'perform'. It's obvious that the majority of these models are doing it for kicks, not just for money (that's bound to be insignificant) but for fun.

Of course there's another complete world of difference from paedophile pornography. The exploitation of children is disgusting, and revolting and completely unacceptable.

But I don't see why we have to accept the feminist sermon on pornography for gay men. Feminists must stand up for their wishes and we must stand up for our wishes. Gay rights are not the other side of the feminist or lesbian coin. Too many gay men believe that.

What is needed is a critique on gay pornography. And I would like to see a sort of separatist movement for gay men. Self rule for gays! At the moment we pay the subscription for our own oppression and everyone oppresses us: governments, straights, feminists, Christians, Muslims.

Best wishes
Wolfi

Bregenz
18. 8. 88

Dear M –

I'm in the Red Cross Centre in Bregenz where we have our basic training. This is the second letter I've written here and for the second time I've been asked am I writing a love letter. It's hilarious. But they haven't realised yet, I'm not a natural blond.

This is a very 'straight' environment. They do know – in theory at least – that gays exist. It would be impossible not to know in the age of AIDS, but it's something remote, that doesn't affect them. Like a war or an earthquake in a distant land.

One morning I was required to attend a lecture on AIDS. I

kept quiet during the whole thing, feeling as if the *spotlight* was turned on me. But I would have to be in full drag to *come out of the closet* in this group.

Some of them are friendly in their own way. A few of them are quite interesting even. There's one young guy I fancy. He reads comics all the time. He remains aloof. There's not much hope but it's a bit of fun. His name is Engel (= angel).

We disagree completely about *The Iceman Cometh* but my taste is more popular than yours. Having said that, eating at McDonald's is popular. Perhaps the characters in O'Neill are types as you say, but aren't most people clichés? It's more difficult to be an individual than a type. People don't like individuals but they don't realise that.

I don't have much time for reading these days, I'm too tired, I prefer to watch the news on the TV.

Is my written Welsh improving? I don't feel that it is and I have even less time to read Welsh now – apart from your letters, of course, so you have to write often.

Warmest wishes
Wolfi

Innsbruck
28. 8. 88

Dear M –

I had my exam on American Literature this morning. Now I'm on post-examinal high. I liked the first question – 'The New Yorker *asks you to write a short story for them; what criteria would you have to consider?'* I don't think they would have accepted my story.

[–]

There's a saying in German which is quite funny: 'Ich hoffe ich bin dir micht auf den schips getreten' (I hope I didn't step on your tie). I'm afraid I stepped on your tie in my last letter. [–]

I feel *gossipy* now, I'd like to share some *juicy gossips* with you now, but I'm not a good one for thinking up stories myself. Did you know that *gossip* comes from *God's siblings*?

I met these people who are teachers. She's *androgynous* and her husband is *bisexual*. Recently they seduced the son of one of their colleagues and he thanked them for looking after his son and giving him dinner and allowing him to sleep overnight! I like the story but I don't like the people, actually.

I continue to study post-modernism. Some of the ideas appeal to me strongly. According to one critic we are living in a period of *synchronicity* rather than one of *diachronic* mentality. At best people have these visions of a nightmarish future, for example *Endgame* Beckett – fears (AIDS would probably be one of them). Also, the new structural principle, it seems, is Space, but we don't have the appropriate organs yet to steer ourselves in Space! The argument is that this is an age of deconstructed subjectivity. Subjectivity is the result of the interplay between the past – the present – and the future, but once humanity lives in the Now it cannot delineate itself.

Lots of love
Wolfi

Götis
[no date]

Dear M –

This is my marking pen [red ink]. On Thursday my German class will have to write their first exam.

[–]

Walter used to work in the same ward as me. He's not sure about his gayness, and he's afraid people will find out. (I have trouble getting along with homosexuals like this. I don't make a show of being gay but on the other hand I don't try to hide it either. And to say the truth it's not an important thing to me). The funny thing is he's obviously a queen. I've learned that people that feel deeply about their gayness, and who go to great lengths to hide it, are more obviously gay than those that are quite open about it. All the energy that goes into hiding their gayness is wasted because everyone knows they're gay and gossips about them. Like Walter, he's sure no one knows about him and that he successfully fools everyone into believing he's straight – but everyone knows he's gay, and the only one who is fooled is Walter himself!

A sea of love

Wolfi

P.S. I've officially left the Catholic church. I don't believe in a formal religion but in a sort of worldly *secularised*, individual religion that is also aesthetic. I read Saunders Lewis recently. It's hard to believe he's taken as a philosopher in Wales – what philosopher could take the idea of a Pope seriously?

Götis

[no date]

Dear M –

For some reason I've delayed reacting to your letter. I'm sorry to hear things have gone wrong in Cardiff – I'm re-reading your letter – I'm worried your 'love life' has been caught within ironic distancing quotation marks. But to be honest I would have to put my [love life] within square brackets, like that to convey insignificance and absence at the moment. Generally sex is an appendix to life. When it's a natural part of life one forgets about it and only in a case appendicitis do you focus on it. That's a bit of 'wisdom' that is too *obvious* to be of value.

You should socialise more but Aberdare sounds like a bit of

an unsuitable place to socialise. And I know what I'm talking about as I live in Götis and almost never go out. I think you are much more sociable than me and you 'bloom' among people – the right people. But I know there's another side to your personality that tries to withdraw from people for reasons that are dark and unclear to me. I'm trying to project myself into your mind and I ask are you afraid of *turbulence*, afraid of *turbulence* brought about by *contact*, afraid of disappointment? Probably I'm completely wrong. And yet, there's a massive fear of loneliness, obviously, a fear of being overwhelmed by another's love, and the desire for love and for peace. Do you remember mentioning Emily Dickinson? At the moment it seems there is a similarity between your life and hers –

We send the Wave to find the Wave-
An Errand so divine,
The Messenger enamoured too,
Forgetting to return,
We make the wise distinction still,
Soever made in vain,
The sagest time to dam the sea is when the sea is gone —

Work was hard today. I'm tired. One of the nurses was teasing a (male) nurse who plays football. Sue believes football is a homosexual sport because players kiss and embrace every time they score. She is shocked every time she sees men showing feelings. Once she read a book about friendship between men and she whispered she thought the author was very brave in writing about such things as there was a danger people would assume he was queer. Another nurse is reading *Kiss of the Spider Woman* and she shared with me her suspicion that the two main characters were queer. I could list many such examples. I find these situations

embarrassing. The constant conflict between what I should do –
challenge them, tell them I'm gay – and the way I avoid the truth.

[–]

I love the sound of Welsh. Pity there's not much chance of
hearing it in Austria. Welsh is a sort of *luxury* to me.

Lots of love
Wolfi

Götis
9. 6. 89

Dear M –

I have an exam – the last one – on June 27 – think about me.
I work in the asylum regularly now (until August). This only
leaves a little time for my studies, let alone anything else.

[–]

I had to give blood. Or rather I was politely asked to
contribute some in the Autumn. Of course, I knew, being gay,
this would be a problem. However, assuming I am *low risk* (very
very *low risk*) – I decided I would volunteer and let them know
I was gay. I have to confess I hadn't felt like giving blood before
but now it became of enormous importance to me. Anyway,
when the doctor heard I was gay he asked me not to give, no
further questions.

I was rejected. Perhaps I had never had 'dangerous' sex but yet
having declared myself to be gay I had 'caught the disease' as it
were. My blood was already contaminated with AIDS. The
illness was certain to be within me. I was a danger. A threat.
AIDS and homosexuality are synonymous.

[–]

Fondest wishes
Wolfi

Götis
15. 8. 89

Dear M –

I have spent the last few days in the house of my brother and
sister-in-law. (This is my ultimate finding address, by the way, if
ever you need to get in touch with me or lose track of me and all
else fails.) They were on holiday in the mountains and I was their
'guard dog' in their home. Now my sister-in-law is tidy, sinfully
tidy. It's much more than spotlessly clean, it is pristine (good
word), as if no one lives in the house. Even the lawn is flawless,
with no rotten fruit or leaves even. The path to the door is
unsullied with the petals of flowers. No corruption. No impurity.
Everyone who lives in this house is clean. Even her children (all
under eleven years old) are clinically clean, neatly dressed at all
times and perfectly behaved with no slacking off. Everything is
in perfect order and the order is entirely hers. It's almost
horrifying how the whole house, everything within it, is steeped
in Order. It's terrifying to see how the children's toys sit along the
wall, obediently, geometrically arranged, adjusted to coordinate
with the order of the play room. I almost feel guilty because I
didn't wash the dishes straight after breakfast. I tried to use the
smallest amount of space possible so as not to disrupt the order
to the point where it would take hours to restore it – not to
mention making total chaos. I did quite well. Before they came
back I revived a drooping cushion on the sofa and got it to stand
up straightbacked and proud like a little soldier once more.

And yet the children spotted my slovenliness. In the middle
of all this order I had dared to place a small basket of dry clothes
(neatly folded too) on the floor! My dear little nephew
complained (really, he's perfect, almost, and his childish little
flaws serve only to underline and emphasise his perfection),

complained about the 'mess' in his room. I hadn't folded my clothes correctly, so there were no parallel lines, in a word, not sufficient geometry.

But I felt glad to think when the boy went into his room that he trod on my watch – accidentally, I am sure – and that he threw it away for fear of being punished. On the other hand, perhaps he had stolen my pretty little (effeminate) watch because he liked it so much (which is unlikely actually). Whatever, the watch vanished and my sister-in-law slightly lost her head, just a little; she's too sure of the order of her house to have it lost completely. I didn't mention it again so as to protect my nephew from her wrath.

What about my nephew? Will he have to hide his Desire when it unfolds? My perfect little nephew makes me think a little devil sleeps in his heart. What if the demon awakens? What if he comes to think about Freedom and about smashing Order?

Well, I'm happy to be back home again and to leave that house. What would happen if my sister-in-law came to know I was gay? What is so funny is that she looks upon me as a sort of model for her son!

Lots of love
Wolfi

17. 5. 90

Dear M –

[–] Have I mentioned Markus? Markus is 'into leather' and everything connected with it. To begin with the relationship was pleasant but difficult. I fell in love with him but gradually I learned that gay is not the same thing as gay. It's a heterogeneous term in fact.

[–]

599

Since there's no openly gay group here I've begun to explore the hidden, secret ones.

I still follow 'intellectual' pursuits occasionally but I've lost the taste for them. My interests now are the basic elements, I've moved to a personal minimalism.

[–] I'm afraid to be tied to one person. It sounds funny but it's true. When a man shows any interest in me the idea goes through my mind, 'Now you'll have to go on holiday with him, do everything with him, meet his mother...'

[–] The search is difficult. It's hard for me to name what I'm looking for. I've got a magazine from Markus with gay contact ads on it. Not one appealed to me – which makes me worry! Then I got the idea of putting in an ad of my own. But I couldn't think of the right words. Having studied languages for such a long time I can't compose an advert for myself! I don't know myself well enough. It's easy for Markus, he makes a list of colours and that's it! Is this too personal for you? Johnathan would say, 'This is very un-English of you'. I'm glad I'm not English, then. Is it un-Welsh?

Take care

Wolfi

[I did not hear from Wolfgang for many weeks after this letter, which was very unusual. So I wrote to his brother. His sister-in-law wrote back to say that a group of Neo-Nazis had attacked him and a few other people as they came out of a gay club one night. Wolfgang was killed in the skuffle. He was 27 years old.]

MUSCLES CAME EASY
(2008)
Aled Islwyn

Muscles came easy, I said. *Looked like a bulldog at eight, size fourteen collar at thirteen and captain of the senior school rugby team at sixteen.*

He was impressed. I could tell. Shuffled his arse on those pussy-sized stools they have at the bar at Cuffs and offered to buy me a drink.

Now normally, I don't. Don't talk. Don't look 'em in the eye. Don't do nothing once I've fucked 'em in the darkroom. Them's the rules. Walk straight out of there. Maybe have a drink on my own, or talk to Serge behind the bar, as I did tonight. Then go back a little later to see if it's busy in there by then.

Guess this guy just happened to see me there at the bar.

Well! Let's face it. You can't miss me.

French, apparently. From Lyon. A businessman on his way down to Tarragona. Married. I wouldn't be surprised. But no ring. Not your usual Cuffs customer at all.

Asked me if he could see me tomorrow. How naive can you get? Didn't disillusion the sad fart. Didn't seem right to, somehow. Said my day job at the gym kept me busy. Wanted to know the name of the gym. And I told him. Said he'd look it up next time he was in Barcelona.

Yes, do that, mate, I said. But, frankly, I wouldn't recognise him if he pole-vaulted onto this balcony right now. Then – big mistake! – he grabbed me by my upper arm and tried to lean over to kiss me. Jesus, man! How gross can you get? But I still didn't have the heart to tell him to fuck off, or that Serge paid me to prance around in the darkroom with no shorts on. It's Serge's way of making sure the facilities get well used if it's been quiet in there for a couple of nights. I start the ball rolling in there if they seem a bit on the shy side. Pick someone I'd normally go for and give him a blow job. Sometimes it develops into a free-for-all. Sometimes not. But they've got to feel they've had a good night out, these saddos. That's what they're there for... supposedly.

For the most part they've got to grope around in the dark for themselves and find their own bit of fun, but Serge reckons someone like me making himself available for a while helps get things going. And it's always the start of the week he calls me. By Thursday, apparently, they need no encouragement. Never get these club jobs on a weekend.

Wouldn't have touched that French guy with a bargepole in my own time. Just didn't have the heart to tell him the truth. Should have really. I'm just too soft. Always have been, see!

Got up and left him after the kissing fiasco. Went straight back in there and fucked two more. Condoms worn both times, of course. Part of the game ever since I've been at it. Surprised how many of the older ones still ask and check. Guess they remember a time when it wasn't the norm.

Seeing the traffic going backwards and forwards kept Serge happy, I could tell.

Then the last dumb trick I pulled must have had this thing for armpits. Licked me sore he did, the bastard. Not really my thing. But he was good at it, I'll give him that.

Glad of that shower though.

First thing I always do when I come in from these club jobs. Check Mike's asleep (and he always is) then get cleaned up.

Check myself over. Thorough. All part of the routine. Important. Never fail.

And so's this brandy. Part of the routine, like. Just a small one. Few minutes to myself out here in the fresh air. Mull things over. How it all went and that. Well-toned body. Well-honed mind. All that shit they pumped into you at college. Well! When all's said and done, it's right, like, isn't it? When you really think it over. Has to be... for the life I lead.

I refused point blank. Told him straight. I'm not dressing up in cowboy boots and stetsons for nobody – and no amount of extra euros.

O, si, he said, *but line dancing is all the craze now!*

That may be so, I said back, but I told him straight... he's running a great little health studio there, Raul. Legit. The genuine McCoy. Not some poof's palace where a lot of poseurs prance around pretending to lift weights and keep fit.

I'm strictly a one-on-one guy. Personal Trainer is what I'm employed as and that's what I am. Press-ups. Rowing machine. Circuit training. All the stuff I know really works. I work with clients individually. One-to-one. Assessments. Supervision. Even down to diets and lifestyle choices. A proper trainer.

Okay, I do some aerobic stuff with the women clients, I grant you. But they just like to hear the word used often. Don't think half of them know what the hell aerobics means. And told him that's all the pampering to fashion he'll get from me.

Oh Joel, you not mean it! You think it over, Joel... please... for Raul!

Love the way Raul says my name. And he knows it. They're not used to it here – Joel – which is strange. I always find. Spain being a Catholic country and all. You'd think they'd know their Bible.

He makes it sound like Hywel. Reminds me of home. Our geography teacher was called Hywel Gordon. Had a hell of a crush on him at one time. He'd been a very promising full back, but some injury had put paid to that. No sign of injury on him from what I could see. But there you go! Guess it was the bits of him I never did get to see which needed scrutinising the most.

Raul's been good to me these last four years. Him and his missus. Helped me with my Spanish when I first arrived. Fed me. Gave me a job. *I only want best people work with me in my fitness studio*, he'd say. *And I want you.*

They speak Catalan together. Raul and his wife. And their kid gets taught in it at school. Like they do with Welsh back home, I suppose.

Not me, of course.

My nanna could speak Welsh quite a bit. Chapel and that. But I couldn't sing a single hymn at her funeral. And felt a right nerd. If there's anything of value to lose, you can bet your life my mam'll be the first to do so.

Couldn't be arsed with all that, really, were her thoughts on Welsh.

Then one day she lost her purse on the bus. Huge kerfuffle in our house. A whole week's wages gone. No wonder my dad left. *I'd have been okay if it wasn't for her with the glass eye from Tonypandy confusing me with all that talk about her Cyril!* The only explanation anybody ever got from her on that little incident.

Poor cow has even managed to lose a breast. *You're one nipple short of a pair of tits, Mam!* I tease her rotten sometimes. She laughs.

You've got to laugh in the face of adversity, she says... except sometimes 'adversity' slips out as 'anniversary'. It's a miracle I'm as well-adjusted as I am.

And I bet Raul has me taking these bloody line dancing classes any day now. I can see it coming!

Don't know why you won't get yourself a tidy job, she said.

I knew as soon as I picked up the phone she was going to take a long time coming to the point.

Come back home and be a teacher. Papers always say they're crying out for them round here. And there's you there with all them qualifications...

I already got a tidy job, I said. Why I bother explaining every time, I don't know. She'd never heard of a Personal Training Instructor 'til I started calling myself one – as she'll happily tell anyone who's sad enough to listen.

Didn't take a blind bit of notice. She never does. High as a kite 'cos of something. I knew it when she first came on the line. I could always tell, even as a child. Her voice almost croaking with that hysterical shriek she puts on when she's dying to tell you something.

Our Joanne's pregnant again. At last she came out with it. In one great torrent. *The washing machine's on the blink.* And to cap it all, the real biggy was her final punch: *Oh, yes...! And Dan Llywellyn has cancer.*

Then silence.

I felt nothing, really.

Said I was sorry to hear that, like you do without thinking. But I couldn't honestly say I'd thought of him at all for several years.

She didn't know where it was. *Somewhere painful*, is all she'd heard. The talk of Talbot Green Tesco's last Saturday, apparently.

He had it coming, I suppose. But I couldn't tell Mam that.

Wasn't glad. Wasn't sad. Felt nothing.

Still don't know why you started calling him Dan Dracula. She was chipping away on an old bone, hoping she'd catch me on the hop. *Always thought it was cruel of you, that, after all he'd done for you.*

It's because of all he's done to me, Mam. That's what I wanted to tell her. But didn't.

He's also the one who introduced me to weights. Saw my potential. *Dan Llywellyn is the one who saw our Joel's full potential.* That's what he'll always be credited with. Showed me the ropes. Gave me definition.

You're everything you are today 'cos of that man, she declared with conviction.

She was right, of course. And she meant it at face value. Wouldn't know what irony was. Not my mam. If she can't get it cheap on Ponty market, she doesn't want to know.

Her kitchen floor was completely flooded, apparently. Took three bucketfuls of mopping to clean it up. And today it rained there all day.

You call me a Muscle Mary one more time and I'll fucking give you a good hiding, I said.

I haven't called you a Muscle Mary once yet, he replied, playing child-like with my left bicep.

Well! To be fair he hadn't. Not during today's debacle.

Pussy-boys are so predictable, I said. *I always know what's coming next with you.*

You're just a slave to your ego, Joel, he retorted. *And that's a very subservient place to be for a man of your physical stature.*

On the bed, Mike rolled on his stomach as he spoke, and lowered his voice to that detached level which always places him beyond any further verbal bruising. It's a ploy he's mastered to perfection. The aim is to intimidate me and exonerate himself. It's a tactical illusion, of course, rather than a sign of true superiority. It's a part of our game. A futile duel fought in a darkened room, while our neighbours, all around us, bathe in a siesta of rest and serenity.

Maybe that's why we laughed. Lying there bickering in our Calvin Kleins on that vast double bed this afternoon. It was the only thing to do. Our last hope of not looking ridiculous, even to ourselves.

We've lived together long enough to be both comfortable and bored with each other in equal measure.

I slapped his arse and told him to go make a cup of tea. And that's when my mobile rang, just as he opened the door to the living room and let the light in.

This guy's from Valencia, right. The one who rang. Owns a club, it seems, and wants me down there next Tuesday night to work his back room. Personal recommendation from Serge, apparently.

I jumped off the bed and stood upright to talk.

Two things, I said. One: Valencia's too far, man. Must be four hundred kilometres, easily. Don't know how much that is in miles. Gave up converting long time ago. But then relented when he mentioned the fee. Said I'd think it over. Oh, yes! And the second thing, I said: *I'm strictly a top. Hope Serge made that clear. This boy's arse is an exit only. Period.* Silence! Think the aggro in my voice had been too much for him. All I could hear was the amount of money on offer being repeated down the line. And the sound of water boiling in the kitchen where Mike was doing what he does best.

Being English.

I've tried to talk to Mike. But I can't.

The news of Dan Llywelyn's imminent demise has followed me around for days. Ever since Mam told me. *And all the memories slogged me in the guts!*

That's the last line of this poem by a guy called Harri Webb. We did him at college – *You see, it wasn't all boys running around in muddy fields and pumping iron*, I told Mike earlier – and I really loved his stuff.

Mike's painting at the time. What I still call the small bedroom is now his studio. Looks more like a clinic if you ask me. I've never heard of anyone being creative and so tidy at the same time. Whilst the canvas is awash with colour, Mike remains immaculate. But that's Mike for you.

He was only half listening to me, I could tell. He then informs me that he's never heard of Harri Webb. *Another one of your trivial poets*, he insists. But inside I know that he takes it as a personal affront to his dignity as an English lecturer that I've managed once again to draw attention to a lapse in his supposedly superior education.

He was still at it when Mam rang in the early evening. Painting that is.

Things are worse than first thought, apparently. For old Dan. He's at home. But he's shrivelled to a nothing and his hair's all fallen out. Sick every other minute, it seems. All over the bus back from town. So she said.

And what's his wife got to say on the situation? I chipped in. *The usual fuck-all, no doubt.*

Mam tells me to wash my mouth out with soap and water, but I tell you, that woman should have had 'I see nothing, I hear nothing, I say nothing' tattooed across her forehead years ago. She must have known what was going on. Wasn't deaf, dumb and blind through ignorance, I'm almost sure. And I don't think it was fear either. Doubt if Dan Llywellyn ever touched her. It was just indifference. She'd sit there like a beached whale in front of the telly, stuffing chocolates in her mouth, oblivious to the tip around her. And all I ever did was mumble some banality as I passed her on the way to the bottom of their stairs. Dan upstairs before me, usually.

You go on up, love, she'd urge me. And up I'd go.

Twp she was, I reckon. Probably still sitting there right now, incarcerated by her cholesterol consumption and jellied in cellulite, flicking from channel to channel in order to shut out the outrages going on around her.

I reckon our Joanne will go the same way. Already showing early signs of abandonment, despite all this breeding she's intent on inflicting on the world. In fact, I'm convinced it's part of it. All these brats of hers are only an excuse for doing less and less. That's the reality. She has no creative aspirations in her at all. Not for herself. Not for her kids. Never did.

Leave her alone. She only wants to give me more grandchildren, pleads Mam on her behalf. *Since you clearly don't intend to give me any.*

Joanne and Dean already have three. *That was my point*, I said. Why the hell would they want more? Going by the evidence so far, the possibility that some hidden pearl of genius is hiding away in their shared gene pool is pretty remote.

They scream a lot. Mam spoils them. Dean disappears down the pub. And Joanne gets fatter by the day, only admitting when pushed that she doesn't really care what the hell they do with their lives... *so long as they're happy.* This is the happy heterosexual life we're all supposed to aspire to, as lived halfway up a Welsh mountain. I swear the sheep have more fun.

It's all over the *Observer* apparently. The latest Rhondda bombshell. Dan Llywellyn arrested amidst allegations of child abuse. They've torn his house apart. Even removed the telly and the video. So it's a real crisis as far as his missus is concerned.

I chuckled to myself, but felt nothing. Said even less.

You used to spend hours down that gym with him.
I let her do the talking and grunted in agreement.
And round his house! Some weekends, you practically lived there.
Her hysteria was muted for once. I knew there was so much else she wanted to ask, but never would. Some places are too raw for even my mam to venture. I simply coughed. (This cold I've caught has made me croak incoherently when I speak, making my silence sound less guilty than it might otherwise have done.) Mam's voice cracked in unison.

The mirror by the phone was briefly my only comfort. I flexed my free arm. And smiled at myself in approval. For a moment I remember wishing Mike had been there with me. But he wasn't. It was just me and Mam... the mirror and the memories.

Got a worse drenching that night than I thought at the time. Must have. 'Cos I'm convinced that's where I caught this lot. Okay! I know I said I definitely wouldn't do that job. But did in the end, didn't I?

Fancied the run. That's what clinched it, not the money. When you consider that it emerged he wasn't paying mileage for the petrol, it wasn't really that much. But I hadn't been for a seriously long run on the bike for months. So, Valencia, I thought, why not?

The evening went well. Tidy little bar. Changed into my cut-off shorts and leather harness and did a few tricks.

Hadn't even realised it was raining until I came out the back at 4 a.m. If I'd had any sense, would have asked that guy for somewhere to stop over. But in my mind, I'd been looking forward to those empty roads along the Costas in the middle of the night. So wiped the seat, got on and revved my way out of there.

How was I to know the 'Med' was due to have its worst storm for five years that night?

Bloody exhausted by the time I got back here. Had to keep my speed right down, see. Made the journey longer, which meant I got even wetter. Thunder sounding off all around me. Lightning. Hailstones the size of golf balls. Could feel her sliding underneath me. Probably should have checked the pressure before setting out. But didn't. Could feel them tyres fighting the torrent for supremacy of the tarmac on certain corners.

Exhilarating at the time. But glad to get home, I can tell you. It was already light. The sun all bright in the sky as though nothing had happened. Mike still asleep, thank God. Squelched my way to the bathroom to strip out of my bike leathers.

Well! It's been a week and I'm hardly any better. Still coughing my guts up. Sneezing. But the shivering's gone. That was the only hopeful news I could give Raul when he called earlier. Wanted to give the man some glimmer of hope I might return to work before the end of the week.

The things you do, not to do the line dancing, he teased, accusing me of being a fraud.

Cheeky bugger! I leaned forward and pinched his nipple through his T-shirt.

I'm as honest as my prick is long, I said, choking as I coughed as I laughed.

He didn't flinch. Just laughed along. I'm sure he'd be a kinky little bastard given half a chance. He knows I'm gay, of course. Always has. But we've never really discussed it.

That's what made it rather embarrassing when the phone rang. Raul was still here in the lounge when they called. Over there across the table from me. He could tell I'd sobered up pretty quick after picking up the phone.

It was some bloody detective from the central police station at Pontypridd. Well! You don't expect it, do you? Not in Barcelona during siesta on a Sunday afternoon.

It's another world, you see. That's what I keep telling Mam.

Nice for a week, love, but wouldn't want to live there, she keeps replying.

She must have been the one to give them my number. Didn't think to ask him where he got it from. And looking back on it, he didn't really ask me anything either. Confirmed who I was. That I knew Dan Llywellyn. That I'd agree to see them when they came over. And that was it.

Must be serious, mind... coming all that way just to see me.

This coming Wednesday? asked Mike in disbelief when I told him. *They are in a hurry.*

Guess they have to be if Dan is fading fast. They'll want to get their summons served before the death certificate is signed.

Explained very little to Raul after I'd put the receiver down. He had the sense to down the whiskey I'd poured him pretty sharpish. Said he hoped I'd be better soon.

So do I. It's no fun, this sickness lark!

I guess I should have. But I couldn't, could I? Don't ask me why, just knew I wasn't going to before they rang that bell. And all that talk of 'substantial financial compensation' he kept dangling like a carrot in front of my eyes throughout our 'little chat' didn't make a difference either.

This isn't a formal interview, Joel, he said. *I'm not obliged to caution you and you're obviously not suspected of committing any criminal activity yourself. We just want a little chat.*

He didn't have a Valleys accent. Couldn't really tell where he was from, the young burly one who talked. Impressive thighs though. He was lean and well-muscled. Not in my league, like. But I knew he was a fit bastard and guessed he probably punched above his weight. Wore a pair of safari shorts, which looked great on him. And a kind of pink cotton shirt, which didn't.

Found the heat oppressive, he said. Never been to this part of Spain before. Investigating serious allegations made against Mr Daniel Llywellyn who ran the Junior Gym and Recreational Club down Bethel Street for many years.

Well, I knew why he was there! He could have saved his breath on that score.

How is he? I found myself asking.

Poorly, came the reply. God knows why, but somehow I'd expected more.

He already knew I was gay. He told me so when he first arrived.

Yes and very happily so, I fired back with confidence. Thought afterwards that I must have sounded defensive and regretted saying anything.

So I see. Beautiful city. Lovely apartment. Must be a very nice lifestyle.

I like it. I found myself agreeing like a sheep. He was setting me up for compliance and I wasn't having any of it.

He also knew I was now working at a health studio myself. *A bit different from your old haunts back in Wales*, he sneered.

Told him I'd taken time off work especially to see them. He said he was grateful. But inside I knew every word he spoke meant something else.

Should have dropped Dan Dracula right in it, I suppose. The stupid bastard. But just couldn't bring myself to do it, see.

Then he said he knew it was difficult to talk about such things.

His mate, meantime – the little short-arse git who hardly said a word – is still sitting in that armchair over by the door to the spare bedroom. Fascinated by art, it seems. Had a good look inside and his eyes devoured every painting we have hanging here in the lounge too.

It seems I can get back in touch with them anytime... or so the talkative one kept reminding me. No problem... day or night. When I'd thought it over. If I could remember any little incident when I'd felt uncomfortable... I shouldn't hesitate. *Any time. You just call me, Joel.* Like all the other lads had done... the ones who'd come forward and were now in line for *substantial financial compensation.*

Wants us to meet again before they go back. Tomorrow evening after the gym closes. For a drink.

I suggested the Zanzibar bar on Las Ramblas. His tourist attire should look at home there.

We shook hands as they left. And I looked him in the eye. For the first time. Didn't want him to think I was scared of doing that. But it's not something I've ever been good at. Looking people in the eye.

Still have his card here in my hand. Detective Sergeant Gavin Hughes BSc. Can't remember the name of the other one. He never left a card. But I told Mike how besotted he'd been with his paintings.

You see the truth doesn't always come easily in this life, Joel. That must be his mantra. It's his favourite sentence, most definitely. Heard it so many times this evening, it's spinning round my brain. Which would make him happy back in his little hotel bedroom if he knew.

That was obviously his intention – to plant the seeds that would get me to spill the beans. But the truth doesn't always come that easy in this life, does it?

Should have thrown the sentence back in his face... and added 'Gavin' at the end, like he kept adding 'Joel' to the end of everything he said to me. Like one big strapping full stop.

Still, he got more than he bargained for one way or another!

A strange evening really. Don't quite know what to make of it.

Sorry! I just don't do guided tours of gay Barcelona, I said.

Oh, don't be like that, Joel! he pleaded. A wry, old-fashioned smile lit his face.

I gave in in the end. We ended up in Cuffs. Introduced him to Serge.

Shouldn't have really. Gone round clubs drinking, I mean. I'm still taking the antibiotics for my chest infection. Don't finish them till Saturday.

Added to which, Mike went ballistic when he heard I'd shown him some of the nightlife here. *He's a cop, for God's sake!*

He's so paranoid, that boy! It's unbelievable. I know he's a cop, don't I?

I've done my share of hanging around in gay bars, Gavin assured me.

That was much earlier in the evening, when we're sitting outside the Zanzibar, watching the world walk by on Las Ramblas. It's a warm evening. (Aren't they all, out here?) We down a few drinks. Just me and Gavin. His fat-git partner made his excuses after downing two beers in a hurry. Then headed back to their hotel. Needed his beauty sleep, he said.

Slugs do, I thought.

So that left me and good old Gavin, who proceeded to assure me that he didn't intend to talk about Dan Llywellyn all evening. But then again... *the truth doesn't always come easy in this life*... and he knew what I must be going through... how I mustn't feel disloyal... how wishing to put the past behind me was natural... but how I never would until I had all this off my chest. Oh yes, he understood!

Which amused me, really. He was jolly about it all. One of the lads. Leaning over. Sharing a joke, where appropriate. His hand on my knee when occasion allowed. All textbook 'You can trust me, I'm a policeman', stuff. I knew his game and went along with it all.

Why shouldn't I let him ply me with drinks? Buy me a meal? As far as he was to know, my tongue might have started to loosen at any second. The one right word from him could have triggered an avalanche of juicy memories at any moment. My guard could be down. Floods of steamy recollections could be streaming from my lips. Salacious anecdotes. Times and dates and sordid details. All the conclusive evidence that would put Dan Llywellyn away for many years.

I'm the big fish he wants to haul. Worked that one out after he rang to ask to see me. And he virtually admitted as much this evening. I was, after all, Dan Llywellyn's 'star boy'. Played for the county at almost everything. Boxed for Wales as a schoolboy. Very nearly made the British Olympic wrestling team. Got to represent Wales in some World Federation weightlifting tournament in Budapest at the age of eighteen. More trophies than my mam could cope with. Which is why half of them ended up in Nanna's house.

So it's down to me.

You're the man who can nail Dan Llywellyn, he tells me.

Seems to me the undertaker will do that soon enough, I said back to him.

He laughs at that and slaps me on the back. Furious inside, I reckon, 'cos he knows I'm making light of his mission. But he's enough of a professional to know he mustn't lose it. I would, after all, be the dream witness for him, if only I'd play ball. The ending of this dark chapter in the annals of Welsh crime lays in my hands. And maybe old Gavin needs this one for his CV to secure promotion or boost his self-confidence or his reputation amongst his colleagues or whatever else he feels is missing in his saddo life. He knows he mustn't blow it with me.

Daft sod! Does he really think I'm going to dish the dirt on Dan?

Seven-thirty! The traffic's buzzing. And the sun is up.

I'm not exactly suffering. But I can't get going either. This coffee is just about enough to revive my mouth. The rest of me can follow later, once I'm doing some warm-ups down the gym.

Raul will already be there. Cleaning. Setting everything up for the day. He works hard.

It must have been two o'clock when we left Cuffs. Early really, by Barcelona standards. The place was hardly getting going. But I told him I had work to go to in five hours' time and that he was also flying home today.

All in all, he must have been resigned to the fact that his tactics hadn't worked.

Guess I can't break you tonight, Joel, he joked half seriously over our last drink.

You'll never break me, man. All these sad wannabees who made these allegations against Dan, don't know what they're talking about.

Talking about tears in some instances, Joel, he comes straight back at me. *The tales some of those boys had to tell have left them emotionally scarred for life.*

You'll never find me crying, mate, I proclaimed adamantly.

Ah, Joel, the world is full of men like you who've lived to swallow bitter tears.

Tears are totally feminine things, I tell him. *They're void of any maleness. It's a clinically proven fact. No traces of testosterone have ever been found in a man's tears. Only feminine hormones.*

He was stunned for a moment and didn't know whether to laugh or not.

Oh! Men have the capacity to produce them, I said, *but no means of instilling them with any masculine traits. It's a fact.*

When the taxi pulled up outside, he placed his hand on my knee once more. Just as I was about to open the door. He half turned to face me full on and willing sincerity into his eyes with all the power he could muster, he said, *Remember, Joel, I'm on your side.*

I'm convinced the line about 'truth not always being easy' is about to get another airing and in a sublime moment of panic, I kissed him. A smacker on the lips.

Think I meant it as a joke. Can't really remember.

Well! Yes, I can. It was and it wasn't. A joke, that is. I was confused. And high. And horny. And he responded. Old Gavin. There, last night, in that taxi his lips went 'Open sesame' and his hand moved up my thigh.

The taxi driver just sat there not caring a damn. He's seen it all before. And besides, the meter was still running. Why would he mind?

Eventually, my tongue slid free and I got out without a word. Just stood there gobsmacked on the pavement as he's driven away. My hand clutching the card I'd felt him slip into my pocket. It's the second one he's given me. I now have a pair. Only on that second one he's written his personal email address in biro on the back.

It's here in my wallet, hidden away.

I've no idea how he got my email address. My mam is off the hook this time. Telephones are an integral part of her communications system. It's a well-known fact. But an email remains a mystery to her.

However he got it, there it was this evening. Waiting for me.

Thanks for seeing me. I appreciated it and respect your position. But if you ever want to relieve yourself of anything, you know how to get hold of me. My investigations continue. It's a sad and sensitive business. Hope we get to meet again, especially if things get clearer in your mind. Regards, Gavin.

I couldn't reply immediately. What a relief!

Mike has had several of his paintings accepted by some prestigious gallery. He needed the computer urgently. I was banished out here on the balcony. No! Correction. I banished myself.

Hate these days when I've been for a check-up. So fucking humiliating. And six months seem to come around so quickly. Condoms and care are all well and good. But I'm wise to stick to my routine.

Mike pointed out that I wouldn't need to go if I didn't play around. The darkroom work really bugs him. He suffers from selective memory. *We met in a bloody darkroom. Mike*, I said. *Remember?*

You're thirty-three now, was his response. *Time you grew up.*

Perhaps he doesn't want to remember. It was ten years ago. Not here, of course. Not Cuffs. Ibiza. Another club. A holiday. Our first shag. No condom. No cares.

And now, it's not even a memory.

He'll still want me to accompany him to the opening of his exhibition. He told me all about it as he broke the news. 'Launch party' it's called. More of a small reception, apparently. Just critics and friends. He told me the date and to be sure to keep it free.

I'm still good for wheeling out as the trophy boyfriend, it seems. And don't get me wrong, that's fine by me. So long as Mike doesn't forget at which bring-and-buy he picked me up.

Being told you're all clear should give you a high, I suppose. But curiously, it doesn't. There's relief. And then this empty feeling takes over inside, as you stop off in reception before leaving to make your next appointment in another six months' time.

Raul's missus made such a fuss of Mike last night it was almost embarrassing. Her wonderful meal was already enough of a contribution to the celebrations. She's generous to a fault and I can understand why Raul lives in awe of her every act of kindness. I have never in my life lived with anyone who oozes so much goodness with such grace and I understand that it can't always be easy.

It's only two paintings, Mike insisted repeatedly every time she mentioned his triumph.

Still two more than Van Gogh ever sold in his lifetime, I kept chipping in, playing the proud partner.

We'd taken the champagne, of course. Not cava, Raul noted, tossing the bottle in the air when we first got there and catching it again behind his back, much to Mike's relief. Things are pretty tight on old Raul, I think. His overheads are high and with another bambino on the way he can't have much money to throw around.

As we sat down to eat in their tiny kitchen, Mike ceremoniously popped open the bottle. And the kid starts throwing his pasta across the room in excitement. The rest of us just laughed and made a toast of Mike's success and cleared off that first bottle without a care in the world.

Raul suggested a spot of line dancing to follow and I told him to bugger off.

I flexed my biceps to amuse the kid and he in turn tried to knock the muscles back into place with a plastic hammer which must have come with the set of plastic blocks I kept tripping over underfoot.

As the evening drew on, we all seemed bloated and bubbly and larger than life. And I really hated the moment when I knew I had to tell Raul I'd be away another week. It seems so soon after the week I lost when that bug laid me low.

Needless to say. I needn't have worried. His handshake was flamboyant in his sympathies. He knew. He cared. He caressed.

Si, si! You must, you must, he said. And with that he fetched the second bottle from the fridge, saying such sadness had to be drowned immediately.

He indulges you something rotten, was Mike's verdict on the way home last night. *You're like a great big toy he just can't get enough of.*

You used to be like that towards me once, I replied. *What happened?*

It's not good that it's back.

Mike made all the right noises last night after Joanne rang, it's true, but he's so buoyed by his newfound success, his words just sounded empty and devoid of any feeling.

Even Joanne's voice rang hollow as she tried to speak through the tears. A combination of the waterworks and the Welsh in her voice. Like a drunken sailor trying to sing a shanty aboard a sinking ship on a stormy sea. The meaning made no sense at all, but you could still taste the salt on your lips as the song slapped your face.

It will be two years since I was last at home. That's the trouble. I've started to forget.

She won't come over to see me. Our Joanne. I've asked her. But she won't. Says she doesn't like the food.

Bloody ridiculous excuse!

The truth is, she's never been anywhere much, our Joanne. No further than the prenatal clinic. And even then, our mam has had to go with her every time.

Not the next time, though! The thought struck me like a left hook. Not if it's back.

Knew immediately I had to do the same. Go back. Take charge.

I had no chance to even ask how Mam was. Dean has a go at me as soon as he picks up the receiver. It was late, apparently, and I'd woken up the kids. He's always hated my guts. Likes to think he's something special with his fists. And he'd love to take a pop at me one day, I know. But the sad wimp has never quite been able to pluck up the courage, 'cos he knows I've won prizes for it. So it's hands buried deep, whenever we meet. Pocket billiards and a mouthful of abuse.

I know I wind him up, which doesn't help, but he's such an easy match to light, I can't resist!

What are you doing sleeping round Mam's house, any road? I said. *Can't you provide a house of your own for your family?*

Very compassionate, Joel, he retorts, except he can't really do sarcasm. He has to scream it at me, thereby missing the advantage of the higher moral ground which had subtly been his for his taking if only he'd played his cards right.

You boys fighting again? You'll be the death of me!

Mam could be heard almost physically wrestling the receiver from Dean's hand as she talked. Her voice was full of sniffing. More tears. I sighed and start to feel depressed.

It seems that she hasn't had the test results yet. I tried to interrupt the moist flow of pessimism by looking on the bright side, but she was having none of it. Easier to wallow in anticipation of the worse scenario than hanging on to hope, it seems.

I was glad to get off the phone.

So much for 'The old town looks the same...' It doesn't.

They've knocked half of it down. And the other half's boarded up.

I'll be next, said Mam. *Already feel as though I've been knocked down by a bus. And I'll soon be boarded up. Eight nails in the lid*

*should do it nicely... with some lily of the valleys from you and
Joanne resting on top just to set it all off!*

She chokes me when she speaks like that.

Don't go wasting your money on me now, mind, she continued.
*So long as you keep it dignified, that's all I ask. I don't want
anything tacky. And make sure your father doesn't put in an
appearance at the last moment. Don't want him ruining my big
day. He ruined the last one I had in that chapel.*

Mam, don't talk like that, I said.

Well, the bastard turned up, didn't he? Her loud voice brings
high camp comedy to the cancer ward. *And don't think I'm the
only woman who's ever wished her husband had jilted her at the
altar with the benefit of hindsight. The world is full of us.*

*And if you hadn't married him, I wouldn't be here now, would
I? Have you thought of that?* I said.

She's only trying to be cheerful, she answered, expecting me
to laugh along. But of course, I don't. I didn't. And I can't. Can't
cry either. Won't allow myself. I never can. Ended up just sitting
there, telling her not to be so daft.

Had a long chat with the doctor a little later.

He'd no office to take me to. We stood out in the corridor out
of earshot, keeping our voices down and shifting sideways
whenever anyone walked past. The staff use that corridor as a
short cut to the car park when they go for their illicit fags. It sees
a lot of traffic. Our whispers had to blend in furtively with a sea
of uniforms, camouflaged by smiles and the slight whiff of smoke.

She's been slightly overly pessimistic, apparently. That's what
he told me. It turns out he's more worried by her mental state
than by the cancer. Well, not more, maybe, but as much.

You're going to be okay. I tried to reassure her when I finally
returned to the ward to sit with her a little while longer.

The doctor had just told me her depression manifested itself in laughter, so my heart sank as she roared hysterically in response. She lunged at me sitting in my chair, before throwing her arms around my neck and all but falling out of bed.

It's back, my boy, she howled. *It's back. And so are you.*

Listen to the darkness.

You can't, of course. That bloody clock won't let you. Like it won't let me sleep. Five nights I've been back home and five nights I've just been lying here contemplating how much I hate that clock. I've always hated it. When it chimed away in Nanna's house, I hated it. And now I hate it here.

To put it in boxing terms, it seems to punch above its weight. Stands there in the corner. Looking petit. A wallflower with time on its hands. Delicate casing and a poofy face. Calls itself a grandmother clock. *The only thing of any value I ever got from my mother*, Mam says. It may be old, but I doubt it's worth much. Just a clock with attitude. A wedding present to my grandparents, in the days when even the cheap pressies outlived the marriage.

Hear that tick-tock measuring the emptiness; its tenacity audible above all the other anxieties throbbing in my brain. Like a bantam fighter, it just keeps coming at you. Wearing you down. Numbing your pain. Making you oblivious to the killer punch that's about to get you on the blind side.

Curiously, Mam asked about it tonight. The clock. She wants everything to be in full working order if she's allowed home tomorrow. Had I wound it up?

No, but it's winding me up plenty! I replied.

She laughed that exaggerated laugh the doctor seemed to find so worrying.

I've thought about it. That chat I had with him yesterday.

She's not suppressing depression. More like celebrating her inherent over-optimism.

Mam will always laugh. She always has. It's what pulls her through.

I've made her bed up. Ready for tomorrow. Hoovered round a little. Even wound up that bloody clock for her. Well! It's what she wanted.

It hasn't happened, has it? Mam isn't home tonight, as planned. I'm still here on my own. Just me and the clock.

More tests are needed, apparently. They want to be absolutely certain. Of what, I'm not too sure. But it seems they can't decide what to do. The consultant has been consulted and the specialist has had his say. And the doubts that are mostly left unsaid are deafening.

I could tell she was down, bless her. And when I rang Mike earlier, he said I sounded down myself.

I can feel the despondency in your voice, he said. How profound is that?

Well, is it any bloody wonder? I bellowed back.

He always has to use big words to deal with any gut feeling anyone may ever have. It's his defence against any genuine raw emotion. Yes, I was pleased to hear the exhibition continues to be a great success... and no, he doesn't really care a damn about what I'm going through here. I could tell by his voice. He never has cared. That's the truth. Not about me, where I come from, or my family.

The trouble is. I don't really miss him. It's been ten days and I've only made contact with him twice. Both times, what I really needed to find out was how everyone was doing; Raul and the gang, etc. Things in the flat. Not Mike.

Dan Llywellyn turned up a lot tonight. Not in the flesh, of course – what's left of it! In conversation. A verbal resurrection from Mam.

I know he's there, of course. Same hospital, different wards. He's in a lot worse state than her. She kept repeating that. Never mentioned dying, but I knew that's what she meant.

He'd love to see you. Why don't you pop along and have a chat?

She needn't have bothered naming the ward. I've known which one it is since I first went to visit Mam. It's where the terminally ill are kept. 'God's waiting room' the staff call it on the sly. It's out on a limb. The ground-floor ward nearest the gardens.

One of the cleaners I got talking to the other day told me it was to enable the earth's gravity to make their journey easier at the end. Dust to dust, earth to earth, ashes to ashes... she could quote the lot.

By the sound of her, she'd caught religion and I didn't have the heart to tell her it was probably more to do with the fact that they built the mortuary round the back.

I wound that clock in vain last night. And now I wish I hadn't. Really only did it for her. And she's not here.

A torture for my own insomnia. Should have left it to its own devices. Do unto time as time does unto all of us.

When I next see that cleaner, I'll tell her that. She looked easily impressed.

It's all right for you, Joel, he said. *You're one of the lucky ones. You got out. Looked after yourself. Made something of yourself.*

I told him to go to hell.

I know you don't mean that, he said, eyeballing me like a pneumatic drill as he spoke.

Then he went straight into this sob story about Darren Howley.

That was his name apparently; this gawping, chubby geek I'd noticed in Spar this afternoon. Looked around forty. A beer-bellied no-hoper. The valley's full of them. Except this one had a real talent for staring. I wasn't flattered. I wasn't angry. I just wanted Mam to recover quickly so I could catch the first plane back to Barcelona.

Well! It seems he was once a promising football player.

Went to Dan Llywellyn for coaching. Ended up on drugs and off the rails.

A life blighted, Gavin called it.

It seems this Darren called him on his mobile after stalking me round Spar.

I keep in touch with many of those boys, Gavin explained. *Or at least I allow them to keep in touch with me. Feel protective towards them, you see. Seen so many lives destroyed.*

Mine's not destroyed, I started to protest.

No, quite, he interjects. *Like I said, you're one of the lucky ones.*

Made things happen for myself, I said. *No luck about it. Stuck at it in school. Went to college. Learnt Spanish. I'm a self-made man. Made things happen for myself.*

The trouble is, the Darren Howleys of this world are wondering why the hell you didn't make things happen for them as well, Joel, Gavin continues. *Or stopped things happening to them, is more to the point. Do you know what I mean?*

I knew by now that he was intent on saying his piece, so I stood there with my back to the wall and my hands deep in my tracky bottoms.

They know you see. They know what you went through. The verbal assault continued. I held my ground in silence. *And they can't for the life of them work out why you didn't put a stop to it. Back then, they didn't have your balls, Joel. They didn't have your brains. They were dependent on a bright lad like you to speak up and save them further misery. Speak up and break Dan Llywellyn's vicious circle. But you didn't, did you, Joel? Why is that, Joel?*

I still don't know what you're talking about, I said. *No one ever messed with me I didn't want to mess with me.*

I know you, Joel. I just know.

You don't, mate! You don't know me at all...

And I'll get it all out of you too, one day – the hard way if I have to. But it will out. You listen to me good... He paused a moment while a distraught-looking relative went scuttling past in pursuit of a member of the medical staff. His half-turned eyes judged when she'd be out of earshot and, before continuing, his voice lowered an octave, just to be on the safe side. *One day, I'll have you there in front of me, just like you are now. Only it won't be a fuckin' hospital corridor. And you won't be looking so smug. You'll be crying your fuckin' eyes out, Joel. Just like all those other sad bastards I've met on this investigation. You'll be so relieved to have all that shit of years ago out of your system, you won't know whether they're tears of joy or anguish sobbing down your cheeks and nostrils. You'll just know that you've wrenched out a gutful of pus that's been there hiding inside you all those years, Joel. And I'll be the one you'll be grateful to for giving you the best feeling of relief you'll ever know in your life.*

Dream on, sunshine, I said. And he sort of smiled. Knowing it wasn't the place or the time to pursue it further. The worried lady was making her way back from the smokers' den, the nurse she'd managed to collar barely hiding her annoyance at having her fag curtailed.

Can't pretend it's not good to see you again, he chips in casually as the two women made their way back towards the wards.

Really? Gee, thanks!

How's your mother?

As if you cared! I retorted sharply.

Well, I sort of do, really, Joel, he replied. He'd moved from menace mode to vague benevolence with barely a facial distortion, only the subtle shifting of the balance of his body weight conveying his newfound mood of conviviality. *How is she?*

If the mood had changed, the persistence hadn't.

You're only here 'cos Darren what's-his-name's call reminded you that I'm still in town, I said. Equally calm. Equally polite. I put a jokey lilt in my voice to neutralise the tension. *You knew I'd be up here at visiting time.*

So how is she?

Coming out day after tomorrow, I replied. It was like giving in, really. Telling him that which I'd only just heard myself from Mam. But what could I do?

So you have tomorrow to yourself then?

Found myself agreeing that I did, without thinking through any implications.

Come play a game of squash with me tomorrow afternoon, he says. *At my club. I'll sign you in.*

Played a little at college, but not really a game I ever got into. I'm built for bulk sports, not speed. Had to say yes though, didn't I?

The trouble is, these old routines of mine don't work here. This view's all wrong. This brandy doesn't even work the same. Not like it does when I unwind in the early hours at home in Barcelona.

Mam's lean-to isn't quite the same as our balcony. No warm night breeze. No sound of a city still throbbing somewhere in the distance. Just Welsh rain on the windows, so lacking in force or purpose, you can see how it leaves the bird-shit untouched.

Beyond Mam's ramshackle excuse for a garden, I can glimpse the dawn creeping its way up the mountain. Typical of life here – all routine and no passion.

Except old Gavin's left me knackered tonight. So I guess the passion's always there, if you know where to look for it. He thrashed me at squash, of course. No surprises there.

I could barely remember the rules. Not that that mattered much. When you play with Gavin there are no rules, it seems. Almost five when I got in. Coming out of his car, I could see some lights just going on in other houses. People getting up for work, I suppose. Routines.

As we drove back from Cardiff, I told him all that heavy stuff he tried the other day in the hospital wouldn't work with me.

He laughed with condescending candour and said, *No, I know*, as though none of it mattered after all.

God, his wife must be a tolerant woman, I told him.

He didn't say a word to that. Didn't even smile. Just drove.

You never said nothing.

The police had apparently told him of my reluctance to testify against him. And that was the most he had to say to me. Almost all he had to say to me. An anticlimax in the end. It was bound to be.

I knew it had to be today or never. Mam came home this afternoon. And no way am I going back to that place just to visit Dan Llywellyn... even a dying Dan Llywellyn.

I don't know why you don't do the decent thing and go see him, Mam's been nagging ever since I came home to see her. *After all he did for you...*

Sat her down in that foyer place. The concourse they call it. Large waste of space designed to delude you into thinking you're entering or leaving a grand hotel. Placed her bag by her side and told her I wouldn't be long.

The taxi was already late.

The bus would have done me, of course, she proceeds to tell anyone within earshot daft enough to listen. *But our Joel wouldn't have it. He's very good to me. Come all the way from Spain to look after me, he 'ave.*

I tell her to wait. Though God knows where I thought she was going to go without me.

Such a sensitive boy. He loves poetry and all that stuff, you know. Won prizes for all sorts of things at school. Don't be fooled by all that brawn... he's a sensitive boy.

Mercifully, her voice drifts to nothing as I disappear down the corridor. The relief I feel is short-lived, as I see Mrs Llywellyn coming towards me. On her way to sneak a fag, apparently. After years of chocolates and the telly, she's succumbed to the joy of a new source of brain death, it seems. A packet of twenty and a gaudy-looking lighter were clutched in her fat hand.

Oh! What a good boy you are! She oozed all over me. The sentence that followed the most she's ever said to me. *Your mam said you'd go to come see 'im before he goes. I know you'll do him no end of good. In there, sixth door along.*

All those visits to her house! Out the back with Dan. Upstairs with Dan. Picking up some piece of kit I'd left there. Dropping off some piece of sports equipment I'd borrowed to work on at home. He and me in our man's world. Her, silent and redundant.

She shuffled down the corridor towards the smokers' yard.

Won't be here long, are the first words I say to him. Could have kicked myself, of course. But take comfort in the fact that he never has had much sense of humour. ('Getting to be perfect is no laughing matter,' he'd say to me as a boy whenever I started messing around during any sort of training.) So the irony, like so much else, is lost.

He didn't really seem to be suffering. I felt a little cheated. But he's gone to nothing. That much is true. Just a sad shadow staring at me from the pillow.

You didn't squeal. He made his voice as loud as he could muster. *You never told 'em any of our little secrets.*

It's a long time ago now, butt! I said.

He struggled to move his right hand from where it lay on top of the bed, finally lunging for what he thought would be the safety of my forearm. When I pulled my arm away in rejection, it fell back on the blanket again without a murmur. His face remained unmoved. No sign of disappointment touched those dark sunken eyes. He'd managed to sense my meaning without as much as a lilt of the head. All shows of remorse were held in reserve, ready for the big one.

You moved far away, didn't you? Spain, is it? They told me you were far away... and wouldn't talk...

Each little verbal outburst came shrouded in a silence with which he seemed ill at ease. Like memories of a life once fully lived. Once vibrant and clandestine. Now, dribbled onto pale pillows. Like small deaths.

They kept me there. Transfixed by curiosity. Those little words of nothing.

A gargle from his throat made me lower my gaze for a moment from his hollow eyes to his dead man's lips. The two thin lines quivered slightly, but remained perfectly dry. And I remembered the time he'd tried to kiss me. The only time.

I'd flinched in repulsion and lashed out with my fists. Kisses were for girls and proper poofs, I'd thought.

Today, I know differently. My stomach muscles tightened, squirming at my adolescent reasoning. I drew in breath. The way I would before a lift.

There was no one there to see me. He has a room to himself. The dying do, it seems. It's a private affair.

When the taxi finally drops us off, it turns out Joanne's long since let herself in. What you call a surprise party, apparently.

The kids ran around like idiots and shouted, *Welcome home, Nanna!* when prompted.

To crown it all, when Dean arrived from work at the end of the afternoon, a dirty big cake appears. It's candles. And streamers. And most of all, it's a load of bollocks.

She's in cancer remission, not joined the circus, I shouted. Mam didn't want that crap. I could tell.

But she's laughing as I went upstairs to change into my jogging suit.

Four hours later, it's her and me again. The remnants of a cake and a pile of dirty dishes in the kitchen.

She's gone to bed, exhausted. And I'm lying here in the bath.

It rained solid for the two hours I was out. And Gavin had his mobile phone switched off, it seems.

He caught me unawares. I'll give him that.

That first punch to my belly stopped me in my tracks. And I never saw the second coming, either. His fist colliding with my face with such clarity its terrifying thunder still throbs from the pit of my jaw to the top of my skull.

Floored in one fell sweep, he towered over me, asking repeatedly. *You were abused, weren't you?* His voice intense and calm. The emphasis placed on a different word with almost every repetition. It isn't a passion on his behalf; it's a technique put into practice.

In intent, my *Yes* was a defiant shout, but gasping as I was for breath, I know that the reality of my utterance was nothing more than a whisper in the autumn air.

Barely a mile down the hillside from the scene of my humiliation, Dan Llywellyn's remains were burning in the municipally-approved manner. Even as I lay there, stunned into neo-silence, I remember noting that I was thinking that thought.

Conspicuous contempt had been the motivation for our run. Or so I thought. His idea, of course. *Let's run while old Dan burns? I'll pick you up!*

Our fun run through the Pencwm woods high above the crematorium was planned to coincide with the very hour of his funeral. A show of disrespect. A symbol of indifference. In reality, it was nothing of the sort, of course. It was his planned revenge. Now that it's too late for me to add a gold star to his CV. Now he's been humiliated by a high-profile investigation that's come to nothing. Now that promotion is that much more difficult to achieve.

Yes. I desperately tried to articulate a second time as I felt his trainers thundering into my ribs.

And he buggered you? Go on! Say it! Tell me what I already know, you piece of shit.

At that point, my hands tried to stabilise the floor. And failed.

I flinched as I saw his right foot raised again and aiming for my face this time.

Once again, *Yes* formed submissively in my brain. The trees above me swayed. The sky-blue faded. Pain was all around. Rolling over on the earth, my capacity for thought was consumed by it.

Then why the fuck wouldn't you tell me? This time, his voice doesn't come from far away. He's in my ear. I smell him close. Feel him grab me by my vest, dragging me to my feet... *You stubborn Welsh bastard!*

Instinctively, I aimed a fist to ward him off. But one arm was already planted round his neck for balance and, staggering backwards, I dragged us both down. Drops of blood spraying both his face and the leaves beneath.

It's a long time later that I laughed. His outstretched arm ignored as I fumbled on the ground for a wristwatch that somehow managed to get dislodged in the assault.

He only allowed himself a smile.

Finding the watch, I stagger to my feet of my own accord and follow him to the car. We're both mute.

My senses remain disconnected. Even now, hours later, the pervading pain is the only message any of them will carry to my brain with any conviction. All else is fluff. Pain stands alone. Still throbbing, black and sore. Thorough and unrelenting. Worse than anything my memories of a bruising youth can bring to mind.

Mirrors have always been my friends. Until tonight. The wardrobe door's been left unlocked, allowing the reflective facade to swing away from the sight of me.

I can bear no light. I can bear no blanket. Tonight, I lick wounds. And curse.

Just leave it there... and... and go away, I said, straining to be civil to her.

If I've said I tripped and fell while out on my run then that is what she will accept as truth. That is what she'll tell the world. After all, that's what she told Mike. I know how Mam works.

What exactly happened? he asked in that tone of voice he reserves for cynicism.

Oh! Mam exaggerated as usual, I said when I eventually decided to ring him back. *You know what she's like. It's just a scratch.*

It was two days ago that he spoke to my mother. He just happened to ring almost as soon as I'd come into the house. Bad timing. I'd hardly had time to hobble to the bathroom to clean up before Mam could take a proper look when I heard the ringing.

Made the effort to take myself downstairs last night to ring him back. My mobile won't stretch as far as Spain. But I'm struggling for normality.

That's what you get when you hide yourself away in a darkened room. Self-absorption becomes self-destroying. Self-pity dulling your ability to deal with the world.

The telephone rings. Not often. Just once or twice a day. Joanne. Some of Mam's cronies. Mike. A social worker. The front door bell goes too. But that's an even rarer event. No symbolic roses have arrived to put my bruises in the shade. No perfumed bloom has been forthcoming to make tender my unsated nose.

A good bottle of brandy might have been the manly gesture. But, no. Nothing has been forthcoming from him. All I get are trays. Left on the landing by my mother as instructed. A knock on my bedroom door heralding each arrival. Mere supplies for a self-imposed prisoner.

I'm okay. Honestly. Just leave me alone. Had to shout at her several times before I heard her footsteps retracting that last time.

To all the world, I'm here to look after her. But the will to nurse anything except my own ego has left me. I just lay here on this bed, thinking that after this fiasco's over, I never want to come back to Wales again.

Okay! I'll go back for Mam's funeral, I conceded. *But that's all.*

Mike just smiled over his cup of tea. I smiled back.

He doesn't believe me regarding almost anything I've told him since my return. But it's all true.

We were both up early this morning, Mike and I.

He had some faculty meeting at the university. Wanted to know if I'd met Gavin back in Wales. *You know, your gay detective friend*, he said, pretending not to remember his name. *The one who came here that time with his fat colleague with a taste for fine art.*

Oh him! I replied. *We collided once or twice in the corridor. But he never got what he wanted from me.*

Serge wouldn't believe me either at first, when I said I wouldn't work the darkroom for him any more. But wasn't too concerned. *Don't worry. I find someone else.*

Maybe I wasn't that sensational after all. But maybe it's just that there are always others. Others who'll come do what we do after we've long since given up. Moved away. Moved on.

I figure darkrooms are like Wales. I won't go there again. Well! Only in my memories.

THE LARGEST BULL IN EUROPE
(2014)
Kate North

I was watching the children in the square behind you when I noticed that the waiter was on his way over. You sat straight, a dart up to heaven, and placed your hands on your thighs like when you're expecting news. The last time you sat like that we were in the hospital waiting to find out whether I'd fractured or sprained something.

The waiter placed our second dish on the table. We had decided to order a number of starters rather than a main meal each. You don't eat meat and there's no way of knowing what's really a vegetable and what's masquerading as one on menus this far inland, this far away from what we are used to. You had ordered in French because we don't speak Spanish and I liked the way you said 'pour le plat principal'. I was proud of your accent even though it was in the wrong place.

We looked down at the fresh plate together. There were six or seven items that had been deep fried in breadcrumbs. They were each the size of a baby's fist and they nestled next to a handful of fried potatoes with a large dollop of garlic mayonnaise.

'This could be a main course,' you said, then smiled. Taking a knife and fork you split open one of the fists, sniffed at it then pushed the plate towards me. They had sounded vegetarian on the menu, stuffed peppers, but they were filled with a meaty mince.

'You'll have to eat all of the aubergine yourself,' I pointed as it arrived. You pouted at me, aubergine is your favourite. When you first told me about your love of them I remember being fascinated. You consider it the most versatile vegetable as it can be fried, stuffed, baked, pureed, mashed, roasted, grilled and stewed. However, it is one of those vegetables that is actually a fruit, like the tomato. You told me you liked the way the texture varied so much according to how it was prepared.

You gave me a lengthy description of the aubergine when raw, dense and light like some industrial foam clothed in a wax jacket. Then, commentary style, you talked me through the breakdown of this ingredient when used to make a dip. From the charring of it over a flame when the skin peels and splits to the glossy ribbon of goo it becomes when mashed and blended with garlic and rock salt. You let me know that the largest producers of aubergines in the world are the Chinese followed by the Indians and that you have been to China and your sister has been to India.

This particular plate of aubergines looked like a nest of fat snails. The chunks had been coated in a cumin batter and deep fried, then glazed with a thick honey that was starting to set as we stared down at it.

'Go on then, eat one.' You stabbed a chunk with your fork and it made a moist crackle, opened your mouth wide like a chorister and placed it far inside before closing your lips around the fork then pulling it away. 'Mmmm', you said, 'mmmm.'

'Nice?'

'Mmmm, nice.'

Good, I thought. They didn't look to my taste. I bit into a meat fist and dipped a potato slice into the mayonnaise.

'Really, really, really excellent.'

'You'll have to look up the recipe when we get home.'

'Mmmm.'

When the time came to pay I reached into my new leather handbag and pulled out my new leather purse.

'I'll get this,' I said and I unfolded the note section of the wallet. I took out all of the notes like I never would at home, and flicked through them until I had selected the right amount. I fanned them out on the saucer that came with the bill and weighed them down with a sachet of sugar.

'We still have some wine to finish,' you said as you wiggled the half-full bottle in front of my face. I slid my glass to you and you refilled it. We both sat there taking in the couples and families on the tables around us. After a while, when nearly all of the wine was gone you said, 'I wouldn't mind going to see that bull.'

A circus had appeared on the edge of the village where we were staying. We drove past it the previous afternoon when they were hoisting the tent poles. In the evening when we came out to the square for dinner, we noticed lots of posters had been put up. They were on telephone poles, bins, swinging from streetlights, there was even one across the doors of the town hall. It read in Spanish,

For one night only El Circo Ronda brings you
the largest bull in Europe – 750kg!

'They're showing it tonight.'
'It would be a shame to miss it.'
'I didn't think you'd be that interested, I must admit.'
'I am an animal lover.'

Throughout the afternoon and into the early evening one of the circus workers had driven through the streets in an elderly truck with a loudhailer attached. It blared out tinny classical music that was interrupted frequently with a recorded announcement detailing the time of the show. You looked at your watch, then at me.

'We can still make it if we get a move on.'

'Are you sure you're up for it? I mean, it could be cruel.'

'We're in Spain,' you said and stood up as if about to burst into song.

On the way there we discussed what they would actually do with the bull. Would they make it do tricks or simply parade it about? Would it be trained and part of an act? We carried on down the hill to the edge of the village. There was a queue of locals at a ticket kiosk that had been set up on the scrubland by the tent. We joined the queue.

'Dos,' I said to the ticket clerk when we reached the booth. He was smoking a cigarette and he allowed the ash to fall on two tickets before handing them to me. He pointed towards the tent and told us the time of the show in very slow and enunciated Spanish. It didn't start for another twenty minutes so we headed to the other stalls that circled the main tent. There was an old lady selling children's toys: balls and sweets with trinkets inside them. She looked ancient and the lines on her face were like troughs in the land in which you could deposit seeds. There was another stall selling toasted almonds and polythene bags of peeled and sliced fruit. You bought some almonds in a rolled paper cone that looked like a miniature Ku Klux Klan hat.

Inside families were taking their seats. Some were firmly installed and passing foil parcels of pastries about. One family entered through the curtain flap, looked around and waved at another family who beckoned them over to join them.

'Front, middle or back?' I said and you pointed to the front row where there was room at the edge of the bench. We took our places and you munched on the almonds.

'Mmmm, mmmm,' you said.

'Nice?'

'Mmmm, excellent.'

That's when the band started to play. I hadn't noticed it on the way in. A blast of trumpets made the audience look up and focus on the small but significantly loud five or six middle-aged men who made up the band. They were all round and sported extravagant moustaches like old cinema villains. As their first number built to a swell, so did the audience, who started to clap in time to the music. You patted your knee with your free hand and continued to clutch your almond cone with the other. By the end of the piece the audience had filled and the entry flap was pulled shut. A drum roll began, the lights were lowered and with a cymbal clash a spotlight appeared in the centre of the ring. A voice flared through the speakers and a traditional ringmaster with red coat-tails and a top hat ran out into the spotlight as we made our applause.

After a brief introduction the performers paraded into sight one after another until they lined the entire arena. Marching and dancing, jumping and rolling in time to the music there were a number of clowns, a dog wearing a necktie and carrying a bone, an acrobat on a large ball, stilt walkers, a couple of people on unicycles and even a juggling dwarf in a unitard.

The first act was the acrobat walking on the ball. I didn't think much of him but I suppose he was just warming things up. He manoeuvred his way through an obstacle course of large foam objects that had been laid down by the other performers before they left the ring. I could see that it took a lot of balance and a huge amount of leg strength, so I did clap.

The next act was a clown. He appeared from somewhere in the audience and there was a yelp from a grandma. She was sat next to him when he stood up and started to shout at the man on the ball. Everyone around him burst out laughing and then eventually, once she had realised what was going on, so did the grandma. He seemed to be telling the performer with the ball that he could do just as well. The man left the ring in a faux state of despair and before going to claim the ball as his own the clown bent down to the grandma, pulled a bouquet of weeds from his jacket pocket and presented them to her with serious decorum. She took them and also accepted a peck on her cheek.

After trying to roll about on the ball and falling over a number of times, he made his way to the centre of the ring and motioned for silence. Then he pulled a violin from his extremely large trousers. The lights dimmed and he was lit by the spot. Taking us all by surprise, he suddenly charged into a very skilled performance of Vivaldi's Summer, presto. He played with raised eyebrows and concentrated eyes focussing on an unknown point at the back of the tent. I looked around and saw that most of the audience had a similar expression on their own faces. We were all in his moment as I felt your hand squeeze my knee and, even though I couldn't bring myself to turn and look, I knew you were smiling. As the rendition built I could feel all the breath in that tent, the whole audience inhaling and exhaling slowly, the way you do when you're concentrating so hard that you don't want the sound of your gulp to interrupt what's in front of you.

As the performance was reaching its climax we began to lean forward. I was clenching my fists as if I were a mother urging my child on to make the high note. The clown was starting to perspire, I could see the beads forming over the white of his makeup. That was when the violin burst into flames as if through the audacity of his playing. It was perfectly timed and the audience gasped before realising it was part of the act. The clown ran about the ring waving his musical flame until diving for a large trough of water in which he threw both the violin and himself. The applause was solid and didn't stop for a good two or three minutes. The clown was fished out of the trough by some performers and dragged to the back of the ring. He was propped up and he rolled his shoulders as if he was going to be sick. Then he coughed a lot of water onto the floor followed by a few fish. He straightened himself up, gave a long, low bow then disappeared behind the curtain.

The clown stood out as the best performance of the night. When he left you noted that the bull still hadn't made an appearance. I suggested that it would be saved for the finale, given it was the focus of the advertising. The following acts were fair, the dwarf juggled a number of things: clubs, saucers, torches, vases and so on. But she was at her best when balancing a sword on a dagger on her chin while climbing a ladder. A trampoline was brought out at one point and most of the performers did something on it. More clowns showed up and bashed into each other mid-air, some acrobats combined trampoline leaps with trapeze work and the dog with the bone did a few back flips. The final act involved performers dressed as bandits on galloping horses. The horses were as large as minibuses, but they were no bulls.

The end was much like the beginning with a parade of performers, only now there was more applause as the audience had become familiar with the cast. They gave farewell waves in time to the music and proceeded back out behind the curtain. When the house lights came up you turned to me and asked, 'So, what about the bull?' I shrugged then you grabbed my hand and said 'Look.' You pointed to another curtain flap that was open on the opposite side of the tent. People were leaving their seats and heading for it. We stood up and you handed me your empty almond cone. I made space for it in my handbag and we moved towards the new exit. A queue was forming and we joined it dribbling forward.

'Do you think this is where we'll see it?'

'I suppose.'

As part of the queue we made our way out of the tent to a

space where I could see a number of animal pens in a row. The audience was snaking past them in line. Fathers picked up toddlers and leaned them over the rails, behind which various animals were housed. In one pen there was a selection of unusually large rabbits that looked like they were on steroids. They had bulging eyes and long wavy hair in a variety of browns and greys. Next to the rabbits were some goats. Nobody seemed that fussed about them and the queue moved along swiftly. Then came a solitary llama who was marching back and forth along the length of the barrier. It stopped intermittently and shoved its head forward at the crowd who were laughing and squeaking at it. One small girl burst into tears, which provoked further gentle laughter, and her mother scooped her up onto her hip for protection. The crowd stopped moving at this point and we halted right by the llama.

'Give it a pat,' I said.

'No way. That's cruel.'

The llama looked down at us and batted its eyelashes. It had goofy teeth that pushed through what I made out to be a smile.

'Awh, it's smiling at us, go on, give it a pat.'

'It *is* smiling isn't it?'

You reached toward it, your hand flat and calm. Then, just as you were about to make contact with the top of the animal's head it pulled back its lips, nodded towards you and hissed a large gob of spit in your direction. You shrieked and people turned to look at your stunned, wet face. There was quite a bit of laughter and you did your best to smile, when I knew what you really wanted was to scream and to run, run, run, keep running. I fished out a tissue from my bag that you snatched from me.

'Thanks.'

I slipped my arm around your waist and squeezed on that bit of muscle, your oblique I think, that you always insist is fat.

'Stop squeezing my fat,' you said but I didn't. I just hung in there until you let it pass.

'This bull had better be worth it.'

Then we pushed forward. I could hear the gasps from those people in front of us who could now surely see the bull. There was a reverential beat of quiet and a few more gasps until we found ourselves at the barrier in front of the beast.

'Shit!' I said.

'What?'

'It's big.'

'Massive.'

'Shit!'

There, in a pen almost as big as itself, rather like one of those bed-bound obese people they make documentaries about, knelt a bull that was so huge the spectacle felt like witnessing the sheer face of mountain for the very first time, or like the view from a ship when there is no land to spot, only ocean and ocean and ocean. Everywhere was bull. I squeezed at you harder.

'750 kg, what's that in stones?'

'It must be over 100.'

The bull was totally black and snorted loudly. It had a ring in its nose and a large rosette pinned to its back. Its horns were two perfectly symmetrical protrusions either side of its head, which looked a bit like a giant shoebox. Its plum eyes were shifting nervously, though it had a chest that looked proud and brave like the bonnet of a sports car. The crowd moved on. I looked to the bull and felt the need to stay with it. I remember thinking that I wish I could talk to it, just say hello or ask what it is like being *it*, a bull, that particular bull.

'No wonder it wasn't part of an act,' I said as we walked back up the hill toward the village square.

'Too big for that. It could kill.'

'Do you think they are that big in bull fights?'

'No chance.'

We reached the square and took a seat outside a bar under an orange tree. A waitress came and took our drinks order.

'I'm still in shock to be honest.'

'It was massive.'

'The largest bull in Europe.'

'And it was *so* still. Big and still.'

'Unnerving.'

'But fascinating at the same time.'

Our drinks came along with a bowl of olives. The olives had been marinated in garlic, oil and a herb I couldn't make out. You popped one in your mouth.

'Mmmm, mmmm,' you said.

'Good?'

'Mmmm, excellent.'

'There's something I'd like us to do before we leave.'

'Mmmm. Mmmm?'

'You might not like the sound of it.'

'Go on,' you said, then you spat an olive stone into the palm of your hand and placed it in the terracotta serving dish on our table.

'I'd like us to go and watch a bull fight.'

You took another olive from the dish and put it to your mouth. Sucking on it you looked up to the tree above us, then back down at me. You nibbled at the flesh of the fruit like a squirrel on a nut, then you held the stone in your hand between your thumb and forefinger and said, 'Okay.'

It was mid-August and we had unknowingly purchased the best seats for the first show of the season. Tourist's good fortune.

'What will you wear?' you asked. I hadn't a clue. 'Do we need to dress up?' I said.

'Well, I intend to.'

We got there early and sat outside a café where everyone else was sat. We ordered two sherries and some water like everyone else and sat back with our matching shades balancing on our noses. It was about an hour before the start of the show and perhaps thirty minutes before the gates opened. I took out the tickets and double-checked which entrance we needed. Two elderly ladies strolled past arm in arm and you grabbed my hand, widened your eyes and said, 'I'm so excited.' They were wearing patterned dresses and large flowers in their hair. One held a scarlet fan in her hand and you said that I should have one to go with my lipstick.

'This is just like a night at the theatre. Everyone's dolled up.'

'I'm glad we made the effort.'

There were clusters of people on the tables around ours. It was a predominantly older crowd but the youth were not entirely absent. The thing that unified everyone was the style of dress – certainly the very, very best. High polished shoes cut past proud pressed chinos, tight black skirts accompanied expensive jeans and deceptively relaxed linen shirts.

The twenty-somethings butched-out their chests and primped-in their buttocks. The thirty-somethings slanted in their seats while sucking slender cigarettes and taking sultry nods. The forty-somethings relaxed against the street, the rare flicker of a significant signet ring or the practised savvy of an arriving heel occasionally causing the crowd to turn. The fifty-somethings communicated with their hands, fondling cigars, pinching cheeks, stroking palms, grasping shoulders. The couples in their sixties fussed with handkerchiefs while those in groups laughed in low rolls and pointed or waved at each other. The oldest people came as part of family arrangements where each generation had at least one representative present. These families took up two or three tables each, the waiters pushing them together and separating them as the afternoon required. Plates of food were passed about, uncles casually served grandmas, teenagers fed babies and parents loomed between mouthfuls in order to quietly air their presence.

One such family arrived shortly after us. They sat opposite our table on the other side of the thoroughfare that was encouraged by the break in seating to the front of us. They were in the kind shade of a kiosk that formed an arc over the pavement with the help of an old oak tree. Dishes came and went, napkins were flapped and flourished while toddlers crawled on laps and escapees rolled toward strangers.

'Should we eat something?' you said.

'Yes, but maybe something small. We don't know how you'll feel later.'

'Yes, something small.'

We both liked the look of the thick purple salsa that came in a small oval tureen. It sat in the middle of the family's table and each person punctuated their meal with regular dips of bread into it. It was the last thing to remain on the table and arms reached for it solidly with javelined breadsticks and swinging forks until it was emptied.

'It looks delicious,' you said, 'I wonder what's in it?'

'Maybe tomatoes blended with black beans and oil.'

'Mmmm, yummy,' you said.

When the waiter came we pointed at the empty tureen and ordered our own along with some bread and another two sherries. It was served quickly and you submerged a torn chunk of bread into the slush immediately.

'Mmmm, mmmm,' you said.

'Good?'

'Mmmm, excellent.'

I took a piece of bread and did the same. It wasn't what we were expecting, but it was perfect. A messy, oily, spicy, chilled concoction of the freshest unidentifiable ingredients I have ever tasted. It sang in my mouth the way a strong cheddar vibrates against one's gums. It clung to the insides of my cheeks like an obedient ice cream and dissolved the bread slowly on my tongue like a saucy communion wafer.

'There are definitely tomatoes in it,' you said before pausing to dislodge a thin fibre that had got caught between your teeth. Pulling it out then dangling it in the air in front of my nose, you giggled.

'What makes it so dark and gloopy then?' I asked.

'Must be beans. All whizzed up then mixed in.'

You clearly didn't care what the tureen contained and I didn't blame you. We were in the place for such a dish, we were eating it like all of the other people around us were. It suited the temperature, it tasted divine and it felt like the only thing to be doing. We didn't talk again until the tureen was empty and then only to agree on a 'yum' or unite in a 'gorgeous'.

After a while the family opposite us prepared to depart. Men nearby stood up from tables and took their places under trees while they waited for wives to use the toilets inside the café. I asked for the bill and the waiter was so impressed with my accent he performed a kind of mini-flamenco clap on the heel of his palm and I blushed.

Outside the gate there were stalls with refreshments. I wanted some water and you insisted on cigars because everyone else was queuing up for them. We made our way to gate number three, a bulky cavern set into the round of the building. I felt like a peasant walking into a cathedral in the Middle Ages. We both looked up instinctively, awestruck with the height of the corridors containing the babbling brook of people in which we swam without control. I grabbed your hand and reached us toward a man who was tearing tickets. He glanced at us, then the tickets in my hand, took them, gave them a rip and motioned for us to follow him.

CHRONOLOGICAL INDEX

CHRONOLOGICAL INDEX

CHRONOLOGICAL INDEX

AUTHOR BIOGRAPHIES

Deborah Kay Davies (1956–) won Wales Book of the Year in 2008 for her collection of short stories, *Grace, Tamar and Laszlo the Beautiful*. Her novels include *True Things About Me*, *Reasons She Goes to the Wood* and *Tirzah and the Prince of Crows*. She received a PhD in Creative and Critical Writing from Cardiff University.

Lewis Davies (1967–) was born in Penrhiwtyn, south Wales. He is a novelist, playwright and short-story writer. He has won a number of awards for his writing including the Rhys Davies Short Story Award.

Pennar Davies (1911–1996) Born in Mountain Ash, a coal miner's son, Davies had a distinguished academic career at Cardiff, Oxford and Yale. He was a minister for a time in Cardiff and then Professor at the colleges of Bala-Bangor and Brecon. He was appointed principal of Brecon (until that college moved to Swansea) and remained in that post until his retirement in 1981. He was a prolific poet, short-story writer and novelist and theologian.

Rhys Davies (1901–1978) was among the most dedicated, prolific, and accomplished of Welsh prose-writers in English. He wrote, in all, more than a hundred stories, twenty novels, three novellas, two topographical books about Wales, two plays, and an autobiography in which he set down, obliquely and in code, the little he wanted the world to know about him. He was born at Blaenclydach in the Rhondda, in 1901. Leaving school at fourteen, he had a few menial jobs until, at the age of twenty, he moved to London. He began writing in the 1930s, primarily in the short-story form, of which he was soon hailed as a master, publishing widely in the UK and the US.

In 1971 he was awarded the Arts Council of Wales' principal prize for his distinguished contribution to the literature of Wales.

Stevie Davies (1946–) Emeritus Professor of Creative Writing at Swansea University; a Fellow of the Royal Society of Literature and a Fellow of the Welsh Academy. She has published widely in the fields of fiction, literary criticism, biography and popular history. A collection of her short stories, *Arrest Me, For I Have Run Away*, was published by Parthian in 2018. Parthian reprinted *The Element of Water* (2001) in The Library of Wales Series (2019): the novel was long-listed for the Booker and Orange Prizes and won the Arts Council of Wales Book of the Year in 2002. Stevie's most recent novel is *The Party Wall*.

Amy Dillwyn (1845–1935) A novelist, industrialist and iconoclastic campaigner from Swansea. Three of Dillwyn's seven novels have been reissued by Honno Classics: *The Rebecca Rioter*, *A Burglary; or Unconscious Influence* and *Jill*, all of which have queer themes.

Dorothy Edwards (1903–1934) A modernist writer from the mining valley of Ogmore Vale where her socialist father was a schoolmaster, Edwards published a short story collection *Rhapsody* (1927) and a novel *Winter Sonata* (1928). The former is part of the Library of Wales series of classics, and the latter was reissued by Honno Classics.

Jane Edwards (1938–) Born and raised on the isle of Anglesey, Edwards has had a long and notable career as a novelist. Her first novel *Dechrau Gofidiau* (Troubles Begin) won a prize at the National Eisteddfod under the adjudication of Kate Roberts. Since then she has published many novels and short stories, some for younger readers, and some poetry.

Ken Etheridge (1911–1981) Playwright, artist, poet and teacher. He was born in Ammanford and taught art at Queen Elizabeth Boys Grammar School, Carmarthen. He wrote in English and Welsh.

Margiad Evans (1909–1958) Margiad Evans was the pen name of Peggy Whistler, who adopted the border country around Ross-on-Wye as her home and the setting for her novels and short stories, including *Country Dance* (1932). Her novels include *The Wooden Doctor* (1933), *Turf and Stone* (1934) and *Creed* (1936). She published her short stories in *The Old and the Young* (1948) and was the author of two autobiographical accounts of epilepsy: *A Ray of Darkness* (1952) and the posthumous *A Nightingale Silenced*.

Kathleen Freeman (1897–1959) was a British classical scholar, short-story writer and author of detective novels. Her detective fiction was published under the pseudonym Mary Fitt. She was a lecturer in Greek at Cardiff University between 1919 and 1946.

Jon Gower (1959–) has over thirty books to his name, including *The Story of Wales*, which accompanied the landmark BBC series, *An Island Called Smith*, which won the John Morgan Travel award and *Y Storïwr*, which won the Wales Book of the Year award. He has published five collections of short stories, in Welsh and English.

Emyr Humphreys (1919–2020) was born at Trelawnyd in Flintshire, and attended the University of Wales, Aberystwyth, before registering as a conscientious objector at the outbreak of the Second World War. After the war he worked as a teacher, a drama lecturer at Bangor, and as a BBC producer. During his long bilingual writing career, he published over twenty novels, which included such classics as *A Toy Epic* (1958), *Outside the House of Baal* (1965), and *The Land of the Living*, an epic sequence of seven novels charting the political and cultural history of twentieth-century Wales. He also wrote plays for stage and television, short stories, *The Taliesin Tradition* (a cultural history of Wales), and published his *Collected Poems* in 1999 and *Shards of Light* in 2019. Among many honours, he was awarded The Somerset Maugham Prize, The Hawthornden Prize, and the Wales Book of the Year Award.

Dylan Huw (1996–) Originally from Llandre, Ceredigion, Dylan Huw is a Cardiff-based writer of fiction, essays and criticism in both English and Welsh who won the crown at the Urdd Eisteddfod in 2015. He holds an MA in visual cultures from Goldsmiths, University of London, and works as part of National Theatre Wales' creative development team.

Aled Islwyn (1953–) was born in Port Talbot, south Wales. He writes primarily in Welsh. He won the Daniel Owen Memorial Prize at the National Eisteddfod for *Sarah Arall*. A collection of short stories *Unigolion Unigeddau* was published in 1994 and a first collection in English *Out With It* in 2008.

Siân James (1932–2021) published thirteen novels since her first, *One Afternoon*, won the Yorkshire Post Prize in 1975. Her third, *A Small Country*, was adapted for film by Stan Barstow and Diana Griffiths and televised in four parts by S4C. Her last was a sequel, *Return to Hendre Ddu*, published by Honno. Two volumes of her short stories have been published and a memoir of her childhood, *The Sky Over Wales*, won the Arts Council Wales Book of the Year. With Tony Curtis she compiled the much-loved anthology *Love From Wales* and she translated *Y Byw Sy'n Cysgu* by Kate Roberts. Siân James was a Fellow and an Honorary Doctor of the University of Wales. She was married to the actor Emrys James.

Crystal Jeans (1988–) is a short-story writer and novelist. She won the Wales Book of the Year for her second novel *Light Switches Are My Kryptonite*. Other books include *The Vegetarian Tigers of Paradise* and *The Inverts*. She lives in Pontypridd.

Glyn Jones (1905–1995) entered the Welsh writing scene in the 1930s and continued to publish novels, poetry, short story collections, translations and works of criticism throughout his life. He received several awards for his contributions to literature in Wales. Brought up in a Welsh-speaking, chapel-going family, Jones was educated in English, which remained his primary writing language, although he read and spoke fluent Welsh. The first chairman and then vice-president of Yr Academi Gymreig (English section), he was deeply concerned with supporting the literature of both languages. His novel *The Valley, The City, The Village* is published in the Library of Wales.

John Sam Jones (1956–) now lives with his husband in a small German village a stone's throw from the Dutch border, where he moved from Wales following the Brexit referendum. In 2001 he became the first co-chair of the LGB Forum Cymru (which was later renamed Stonewall Cymru), set up to advise the Welsh Government on LGB issues. He studied creative writing at Chester. His collection of short stories – *Welsh Boys Too* – was an Honour Book winner in the American Library Association Stonewall Book Awards. His second collection, *Fishboys of Vernazza*, was short-listed for Wales Book of the Year and was followed by the novels *With Angels and Furies* & *Crawling Through Thorns*. He published a memoir *The Journey is Home, Notes from a Life on the Edge* in 2021.

David Llewelyn (1978–) is a novelist and script writer based in Cardiff. He grew up in Pontypool and graduated from Dartington College of Art. His most recent novel, *A Simple Scale* was shortlisted for the Polari Prize.

Mihangel Morgan (1956–) was a lecturer on modern Welsh literature, folklore and creative writing at Aberystwyth University. He writes primarily in Welsh. He won the Prose Medal at the National Eisteddfod in 1993 and has published many poems, stories and novels, including *Melog* which was also published in English, translated by Christopher Meredith. He writes a regular column in the Welsh language magazine *O'r Pedwar Gwynt* (From the Four Winds).

Thomas Morris (1985–) is the author of the short story collection, *We Don't Know What We're Doing* which won the Wales Book of the Year in 2016. He is a recipient of a Somerset Maugham Award.

Kate North (1978–) was born in Glasgow and moved to her family hometown of Cardiff soon after. She studied English in

Aberystwyth then Creative Writing in East Anglia and Cardiff. Kate is currently the Programme Director of the MA English Literature and Creative Writing pathways at Cardiff Metropolitan University. She has published a novel, *Eva Shell*, and several collections of poetry.

Kate Roberts (1891–1985) Born and raised in Rhosgadfan near Caernarfon, Roberts is considered the most significant writer of fiction in Welsh in the twentieth century, known during her own lifetime as Brenhines ein Llên (Queen of our Literature). She graduated in Welsh at Bangor, worked as a school teacher in Ystalyfera and Aberdare before she and her husband bought Gwasg Gee printing press, publishing the Welsh newspaper *Y Faner* (*The Banner*) for which she wrote regular columns. Many of her short stories were translated by Joseph Clancy into English as *The World of Kate Roberts 1925–1981* (1991) and a new translation of *Feet in Chains* (translated by Katie Gramich) was published in 2012.

Bertha Thomas (1845–1918) The daughter of Canon John Thomas, originally from Llandeilo, and Maria Bird Sumner (daughter of John Bird Sumner, Archbishop of Canterbury 1848–62). The author of nine novels, two collections of short stories and a biography of George Sand, her last book, *Picture Tales from Welsh Hills* (1912), was reissued with additional material as *Stranger Within the Gates* (Honno 2008).

ACKNOWLEDGEMENTS

A number of the short stories included in this anthology were brought to our attention by Michelle Deininger, Tony Brown and Norena Shopland; their generous support has enriched this anthology. We benefitted from the research of Liza Penn Thomas on Ken Etheridge, M. Wynn Thomas on Pennar Davies, and Claire Flay-Petty who with Michelle Deininger is researching the modernist network of women based in Cardiff of which Kathleen Freeman and Dorothy Edwards were a part. Several authors shared their work with us pre-publication and Katie Gramich undertook a translation of Kate Roberts's 'Nadolig' in the very early stages of this project which helped to shape the direction of the anthology. Masters students at Swansea University have contributed directly and indirectly to this anthology through their lively discussions of many of the stories. In particular, Lisa Bittner identified and documented the German tradition of the Liebesmaie and Eleanor Fraser worked on an early version of the anthology during an internship at Parthian Books.

We are grateful to Ruth Jên Evans for the cover picture, 'Merched Becca', and to Mihangel Morgan for his translations of 'Parting' and 'The Formations' as well as the translations of his own stories 'Posting a Letter' and 'Love Alone Remains'.

Thanks also to Kathryn Tann and Richard Davies at Parthian for seeing this huge manuscript through the publication process and for suggesting a few extra stories at the last minute.

Modern Wales by Parthian Books

The Modern Wales Series, edited by Dai Smith and supported by the Rhys Davies Trust, was launched in 2017. The Series offers an extensive list of biography, memoir, history and politics which reflect and analyse the development of Wales as a modernised society into contemporary times. It engages widely across places and people, encompasses imagery and the construction of iconography, dissects historiography and recounts plain stories, all in order to elucidate the kaleidoscopic pattern which has shaped and changed the complex culture and society of Wales and the Welsh.

The inaugural titles in the Series were *To Hear the Skylark's Song*, a haunting memoir of growing up in Aberfan by Huw Lewis, and Joe England's panoramic *Merthyr: The Crucible of Modern Wales*. The impressive list has continued with Angela John's *Rocking the Boat*, essays on Welsh women who pioneered the universal fight for equality and Daryl Leeworthy's landmark overview *Labour Country*, on the struggle through radical action and social democratic politics to ground Wales in the civics of common ownership. Myths and misapprehension, whether naïve or calculated, have been ruthlessly filleted in Martin Johnes' startling *Wales: England's Colony?* and a clutch of biographical studies will reintroduce us to the once seminal, now neglected, figures of Cyril Lakin, Minnie Pallister and Gwyn Thomas, whilst Meic Stehens' *Rhys Davies: A Writer's Life* and Dai Smith's *Raymond Williams: A Warrior's Tale* form part of an associated back catalogue from Parthian.

the RHYS DAVIES TRUST

PARTHIAN

MODERN WALES

WALES: ENGLAND'S COLONY?

Martin Johnes

From the very beginnings of Wales, its people have defined themselves against their large neighbour. This book tells the fascinating story of an uneasy and unequal relationship between two nations living side-by-side.

PB / £8.99
978-1-912681-41-9

RHYS DAVIES: A WRITER'S LIFE

Meic Stephens

Rhys Davies (1901-78) was among the most dedicated, prolific and accomplished of Welsh prose writers. This is his first full biography.

'This is a delightful book, which is itself a social history in its own right, and funny.'
– The Spectator

PB / £11.99
978-1-912109-96-8

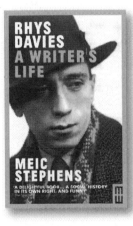

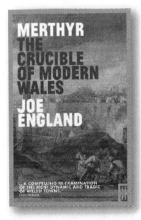

MERTHYR, THE CRUCIBLE OF MODERN WALES

Joe England

Merthyr Tydfil was the town where the future of a country was forged: a thriving, struggling surge of people, industry, democracy and ideas. This book assesses an epic history of Merthyr from 1760 to 1912 through the focus of a fresh and thoroughly convincing perspective.

PB / £18.99
978-1-913640-05-7

THE JOURNEY IS HOME

John sam jones

'People like John Sam Jones are the real unsung heroes of society... his own journey is the making of him and it's a privilege that he chooses to share it.'
– Gwales.com

HB / £15.00
978-1-912681-74-7

BETWEEN WORLDS: A QUEER BOY FROM THE VALLEYS

Jeffrey Weeks

'Beautifully written, wise and insightful'
– Jenny White, *The Western Mail*

HB / £20.00
978-1-912681-88-4

TURNING THE TIDE

Angela V. John

This rich biography tells the remarkable tale of Margaret Haig Thomas (1883-1958) who became the second Viscountess Rhondda. She was a Welsh suffragette, held important posts during the First World War and survived the sinking of the *Lusitania*.

PB / £17.99
978-1-909844-72-8

BRENDA CHAMBERLAIN, ARTIST & WRITER

Jill Piercy

The first full-length biography of Brenda Chamberlain chronicles the life of an artist and writer whose work was strongly affected by the places she lived, most famously Bardsey Island and the Greek island of Hydra.

PB / £11.99
978-1-912681-06-8

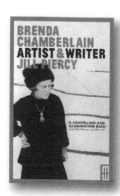